ON THE

NIGHT
PLAIN

Also by J. Robert Lennon

The Light of Falling Stars

The Funnies

J. ROBERT LENNON

ON THE
NIGHT
PLAIN

A Novel

PICADOR USA

A JOHN MACRAE BOOK

HENRY HOLT AND COMPANY • NEW YORK

www.picadorusa.com

Picador® is a U.S. registered trademark and is used by Henry Holt and Company under license from Pan Books Limited.

For information on Picador USA Reading Group Guides, as well as ordering, please contact the Trade Marketing department at St. Martin's Press.
Phone: 1-800-221-7945 extension 763
Fax: 212-677-7456
E-mail: trademarketing@stmartins.com

A portion of this book appeared in a different form in *Harper's Magazine* and in *Prize Stories 2000: The O. Henry Awards*

Designed by Victoria Hartman

Library of Congress Cataloging-in-Publication Data

Lennon, J. Robert, 1970–
    On the night plain : a novel / J. Robert Lennon. 1st Picador USA ed.
        p. cm.
    ISBN 0-312-42086-2
    1. Sheep ranchers—Fiction. 2. Rural families—Fiction. 3. Ranch life—Fiction. 4. Brothers—Fiction. 5. Montana—Fiction. I. Title.

PS3562.E489 O5 2002
813'.54—dc21   2002025153

First published in the United States by Henry Holt and Company

First Picador USA Edition: August 2002

10 9 8 7 6 5 4 3 2 1

To my grandparents,

Robert and Mary Stein

· PART ONE ·

ASEA

1

When the war was over, Grant clipped his hair close and made the long ride out to the flats where the railway ran east-west. He left in the night with the moon near full, taking a horse nobody would much miss if it failed to come back. There was no hurry. The sun and train were hours away, the packed dirt full of hoarded August heat. Stars jumped where the heat met a night breeze. Hoppers beat themselves against his legs and the horse's flank. He had an early apple in the pannier and ate it all but the seeds and stem, which he spit into the weeds. Once he'd spotted the tracks he followed them west to the empty station house and dismounted. He freed up his bag and shouldered it and turned to the old horse.

Hi! Go on home!

The horse was still. Grant made to lunge at him and he backed off a few steps and turned to browsing in the grass.

Go on! Grant said. He took off his hat and swatted at the horse and kicked him gently in the ribs. The horse shied and let out a disgruntled squeal. He rolled his head and let out a snort and turned around north. After an interval he walked off without looking back.

This had been a town called Grissom, but nobody lived in it now. When Grant was a boy two Mexicans had been hanged here for

stealing horses. This was long after such things were decreed by
courts, but the men had no local family and not much English, and no
one who knew of their crimes objected to the punishment. That they
were guilty was beyond doubt. They were found on the range asleep
near the stolen horses, with their Winchesters lashed to the riggings.
Grant was not sure where they'd been hanged, he'd been told the low
rung on the water tower, but he did remember that for some time
nobody bothered to cut down their bodies. Not long after this the last
inhabitants of Grissom quit the town for good.

There was some doubt that the train would stop at all. Grant had
sent a letter saying he would be here to meet it, but he had not
requested a reply. If the train came, he planned to get on it and ride it
as far as it took him, and if it didn't he would go back to the ranch and
resume work as if nothing had happened. His parents and brother
would know what he had tried to do but wouldn't be inclined to mention it.

As it happened somebody was already waiting, an old man wearing
a crisp new suit and clutching a shabby carpetbag. His jaw worked
with an involuntary motion, but he regarded Grant with clear eyes
that followed him as he walked to the only other bench on the tiny
platform. The bench shifted under him then steadied. Above hung a
sign with GRISSOM painted clearly on it. The windows of the station
house behind him were covered by bare boards. Across the tracks
stood a silo with its elevator in ruins at its foot, and behind it in the
indeterminate distance rose a solitary table of earth, disfigured by an
irregular rocky outcrop the wind had spared, that could have served
as a stage where giants performed for travelers of the ancient past.

Grant took off his hat and looked over at the old man. The old
man had been watching. Now he looked away.

Since the victory over Japan Grant had given this journey a great
deal of thought. He had pictured himself much as he was right now,
seated and calmly awaiting his train. He had imagined the rocking
motion the train would make, and the swaying of his fellow passengers with it and the soundless slosh of his breakfast coffee in the din-

ing car. Less clear in his mind was what he might do when he got off. He supposed there would be work wherever he went and people who could tell him how to get it. His only certain intent was to reach the Atlantic Ocean and walk barefoot into it, his shoes and socks behind him on the beach. Beyond that imagination failed him.

Something moved in his peripheral vision and he looked up to find the old man coming toward him, holding his bag close as if somebody might take it.

Time? the man said.

Grant had no watch. He said he didn't know. This didn't seem to satisfy the old man, but he asked nothing further and remained standing between the benches, as if to return was more than he could manage. A strong wind passed like a ghost train through the station and both men touched their hands to their hats. Light began to gather as if pulled by the wind. Grant offered the man a seat on his bench.

'Bliged, said the man.

He was on his way to Chicago, he said, to visit with a son and the son's wife and children. But the visit filled him with dread. He could not remember the name of his son's wife, nor the names of his grandchildren or even how many of them there were. He feared that he wouldn't recognize them at the station and that they would turn him away. And the ride in his son's car to their home outside the city: he'd seen pictures of the thousands of cars that raced along the highways and worried about an accident. Grant didn't know what to tell him. These seemed like valid fears. He asked the man where he lived.

Oh, right 'round here.

Grissom?

The old man frowned without meeting Grant's eyes. Not no more, he said.

Some time later the train came into view in the distance. It came slowly and didn't seem to get any larger as it approached, so that when it stopped before them it appeared a small thing to Grant, powerless to bring them any significant distance. Its doors fell open but no one emerged to usher them inside. Grant stood up and asked the old man if he'd like a hand with his bag, but the man ignored Grant's question and made his own way onto the train and disappeared.

Grant followed with neither reluctance nor eagerness, mounting the three steps because it was what he had anticipated doing. Though the day was now bright, the car was dark. A few passengers sat in grimy pools of light cast through soiled windows, while unoccupied seats remained shadowed by heavy opaque curtains. The passengers were asleep. Grant walked to the center of the car, raised his bag to the overhead rack, then thought better and set it down on a nearby seat. He slid in after it. No pull was visible for the curtain so he grabbed two handfuls of fabric and pushed them aside. Already the train had begun to move. He watched the strange butte roll out of view, then brought his bag onto his lap as if he might open it. But there was nothing inside that he needed and he put it back.

He fell asleep. He sensed the braking of the train and the passage of people in the aisle. Around him more curtains were opening and whispered conversations grew louder. He felt a hand touch his shoulder and opened his eyes to find the conductor standing over him, one hand holding his tickets and punch and the other in his change pocket. He asked how far Grant was going.

Where's it headed to?

Chicago.

Okay, Grant told him, and paid. Then he fell back to sleep.

When he next woke the sun was high over a miniature range of hills with cattle walking on them, and a heavy man of about sixty sat beside him. The man had one hand in Grant's bag, which Grant had left open when he paid the conductor. Now the hand withdrew.

Where're you headed, soldier?

Grant met his eyes, which were small and hard like plum stones. Chicago, he said.

You ought to know better than to leave your belongings unguarded beside you like that. You may find them made off with.

Grant zipped the bag shut and pushed it under the seat with his calves resting against it. The older man settled himself, stretching his body out, shoving both feet beneath the seat in front and nudging each shoe off using the toe of the opposite foot. With his creased wool trousers and starched shirt mussed by travel, he carried the air of a modest businessman, of monotonous work reluctantly done. An occasional tic wrinkled his nose and mouth. He was ewe-necked, with a large head that nodded like a daisy when he talked. He had not taken his eyes off Grant.

Been on the Pacific coast, have you? Back from where?

Grant glanced out the window. A motte of tall leaning cottonwoods passed, cupping a cluster of what could have been broken tombstones. Though he'd just woke up, he felt played out. He would have been riding line right now, seeking fence to fix. Instead his brother Max was likely doing it. About now they would all be acting like Grant had never been.

Okinawa, he said as the graveyard hove out of sight. Peleliu.

The man nodded. Not Iwo, huh?

No.

Ever eat dog?

No, Grant said.

The man was laughing. Damn good thing, he said. These boys come back saying they ate dog as if it's a admirable thing. God damn. He stuck out a bent hand, the knuckles tough and enlarged like knots in a branch. Sam Kroch, he said, high at the end like a question, so that Grant did not immediately know it was his name the man was speaking.

Grant Person, Grant said presently and shook the hand.

You a farm boy, son? You have got a sunpecked look to you.

Yessir.

You going home? Indiana? Illinois?

Indiana.

So you're a hero back home, are you. Look at you, all in one piece. Some of these boys come back all tied up together like a pot roast. You get yourself shot?

The wound grew hot at the question, the one thing Grant had as evidence if he needed it. He had suffered it when a neighbor's cow wandered onto their land and mired herself in mud. Grant pulled her out and she bolted, jerking the rope from his hands. The rope whipped around his calf and cut a channel through his trousers and into the flesh. This was four years ago. Scarred white and without hair, it could pass for a bullet wound if it had to.

I took one in the leg at Peleliu, he said. Healed up good. He cleared his throat. I still favor it some, he said.

Kroch laughed as if at a clever joke. I don't doubt that, he said, not a bit. And he tipped his head back still smiling and went to sleep.

·

For a short time there were six of them, all boys. The oldest was called Edwin. He was eight the winter Grant was seven, naturally broader in the shoulders and face and taller due to his age. This was at the onset of the Depression, and of all the children only Edwin seemed to understand the gravity of the situation. Under it he grew serious and sure, like a person expected to take control of the outfit at any moment if necessary, which in fact he was. At seven Grant was still thought of as a child, his horsemanship a form of play, not work, his assigned tasks around the place chores as opposed to duties. The others truly were children: Thornton was slow even for a four-year-old; Robert, at two and a half, was his playmate and protector. Max could barely walk yet and Wesley, a newborn, was already sick. In which way he was sick was initially unclear. He was declared to be colicky and cried evenings for many hours before sleep. He refused the breast. When Grant thought about this time, which was not often, he remembered Max sucking greedily, his shod feet dangling off their mother's chair, while Wesley lay silent and watchful nearby in the bassinet. Wesley was born too small and never grew significantly.

Their mother's name was Asta. Their father was called John. He was raised in the north of England and collected her from her home in Iceland during the first war. She had kept house with her mother there while her father raised sheep, and now in America she kept house and bore sons while her husband raised sheep. Growing up Grant never heard a single word of Icelandic from her and few of anything else. Nevertheless her English was good. Although she would not have been called beautiful, she stood apart from other women in the clarity and fullness of her features and by her great height, nearly six feet. She was feared and respected by the ranch men, most of whom were not as tall. Among those who feared her was John, who was short and talkative and boastful and whose strange skills, such as carving toys out of pinewood and playing the fiddle, distracted him from ranch work, at which he was mediocre at best. Away from Asta he seemed to blame her for his ineptitude. He could often be heard wondering what good she had done him, with all of her supposed sheep smarts. In her presence he would blame the shiftlessness and disobedience of the boys, once they were old enough to blame. Asta ignored him and continued to provide him with sons. She knew as well as he did the worth, on a ranch, of six boys.

On Christmas night 1929 they ate dinner together alone, without the hands. This uncharacteristic family privacy made them all uncomfortable and they struggled for things to say. Wesley nursed weakly for a short time, then once laid down began to cry, and the sound seemed to unhinge Asta, who held her knife and fork tightly but didn't touch them to her food. When John told her to go quiet him, Edwin got up from the table, went to the bassinet and whispered in the baby's ear. In minutes he was asleep.

The following morning Wesley woke congested in the nose and throat and spent the day facedown on their mother's lap, expelling mucus. Two days later he began to turn gray, then dull purple in blotches, and his fingers went cold and stiff. The following afternoon his head began to bulge at the fontanel. He stopped crying. That night he fell into a coma and he died under the doctor's care in the late morning of January 1.

Grant dreamed that a gentle horse, a blood bay, had entered the house and knelt before the bassinet, and tiny Wesley had climbed onto its red back and ridden away into the night. That afternoon he went to his mother where she lay next to the baby's still body and told her what he had dreamed, and without turning over to face him she reached back and slapped him hard enough to knock him down. In the morning they buried the baby in a wind-scraped corner of the starveout. John enclosed the grave with fence, leaving ample room around it as if he knew what was to come.

·

While Kroch was sleeping, Grant tried to imagine what life in Indiana might have been like had he actually lived there. He expected it was gentler, with more time for sleep. The animals were healthy and tractable and crops always brought a good price. The train was nearly to Minnesota now and night was falling. Passengers filled the compartment. The look of them made Grant glad Kroch had chosen him. It was not uncommon during the war to see women alone or alone with children, but the women in this car were accompanied and all the solitary travelers were men. The men varied in age and appearance but all had the eyes of outlaws, or so it seemed to Grant. They carried bought bags with few signs of use, as if they were only props for some private performance. Activity in towns they passed looked staged, and of course with his first lie Grant had become an actor. This was not a simple matter of making up a story and telling it to whomever he encountered. It was himself he was inventing, a version of him who had spent years in the company of other young men and had known the drudge and racket of war.

But he hadn't. He had lived in increasing solitude without reference to anyone. He had gone among the men back home without making an impression and he had never paid his own looks or talk any mind. He could vanish in the creases of land and not be thought of at all. Now suddenly he was traveling in a landscape of eyes, and he wondered for the first time what he had done to himself, wondered if the part of him he had hidden from the world could ever be found.

He was able to sleep with his heels clinched tight against his bag for safekeeping. When he woke it was to a scene of straight flat paved roads and cars that waited at intersections for the train to go by. Towns flashed past until they ran together, and this was the city. Passengers woke as if by a sixth sense. Kroch was among them, his clear eyes on Grant.

There she is, son, he said.

Grant looked out to make sure he meant Chicago and not some specific structure. A sign read UNION STATION. I reckon my daddy's here to meet me, he said.

Maybe I ought to wait around and see that. A hero's welcome.

Grant reached out and steadied himself against the seat in front, quelling nausea. The train was slowing. I ain't any kind of hero, he said.

Kroch was laughing. The way you tell that story, I believe it.

I don't follow, Grant said without looking.

Kroch was close now, right up at his ear. You have got to convince yourself before you can convince other people, boy. You don't even say your name like you mean it.

Grant felt him retreat, felt his body rise from the seat. He turned fast and found Kroch in the aisle peering down at him.

It's my name, Grant said. People turned.

A smile discovered Kroch's face and warped it. Okay, Grant Person. Now you sound like a honest man.

The train moaned and stopped. Kroch kept his balance like a steel beam. People got up all at once, but Kroch was ahead of them, down the stairs and across the filthy platform.

◆

He followed the other passengers through heavy glass doors into a room of stupendous size crammed tight with the sounds of footsteps and their echoes. It was like a cathedral where you worshiped by walking. He stood with his eyes shut while people arced around him from behind. He wondered if they would crush one another to death if obstructed, as sheep were known to do. His bag, bumped by passersby, tugged at his hand like a leashed dog.

He found a place on a long high-backed bench and caught his breath. In time a man and woman and child sat down nearby and he looked toward the woman and said, I want to get a train to New York City.

She wore a pink dress with frills and a hat with fake flowers on it, and her hand went to her child's shoulder and then her husband's.

What? the man said turning. You said what?

I want to get the train to New York.

The man was holding a cigar, rolling it in his hand. Well, you go to New York, soldier. It isn't any of my business. He brought out a silver guillotine from his coat and sliced the cigar end clean off. The cut end dropped to the floor.

Where? Grant asked him.

What!, now with the cigar between his teeth. The child, a boy, was staring.

Where do I get the train?

The man snorted, then pointed, shaking his head as if to fling Grant free of it. The woman stood, pulled her son from his seat, walked to her husband's opposite side and sat down.

The man lit his cigar. Well? he said.

•

There was a train leaving on the hour. He bought a ticket and was shown where to go to get on. While waiting he came across a machine that dispensed sandwiches and he put his coins into it. The carousel turned and he opened a door, then he thought better of his choice and quickly shut it. But the next door he tried wouldn't give, and neither would the first one when he tried it again.

Nearby two doors yawned into light and he could see cars moving on a street. He went out. The city looked like it did in pictures, except lived in, with buildings faded or crumbling from use and the cars nudging around one another with the scattershot instinct of insects. The order of city streets now seemed an illusion, like the smooth contours of rough land viewed from a distance. In each direction traffic lights changed abruptly, flashing red and then green between the buildings. A taxi stopped before him and a man dashed toward it and climbed in. Grant watched the taxi pull away. He was hungry.

The train stopped frequently at stations and sometimes stood still in lush countryside for no apparent reason. When it moved it moved slowly. Grant's compartment was full. He washed himself in a rural station bathroom and changed his clothes. When he learned the price of food in the dining car he tried to abstain from regular meals, but at times hunger overtook him and he ate without concern for money or manners. The men and women who shared his table didn't speak to him and he offered nothing to their conversation. He listened while they talked about Atlantic City. Men spent entire days making sand castles there, they said. One could witness a seven-foot shark in a glass tank and a horse that jumped from a great height into the ocean. This last seemed hard to believe. His fellow diners asked their waiter if he knew the city, and when he said he did they asked him if there really was a beach for coloreds and special entertainment for them as well. The waiter said that indeed there was, it was the hottest spot on the coast. One woman in the group occasionally met Grant's eyes with a kind look, and he thought of her soft features and long neck as he went to sleep that night.

•

By the time the train reached the station, Grant understood that he didn't want to be in New York after all. He considered the cars and lights he'd seen in Chicago and the thought made him very tired. For a while he sat on a bench much like the one he'd sat on there, and he closed his eyes and daydreamed about home. The routine that milled his days was absent utterly, like a cycle of weather going on halfway around the world. He wished he had a horse to ride. He would find the beach, and the horse would test itself on the shifting sand like a horse in a storybook. It would shy at first from the advancing water, then master itself and crash through the tide, leaving prints that washed away behind it. When he opened his eyes he watched his dining companions pass without noticing him. Once they had disappeared he made his way to a ticket window and asked how to get to Atlantic City.

He was told he would have to get a bus at Grand Central.

Which way? he said.

But when he went outside and saw the whole of New York he forgot the directions he'd been given. He watched travelers motion to taxis and tuck themselves inside and the taxis fold into the flow of cars. He took his money from his bag and counted it.

How much? he asked when he got in. The driver told him and Grant considered getting back out, but the driver was shrewd enough to have already started moving. Anyway he'd made his decision and ought to stick to it.

At Grand Central Terminal he paid all but three of his dollars for a ticket. The bus took him out of the city and along a busy road where identical housefronts crowded together like men lined up at a bar. They were traveling south, so he looked left in the hope of seeing the ocean. He couldn't. Soon they turned away from the evening sun, and sand began to appear along the road. Everything inside the bus turned to gold. Where the bus stopped he saw the backs of tall buildings and between them a mass of people walking. He heard the odd cacophony of a big band and smelled fried food. On the other side of a packed parking lot rose a flight of wooden steps. He went to them and climbed them and found himself on a wide wooden boardwalk, where people laughed and clutched one another falling down drunk in fine clothes, and publicly embraced in the backs of carts towed by running men, and pushed in and out of penny arcades and theaters and bars. Beyond all this was a cloudless purple sky that grew darker as it descended to the horizon. The horizon was flat and absolute, the authentic edge of the world. This at last was the ocean.

•

He sat shoeless mere inches out of reach of the ocean's tongue, eating from a paper plate of pierogies. He had wanted meat but ended up buying the first thing he laid eyes on. Beside him his lemonade was already empty. He had two dollars and ten cents left and all his clothes were foul and wrinkled.

Night came sooner here, so back at home his mother was likely cooking supper for the men. By now they would have stopped wondering about him. Less than a week ago the house had been emptier at night than Grant could bear. Now, without him, it was emptier still.

He would not have thought it possible for an entire family to go wrong. They had been strong and abundant and lived in a valley that seemed theirs alone: when anyone entered, the dust they raised was visible for miles, and even unexpected visitors could be met on the road. Home was sacrosanct, permanent and unbreachable. In retrospect this seemed a childish way of thinking. Families die out, even the hardiest lines. No blood can resist bad luck.

Robert was the second to die. He turned six on the same June day in 1933 that Edwin turned twelve. That month a man just hired had fallen drunk off the back of a truck and for several weeks afterward walked with a crutch. The boys were poking fun out in front of the house, with Grant dramatizing the fall and Thornton looking on from under a shade tree, laughing appreciatively in his strange husky voice. Robert impersonated the remorseful hired man stuttering apologies and jerking his crutch about, using as a prop the shotgun he'd been hunting pheasants with earlier in the day. He had forgotten to engage the safety and when the stock struck his boot top something caught the trigger and a barrel discharged under his arm and nearly took it off his body. No one appeared at the noise. There were a lot of people on the ranch in those days and a lot of reasons to fire a shotgun.

Robert didn't fall, not yet. His shirt swallowed up blood like a patch of dry ground and quickly turned black. He held the shot arm with the opposite hand and dropped to his knees.

Thornton had continued to laugh after the shot but now he perceived something amiss and fell silent. Grant ran to Robert, who had pitched onto his side. He took the boy's gray face in his hands, telling him stay still, don't move. Then he ran to the barn screaming to his father to come hurry, grabbed a rotted wool sack and balled it up as he ran back to Robert's side. Robert had his eyes shut and his dry lips together. Grant shoved the sack under the bleeding arm and pressed it there to stop the flow. If this hurt Robert he made no sign. Bits of grease wool were poking from the sack and lapping up the blood and shrinking to slick strands with it. The shotgun lay in the dirt nearby and Grant snaked out a foot and kicked it away. Thornton sat blubbering in the shade. Their father arrived cursing, and Edwin behind him with a face that seemed already to have considered the possibility of such an incident and fully accepted its inevitability. Unlike their father, Edwin was not surprised.

And neither was their mother, when John returned in the truck with Robert's body to bury it. They had aimed for the hospital in Ashton but Robert died on the way. John didn't stop at the house, only drove across the bare dirt of the starveout to the corner where Wesley lay, and waited for Asta and the boys to follow.

She was not seen to cry then or ever again that Grant could recall, not even when Edwin shot himself in the stand of lodgepole they harvested from the hillside or when the soldier came to inform her that Thornton had perished at sea. The years those incidents spanned were compressed in Grant's memory like frayed patches on a coiled rope. Certainly there were other things in between, his childhood adventures and schooling and the reckless driving of gravel roads, but these recollections faded quickly in the intense tragic light and made his short life seem worthless and futile. When he thought of his mother her face bore the stoic glare she had adopted, a figurehead's face of the sort a person might contrive for staring into a wild wind, as if it was possible to find the source.

Night fell and the noises behind him died. The ocean crept up toward where he sat, and he moved himself back. When it approached a second time he stood and turned toward the city. The sand was treacherous, with broken bits of shell and rotting crabs that he could see in the light from the moon and from the buildings ahead. A sign was posted at the base of the steps that read SHOES MUST BE WORN ON

BOARDWALK. He sat down and put his on. A group of young men passed behind him singing. On a bench a man was kissing a woman. After a moment Grant took his shoes off again and climbed back down into the sand. The boardwalk was built on wooden pilings that created a sheltered space, and he ducked his head and situated himself in it, with a mound of sand as a pillow and his bag close beside him. He fell asleep to the sound of footsteps overhead.

·

It had to be noon, or nearly so. The traffic on the boardwalk was a relentless rumble and the air hot even here in the shade. He came out into daylight. People in various states of undress sunned themselves and leapt in the surf. Women's arms and legs were bare, and men walking along the water's edge held them close. A tall Negro was building a sand castle and had already finished one just beside it. Grant recognized the completed castle, from pictures he'd seen, as the Roman Coliseum. As he watched, two men approached the Negro and dropped money into a nearby paper cup, and he responded with a nod, not taking his eyes from the work. It seemed to Grant that the war's end had driven people to forget who they were and where their lives were leading, to relinquish their money and secrets as if now there would be an unlimited supply. He wondered what the day of the week was—he had forgotten—and if it mattered to anyone.

On the boardwalk he bought a breakfast of sausage and eggs and toast for one dollar and ate it standing up, under a colorful umbrella. He walked as far as the boardwalk would take him, peering down each extravagant pier through its gaudy archway, to the massive halls and costumed people passing handbills, and food stands and games of chance. Graceful dirty gulls swooped in loose formation around small children, who tossed bread in the air for them to catch.

Walking back he stopped before a small crowd of people playing ball and ring-tossing games, at a little concession that also included a burnt-out frypit and griddle and a shabby parrot on a perch. One game involved throwing a baseball over the wooden counter and into a shallow basket with a convex bottom. In another game players tried to yoke a milk bottle with a wooden ring. Both games were cheats. The ball reliably bounced out of the basket every time and the rings were too small.

But the parrot was interesting. One foot was tied to its perch with string. The parrot tottered back and forth on the perch, two steps one way and two the other, as far as it could go in either direction. It did this compulsively, silently.

Give him a coin, the proprietor said. He was ropy looking, with a crooked nose and a frayed straw hat, and his black eyes, which rapidly blinked, were like the parrot's.

Go ahead, he said. Give him a coin, see what he does.

Grant placed a penny on the counter in front of the parrot.

It'll take at least a nickel, the parrot man said. As if in agreement the parrot made a strangled sound, like a squawk.

Grant replaced the penny with a nickel. The parrot grabbed the nickel in its beak, flapped its wings and flew to the rim of a tall glass container standing behind the perch. The string went nearly taut. Having steadied itself the parrot dropped the coin. It landed with a dull sound on a pile of nickels, dimes and quarters at the bottom of the container. Then the parrot returned to the perch. Behind Grant someone applauded.

Hey, is that something else? the parrot man said.

Ain't it supposed to talk? Grant asked him.

The parrot man glared. He's supposed to do exactly what he just did.

Parrots are supposed to talk.

Well, this one does exactly what I tell him to, mister. He's supposed to fly over there and drop that nickel and that's exactly what he did.

Grant gave this some thought. All right then, he said, and deciding he'd been duped like everybody else, moved on.

He bought dinner. This left him with thirty cents. The afternoon passed and he considered that he might skip supper and sleep again on the sand, but what then in the morning? He went back to the parrot man and asked him if he had any work. Nobody else was at the stand.

The parrot man blinked. Do I look like I got any work for you, mister?

I just got here. I don't have any money.

What do I care? the parrot man said, but then, Where do you come from anyway?

As if to balance against future lies, Grant told him about Eleven, the nearest town to the ranch. It was no home town but it came close enough.

You fought the war?

Yes.

The parrot man nodded. I was a cook over in France. Boy, I don't ever want to pick up a fry pan again.

How about that cooking spot? Grant said, an idea beginning to form. The parrot paced, occasionally opening and closing its beak.

What about it? It's ruined.

What if I clean it up and try and get a little extra business going?

The parrot man frowned. I'm going to get myself some skee-ball for over there, he said.

Well up until then, Grant said. I'll clean it up free. You don't have to pay me nothing until I get it working. I'll take whatever you can give me, I don't want for much.

You're staying someplace respectable, right? The skin seemed over-tight across the parrot man's face, a chart of all the fretting he'd done in his life.

I got a room, Grant lied.

The parrot man paused to take somebody's money. For a minute he appeared to have forgotten Grant. Then he held out a bill and said, You go get something to scour it with and come back here. Tomorrow morning I'll get the truck to bring the food. You know how to cook, don't you?

Grant put the bill in his pocket. Sure.

All right, the parrot man said. He looked more worried now, as if he thought he'd made a mistake. Grant smiled at him but the parrot man took it wrong and scowled.

There was not much in the way of rooms. As he walked west the rates dropped. When they got low enough he walked north until he found a landlady who would let him wait until the next day to start paying. She was heavy and old with a pale expressionless face like a reflection in a china plate, and she sat in a wooden folding chair behind a grimy linoleum counter. A scratched glass bowl was sitting on the counter with a handlettered sign: DO NOT HAND ME YOUR MONEY PUT IT IN THE CUP. From an open door behind her issued the sound of a radio. She dropped a key into the glass bowl and Grant took it out. He had better pay two nights tomorrow night, she said, or she would send her husband up to kick him out. Grant told her he understood.

She leaned forward ever slightly and said in a low voice, This place is full of niggers. They will steal the fillings out of your teeth.

Yes, ma'am, said Grant.

The lobby was painted with what might once have been a cheerful yellow but had been corrupted by water stains and the husks of dead insects. A low table had old magazines on it and there was a dry astringent smell as if hundreds of newspapers were stored nearby.

He went to his room. It was about six feet by ten with a high ceiling and a narrow mattress bowed in the middle like a phantom boarder was asleep on it. There was a chair and a small table and a tiny closet with three wire hangers inside. A shallow sink had a sliver of soap on the rim and a square mirror above. The walls were stained but not too badly. His window overlooked an alley and a smaller building, and if he leaned to one side and pressed his head to the glass he could see a strip of beach far off to the north. For awhile he watched the strip of beach until the shadows of the fancy hotels threw themselves over the sand, obscuring its bathers. Then he lay down on the sunken mattress. It was not uncomfortable but he doubted its strength. He lay gingerly, trying not to move around.

The room was all right, though it had too much in it for its size. He looked up and considered the ceiling, where a specked length of fly-paper dangled from a nail. All that empty space up there with no way to use it. He closed his eyes and reviewed his war story. Japan. He pictured palm trees and little flat thatch houses, and the Emperor's men peering out of them with their rifles.

He should have gone. The local board had considered their defer-ment applications and told John to send one of the boys, one only. Max was too young to go, though he begged. Thornton had no idea what he was getting into. It ought to have been Grant who went and who was sunk in the South Pacific. But their father kept him, because he didn't trust Max to work reliably and because Thornton was the kind of help he could easily hire. With Edwin dead he needed to teach someone to run the ranch. Max argued that he could take Thornton's place, that he could go and call himself Thornton Person and pass for eighteen, but John would have none of it. I won't have my sons lying, he said, there's no honor in a lie.

No honor in staying home, Max said.

Grant might have said anything at all but he kept his mouth shut. It is awful quiet around here, Max said to him. Their father did not speak up in his defense.

I got work to do, Grant said and got up from his chair. They were all in the kitchen, the three boys and their mother, her back to them, washing a sinkload of dishes.

Hey Grant! Thornton said. Hey, where you going? We're just talk-ing. It was intolerable to him that they quarreled and intolerable that their father's will be questioned. The boys towered above John Per-son like miraculous crops.

It was never clear why their father mistrusted Max, who was fifteen in 1943 when Thornton was sent away, and who had never once appeared late to do his work or skipped school or engaged in any foolish thing that most boys were forgiven for instantly. But John dis-liked him. He made no effort to conceal it. Every time he opened his mouth in criticism of Max he would praise Grant before he closed it, and while Grant had no use for this misplaced attention he was powerless to refuse it, the way a thirsty man can't help drinking bad water. John acknowledged the rivalry that sprang up between them but did nothing to set it right, believing the boys ought to be able to work out their problems themselves.

John often said with apparent disgust that Max took after his mother, and this was true. Like her, Max was competent and self-reliant. She was the braver of their parents, Grant saw now, because she never hesitated to love them and did not stop when they began to die. She once surmised to Grant that she was chosen to lose her children because she was strong enough to withstand it, which gave Grant to wonder if he then was chosen to be lost.

He had let Thornton go because he valued his life over honor, he valued his life over Thornton's life. He had got what he wanted. He was alive.

He returned to the stand just past dark with a soap bucket and some steel wool pads from a grocer's. The parrot man was surprised to see him. I thought you'd gone and run off with my dollar, he said. I was feeling like a goddam fool.

Sorry, Grant said, and handed the parrot man the change. The parrot man counted it carefully.

He got to work straightaway, grinding off the blackened crust and the years of grease glued up with dust and sand and salt. There was a basket for dunking potatoes in the hot fat and he toiled at this for hours, gradually exposing the steel mesh until it gleamed. When he looked up it was late and the parrot man was watching him. The parrot was in a cage up on the counter, talking quietly to itself.

What's it saying? Grant asked.

The parrot man paused to listen. I don't know if it's foreign or if it's something he made up himself. Anyway, I don't understand a word of it.

Has it got a name?

Who? Him? He crossed his arms over his skinny chest and his eyes grew limpid and sad. You know what, I guess I never call him a goddam thing. I just talk to him. I don't call him nothing at all.

Grant cleared his throat. I need some money.

The old tight face snapped back into focus. You ain't cooked a thing yet.

You'll pay me tomorrow? My landlady needs her money.

The parrot man backed up a step as if he thought he was being tricked. You come in here tomorrow and fire up that frypit, you'll earn your money.

Grant nodded, satisfied. He and the parrot man swung down the boards that served as an awning and latched them in place over the windows. Then the parrot man locked the door. He took a key off his ring and handed it to Grant. You'd better be in early, he said. I got the truck coming here at six with your supplies, and you got to put up some kind of menu. There's going to be potatoes and pierogies and the like. You'll see it when it gets here.

All right.

The parrot man draped a purple cloth flecked with yellow stars over the cage, an artificial night. The parrot was silenced. For awhile they stood there, Grant waiting for further instruction. None came. He said goodbye and set off down the boardwalk.

When he reached the stairs down to the street Grant looked back at the game stand. The parrot man still stood in front, the cage on the counter beside him, staring off at the starlit outline of the sea. Grant raised a hand to him but the parrot man never turned.

•

The next morning he unpacked the boxes that waited for him and stashed the raw food in the cooler. He dumped several blocks of cut fat into the frypit and fired up the gas. Then he found a grease pencil under the counter and wrote a menu on the back of the supplier's receipt. He raised the awning and hung his menu on a nail. Fifteen minutes later a man asked him for eggs and potatoes, and he made them and took the man's money. It was easy. At the day's end the parrot man tore down the menu and wrote up a new one, with higher prices.

The parrot man allowed him breaks, which he spent exploring the boardwalk. There was a hotel for rich people that looked like a wedding cake and a place where cars of the future could be seen and touched. And of course there was the horse, which as promised leapt into the ocean hourly with a girl on its bare back. The girl wore a bathing suit and smiled all the way down, even as the water came up to engulf her. Grant thought she must be brave and dreamed of meeting her, but he couldn't imagine how to approach her or what to say if he did. The horse, on the other hand, although it possessed a beauty flying through the air, up close proved old and tired, its coat coarsened by the salt water.

He sent a postcard home. It had a picture of the diving horse on one side and on the other he wrote:

> I am well here and have seen many amazing things. There is
> not a single hill anywhere. You can write me at this address.

And he gave the address of the rooming house. What he had written dissatisfied him, but it was his only postcard and he sent it without giving the matter much thought.

Business was often slow. It seemed there were plenty of other places to get fried food, most of them newer or cleaner-looking or with a larger menu. For this reason Grant's job did not feel secure. It was obvious the parrot man lacked much sense: it would have been easy to give the stand a coat of paint or pass out handbills or expand the menu, but instead he griped, asking Grant where all the customers were. Grant could only shrug. When idle he leaned against a post and watched the parrot moving back and forth on its perch. The bird seemed perfectly accustomed to this circumscribed life. Sometimes the parrot man allowed Grant to feed it a shred of lettuce, which the parrot accepted silently, champing on it for a minute or so until it was gone and then returning to work. Afterward Grant always lost interest in the bird and turned to face the ocean, another entity with a singular aim. Occasionally the sight of it sent him into a kind of trance, difficult to rouse himself out of. Sometimes he couldn't understand how people went about their lives in its presence. A thing so drastic, mocking them like that.

.

After one September night Grant woke earlier than usual and left his room to sit on the beach and plan or at least imagine what he might do next. Though it was before ten in the morning hundreds of people were out in the cool air, standing on the sand in their street shoes. There were no bathers at this hour. He walked through the crowd listening for clues to their purpose here, but learned only that something was expected to happen, some kind of show, and it would happen out at sea. The presence of these people on what he had come to think of as his beach irritated him and he found their proximity unnerving. Still, he chose a spot and waited.

Pretty soon a dot appeared out on the water and resolved into the shape of a boat. The static of conversation became a thrum and dropped off entirely as more boats bulged onto the horizon and drew into clear view, as if brought by the tide. From newspaper photographs he'd seen, Grant was able to identify these as transports.

It was in one like them that Thornton was killed. The ship had not been attacked but had suffered an explosion on board and sunk. It wasn't hard to imagine what this must have been like. The death was Grant's after all and had simply been lent to his idiot brother, who gratefully wrapped it around himself like a poisoned blanket. He imagined Thornton hunkered in his tiny cabin, straining to assemble in his mind all the evidence of danger; the deadened blast and the rushing water and the sudden darkness, the slide of objects from their customary places, and finally the ocean's blind hungry clench.

Just offshore now, the ships yawned open to frenetic applause, and from the guts of them came soldiers who knelt in the surf and fired upon the onlookers, and got up and ran, heavy with seawater, onto the hard wet sand and fired again. Women screamed and a few fainted dead away. Soldiers pulled up short and theatrically fell, writhing in mock death. And Grant knew genuine pain as the bullets entered him, even as he understood them to be imaginary; they found his heart and pierced it, tore the breath out of his lungs, swept his legs out from under him. They glowed inside him like irons. He was branded from within: the destruction his brothers had claimed was also his, was Max's and their mother's and father's.

He lay contorted in the sand forcing sobs from his body, oblivious to the sympathetic shadows falling across him, to the hands on his arms and back and head. He would not be helped. Instead he wanted to fill this ground with his tears and claim it as his own. He wanted to make himself an impossible promise, one he would sooner die than break but which he knew was already as good as broken, that he was never going to go back.

2

The parrot man fired him. It wasn't hard to see it coming and Grant had been prepared. By eating at work he had saved enough money to last him through several days of looking for a job. Nothing much had happened out of the ordinary, the parrot man had just finally had enough. He berated Grant, telling him he was a bad influence. The way Grant figured it, though, the parrot man had got it in his head to sell the frypit and griddle, which looked practically like new, and then use the money for the skee-ball game he wanted. Grant didn't blame him, much as he hated being shouted at.

I didn't do anything wrong, he protested, even as he untied his apron.

The parrot man's face swelled and darkened. It don't matter! he shouted. It's you! It's just you!

That night Grant washed his clothes in his room's small sink and hung them to dry in the narrow closet. The hangers there were rusted and the wallpaper soiled, so that the otherwise clean shirts bore crooked orange lines down the shoulders and a smear on one upper arm where the hanger butted the wall. To some extent these stains could be brushed off, and in the shifting colored lights of the street they were not easily detected. Tonight Grant had one clean dry shirt.

He put it on and went for a walk, determined to investigate the city's night life.

For a time he watched people shoot air rifles at wooden ducks. Winning the game earned them tickets which they could exchange for stuffed toys, gag items or small trophies. Later he sat on a bench facing the sea. Below him children played tag on the sand, lit by the bright city. But the activity around him only served to deepen his solitude. He felt like these people were stealing something, something he was unaware he had possessed or relied upon but which, once taken, seemed to represent a grievous and irrevocable loss. It was as if some integral, helpless part of him had been exposed and seized. When a group of young men passed him laughing he could practically see them reaching out toward him with greedy hands. Impulsively he leapt to his feet and trailed behind them to see where they would go.

There were four of them, pale bedraggled men with the weight of hard work on their faces like a heavy curtain. He could see that they were drunk. They left the boardwalk and entered an alley behind a hotel, where they vanished through an unmarked door. Grant lingered nearby. Voices, the smell of cigarettes. There was a bar in Eleven that Grant used to go to, all the time before the war but less often the longer he failed to enlist. Still, he felt at home among drunks.

He went in. It wasn't much different from the bar he knew. Dark walls and floor, the row of men's backs, a picture of the Sioux killing Custer. No music played. The men he had followed sat at some tables among girls and were already engaged in casual embraces with them. A woman served them all drinks which they set upon at once without looking up to acknowledge her.

Grant's entrance had brought no reaction whatever. He might not have been there at all.

At the bar he bought whiskey and sat facing the door at a table near the men. Behind him they cajoled and exclaimed and the girls laughed. For a short time he suffered in the wash of their voices, but before long the drink insulated him. He had no idea what he was doing here.

Someone bumped his table and Grant's hand shot out to steady his drink. 'Scuse me, buddy, the man said.

Grant looked up and answered, No harm done.

The man hesitated. He was big and full-bodied as a bull, but he had a frightened aspect, an incongruous nervousness around the eyes and mouth. He was one of the men Grant had followed. Whassat you're drinking there, he said.

Whiskey.

The man nodded and went to the bar. He came back with two glasses and set one on the table, leaving his fingers on the rim while he appraised Grant frankly.

After long consideration he said, Where you been, soldier? While he waited for an answer he licked his lips, pink and full like a woman's.

Peleliu, Okinawa, Grant forced himself to say.

Regular army?

Grant told him yes.

The man let out breath with obvious relief. I'm a navy man. Got myself discharged awhile back and couldn't wait to get back on a boat, if you can believe that. He pointed to the others. We're on a crew out of Boston, codfishing on the Grand Banks.

Grant nodded.

I bet you saw some action, the man said after a moment.

Saw my share.

Yeah?

Again Grant nodded, wary of where this was going and determined to keep it where it was. He said nothing.

Well come on over and meet the boys. We're just making some friends.

Grant joined the group. He finished his drink and soon another was put before him. He finished that one too. Everyone told him their names and he gave them his, but he couldn't keep straight who was who. Their personalities and faces ran together. A squared-off chin, a cauliflower ear, a round bosom under a cotton blouse. They asked him a lot of questions and he answered them, and sometimes they laughed at the answers. At some point one of the girls began to cry. One of the boys led her off and the two never returned. There was talk of fish and fishing and he must have told them about the parrot man, because that's what they were calling him by the fifth or sixth drink. Somebody shoved a crumpled paper into his shirt pocket and then he was alone on an empty street, and he was vomiting into the gutter underneath a flickering streetlamp. Next he found himself in bed, his hands gripping the mattress as if it was a raft asea. A certain water stain on the ceiling looked like a barren island. He bobbed around it as it spun above him and he vomited again, into the sink. After that he felt much better, and he cleaned himself up and looked out as the sun rose over the rumpled strip of visible beach. He brushed his teeth and noticed, in the mirror, the paper sticking out of his pocket. It was smeared and damp and read: CHALFONT HADDON HALL BACK ENTRANCE 8 AM.

Now he remembered. They were going to find him work, on their boat. He'd told them no, he was going home. That was his plan anyway. But he felt like a fool standing before the mirror, looking into his own drink-wracked face, he felt like he'd failed at whatever it was he set out to do. Here was a reason to wait: a way to buy time, the only thing he could afford. He wouldn't go back, not just yet.

He didn't know what time it was, he guessed five. He took off his clothes and washed them, then waited in his undershorts while they dried. In an hour he put on his one dry shirt and pulled on the pants still wet, and he packed the wet shirt and left. He dropped the key in the glass bowl at the unmanned counter. Out on the boardwalk he ate sausage and eggs and sat awhile to calm his stomach. He asked somebody where the hotel was, and then he went there. The rear entrance had a circular drive for cars and an area of white gravel with tropical plants growing in it. The seasons were changing and the plants were half dead.

They came in a black sedan without the girls. Somebody opened a back door and the men made room on the seat. Grant got in and shut the door and the car pulled away.

Holy Jesus, Parrot Man, what a night, someone said.

Hurts, was his reply. They laughed as if this was a joke. Then they exchanged stories about their drinking and about the girls. One said he couldn't get the dress off his.

Prude? asked another.

No, I mean I was too drunk. They laughed again. Meanwhile the buildings were shrinking outside and the sand thinning at the road's edge.

Where are we going? Grant said.

The driver was the bullish man who had bought Grant's drink. New York, he said. Fish Express.

Are we going to make it? someone asked.

Does Betsy have tits?

Their laughter died down and for awhile everyone seemed to be sleeping. Then they were in New York. The car was parked in a crowded lot. It had been rented. Pony up, one of the men said, and everyone gave him money. Grant counted out his share, half of what he had to his name. They shouldered their bags and walked dozens of blocks in silence. The sun was overhead and the tall buildings swallowed their shadows.

They arrived at a warehouse and walked around behind it where a train waited, its tank cars expelling a brilliant liquid like half-molten metal, which the afternoon sun shuddered upon as it flowed down troughs into the building. The liquid was fish. Grant stood and gaped as the others continued down the train's length. He had caught trout in streams but had never known such abundance of fish. They couldn't have been alive, nevertheless they roiled like a simmering pot. The hole they plunged into was black around them and they pulled the sunlight in their slipstream and reflected it from inside the darkness, like faceted gems.

Up ahead the men were signaling to him. He followed, ducking under the flowing fish, their scales rasping terribly against the trough bottom. The others were nodding to some men smoking outside a boxcar. Grant hurried to meet them. They climbed into the car and the smokers climbed in behind. The boxcar was equipped with benches bolted onto a rickety pine floor. Sunlight shone in strips through the narrow slatted walls and floor and spread across the car. The men found seats and smoked there, cleaved by the light.

There were maybe fifteen men altogether. They greeted one another with nods. Each had the pallid complexion and rimmed eyes of someone who had enjoyed himself to within an inch of his life. Some sipped from thermoses of coffee, a few ate sandwiches wrapped in waxed paper. Grant's breakfast had long since exhausted itself and he was simultaneously hungry and too nauseated to eat. He closed his eyes and fell asleep.

The movement of the train woke him. Men were starting to speak. They weren't all young as he was, most were too old to have been in the war and talked about other things. His companions were still on last night's girls. Grant had nothing to say at all and might not have even if he'd taken a girl home. He might like to talk to a woman but didn't see much point in talking about one with other men. He had dated when he was in school; there was a dance in a nearby town that once a year he rode to all day to get to, and all night to return. On those rides he liked the company of his own mind, liked to let it go where it wanted, to hypothetical situations and acts, perhaps with a girl he would meet that night. Sometimes he did meet a girl, but nothing beyond that night usually came of it. Mostly there was talking and some kissing. One time he met a girl with a reputation and she took him off to a riverbank for a couple of hours, and he often thought about that experience. He reckoned such a night could easily be had any time, it was what people liked to do after all, but he didn't care so much for afterward, when it could be hard to find anything to say. If he wanted to go to bed with a woman, he was going to have to find one he could talk with. But in his experience the ones who would talk didn't want to do it, and the ones who wanted to do it wouldn't talk. Maybe the two things simply did not go together. His mother had plenty of children but not much to say. He didn't want to meet a girl like his mother, so tough and unhappy.

Then again he didn't see himself meeting a girl at all. He felt very far from desire. Even so, he was lonely.

He looked at the men around him. Solitude hung on them like a soaking coat. And then he thought he could feel it on himself, leaden and cold, and suddenly he was no longer among them but with them, and of them.

Conversation waned. Some of the men peeked between the slats at what passed. From where he sat in the center of the car, Grant could distinguish bright sky from ground and ground from water, but little else. Instead he leaned forward with his elbows on his knees and watched the flickering railroad ties filled in between with gravel. This quelled his nausea and hunger, and from time to time, when the train crossed a river and the ground dropped away beneath him, a lightness overwhelmed him as if he was in flight.

They arrived at evening and leapt down onto a massive rail yard where freight cars surrounded them on every side. The men spread out and picked their way among the cars with the sun at their backs. At the yard's edge was a road and Grant followed the men along it. Gulls dangled overhead, tufted and greasy like dead wool, or stepped along the roadside in ragged regiments. The men turned onto a smaller road which led them to a wide and boat-strewn bay. Here the group wordlessly dissolved. Grant's companions led him around the bay's great arc to a ship of considerable size, as far as Grant could tell. They boarded via a gangplank that thundered with their footfalls. Men clinging to ropes that hung from the deck were scraping a barnacled crust off the hull. Once on board Grant was asked to stay where he was while the skipper was fetched.

From here it was possible to see where the bay emptied into the ocean, and the low land that curled back upon itself to admit it. Clouds massed to the north, and to the south the sky was slowly sinking deeper into blue. Behind Grant lay a huge city that until now had somehow escaped his attention. It had to be Boston. Sunlight careened through its buildings and they pulsed with an almost bodily translucence, like living things. All around him were men in unhurried action, coiling ropes (he would later learn to call them lines) and mending with large meticulous hands a vast sisal net threaded with glass bobbins. Cigarettes hung from their mouths. There was a sense of deep calm, as among pastured horses. He stayed very still, afraid of breaking it.

The skipper was short and thick and gave the impression of tremendous density, like he was full of lead. He arrived shaking his head no. Grant offered his hand and the skipper took it and held it for a scant moment, then dropped it suddenly so that Grant's surprised arm swung free at his side. Despite what he had been told, the skipper said, there was no work. But he knew a Brit who needed men.

It'll be trial by fire, though, the skipper went on. His crew took violent sick, there's hardly any of them left.

All right, Grant said.

You boys did good work over there, the skipper said with the tone of a man relating something he's just looked up.

Pardon?

Okinawa.

Thank you, sir, Grant told him and looked up and then down the shoreline, along the confusion of mastheads. Which way do I go?

There, I'm pointing at her now. She's the *Rose Adams*.

I'm real grateful.

Alone on the gangplank his footsteps made a disconsolate clang, and he wandered along the docks unsure of where on a boat to find its name. He asked passersby, some of whom pointed him so far one way or another, and at last he stood before the ship, and found his way aboard and asked an unoccupied man for the skipper.

You come to work? the man asked him. He spoke with an accent Grant thought might be French and wore his hair gathered underneath a black cap. A tidy ring of graying beard encircled his mouth and chin.

Yes.

The Frenchman nodded. For that you don't need the skipper, he said. He led Grant into a warren of steel passageways, through a lightless chamber full of tables and benches, through a low hatchway into a dim close hall lined with doors. The Frenchman opened one of these and motioned to Grant with an impatient hand.

Your bag, he said.

Grant gave him the bag and the Frenchman flung it onto the lower of two metal bunks. Each bunk was barely two feet wide, fitted with a thin cushion and two blankets, one for warmth and one folded as a pillow. A canvas belt was attached for keeping the sleeper in. Grant saw that he couldn't sleep here in the manner he was accustomed to, he would have to find a new way. There was a polished metal mirror in the berth and a low open sea chest on the floor divided in two by a board.

Come, said the Frenchman.

Grant followed him onto the deck. Here men were at work on a net much like the Americans', with bright golden-white patches gleaming among the dark sea-battered strands like late sunlight through a barn wall, the whole bunched across the deck and trembling under the sailors' fast hands. The net was woven of ropes in various thicknesses and in many patterns, with an obvious order that was nonetheless incomprehensible to Grant. He would learn this was the trawl, and that its use and care made necessary a vast new vocabulary that would become the core of his everyday speech. The trawl was as integral to this work as the ship itself. Even now Grant understood this: fish couldn't possibly have been caught from deep water until such a thing was conceived and fabricated. The Frenchman said something Grant didn't hear.

What?

The knot. You tie the knot? His fingers casually knitted the air in illustration.

No, I've never done this in my life.

There was no evidence that the Frenchman was surprised or annoyed. He nodded, taking Grant by the arm. They sat on lidded wooden buckets with the trawl on their laps and the Frenchman showed him how. As it happened he was not French but Belgian, and his name was Luc. The words eluded Grant but slowly he came to own them: becket, codend, belly, warps. They sat for hours until the sun was gone and then mended the trawl by moonlight. From time to time they moved to another section and Luc demonstrated, stringing the heavy iron bobbins onto the ground wire, repairing the frayed headline with fresh supple hemp. There were a dozen men around them, silent or whistling or singing quietly, speaking soft words to the trawl in accented English. They seemed to be from everywhere and nowhere, their foreignness a kind of commonality. They were thin, their motions sure. Grant pulled and wove the mesh slowly under Luc's eyes, aware the others' work depended on the strength of his own. For some reason this fact filled him not with anxiety but with clarity, like a sharp steady light. He tied and tested. Luc sat nearer than would be appropriate on land, touching the back of Grant's hand when it faltered. A boy named Brian with a narrow nose and large crooked teeth brought them coffee in a huge dented pot, coffee that tasted faintly of tea, as if the same pot was used for the two. The men whispered their thanks to him. He was the steward. Grant shook his hand and found his own fingers weak with pain. It would be three years before he went home.

·

The ship was a creature that lived on fish. It sailed to bitter and awful places, hauling fish out of the ocean, digesting them with its hands and knives. The Georges Bank thrashed it with storms and cold and tucked it away into epic fogs. It was flung and shaken by implausible waves, rolled by mad winds. Icebergs the men called growlers threatened to gouge them as they passed, and on calm days puffins sat on the water bobbing like buoys with the undulations of sea. There were many seas, some so flat and regular they seemed plowed, some violent and white as an avalanche. Calm seas changed color and texture from mile to mile, as range grasses thrived or foundered over the shifting character of soil.

As at home, life on the ship consisted of work and its consequences. Even the strongest bodies couldn't escape the pain of repetitive action. But the understanding among the crew was that work was preferable to repose. Rest meant less money. If this seemed a dreary kind of life, it could be said that few thought of it as life; rather the voyage served life, as it was lived elsewhere by other people. Though none of them ever said as much, they had come from the land and would always return to it. It was land they sought when they looked out over the water, however far away they knew it to be: land and its inhabitants: the people they hated or loved, who gave their lives meaning. And so much of the time that passed, heavy as it was with men's yearning, was dull. Dragging to and from port the men could find nothing to occupy themselves with, despite the crate of paperbacks that never left the boat and which few had read his way entirely through; despite the bottomless trough of personal tales they had brought which they told and retold and nobody seemed to listen to. The sea's cyclic fierceness murdered narrative. Instead it was superstition that gripped their imagination, a periodic terror fueled by the vagaries of nature. The behavior of birds and fish, the character of winds and waters, all were portents. Fear loved an idle man.

One man confessed he couldn't sustain an erection. He was the splitter, whose job was to debone and decapitate cod. He did this with such speed and agility that he frightened the others, some of whom confessed to nightmares about him and his knife. This man told them he had never made love to a woman, had tried but could not. A merchant he knew in Boston, he said, got him fresh ginger from Japan, because it was thought to be an aphrodisiac. He sucked slivers of it while he worked, occasionally stopping to chop off a fresh piece and spit the depleted one into the sea.

The chief engineer told them that he used to write daily letters to his mother, saving them in a velvet bag during each voyage with the intention of mailing them at once when he returned to port. On one voyage he argued with a Portuguese who beat him and flung the bag overboard. Now the engineer wrote no letters at all.

One man, the gogotier, who excised and preserved cod livers, never spoke at all. It was to his stoicism that Grant aspired—he didn't wish to tell his or any story. But Grant learned that he could be drawn out, and in the captive intimacy of the boat sometimes allowed himself to be. He revealed only the barest outline and the men filled it in with what they liked. By his silence Grant confirmed their versions of events. They made him into a marine of the Seventh Division and had him storming Orange Beach on D-Day. He fought bravely, and miraculously wasn't hit. At Okinawa a sniper nicked him. He showed them the rope burn and they held silent witness to it. Grant would hear of himself capturing and executing the sniper, would learn he had taken a Zero out of the sky. Over time the crew lost its veterans and took on younger men who had missed the opportunity to fight in the war, and these men held Grant up as a hero. It was thought that he had chosen this desolate life at sea as an antidote to the horrors of war. After awhile he began to act like this hero, speaking solemnly when at all, accepting without contradiction the respect of those he knew were his betters. Only the gogotier seemed to know the truth, or at least Grant feared that he did, seeing reflected in his hard hooded eyes the liar Grant knew himself to be.

He read his way through the crate when there were no fish to haul. The paperback mysteries, with their haunted heroes and wrecked lives, made his own life seem austere and pure, and the resigned French heroines of the pornographic novels filled him with a sick yearning. Like the engineer he wrote no letters.

By the change of seasons he could tell how long he'd been at sea, but the specific date was never clear. Time only mattered once the trawl was shot. Then, the roof of the water flashed under the projector's beam and they watched as the threads melted into it. Grant's heart learned to tick off each moment until the skipper called Let go everywhere!, and the boat levered like a jet underneath them and drummed full ahead. And then for two hours they ate flounders and drank coffee and the *Rose Adams* rolled through space.

They would wait on deck then, watching the winches turn until the beaded line of floats grinned on the water and the whole of the trawl outlined itself, humped beneath the surface like a grave. Boys at the gunwale hooked the trawl's fat body and the great boom swung out to pull the catch home. The bladder of fish climbed the hull and at last swung heavy above them, the terrible mass writhing in its mesh skin. Then Luc stepped forward and yanked the drawline and the fish flowed down and out around their feet, up to their waists, the cod's bulging eyes twitching against the caustic air.

Only then did work begin. They worked for eighteen sleepless hours at a time, sorting and gutting and salting the fish. Men went down into the hold where the cod were thrown and didn't come out until the following day. And on deck it was rarely a clement sky they worked under. This was the North Atlantic and the boat pitched and heaved like it was trying to slough them off. Waves washed the catch overboard or picked men up and flung them and knocked them out cold.

This happened to Grant. He remembered he was piking with the other men and next thing he knew he was sitting with them around a table, laughing at somebody's joke. He would discover that more than a week had passed. They told him he cracked his head on the outrigger. He fell unconscious, awoke in bed, recovered, went back to work and, when they had finished with the haul, spent several days reading books in his cabin. He never could remember so much as a minute of that week, up to and including the joke he'd been laughing at when he finally came to.

He visited countless port cities throughout Europe and North America. Sometimes he drank to excess and passed out in cheap motel rooms like everyone else. But mostly he walked through the filthy streets of foreign places wondering what living there would be like. He understood there was much to be learned by talking to the residents of these places, but could never bring himself to start conversations. Women came to the bars he visited and some of them were beautiful. Still he didn't approach them, for some irrational fear. He had a sense that he would be discovered, not simply his invented combat record but something terrible and empty that was inherent to him, some unsprung trap a woman might unearth and hold up inquiring before him.

One day he woke and saw his father's face in the mirror. He touched his lips and nose, the ridges under his eyes. A lock of hair formed a sleep-stiffened arch over his forehead, exposing the fine familiar lines there which deepened as he watched. Curiosity gave way to anger and he spat at his image. A ridiculous thing to do. As he wiped the mirror clean his throat burned with emotion, and he knew it was time.

The skipper was a rangy Englishman with an elusive kindness of face you had to search for to see. Whenever Grant encountered him, the skipper looked like he'd just heard a good story that he didn't have the time or inclination to repeat. On this day Grant found him alone on the bridge, staring into the wind as if calculating how it would turn. The hold was full of cod and they were headed for port in Canada.

I believe you have something to tell me? the skipper asked him. His prescience did not seem odd to Grant, only reassuring.

Yessir.

The skipper's thumb and index finger brushed against each other in a silent snap. You're leaving us, then? When?

In Halifax, I believe.

You have some plan? the skipper said.

Only to go home, sir. I got family I ain't seen in a long time.

Where is home? I don't remember.

I don't think I ever said, Grant told him. It doesn't matter.

The skipper nodded, his head aslant, listening to the sea. I don't suppose it does, he said.

As they drew closer to port a few of the men approached him to say goodbye. Luc gave him a compass he said he had gotten from his grandfather. Abashed, Grant accepted the gift.

But no one else came to him when they docked at Halifax. It wouldn't be a long stop and the boat had to be readied for another voyage. It was late summer now, and though the air here was clean and warm, the smell of habitation lay on it like a sixth sense, a mix of milled lumber and frying grease and automobile exhaust. The oddness of it was striking. He had smelled it in port before but this time he was part of it for good. He braced himself for contact with unfamiliar people. When he turned on the quay to raise his hand to the men, there was nobody at the rail. To them he was already gone.

A train brought him down the Canadian coast and all the way to Boston, where he ate fish in a seafood restaurant and spent the night in a familiar hotel. His bag held new things. He'd bought a carved whalebone box in Iceland. He had an ivory-handled flensing knife he won from a whaler in a card game. There was a corroded antique wristwatch he had pulled from a live fish, and Luc's compass, and his money, a thick sheaf of bills rolled up with an elastic band and stuffed into the toe of a black sock. He had made a lot of money in three years and spent nearly nothing. There might have been as much as ten thousand dollars, he didn't count it. During the night he woke in darkness and sat listening to the city. Tomorrow he would go.

•

But not home, not yet. First south by train to New York. There he bought a ticket west for two days later. Then he continued by bus to Atlantic City. He arrived after dark and carried his bag up and down the boardwalk, remembering. He'd thought he would never forget the diving horse, but the one diving now may or may not have been the one he'd known before. The girl riding it was different, that much was certain. The parrot man was also gone, the space he'd held converted to a taffy shop. The glass canister was still there, filled to the rim with gumdrops.

He walked inland. The shabbiness of the west side seemed to be creeping toward shore. The roll of bills glowed like a coal in his bag. He thought he was wandering, but soon he found himself at the door of his old boardinghouse, his fingers around the handle trembling with a child's anticipation. He didn't understand why. He hadn't been happy here.

The old woman was right where he'd left her, the glass bowl still in place upon the counter, the radio still playing in a back room. She looked up at him without recognition and he mustered a smile. She gave him the price of a room.

I used to live here, he said. About three years ago.

Looks like you're back, she said.

Just for a night.

Suit yourself.

He wrote his name on an index card and paid her in advance. She dropped the key into the bowl and he took it and headed for the stairs.

Hold your horses, she said. You got some mail. She rooted under the counter and brought out a basket of envelopes, then sorted out one, two, three of them and laid these on the counter next to the bowl. Name rung a bell, she said.

Grant went back and picked up the letters. He recognized his mother's handwriting on one and Max's on the others. His mother's had been posted some time ago, Christmas 1945. Max's were more recent. Holding them in his fingers, he thought they must be impossible.

His room was just like his old one except with a better view. Outside, the boardwalk glowed under a new profusion of lurid colored lights. He set his bag on the bed and sat down next to it. Then he opened the letters.

Dear Grant,

I hope you are well. Your father and brother and I are work very hard and the flock is pretty healthy. We hire an extra man but he is a drunk, so now we are looking for another. I hope it might be you but your father will not hear of it.

I do not know exactly why you left from home but I think I understand. Sometimes in life I thought I should leaving if I could, but I never did. But I have to ask you please to come home. It is important I know that you are all right.

My thoughts are with you.

Sincerely Mother

Grant

Mamas sick. A hired man is cooking the food and tending the cows and chickens, but she is very sick and you better get back. She is in her bed day + night and doesnt get up. Daddy yells at her to get up because he thinks shes faking and it is no good for her condition, despite that he is just a bastard all the time.

Dont think Im writing this because we need you to run the place because we dont. I could care less if you come back but Mother wants you so I am writing this for her.
Max

Grant

Mamas dead and buried here at home with the others. I wanted to bury her somewhere else but Daddy insisted. Enclosed is death notice in the paper. I thought you should know.

The letter was unsigned. He pictured his brother, pale and black-haired, bent twiglike over the old office desk in the shed writing to him. He read the letter again, making sure he had gotten everything right.

Grant unfolded the notice. On the back was half a coupon for whole cut chicken from a grocery.

PERSON, Asta, née Einarsdottir, died September 5 at home near Eleven. The deceased was born in Iceland in 1897 and came to the US with her husband John Person at the close of the first World War. She is survived by John Person and two sons.

He put the letters back in their envelopes and set them aside. After a time he lay back across the bed and later fell asleep.

In the morning he woke and took up his bag and went out, leaving the letters on the hopeless mattress for whomever might find them. He dropped his key in the bowl and walked to the beach. Dawn had broken and had begun to uncover the night's activity. No footprints marred the surf-dredged sand. Slick dark branches and clumps of seaweed dotted the shore, as if there'd been a storm in the night. Maybe there had been. He weaved between pilings under the piers and wandered onto a stone-and-cement jetty to look out at the sea.

He had meant to say goodbye to it, to the ocean. It was possible he would never see it again after today and it seemed right to take one last look. But the ocean he knew was nowhere evident. Here it had no character or identity. This was where it met the land, nothing more. He watched it advance and retreat then continued down the beach, still gazing out, still searching for its familiar faces.

On the far side of the Million Dollar Pier he saw a group of standing people staring down at a shape in the sand. There was a tall thin man, a Negro, wearing a straw hat and a cream-colored linen suit slightly too small for him. A white woman stood with a boy of about six. Grant came up close and saw that the shape was that of a man. He was heavy, short, his features bleached by the salt water. A gray pin-striped suit jacket and pants adhered to his body, but he wore no shirt underneath. His feet were bare. Sand was stuck to the suit and to his hair and three ragged bloodless holes gaped in his chest, another smaller one in his forehead. A large gold ring with a green stone was on a finger of his left hand.

Mama, that's a dead man, the child said, the words all run together as if they'd already been said many times. He tugged at his mother's hand.

No, she said, that isn't a dead man, now let's go. But they stayed. The woman was young and black-haired and stared helplessly at the body.

The Negro said, turning to Grant, That is a gangland rubout. I suppose somebody ought to be told. He was looking at Grant as if Grant ought to be that somebody.

Without thinking Grant knelt before the dead man and turned back the lapel of his jacket. In the inside pocket he found only sand and salt. The outside pockets were also empty. The trousers stuck flat against the dead man's legs and nothing was outlined in the pockets there.

When Grant stood up the woman regarded him with shock. She gripped her boy's shoulder and pulled him to her. He is, the boy said, he *is* dead.

Come, she said, and turned, tugging him along with her. He stumbled and fell in the sand. Wordlessly he picked himself up and followed her toward the boardwalk.

This city ain't the same, the Negro told Grant. I was a boy during the prohibition. You expected to see this kind of thing in those days, but now we're supposed to be in another sort of era.

Nothing'll stop a body from dying, Grant said.

That ain't what I mean, came the terse reply.

Grant left him there and walked up the beach a ways before heading toward town. The dead man's waxy face followed him as he walked, a terrible face, Grant thought, that might not have been improved by life. Its features were spread flat as if pressed into glass, the mouth and nostrils wide and black and the chin smoothed over, by fat or the effects of water he didn't know. The face was so unlike his mother's. Her fine features barely registered, like quick strokes of a pencil. She could never occupy the same state as this man, her flesh never take on the mass, the burden of death.

The boardwalk seemed tainted by false optimism, its proprietors brisk and enthusiastic in their preparations. They reminded him of farmers he'd known, steadfast men who believed that God and the land would provide. He remembered his father, who had left his home country and never returned, in his struggle to live having lost the opportunity to do so. Obligation pulled Grant and he grew eager to leave.

He walked west until he found a diner, where he was served black coffee and a thick slice of moldy cake. When he complained the waitress reached over the plate for his fork and took a sizable piece into her mouth. She chewed it and swallowed and said she didn't taste anything funny, so he took her at her word and finished the rest himself. It seemed important to have faith in her opinion.

There was nothing left for him here. He paid and went to the bus station to wait. So far the weather had been fair but now a cold wind picked up and chilled him. He pulled a jacket from his bag and put it on. The world was still, the sun steady in the sky.

He wondered how they got his mother into the starveout. Probably his father and Max lifted the casket up onto the truck and drove there, with the box clattering on the bed behind them. And then what? Did anyone else come for the burial? There were ranch women who when they went to town were greeted and talked to and touched, but his mother had never been one of them. It was possible that none of these women went to pay their respects or even sent condolences to the house. They may not have known she was dead until they read it in the paper. This is the way their father would have handled the matter. He needed them now, his living sons, both of them.

Some hours later a bus came and took Grant to New York. He ate and slept at the station, his fingers tight around the handles of his bag. In the morning he bought a newspaper and found a story about a body washed ashore in New Jersey. The deceased was thought to be a minor mob figure. No other details were provided about the man, save the peculiar shambling walk he was known for when alive. It was unclear who killed him or in retaliation for what offense, but an investigation was being opened by the police.

Grant inspected his fingers where they had touched the dead man's coat. There was nothing unusual about them. Even so, he felt defiled by his involvement, peripheral as it was. He felt that something of the dead man had seeped through the skin and was running now in his blood. He flexed the muscles in his fingers and watched his hands open and close like machines.

When the train came he folded the newspaper and stood. The events of the world were unimportant now; all that mattered to him was his place in it. He threw the newspaper into the trash and climbed on board.

3

He woke before Chicago certain someone had taken the seat beside him and was gazing at him with malevolent intent. But it was an old woman, seemly and upright, staring straight ahead. He blinked. In his ebbing sleep the world was all stirred up, its visible parts set off strangely against one another. He sensed that he'd dreamt but could not remember what.

The train was moving west. Though he had passed by here before, the towns outside looked flat and alien, the light dimensionless. He felt with his feet for his bag and found it under the seat, right where he'd left it.

It would have been easy to get himself a berth to be alone in. He had the money. But this would have seemed a waste, and he'd have wished he was out among the other passengers. Solitude was polluted; he'd had enough of it. He could smell fish on his clothes: there was nothing to be done but throw them out and buy some new. He wondered how long until Chicago and asked the woman beside him if she knew the time or where in the world they were. She examined the back and then the palm of her small white hand, then told him she was afraid she did not know.

As it happened they were very near Chicago. Grant disembarked with some relief. He bought a basket of fish and ate it on a bench next to a trash can. The fish wasn't fresh and had been cooked in old grease, and he could smell spent cigars and discarded lunches in the garbage, but there were no other benches in sight and he was too tired to stand. He was the first to board the train home. The seat he chose lacked adequate leg room, though by the time he realized this the train was full. He stayed there for the next day and a half.

Twice he was gripped by strange fears. The first came as the train left Chicago. He was watching the stockyards the tracks snaked through, the animals inside them so unlikely against the backdrop of warehouses and tall buildings. The wheels moaned, and suddenly he believed he had left something behind on the platform. He panicked, his hands flew to his bag. Again he found it where he'd left it. But this gave him little comfort, even though he hadn't carried another thing since he left home three years before; and for much of that first day his legs ached and twitched, yearning for the station and whatever it was he had abandoned there.

Then, that evening, he looked up and saw a small pale face regarding him from outside the cabin. Its eyes were in shadow and it raced alongside the train. But it was night and the compartment dimly lit, and the face proved to be another passenger's reflected from across the aisle.

The train couldn't be stopped at Grissom except to pick up a new traveler, and since there was none he would get off at Ashton, a city of about twenty thousand that lay an hour's drive from Eleven. It was just as well, there would be no one to pick him up in the ghost town, nor any telephone to call for a ride. Ashton was where the hospital was, the one Robert hadn't reached in time. Their lambs went to market in Ashton and the wool was graded and sold there.

It was late September, still warm. A wind lashed the Ashton depot that in January could freeze a man to death. Grant stepped off the train and leaned into the gale, his bag and arm with it driven out behind him. Men staggered past in city dress, clamping their hats to their heads. The streets seemed abnormally wide and the cars more and newer than he remembered. He went into the Ashton Dry Goods, bought new clothes and changed into them. The old ones he left behind, in the trash. He entered a steakhouse and ate a steak. Then he turned back toward the station, walked several blocks along the tracks to Ashton Supply, and pushed through the door. He looked up and down the feed and seed counter for anyone he knew. Only the proprietor, bald, narrow-eyed, was at all familiar.

You know of somebody headed for Eleven? Grant asked.

The proprietor's eyes took in Grant's new clothes and landed finally on his face. What's your name? he asked, as if he ought to have known it but had momentarily forgot.

Person.

Person, okay. Your people was here not long back. But no, I don't believe nobody is headed out that way.

I just got off the train.

Looks like you have, he said. Tell you what. There's a dude around here somewhere who I bet'll take you where you want to go. I believe I seen him putting on every hat we got.

Grant thanked him. He found the dude as promised, standing before a window trying to discern his reflection in the dusty glass. He was tall, about thirty-five, with the rumor of a yellow beard and fresh-bought ill-matched clothes. But there was a tragic leanness to him, and a sharpness of eye that marked him as smarter than he looked from a distance. One of his hands adjusted the hat on his head and the other held a folded-up map.

Pardon, mister, but I been told you might give me a ride.

The dude twitched. His map rattled in his hand. Me? Really? he said. The hat had a price tag attached to it which lay against his ear on a string.

I need to get to Eleven.

The response was an apprehensive glance. He unfolded the map and turned it around in his hands.

It's right the other side of the flats, Grant said, here. He leaned over and put his finger on the place. The dude had a scent to him, a boozy sort of perfume.

Well, that isn't on my way.

Where're you going?

He fingered the cuff of his coat, lambskin with wool on the inside, too hot for the weather. Nowhere, really, he said.

•

The dude's name was Ted Purcell and he came from Peoria, Illinois. He seemed to name the town not with the expectation that Grant would recognize it but to impress upon him the great distance he had come. People from the east had a tendency, Grant noticed, to consider travel by car or train or airplane rigorous and brave. Knowing what he did about life there, Grant supposed this was a sensible thing for them to think. Still, he only gave Purcell his name and offered no congratulations. They were riding old route five in Purcell's new red Ford pickup, its elaborate radio failing to draw a clear station. Purcell had bought the hat and was wearing it now, the thong cinched tight under his chin.

So what do you do out here, Grant?

Raise sheep. But I been away awhile.

Is that so? I'm away myself.

Grant could only nod in answer.

You could say I'm on a little vacation. I'm a salesman, not door to door, or rather I go door to door you could say to big companies, and sell them the numbers they need to operate. I sell information, statistics. That might seem funny to you.

No.

Oh? Purcell said. Okay, good.

He reached out and turned off the radio, but by now the static had fused with the sounds of the engine and asphalt, and its sudden absence shocked them into silence. It felt like they had taken flight. A while later a truck with a wide wooden bed clattered by, heaped with hay bales. Some of the hay fluttered against the windshield and Purcell ran the wipers, though the hay had already blown away by itself. White-faced sheep were clustered on a distant hillside. Breeding season was long under way, and a current of emotions roiled through Grant, dizzying and strange. His palms and forehead perspired.

A kind of vacation, Purcell said. Usually, since I travel a lot with my work, I take my vacations at home. With my wife and daughter. I'm married to a terrific lady.

He held up his ring for Grant to see.

But this time I don't know. I just don't know what I'm doing out here, I really don't.

He continued: It's beautiful country out here, don't you think?

I don't tire of looking at it, Grant admitted, and this was exactly what he had been thinking, that to see a hillside covered with sheep filled him up near to overflowing. He licked his lips, sitting straight as if to keep from spilling.

Purcell said, How much farther along here are you?

Not much.

The first buildings came into view a good two miles out, wind-raked board structures half leaned over and filled with weeds. It was as if Eleven had tried to grow once, but its extremities had shriveled and died of their bloodless distance from the town's weak heart. There were probably old men who could tell him who had lived out here. Now cattle were grazing around and in the wasted buildings.

Here were a couple of farms run by drunks, with their ragged mongrel stock rooting in the trampled pastures. Whenever Grant's father culled a ewe with a bad jaw it was to these men he sold it cheap. And then came Eleven itself, low, blown dry, its paint peeling. Patchy-looking bored horses foraged out behind the post office and market and garage. Grant signaled to Purcell to pull over in front of the bar, marked as such only by the chipped tiles set into the front stoop which crookedly spelled out the word BAR. Purcell obliged and shut off the truck. Stillness settled over them like a tarp.

Wow, Purcell said. This is your home town?

Not strictly speaking. It's the nearest town to it.

A couple of men had come out of the bar and were gawking at Purcell's truck. Grant knew them. One he had finished high school a year behind. The other was the first one's father. They owned the garage across the street, but the bar was where you had to go to pay for your gas.

I appreciate the ride, Grant said.

Purcell flicked his finger at the keys where they hung from the ignition. Are you going in for a drink? he said.

In fact Grant had thought he'd just ask somebody for a ride home. Some part of him didn't want Purcell to know exactly where he came from. But as his hand tightened around the door handle he told Purcell that he could stand a drink.

I believe I'll join you then, if you don't mind.

All right, Grant said. But lock these doors. My bag.

The father and son looked them over good as they passed. Their name was as lost to Grant as he imagined it was to others, but it didn't matter. One could be identified with respect to the other—the son, the father—like a couple of undistinctive boulders notable for lining up in a particular way. They were a landmark, a point on the map.

Inside, Grant discovered that a radio had been added to the bar. A Maddox Brothers song was playing. Nobody danced. Instead there was a rhythmic sort of drinking, a methodical scrubbing away of all memory of work. It made a sound, a throbbing human static of brittle voices. He knew the sound pretty well but in his absence it had taken on a humorless intensity he didn't like. He recognized men who had been in school when he left town, whose eyes, in the interim, had crystallized into malevolent little pearls. All this he appreciated in a matter of seconds, a few steps beyond the threshold of the bar. He stopped Purcell with a hand.

I ain't leaving with you, he said. Don't get caught short in here. Some of them come in looking for a dog to kick, and you don't want to be it.

This is really something else, Purcell was saying. Wow.

Grant saw two men looking at him from a table, one seated and one standing. The sitting one was named Cotter. He was a towering hand of about sixty with an exhausted, disproportionate face, who had occasionally worked at the ranch. The other man fixed things, Grant couldn't recall his name. This second man had been getting up and now he walked past them and out of the bar.

Grant met Cotter's eyes. I'm gonna talk to that man there, he told Purcell.

Okay, go right ahead.

He went to the table and sat down. Working for my father these days? he said. Cotter had a glass of something black and viscous-looking in front of him. His eyes tumbled over Grant's face.

Up until recent, he enunciated, like they were foreign words from a book.

You quit?

Cotter smacked his lips. Been away, have you?

Yep.

Where to?

The Atlantic Ocean. I fished out at sea.

You want to know the truth? Cotter said. I'm still working at your place. But I ain't working for your father no more, cause your father has gone and quit this county, just like you done.

Grant waited a moment before saying, Quit where to?

I ain't with him, so I don't know.

I'm coming back, Grant said, and since it didn't seem like enough added, I'm back for good.

Cotter nodded, examining him as if he was some rare animal, subtly different from the common variety. If Grant remembered right, Cotter had a wife once who quietly walked out on him. He moved onto the ranch and worked there two years, frequently neglecting the animals and buildings and pens and fences he was supposed to maintain, in favor of a lot of private drinking. During the second winter he nearly froze to death, after which he was fired. Grant might have been ten at that time. Cotter said, Who in the hell is that you come in with?

A man who gave me a ride from Ashton.

Looks like he needs a wet-nurse. He turned to Grant. And you look awful pretty yourself. A smile seemed to be thinking about appearing on Cotter's face, but it never arrived.

Grant opened his mouth to reply but the new clothes were too complicated to explain. Already he was changing his mind, wishing he had asked Purcell to take him all the way. So are you headed out there? he asked Cotter. Out home?

If you could call it that, Cotter said nodding.

But you're going.

Wouldn't be in such a hurry if I was you. He leaned back in his chair. You had better drink something.

Grant obeyed. They sat and watched Purcell as he fell in with a couple of show riders at the bar. The riders were lanky and polished, kids by the look of them, shooting glances at one another behind Purcell's back. They were buying him whiskeys which he haggled over with the bartender, demanding he bring the bottles up close so he could look at the labels. The riders had a great laugh at this and slapped Purcell too hard on the back.

Grant fell into a protective frame of mind. Plenty of people were laughing in this bar tonight but all of it seemed to be at somebody's expense. At every roaring table was a man with his chin in his lap. Just once, Grant thought, he'd like to hear a good joke. He would enjoy a good gentle kidding.

His mother used to be funny, before Wesley took sick. It was no specific memory that told him this but a general sense of absence, like a room shut for winter that nobody remembers to open back up. In fact he couldn't place a smile on her face in his mind, nor could he recall the face entirely, only its individual features, without particular expression. He could remember the sound of his own high laughter, and Max's strange chuckle, knowing and sharp for a child of two.

Cotter must have come the spring after Wesley died. The chinook ought to have brought them some kind of hope and instead it brought Cotter. He arrived on foot having got a ride as far as the crossroads.

Grant was playing on the front porch with the younger boys and Cotter simply walked up the road and asked for their daddy. It was never clear how the men knew each other but John Person must have owed Cotter a chance. In any case their mother didn't like him and never once looked him in the eye. And here Cotter had outlived her, against all reason.

By now Purcell had put on a talking load and was audible where Grant sat, not in sense but in tone. The riders asked him questions and Purcell blurted answers, slurring and spitting his words. The three of them seemed to come to some agreement. They headed for the door, Purcell in the lead and the riders behind him with their fingers twitching at their sides. Grant didn't like the look of it. He was angry at Purcell for coming in here and angry at himself for letting him.

He got up and Cotter followed. Outside Purcell was fishing in the glovebox of the truck. The riders leaned against the bed waiting, one with his boot on the runner, rubbing the toe back and forth over the bright paint. They regarded Grant with proprietary glances but turned away entirely when Cotter filled the doorway behind him.

Grant said, Purcell, what in the hell are you doing?

Got to show these fellas something.

He turned around holding a gun. It dangled in his hand like a rag: an old-fashioned revolver, something he might have got at an antique store. He said, It's this thing I've been working on. Okay, where do we go to do this?

One of the riders motioned for him to follow. Grant put his hand on Purcell's arm and Purcell trained a dark look on him, a thing outside common understanding, intense and prophetic like a ewe in the bloody heat of birthing. It occurred to Grant that a man ought not to remind him of a sheep. He tightened his grip.

Leggo, Purcell said and jerked away. He turned to the riders. Okay, fellas, come on.

Cotter followed the three of them but Grant stayed behind to lock the door of the truck. Only while slamming it shut did he notice through the window a busy ring of keys splayed on the seat.

They went around back where beyond a half-acre square of weeds lay a dark and empty pasture, grown over with the baked bloomless stalks of wildflowers. They climbed a split-rail fence where a beam had slipped out of its notch and under moonlight gathered around Purcell while he fiddled with the gun. Off to the west a long hill was humped like a spine. Behind it lay home.

Okay, you ready? Purcell asked. He must not have expected an answer because he lifted the gun and started firing, pulling the trigger with a spasmodic motion and bringing his open palm down on the hammer for another round, a flip-cock, like a movie actor: one, two, three and four almost at once, five, and he staggered back on the sixth. His heel struck a clump of earth and he fell, and the shot went wild, straight up in the air. In the long seconds after, as the last report decayed, Purcell moaned and stirred and patted the ground around him for the gun. Cotter was the one who stepped up and moved it out of reach with his boot. The two men regarded each other. Under the moon Purcell's eyes were clear, and he blinked and a smile spread over his face like a stain. Then the riders laughed and one of them made a kind of rodeo holler, and Purcell sat up and shook his bare head. It was not clear what had become of his new hat.

He extended his hand, and there was quiet again as Cotter clasped it and began hoisting Purcell up. Then they all heard the whickering whistle and felt a sharp snap conducted through the ground to their feet. A little cloud of dust leapt up six inches to the right of Cotter where the bullet had hit.

Cotter paused to glance at the dust cloud moving off, then he pulled Purcell closer with one hand and used the other to knock him back down again. No insects were chirping in the wake of the shot, and the blow made a clear wet crack like a piece of meat hitting an iron pan. Purcell stood his ground a moment until Cotter let him go, and then he folded over and lay flat out on the ground. Cotter bent down, prised the slug out of the dirt, and tossed it onto Purcell's chest.

Maybe the riders had anticipated beating Purcell themselves. Their dejection was plain as they cleared their throats and turned back toward the bar. After a minute Cotter left too, and so did Grant. He felt bad for Purcell but what the Peorian had done was stupid.

In front of the bar Cotter was getting into a truck that Grant recognized as his father's. When he asked Cotter to wait, Cotter glared at him. I thought you wanted a ride home.

My bag, Grant said. It's locked up in his truck.

The two of them stood looking in Purcell's window awhile, at Grant's bag and the keys on the seat. Cotter said, How bad you need that bag?

It's got a lot of money in it.

Cotter nodded. He went over to the stoop, where he asked a couple of sitting women to move. They did, and he pulled a loose wedge of cement from the step. Then he turned around and flung it through the truck window. Glass splashed across the interior. He reached in and pulled out the bag and tossed it onto the bed of Grant's father's truck, then carefully replaced the chunk of cement.

I got work in the morning, Cotter said, let's go. He got in behind the wheel.

Grant wanted to rouse Purcell or at least put the keys in his pocket for when he came to. But his bag had been moved and he realized the necessity of moving with it. He took a last look at the bar's open door and got in the truck.

•

Cotter drove fast enough to kill them both. They climbed the hill obliquely and crested after several switchbacks, then briefly followed the ridge and angled down into the valley. The road ruts gripped and expelled their tires, flinging them from side to side. Whitetail deer leapt in the grass behind a roadside fence, and when the fence disappeared the deer came in slow motion across the road. Cotter missed them and swore. Grant didn't know if this was due to the close call or because he'd half hoped to strike one a deadly blow and bring it home to slaughter.

He felt the turn with his body's memory before Cotter spun the wheel to make it. They came to a stop in front of the gate and Grant got out to pull it open. When Cotter had driven through, Grant shut the gate and climbed back in. The road was deeply furrowed and uncared for. Grant's teeth knocked against each other and he understood for the first time how distant this place was from the one he used to know. On either side, beyond the headlights, the land was swallowed by darkness, as if the moon had been extinguished. Fixed above them, it was like a moon in a painting, illuminated without casting light. The land rose in front of the truck, and then the rise was behind them and the ranch stood blackly, outlined by a less comprehensive darkness. No lights shone in the windows. Cotter pulled up and turned to him and said, Good night, boss.

I ain't your boss, Cotter.

You're gonna be. The wound of his mouth took on a grin's shape. Don't get on your high horse and fire me.

Grant was left holding his bag in a still cloud of blue smoke near a dry tire-carved trench in the yard. The buildings were beginning to etch themselves into a sly clearness around him. Off to his left was the sheep shed, and he could tell at first by scent and then by sight that the animals were in it. Ewes spilled out along the fences like snow-clumps, sleeping. Beyond the shed the rams were likely penned, as the ewes by this time had been bred and would be coming down out of heat. Pretty soon they would go to winter pasture.

Up ahead at a bend in the road was the equipment shed and to its left the horse barn with the chickens penned up beside it, and a small yard. Rising on the right, hugged by the road, was the hill that ran up behind the house; past that was where the hands were quartered. On the hill was the pasture and starveout, where nothing was moving that Grant could see. The house stood at the base of the hill like a wagon that had careened down it and never again been touched. It lay barely held together by force of habit alone. Grant entered it, passing the woodpile arranged beneath the eave. The pile was insufficient to last the winter. He would have to go up the hill and skid down some logs as soon as he was settled. Inside, the house was cold and dark. He moved to the stove by memory and touched it. No heat.

Surely Max was here. But the house seemed empty, emptier than it ever had when he was the only one in it. He breathed the stagnant air and it smelled arid, like the outdoors. His quick breaths made him cough. The cough echoed.

He skirted the tables and chairs and felt his way up the stairs. At the top he found the hallway lit by that painted moon, suspended in the exact center of the paneless window at the hall's end. Two doors on each side, all shut. His own was on the left, nearest the window, with Max's across the way. The room that had been his parents' waited for him behind its warped door. A layer of dust coated the hall floor, with a scuffed track leading through it, ending at Max's room. Grant stood still listening and could hear neither his brother's breathing nor the movement of his body in the bed.

His own door yielded to a gentle push and cracked open with the small sound of a breaking seal. Bitter air flowed out. It was as if the room had preserved the cold from winters past especially for his return. He left the door open and went inside.

Nobody seemed to have been in here while he was gone. Enough grit had coated the windows to render them near opaque to the moonlight, and his bed was made in just the formal manner he would have made it were he planning to leave for a time. A couple of Indian arrowheads lay on the bureau, a folded handkerchief, a jawbone shaped like a crooked finger with a few teeth adhering to it, which he had found on the range and believed had come from an antelope. He set his bag on the bed and opened the dresser drawers. There were his clothes, and a few rocks with the shapes of ancient shells and leaves embedded in them, and a pack of cards depicting a tropical beach scene, and a photo of a girl he had gone to a dance with once and who had died of pneumonia not long after. He took off his clothes and dropped them on the rug, a crooked gray thing his mother had made out of rags, and put on a red union suit and a pair of woolen socks with holes in the heels. He shivered while his body warmed the fabric. Then he pulled the stale sheets back and got in under them, and stared at the wall at the bed's foot where a pencil picture was tacked. Max had drawn it as a child. It was a picture of the doglegged U of the valley with the house and the grounds nestled in the middle, from the vantage point of the hill out back. He put himself in the drawing, here in this bed under the northeast roof corner, and imagined himself to be asleep there, and soon enough he was.

·

He opened his eyes to the sight of Max in the doorway watching him. His brother was narrower than he was, his dark hair parted in the middle, his face stern and shaven and watchful with the clear blue eyes of their mother. He had the artificial stillness of a sitter in an old photograph. It seemed to Grant as the sleep left him that Max had likely been planning this meeting for years, and it was part of the plan that Grant should speak first, so he did.

I got your letters all at once. It was after everything happened. And then, when Max's expression failed to break, he said, I'm sorry.

Max raised his arm and rested it on the jamb. He was wearing his jeans and stocking feet and a wool shirt, and he sniffed in the way he always had on cold mornings.

Dad ain't here.

Cotter told me. Grant sat up and the dust came off him and the bed. Where's he got to?

Damned if I know.

How long's he been gone?

Couple of weeks.

Grant swung his feet out from under the bedclothes and set them on the floor. The boards chilled his heels. So where are we then? he said. We got a herder still? They ready to go to range?

Max met the questions with a hard glare and Grant saw how it was going to be. It ain't my problem, Max said. It ain't my goddam problem because you are on your own here, brother. Because I am planning to disappear myself.

Grant got up and pulled his pants on. Max had turned twenty this year, if he remembered right. Okay, he said, where are you off to?

Damned if I know, Max said.

There was not much of their father in Max's face. Some, though, at this moment: a studied expressionlessness which failed to conceal his satisfaction that things had gone bad in much the way he'd anticipated. But mostly Max was a ghost of their mother, with his high smooth brow and small mouth and thin nose that drew the eyes close together. In fact he might have been called feminine if not for the way the flesh gripped the bones in his face. If Grant squinted he could almost see her, waiting in the doorway for him to leave the room. This is what Max was doing, waiting. Grant obliged. Max led him down the hall and set his hands on their parents' bedroom door. He pushed it open.

It was me and Dad and Doc Lafitte, he said. Dad over on her left side there and Doc holding her by the wrist on the right, and I was in this chair at the foot. Just so you know exactly how it happened.

The bedclothes had been left mussed, the chairs off true in their places as if they'd just been got up from. The little closet was open and her handful of dresses hung up in it, a big straw hat on the shelf above them and shoes on the floor. The bureau that had been filled with their father's things was partly emptied, the drawers gaping, his wallet and comb gone from the top.

I think I got the picture, Grant said.

Max went back to his room and came out with a suitcase in one hand and a paintbox in the other. The box had an easel attached that could be unfolded and set up out of doors. Max had gotten this as a gift for his fourteenth birthday and occasionally took it out and painted pictures with it, but rarely had he offered to show them, nor had anybody asked to see. He passed Grant, who still stood at the open door, and vanished around the corner of the stairs. Grant went down after him.

Max was sitting on the floor pulling his boots on.

Who's the herder? Grant asked from the bottom of the stairs. Is it still Murray?

Yep.

He's coming?

Said he was.

Grant went over and stood by his brother. How about the record books? They out in the shed?

Max said, I ain't touched 'em. He stood up and took his coat off the hook and put it on.

How about the flock? Grant said.

Max grabbed his hat. He turned to Grant, putting it on his head. I would have to say the flock has seen better days. But like I said. It ain't my problem. He bent down for his box and bag and grinned without particular scorn. Maybe you'd like to open that door for me.

Grant opened it.

Cotter was outside standing by the idling truck. Behind him the sheep were bleating on the browsed muddy grass and the sun was beginning to ignite the ridgetop on the opposite side of the valley.

Grant called out to Cotter, You're coming back?

So long as you can pay me, I'll be back.

Max had set the suitcase down and was sticking out a hand for Grant to shake. Good luck, brother, he said.

Grant's hands were under his arms against the cold. Suddenly angry, he kept them there. This is what you really want to do? I don't know what there'll be for you when you come home.

Max's smile remained but lost its carelessness, tightening up at the edges, showing signs of effort. Didn't say nothing about coming home, he said, his hand falling. And he walked out to the truck.

Grant watched it pull away and over the rise, and then he was alone. He blinked at the gathering light. The sunline was creeping

down the mountainside. More ewes emerged from the shelter and
jostled one another looking for a clump of uneaten grass. He went to
the fence. Here it had come unfastened from a post and gaped out
like an old boot top. He pushed the wire up against the pine and bent
a rusted staple around it, and when he let go the staple gave way and
rattled on the freed wire. He ran his tongue over his thumb and tasted
the pitch there.

He did not know where to begin.

•

Cotter set to work as soon as he came back. He parked the truck
directly in front of the barn and released the horses into the pasture
behind it. Grant called to him that he would be in the shed seeing to
the books. Cotter nodded and continued working.

The equipment shed housed a rarely employed tractor, fencing,
feed, paint, water pipes, tools for shearing and the collapsed wooden
pens for lambing and a lot of rusted junk. The lights still worked.
Grant slid the door shut behind him and picked a path to his father's
desk. There were shelves bolted to the walls with ledgers and manuals
lined up on them. A lamp with a cracked green glass shade leaned
over a tin cup full of pens. The calendar his father had used for a blotter showed the month of June.

The oaken chair at the desk was worn smooth around the seat and
armrests, and when Grant sat down on it the joints adjusted soundlessly like a man's. He opened the desk drawers. One was packed with
files marked by year with that year's tax forms inside. The other drawers had tools in them or machine parts.

He reached up to the shelf and took down the last few years'
books. Each began with a penciled inventory of land and stock and
feed, followed by all bills outstanding and accounts unsettled. Then
came the year's receipts and expenses and a record of production.
John Person had run the ranch on a cash basis and the numbers ought
to have been simple and clear. But for some reason the books had

gone slovenly in recent years, with question marks appearing at the ends of columns and some not filled in at all, the penmanship itself staggering above and below lines and the totals at year's end left uncalculated. The erratic accounting dated from before the war and only intensified in the years Grant was gone. In the column marked STOCK for 1946 there was a barely legible notation—

circling 80? 100? 120?

—meaning, Grant guessed, that a hundred or so head had been killed by an infection of circling disease. It was bad that the sheep had been lost but worse that his father couldn't figure out how many.

He saw that a solid inventory of stock had been taken in January, one of the few sure figures in the ledger. The number was a full third less than five years before. They appeared to have under a thousand head now.

He took out a stack of files and read the tax forms of the past three years. They looked clean. He didn't see how they could be correct but there was no use worrying about that now. Instead he spent several hours estimating what they were owed and what they hadn't yet paid, and made a list of names of clients and creditors. These he wrote right into the ledger. The figures came out crooked from his unpracticed hand which had written near to nothing for a long time: the muscles remembered their fishing work and let him know they preferred it to this. In the end he came up with two figures, bound to be wrong: $2,100 and $9,700. The first was what was owed them, the second what they owed.

The men he spoke to on the telephone were brusque and polite, reading the numbers off to him without judgment. He didn't tell them whether they would soon be paid and they didn't ask. Grant made the calls sitting on a kitchen chair, and while he waited for responses paged through a four-year-old Montgomery Ward catalog hanging from a nail on the wall nearby. Somebody had bored a hole in the upper left-hand corner of the catalog and threaded it with twine, thinking to do exactly what Grant was now doing. Grant guessed that not much had ever been ordered from it.

The kitchen and supper room were all of a piece, the kitchen floor fitted with narrow dark boards and the eating area with cheap pine planks. Once the entire floor had been packed dirt, up until Wesley died. Soon afterward, Edwin got the idea that his brother's death was attributable to dust and vowed to raise the kitchen floor up off the ground. He learned how to cut and fit floorboards from a book and worked sporadically on the project for seven years, until he shot himself. The floor was never finished. For some time the table stood half on the new floor and half off, with cement blocks propping up the orphaned legs. The pine planks had been nailed down since Grant left. They were poorly measured and a gap of several inches between the wall and floor ran along the far side of the room.

Not long before his suicide Edwin confessed to Grant that he believed he himself killed Wesley, by whispering in his ear that night during supper. Though Grant begged Edwin to tell him, he never learned what it was he whispered.

By the time Grant finished his calls it was one in the afternoon. He'd been slightly wrong about the figures. They were owed less than eighteen hundred and had fallen almost eleven thousand behind. That he could use the money he'd earned to settle nearly every outstanding account seemed a fitting penance, but the decision to do it was slow in coming. It was also possible to sell the ranch and everything on it, but this raised the problem of finding their father, who owned it. Or he could keep his money against future catastrophe and run the outfit as if he had nothing whatever to his name.

He might have decided right then had the door not crashed open and the herder appeared. His dogs rushed in around him and stood sniffing the air, bristling with suspicion.

I'm taking the flock, Murray said. He gazed at Grant, seeming not to register who he was or who he was not. Confident now that Grant was no threat, the dogs came to him and smelled his open palms.

Let me come have a look first. I been away.

Murray blinked at him as if he couldn't see the point. He turned and walked out into the yard.

Grant put the ledger down on the table and followed. There wasn't much to Murray, a snarl of dirty black hair, brown trousers and vest, a nervous little face that looked like it had been out in a lot of bad weather. Around him hung an air of physical weakness and ill health. But in fact he was strong as an ant, able to perform without effort tasks a man twice his size would need a machine to do. Grant had seen him lift up a sheep and dunk it in the insecticide, the pasty bare arms holding the struggling animal in place for the requisite time, and then hoisting it back up and out of the tub as if it were an infant and doing this over and over for hours, without anyone's help. He was powered by will, violent and potent.

Now he was inside the fence with his dogs, and the ewes moved like blown smoke to the back gate. Murray called out to the dogs and they came around the flock and lay down by the fence. The sheep stood at anxious attention; a gentle wave of baas rippled over them. Murray stood with his hand on the back gate waiting as Grant came in the front from the road.

The sheep were Rambouillets and crosses, mostly white-faced, some black. They cleared a space around him as he entered, sidling almost, seeming to pretend that it wasn't Grant's presence but some random whim that made them go. Grant found himself ill at ease among them. From a distance of several feet they didn't look good: he saw long necks and paunches and patchy fleece. There were surely culls here, ewes that oughtn't to have been bred but had been bred all the same. He caught one by the neck and dock and moved her out of the band. Her head was scurry, the chest bony and thin. Others had weak or crooked legs or showed signs of disease.

One year could not have done this to them. His father had been letting them go bad for some time, at least since Grant had left, probably before.

He walked through the front gate and around the fence to Murray, who was letting the dogs lead the ewes out the back. Beyond the property Murray's piebald horse was hitched to his camp wagon, a rickety thing in a half-barrel shape fitted with truck wheels and a high stovepipe. The sight of it angered Grant, it seemed to speak to the whole rotten state of the outfit, and he said to Murray, It looks like a goddam hospital in there.

Murray swung his red face around and replied in a mutter. I bring 'em home at least as good as when I come for 'em. Whatever happens happens when I ain't here.

He didn't look at Grant while he talked. His mouth barely moved to let the words out.

I don't care a whit for you or your brother, he went on, his brogue like a marble in his mouth. I used to been working for your father and now I'm working for the sheep. When you got 'em they're your own responsibility. That's all I care to say.

He moved off calling to the dogs. When he reached the wagon he mounted it and led the flock out across the valley floor. Grant watched him awhile and then went back in the house. Upstairs he took the roll of bills from his bag and stuffed it into his shirt pocket. Then he collected the record books from the table and brought them back out to the shed. With the sheep gone the yard seemed deserted. Neither Cotter nor the truck was anywhere in sight. The horses stood flank to the sun in their pasture. Inside, at his father's desk, Grant found a box of envelopes and wrote a name and an amount on each. When he was through he counted out the bills and sealed them inside.

4

It was evening when he next approached the house. He could hear
the unfamiliar voices of two men behind the door, one of them talking
and laughing at something, the other one hoarsely mumbling back.
He stepped up onto the porch and the boards creaked. The voices fell
silent. After a moment he opened the door and walked in.

They were seated across from each other at the table with a deck of
cards spread between them face up and scattered, as if the game was
long over. Both looked up at Grant, one smiling and the other with a
stubborn sort of incomprehension. The smiler wore a felt hat which
he took off and set on the floor by his chair. The other one had his
chair tipped back. He pushed himself forward and the legs struck the
boards with a hollow sharp crack.

I'll bet you're Grant Person, the smiler said. He was about forty,
lanky and coarse. His had been the mumbled voice. It put Grant on
edge, seeming with each word about to give way to a cough. The
other man was half the smiler's age. He looked down at the table and
began pushing the cards into a little pile in front of him. His big still
shoulders and hung head gave him the appearance of a stump that
had begun to grow back.

Grant stood on the threshold, cool air sweeping in behind him. He leaned back out and collected some firewood, then dumped it in front of the stove and shut the door with his foot. I don't believe I know you, he said.

Kittredge, said the smiler, and raised up a hand like a calling card. It was the left and was missing its middle finger at the first joint. Obviously it was the man's habit to present the injury baldly, in order to preclude discussion of it. Grant was sympathetic to this tactic but wondered how a man could lose a middle finger without doing any damage to the other ones. Kittredge gestured with the hand toward the younger man and said, Petey, you ought to give Mr. Person your name.

Pete Neeler, he said without taking his eyes off the cards.

We're in your kitchen, see, Kittredge said, because this is the usual time supper gets eaten. I suppose your brother has took off, has he?

Yes he has.

I wonder if Petey and me even have employment to look forward to.

At this Neeler raised his head and gawked at Kittredge. We sure better, he said. God damn we better. Even if we don't we got some money owed us, that's for sure.

Grant decided to ignore Neeler and direct his inquiries at Kittredge. He said, You two been staying out at the quarters?

Yep.

Is it just the two of you and Cotter out there?

Kittredge nodded. Your brother brought in some Mexican shearers, and there was some men helping out at breeding, but now it's just us all. No dogs, no girls. And he smiled again, or rather widened the grin that seemed to be the natural state of his mouth. Grant found himself returning it by instinct. It struck him that he hadn't had occasion to smile at anything or anybody for more than a week, and he remembered that a week ago he had in fact been out on a boat in the Atlantic Ocean. He thought that he might have an ally in Kittredge.

Well, he said, there's always enough work that wants doing. I don't know how long I can pay you to do it though.

Fair enough, said Kittredge.

Somebody's going to need to bring down some firewood. And I ain't been up to the ditch yet, but how's the headgate looking?

Could use cleaning up, I'd put money on that.

Okay. Okay, we ought to get that taken care of before the freeze. So there's some work for you.

At this point Neeler reared back and looked clearly at Grant for the first time. Out of the corner of his eye Grant saw Kittredge go rigid in his seat.

Your brother said you was in the war, Neeler said. You took a long time coming back, didn't you? Where you been, then?

It was possible to believe in the innocence of the question, judging by the voice alone. But Neeler had a challenge in his eye even if he didn't know its full import. His eyes were set far apart under wild thick brows, his face was a knot, pocked and blunt and dumb. Grant said, I was doing some work on a boat off the Atlantic coast. I didn't fight in any war.

But your brother said—

He wasn't talking about me. He was talking about our brother that didn't make it back. Grant gave Neeler a minute to register some remorse or at least embarrassment but his face remained vacant. So what do you like eating, Grant said, and maybe I can try fixing it.

Your brother makes beans with bacon and good biscuits, Neeler said. And coffee.

That so? Grant asked, directing the question at Kittredge.

Kittredge nodded.

Well, that is something I can do, anyway, Grant told them and moved to the pantry for the food.

•

That night Grant found the broom leaning up against a wall of the pantry and began to sweep the dust out of the house. He did the kitchen and his own bedroom and then Max's. Max had emptied his bureau drawers but left much of what hung on the walls, drawings he had done in pencil, watercolor paintings of things Grant recognized from the valley, such as a certain rock set into a hillside or water flow-ing out of a spring. The pictures were spare and haunted, rendering the land as a scattering of crisscrossed lines and colored fields. Grant didn't know if they were good, only that they didn't represent his own understanding of the place. When he left the room he shut the door tight behind him.

He swept the hallway, erasing footprints: his own, Max's, maybe their father's. Then he moved into his parents' bedroom. He worked quickly, jabbing the broom into the visible spaces and pulling out the dirt. A presence here was urging him to finish the work and leave. At first he identified it as his mother's. But he trusted her death now and knew there was nothing left of her here. Not until he was through and the door was shut behind him did he understand: the presence was his father's, the presence of his absence, of his inevitable return. The house, the ranch belonged to John Person, and surely he would come back to it and would condemn Grant for what he'd failed to do, as he never had years before.

Before Wesley, Thornton had shared Max's room, and Robert, Grant's. Only Edwin had his own. This was the room still unswept, and Grant hesitated to enter. The window at the hall's end framed a moon barely changed from the night before. Its cold light threw the tendons and veins of his hand into sharp relief, into a landscape lunar in character. He wiggled his fingers, putting shadows into motion, and finally pulled the string that brought the hall light to life. The moon was lost in glare. Grant pushed open the door.

Only Edwin's bed remained, supporting a bare lopsided feather tick and surrounded by chairs, as in a theater. He recognized the chairs. They had come from the kitchen. As many as fifteen people had eaten there once, when the family was larger and there was more work to do, and someone, probably their mother, had hidden away the unoccupied chairs when the extra hands disappeared. Against the bare walls the chairs looked penitent and skeletal, locked outside time. The sight of them made Grant think of the men who had sat on them, gone from his memory until now: the haggard truckster who came with week-old city newspapers and left a day later with wool, a chore boy who carried water and kept the woodboxes stocked, the extra herders and camp tender, men whose names were lost to him but whose faces could be recalled piecemeal: a knobbed drunkard's nose, a drooping gotch ear that came from sleeping flat in the dirt and never washing, a row of yellow teeth with a laugh behind it. Then, he could not have imagined running the place without them. But they had made do when it was necessary, and when a brother died they did without him too. When Grant left they did without even him.

Now it looked like they hadn't done well enough. The ranch was dying, there was no getting past it, drying up under a thirsty sun, and no simple ministrations would set things right. He would send away that money in the morning but this was a mercy, not a cure.

Or so it seemed to Grant. It was best to avoid much hope. He backed out of Edwin's room and shut the door, leaving the chairs in their lifeless attitudes and the dusty floor undisturbed.

·

There was a light above the front door, cobwebbed beneath the eaves, and when he went out Grant switched it on. The yard came into view around him. He walked up behind the house, through the pasture, until he came to the starveout fence. The rusted wire bowed as he climbed over and stayed bowed when he was past. No grass grew here and the dust shifted underfoot like sand. He followed the fenceline up over the rise until the house was out of sight and the headstones of his mother and brothers shone like open palms under the moon. There was a gate, which he opened. Beyond the graves the hill dropped off into a coulee and it was here that a night wind struck the bank and crept up over its lip. Grant was standing in the wind's path. His pantcuffs shackled his ankles. His mother lay under him.

They had paid for a properly engraved stone, same as they had for the others. Just her name and dates. He crouched and ran his fingers through the cuts. The ground was gently mounded but likely had been more so, not long before. He thought they ought to have covered her with boulders to keep the dirt from blowing away. The other stones stood pitched forward in the wind, all but Wesley's, which somebody had piled the dirt back around and tilted windward as a precaution. It appeared to Grant that the graves were creeping closer to the bank, and in fact a fence post already hung by its staples over the edge.

He peered down and then lowered himself into the creekbed. Rocks half buried in the bank were blown smooth. A few desperate patches of brush clung to the loose dirt. Above them he could see something else jutting, a split plank with a nail head protruding, another one a few feet past it. He realized these were the boxes that contained his brothers, the ground around them eroded away. He stood on tiptoe to touch the wood. Blown grit had sanded the varnish off a corner of one box and much of the lower edge of another. The one exposed longest was worn so far through that soon there'd be a hole and the coffin would fill up with dust. He pushed his fingers into the earth and pulled away a clayey lump, which he pressed against the corner, trying to make it stick. But it fell off and scattered around his boots. The hungry wind thrashed at his back. For a minute he let it press him to the bank, and he smelled the dirt and felt the ground strain against the punishing wind. Then he reached up and seized the hanging post and pulled himself back up onto the hill.

·

When he got back to the house, Kittredge was waiting for him with a bottle in his hand and an apology on his face. He said nothing until they were at the table with glasses in front of them.

I'm real sorry about all that. He ain't mine but I got no choice but to keep him, y'see. It was with some embarrassment that Kittredge said this, his eyes averted, his jaw taut.

You're only responsible for what comes out of your own mouth, Grant told him.

Well, it sure don't hurt nobody for me to try keeping him in line.

Whose is he? Grant said, as if Neeler was a child. But that seemed to be how Kittredge regarded him.

A woman I used to know. She died of a tumor in her belly and she asked me would I look after Petey for her when she's gone. Well, I told her I would. That must have been about eight years back. I believe he's a little bit slow. Didn't seem that way when she passed on, but I suppose seeing as he was her boy and not mine I wasn't paying much attention, y'see.

You wouldn't of said no even if you knew what he was like.

No, that's right, Kittredge said nodding. You're right about that. Her husband lit out a long time back and nobody seemed to know where he was at. I wouldn't leave a boy to be no orphan, that's true.

Kittredge drank in little sips with his mouth barely opened. The two of them listened to the wind coming down on the house. Then Kittredge said, Petey didn't have no respect for your brother, maybe because they was the same age. I wouldn't put it past the boy to twist around his words.

Grant took his time replying. Our brother Thornton went instead of me, he said. His ship got sunk. My brother considers me to be a coward and I can't say I blame him.

Kittredge received these words without evident judgment. He nodded. My daddy died in the first war. Ain't no shame in keeping alive's what I say.

That's kind of you but it's not the full truth.

I don't suppose.

Grant could have argued further, he had it in him. But he kept silent. Without even trying he had befriended Kittredge and there was no point in riling him. They continued to drink as the house shuddered around them.

Nothing was worse to an easterner than silence. He would see in their eyes while he was talking that they were only half listening to him, because they were busy working out what they were going to say back. And if after they finished talking he tried to think through what he was going to say, they wouldn't give him time, they would just go right on ahead and say something else to fill up the empty space. Grant couldn't have said why this should be so but he guessed it was too much like dying. For them, being with another person without talking was like being side by side in the ground.

But he had gotten used to it, so much that Kittredge's silence seemed heavy with significance, and he turned an eager face to the older man. Kittredge smiled, confused. Grant realized he was going to have to watch himself while he got reacquainted with the customs of the region. His mind raced with the ugly sound of his own voice as he said, How long you been working here?

Two years, Kittredge said.

You were here when my mother died.

Kittredge looked into his glass and turned it slowly on the table-top. I kept myself out of all that, he said.

Grant got the message: Kittredge wanted it kept that way. But he had to know, he had to find out what he could. And my daddy? he said. You were here when he left? He say if he was coming back ever?

Kittredge wiped his tired face and got up from the chair. I just came by to apologize is all. If we're gonna be working together, I just want to let you know how it is with the boy.

At the door he turned back to Grant, still at table, and spoke. One day he just weren't there no more. He didn't say nothing to me. Horse came back from town on its own.

Good night, Grant said to him.

Kittredge pulled his hat down tight and nodded. G'night.

·

It was hard sleeping in the familiar bed. The house complained in the wind. Every sound carried clearly through the old dry boards. Surely he would have woken his father leaving here that night. Grant could see him: propped on one elbow with Mama asleep beside him, he would have remained still and alert for hours, waiting, and then given up for good the second the sky lit. Going to town his father would have been ashamed of him, even more than he'd been during the war.

Grant rarely went to town in those days, once Thornton was dead. He usually let Max and his father go alone. Then, when it was just him and his mother at home, he would find a reason to go into the house and talk with her. By this time her hair was white but she still pulled it back in a ponytail like a girl. She sat at table mending something or making a list, her hands doing the work with what seemed excessive strength, the needle or pencil jabbing purposefully and calmly. She was calm even in grief. She asked him about whatever work he'd done that day and he told her. Sometimes he asked her about life in Iceland, but she only nodded as if it was a yes no question and said that it was no easier there than here. Until he was fifteen he didn't know the names of his grandparents, Einar and Finna, and by then they were long dead.

He believed he was the person closest to his mother, closer even than his father was. There was little evidence for this, their conversations could not have been called personal. Nor were they affectionate: she touched him only when he was sick or hurt, and when the rope cut his leg she held his hand while the doctor applied a stinging poultice. She held him after Robert's funeral, or he assumed it was her, he could only remember being held and not who was doing it.

For no reason he remembered a textile dealer in Eleven who used to bring his mother an orange on her birthday. Maybe he did this for all the ranch women, to lure them into town to buy cloth, Grant didn't know. But nobody else had ever brought his mother gifts. He realized he would never again see her peel and eat an orange.

He was cold, so he got out of bed and took another blanket from the bottom bureau drawer. Under the blankets, he considered that come winter and the real cold, he would have little trouble keeping warm. There were many blankets in the bedrooms and all of them were his now.

·

He woke before sunrise and went down to the kitchen. The moon was gone and the house had purpled in the near-light. He lit a fire and set water on to boil. Into a handled sieve he folded a clean cloth and he shook coffee from a canister kept out on the counter. When the water was hot he let it trickle through the grounds and into a cup until it brimmed over. He brought the cup and a kitchen chair out to the front stoop, and he sat there and sipped the coffee as the day brightened around him.

In time the far hill came into clear view and with it a moving dot on its face, following the lumbering trajectory of a bear. He watched it descend. It came in a zigzag, switching back here and there with the folds of the hill. For awhile it dropped out of sight beneath the slight rise of the nearer land, and Grant forgot it. But then it returned, visible between the sheep shed and barn, in the unmistakable form of a man afoot. Soon it had topped the rise and started down toward the fence. Grant leaned forward in his chair and brought the coffee to his lips. It was cold now. Could the man be Murray? If so, something bad had happened which had separated him not just from the flock but from his dogs and horse and wagon as well.

It wasn't Murray. This man was fat; his body swayed as he walked. When the man had nearly reached the fence Grant could see that he was wearing town clothes, a suit and no hat. He started to get up to meet him, but changed his mind. Any city man who'd walked down off that hill and come all the way here could take the extra few steps onto the porch. The sun was just starting to climb the hill behind him and its first rays to strike the distant ridge, and unless he missed his guess it had been fifteen or twenty minutes he'd been out here watching. Which was funny, because he couldn't fathom a man making it down off that hilltop in under an hour.

The man was in the road now, twenty yards away. Grant was almost grateful when he realized that it was the dead man he had discovered on the beach in Atlantic City.

He was much the same as before, corpulent and white, his eyes eaten raw by the salt water. He soundlessly mounted the steps and stood still before Grant, drawing no breath. Grant sipped his cold coffee.

So what'd you come for? he said.

The dead man's lips had retreated and two brilliant rows of false teeth arrayed themselves across the opening. An arm rose and the bleached hand at the end of it pointed to Grant's cup.

Grant looked down into it. The coffee had spilled over his fingers and clothes and patterned the porch underneath him. Suddenly it seemed to be burning. He dropped the cup and coffee fanned out over the boards. Full day had broken and Grant could see clearly now that it was in fact blood.

When he woke it was still night. Dread gripped him as he considered having to get up and go through it all again. He sat up in the bed panting. In time the dream lost definition, and he went down and made coffee in much the same way he'd dreamed. It was his mother's method, most of the men boiled theirs. When the sun came up he pulled on his boots and walked up around the back hill to the hands' quarters, a little row of plank shacks with chimneys sticking up out of them. Smoke was coming from one chimney and Cotter was out in front of another cutting wood with an ax. His breath formed clouds that hovered over him, and steam poured off his hands and out of his collar. Grant said, I got to go to town to pay some bills.

Cotter looked up, then went over to the truck and opened the door. He reached in and pulled out the keys and tossed them to Grant. Grant passed them from hand to hand while Cotter returned to splitting wood. He wondered if he should address Cotter as he would a friend or just tell him what to do. The latter, he supposed. They had nothing in common but work.

You got any particular plans for today?

No, Cotter said.

How about fixing up the sheep shed? Mays well get it out of the way before the cold.

Cotter nodded. He looked old in this infant light. Grant put the keys into his pocket and called on Kittredge.

It was Neeler who answered the door. He wore no shirt and his hairless chest looked stove in. Grant couldn't understand what he was doing here, there were two unoccupied cabins and he could have his own. Neeler stood staring at Grant until Kittredge came to the door behind him. Grant said good morning and suggested they get up on the hill and start skidding some logs down for firewood. He told them he would join them when he got back from town.

Okay, Kittredge began, you want we should—

We already got wood enough for our ownselves, Neeler said.

Petey, said Kittredge, stepping forward into the light. Neeler's hands were on the jamb and he filled up the opening, keeping Kittredge behind him. The boy's eyes were on Grant, as deeply interested as Grant had yet seen them.

Grant said, I'll barely fire up the cookstove except for your breakfast and supper. So you've got a responsibility. I'll meet you up the hill when I get back.

All right, Kittredge said quickly, sounds good to me. But Neeler stayed where he was, saying nothing, until Grant turned to go.

The truck still worked the same, turning over with a couple of coughs and a tap on the gas. He stopped it in front of the equipment shed and went in and got the envelopes. The ones that were going to Ashton he had written addresses on and the others he planned to deliver by hand. The sun lit up the windshield dust as he topped each hill, and behind it the valley shone like a haunt. On the county road he passed a brand-new rig he didn't recognize, but he raised a hand in greeting that the driver returned.

His coffee was rolling in his gut and refused to go to his head, where he wanted it. The dream had soured him. He put on the wipers and the dust streaked across the window and blew off. The radio said frost. Town came into view and he pulled over by the Sunrise restaurant and went in.

All six people there were familiar to him. Jean Tate was cooking. She was the sister of the girl whose picture he had in his bureau drawer, the girl who died. At the counter were the father and son drunks from the gas station. Three others shared a table, an old man and his sons. Grant knew the sons. All of them looked up when he came in and then turned back to their breakfasts. He sat at the counter, leaving a stool empty between himself and the drunks.

Welcome back, said Jean Tate. Want a couple of eggs?

Please. He turned to the drunks beside him and said good morning.

The younger said, A lot of coming and going up at your place these days.

It was uncertain if Grant was to take this as meaning, among other things, his mother. He chose to see it as an indiscretion and didn't pursue it.

Afraid so, he said. There was an Ashton newspaper on a nearby stool and he picked it up and read a few headlines.

Your amigo left here with a hell of a headache, the young drunk said, that pretty boy you brought in the bar. There was a certain wistfulness to his voice, as if he wished Purcell was still here to ridicule but would have to make do with Grant. Grant turned. The father slurped his coffee, wincing. He made no sign of noticing the conversation. Booze had seemed to loosen his skin and his face sat low on his skull. It was easy to see the son going the same way, in fact it was starting already, his features in the early stages of slipping off.

That so? Grant said.

The son laughed. Where in hell'd you pick him up, I want to know.

Ashton.

He snorted. Could of guessed as much.

Across the room, the old man and his boys got up. The old man threw a few bills onto the far end of the counter. The three nodded at Grant as they left and Grant nodded back. One of the boys looked over his shoulder as he passed through the door, and it wasn't clear to Grant who he was looking at, the drunks or him.

When Jean brought out his food she met his eyes. You ready for winter? she said.

Nope.

He ate in silence and left while she was cleaning up in back. The truck was still warmer than the air. He drove out to the grocery and paid Mrs. Healy in full, and she gaped at him as if he'd just handed her his own head. The horseman Klopfer counted out every bill right there in front of him. The man at the farm supply only nodded and said thanks. He saved the drunks for last to give them time to get from the Sunrise to the bar. It was there that he handed the old man his money. The old man took a single bill out, turned in his stool and gave it to his son, then he folded the envelope once without looking and shoved it into his coat pocket.

The rest he mailed at the post office. The clerk was a young man Grant didn't know, but Theroux the postmaster could be heard in back shouting bets into a telephone. Grant got his receipt and stood out on the sidewalk looking at it. It was done now, the money was gone. After awhile he went back to the Sunrise. Jean was alone with the paper spread out on the counter. He sat in front of her and she looked up.

How's your mother? he said.

Okay, she said. Daddy's all right. I'm living up above. She pointed at the ceiling.

You're making a living on what Nellie pays you?

Nellie's dead. I bought the place.

He nodded. It took some effort to say what he was thinking. Maybe I could come into town some night and see you.

Yeah, okay, she said simply. She looked like her little sister around the eyes and nose, except that her face was full like her mother's where her sister's had been sharp. She'd survived the same pneumonia that killed her sister. Grant was surprised she wasn't married to somebody. Maybe she had been.

What night?

Just show up. I won't be anywhere special.

When he got back to the ranch he could see Kittredge and Neeler up on the ridge at the edge of the trees. Kittredge jerked his arm and in a second or two Grant heard the rattle of a chainsaw. Across the yard Cotter was at work on the sheep shed. The sun had burned the clouds out of the sky and Grant was getting hot standing under it. He took off his jacket, went to the barn and saddled a horse. It wasn't one he knew but it let him on easy. He rode up the hill along a trail that had been there since before his parents came, worn by the home-steaders or the Indians or whoever came before them. The trail led him across the bald stumped hillside where the forest used to be, creased now with dry shallow ravines. A few of these had dugways cut on either side to let the horses through. Others he had to goad his horse into crossing. He came upon two horses tied to the ground, too close in his opinion to a cliffedge. He dismounted and peered over. Maybe twenty feet down. He went back and looped his reins around a stump, then continued to where the men were working.

Kittredge was cutting and Neeler sawing the branches off the felled trees. Logs were lying about along the treeline, too puny to have bothered with. The noise of the chainsaw stopped.

I'll start skidding them out, Grant shouted. Move into the woods a little and get some of the big ones.

Kittredge nodded. If he thought this suggestion a slight, there was no sign. But Neeler looked down at the tree he was sawing and then up at Grant as if comparing the two. Grant went back for his horse, tied a rope around a log and dragged it down the trail. He left it in front of the house and returned for another. They worked in this man-ner until two, when Grant made them dinner. Cotter had already come in and left an empty bean can behind, with a crusty punched-tin fork sticking out of it.

After dinner they worked until sundown, and all the next day. Sometimes the sun was covered by a cloud but mostly it stood out naked and fierce. It burned them and so did the wind.

That night Grant went back to town with Cotter, who was headed to the bar. When they got there Grant turned and started to cross the street. Cotter asked him where he was going.

I'm meeting Jean Tate.

Jean Tate? he said, as if he didn't know who it was.

Grant stood embarrassed, his desire exposed. But it was of no con-cern to Cotter. He shrugged and continued to the bar.

The Sunrise was open but it was a skinny kid working there, his scoliotic back straining over the grill. Grant went around behind the building and found a lighted door. He knocked twice and went in. A flight of stairs led him up to another door, standing slightly ajar, a thin strip of light from inside illuminating the stairwell. He knocked again and the knock forced the door open another inch. From inside came a voice too faint to understand. He pushed and the door gave way onto a simple apartment with a bed and chair and a radio on a round table. There was a sort of alcove with a stove and sink in it, and she was standing there cooking. He'd already eaten but when the smell reached him he felt compelled to eat a second time.

Eaten? she said. She had a wooden spoon in her hand and an expression on her face that neither welcomed him nor fended him off.

No, he said.

She reached up and took a plate from a doorless cabinet and set it on the counter next to another like it. Then she emptied a boiling pot into a colander and the colander onto the plates, and covered the noodles with whatever was in the pan.

Sit down, she said, and put the plates on the table. I'll be right back.

When she was gone he sat down. A sort of stroganoff. He was near to pitching over onto it, he was so hungry. It was as if all he'd eaten an hour ago got lost on its way to his stomach. This was a familiar kind of hunger, he'd felt it time and again on the *Rose Adams*, when a twelve- or eighteen-hour shift came to a close and his body suddenly remembered that there was such a thing as food. He strained to think about something else while he waited for her to return. What he thought about was kissing her. He had kissed her little sister, who slapped him and then kissed him back.

She came in with two pint glasses. They all know you're here, she said. They gave me hell about it.

Probably think we're up to something, he said.

Aren't we? She gave him his beer and sat across from him. Round-faced, small-breasted, shoulders wide for a woman, she looked like an owl. She shot him an owl's look, surprised and puzzled, like she'd just tricked herself.

I admit that crossed my mind, he said.

Eat, she said. They ate. The food was almost good enough to make him cry. It had been a long time since he'd eaten anything with seasonings in it. Neither of them looked up until they were through. Then she came around to his side and took him by the hand over to the bed.

•

I'm not ever marrying nobody, she said. I got myself engaged to Claude Miller, did you know him?

A little, he said. They were still in the bed, the sheets half on them.

He's in college, studying veterinary doctoring. Anyway, once we were engaged he made it pretty clear he didn't approve of my living by myself, and he said while he was at school I'd go live with his mother. She had a room ready for me. Well, I had to tell him to forget it. In fifty years I'm going to be in this very room, smoking a cigarette and looking out that window at what's left of that street. Mark my words.

Reminded of cigarettes she took a pack off the night table and lit one. The apartment was dark and the orange glow of the match danced over her skin. Grant wanted her again. But she said, Did you and my sister ever do it? She spoke in a low quiet voice, almost as if he wasn't supposed to hear. He considered how to phrase his answer, unsure of what kind she wanted. People aren't very sturdy inside, he thought; there are a hundred things either of us could say that would break the other. People shouldn't have that kind of power, they ought to have strong walls and no weapons. At least it seemed so at the moment.

We had a little tussle once, Grant said. But nothing came of it.

She opened up her mouth and closed it again, then burst out crying. He put his hand on her thigh. She said, Oh, hell, I was going to say I wish you said yes, so you could tell me about it. Then I thought better of saying something like that. She laughed.

You miss her.

Claude might not of seemed like such a terrible idea, she said, if I had her to talk to.

He said, Did you see my brother much while I was gone?

Her breath caught. She released it slowly and the air filled with smoke.

Not like this, she said.

He laughed. No.

She cradled her chin in her hand. I guess this town hasn't got whatever it is he thinks he needs. He never much liked the kind of talk that goes on around here. Folks look at him as funny, and I think he looks down on them.

You know he's left.

Heard it.

He said, You think he'll come back?

You did.

He moved his hand over, and into her. I did.

Don't get comfortable, she said.

.

That fall they did a lot of work, and by the time it snowed the fences and buildings were fixed and a little money was coming in. Kittredge said that he and Neeler were going to Colorado to help out his mother. Grant drove them to the bus station, dreading a winter alone with Cotter.

Sometimes he saw Jean, never consistently, never once calling her first. The telephone was connected up with a lot of other people between here and town and somebody was always listening in; and though he didn't care what any of them thought about him he considered it unfair to subject Jean to their scrutiny. Besides that, she seemed satisfied with this arrangement. He would just go down to the Sunrise and eat dinner at the counter, then go over to the bar. After awhile he'd come back with a couple of glasses and they would drink them and then go to bed. Jean was solidly built, he liked the way she felt under his hands. Sometimes when Cotter wasn't along he'd stay the night and drive back in the morning.

He supposed he preferred her company to nights alone in the empty house. But mostly it felt like a cheat—it'd be wrong to rely on the pleasure of a temporary thing. She never said what she thought of him and he didn't want to know.

He did learn a lot about her dead sister. Claire had worn mud on her face nights. She tried to learn the piano but had lacked the aptitude. She'd been a fair cook and a good rider and had aspirations to own her own store, a dry goods or the like. Jean had the idea that she herself had only won her independence because Claire never got hers.

I wasn't made for leaving home, she told Grant. Not until she was dead did I start thinking I might. I can't explain that.

I don't guess you ought to.

She asked him if he felt the same way about his dead brothers. For some time he considered how to answer. The way he saw it, there wasn't much point in worrying about what might have been, not just because it's never going to be but because you're bound to be wrong anyway. All he felt about his brothers was that they were gone. He wouldn't have done some of the things he did if they had lived, but for all that, he might have done something even worse.

No, I don't, he said finally.

The answer silenced her a moment. I expect it would be different for you, she said.

Only once did he ask her if she wanted to come out to the valley with him. A kind of curtain came down over her face and she said no, she would have to be back at the restaurant real early. Of course he could have had her back in time, but it was obvious she would never spend a night in his house regardless.

That suited him. There was no need to get closer. Death had darkened the air between them and neither wanted to see the other too clearly.

Around Christmas one afternoon he stood in the road by the house and noted a certain blankness of sky to the north. It was coming on four o'clock and what sun they'd had that day was near to gone in clouds. Snow covered everything and the air was uncharacteristically still. He didn't know what his eye was telling him. December, blank sky. Nothing to get surprised at. He went in and lit the stove and cooked his supper with the radio playing. He tried to hum along to the holiday music but it made a hollow sound and he stopped. In awhile he'd finished with the food and prepared two plates and sat down at the table. He ate his dinner and thumbed through an old magazine. Then he got up and looked out the window. Beyond the swell of hill there was only blackness, not a single star in sight. He had stood here this morning and the sky had been clear and blue for a long time before it clouded up again. He pulled his boots on, went outside and walked up the road. It was cold and he wanted to fold his arms against it, but even alone after dark he wouldn't, ashamed for no good reason to be moved by weather. Halfway to Cotter's shack he realized what had brought him out here, and he ran. Cotter's door was slightly ajar. He pushed it open. Inside, the stove was cold and Cotter lay on the floor beside a fallen chair and an empty liquor bottle. He had pissed himself and vomit stained his shirt. Grant watched his chest until he saw it rise and fall. There was a pile of wood by the stove that Cotter must have brought in and forgot. That was what he'd noticed—no smoke. Grant got the wood lit and stripped Cotter and covered him up with bedclothes. He wiped his face with a wet cloth and tried to pour water into his mouth. Cotter sputtered and coughed as the fire took on life.

Grant pulled up the fallen chair and sat over Cotter, giving him water every few minutes and staring into the stove's open door. In half an hour Cotter opened his eyes. They came to rest on the fire as well. Grant handed him the water cup and he took a few sips. Then he rolled over wincing, scrabbled his fingers until they found the liquor bottle, and swallowed the few drops left inside. He blinked and sat up.

Get me some clothes.

Grant pulled a few things from a pile on the bed and handed them to Cotter. He got dressed, his back to Grant. There was a scar beneath the ribs, whether a doctor's or attacker's Grant couldn't tell. When he was done Cotter took the water from Grant and drank some more of it.

Why don't you move up to the house, Grant said.

Cotter shook his head no.

Plenty of room for you.

Them rooms belong to other people. It ain't my place.

Grant stood and went to the door. With his hand on the latch he said, Don't feel much like my place, neither.

Longer you live, Cotter said, the more it'll feel like yours and the less it'll matter to you. I can make myself at home anywhere. This here's fine.

He waved a heavy hand at all that was around them, the smoke-brown windows and walls, and the dirty sheets and the stiff sick-soaked clothes in a heap on the floor. Grant nodded and opened the door and the winter rushed in, fanning the fire.

Good night, Cotter, he said, and stepped out into the cold.

·

In January of that winter he rode south over the government land to check up on Murray. It was a good day's ride and he counted on having to camp somewhere for the night. He knew a few outcrops that could pass for shelter. With him he brought a bottle for the herder and a mystery book to read. The hills were lower and more narrow and jagged to the south, as if a great fist had come from the east and struck at Eleven, bunching the land all up and down the Post Range.

Why these mountains had that name depended on who you talked to. One story had homesteaders fencing a pasture when Indians killed them and bound their bodies upright to the posts they'd been driving. Mostly this story was used to scare children, to keep them from getting lost in the hills. Some people thought the name referred to settlers' outposts once built on the ridgetops, now gone. There had also been a mail route through here which was often attacked. It was true that people used to find decaying letters scattered through the passes, though Grant himself had never seen one. The Indians had had another name for the range that meant surrounded by rivers, because its boundaries could be marked by the streams that flowed around it. Now and then you heard old people call it by that name.

The folded land offered long changeless channels of astounding length. Over years Grant had learned to mark the distance he'd gone down them, the way long study of a clockface can make detectable the hour hand's motion. When he was younger he would pass the time on long rides by imagining attacks by animals or Indians and devising ways to defend himself against them. If he was alone he might take a few shots at a tree or rock, for fun.

He left in late morning. By midafternoon the flock came into view in the distance, languidly shifting, a gray stain on the snow. The sight reminded Grant of the carpets of seaweed that spread just beneath the ocean's surface, swelling with the currents. Murray's wagon punched a dark pinhole in the white beyond the sheep. Its chimney emitted a thin line of smoke that rose straight up in the windless air. Grant's horse snorted and quickened. A pan and cup clanked together in the pannier.

When he was halfway down the incline two dark shapes broke away and moved toward him on a swift parallel path. Soon they sharpened into dogs. Grant slowed to give them a chance to smell the horse. When the animals seemed satisfied with one another, the dogs led him down into the valley.

Against the trampled white the sheep looked jaundiced and sick, their bellies stained by mud. They were eating grass through the snow. Grant believed he knew this area and thought he could remember a cutbank running east-west beyond Murray's camp. He rode down toward it and the dogs followed as far as the wagon, where they waited to see what Grant would do. In a minute he pulled up short a few lengths from the bankedge, acting on intuition alone. He hadn't seen it and would have fallen over had he kept on. He dismounted and looked down at the ground ten feet below. It rose to about twenty feet off to the west before the lower ground came up to meet the higher. The undisturbed snow below rendered the drop nearly invisible. He rode back to the wagon, the dogs picking him up halfway and trotting intently beside him.

There was no door on the wagon but for an elkskin tacked across a sidewall of sheet metal. Without mounting the buckboard he rapped on the metal and felt rust flakes scrape his knuckles. He called out Murray's name.

The herder pushed the skin aside with a rifle barrel which came to rest aimed at Grant. Grant could hear the dogs growling, suddenly anxious. Murray looked at him with eyes shielded by colored glasses. Behind the lenses the eyes were small and wild, like poison berries. It occurred to Grant that Murray didn't recognize him.

It's Grant, he said. Grant Person. Come to see how you're doing.

Murray stepped out and hopped to the ground and Grant backed up to admit him. The rifle barrel did not waver in its aim. Murray had grown a beard which had filled in unevenly, leaving bare rough skin at the corners of his mouth.

Grant said, Flock's all right, is it?

'Sfine, Murray said. His Adam's apple quivered high on his throat.

You know there's a little cliff a quarter mile south of here. You'd best bed down beyond it on the low side. So the sheep don't wander over the edge. Don't you think?

Nope, Murray said, keeping his eyes full on Grant.

In this blinding white landscape, Grant figured, every foreign shape has got to shake a man deep. He suddenly remembered the names of the dogs, Cootie and Mitch. Assuming they were the same dogs. He felt like a fool with this rifle pointed at his chest and the silly dogs behind him.

How about you put that thing down, Murray? I ain't armed. My rifle's still in the scabbard. He pointed to the horse but Murray didn't look where he was pointing. There's nothing to get upset over.

Murray lowered the rifle and blinked, as if waking up. One of the dogs came over and stood by him.

You all right? Grant said.

Aye. He looked south. I don't see no cliff.

Look where the grass stops. A quarter mile. It's a ten, fifteen foot drop.

Murray leaned a little forward. Aye, I see it now. I mean to take 'em there tomorrow.

Grant wanted to suggest he take them there today but he said nothing, not yet. He understood these were too many sheep for one man, this man in particular. Looking out over the flock Grant felt the burden of owning it and wished for the first time since returning that he might find some other endeavor broad or deep enough to absorb him. As a child he would ride out far enough so that he couldn't see the house anymore, and the largeness of his surroundings would make him feel larger himself, and it was possible to believe it was all his: that he had subdued it, and everything he could see was under his control. Now the sight of the flock alone filled him with feelings of powerlessness, and all the human influence he had seen in the east, all the evidence men had fabricated to prove to themselves they existed, seemed little more than a brittle crust that would one day be scoured off the earth. In the world of men, in buildings and on streets and under the influence of commerce, maybe it was possible to see it differently. But here it no longer was, not for him.

He camped that night cupped by a cretaceous overhang eroded under, he guessed, by pooled ice some fifteen thousand years or so back. Nearby stood a cairn of rounded stones herders used to stand upon to watch sheep. He didn't know how old that was, it had been here when he was born. He built a fire and ate bacon and beans cooked over it. The grease left over went into a tin cup, and he dredged a lampwick through it, which he held upright while the grease hardened in the cold air. When the fire went to embers he wrapped himself in his sougan, lit the wick and read his book until he couldn't feel his fingertips anymore. Then he blew out the flame and covered up his head and hands.

The virgin world he woke to didn't seem so oppressive and he found his confidence in the herder renewed. He had left Murray his bottle of booze and promised to bring him the mail, if any came. Riding back home he made a model in his head of each day of the coming year, through the winter and into lambing season and shearing and on to fall. There was some solace in the anticipation of work, and punished hands and feet and the inevitability of injury and illness. But he dreaded restoring ties to the market. Either he would not be remembered by his buyers and thus susceptible to swindle, or remembered as the one who had left and come back, and thus the object of their disdain.

Regardless, there was satisfaction in the planning, in the imagined days darkened with instructions on his imagined calendar. It had a different picture above each month, of one idyll or another, a silhouette of a man among animals or a sentimentally lit landscape.

When he got home he read his book and fed Cotter, and he worked in the morning and on subsequent mornings and read and ate and listened to the radio, and in this way he passed through the winter.

By spring he had convinced himself some change was imminent, but it would be another year before Max returned.

·

It was a year of holding on. In spring Murray came back thinner. He said he had run out of food. Grant suspected him of slaughtering a ewe but didn't mention it. He plied the herder with a little extra money to keep him working a few days longer, to get the flock ready for lambing, and with Cotter they tagged each ewe and clipped the hair around her teats. The lambing pens had long been set up in the barn and they stocked each with good clean bedding.

When the lambs started coming the men eased into the work as into cold water, tentative at first and then later without even knowing they were doing it. Cotter and Murray, near drunk, gentled the ewes like mothers. Murray kept a washtub warm with boiled water from the house, and carefully dipped chilled lambs up to their necks and rubbed them dry one after the other. When it got to be too much for the three of them, Cotter went into town and brought back a couple of men from the bar. Grant didn't know them, a husky teenager with bloodshot eyes and a Crow Indian named Charlie, who spoonfed orphaned lambs with a nurse's steady hands. When once a ewe nudged its teats against a stillborn lamb, they watched Charlie lift the dead animal from the pen, slit it throat to dock, pull it out of its skin and wrap the skin still bloody around a wobbling orphan, which suckled at the mother as if she were its own. All of them had seen this before, but never done so swiftly or with such gruesome kindness, as if the Crow was dressing a child for school.

Some of the dead lambs were born amputated, without hooves. Some curled up like oak leaves, their bones bent against the rigid muscles. Living lambs lay shaking themselves to death or stood paralyzed until they perished on their feet. Among the dead and dying and newly living animals the five men worked without speaking to one another, sometimes lying down right in the dust and sleeping. Half awake one night with his head inches from a newborn lamb, Grant believed he was among his brothers, all grown and familiar beyond the necessity for speech. When he woke fully he held back tears and touched the weariest man, the teenager whose name he'd already forgot, and the boy filled Grant's shape in the dirt, as if this spot, once occupied by someone else, was therefore now more acceptable as a bed.

Grant would forget the boy's face within weeks, and the Indian's not long after. The intensity and intimacy of these days would bleed in his memory into similar days of other years, until no particular recollection could be extracted from the ones that surrounded it. Soon after they were finished Grant would sense his memories losing definition in just this manner. Alone in the barn he would struggle to retain them, believing that what they had done should seem, years from now, more essential, more particular, than other days among other men. It should have created between them some uncommon affinity. But Charlie and the boy he would never see again, and Murray and Cotter were not inclined to reminisce, and he would allow his memory to erode as it always had, leaving him with only the contour of the thing, a kind of haunting, which came to him in odd moments like a draught from a previous life.

On a day when they were near done, Grant stepped from the barn to find a warm and cloudless spring evening. The light was like an heirloom taken out of storage and spit-shined. He rolled up a cigarette and smoked it. Almost eight months he'd been home and only now was the last piece of him truly back, as if it had taken the bed and body of Jean Tate and the blood of the birthing ewes to root him at last. After awhile the other men joined him. When they had all gone in and eaten, Grant counted out their pay and Cotter drove them back into town.

Murray would return in a week to take the flock onto spring range, and Kittredge and Neeler would come at shearing. But for the moment Grant was alone, and his past, which before had seemed like a fierce intractable living force, reminded him now of the herders' cairn on the hillside, something cold and inert he could stand upon to see what was coming.

Later he would wonder how his imagination had failed him. But for now there seemed nothing in front of him that wasn't simple and familiar. His life's odyssey was over and he was where he'd always be. Such were his thoughts on this impossible first warm evening of the year. In four days he would be twenty-seven years old.

PART TWO

AFOOT

5

A year later he came back from riding the ditches and saw, standing on the sill of an upstairs window of his parents' bedroom, a square bottle of blue glass catching the late-afternoon sun. He pastured the horse then returned to the yard to stare at the front door he was going to have to walk through. A blue glass bottle in the window. It would be casting a long shimmering colored shadow across the floor and bed. He entered the house as if nothing was out of the ordinary.

You need to get an electric refrigerator, Max said. He was sitting at the table with a bottle of whiskey in front of him. A cloudy shard of ice poked up over the rim of his glass. He swirled it around with his finger. Sawdust, he said. It gets in your drink.

When'd you get here?

I got a ride out from Reese Hamlin. He said you had something going awhile back with old Jean Tate.

Grant sat down and took his hat off.

Have a drink, Max said.

I might at that. He stood up and got a glass. Do I want to know where you been?

I don't know. Do you? Max looked different. He was wearing

clothes a city laborer might wear, his head bare, his face thin but soft, gruel-fed.

You been to the city.

Max said, New York.

You like it much? Grant asked. He sat down and put his empty glass on the table.

You meet a different breed of people there, I can say that.

At this, the groan of a mattress sounded from just above them, their parents' room, and then light footsteps. Grant hadn't heard such a sound for nearly five years. Max was grinning now, but not for Grant: a private grin. His eyes were somewhere else entirely.

You bring somebody along?

Sophia, Max said.

Sophia, Grant repeated.

She came down the steps wearing a black dress, though Grant understood this to be a city style and not mourning clothes. Nonetheless the sight of it reminded him of his mother. The girl was barely there, a bending branch wrapped in a twist of rag. Her skin was white and lucent, like the open palm of a candle which held the melted wax. Her nose was long, her eyes dark and large and far apart. Long hair tied back onto itself. Face fearful and unbeautiful.

Sophia, my brother Grant. Grant, Sophia.

Ma'am, said Grant.

She snickered. Oh boy, she said, a woman's voice filling the room. I can't believe this.

We met in the city, Max said. Her daddy sells radios.

He's a retailer, said Sophia. She blushed.

Grant let his eyes stay on her a moment. The oddness of her voice had seemed to amplify it, he could hear it still.

Help yourself, he said to her and nodded at the bottle. She went to the counter and took a glass without hesitation, then sat down at the table. In a moment Max took his eyes off her and asked how the outfit was doing.

A lot had been done, the flock culled and bred, repairs made around the place. Grant told him this knowing that pride was creeping into his voice, pride he knew his brother would be listening for. Max's face maintained a kind of imitation attentiveness: but this was Max, you never saw the whole of him. There was the face he was showing you, which stood for what he thought you wanted, and there was the real face you could only see when the other one slipped off by mistake. Looking at his brother and at the girl and back, he saw that Max had a hidden beauty, something about him almost womanly, the pale ears and the softness of his skin. It took a woman's presence to bring it out, or at least this woman, who looked gripping her whiskey as if she'd fight you for him and expected she might have to. Her glass was empty. With a start Grant noticed that his was too. He'd never filled it up. Sophia said, Did you show him your paintings?

Max coughed. He just got in, he said a little loudly.

Grant watched Sophia. A change in her posture told him she was nudging Max with her foot. She turned to Grant with an underhand grin.

He isn't telling you he's been painting. That's what he's been doing all this time—she turned to Max—haven't you? He's the real thing, she said now to Grant. No kidding.

He looked at his brother, glad to have her out of his sight.

Yeah, Max said, and here was an answering look, dirty and conspiratorial. The girl didn't seem to catch it.

You were always good at art painting, Grant said.

She snorted. He sure is!

Then they were silent. A raven's cry broke through a window and across the room and was rebutted from someplace distant. Grant was looking at Sophia and her entire mien split wide open, as if in the birds' calls she had heard a scrap of her own tongue telling her she was farther from home than she knew. And like that she sealed back up, and whole again punched Max in the shoulder, and laughed.

Grant had seen the truth. They hadn't told him yet, but they weren't planning to go back to New York.

•

Sleep was next to impossible with other people in the house; it cried out as if changing size in the night. And in fact it was: huge when Grant was a boy and small when he left, large when he returned and small again tonight. Voices came to him from Max's room distorted by space and by walls: Sophia's in the shape of desperate queries, and Max's, curt replies. She was feeling around the edges of her situation, he guessed, a blind woman tossed in a cell. Max, reluctantly, would be telling her how it was going to be. Earlier, when she was sleeping off her drunk, he had walked with Max around the yard and Max told him all he'd done in the city. For the first week he slept on benches and bought hard rolls and bottles of milk at a bakery. Then he found this bar where the famous painters drank and he met Sophia, who bought him liquor and introduced him to important people. She set him up in a warehouse her father owned and he got a job washing dishes for some Greeks at a diner. At night he went to jazz clubs and drew pictures of the players and sold them the drawings. He painted with watercolors because they were cheapest, and when he had no money he found scraps of paper in the warehouse to paint on or else went out in the street and tore broadsheets off walls. He told Grant he tried to paint a certain horse a thousand times and never once got it right. Once a week he took a shower at the YMCA. After awhile he moved into a room with Sophia and her father quit talking to her. One night somebody discovered his things in the warehouse and threw out his paints and easel and everything he'd done, and after that he had to paint in the tiny apartment.

So what are you doing here? Grant asked him.

For a minute it seemed there would be no answer. Then it came fast, spat out. There's something fake about those people, those painters. They pretended like they were dock workers. Half of them are rich off art and they can't even paint a goddam picture.

They think much of you?

How in the hell should I know, Max said, sounding like he knew all too well. The two of them had been leaned up against the sheep fence where the strongest ewes and lambs were walking, and Max shook his head and went alone to the equipment shed and poked his head in the door awhile. For a few minutes he disappeared inside. Then he came back out and approached Grant with his hands in his pockets.

Hear anything from Daddy? he said.

No.

He nodded, unsurprised but seemingly embarrassed to have asked. Grant said, You planning to stay long?

Max was looking up over the house at the grinded-down hillside, grimacing at its wasted brightness. Might, he said finally.

She gonna stick it out, you think?

I expect. Ain't much for her in the city. Her daddy cut her off when she moved out.

How old is she, Max?

Plenty old. Nineteen.

I wasn't suggesting anything funny, Grant told him.

A mirthless smile cracked Max's lips. Maybe you ought've, he said. There's plenty that's funny.

Now, in the room at the end of the hall, Max and Sophia had fallen silent. The house still shivered around them as if trying to expel them all. Grant wondered what his brother had told her she was going to be able to do all day long. He could feel the panic in her, in city people, their crushing need to keep themselves occupied. Now that the sod was giving up its freeze there would be plenty of work, especially at a shirttail outfit like theirs, with the lambs here and summer ahead of them, but he guessed none of it was anything she'd be willing to do. He bet she didn't even have a decent pair of shoes.

Minutes passed or maybe hours. The moon soared up out of sight over the house. Coyotes cried and he thought of the sheep on spring range, where Murray'd take them soon, and he hoped they'd be as lucky this year as last. Listening to the coyotes he doubted it. In awhile their cries grew faint and a closer sound reached him, which he recognized as the sound of floorboards straining under somebody's weight. The footsteps were in the hall and they stopped outside his cracked-open door. He could see a figure there darkening the threshold and he sat up in bed with the blankets spilling off him.

The door opened and the figure stepped in soundlessly and shut it. Outside, the coyotes again took up their barks. He spoke his brother's name into the darkness.

In response the figure moved closer. The room's only light came from the moonglow the hillside reflected. Its intensity was insufficient to show the visitor's face.

Sophia, he said, much quieter now, and the figure stepped forward into the light. Grant saw the smooth sleeve of a suit jacket. A bead of water collected at the cuff and fell, and it thudded on the floor like a bomb. The dead man's face came toward him, a bloodless wound cracking its cheek.

Sssh, the dead man said. Grant was very still. A cold finger reached out and touched his lips. The touch froze and sealed them. He woke frantic, his fingers in his open mouth and then over his eyes. He began to forget. Suddenly exhausted he fell back to the bed and into dreamless sleep, with his face cradled in his hands.

◆

Yearling lambs had to go to market. They'd be trucked to Ashton and from there to Denver for slaughter. Lambs were too valuable to eat on the ranch: maybe once in the spring, a skinny or sickly one they couldn't have got much for. Otherwise the animals they slaughtered here were past the breeding age. They ate mutton or sold it in Eleven, where people didn't so much mind the flavor and texture of mature flesh. Grant woke to find the house still quiet and innocent as a contrite child. Downstairs it was cold. The door had been left open, or had blown open in the night. Out in the road ravens paced, peering in. He shut the door and lit a fire in the stove.

He'd made arrangements with a man named Teabow, who owned a truck, to come help them haul the lambs to Ashton. As the kitchen warmed this was who he phoned. Teabow said he would be late. He would have been later still had Grant not called. They would get better prices for their lambs the earlier they came in the day, but there was nothing more that Grant could do. He hung up the phone and set to fixing breakfast.

Through the window he could see Cotter hitching their trailer to the pickup and bringing it around to the yard, near the shed gate. The lambing pens could be rigged to create a chute to drive the lambs through, and this is what Cotter did next. Then he came in to eat.

Cotter had not been around, having taken a few days off. Grant put his eggs in front of him and said, He's back.

Your daddy?

Max.

Cotter put his egg in his mouth and chewed it, thinking. He said, We could sure use him.

It was true. The work would take all day. When Cotter was done eating, Grant said, He's brought a girl with him.

What kind of girl? Cotter said. He stood and put his plate and his coffee cup in the sink.

From the city. New York. That's where he's been.

Cotter crossed his arms and let out a breath. He pursed his lips and appeared to think it over. He ain't gonna work a lick, he said.

They went out and spent some time looking over the ewes they planned to keep. Grant went into the shed for a notebook and pencil and came out to the chute where Cotter had chased a few ewes and wethers with a stick. Cotter opened up the gate and Grant ticked them off as they went through. The trailer filled and Max still hadn't appeared. A few times Grant looked up at the corner window but nothing was moving there. Eventually Teabow showed. He was stooped at middle age like he'd been living in a burrow, and his eyes bulged and blinked unceasingly. The three of them filled his truck and gathered in the yard a moment to smoke. Grant wanted to get moving, they could smoke in Ashton. But the break only seemed fair.

It's gonna freeze again yet, said Teabow.

Can't argue that, Cotter said.

Teabow turned to Grant. Them sheep look better'n last year.

I'm trying to grade them up. How's your missus?

Teabow shook his head. He had got a Mexican bride, who had registered with a marriage bureau in the hope of finding somebody more well-to-do than was locally available. Teabow had chosen her off of a list. He'd gone down there and picked her up and they got married on the way, somewhere in Arizona. She was a nervous woman to begin with—whether this was her regular nature or on account of marrying Teabow nobody seemed to know—but had not come to town much at all lately and was thought by a few to be sick in the head. It was rumored that her mother had been shot or stabbed in some kind of bar fight, and that Teabow may have misrepresented himself as a wealthy rancher. For this reason people felt some sympathy toward her, strange as she was. The Teabows lived on the far side of town, out on the flats, and raised a few animals. She pretended not to know much English though Teabow said she spoke it good.

Grant had inquired after her in the hope of getting things moving, but now he regretted bringing her up at all. Teabow looked hurt and Grant had a sudden sense of his desperation, of his shock and puzzlement at the unexpected turns his life had taken. He saw himself years in the future, driving south in the blue pickup to meet his own catalog bride. Teabow said, Aw, she's all right, she's a little barn sour, is all.

Maybe we ought to get going, Grant said.

He rode with Teabow in the cab of his truck. They didn't say much except to comment on the weather, which was unremarkable. Grant wanted to apologize for asking about Mrs. Teabow but he knew it would likely compound Teabow's embarrassment. Now he would always be the man who had said that, and Teabow the man it was said to. That words couldn't be taken back was simple and obvious, a feature of passing time, but the idea filled Grant with despair.

When they arrived in Ashton they had to wait for another outfit to unload its stock. A good half hour passed. Finally they drove in the sheep. The price was lower than expected. Grant tried to haggle up but his heart wasn't in it. They got back to the house after noon and Teabow wanted dinner, so Grant figured he might as well make it. In the kitchen he found Max and Sophia sitting at table as if waiting for him. Introductions were made.

We got to get Sophia some shoes, Max said. You going back into Ashton?

Grant said, Well, what do you think?

I'd guess you are.

All right, then.

But the two of them stayed inside while the trailers were loaded, and only when the work was finished did Max lead his girl down the steps and across the muddy road. They got in the pickup with Cotter.

That's a real pretty girl, Teabow said to Grant out on the highway. How long them two been married? I didn't hear nothing about it.

I don't know that they are married, Teabow.

Well! Teabow said. That seemed to hold them until Ashton.

Max and Sophia slipped away when they got to the market and came back later with her new clothes. In work boots and dungarees she looked like a toy, her legs spread slightly as she walked and her hands stiff and open at her sides. Men stopped what they were doing and gawked. Grant was embarrassed for her—their stares were mean—but something told him she wouldn't have cared what they thought. When she smiled at them, most of them smiled back.

They returned too late in the day for another run. Grant told Teabow he'd handle the rest himself in the morning, and paid him cash. He watched Teabow's rig disappear over the hill. Cotter had been backing the trailer around the side of the shed and now he came to join Grant where he still stood in the road. Grant said, You were right about Max. He didn't lift his little finger.

Can't say I blame him.

Grant looked at Cotter but the face betrayed no especial hostility. What's that supposed to mean?

Just what I said.

Grant kept looking at him. Cotter hitched his shoulders and sniffed, and finally added, Hell, I ain't never blamed you for nothing, did I. Let's drop it and go eat.

All right, Grant said, and they went in the house.

•

Over the next few days Max and Sophia seemed to be spending a lot of time out in the equipment shed, moving things around. Now and then Grant went in there for something and noted that a space was growing in the back, by the desk. One afternoon he found that the desk itself had been moved, the shelves taken down and stacked on it. Max was kneeling on the cement floor banging something together out of old boards. Sophia stood off in a corner holding one of Grant's mystery paperbacks in front of her face.

What're you working on? Grant asked.

Easel, Max said.

Plan to do some painting out here, do you?

Yep.

Grant looked over at Sophia, who lowered the book and met him with a smile, the one she'd given the ranch men in Ashton. It was common, like a knickknack, something she'd learned to do somewhere. Yet Grant found himself returning it. Embarrassed, he walked out.

When they came in the house that night only Sophia climbed the stairs to her room. Max sat down at the table with Grant. When she was gone Max said, She's bound to run out of books pretty soon.

Max had picked up an air of complaint in the city which Grant didn't much like. You're gonna have to go down to Ashton and get some more then, he said back, too harshly. Max got up and poured himself a drink. He looked at Grant, gesturing with the bottle, and Grant nodded. Max put the drinks on the table.

Looks like we're drinkers now, Max said.

Looks like.

Max drew breath and let it out. We're clean out of Sophia's money, he said. It took most of what she had just to get here. It was a long time coming with her and her daddy. She was supposed to enter into girls' college last year and she never got on the train. And then I met her. He shook his head and drank.

Grant said, You're going to have to pull your weight. You know how it is.

Mama asked for you every day she was dying, Max said suddenly.

It was so clumsy a weapon that Grant couldn't even get himself angry over it. The words sat there orphaned between them. Max swirled the drink around in his glass and held it up to the light. Then he went on.

Sophia says she can cook. She taught herself a couple of things. She can take over for you, and wash the clothes and such.

Get her a library card.

I believe I'll do that, Max said. So. The lambs, did they go high?

No they did not. And it wasn't me that made Mama sick.

No, Max said. It was Edwin and Robert and Thornton and Wesley. You didn't have a goddam thing to do with it, did you. No, you're right.

I'd best turn in, Grant said standing.

You still got whiskey there.

I'll leave it to you to pour it back. Or you can have it yourself. That'll be your first job. And he pushed in his chair and went quietly up the stairs, pretending to Sophia that he thought she wasn't listening to all that, that she was trying to go to sleep.

·

They were lucky to own their spring range outright. This was the gentle clump of foothills to the north, close to home and at this time of year covered in lush grass. John Person had bought the land from a Norwegian homesteader who couldn't hack it and was moving to Minnesota to find a wife. He'd got it for next to nothing and paid it off by the beginning of the war. They started out with a hundred and fifty head and added every year, creating more work for themselves as they went. The extra children—Thornton, Robert, Max, Wesley— were supposed to make up for it.

Grant expected Murray back in the morning and woke intending to get a good breakfast together. When he got to the kitchen he discovered Sophia already there. She was wearing an apron, his mother's which she had found in the pantry. The apron was bleached white but Grant could remember it spattered with blood as his mother stood hacking at a knot of meat. She had made it herself out of tarp canvas. On Sophia it nearly reached the floor. Her booted feet poked out from behind it.

Max'll be down, she said. He was up late getting his studio finished.

You mean in the shed.

Yeah. So I guess I've cooked a little, before. I mean, I know my way around a kitchen but I don't know how you do things around here. So maybe you could get me going.

Grant said, There's five of us this morning and I was going to make some potatoes and eggs.

Okay, I think I can do that.

One of your jobs is gonna be the chickens. You know how to get eggs from the henhouse?

No.

He led her out across the yard to the henhouse. Inside she made a face at the odor in spite of her obvious efforts not to. He showed her how to tell if a hen is setting on anything or not, and how to reach under her and get the egg. They brought twenty or so inside in a bucket and he got her cracking and scrambling them, which it looked like she'd done before. He told her how to clean potatoes and cut them up. While she did that he made the coffee.

Cotter came in with milk frothing in a pitcher and set it on the table. He gave Sophia a long look. Her new trousers were hanging off her narrow body. She said good morning and Cotter nodded. Grant put a cup of coffee in front of him and Cotter poured the warm milk in.

Grant took some fat out of the can and melted it in a skillet. Then he fried up the potatoes and added the eggs. She stood close and he felt her eyes on his work. When he was finished she put the food on plates. By then Murray had walked in and Max was on the stairs.

He came up behind her and grabbed her around the waist with a hand coming up just under the breast. The men watched him do this, abashed and transfixed. How's it going? Max asked her.

Oh, you know.

He didn't let go of her until Grant took the plates and set them on the table. Let's eat while it's hot, he said.

They all sat and ate, and drank the milk and coffee out of good chipped china. Murray looked a long time at Sophia and at last asked Max who she was. The question seemed to please Max but it was Sophia who answered. She stated her name, staring Murray straight in his eye. Shocked, the herder turned away, and the other men laughed at his discomfort and at their own.

Grant couldn't remember anything the herder had ever laughed at, though he'd seen him smile at something said in a bar once or twice. Maybe he laughed when he was by himself. Sophia looked up a couple of times while they ate, as if making sure it was all right not to be talking. He could hear the meal through her ears, the uncivilized chomp and smack of people who had better things to do, and he slowed himself down. She was still wearing the apron.

When they were finished Grant sent Max to help Murray move the ewes out, and he showed Sophia to the animals and them to her. She seemed to regard them with a fearful respect, as if she was encountering them in the wild. In the barn he sat her down and made her milk the cow. The cow kicked and complained. Sophia slipped backwards off the stool, alarmed. He helped her up, taking her hard round elbow in his palm. He explained the routine of feeding and milking and cleaning.

What about the horses? She looked at him frankly. I'm afraid of horses.

Cotter takes care of them. But you ought to learn riding.

It had never been Grant's role here to instruct or advise; he felt funny telling somebody what to do. You couldn't live comfortable with a person you knew too much more than. It wasn't a balanced kind of life. Sophia threw things off, made him take note of how he looked and sounded, and that scrutiny of himself, not in his nature, made him long to be alone. She cast the ranch in a new light: she wasn't of them, she was an envoy of the larger world that also wasn't of them, and without even trying she made them an object of the world's judgment. Of Max's judgment.

That was the real difference. The opinion of a girl from New York City didn't mean much to him but his own brother's did. Max had a critical streak the east hadn't put in him. He was always like that. Edwin had been too, and their father. But there was something different about Max. He measured them against his own fledgling consciousness and seemed to find them lacking. It wasn't their actions or lack of them that bothered him but unseen, inherent flaws, things over which they had no control. They were powerless to please him.

Why had Max come back, and why had he brought this girl with him? Was she a keepsake of his failed escape, or was she here to bear witness to him, to the spectacle of his indecision? Grant would have wagered that Max never had this picture in mind, of the poor girl slapping dust off her skinny backside, standing in fear of a cow. It was almost funny, or would have been if he didn't know so well the shape of his own meager heart: the very shape of this valley, a bleached-out miniature clenching in his chest.

.

That night Max and Sophia turned in early, so Grant went out to the equipment shed to see what they had done. The easel stood in the center of the empty space, a wooden cross with a narrow ledge to support a painting. From the ledge hung a little tin bucket with paintbrushes poking out of it. In front of the easel there was an upturned fertilizer drum covered with a tarp, he guessed a place for Max's subjects to sit. A lamp had been rigged, a bare bulb on a long cord slung over a ceiling beam, which exposed the tarp and the gray cement floor to a naked unrefined light. Grant crossed the space to a far wall where four thick cases were standing, cracked leather portfolios with taped-up handles. They must have dragged these onto the train with them, or the bus. He opened one up and spread its contents on the floor. Paintings, drawings on paper, smudged and torn around the edges and in some cases creased twice from folding. Here were the jazz sketches, wandering lines of ink that suggested the outlines of things: drums, a horn, the glow of a spotlight on a slick forehead. The pages were nearly blank, so minimal were the lines. But somehow the empty space stood for darkness or light or the sound of music. They were hurried and sloppy to Grant's eye. But their birth under his brother's hand chilled him. He didn't understand why.

The paintings were of gray city buildings and the stairstepped V of light the street cut between them. There were nudes, distorted and sexless, arched across sofas or floors like caught fish, their flesh the color of sinew and bone. He believed he recognized the body as Sophia's, or maybe that was only a suggestion his head was making to his eyes.

He gathered up the papers and put them back into the open port-folio, then leaned it up against the wall with the others. Afterward he sat on the barrel awhile staring at the darkened space behind the easel where Max would stand.

Grant knew what it was to be looked at: a kind of mirror, a way of seeing his own foreignness in others' eyes. He felt it when an animal he was hunting turned its head and regarded the hole he made in the landscape. He had felt it on the *Rose Adams*, when they called him a hero. He wondered what his brother saw when he looked at him, what Sophia saw.

But there was no point in contemplating what he had no way of ever knowing. He reached up and switched off the light. Then he stood still in the total dark for a moment, listening to the sound of nothing.

Coyotes came down out of the hills. This was early April, when the snowline was retreating up the hillsides leaving good grass in its wake and pulling the sheep up after it. A clear moonlit night brought the first kill. Grant heard the animal's screams from his bed and the blast of a rifle after it, and he got up and went downstairs to look at the clock. It was four in the morning. He went back up and dressed and as he passed Max's room he heard them stirring in there as well. By the time he'd got the coffee going Max was on the stairs and Sophia behind him rubbing her eyes. What's going on? she was asking.

You heard it? Max asked.

Yeah, Grant said, and to Sophia, Coyotes.

She went to the cupboard and set to work with a reluctant air. When they had eaten, Cotter showed up and Grant asked him to go get the poison out of the shed. Then he readied the provisions for a night's vigil.

Max watched him. I'll be sleeping here tonight, he said.

Grant could picture them in the bed together, his brother's hand at rest on her hip, her arm dangling off the edge. It won't get done in a day, he said.

Sure it will. We'll track 'em and dig out the den. Nothing so hard about that.

Grant said, We're out of practice.

He went to the shed and packed their bedrolls while Cotter rigged up the horses. They met Max in the yard. He was rubbing his hands together. Shit, it's still cold, he said.

Cotter handed the strychnine tablets to Grant in a candy tin which Grant slipped into his shirt pocket. Then they got on the horses and rode out over the hill following the sound of the dogs. Murray was circling the flock on his horse, a rifle under his arm and his colored glasses on a string around his neck. He was still cursing when they got to him. A bloody gash was on his lower lip where he appeared to have bit himself. I nicked 'im, I nicked 'im, he was saying.

Murray led them to the carcass. A back leg was broken and stripped to bone, and the ewe was torn open through the anus with its innards spread out on the spongy earth. He pointed up the hillside where the grass was bare. Fleeing, the coyote had avoided the snow until it was out of sight around the south side, leaving no visible tracks.

Grant dismounted and sliced the ewe open along her belly. He cut out rough cubes of flesh and slit them down the center, then pushed a tablet of poison deep into each. He handed some to Max and kept the rest. The dogs, quiet now, circled around them smelling the air.

Keep the dogs back, Grant said to Murray.

They took off in opposite directions around the hill, dropping the poisoned meat above the snowline. To the north Grant found a scrub pine that had been pissed on, but the tracks, clear in the shade, had melted nearly to nothing out in the sun and wind. At this altitude the sun had already risen and he had begun to sweat under his hat. He rode up among the rocks looking for further sign. But there was neither scat nor tracks.

When the meat was gone he rode back around the hill and met Max down in the canyon. Grant told him about the markings under the tree.

Might be looking at the wrong hill, Max said.

Doubt it. He wouldn't go off south if he didn't have to.

Max looked up at the hillside, brilliant now in the sunlight. Murray's kidding himself about that shot. We would of seen blood.

Maybe, Grant said.

They ate dinner with Murray in his wagon, where they could sit down without getting wet. Grant had never before been in it. It seemed larger than it did from outside, with a miniature cookstove and a wooden bench and a man-sized space on the floor where Murray could unfold his cot, which hung from pegs on the wall. The smell was of old meals and the herder's unwashed body. A lantern that hung from the ceiling was the only light. Grant imagined that in winter a man could go mad. When they'd finished eating he suggested Murray move the flock over the next hill while they hunted the coyote. He was surprised when Murray agreed. Then they cleaned up and stepped out into the daylight, which fell on them now with unusual intensity. In the still air it felt like a summer day. Murray called the dogs, and the sheep looked up and began to gather on the hillside like droplets of oil in a pan of water.

Grant and Max mounted and again circled the hill, this time higher up past the snowline where the rocks were larger and broke out through the ground. Twenty minutes later Grant heard his brother's whistle and moved ahead until he could see Max afoot on the western slope, standing over a shape in the snow.

The shape was the front half of a mule deer eviscerated by a coyote. Its dragging tracks came around from the south accompanied by the coyote's pursuing trail, its prints spread out and staggered in a casual walk. Alongside the trail was blood. From his saddle Grant took a shovel and shotgun, and they followed the trail up and around, back to the eastern face, which by now was in shadow and cooled by a wind. The snow had a crust which their boots crunched through as they walked. They were led to a gap among rocks, where the burnt-meat reek of the animals was drifting. Max stuck out his hand and Grant gave him the shovel.

No, Max said. He took the shotgun and jammed it in the hole and flicked off the safety.

How much good you think—Grant said, and Max fired. A single scream followed the shot's echo out across the canyon. Grant's bowels loosened at the sound and he crouched with one hand in the snow to keep from emptying himself.

Let's dig 'em out, Max said.

It was hard work. The ground was rocky and they had to roll big boulders out of it to get to the den. In a few hours it was exposed: a mother and six pups, most of them wounded by the shot, the mother glasseyed and panting, bleeding from the face and flank, and the blind pups squirming like mice underneath her. She tried to snarl. The shotgun lay next to Grant on a flat rock. Max pointed to it.

You want to finish them off? Or else hand it to me.

Grant bent down and picked up the shotgun and reloaded the empty chamber. He walked to the exposed den and aimed and the mother's eyes turned up to him. He saw that her legs didn't move, the shot had paralyzed her. He looked in her eyes and it was like looking into the night sky, at starlight that has taken a thousand years to reach the earth. He fired one barrel and killed her, then turned her over with his foot and finished the pups with the other.

When the echo died out Max stepped up and pushed the animals around with his boot. That's a goodly amount, he said.

Grant's eyes were on the dead pups. He said, He's still out there somewhere.

Drop bait ought to get him, don't you think?

Ought to.

Told you we would do it in a day.

Grant looked up and faced him. Max was grinning and the grin filled Grant with a rage he neither understood nor felt able to control. He was still holding the shotgun. Max looked down at the barrel and quit grinning and walked up to him. His boots dislodged a fist-sized rock that went tumbling down the hillside, skittering over the crusted snow. He grabbed the shotgun and Grant's hand loosened to let it go.

Without it his palm felt the cold and suddenly he could feel the cold all through him, in his joints and his gut and throat. He said, I think I may be coming down with something.

That must be it, Max told him, their eyes locked.

By nightfall Grant was feverish and by midnight he could barely stand up from bed to get a drink of water. He must have slept because at some point it was morning and his throat was a burning log, and a dark-faced man he recognized as Doc Lafitte was looking into his open mouth. Lafitte's strong features betrayed nothing, his big fleshy ears and bent nose, the dark smears under yellow eyes which had the lifeless appearance of things that were tacked to a wall. Figures flitted behind him: Sophia, his mother. Grant remembered that his mother was dead, declared so by this very man. Or was it Lafitte who had died?

Doc, he croaked. His throat swelled and contracted to a tight agonizing point.

Lafitte's hand drifted to Grant's forehead and then felt up under his chin. Grant shied away from the contact and a new pain exploded in the back of his head. Last night, the doctor said. They tell me you are having a terrible dream.

Grant remembered no dream and tried to say so. He opened his mouth and some air made it through but the words were lost in pain. Then it was night and moonlight was heavy in the room. He sat up. On the bedside table was a water bowl with a sponge in it, and a pill bottle and a glass of water. He sipped from the glass and coughed some of the water out. Then he put the glass down. From somewhere he heard the sound of someone sitting up in bed. Next he found himself flat on his back again with a screaming pain in his head and neck. After that time seemed to pass and it was morning again and there were eyes staring down at him. Sophia's. He was hungry.

I'm hungry, he said.

You look a lot better. She was wearing his mother's robe over a nightgown and her bare feet were flat on the plank floor.

My throat, he said. My head hurts like hell.

Here. She gave him the water, put it to his lips though he could have held it himself. Some of it dripped down his chin and neck and she wiped it dry with her sleeve. He smelled his mother's scent. Sophia stood up from her chair.

I'll make you some toast, she said.

Eggs, he said. Meat. What time is it?

Ten o'clock. I don't know if you can keep all that down. My daddy always eats a big breakfast the day he gets over being sick, and it always comes back up. A look crossed her face like it was on the way to somewhere else: rueful, repulsed.

If I can get it down I can keep it down, he said. Her answering expression was wary. He tried to remember. How long's this been going on? he asked.

Two days, she said. Max said not to worry but I thought you were going to die.

She looked at her hands, which were white and knit together. You had some kind of fever, she went on. Since you went to sleep last night it's been holding steady and it broke sometime this morning. The doctor gave you aspirins. You should take more when you eat your food.

Hair was growing on her ankles, a fine dark stubble. The toes curled and made a cracking sound.

I shot those coyotes and got a chill.

I know. Max told me.

Where is he?

Out working. Doing my chores, I guess. I said I would stay in and look after you.

That's real nice of you.

She blushed. I'll get your breakfast.

He listened to her going down and after awhile smelled bacon cooking. He took two of the aspirins and choked down a little more water. Then he got out of bed and went to the kitchen. His own body smelled of the sickness. She had the door propped open with a chair and sunlight was bleaching the room. The light was on the table and floor and her face at the window. She was looking out at Max working with Cotter in the yard. When Grant sat down she jumped.

Holy Moses, you scared the crap out of me, she said.

Pardon.

She turned back to the stove, moving quicker now, banging pans and dishes and spilling coffee over the counter. She muttered an oath and poured his black. Then she put food in front of him and sat with her legs crossed while he ate. When he was through she took the plate away and poured him more coffee, then rolled a cigarette from the makings in the pantry and smoked it sitting across from him.

There milk for this? he said, raising his cup.

She shook her head. Besides, she said, in your condition you don't want it.

Thanks for looking after me, he said.

She shrugged. How're you feeling?

Weak. I'll go out later.

You ought to stay in bed.

He could feel the food sliding into his stomach and his stomach reacting with a kind of astonishment. He closed his eyes. Maybe you're right.

You had brothers, she said suddenly. You and Max.

Four, he said.

She was looking past him at a corner of the room. They died. What happened?

You ought to ask Max about that.

He's told me.

Ain't anything else I can tell you then.

She was silent a long while. He wanted to get up but the breakfast was pinning him to the chair. He watched her because there was nothing else in the room to look at. The sun blazed behind her and he could see the outline of her scalp, round and helpless like a newborn's.

So, he said. You got any?

Sure, she said. Brother and a sister. Both older. My sister's a lot older. She's got a family. They live in the city but I hardly ever see them. My brother's married too. He lives in Chicago.

I've been there.

She smiled. Then the cigarette burned her fingers and she yelped and tossed it on the floor. It smoldered and went out and she cleaned it up with a rag. She threw the rag into the sink, and when she turned to him he could see tears forming in her eyes. They didn't fall.

I don't know how you can stand this place, she said.

Nobody's keeping you, he said. It came out angrier than he meant it, owing to the headache which only now was beginning to subside. But it was as if she didn't hear him.

Never seeing a soul except each other, she said, it's nuts.

It's a certain kind of living.

An idea seemed to occur to her. Where's the closest city?

Ashton's an hour's drive, he said.

Ashton! And she was up and past him and climbing the stairs.

When she came back down she was dressed in work clothes. She sat on the floor by the door and put her boots on. Just bought these, she said, and already they look like hell. She laughed. Of course they weren't so pretty to begin with, were they? She laughed again. Then she got up and faced the open door.

I'm sorry, Grant found himself saying, though none of what she'd said was on his account.

But she didn't answer. She turned her tight unhappy face on him for a moment and went out into the light.

·

He read and slept the entire day and dressed to eat dinner with the rest of them. Cotter and Max nodded when he came down, then turned back to their meals. This had a strange effect on Sophia. She looked from one to the other, asking them why they didn't so much as inquire about how Grant was feeling, her voice offended as if they'd failed to notice something she herself had done. Max said Grant looked pretty all right to him, no need to inquire, and the subject was left there.

Grant quit taking the aspirins. It didn't sit right with him. He slept uncomfortably and dreamlessly that night. In the morning he dressed straight off and after breakfast went to town for supplies, groceries and nails and meal for the chickens, because going to town wasn't too hard and could take up the time. His hunger of the morning before would not subside no matter what or how much he ate, and he was beginning to think the fever had undone something in him permanently, had hollowed out a place and sealed it off for good so that nothing could satisfy him. He ran through his errands and invented a couple of extras to keep from going home. When he'd truly run out of things to do he parked in front of the Sunrise and sat down at the counter.

Jean didn't say anything to him but when she brought his sandwich there was a plate of potatoes beside it that he hadn't ordered. He peered at himself in the napkin dispenser and found his reflection a little wan, the cheeks sunken, though that could have been the metal distorting him. He read the newspaper through the lunch hour and didn't look up until everybody had left the place. Then he saw Jean's eyes on him and watched as she went to the door and turned over the sign to read CLOSED. She stood and waited for him. He put down the paper and followed her upstairs, where she undressed him and then herself.

It seemed to take hours, like all goodbyes. He knew even as she moved under his hands, her flesh was somehow heavier, as if the lightness of passion had gone out of it and it was only a human body now, living but unpossessed. They lay listening to dogs barking outside and she told him all of what was going on in town, who was selling out to a cattle company, who was cheating who, an appearance of Mrs. Teabow buying bread at the grocery. Grant told her that Kittredge and Neeler were coming back from Colorado in a few weeks, he'd got a postcard saying they'd buried Kittredge's mother. He told her about the coyotes, and his fever.

What about the girl, Max's girl?

What about her, he asked.

There a story behind that? Or did she just appear out of nowhere?

He told her what little he knew. She thought the girl wouldn't make it very long. Grant couldn't disagree. But he didn't want to be talking about her like that, as she'd treated him kindly when he was sick. Instead he reached for Jean and she kicked off the bedclothes for the last time. During it she pinned him down and looked at him hard and said, You watch yourself, you don't look too good.

I don't feel quite right yet.

No, she agreed.

When he left her she said goodbye and shut the door behind him. He sat unmoving in the truck awhile, staring out at the filthy street, feeling the ghost of her under his fingers. He was hungry.

•

In the beginning of May Grant drove to Ashton to pick up Kittredge and Neeler. Kittredge had phoned the morning before to say they were coming by bus, and he was sorry if they were coming early but he was awful anxious to get out of Colorado. Petey's a little agitated, he said. He and my mama didn't much care for the other and we had a hell of a time down there. And then she passed on, Kittredge continued, and it just seemed to me it was time to get out.

Grant said, That's all right.

We finally got her trailer sold, though if you ask me we got skinned on account of we wanted the quick sale. Anyway it's no trouble if you ain't got work for us yet. We can put in our share for room and board if that'll help matters some.

Don't worry about that now, Grant said.

Well, I'm much appreciative.

Now the May sun was hot and dry and it chased the road dust through the truck window and muddied his throat. He thought he might get himself a bottle of pop in Ashton and drink it on the way back. Off to the south the mountains were indistinct, blazed and blurred by snowcaps. A man could be standing up there, Grant thought, with nothing but air between you and him, and still you could barely see him. For a moment it seemed strange that distance could render a thing invisible, that a man standing on the mountain could go unnoticed from the road. He thought about Kittredge, saddled with that fool boy, putting his mother in the ground. He could imagine what that felt like, but it was only his own memory he was thinking of, his own experience of death. The actual contour of Kittredge's pain was as distant to him as the mountaintop.

The bus station was an exposed wooden enclosure in the dirt lot behind the Ashton Supply. When he got there, nobody was in it. He parked the truck and walked in the back door of the store. Kittredge was folded into a metal army chair, tired as a rag blown up against a post. His hair was whorled across his scalp in a thumbprint's pattern and appeared brittle and gray, the hair of a much older man. Neeler'd gotten a haircut and was sitting on a shoe salesman's stool violently pulling on a pair of red Justin boots with fancy stitching up and down the sides. Grant took a chair.

Oh! Kittredge shouted. He plucked Grant's hand off the armrest to shake it. We got in a little early, he said, and Petey wanted to take a look at some boots—

I'll take these here ones, Neeler said without turning toward them. There was a slickness about him now, his shirt buttoned up to the collar and the red boots on his feet.

Hell, Petey, Kittredge said to him, they ain't worth nothin' for real work. You'll just rub out all that bric-a-brac.

They ain't for work, came the reply. They're for me.

Hey, look at who you're ignoring here, it's Grant, come to pick us up.

Neeler tilted his head halfway in Grant's direction and nodded once, a slow rote thing he must have seen in the movies.

Truck's out back, Grant said, I'll just meet you there when you're all finished. He saw their bags between the chairs and he picked them up and walked out. Funny how he had got used to wordless Cotter being the only one around; the population was doubling and tripling. He laid the bags in the back of the truck and went around to the front of the store, where he got a cola out of a machine. He stood drinking it a minute then went back to the lot to wait. Not much later they came out, Kittredge first, fingering his hat brim, and Neeler ten feet behind him wearing a new pair of brown work boots. Kittredge opened the passenger door and got in, leaving a space for Neeler. But Neeler jumped in the bed with the bags. Kittredge shut the door and Grant started the engine.

God damn that boy, Kittredge said with an uncharacteristic vehemence, still wearing his flat smile as if it was the only thing his face could think to do. God damn him, I don't know what's his problem. I ought to just cut him loose.

Grant steered them out of the lot and onto Main Street, slowing for the blinker. Why don't you? he said.

I can't. I can't, Kittredge said sighing. You ought to see him some nights, balled all up in his bed like a baby, it'd be like putting a gun to his head, it sure would. I'll tell you what, I feel sorry for that boy, I really do.

Out on the highway Grant took a draught of the cola and put it back between his legs. Max came back, he said.

Kittredge looked at him. That so? Where's he been all this time?

New York City. He was painting pictures.

Kittredge squinted out over the hood at the coming road. Painting pictures! Well why'd he come back then?

Same reason anybody does, I guess.

There was a knock on the cab window. Neeler was pointing and making a gesture, drinking from his thumb and little finger. He had a look on his face like something'd been stolen from him. Grant drank from the bottle once more and then held it out the window, and Neeler leaned over the side and took it. Through the rearview Grant saw him empty the bottle into his wide cracked mouth and fling it out behind them, where it bounced and shattered on the black macadam. The glass receded, glimmering like a liquid.

He drove them straight to their quarters. Come up the house when you're ready for some dinner, he said. In fact they were late, it was after two and Sophia'd likely cooked it and left it, if she'd cooked it at all. Neeler beelined to the cabin empty-handed and Kittredge humped their bags to the door.

Back at the house he found himself alone. He buttered some bread and sat down to eat it. His eyes moved to the kitchen window. As he watched, Sophia came out of the barn slapping dust off her clothes. She looked up and saw the truck and then turned her head to the window Grant was looking out of. With the sun above and behind her reflecting off the house, he doubted she could see him there, yet she stood frozen for long seconds before she went into the henhouse.

Ever since he was sick she'd been striking up conversations, at first asking him practical questions about the animals and later inquiring about him personally, about their childhood here and his years at sea. Initially he was reluctant to discuss either, but since they were often on his mind he came to think there was no harm in it. Now he wasn't sure. Talking about a thing, he'd learned, could freeze and focus the memory, sharpening some parts and obscuring others, as in a photograph. He didn't want his memory to be like a box of pictures, a set of little truths that didn't add up to a life. Yet he kept talking to her, trying to ignore what he was saying, because he found he liked her brand of talk, liked the company of somebody who wanted to hear.

She told him about her girls' school in the city and all its pettinesses and trivialities, which struck him as absurd, the way they taxed and strained the emotions. It made him think of his own school, the one they went to before the new elementary was built in Eleven, a single brick room under a crumbling roof which now stood slumped and empty along the road to town. Their teacher was a tiny lady from Eugene, Oregon who had married a local cattleman and had used to play in an orchestra. Half of every day they spent practicing on musical instruments, whatever ones the students could find, harmonicas, flutes, a concertina, a fiddle. A dented trumpet that had a shivery, addled tone like the bleat of a goat. They played in concerts for their families, though only when the weather was fine and they could do it outdoors. There was no room in the school for both performers and audience. Grant had learned to play a borrowed flute and Max a guitar. Sometimes there was a girl singer. A passing truck might pull over to listen. It seemed a strange way to occupy schoolchildren, though nobody questioned it at the time. The teacher would be sad to know that he no longer played music, and to think of it made him a little sad himself.

When he talked, particularly about things he'd done with Max, Sophia sometimes sat up suddenly or spoke a wordless note as if she was amazed, even at such plain recollections as a hunting expedition or fistfight. He got the sense that she was remembering it all for some future purpose.

They didn't ever talk about Max directly, and when Max was with her she didn't say much to Grant. Instead she directed what she said to Max, who might look at Grant to include him or might not. For awhile Grant didn't notice this was going on, not until he'd begun to speak to her in private, and he began to wonder whether Max knew the two of them spoke at all, so different was she in his presence. Only when he was alone, out riding or lying in his bed, was Grant fully at ease, when he could forget and didn't have to keep track of who was around him and who wasn't, and what he could say and how he could say it. Yet at these times he missed her, anyone's, company.

Now he got up from the table and went out to her and asked if she could fix something for Kittredge and Neeler to eat. I'm sorry to miss you earlier, he said.

You didn't. Max and Amos wanted to wait.

It took him a second to register this name: it was Cotter's. Where are they? he asked.

Shed, she said scattering meal on the ground for the chickens. Her eyes were on the work, her movements dismissive, like she was shooing him. He went to find Cotter and his brother. They were in the shed as she told him, examining a canvas tarp for wear.

Christ, Max said to him, you have got to get some rat poison out here. He waggled a finger through a round hole that had been chewed in the tarp.

I've done it. It doesn't seem to do much good.

They'll get into my things, Max said.

Grant shrugged. They were expecting the shearers soon, a band of Mexicans who worked their way north following the season, up into Canada in summer, visiting outfits like theirs who didn't have the time or skill to do it themselves. There was no permanent shearing shed here, so the lambing pens were nailed together and covered with a treated tarp to keep the rain out. This was the tarp Max and Cotter were working on.

You hear from the Mexicans? Grant asked.

Max let him wait for the answer while he fished in a metal box for a roll of gray tape. He tore off a length with his teeth and fitted it over a mousehole. Called from Gillette while you were out, he said. They ought to be in tonight late.

Grant wondered when Max had been planning to tell him this. He said, You get the rooms done up?

Max treated the question like an accusation. Don't I look busy enough already?

Cotter caught the tone and lifted his head. He turned to Grant to see what he would say.

Only asking, Grant said and a split second later made an error in judgment and added, You're near to boiling over, Max. Maybe you ought to tell me what's going on.

Max stood.

Grant said, It ain't my fault I got sick. I'd've liked to be out here helping you—

That's right, Max muttered, nothing's your fault, is it. Everything just happens.

His hands seemed to be shaking. The sight of them filled Grant with remorse for everything he'd done and said, the way seeing a quaking tree branch can bring on the instincts of winter. He shivered without moving. He wasn't sure what was happening.

Cotter moved suddenly and the both of them turned as if they'd forgot he was there. He was holding a set of pliers and stood framed by the painting tools behind him, the easel and the model's platform. In the dim light, by a trick of perspective, he looked to Grant like a giant, the subject of some myth.

What! Max barked, and Grant felt himself twitch.

Cotter coughed. I was just thinking, he said. When you two was boys you used to pretend you was fighting, remember that?

He was turning the pliers over and over in his hand. A bent nail fell from their grip and rang out against the cement. He put the pliers in his back pocket as a man sure of his safety holsters a gun.

No, Grant said.

That was your way of fighting, pretending a fight. One of you got mad, the other one would get his dukes up and start scuffing like it was some kind of joke. He looked from one to the other and let out a laugh. You'd think from looking at you that you was afraid of killing each other.

Grant turned his eyes to his brother but Max wasn't looking back. He appeared to be in a trance. Grant remembered now, the bogus dustups out in the barn. They'd got started because of an incident when Max was seven or eight and Grant thirteen. Robert was two years dead, they were arguing over something of his, maybe it was a saddle. Max was cleaning off a knife or sharpening it on a stone, and Grant came over and took the saddle from nearby for some reason. And then—he couldn't have explained why, maybe Max was entertaining some fierce possession of the saddle in his mind at that moment— Max came up behind him with the knife and stabbed him through the side just below the skin, so that the blade sunk in under the ribs, pierced the fat and came out again a couple of inches beyond at the front side of his flank, never going more than a fraction of an inch deep. He couldn't have said what Max had been thinking to do when he got up off his stool. Probably not what he ended up doing. But Grant had half turned when he heard him coming, and the knife went in hard and smooth and easy. Max's face was bent in a theatrical fury that Grant had sometimes seen since Robert died, when Max thought he was alone. He was only a little boy, Grant remembered, barely beginning school and already with two dead brothers behind him.

The two had stood still, regarding the knife sticking out of Grant, the blade clean where it met the hilt and streaked with blood where it emerged. After a silence of seconds Max began to cry and Grant dropped the saddle into the dirt, or must have, because he used one hand to press the wound and the other to pull out the knife. Afterward Max helped him to disinfect and bandage the cuts, his only apology. At the time, Grant's impression was that Max had no idea what he'd done, or even that he'd done anything. They told no one. From then on their skirmishes were faked.

It was strange. A kind of animal readiness came over Max, his eyes grew wild. Grant learned to drop whatever he was doing and take him on. They batted at each other and rolled on the floor in a feral clinch. Max always held on longer, even when Grant loosened his grip and tried to roll him off. In due time the aggression drained out of the embrace until, in its greediness and desperation, it began to resemble an act of grief. Max bit him, sometimes breaking his skin through the clothes, and Grant held him until at last he grew limp in his arms. This went on a month or two until Edwin shot himself. After that Max began to teach himself and Thornton the rudiments of work, and what peculiar intimacy he'd shared with Grant was gone.

How Cotter had managed to see them doing this, Grant had no idea. They had carried on in private. But Cotter, who they'd not thought of as real, had seen and remembered, and he had them now in thrall, like a magician.

Cotter bent over and pulled another nail out of the plank he was working on. The sound of his breath shook them awake. Grant hazarded a glance at his brother and Max fixed his eyes on the floor where the tarp lay crumpled. His hands were still. It was obvious he was waiting for Grant to go.

I'll go fix the rooms, Grant said, and he left the shed for the house to get the linens.

•

He hadn't been in his parents' bedroom since Sophia had come to occupy it. Little was changed. A photo of some girls, Sophia among them, was thumbtacked to the wall; a scarf hung over a lampshade; the bureau was covered with small things, perfumes he hadn't known her to wear, letters, jewelry. He picked up the blue bottle from the windowsill. The glass distorted and discolored his fingers. Some tonic had been in it once, he could smell the astringency and make out the antiquated type on a half-gone label. The sight of his shriveled hand made him think of Wesley. He put the bottle back. From this window he could see the road vanish beyond the rise and reappear as it climbed up out of the valley.

The extra linens were kept in the closet, folded and stacked in a far corner behind the hung clothes. This was the only upstairs closet and it had been his mother's alone for as long as he could remember. It wasn't in her nature to be especially private or possessive, but it was understood in this house that the closet was all she had to herself. He opened the door and took note of what Sophia had done. Her few clothes—an extra pair of dungarees and several work shirts of Max's, a few dresses too fine to wear and which he had never seen her in—hung on the right side with more than six inches separating them from his mother's. His mother's dresses she had not disturbed. He widened the gap to see where the linens lay and the back of his hand brushed the waist of a dress, Sophia's. He pulled the hand away like he'd been shocked. Reluctantly he brought it to his face. After a moment he took the fabric between his thumb and finger and leaned forward to breathe through it. The air trapped inside smelled of her powerfully, a concentrated scent he knew from passing her. It reminded him of the ocean, not for the specificity of the fragrance but for its intensity, its separateness from the smells ordinarily around him when he worked or slept. It was like looking at photographs of a place he knew he would never go to, someplace foreign and lovely. For a moment he missed the sea and the man he had been then; their distance from him filled him with longing. Not that he would prefer to be there now, to be that man. He had not been happy. But he longed for the inevitability of those days, the impossibility of leaving the boat, the certainty of some hardships, the necessity of other people. He let go of the dress but allowed it to brush his face when he bent down to pick up the bedsheets, and he closed the closet door firmly behind him.

In the shearers' quarters, fitting the narrow beds with sheets and inhaling the old woodsmoked air, his concentration left him and he envisioned Sophia posing for his brother, undressed before the cold corrugated metal walls, and he sat down on a freshly made bunk and for several minutes held his face in his hands.

•

Max rode out over the hill to bring in Murray and the flock, and by the time the sheep were back in their shed, clouds had begun to mass over the mountains to the north. By nightfall Cotter had the shearing shelter assembled in the yard. Grant woke that night to the sound of the Mexicans' truck and the near-silent swipe of drizzling rain on the windows and roof. He dressed and went down to meet the men. There were five of them, all small and muscular. Their reticence and similar build made him believe they were brothers. Each had some English but it was the oldest, Jorge, who spoke for the group, and when he met Grant he clasped his hand and pointed at the sky. Grant nodded, telling him the tarp was patched and sealed and the flock under cover in their shed. But he knew the shearing would be hard in rain. Though these men were professionals who could each get the fleece whole off two hundred head in a day, the wool couldn't be bagged wet and there would be a delay as each sheep was toweled off and the towels dried. Grant was ashamed of their makeshift shelter, he dreaded ushering the workers into it. To Jorge he said something to this effect, and the smaller man shrugged and said it was okay because their ranch, unlike most, had good beds. Elsewhere the flock was given the better roof. Somewhere in this comment Grant thought he could hear a slight, but one so oblique and blunt-edged as to be inconsequential. He nodded and pointed them toward their quarters.

The rain picked up as the truck's lights receded into mist. Grant thought about what they would need to combat the rain: every towel and blanket in the place, a barrel they could start a fire in and scrap wood to burn, another good tarp to keep the water off the gas generator that would power the electric shearers. It couldn't have been much past two A.M., but he turned back to the house to wake his brother up.

•

By morning the rain was a steady torrent under a black sky cut at intervals by lightning. But the shearers seemed oblivious to weather, going at their work with silent determination, the fleece loosening itself from the sheep in thick intact mats. Max rolled the fleece and gave it to Neeler to examine and stuff into sacks; Neeler rushed the sacks to the equipment shed. Kittredge and Murray and Cotter led the shorn sheep to their shed, wrestled each into a dipping vat and let it loose to huddle with the others. Grant was rubbing the unshorn animals dry as fast as he could, trying to wick the rain off the fleece without pressing it deeper down, and Sophia ran, frantic, to the fire and back, trying to keep the towels dry enough to do him some good. But they were losing. They would need to empty out the bags and air the fleece, it was inevitable. Sometimes Grant looked up and saw one or two of the shearers standing idle, somehow smoking a cigarette in the awful wet, and he understood that they wouldn't be finished by nightfall, that there would be at least another half day, and though the shearers weren't union workers Grant had promised them union wages because they were better than the local men. It was more than he could afford. By noon Neeler had begun to complain that the fleece was giving him a runny nose and making his head ache. Sophia traded jobs with him. But after that the towels came to Grant still wet, and the shearers looked up from the damp animals annoyed at the sudden change. By late afternoon the shearers had their shirts off and were using them to dry the sheep a second time. Throughout, the roar of the generator filled the air, punctuated by the crash of thunder and the occasional frenzy of barks from Murray's dogs.

All of them took supper together. Grant went up to Edwin's room and brought down the chairs, which by seven o'clock were again occupied by brothers. Max finished eating first and said, in a hoarse disgusted voice, What a goddam mess.

No kidding, said Neeler, rubbing a handkerchief under his nose and looking at it.

Max went on, ignoring him. This cheap shit won't work, he said. A few of the shearers looked up. All that goddam work for what's going to be a rotten soaking load. I seen 'em going in, the wool's all taggy and grimy. He threw down his fork. We got to start bringing them in before lambing.

He hadn't been looking at Grant, but it was for Grant the words were intended. It's too cold before lambing, he said.

Too cold for that slapped-together shack, maybe.

Jorge was sitting beside Grant and touched his wrist with two thin fingers. Maybe you build a permanent pen next to your shed, he said quietly. With wood floor. And a chute that come up to it, with a roof. Not so hard to do.

No money, Grant said.

Sophia came up behind Max and spooned food onto his plate. Max turned his head and pushed the plate away. She paused a moment and moved on to the Mexicans, who nodded their thanks.

Grant's arms and fingers ached from working the towels over the animals and his eyes were red from exhaustion and cut fleece. It seemed they might all be at this table forever, so powerful was the disinclination to move. Sophia sat down in front of her empty plate and looked at it, keeping a distance between herself and Max. Some time later Jorge cleared his throat and stood up, and the other shearers followed him to the counter where they left their plates in a neat stack. Then they went out into the rain for another few hours' work. Not long afterward Cotter got up too, and then everyone else.

•

The Mexicans were paid and gone by midafternoon of the next day, and while Sophia slept, the rest of them tore down the shearing shelter and dragged the pieces into the shed. The sun had arrived as if it had been waiting for them to finish. Shorn sheep were wandering out into the light. Cotter and Murray went to give them dry bedding and feed. In a few days they would be on summer range.

Kittredge sat on a fence rail rolling a cigarette with shaking hands. Grant watched, wanting to take the paper and tobacco from him and do it himself. When Kittredge had finally got it Grant went to him and asked if he wanted to go get some sleep.

Nah, Kittredge said without elaboration. He looked peaked. He rubbed his forehead with the stump of his missing finger, still shaking but less so now that the smoke was in him.

Maybe you'll want to take a little rest, Grant said. Stay here and heal up some. I wouldn't ask you anything for the bed but if you could get some of the food when—

Nah, now all *that's* done—he pointed with his thumb in the direction the shearers had gone—it'll get easier around here, ain't that right?

Sure.

Unless you can't keep us on here, that's a different matter, I understand that.

No, that ain't it, Grant said, though it was. He owed again, a few hundred here and there. The fleece would cover it but beyond that he didn't know. Once the fleece went to market Kittredge and Neeler were no longer necessary. Kittredge's free hand gripped the rail steadily, but the hand he smoked with still shook. He tried to keep the arm pinned to his side. It gave him a winter look, like he was protecting himself from weather. Grant said, I just thought you might use a break, that's all.

Kittredge nodded. Maybe, he said. Maybe soon. I think right now I'll just smoke this here cigarette.

Grant left him there. Murray and Cotter were tending to the sheep themselves now, salving shear cuts and guiding the animals out of the sun to spare their skin. He remembered he'd sent Neeler into the shed to air out the fleece. When he went in he found it unrolled across the floor, much as he would have done himself, covering every inch of space, filled in among the equipment and over Max's area like a moss that had sprung up. The scent of wet wool filled the room. Neeler was bent over at the shed's far end, opposite the easel, one hand pressed to the metal wall, a burning cigarette in the other. Grant said to him, Good job, Pete, and Neeler almost jumped out of his skin, dropping the cigarette onto the fleece and quickly stooping to pick it up. He'd never looked to Grant so much like a boy, so inessential, as he did now, still half-crouched, a crosseyed cornered look on his face like a streak of mud. He said nothing.

Good going, Grant said. This'll do the job.

In the rusted wall behind Neeler, Grant could see a small hole where Cotter had once backed the truck up too fast with a length of copper pipe in the bed. The pipe had torn through and left a corroded flap that had since fallen off. Neeler had been looking through the hole. Grant said, If you want to fix that I won't stop you.

Neeler closed his mouth and stood straight, a hint of swagger returning to his frame. Hey, all right, he said. Maybe I will, sure.

You might find a little scrap metal in the fire cabinet, or else you could go to town and bring back a sheet. There's a torch in there too. You know how to use a torch?

I think I used one once.

You put the mask on, and then there's a lighter in there.

Neeler nodded, his whole upper body moving with it. Okay, I can get to that maybe.

But something told Grant he wasn't going to do it at all and possibly didn't even know what Grant was talking about. There was a deep meanness and stupidity to the boy which no good will could touch. He doubted Neeler even knew what was in him, no more than a house could know who was living in it or a stream know where it was flowing to. He was like a force of nature, dull and destructive.

That was a heavy load to hang on this dumb motherless boy, Grant knew, but it was hard to shake the impression of malevolence, to believe there was a decent man under there who could do the outfit some good.

There was nothing else to say. Grant touched his hat and nodded at Neeler, leaving him standing on a tiny patch of exposed cement, the only thing he'd left uncovered. He looked back again from the doorway. The boy stood helpless on his little island, wiping his nose with the back of his hand, fleeced in.

In a day, when the fleece was dry, the men and Sophia spread themselves out through the shed rolling and tying it up, picking out burrs and bits of skin. For the most part it had turned out better than Grant expected, and with the weather mild and clear in the wake of the rain he let himself be filled up with optimism. Neeler had stacked the empty bags still damp. They had not fully dried and smelled of mold. So Max and Sophia aired them out in the yard, running in circles, holding them over their heads under the bright sun. Cotter hitched the trailer onto the truck and with Grant loaded the bagged wool to bring it to the merchant's in Ashton. They rode with the windows open and the cool wind along the ridge rushed in. Aspens glittered at the roadside like pinwheels. Between the men lingered that strangeness with Max in the barn, but Cotter was unlikely ever to mention it again. Once they were down on the flats Grant fiddled with the radio knob until something came in they could both stand to hear. The music was like an unexpected and not unwelcome passenger, evidence of life elsewhere. It eased Grant, the remedy for an ailment he hadn't noticed he'd got.

The Merchants' Hall in Ashton was a brick warehouse with tall windows set close together on the north side. When they pulled around they were momentarily blinded by the sunlight glancing off its face. Nobody else was here. A wooden chute marked where to back up the trailer. Once they'd done so they began unloading the wool bags through an open steel door. Inside, a fan was moving. Over its roar they greeted the grader, a high narrow man of about sixty Grant could recognize but not name. They all said good morning and Grant shook his hand, and the grader's eyes rested on him a moment longer than was necessary, apprehending and judging him. But the grader said nothing. He stood behind a long wooden table, and behind him stood a dozen wicker baskets, each about the size of Grant's cabin on the *Rose Adams*, into which their wool would be sorted. The grader plunged his hand into the first of the bags and let it linger there. He glared blankly, lost in a private tactile world.

They brought in more bags, stealing glances at the grader's work as they heaved them onto the table. With quick fingers the grader was tugging at the fibers, holding them up to the light. Shortly an assistant arrived, a man of about thirty, shorter and rounder in the face than the grader but nonetheless his very image. His son. Now the work moved faster, the son opening their bags along the seam and, when his father was through, tossing the graded bundles into the bins behind them. Meanwhile the grader made notations with the stub of a pencil on a yellow form.

Their demeanor made Grant uneasy. The son accepted mumbled assessments from the father and flung the bundles with a studied carelessness. For a moment Grant had the notion that he wanted them back, he felt his body tugged toward the bins each time he stepped through the door with a new bag. The bags were heavy and unwieldy and his back was beginning to ache.

Grant and Cotter were finished long before the grader and his son, so they stood inside with the windows behind them and watched the men work. Most of the bundles went into one of two bins close behind the tables. The bins weren't marked but Grant knew that each represented a grade of wool. Outside more trucks began to arrive and Grant could hear men talking to one another just outside the door. After awhile the grader spoke to Grant without looking up.

Your daddy used to raise a fine wool.

Yes, he did, was all Grant could say.

How's he doing? the grader asked. Your daddy. He looked up and met Grant's eyes, and Grant knew he knew that John Person was gone. Panic began to well in the hollows of his body.

Couldn't say, Grant said finally. He peered at the grader's son and found him looking back, and in that moment Grant knew him. Only the last name would come to him. Burt. Their name was Burt. This junior Burt had come back alive from the war. He had a brother who hadn't. Grant held his eyes until Burt turned to his father.

Oh, he's away, is he? the grader had gone on. Now you're the older boy, is that right? You were away yourself awhile.

That's right.

I imagine it's hard coming home to us after seeing the world.

I didn't see much but the inside of a boat.

The grader was finished, the tables cleared of fleece. The young Burt began to fold and stack the empty bags. Grant's eyes lingered on the older man, who stared furiously back, then at last bent over his adding machine and punched in the numbers he'd written. He marked a total on the yellow sheet and handed the carbon to Grant. They'll cut you a check at the office, he said.

Grant looked at the form. Only about a third of what they'd brought had been marked fine, the quality numbers just over sixty. Much of what he used to bring here with his father was far finer, usually in the seventies. The other two thirds was marked half or three-eighths blood, not the typical numbers of a professional outfit. In fact they were worse than last year's: not just disappointing but wrong.

Is something the matter, Mr. Person?

Grant looked up into the grader's eyes but could not comprehend what he was looking at. The man's judgment of him was extraordinary, even absurd. Nevertheless Grant couldn't help feeling it was correct. He grew hot with shame and rage and felt Cotter's hand on his arm.

Mr. Person? the grader asked again.

No, Grant said. Nothing's the matter, Mr. Burt. Burt's son stood frozen now, unsure of what was happening, and the older man himself seemed stunned by the mention of his name, as if suddenly reminded that it was indeed he who had cheated a customer. He hung his head. Grant had it figured now: the bins closest to them were likely reserved for fine wool, the commonest grade received here. Much of his own wool had gone into them. The younger Burt began almost imperceptibly to pale. He hadn't known what his father was doing, nor who Grant was. After another moment Cotter turned and left and Grant followed him out.

Cotter moved the trailer out of the chute and met Grant at the office door on the west side of the building. He took the form from Grant's hand and read it.

He won't do it again, Cotter said. He knows it was a mistake. There's other places to sell wool and he's got a reputation to keep.

Cotter handed back the form. I ain't surprised he done it, he went on, fingering the collar of his shirt where it curled under. The morning sun was throwing the shadow of the hall over and past them, across a gravel lot and up the wall of an apartment house, where it gave way in the middle of a window to a blinding reflection of the sun itself. Cotter said, I figured you was no damn good myself, when you got back. People don't see how complicated a thing is. They think if it was them they'd of done something different. They don't know how weak they are until something happens that's stronger than them.

Cotter held Grant's forearm loosely in his fingers. Grant watched his own fingers creasing the form, the sweat smearing the numbers on it. Cotter said, I ain't saying you always done the right thing, but you never done what that Burt just did. You never cheated an honest man.

For some reason these words evoked Grant's father, a trip Grant took west with him once, over the divide to look at a tractor somebody was selling. They'd been thinking of growing alfalfa on a section of their pastureland, to feed the flock cheaper during lambing. As they topped the mountains and descended into the lushness and warmth of the western slopes, John grew morose and finally pulled over and collapsed onto the wheel.

Grant was still a boy, he didn't understand. What is it? he asked, shaking his father by the shoulder.

Sometimes you want to go back where you came from, his father said through tears. He fished a rag out of the glovebox and wiped his face with it. Then they turned around and drove home, the tractor and alfalfa forgotten.

With Cotter's hand still on his arm, Grant wondered out loud if he would ever see his father again. And Cotter, as if following perfectly this wayward train of thought, said no. Grant's hand fell to his side. He could release the paper he was holding and watch the wind carry it out into the street, and they could get into the truck and leave here. But he didn't do that, it would be crazy. Instead the two of them walked wordlessly into the office to collect their money.

•

He woke that night to the sound of scratching above him, something moving around. A vague memory of past dreams crossed his mind and frightened him; he drew breath and threw off the covers. But the memory was gone. The scratching continued, rhythmically: there was a sentience to it. Animals up there. They had an attic he'd forgot about. He lay down and tried to sleep, the pillow clamped over his ear, and in the half-dream that followed, the muffled scrabbling became a man's heavy tread, monotonously pacing as if in anticipation of terrible news.

Morning brought naked daylight and the hotness of summer. The night's noise came back to him. When they were boys he and Max and Robert used to climb up and pretend to guard the valley against the Germans their father had sometimes told them about. Grant couldn't recall if anything was up there now. He could remember no floor, only planks laid loose across the joists. The sound they made when he and his brothers ran across them was like an artillery barrage, or what they imagined one to sound like.

He sat up in his bed feeling the attic's presence like days of unfinished work. The light outside was still new but pressed him to get up, so he did, glancing occasionally at the cracked plaster ceiling.

On the floor next to the bureau Grant had left his bag, the one he traveled with and hadn't touched since he took his pay out of it nearly two years before. When he had first returned it reminded him of what he left behind, and he'd no desire to open it. In time it had become part of the room's landscape and his eyes passed it over without catching.

He dressed, then lifted the bag onto the bed. After a few seconds he sat down beside it and undid the latch. Folded on top was his shirt, the one he'd left home wearing, which had wanted washing and still did. He took it out and laid it aside. Only a few other objects remained. A single black sock whose twin he'd kept his money in. The whalebone box, hexagonal with a carved lid. After a moment's consideration he brought this over to the bureau. It had come from Iceland. A sailor had been peddling his possessions out of a sack on the dock. The man spoke no English but managed to explain with his hands that he was to go to sea and didn't wish to be encumbered by his things. Grant paid him and took the box. Iceland was his mother's country and he'd wanted to bring her something from there.

Now he went back to the bag and removed a wristwatch and Luc's brass compass wrapped in a soft gray cloth. The wristwatch had come out of a cod. It was old and eaten away by salt water and by the chemicals in the fish. Its face was stained and buckled, the glass gone, the hands crooked and corroded into place. The word DEUTSCHLAND was engraved on the back.

The compass had been Luc's grandfather's. Grant wondered where his friend was now. Probably still at sea or back in Belgium. Luc had been too personable for the fishing life: Grant would not have been surprised to learn he had quit. The compass was tarnished by years of neglect, but he could polish it. It seemed to work.

The whaleman's knife, the one he'd got in a card game, still glinted at the bottom of the bag. He reached for it, then thought better. Instead he picked up the bag and brought it to his bureau. He opened a drawer and upturned the bag over it, and the knife tumbled in, to rest in a gap between shirts. Then he shut the drawer and returned the bag to the floor.

Later in the morning he had occasion to go out to the barn, and he took his pannier off the nail where it was hung and added the compass to his camp supplies. There wasn't anyplace within fifty miles of here where he'd need it, but knowing he would have it on hand calmed his nerves, as if now he was ready for anything.

•

After supper, when Max and Sophia went out to the shed, Grant entered her closet and looked up into the darkness. He could make out an opening in the ceiling covered by a board. Standing on his toes he fingered the board aside and began to hoist himself up. But his grip was poor and he came down on his feet. He tried again, jumping this time and hooking his elbows into the attic space. From there it was easy.

The attic was boiling hot, the setting sun outside drowning it in an orange wash. His eyes were drawn to the semicircular vent on the west wall; they fixed upon a distant passing cloud, blazed pink by the oblique light. Only when the cloud left his sight did Grant turn around to see what was here.

Not much. Even the planks were gone, probably taken down and used for something. There were leaves blown in by storms and a raven's nest that looked long unoccupied. The nest had been built in a corner, down between two rafters. He goosestepped over to it, ducking his head away from the ceiling beams, and leaned close to peer at a bright thread running through. Ribbon, the sheen still on it, the kind a girl might put in her hair. He tugged at the free end but the nest had been woven too tightly.

In another corner, the one above his bedroom, was a mound of household debris—bits of cloth and paper, thread, and hair—with a depression in the center. It smelled of rodent. Mice. He lifted this second nest and shoved it out the vent. It quickly fell from sight.

The wind picked up and a meaningless breeze pushed through the empty space. Grant's heart was heavy. He felt bad for throwing away the mouse nest. For the next several weeks, as he tried to sleep, he could hear a new one being built.

•

It was July of 1950. The Fourth had passed. The only thing that happened in Eleven all year was the rodeo, and it was about to start. Merchants who wouldn't ordinarily have bothered sweeping their own stoops were out painting the clapboards. Roads were oiled and graveled and trucks came rumbling over them full of boxes from Ashton. Unfamiliar pickups and trailers began to appear, and in a trampled pasture outside town tents sprang up, spilling out calf ropers and bulldoggers who were louder than locals and had more money. The bar was always full. This year it was selling beer in screwtop motor oil cans, and the cans made their way out into the street and started piling up in the gutters and flattening under truck tires. Every night there were good-looking girls crying drunk on curbs until somebody came for them and escorted them back to their tents. They had come with their men from California and had been on the circuit more than two months, with at least three more to go. From here they would go to Cheyenne or Pendleton and after that a lot of them would just go home. The riders would continue without them all the way to New York and Boston.

Every year somebody was seriously injured or killed. Grant had seen a local boy get himself landed full on by his quarter horse about a dozen years back, and the boy had stood up like nothing had happened, walked ten feet holding his head with both hands, and fell down dead in the dirt. People got run down by drunks or drove into trees or phone poles. Occasionally somebody got shot, either by accident or in a fight. Typically the county gave badges to a lot of local men and trucked them down to Eleven for the duration of the rodeo, and often these men got involved in the drinking and shooting. The town's own police department, which consisted of one retired cattle rancher and his son, tended to stay at the office and wait for the criminals to come in on their own.

As a matter of habit Grant didn't go to the rodeo, not since he'd seen the boy die. The immodesty of cowboys didn't endear them to him, either, and the events they competed in seemed less like sport than a brutal parody of work. There was a long-standing rivalry between cattlemen and sheepmen that had its origins in territorial disputes. But it endured out of taste. Grant found the cattlemen brutish and arrogant and their games disrespectful to the animal. It was wrong to mock the thing that gave you life. The sheep was not an intelligent beast but in great numbers achieved a kind of elemental dignity, like an air mass. Once he'd seen a flock move across a hillside and mistook it for the shadow of a cloud. He had watched sheep gather where they once found a salt lick years before, even the lambs, who hadn't been alive to see it. A sheepflock seemed to pulse with purpose almost as if it was one creature, a vast and simple mind that understood its relationship to the land and to man, while a herd of cattle was nothing more than a vegetable garden with hooves, a lowing orchard, inefficient and dumb.

But Neeler wanted to go to the rodeo. Since the shearing, the boy had little to do and had grown bored and hostile. Earlier and earlier each night he slicked back his hair and demanded that Cotter drive him to town, and often he stayed there until morning, spending pocketsful of Kittredge's money on drink and getting himself into fights and once into jail. If Cotter refused him his ride Neeler would take a horse and run it to exhaustion on the rangeland. When he got back he would leave it unstabled in the yard. While drunk he jeered at them openly, everyone but Max, who he was afraid of. Max, for his part, never spoke to Neeler at all.

The night before the rodeo began, a thick wind was draining out of

the northwest. Dust roiled on their road. From his room Grant watched it eddy and sway in the porchlight, the very air given shape. Its deftness and power were frightening: he was grateful that it was ordinarily invisible. He almost failed to notice the shape moving along the back wall of the equipment shed, hunched over in the dark. A bear? Max and Sophia were in there.

He pulled his boots on and brought a shotgun out into the yard. Hi! he shouted, the word nearly lost over the grinding of the wind. Cautiously he moved closer. The shape was a man's.

He recognized Neeler's posture first: the same stoop Grant had caught him in before, inside the shed. Then, Neeler had been examining the hole in the shed wall. He was doing the same thing now. Not to fix it, to look through it. To watch Sophia being drawn or painted.

Naked of course. Grant had tried to keep himself from thinking about it. He supposed it was only natural for such a notion to cross his mind, but somehow, with Sophia, it seemed wrong. Now Neeler had his eyes on her and Grant wanted to get him. He realized that he'd wanted him for weeks. Everything suddenly seemed to be Neeler's fault, all the ugliness of life the product of his ugliness. Grant shouted and his legs carried him to the shed, the weight of the shotgun asserting itself against his palm.

Neeler stood up with a forced slowness, like a man asked to put down his drink and meet guests. Grant was enraged.

What in the hell do you think you're doing? he shouted, and the wind snatched the words and carried them off. He stood as close as caution allowed.

There was a cigarette in Neeler's mouth which, no longer shielded by the bulk of his head, glowed brightly, releasing a stream of white ash into the air. He said, See for yourself, partner, and pointed at the bright hole.

Grant's right hand twitched and discovered it was holding the shotgun. It was the left that opened wide and struck Neeler in the mouth. The slap was loud even over the wind and knocked the cigarette into the grass. Grant leaned into him now and the boy's fat stunned face filled his vision. You're one move away from gone, you understand me? he said, and Neeler blinked and blinked again.

Maybe you wouldn't be so brave without that shotgun, Neeler croaked. His red lips were split and scabbed and his tongue emerged to wet them.

Grant flung the shotgun into the dirt.

Neeler backed off a bare inch, making room to swing. Grant shifted one leg to steady himself. He could remember every single punch he'd thrown in his life: every schoolhouse brawl and sloppy drunken cuff, every shoving match over whatever stupid slight. In the past he'd regretted each of them. Now they seemed justified, even necessary. Neeler stood three or four inches shorter than Grant but his arms were thick and dense as firewood, and when the fist arrived it had that weight behind it. But it was a bad punch, overcompensating for the difference in height, striking Grant on the cheekbone and glancing off his nose without breaking it. Grant's head shook with the blow's force but he had no trouble righting himself and jabbing at Neeler, whose nose instantly gushed blood. By gripping his neck Grant was able to force him to the corrugated wall and the shed rumbled like an empty truck on a rutted road.

Neeler had already given up, though he was stronger than Grant and could have won. He clutched his face as though it was in danger of coming off.

Tomorrow, Grant said into his ear, you get out.

Neeler said something but his words were lost to the wind. Grant tightened the grip on his neck unnecessarily. His cheek burned from Neeler's blow and a headache flickered to life behind his eyes. He wanted to be in bed.

He'd hit Thornton once. Thornton had hit first but that wasn't the point. Grant had made fun of his laugh—mimicked it actually, still angry over whatever embarrassment had made Thornton laugh in the first place. Guileless Thornton had gone pink as a squalling baby and set upon Grant with his clumsy blows. And Grant had hit him, hard.

How joyful it felt to make contact, how awful the moment just after. He told himself this wasn't like that. He tried to hold on to his righteousness.

A floodlight filled the yard and Max shouted into the night. He was standing under the glare in paint-spattered overalls and an undershirt. Neeler raised up his bloodwet face and Max's eyes fell onto it. Max turned to Grant and back, and Grant released Neeler, letting him slump full against the wall. He was seized by a feeling of unreality and for a moment did not know who he was: his hands sticky with Neeler's blood, the left still stinging from the slap, the headache a black cowl gripping his skull.

Max's lips curled, amused. Which of you's the peeper? he said.

Grant was shocked back into himself. His headache retreated a bare inch. Goddam, he said, who do you think?

I think if I asked, you might both say it was worth looking. He was pleased. Grant noticed his hands, fine and filthy, half in half out of his pockets.

It ain't me. What's got into your head?

Max laughed. The wind had calmed, as if to taste him. Okay, then, he said and turned to Neeler. Get yourself a good look, Pete? You get your fill of her?

Neeler stood, looking at one brother and then the other, trying to figure some advantage. Blood still foamed over his mouth and chin and down into his collar, and he brought up his arm and wiped the blood away with his sleeve.

Now Sophia appeared, dressed in her jeans and a shirt of Max's, and glared at the three of them with her arms crossed. Neeler hung his head and half turned away. When nobody said anything Grant spoke to him.

I want you gone by breakfast.

Max didn't change his expression. He seemed to find Grant's command entertaining.

What happened? Sophia asked.

Grant tried not to look at her. Nothing you want to know.

Max said, Pete got an eyeful of you, through the wall.

Sophia flushed and her eyes caught fire. She looked at Neeler. But it was to Grant that she said, You shouldn't go hitting anybody for me.

He nodded, though it had been for himself, not for her. After that she walked barefoot to the house and went inside.

•

Grant knew she slept in Max's bed most nights, but for whatever reason they carried on elsewhere, never in the house when Grant was there. Tonight however he could hear them, a rapid exchange too faint to understand but with the quality of argument. This gave way to a silence, and then an audible breathing that quickened into a whine, hers, and he heard them wrestling on the bed, her voice struggling to contain itself, now and then breaking free with a shout that might elsewhere have signaled offense or distress. Of his brother he could hear nothing. It was a message from Max, but what sort of message he didn't know. The deep soundlessness that followed seemed, at this late hour, a conscious compensation for the disturbance. But after an eternity of listening to it Grant realized the silence was only sleep. In time he slept himself, briefly and unrestfully, and then morning had come.

Eyes open, he remained in his attitude of sleep, the sheets bunched around his chin. He heard Max's voice in his head, telling him what he already knew: You love her.

•

In the kitchen he tried to keep his eyes off her. It might've been his imagination but her movements, seen out of the corner of his eye, seemed to favor him, as if in apology for scolding him the night before. Politeness demanded he acknowledge her but he didn't. He could only nod a directionless greeting and sit down to breakfast.

It was a clear dry cold summer morning. Sophia had the door propped open, gathering the cool in anticipation of the coming heat. Shortly Cotter and Kittredge walked in and sat down. No words were spoken. There were things that ought to be done today but none seemed inclined to do them. The work would be done, though Grant couldn't have said what harm would come to them if they each went his separate way on this day, if time's passing were simply ignored and the whole of future work pushed forward twenty-four hours, never to be caught up on. They ate silently and Grant imagined the rest of them thinking the same thing. Then Sophia sat down across from him and her feet bumped against his where he had them extended beneath the table, and both jerked away.

Kittredge looked up and they all turned to him. He had his hands on the table to steady their trembling.

Say, any of you all seen Petey this morning?

After a silence he went on. I heard him come in last night and then stir real early, I don't know how early, and when I got up he was nowhere atall.

Cotter's eyes were searching their faces. I seen him carrying a bag around daylight, he said.

Yessir, he got himself a kind of a suitcase, and I seen it wasn't in the customary place he keeps it. Kittredge was looking from one to the next of them, his white hands now gripping the table's edge. Grant thought he heard real fear in his voice, and he turned directly to Sophia, who stared openly back at him, her face full of nothing, waiting to hear what he would say.

But Max spoke first. Why don't you ask Grant about that? he said.

Kittredge turned eagerly to Grant. You know where he got to?

Grant set his fork down and leaned back in his chair. I got to be honest with you, he said. I caught him last night spying on the lady here, and me and him got into a fight. He paused, trying to read Kittredge's empty face. Ended up I told him to get out.

He waited. When it appeared no change would come over Kittredge, he went on. I regret the fighting but I ain't sorry for what I said. He wasn't doing nothing around here and wouldn't listen to a damn thing anybody told him. And he ought to've shown Sophia a little respect.

After another moment he added, I didn't really think he would go. And then: I'm sorry, Kittredge.

Kittredge blinked, scanning their faces. He stopped on Sophia. Spying? Spying on you doing what?

She cleared her throat. Sitting for Max's painting. Posing.

For a painting?

Grant said, Kittredge, it was a private thing and he shouldn't have been looking.

Kittredge shook his head. I don't see what harm—

She was naked, Max told him levelly. He was peeping on her while she was naked, that's what Grant got bent out of shape over.

Sophia had no visible reaction but Kittredge blushed deep into his collar. He slid his hands into his lap and looked fiercely down at them.

Well, he said, and it wasn't certain what he meant by it, if the word constituted resignation or forgiveness or a commitment to anger. In any event it was probably the least Kittredge had ever said. Grant looked over at Sophia. It was getting easier to do now. She was still looking at him, glaring maybe, and he started speaking before he had a chance to form the words in his head.

I imagine he's over at the rodeo. I could stand to go to town and do a few things. He turned to Kittredge. I'll ask around and see if I can find him. See if he's coming back.

Kittredge nodded his thanks.

You want to come with me?

No, said Kittredge, I reckon I'm still a mite tired. Maybe I'll just head back into bed. And having said that he left his breakfast uneaten and walked out.

◆

By the time he set out on the road he was hungry and the sun had gotten the kind of hot people would be comparing hot days of the future to. He turned on the vents and let the moving air burn the sweat off him, and by staying extra still he almost got comfortable enough to forget about it.

He felt foolish with his impulses and passions behind him now, shrunk to nothing in the heat. To get hit was just what Neeler wanted. The to-do of it. And the girl: the thought of her now made him half sick with shame, he didn't, couldn't, love her and he'd prove it by sheer coldness. He thought of all the thickheaded talk he'd made with her, all of his prideful mouthing in the kitchen when his brother wasn't around, and it made him furious at himself and at her too, because surely she was going back and telling it all to Max. They were lovers after all and lovers had a way of telling each other whatever popped in their heads, however stupid or secret.

The hell with them all.

In Eleven he navigated the sudden traffic and the misparked pickups and pulled over on a patch of ruined grass half a mile past the center of town. Walking back he could hear the sloppy mob hollering behind him at the arena and could smell the roasting meat. He pitied whoever was tending the fire. At the post office he mailed bills and collected more from the box, then took them over to the Sunrise. At the door he hesitated. Then he went in and sat down. Jean didn't say hello but gave him a piece of meatloaf, and he accepted it with thanks. He shuffled through the bills. When he raised his head to look for the newspaper she was still there, her eyes on him. He had a sudden memory of her and shook off a shudder.

How're you doing, Grant? she said, the way a doctor would ask.

Not bad.

You don't look it.

He shrugged. It's hot, he said.

While he ate she hung around wiping down the counter and looking out the window. A couple other men were here, drinking coffee alone at their tables. Finally Jean said, Okay then, and walked off. He found a newspaper on a stool and read the rodeo standings. Damned if he was going to go looking for the boy there, if he happened to come across him, fine, but nothing would make him look on purpose. Kittredge would get over it, possibly thank him in due time. Maybe punching Neeler wasn't so bad an idea after all. Grant squeezed his eyes shut. He was having a hard time keeping hold of his convictions. When Jean was back in the kitchen he paid and collected his mail and left.

The heat drove him to the Eleven bar. Inside it wasn't simply crowded but full. Men inches apart were shouting conversations, their stiff widebrimmed hats knocking together, their hands in constant motion adjusting the hats, raising cans of beer to their lips. They ought to've been bareheaded but the pegrack had come off the wall and a pile of trampled hats lay on the floor underneath. Grant plowed into the mass of riders and ropers and met with a strange resistance around his feet. He looked down to find the floor covered with empty cans, which reluctantly parted as he slogged through as though against flowing water in a fast stream. Some time later he reached the bar, where a seat opened itself for him. When he was settled with his own can and his pile of envelopes he looked down the bar and saw Neeler, staring back at him with a bleary intensity from the far end, his suitcase standing upright on the bartop beside him.

Grant pulled on the can and turned his attention to opening the envelopes one by one, tearing a strip off the stamp end and making a pile of the strips on the bar. Men were stumbling against his back in a constant rhythm and their feet shook the floor. Now that he'd actually found Neeler he didn't know what he was supposed to do with him. Apologize? Bring him home? He couldn't imagine doing these things. As he took a folded paper from an envelope he sensed a motion at the bar's end and looked up to see Neeler's seat occupied by someone else. The suitcase remained on the bar. The cowboy who'd taken the seat bumped the suitcase with his elbow and it toppled into the darkness. In a moment Neeler appeared beside Grant breathing gin and speaking in a fumbling near-whisper. Grant tried to read his lips.

I could put you down right here, he seemed to be saying.

No, Grant told him simply, unfolding the paper.

You're a coward. I could put you right down. Nobody'd stop me neither. These words were audible; Neeler had begun to shout.

Grant concentrated on the paper he'd unfolded. He flattened out the creases against his leg and brought it up into the light from the open door. So focused was he on the appearance of imperturbability that the words took several readings to sink in, and even once he understood their meaning he had to read them again to make sure.

If you are a relation of John Person, I regret to inform you that he has passed on. He was delivered to me today and has been prepared for burial. This was done at some expense but the alternative would have been immediate burial without your assistance. Please come to retrieve him or instruct me otherwise via correspondence as to the disposal of his remains.

If you are not a relation of John Person I regret the inconvenience.

The letter was signed above a typed name: Lawrence L. Furness, Director of Funeral Services. And below that an address in Lewiston, Idaho.

Grant tried to fold the letter again along its creases, but somehow it eluded his efforts and would not fit back in the envelope. The paper was too large. He closed his eyes. He was not precisely surprised at the news but realized he had harbored some expectation—not hope exactly—of his father's return to the ranch. He couldn't put his finger on exactly what he expected, there was only a vague need anticipating fulfillment. Now the prospect of that fulfillment, whatever it was, was lost. He began to grow afraid.

It was in this state that he felt Neeler's fingers jab his shoulder. He started, nearly losing his balance, only staying on the stool through willful effort. When he looked up, the sight of the stupid boy kindled a horrible fury, much like the previous night's. The fury filled him up. It felt wonderful. He dropped the letter on the bar and clamped his teeth together and might have killed Neeler had not some commotion erupted by the door. A shadow fell across the already dark room and a wave of men staggered toward them, pulling Neeler in its undertow and out of Grant's sight. It was the last Grant would ever see of him.

A horse was standing in the room flinging its head from side to side, lunging forward and retreating, its hatless rider slumped over apparently unconscious on its back. Men were crushing into the corners of the place, upsetting tables and chairs. The horse reared back expelling its passenger, neighing in terror, cans clashing under its hooves.

Grant pressed himself against the bar, stricken with a fear far out of proportion to the danger the animal posed. The horse seemed portentous somehow, the first landmark in this new chaotic world. Grant reached back and grabbed the bundle of papers. He edged along the row of men, Neeler forgotten, aiming for the door and the necessary bearing home of his news. The horse kicked as he passed but Grant dodged, stepped over the fallen rider and slipped out the open door to the street. He hadn't paid for his drink but had not drunk much of it, either.

·

I'll go, Max said to him. Unspoken but implied was the notion that he would do so alone. Grant had found him up on a ladder replacing a rotted beam in the sheep shed. Now they were in the yard. Max held the letter in his pitchblack hand, squinting against the glare it made in the sun. What's the time? he asked.

Near four.

Max handed him the letter. I'll go clean off and leave.

I'm coming with you.

You got to stay here with Sophia.

Grant let out a mirthless laugh. He felt a weakness in his knees and ankles and shifted his body. She can be on her own, he said. She ain't a child.

Max said, Did you find Neeler?

Didn't look.

He nodded, walking past Grant toward the house. Grant followed. Sophia can come with us, then, Max said.

I don't see . . .

Max stopped on the road and faced him. I wonder what your problem is with her.

I don't much care one way or another, he said carefully.

Max was staring, his chest heaving. Grant could see he was stricken, wracked, and he wondered what form John Person had taken in his brother's heart. Max opened up his mouth and said, Go tell Cotter to look the truck over for us.

The order was issued with the same tone their father would have used, long-suffering and hopeless, as if he knew even as he spoke that it would be carried out wrong or not at all. It was pointless to disobey. He watched his brother go inside, then headed off toward the quarters to find Cotter.

They set off at five with bread and jerky and canteens full of water, Max behind the wheel and Grant half leaning out the passenger window. Sophia sat between them wearing one of their mother's dresses. Whatever had made her do this, she seemed to be regretting it now, her knees pressed together and her hands folded over them, her eyes trained straight out on the road. But Grant was moved by the gesture. It was at least clear she intended some kind of respect for their father. And in fact the first words spoken were hers, nearly lost in the noise of the cab. It was the best thing I could find to wear, she said. Formal, I mean.

Max's silence likely meant he wasn't listening, though Sophia seemed to take it as disapproval. She frowned. The dress was handmade, navy blue, sleeveless and cut simply. Their mother had worn it in the weeks after one of the funerals, Grant couldn't remember which. He told Sophia it suited her.

I had to tack up the hem, was all she said in response.

The sun was still high yet low enough to blind them. A visor hung from Max's side of the cab but Grant and Sophia had to keep their eyes half-lidded, as the passenger visor had long ago broken off. The effort of squinting tired Grant and a fresh headache got going right behind his eyes. When a hill interrupted the glare or they turned north for a time, the headache only intensified in the light's absence. For awhile he fell asleep. When he woke, the atmosphere in the truck had changed. Sophia had loosened her posture, she looked at him with a benevolence rendered motherly by the dress, and he felt he'd been talked about while he slept.

What is it? he said, instantly alert. They seemed to have crossed the divide and were following it north now, the mountains sliding by on the right and the sun fat and hot on the western horizon.

You looked tired before, she said.

That's what my bones were telling me, looks like.

He looked at her frankly for a moment. Something about the artificial closeness of the truck made this possible, even appropriate. Then Max turned and said, You want to know who you looked like, sleeping?

Who?

Thornton. You looked a lot like Thornton.

He was hanging on to an unhappy smile as he said it, a guileless and intimate thing Grant could not specifically recall seeing on Max before. It was possible that Max didn't know how much this wounded him, how it sounded like a gunshot. Grant tried to return the smile. The road pulled them northwest, where their father's body waited for them.

·

In the darkness of the cab, while Sophia slept against his shoulder, Max spoke. They had driven hours in silence since stopping in Montana for food and gas, and now the final stretch of the state forest was disappearing behind them. Lewiston wasn't far. Already the hills were populated by logging roads and cabins and the occasional glow of firelight through windows.

Might be it ain't him, he said.

Fear disfigured the words, rendering them thin and false. But whether Max feared that their father was dead or that he was alive was unclear. At any rate the possibility seemed slim to Grant.

Might be, he said.

Can't think of any reason why he'd of been in Lewiston.

No, Grant said, then added, Can't think of where else he would of gone, though.

Home.

When Grant said nothing his brother half turned to him. England. He'd of gone stayed with his sister, what's her name.

Would of written, Grant said.

Margaret. Could be he's with Margaret.

Could be.

Shortly the city came into view, filling its small valley with tiny lights shaken and doubled against the river water. It didn't look like a place that would kill a man. The hour of sleep Grant had gotten earlier had tricked him and he was wide awake now, his mind clear and broad, with the kind of reach it had when he was out searching the range for lost sheep. He was thinking ahead to recovering the body, securing it in the truck, driving it home and burying it. He could feel its hunger for the ground and he wanted to feed it. But he said okay when Max suggested they check into a hotel for the night. It would be hours before Lawrence Furness woke and there was no point in looking for the mortuary until morning.

When Max and Sophia went to bed he left the room and headed off toward the river. He climbed down its muddy bank and found a flat stone to sit on and listened to and watched the dark water. The air was neither hot nor cold, moving about him and over the river with a kind of sentience. The world seemed full of detail beyond the ability of his senses to perceive: a hidden design he was part of. He could climb down into the water and let it carry him off. It felt like the appropriate thing to do. The impulse, not self-destruction but self-abandonment, was so powerful that he inched back on his rock out of fear, holding himself apart from desire. But the effort exhausted him. He fell asleep with his head on his arms, woke just as the sunrise was getting started, and returned to the hotel. In the daytime the hotel looked cheap and uninviting. He went into their room. Max was curled on his side, his sleeping face buried in the pillow. Sophia lay awake. She was sprawled on her back, their mother's dress flat against her body, the skirt folds draped down between her knees outlining the full length of her legs, and her face, polished to glass by the sweat of a nightmare, seemed not to recognize Grant at all. Her eyes followed him to the bedside. He took her burning hand from her belly and held it. The fingers lay limp in his and then her eyes closed and the fingers tightened, crushing Grant's bones together against his skin. His heart gulped blood. Max stirred. Grant released her and turned and went out to the truck to wait.

•

The mortuary stood on a grassy corner of a residential neighborhood unsullied by dust or noise. It was a one-story structure, windows thickly curtained, with a paved-under archway to keep a person out of the rain between his car and the indoors. Max ignored the archway, parking instead on the far end of a large black lot. The sound of the engine sputtering to a stop rang out across the empty streets, and Grant imagined the civilized inhabitants of these fresh colorful houses waking to their arrival, squinting out at the three of them with pity and disgust.

For a few seconds they sat breathing the damp morning wind that swathed the truck. At last Sophia looked at Grant and gestured toward the door with her sleep-softened face. Their eyes had not met since sunrise. Hers were hidden in plain sight, as if they were everyday things, things you might take or leave.

He opened his door and held it for her. Then he went around to his brother's side. Max was sitting with his eyes closed, hands still on the wheel.

Grant laid his hand on Max's shoulder. The shape of his brother's bones, so different from his own, filled him with sadness. He turned to Sophia standing with her back to them behind the truck, and turned to Max again. Max was watching him.

C'mon, Grant said.

He stepped back to let Max out. The two of them walked toward the mortuary and Sophia followed, hanging back when they rang the bell. The wooden door, ominous in its oversize and impression of age, opened after an interval with no sound to indicate anyone's approach.

Furness admitted them silently. He was tall, plump-faced; his languorous movements betrayed a secret clumsiness overcome by long practice. The parlor was laid with heavy dark carpet. A low table bearing a vase of lilies stood in the center of it and upholstered chairs were placed in groups of two and three throughout, stations for grieving. The place smelled newly minted, a made smell not of death but lifelessness. They stood bewildered, unsure of what to do. When Furness spoke they reacted with a collective start as though the ground had moved suddenly beneath them.

How may I help you? is what he said. His large unlined hands were folded in front of him, his voice smooth as rancid oil.

John Person, Max said.

His only reaction was a slow nod. Grant surmised he had not expected to hear from them, let alone find them at his door.

My letter reached you, he finally said.

Yes, Max answered.

Mr. Person was—

Our father, Grant said. Mine and his. He extended his hand and Furness took it and clasped it and released it. The mortician's hand was hot and dry.

Lawrence Furness.

Grant Person. Max, he said pointing. He didn't introduce Sophia, who stood behind them, her head hung.

I am sorry. Would you like to see him now?

Grant looked at his brother, who stared blinking at Furness as if he didn't understand the question.

Please, Grant said.

Furness left the room through a curtained doorway. They waited. Voices could be heard, there were footsteps and the sound of wood scraping against metal, an involuntary expulsion of held breath.

Grant was reminded of the last funeral he attended, a sea burial. A young man's heart had stopped. The *Rose Adams* had just reached the Banks, to return to land would be catastrophic, no one would be paid. So the man's effects were collected, the pornography removed and distributed among the men, and the body cleaned and dressed and laid out on a plank. The sky was quiet, the clouds a seamless mass. Prayers were said and the men's feet scuffed against the deck. They said goodbye to their crewmate. His body, weighted with sand, struck the water and disappeared.

Sophia had taken a seat against a far wall, a bright smear against the regal dankness of the place. She appeared to want to hide herself. Grant and Max stood very still, waiting where Furness had left them.

Their father's casket came in on a wheeled platform draped with black velvet. It parted the curtains, reflecting the dim lights in undulating confectionery streaks. The velvet caught the curtains and pulled them taut before they broke free and fluttered back into place. The casket was accoutered with brass fittings and was varnished to a stunning depth, like a window onto death itself. There was no way they could pay for it.

The platform came to rest in a kind of alcove faintly illuminated by recessed lights. Furness opened the smaller half of a sectioned lid and left the room the way he came in.

The brothers stood on opposite sides of the low table glaring at the casket, the spectacle of it, each waiting for the other to move. Grant's emotions, uncertain up to now, were coalescing into shame and rage. The mortician's presumption, the worthlessly prettied box: to conceal death in this fake dignity: as if this monstrous thing wouldn't rot away like the tree it was made from, as if the brass wouldn't blacken under the ground and the body decompose. He was thinking he couldn't step forward, that he might have to leave, when Max moved, practically leaping to the casket. He leaned over it, thrusting his head under the open lid while his hands gripped its lip.

Grant tried to read his brother's posture, but it was no use. Max's body knew only the vocabulary of work. It betrayed nothing but concentration, as though he was contemplating the undone gut of a wrecked car. Seconds passed. From behind the curtain came the sound of shoes against a cement floor. Then Max stood upright and strode past Grant, his face naked and old as the inside of a broken rock.

It ain't him, he said passing, and he pushed through the door, splashing the room with daylight for an instant and revealing its dressings as soiled and common.

Sophia trained an alarmed glance at Grant which he didn't return. Not him? Somehow the news was a greater blow than the letter had been. The fatherless self he'd become had seemed a considerable improvement over the coward son he used to be. His head throbbed and he saw Sophia stand up and then sit again, covering her face with her palms.

Grant crossed the room. No point in waiting, and of course he had to see for himself who was in the box.

But it was him. For a moment no, but then the familiar face rose up out of the powdered waxwhite mask that had been put over it, and he saw his father laid out dead, the features relaxed and flattened by gravity and sapped of all opinion, accusation, emotion. You could have said Max was right. The resemblance was purely mechanical. But their father was surely dead, as this body was where he used to be and now he wasn't there.

Grant moved away from the face and curled his fingers under the larger half of the lid and pulled it open. The body was fattened and bent, before or after death he couldn't tell. The suit he wore was indeed his own, Grant recognized it. Why would he have brought it with him, except to be dead in? Unless he thought he would be traveling. Maybe he really meant to go back to England and never made it. Whatever the case it seemed unlikely that he ever intended to come home.

The hands were gnarled and scabbed. Grant reached out without thinking and lifted one off the other, and it wasn't until he'd let go that the feel of it struck him, unyielding, like something cast from a mold, the skin artificial, cold from refrigeration. The gangster of

Grant's dreams came full and real into his mind, taking shape for the first time outside sleep. He jerked away letting the lid fall shut, and the force of it jarred loose the smaller lid, and it too came down with a thunderous clap as though his father had pulled it closed in anger. Grant backed away, his lungs hollering for breath, and as he steadied himself against a chair the curtains parted and Furness appeared, his eyes dark with suspicion and stupidity, like a goat's.

Pardon, the mortician said, is there anything—

What'd he die of? Grant surprised himself at the question, which he'd not until this moment thought to ask.

Furness took a step back. The coroner—it was in a tavern—his heart.

You got something that says so? Grant said, drawing air. And whatever else he had on him. He carried a wallet.

Yes, of course.

When he was gone Grant remembered Sophia. She was standing in front of her chair bent toward him slightly, her hands bunching the fabric of the dress. Tears drowned her eyes and he could see she was nowhere at all, alone very far from home, the only men she knew transformed in an instant by death and lost to her. Her chest rose and fell and her face glowed with terror.

Well is it him or not? she whispered.

It's him, he said, and he knew he could go to her but didn't.

Maybe—, he went on, and realizing he was still out of breath stopped to draw one. Maybe you ought to find Max.

But why—

I don't know why he said what he did but any fool could see who it is. Don't stay here. Go to him. I got to settle things.

She stood rooted to the spot, her tongue moving across her lips. He saw that she wanted to speak, for him to say things back. But he tried to silence her with his eyes.

Please, he said.

This time she heard. When the door shut behind her he turned to Furness coming through the curtain.

You can get him out of that casket and into something I can pay you money for. And you can seal it up, we got a long way to drive today and there's nobody else needs to look at him.

The mortician nodded soberly as if this was his plan all along, and held out to Grant the death certificate and his father's wallet. Grant accepted them without raising his eyes. The wallet was empty of money but it could have been anyone, the coroner or in whomever's presence John Person had fallen, who stole it. Not Furness necessarily. The wallet was surely his father's though, cracked and stained at the edges by sweat, and crammed inside were photos, brittle as the leather, that showed their family: each of them as children and a portrait of John and Asta at their wedding. Grant had never seen these pictures. He tucked them back into the wallet and gave the certificate a cursory glance. It was just a typed paper really, signed illegibly and pointlessly at the bottom.

Furness was waiting. Grant met his gaze and held it and Furness was forced to speak first.

I trust you wish to take your father now.

Yes.

There is the matter of your bill.

I know, Grant said. He had brought with him all the money he had, but now he doubted it would be enough. And there was the trip home, the cost of gas, and food if they wanted to eat. He said, How much?

For a more . . . economical casket? Furness asked. He named a figure. It was not as high as Grant had feared but nonetheless more than he had. He took his own wallet from his pocket and removed all but a few of the bills, then handed them to Furness. The mortician accepted them reluctantly, with an expression of distaste. This was apparently not the way he usually did business. He fumbled, patting his coat, and at last pushed the bills into an inside pocket.

You can bill me for the rest, Grant said. You got the address.

Yes.

How long'll it take to get him in the new box?

Furness crossed his arms. Not long. Twenty minutes.

We'll come back.

Yes. After a moment he added, I'm sorry.

I appreciate that, Grant told him and walked out.

The driver's-side door of the truck stood open. Sophia's head was framed in the cab window. She sat on the passenger side, her white elbow sticking out into the sun. He concentrated on that elbow. It would be cool and rough if he touched it, despite the heat. He stood very still until her eyes appeared in the rearview.

When he got in behind the wheel she said, He wasn't out here, I looked. He probably found a bar.

Daddy died in one, Grant said. A bar.

She stared at him, seeming to search his face for a foothold. He let himself stare back. He followed the topography of her face as if he was preparing to make a map. His fingers in his lap twitched involuntarily. A breeze lifted the hairs on his arm and fondled the sleeves of the dress she wore. It was a nice day. A lot of people would wake happily to it and go to their jobs as on any other. He wanted her and nearly said so. Instead he said, What is going on between you, Sophia? It was the first time he had addressed her by name.

Some seconds later she said, I don't know. She was biting her lip and he could see the tips of her narrow teeth probing the red flesh. I came with him because I hadn't figured him out yet. I thought that once he was home I could figure him out and he would be mine. She blushed.

They looked out at a mother pushing a pram down the sidewalk. The pram had a hood and the baby couldn't be seen. I don't know, she said again, everything I learn just makes it more confusing. Sometimes I think he must be crazy.

He's not crazy, Grant said.

She sighed and her head dropped to her chest. Oh, Grant, she whispered.

This could be the moment, he thought. She would love me now if I took her in my arms. He looked down at his hands on his knees and commanded them to move.

The hands rose to the steering wheel. In a moment he started the truck and pulled out onto the street.

•

They found him drinking alone in a low-ceilinged tavern near the railroad tracks, illuminated only by the light through a propped-open door. Nobody was tending bar and the two pool tables in the darkness behind him were covered, the cues lined up in a rack on the wall. Grant and Sophia paused on the threshold and then, wordlessly, she stepped back to let him enter by himself.

He sat facing his brother on a wooden stool and waited for him to speak. It might have taken a long time, he expected it to, but Max turned right to him and with an expression drained of pretense or motive said, Didn't bear any resemblance at all. None at all.

Grant said, What are you doing here, Max? It's nine-fifteen in the morning.

When Max didn't answer Grant took the wallet and death certificate out of his pocket and slid them across the bar. Max ignored them for awhile. Then he took the wallet into his hands. He held it and turned it over and over. He looked inside, took out the photos and laid them in a neat row on the bar. Edwin, nine or ten years old, astride a horse. Grant and Max and Thornton together, stiffly posed. Robert standing with their mother dressed in Sunday clothes, somewhere in town. Then the wedding picture, and one, horribly, of Wesley days or perhaps hours from death, laid out in the bassinet, the eyes bulging from the swelling and fever, the skin stretched and shining.

We ain't never had a camera, Max said finally, touching Wesley's image with steady fingers. He picked up the photo and replaced it facedown.

Doc Lafitte took it, I reckon.

Now Max turned Edwin over and then their parents, young and ghostly and framed by a black oval. After a minute he picked up the final picture and folded it under so that only the two of them were visible, Grant eight or nine years old, wearing a pair of angora chaps and a drooping hat, Max clinging to his brother's fringes.

What now, big brother? Max said. At this a door rattled open in the darkness and a figure appeared at the back of the bar and approached. The bartender. He was a tiny man of about eighty with wild white tufts of hair over his ears, a dirty white shirt and a bright red bow tie. He aimed a questioning look at Grant and Grant shook his head no.

We go get him and bring him home, Grant said.

Max was putting the pictures back in the wallet. You think he'd appreciate that, do you? he said, the cut coming back to his voice.

I believe so.

The bartender looked from one to the other. Max laid a bill on the bar.

Okay, he told Grant. You're the boss. He slid off his stool, leaving the wallet and pictures and certificate behind for Grant to collect.

·

The casket fit lengthwise in the truckbed. They wrapped it in an oiled canvas tarp and anchored it fast through the postholes with rope until it was tight against the side. The box itself was square and varnished, no handles, hardwood, not pine. It didn't look cheap. The wood was smooth and strong with a handsome grain, the sort of thing John Person would have liked to make but lacked the aptitude for. They hadn't seen their father in it so there was no way of knowing he was really there, save prying off the lid. The mortician had helped them lift the casket onto the truck, his jacket off and sweat soaking his white shirt, but now he stood back, dismay bunching his face. He didn't offer to shake their hands. When it was time to go Grant nodded at him and he nodded slowly back. Then they climbed in, Grant behind the wheel, and drove away. It was barely ten.

Later, the sun was high overhead and the air roared into the cab hot enough to burn. Sophia slept, touching neither of them, her head tipped back against the seat, baring the smooth hollow of her neck. Grant kept his eyes on the road and the mountains slipped past on either side.

As if from inside Grant's own head, Max said, This land has ruined us for any other kind of life.

Grant said nothing.

I never really lived in the city, Max went on. I was only ever living not here. Every place I ever been was just not here. All those people and buildings I painted pictures of, it was just not mountains, not grass. There was no life in it.

What about now that you're back? What are you painting now?

I'm not painting anything. I'm just painting notness. He tipped his head back laughing and Sophia stirred for a moment. She opened her blank sleeping eyes and then shut them again, quick, against the brazen world outside the truck.

Notness, Max said quietly. I like that.

Grant said, What I seen of your paintings looks pretty good.

No. Dead as our daddy. Dead as us.

Grant took his eyes off the road to train them on his brother. You been painting her, right? That isn't dead.

For some time Max didn't have an answer to that. Then he said, barely audible over the roar of air, I don't know what that is.

◆

Before dark they pulled over for gas. Grant went out behind the station and relieved himself into a junkswept weedpatch. The temperature at last was dropping and the wind beginning to pick up, blowing the stream of piss into an arc, like a tossed rope. When he was finished he felt hungry. He went back to the truck and told them he was going to go find a store. They stayed behind, too tired to move. As he passed the truckbed he gazed along the length of the tarp, imagining he could detect the odor of formaldehyde and dead flesh and face powder in the heat that rose off it.

They were in a little town without much in it, and he moved through its streets making no impression. Soon he came upon a market with a post-office window. The window was boarded over but through the open screen door, scratched raw by a cat, he could see a man working behind a counter. The cat ran out as Grant entered.

The place was lit bright as day, the shelves stocked neatly with boxes and cans and the cooler full of fresh-looking food and cold drinks. He thought of his hands on the casket and approached the counter. The proprietor was bespectacled and fat, wrapped in a white apron. He looked up and smiled hugely.

What can I do for you, son? he said. His voice was cool and clear and for some reason pleased.

You got a sink I can clean myself up at? And then I think I'll get a few things.

Sure I do. Come on back.

The grocer led him down a hallway to a narrow immaculate tiled bathroom with a sink and toilet. Grant washed his hands and after a moment's thought his face and neck and arms as well. When he came out the grocer said, You look like you haven't slept. Everything all right?

The question came as a shock, seeming to arise from a natural and urgent concern. Grant could not seem to answer it.

Look here, the grocer went on, are you on your way to someplace nearby? You are traveling, aren't you?

Yessir.

I can fix you up with a place you can sleep. You look like you just drove a million miles. Are you driving truck, is that it?

No. No thank you, I—

Both of them waited for him to finish.

That's okay, the grocer said. You just go ahead and help yourself. You need anything else let me know.

Grant turned and began to walk down the narrow aisles, drawn to the things on them but unable somehow to touch them. Finally he opened up the cooler door and took out a bottle of milk and a couple of peaches from a basket. When he shut the door he pressed his palm to the cold glass, and then his cheek, and he closed his eyes and all thought vanished from his head. After awhile he brought the food to the counter and took some jerky from a can there and put that next to the fruit, along with his money.

You sure you're ready for the road? the grocer asked him.

Yessir, thank you. But—

What is it?

I can't bring that bottle back to you.

Hell, that's all right, the grocer said laughing. He took a few of the coins Grant had left. That'll do it, he went on. Keep the rest.

Grant swallowed and his vision clouded. He felt the way the grocer looked, heavy yet somehow buoyant. The weight kept pouring into him as he stood there neither thanking the grocer nor taking his change. He knew he must look mad. At last he managed to say thanks and collected the food into his arms. The grocer was saying something to him as he left but Grant didn't answer. He could only pull open the screen door and stumble out into the dying heat.

Outside, the world had undergone some kind of transformation. Everything pulled him with a new gravity. What was left of the sun seemed a wan projection invented by the air. It was clumsy to hold the food to his chest. He realized the grocer must have been offering him a paper sack. Blocks away a dog barked, and the canyon that cupped the town multiplied the sound and drove the dog to more frenzied barking. What was this place called? He couldn't remember seeing a sign. Nothing about it seemed real, the dog or the cat, the bright clean store or the man in it whose kindness was already losing definition, like it was nothing more than printed words on a burning paper.

Now he seemed to have lost his way. Up and down the street nothing could be seen but low houses with flat roofs and silent grass moving in a breeze he couldn't himself feel. The gas station's white glow was not to be found. He set down his things on a hummock of ground near an intersection and stood gazing into the sky where some stars were making themselves visible. He considered what Max had said and felt the sad rightness of it. Both of them had left and come back to find that their home had turned its back on them. And their father would be returning dead. Briefly Grant imagined that the ground would actually reject the casket, forcing it up and out like a wedge of shrapnel from a wounded man. So clear and convincing was this image that for a moment his mind groped for a solution to the problem: maybe they could bury him above the ground in a tomb or in the Indian way, in a tree or scaffold. Then he remembered who and where he was, and he picked up his things, and the route back to the gas station was restored to him.

The last two hours of driving were the longest, with the darkness expanding and the road assuming a frightening sameness, as though it would never end. They were each awake, each aware that a burial shouldn't wait until morning. Grant felt as though his limbs wouldn't respond to the work; his back wouldn't tolerate bending over the grave, his arms and legs could never bear the weight of the shovel or the earth's resistance. But of course work was never far beyond his reach. Sophia would make them coffee and they would just do it. As they drove Grant vainly scanned the sky for the moon. He remembered it was new. They would dig by starlight.

When they got back Grant stopped the truck in the yard. Sophia got out and walked into the house. As they watched, a light went on in the kitchen. She appeared at the sink to fill a pot with water. Seconds passed. It was Max who finally tore himself away and said, Go, and Grant put the truck into gear and pulled it up in front of the equipment shed. He went in and picked out two shovels which he dropped into the truckbed beside the casket. Their clatter cracked the silent black night. In the wake of the noise the silence deepened. Though it was summer Grant could smell woodsmoke: maybe Kittredge was unwell and chilled. They drove into the starveout and Grant backed up against the graveplot gate. He got out and opened the gate and began untangling the ropes from the shrouded casket. Max lingered behind, waiting. Finally Grant pulled off the tarp and heaved the casket out over the lip of the bed. Max moved up to take the opposite end. They set the casket down against the fence and fetched the shovels, then wordlessly chose a spot in the near-invisible ground.

It took them all night. The dirt was loose but rocky. They dug deep until they hit clay, and below it a sandy clumped soil like heavy snow. Below that was rock. They extended and squared the hole and drank the coffee Sophia brought them. By now Cotter had come, roused out of sleep by the sound of digging. He and Sophia stood at a distance as the brothers lifted the casket and brought it to the edge of the grave.

Cotter got the ropes out of the truck. He threaded them under the box and tested them for strength. Sophia had changed into work clothes, her faint outline the shape of Max's when he was a boy. The four of them took hold of the rope ends and together lifted the casket and suspended it over the grave.

If any of them had wished to say something, the time to do so had passed. They lowered the casket and it bumped hard into the open ground. Each rope came out with a sharp tug. Then Cotter took one of the shovels and gave it to Grant, and Max took up the other, and Sophia and Cotter again stood back as the brothers filled the grave. When Max and Grant were finished, the ground was lumped with the displaced earth, and though Grant wanted to tamp it down, to erase its newness, he couldn't bring himself to stand over his father's body.

•

They sat in the kitchen with clean hands and fresh coffee and told Cotter about the trip. It didn't take them long. Ages seemed to have passed in life, but in the telling the journey was lifeless and empty of incident. Sophia, in the silence that followed, looked from one to the other with bright eyes. She said, He didn't have any kind of funeral. Nobody had the chance to pay their respects. The fact truly grieved her. She held her hands out across the table, as if imploring them to reverse it somehow.

The men listened. They turned their eyes to the hands folded in their laps. Grant would put a death notice in the paper but no service would be held. Nobody would come to a service, or if they did it would be out of habit and not respect, because their family was cursed and sheep people besides. He groped for something to say to get them off the subject. At length he turned to Cotter and asked him how Kittredge was getting on.

Cotter looked at Max first, then Grant. He's upstairs sleeping, he said.

At this Max's head came up. A ready, almost eager smirk spread over his face. Grant said, Upstairs?

Sophia hung her head. Grant could see there was something she'd been told.

Instead of answering, Cotter pushed his chair back and stood, motioning for them to follow.

Dawn hadn't touched the yard yet but a starless gray blush betrayed the hilltop. They turned onto the road and walked north. The house light faded behind them and moonlessness took them back in.

I heard him creeping around the quarters late, Cotter said. Two in the morning I'd bet, black out here. I figured he was an animal or something.

Who? Grant asked.

Max, not Cotter, answered. Neeler, he said quietly, and Grant could make out Cotter's nodding head. He was full of questions but decided he'd wait and see what Cotter was going to show him.

But he knew. The smell of woodsmoke intensified. By the time they reached the ruined cabins the smoke was acid in his throat. The cabins had collapsed, the few standing walls punctuated by skewed black windowframes, white smoke hovering above the lot of them, visible against the sky as a ghostly motion of air. The old dry wood had been eager to give itself to fire. Grant walked up and down the row peering into the ravaged interiors where embers still glowed in pockets within.

Once I figured out what he done he was already gone, Cotter was telling them. Or I seen him running anyway. I went and got Kittredge, he's all right, a little burned on his face coming out the door is all.

Sootblack and wrung by heat, a gasoline can lay on its side beneath the last cabin. It looked a hundred years old at least.

How'd he get here?

I reckon horse.

Grant walked back to where they were standing. So what in the hell was he trying to do?

Kill Kittredge, Cotter said simply. He was woke up on account of his shaking or else he mightn't of made it.

There was a fluid pause loaded with significance, like a creek running between two mountains. The clear and quiet middle of something enormous and terrible. Grant had never felt so tired in his life, his legs near to giving way. He sat down hard in the dirt and lowered his head. There had been no sleep for days and not enough to eat. His blood was thin as a gas, whistling through his heart and veins, his body a winter-stripped cottonwood, brittle and hollow and no impediment to the wind and weather. His bed seemed an impossible distance away.

They pulled him up and led him back to the road and into the house. Cotter brought him up the stairs to his room, laid him on the bed and pulled his boots off. Grant hadn't the power to thank them, grateful as he was, not even the power to complete the thought to do so.

·

The dead man didn't frighten him any longer. They were in the yard, spotlit by the porch bulb, surrounded by sheep gently bleating and pressing into them. The sheep were hungry, their wool patchy and thin with gray skin visible underneath. He was trying to explain to the dead man that they had to go out to range, it was long past time, the summer would dry the grass and creek and the flock would waste away.

The dead man smiled. Porchlight pierced his skin. Below its surface Grant could see the blood vessels blackly clotted solid. The dead man's bent white finger said follow and Grant followed, the sheep more urgent around them now, the bleating sharp and irregular like crows' caws.

He was led through the pasture to the starveout gate. There were horses clustered around the fence, colorless and still as if stopped by time itself. They were illuminated by an unseen source, or from within, the light possessing a clinical coldness like the light from an electric sign. As they climbed to the high corner the sheep overtook them. Grant could see they were starving, their hooves rotten and the skin of their legs rubbed down to the briskly glowing bone. Wait, he called out, the sheep— but the dead man walked on, his coat mold- and moth-eaten riding up above his trousers and revealing a deep white fissure in the skin where the salt water had split him.

The dead man passed into the graveplot with the dying sheep all around him. Their sounds were no longer animal but the high reluc- tant strains of a rusted machine. The noise overpowered the night, so terrible Grant could nearly see it. He ran to the dead man and touched him, shouting, but the dead man pointed to an open grave: the neat squared hole they'd dug for their father, empty of any casket and with no visible bottom. The sheep were diving into it, wasting to nothing as they fell.

9

Grant set out early for the summer range. It wasn't far but he intended to take his time and spend a night camped in the hills. A night out might do him good: Kittredge and Cotter were living in the house now. In truth he didn't much like them there. Kittredge in particular was hard to bear. He mourned Neeler as if he was dead, dragging himself from room to room rendered worthless by grief. Cotter on the other hand remained impassive and practical, yet made it clear by his silence that he disapproved of the arrangements. Max had assumed an air of intense concentration, as if he was very busy doing some kind of work, which he wasn't.

The sound of them recalled the sound of the family, of two or more of the boys fighting in the hours between supper and sleep or a baby waking hungry in the night. His father had been habitual. He got out of bed the moment he woke each morning, and he woke without a clock or whether the sun rose into a clear or storm-darkened sky. He woke, the bedboards groaned underneath him, his feet struck the floor at exactly the same moment, muffled by the frayed rag rug. He took four steps across the room to the closet and slipped a shirt off its hanger, which jangled against the others. Then he pulled on the shirt. He took his pants off their hook, then one foot and then the other thumped the floorboards, and he buckled his belt and slapped the buckle. Grant heard the routine asleep or awake. To the older boys it was an alarm: their father intended to wake them. But their mother made no sound at all when she rose. Larger than their father, she ought to have been heard, but she sat up and dressed by stealth and was posed before the stove when the boys came down, and depending on the year she may or may not have had a baby in the bassinet beside her shielded by the pantry door.

Increasingly his memories were confused, who was alive at a specific time and who wasn't, which boys were considered men and which weren't. Some incidents, a fight or an accident, he recalled differently every time, once with Edwin as a central figure, another time with Max. On occasion he would place a brother into memory at an age he had never reached. He maintained a spurious image of a teenaged Robert swinging across the barn on a hanging rope, bellowing like Tarzan; even less plausibly he could remember Wesley taking his first steps. If one brother did something out of character, but in the character of another, Grant might remember the act performed by the second. Occasionally he even remembered himself doing something Edwin or Max had in fact done.

He suspected it was the nature of memory, not his own nature, that caused the confusion. The truth of a thing only existed as long as the thing itself, and afterward it changed with distance or perspective. His own experience of this very moment, a hot fogged summer morning, belonged only to him; it could not resemble the same moment lived by someone else, Sophia for instance.

She was unhappy here in the house, with the men. Grant feared she would leave them and the intensity of his fear disturbed him. After all, he didn't have her now, and if she left he wouldn't have her then either. But still: the sight of her drawn face turning away from his was too much to bear. For this reason above all others he chose now to visit the herder, putting himself into misery in order to put himself out of it.

He rode west toward the low hills in a light rain. The land was barely visible today, disguised by clouds and mist, its hidden edges arched like muscles. He kept his eyes trained on them as he passed the graveplot and burned quarters. For a long while he rode seeming to come no closer to the hills, then he was in among them, his face beaded with haze, his hat dripping water on his fingers around the saddlehorn. The damp got up under his coat and the clothes pressed coolly against his skin.

He was in no hurry to find the herder. Instead he let his nerves read the map of the terrain they had memorized. They spoke the right directions to the horse, guiding him along the trails, while in his mind's eye Grant probed the gullies and creekbeds and meandered through the breaks for signs of bear.

In awhile he dismounted and pissed and clambered up a sidehill to look around. From a little ways up he could see the first sheep a mile to the south, grazing in a lush depression which graduated into a hill, and now among gray rocks he could make out more of them, still and summerfat and out of danger. There was no sign of Murray and no rain either, only a gray wet heat.

Satisfied, he went back and loosened the horse's saddle and sacking and took out the bits. Then he found a dry outcrop and sat. He shucked off his hat and coat and took in the whole living highland.

Yesterday, in the wake of the sheep dream, he'd set to his father's affairs, bringing the will into town for the lawyer and writing a letter to his aunt in England. He'd sat thinking half an hour without setting a word to paper. In the end he kept to the facts: their father was dead, and if she was ever to come to America she would be welcomed. When he told people in town what had happened they offered their condolence. Jean Tate came around the counter and took him in her arms. Her body, though unchanged, was a foreign thing to him, and unforgiving. Surely this wasn't something in Jean but something in him. He felt stunted, impotent. The Persons were like a shrub cut back too far, he thought. His father's sister had had no children he knew of, there had never been talk of cousins. On his mother's side were brothers and sisters who'd resented her leaving Iceland with an

Englishman and never spoke to her again. Grant didn't even know if they'd been informed of her death. He supposed not. He couldn't imagine himself marrying, couldn't imagine his body giving any woman a child.

After a time his thoughts began to embarrass him. He stood and went back to his horse and tightened up the riggings. In a few minutes he was among the sheep and the dogs ran out to meet him. They knew him now by scent and sight and made little noise, careful not to spook the flock as they led him to Murray's wagon.

The herder was inside making his supper, the elkskin door pushed aside to admit the air. He was holding a potato in one hand and a bent table fork in the other. Without his glasses he looked pitifully insubstantial, something that would wilt in sunlight. Grant leaned his head in and asked him how he was doing.

Murray looked up, and then down again at the potato. Not so bad, he said.

The flock?

A couple of downers a couple of days ago. It ain't catching, if that's what you ask me next.

Grant nodded, unsure of how to say what he'd come to say. Then the herder surprised him by inviting him in for dinner. It was only beans and potatoes, he said, but huckleberries were ripe on the bush and he'd gotten to them before the bears and birds. They could have some for dessert.

All right, Grant said. He went to his horse and took a bottle and some letters out of the pannier. Murray nodded as he received them, in acknowledgment, not thanks.

They ate under the tin canopy of the wagon then sat outside on folding stools to drink. Murray glanced at his letters before sliding them in between the buttons of his shirt.

You come to say something, he said.

Yes.

Grant endured Murray's glare for a moment then told him about the fire. Murray had little reaction. It was none of his concern.

And our daddy turned up, Grant went on. He was in Lewiston, Idaho. I hate to have to tell you he's dead. We brought him back and buried him.

The herder nodded patiently, as if he'd already heard this and was only listening to be polite. He sipped the whiskey from his cup and looked off across the valley to where the dogs were running. Murray's odd cordiality settled over Grant, making him a little uncomfortable. He waited with real apprehension for the response.

Y'boys'll sell, will ye?

He followed Murray's gaze to a nondescript faraway grasspatch. Then the men turned to one another at once. In the herder's eyes was a familiar disappointment. Sell the whole outfit? Grant said. No. No, we'll stay. Nothing'll change.

He looked into his whiskey, reflecting rippled sky. There was some sun now and he felt hot. Murray reached into his shirt and took out the letters. He tore one open along the flap and removed a folded piece of paper. After reading it he handed it to Grant. It was hard to decipher, the shaky hand riddled with crossouts.

Dear Thomas, I dont have much to say. The girls are growin. The lettuce is all aten by rabbits but we dont miss it to much. A new calf the girls named it Jenny. Send money please we need it

Sally

This your sister? Grant said. Where is she?

Oregon, Murray said. It's my wife. Them girls are my daughters.

You're married?

Murray frowned. That's what I just told ye.

When Grant didn't say anything further he went on. The hell ye won't sell, he spat. Comin' and goin' the way ye done.

Murray drank his drink and leveled a look at Grant frighteningly direct, the look of a creature ignorant of danger. Y'don't even know who ye are, he said, and he took the letter from Grant's hand.

The herder's silence afterward was unembarrassed. He continued to drink, wincing after each sip with a painful satisfaction as if some loose bone was being snapped back into place. Grant thanked the herder for his hospitality. He felt no malice toward Murray, only a desire to get away. He set the whiskey down on the ground and stood, his knees audibly cracking. It'd be dark in an hour or so, he said, he wanted to get somewhere he could bed down. The undersides of the clouds were pinking up and the brightest stars were visible, and Venus and Mars. Behind him the dogs were egging the sheep back toward camp. He could sense the flock clustering nearby, the way you could sense changing weather.

Murray stayed on his stool, the wrinkled letter still in his hand and the ripped envelope trembling in the windshook grass beside him. He was still there when Grant left, and again when he looked back from the far end of the spur where the horse had led him. Then he was in the next canyon with the bottomland spread out far below, and Murray was gone from his sight.

·

He set up camp in a clearing above a creek where he could wake and look down on the water flowing, a hundred feet downslope. In the morning he would pick his way there to wash. He'd bedded here before, as had others before him. A flat patch had been worn around a rock circle that surrounded scattered ash and bone. Dry twigs and thick branches could be found in a mossy deadfall not far from the camp. It was his favorite time of the traveling day, when there's no reason to wander into dark woods and your horse is satisfied and still, and everything you want or need is inside the circle of fireglow. He'd brought a book to read, but instead he lay in his bedroll and tried to picture the woman who had wed herself to Murray and borne his children. Murray must have thought they would keep him, or he them. Maybe he'd once imagined they would tend sheep together, living off berries and game and potatoes planted in loose soil all across their territory.

But Grant could envision only his own mother, daughters she might have had, hard little girls who would seem to have cleaved directly from her with nothing of his father in them at all. They might have saved her life, daughters. Girls are shrewder and more adaptable than boys, he thought. They wouldn't have succumbed to short lives of risk and pain the way his brothers had. They would be here now, strong and supple as greenwood.

Grant believed he'd been her favorite. Maybe not when Edwin was alive, not then. But after. After Edwin she brought him closer than before and gave him jobs to do that didn't really need doing but which kept him near. It was to him she came in the night to tell him he mustn't go to the war. Leave the killing to the killers, she said. She said, If one of you boys must go, God help me let it be your brother, and he didn't know which brother she meant, and didn't care. Tears were in her voice, though not her eyes, and he reached for her from his bed. But she had backed away. Stay, she said.

He did. He kept his mouth shut when to speak would have meant to leave her. But of course he would leave her himself in a few years and never see or speak to her again.

A part of him envied the squalid herder, his solitude, the simplicity of his work. The herder always knew what he was supposed to be doing. His tasks were dictated by the grass and sky and sheep. The flock wanted the same thing always, to eat and be impregnated, to sleep and to lamb. Love and family, the whole reckless world of men—there was nothing there for somebody so attuned to the gorgeous stupidity of nature.

Thornton could have been a herder. He was at ease among sheep, his empathy for them miraculous, his lumbering-head gait a human analog of theirs. Even his dark hair, curled by some providence, beaded rain like a sheep's. When they were children they laughed at this affinity, and so did he. He understood his anomalous nature. To their father he was worthless, a beast that could neither be taught nor eaten. He terrified their mother, who was bound to receive his love and reciprocate without ever comprehending it. But the boys adored him, he was their saint and foil and secret.

Thornton.

•

Grant, he whispered that night outside the bedroom door, Grant, I want to talk to you. Grant could hear him waiting for an answer, his large body brushing the door. He could wait a long time, half the night if necessary. Once Grant had seen Thornton sit three hours in front of a prairie-dog hole. He'd watched him watch the moon span the sky. He got up and opened the door.

What is it, Thorn, he said. From across the hall came the sound of Max turning in bed.

Let me in. I want to talk.

Grant went back to the bed and pulled the covers up. Thornton sat at the far end. He sat there awhile as if he'd forgotten why he came. Grant passed the time gazing out the dark window at the hillside obscuring the stars. The way the stars seemed to rise up out of the hillside like fireflies.

I don't want you to be mad no more. I didn't do nothing wrong, Thornton said, leaning in close, his hand on Grant's ankle. I didn't.

You ain't done nothing wrong, I know.

Why you mad then, Grant?

I ain't mad, Grant said. He sat up and gripped Thornton's arm. No kidding.

Thornton seemed to calm under his touch. He nodded, believing. Daddy said I'm going in the army.

Yeah, you are.

I ain't afraid of it.

I know you're not.

Thornton was eighteen. He carried himself like a man did, his shoulders had the careful set, his hands were gentle and knowing and strong, a father's. Though not their father's. When Thornton was in town people treated him like a child, speaking slow and loud and high, or in the case of women mother-bright, or they offered him little gifts like a piece of candy, or worse, money. If anything he had become an adult sooner than the other boys. Early on he had the look of intense focus, as if upon something only he could see. He looked like the thinker that he was.

You're gonna stay here, right, Grant?

Yes.

You're gonna take care of Mama and Daddy and Max?

I will.

When he had left home they began to get letters. Another soldier wrote them, a boy named Granger with a florid style, the handwriting slanted and schooled, showing Thornton's words and actions as seen from without. Sometimes, even now, when Grant thought about Thornton it was in this boy's voice. They never met him. Thornton sends you his enduring love, a letter might say. Today he ran the obstacle course it was a spectacular success. His dinner tonight was dreadful, the meat was old and tough. He misses riding horses and delighting in the fresh country air. The letters came three times weekly for the duration of Thornton's training, and Max always got to them first and read them alone, often on the post-office steps. Only when he was through did he hand them over to their parents. Grant got them last.

He would have made a good herder, Thornton, alone in the camp wagon thinking his long thoughts. He loved his family but didn't need their company, only their memory, only the happy fact of them. Maybe to Murray solitude was a bitter retreat from other people. But for Thornton it was the full embrace of a natural condition, his truest state of being.

When he shipped out, the letters stopped. In a few weeks he was dead, drowned alone in his cabin.

Grant? he said.

What is it.

You ain't mad at me?

No.

How come you're crying?

I ain't crying. I just want to get some sleep, is all.

You want me to go now?

Yes, Thornton, I want you to go now.

Okay. Good night. He rose from the bed and stood in the dark room breathing. Grant closed his eyes. In awhile Thornton was gone. Grant could hear him trudging down the hall.

Good night, he said.

•

For all he knew Max still had the letters. He hadn't seen them since the first day he read them. But it was no matter, Grant had what he needed committed to memory, the look of the papers and the writing and the sentences so clear they were almost better than Thornton himself.

The campfire was waning, the wood still piled upright as it had been when lit, as though it didn't yet realize it was only ash and ember. Grant grabbed a branch from the dirt and drove it into the fire. The logs collapsed in a mist of sparks and glowed steady orange. He was hungry already but it was good to sleep hungry, he would wake with a reason to move. He closed his eyes and slept.

In the morning he rebuilt the fire. Then he went down to the creek and threw in a hook with a grasshopper on it. In awhile he caught a brook trout. He gutted and fried it with a few wild onions tossed on top and he boiled coffee and ate a fine, lean breakfast, leaving something to be desired so that he could eat again later with equal satisfaction.

The horse led him up through a timbered stretch of woods and onto a ridge, which he followed south. He could see over the near hills to the flats, and beyond them to mountains a full county away. It was easy to imagine the glaciers moving through, leaving the stones ground smooth, easy to imagine it happening again.

All afternoon he hunted game. When he set up camp two pheasants hung from his riggings. That night he settled down and read his book, an adventure story about exploring the poles. He woke in the morning feeling as good as he had in five years. He rolled up his sougans into the pack covers breathing cold air and exhaling vapor in clouds, and when the sun reached him between the trees he could feel it penetrate right down to marrow.

He took the trails slowly, pausing often to examine a fossil or artifact or to enjoy a good view. For his dinner he ate a bird and some berries he'd found which left a tackiness on his hands. By afternoon he had sweated it off. He avoided the hills the herder was in and circled the ranch, finally coming down upon it from the northeast. The hills were smoother and near treeless with the infrequent outcrop breaking the flesh of grass. He used to come here sometimes with his mother the year after Thornton died. It was as far from home as she would venture on horseback. In Iceland she hadn't traveled much beyond her home valley, and woods made her nervous. So Grant guided her, taught her how to find her way back without a compass by the pattern of hills, to distinguish natural forms and their variations. She liked this land whose characteristic feature was featurelessness. She told him she liked making her thoughts mirror the land. He remembered the way she looked on a horse, post-straight and high in the saddle as if expecting a spill.

They sent an officer from the base to deliver the news. Grant was with her in the yard. They took note of the road dust simultaneously and stopped what they were doing to watch. When the bug face of a jeep appeared on the rise he saw her chest expand with breath. At first he didn't understand, then he did. He went over to her but something kept him back: he stood close without touching, as the jeep stopped and the man got out and came to them.

The officer saluted, then told them. She nodded. Grant looked from one to the other, stupefied, doubting not the truth of the words so much as the uniformed stranger himself, his crackling emotionless voice ringing out over their yard. His face shaven so close he gleamed.

But he just shipped out, Grant said.

His mother's hand shot out to quiet him but didn't quite reach all the way. The thin steady fingers a couple of inches from his shoulder.

There was an accident, the officer said, an explosion. Nobody survived. He blinked, shook his head. I'm sorry.

A pause stretched into seconds as his mother's hand lingered in the air beside him. The sun was wedged between the shed and barn. The officer squinted against it, trying to maintain his composure.

Well, said his mother, you've told us what you came to?

Yes, ma'am.

She swallowed. Thank you, she said simply. The officer handed her a paper. Then he saluted again, got back in the jeep and disappeared into his own still-hanging dust.

Her hand fell but she stayed put, facing but not looking at the road. Grant stepped in front of her, into the path of her eyes. They moved to him reluctantly. That ain't right, he said, he just shipped out. Hell, he didn't even get to the war yet. Mama—

Ssh, she hissed, angry. That was you. It could have been you.

He looked into her face for direction, for what to think about what she had said. The sun lingered behind her and her stray hairs shivered in its light. She seemed insane, and as if to confirm this flung herself at him and wrapped her arms around his shoulders, wordlessly shouting. He stood horrified, Thornton's demise suddenly plausible. She crushed him to her. Over her shoulder he could see Max, emerging from the barn with a rusted hackamore dangling from his hand. He was headed for the starveout and the new colt running there, and then he stopped—stopped in front of the barn and leaned toward them— and took a step and finally ran, his burden jingling with each footfall until he reached them.

And what he did then—at the time it seemed natural to Grant— was to take his mother's shoulders and pluck her, pull her sharply, away from Grant, and turn her around and embrace her. He took her from Grant and held her: and why not? Max was her son, certainly he had figured out what happened, he would give her comfort. Why not?

But as Grant stood watching them he saw the strain in Max's face, saw his arms tighten around her. He was trying to lift her off the ground, almost as if to pour her grief into his open mouth. She cried out and bit his shoulder. Max's narrowed eyes, turning to Grant, appeared to say, She's mine, her sorrow is mine. And shocked at what he thought he saw, Grant turned away from them and went off to find his father.

That was me, Grant thought now as the home buildings came into view. Always going off for something, leaving to other people whatever needed doing. But what choice did he have? His parents, his brothers: they were forever around him, more ardent, quicker to understand, to desire, to act. He lacked Max's aggression, Edwin's skill, Thornton's determination. Their mother's responsibility. His obsessions hadn't the strength or specificity of his father's. His affinity was with the soonest dead: Robert might have made him funny; Wesley, patient. But neither had ever got the chance. What choice did he have but to leave?

So he left, and found no passion, and returned to nothing at all. He wondered what he had been doing when his mother died. September 5. He would have been asea, but where? Engaged in what? He struggled to remember. The years had lost definition in his memory, had flattened into a uniform gray, the color of ocean and sky, the gray of his lies. Probably he'd been eating or sleeping, it didn't matter. No dread sensation came over him. He was overwhelmed by no sudden terrible knowledge.

He had betrayed her by failing to stay, she had betrayed him by failing to live. Only he was left to atone, and so he would stay. He would live.

•

When he got back he found Cotter and Max at work on the barn. It had stood unsteadily for years, always the next thing they'd see to when whatever they were doing was finished. Now they had it stood up straight with heavy beams propped against the lean. Max was inside nailing new supports to the roof joists, while Cotter cut and fit new planks to replace the rotting walls. The horses watched idly from the pasture, the cows grazed in the yard. Grant watered his horse and led him over to the others. Then he went back to the barn.

Cotter nodded hello. Grant said, Long time coming.

These ain't the only hammer and saw, was the reply.

He went to the shed and got the tools then began tearing away the bad planks and measuring the new ones against them. They worked side by side for an hour. The repaired wall quickly took shape. Cotter said, How'd he take it?

Grant fitted a new board into its place. We got paint?

Cotter nodded.

He thinks we're gonna sell, Grant said. And like that, for the first time, the notion did not seem unreasonable. After awhile he added, You know he has a wife?

Two girls.

I had no idea.

He went around to the back where the wood had been baked and warped by years of sun and rain and the paint lay in brittle strips on the ground at its base. He surveyed the whole, wondering if it would be possible to choose planks to replace, or if he would have to choose between taking it all down or doing nothing.

Cotter appeared at the corner and said, So will you?

Will I what?

Sell.

He turned to face Cotter. The older man's eyes were stony, as if the place was already sold and his feet tainted by trespass.

What in hell would I do with myself then, do you think? Move into town? Nothing there for me.

Inside, the hammering stopped. A hawk cried. The rustle of hoppers in the grass seemed to amplify. The answer wasn't enough for Cotter, he stood tapping the hammer sidelong against his thigh, waiting.

No, Grant told him. We ain't selling.

Cotter appeared to consider and at last nodded. I'll go get

Kittredge, he said. He can start painting what we already done. And he disappeared around the corner of the barn.

•

That night at supper they all seemed improved. Kittredge ate his food. He was shaking less or hiding it better. Sophia had on a dress, it was too hot for pants, she told them. She didn't know how the lot of them could stand it.

You just think about winter, miss, Kittredge said, and they all laughed at the joke.

When they were finished Max went out to the equipment shed. Through the kitchen window, as she washed the dishes, Sophia watched him cross the yard. The other men drank coffee and talked, Kittredge telling some story involving a drunk and a priest. Cotter grunted appreciatively now and then, his eyes on his hands on the table. Grant wanted to go help her—take up the plates and dry them and put them in the cabinet—but he stayed put and watched her work. When she was done she stood with her head hung, seeming to gather herself. Then she went out to the shed. Through the window Grant saw her stepping through the weeds, cautious of the spines against her bare ankles.

He turned back to the table to find Kittredge looking at him. You got eyes for her, he said. It was a kid, but there seemed to be a knife hidden in it somewhere.

Nah, he said.

You got to watch yourself, Kittredge said smiling. I don't know that her and your brother's getting on so good.

It seemed to Grant that Kittredge was looking for information. He wanted to gossip. Grant said, It's nothing. Nobody's getting on so good lately.

Cotter was still looking down at his hands but with greater intent. All were silent until footsteps landed on the stoop and Sophia walked in, her color high and breath heavy. She stopped and composed herself as if for a speech. But instead of talking she looked at each of them, swallowed and went to the stairs. Before she disappeared Grant stole a glance. Her eyes were on him, narrowed in a state of accusation but lacking any specific charge.

We still got some daylight, Cotter said and got up from the table. He nodded at Kittredge. You good to work some more? Above them, the sound of a body falling on a bed.

Course I'm good, Kittredge said loudly. I can go till dark. He stood, stretched his arms out behind his back and left them there with the hands clasped. How 'bout you, Grant? Or are you tired out? He gazed at Grant intently, waiting to be surprised.

I'm okay for it, Grant said, and the three of them went out to work.

·

The rest of that week Sophia stayed in after dinner, or else went out to tend to the animals before going to bed. She didn't follow Max to the shed. Grant lay in his room nights listening to her silence, until Max returned and the two of them spoke. But he couldn't tell what they were saying or even what sort of discussion it was. He couldn't sleep until he heard them. Often he couldn't sleep after that either.

One night he went out to the shed to see what Max was up to. The building was lit up from inside like a private sky, the rusted pinholes in the walls a human starlight. He guided himself across the yard to the door and pushed it open. Behind it a paint can clattered on the cement floor. Max was at work on a painting, his back was visible and his raised arm. The painting was four feet square, a field of crosshatched streaks with bare white canvas along the edges. It didn't look like much of anything. At any rate Grant's view of it was brief. Max gasped at the intrusion and pulled a tarp down over the canvas as if the painting was some kind of dirty secret. Once the easel was covered he spun on his heels, his glare a mixture of fury and shame. The paint can had been a makeshift alarm. Grant snorted in surprise.

What do you want? Max asked him.

For a moment he had no reply. And then: You know, we barely been saying anything to each other since we came back with Daddy.

Max looked tired. He was holding his paintbrush like a weapon. Reckon we haven't, he said. Then he turned and dunked the bristles into a housepaint can and fixed the brush to the upright handle with a clothespin. He wiped his hands on a rag and came limping toward Grant.

What you working on that's so secret?

Nothing worth asking after, Max said.

For all his childish moping Max didn't look twenty-two but a boyish forty, his hair thinning as their father's had, fans of wrinkles framing his eyes. And his stoop. That's what it was, not a limp. Grant said, You look like an old man.

Our old man?

The old man you're gonna be someday.

Max smiled. Don't count on it.

They went out in the yard together and Max rolled a cigarette. He lit it with difficulty in the viscid air. Clouds had been massing all day, now they were crowded into every available space so that it felt like a rainstorm in every aspect but the rain itself. Grant felt less solid out in it, as if he too had drifted here anticipating release. His brother was an orange dot of ash in the dark that seemed itself to breathe as Max smoked.

She seems broke up over your keeping her out, Grant said.

Max took his time replying, so long that Grant wished he hadn't spoken at all. At last he said, She knew what she was getting into.

Did she?

To this Max said nothing. Grant held out his hand for the makings. The tobacco was fresh and the cigarette tasted good. He said to Max, Is he on your mind?

Sure.

I can't seem to think on him directly, Grant said. I remember Mama easy, and the boys, but even that's all fouled up. I can't get nothing straight in my head.

Max seemed to be turning this over in his own mind, through two or three flares of the cigarette's end. Don't see why you need to, he said.

Grant didn't understand. Was he saying there was no point in remembering, or implying that Grant had long ago left off caring about the family anyhow? It was typical of Max to speak plainly without actually saying anything that made sense. His face was near invisible in the compressed darkness.

You plan to show them paintings to anybody ever? Grant asked. Put 'em in a museum?

A chuckle came from Max's direction. A museum. I don't know about that. Ain't thought one way or another to do something with 'em.

The orange light brightened. You keep a diary? Max asked.

No.

Me neither. But it'd be like that, asking me if I'm gonna put my diary in the newspaper, or was I just gonna let it go moldy in a drawer somewhere. It ain't nobody's business and it ain't something I expect other people are gonna appreciate.

Okay, Grant said.

Like asking me if we ought to leave Daddy in the ground or should we prop him up in the town square.

Grant waited awhile before he said, A good forty miles to the nearest town square.

Max's laugh was sharp and quick, a snapping twig. That's good, he said. You can always change the subject with a joke. That's a valuable thing to know how to do.

I don't like how we got on that subject.

Yeah, well, me neither. He tossed his cigarette into the weeds and stamped it out. Old Petey did a hell of a job, didn't he. I don't see rebuilding those quarters.

No need of it.

Unless you and me get ourselves married and start fathering some babies. What do you think?

I don't know, Grant said. He backed up half a step. He felt cracked open, like Max was rooting around in him for something he'd lost.

Well, Max said suddenly, it's been real nice talking to you but I got to go write in my diary now. He reached out and clapped Grant's shoulder. The fingers were hot through his shirtsleeve. And then he was gone, and Grant stood alone in the yard feeling the coming rain. Standing there it occurred to him that there was someone living in his brother he didn't quite know. A seventh brother, at once enigmatic and familiar, that had taken the place of the one he'd grown up with. Or perhaps he had never known that one, not really.

When at last he turned to go back in the house he saw her, white as a puppet in the kitchen window. He didn't think she could see him. When he came closer to the house she backed away.

•

She was waiting when he came in, facing the doorway with the fingers of one hand curled over the rim of the sink. Her hair was longer than it had been. It hung over both sides of her face and lay against her shoulder like a hand. The light was off but she had lit a candle and put it on the table.

The bulb was too bright, she said. I couldn't stand it. Her voice had a quality of suspended motion, like a spun dime.

We ought to put a shade on it, Grant told her. He sat down to take off his boots.

She leaned back against the counter and faced him. She wore a nightgown with a robe pulled loosely around it and her face was thin and starved for sleep. I don't know what in hell I'm doing here, Grant.

He didn't answer, instead set his boots on the mat by the door, toes to the wall as if a penitent was standing in them.

I used to have friends, girl friends. I don't know if you know what I'm talking about. I had a dozen of them, people I saw every day. You know what I mean?

He said, When you work around sheep you get used to being alone.

How long's that take?

Grant stood and pressed his shoulder to the wall. You knew it was going to be different.

I didn't know Max was going to be different.

Her eyes were right on him. He wasn't sure what she wanted. He said, So what do you want to do about it?

In his head the words had sounded innocent. But on his lips they betrayed him, they implied that he had something in mind. He did have something in mind and she heard it. She took her hands off the counter and a step toward him, and he pushed himself off the wall and stood straight. There was a second then that might have stopped it, had one of them glanced away or spoken or stepped back, but they didn't and the opportunity to stop passed them by. She came into his arms and they kissed. His one hand found her face and the other the gap in her robe, and he stroked her back through the cotton of her gown, pausing at each vertebra and pressing gently into it and into the muscled concavity around it. They shifted their weight and the boards strained underneath them. Her lips and tongue were cool from just-drunk faucet water and he touched her face and her hair and body and she brought her mouth to his ear and whispered, Now.

It'll knock you up.

No it won't. Not tonight.

The men are upstairs—

We'll be quiet.

They were. They barely moved from the spot, falling against the wall in an ecstatic discomfort, making hardly a sound. When it was done she stepped away from him, the nightgown still bunched around her waist, and he saw her nakedness and the high color of her face in the candlelight, and the world tripled in size. He knew nothing about her, he thought as she leaned over the table and blew the candle out. Yet now he had these minutes of her that nobody else did, the hand that held her hair from the flame, the bare foot a ghostly blur against the floor. She said, You must think I'm heartless.

No, he said loudly.

Good.

She leaned into him and kissed him quickly and her fingers touched him where he had loved her. Good night, she said, and he said it back, and she disappeared up the stairs. He had no idea who she was. Possibly neither did she. It would be nearly three weeks before he touched her again.

PART THREE

ICE

A hot morning in early August, damp and heavy from a night rain. They had decided to build a chute for shearing as the Mexicans suggested, and to replace a few of the lambing pens which had rotted in the wet. There was no money for this, but a dreamy recklessness had possessed Grant: all that mattered, he thought now, was the betterment of their situation. He sent Max and Kittredge to town early for lumber and hardware and instructed Cotter to fix the fence where a bank had eroded under a post.

He hadn't been alone with her since their first encounter, though that needn't have kept them from meeting. They had all the space in the world to disappear into and wouldn't have been caught. But she had avoided him. Every word they exchanged in those weeks he could recall at will and did, mining them for innuendo. There was none, though: only the words themselves. Do you want coffee? she said. That old mare has a limp. What's today's date? Three times he'd listened to her make love to Max. He had begun to think that what had happened was a piece of mischief, the scratching of a frivolous itch. But if she loved Max, why would she have taken such a risk? But if she didn't love Max, what was she doing in his bed?

On this morning he saw her through his bedroom window, throwing meal to the chickens down in the yard. He yearned for her. Then she turned her face up to his window. The yearning gave way to anger. He pulled on his clothes cursing his body, dashed from the house. He walked straight past her into the barn, looking at her once with his eyes full of cruelty and lust, and shut the barn doors behind him and waited panting in the shallow trough that feet and hooves had cut in the dirt floor.

The animals stirred. Horses nickered and shuffled in expectation of a run. He kicked his feet on the packed dirt. If she didn't come he was giving up for good. Maybe he would leave here altogether. But she came.

He turned to her. She kept a distance, back to the door and head low, but her panicked eyes were on him.

I'm sorry.

I don't understand, he said.

It's hard to explain. None of this is what I expected.

He waited for more but nothing came. To expect a thing and then get it was an inconceivable luxury.

You love him, he said.

I love what I thought he was.

What in the hell's that mean?

I can't explain.

It was true of course, he knew that. Could he have explained his own life, his reasons for doing what he did, to anyone? Still, the explanation was in her somewhere. He wanted and deserved it. He said, You don't get to have what you make up in your head. You get what a person is or you don't get nothing.

Before she could reply he added, All you want's yourself.

He spat this as if it were a sucked venom. It made him feel awful. She was crying openly and he loved her. He took a step toward her and another. He said, I want you.

Yes, she said.

He went to her and held and kissed her, and they went to the mounded hay in the corner and undressed. Her body couldn't have been more different from his own, the uninterrupted paleness of her skin and the plainly described structure of muscles and bones. Like a sketch of herself. Without concern for who might hear, she cried out. In her cry Grant heard the torment of indecision for which he could be no help.

He had one thing that Max didn't: her secret, the secret that was him. What this meant was uncertain. He knew only that he would live here with her or he wouldn't live here.

·

Still it kept on as it was, without relief. From time to time they met. His head filled up with speeches and ultimatums but he hadn't the courage to speak his mind. He believed now that she loved him, believed he had no need for her to say so. Nonetheless he told her he loved her, however much he pleaded with himself not to, and her responses, passionate and sometimes violent but never spoken, left him longing for the covenant of words. It was words that married people and words that pronounced them dead. His desire for them overwhelmed him, caused him to shake and howl, to pound the ground like a primitive. Regularly he took himself off to lonely places to let the emotion spill out of him.

She would long ago have left the ranch if not for him. She told him so. He considered offering to go with her. But he wasn't confident she would say yes, and he feared that in the wake of his offer she would leave without him. And it was here that he wanted her, in this valley, without the foolishness of girls and parties and the distraction of city life to share her with. In the city he would lose her attention and ultimately her love. He would be left alone there with no way back to the life he knew: much the situation she was in herself, right now. If that happened he would have to return to fishing. His only home would be a steel-walled box, or the dreary flophouses of port cities. Or he could go to Iceland and find his mother's family, and they would take him in. He wouldn't have a word of the language, so he would herd sheep, the one thing that didn't require talking. In the harsh endless winter he would wear a lambskin coat he sewed himself with a bone needle.

He would sleep with his dogs and people would think him strange for never taking a wife.

That was how it was. He made these plans, and then, when it seemed like he would never again have her, Sophia would come to him and a life together would seem possible, even likely. Even inevitable. But not for long. That was how it was.

In the fall they let the rams have at the ewes. For the first time he found their rutting comic and horrible. The ewes cried out as the hooves gouged their backs and legs, their eyes filled with elemental terror, and all of sex and birth and life in its redundant splendor seemed a foul joke. When it got cold they pulled up the potatoes and carrots and put them by in the cellar, and this act of faith—faith that they would be here to eat them—seemed tragically proud. He felt the end of everything looming nearby, death and ruin absurdly amplified by the intensity of his love.

He understood that this living couldn't be sustained, that something would happen to change it. In the end it was two things at once.

·

One morning the first week of November they woke up sick. Grant knew it even in his sleep. He shed his blankets one by one and finally the bedsheet, and woke up afire with the window cracked open and snow blowing in and mounding on the sill. His throat felt like a man's hot hands were pressed to it, his legs were splayed out before him white and dead-looking. Outside the sky was thick with resolve, the snow so heavy that clouds couldn't be seen through it, the flakes huge and clumped together. He tried to raise himself up to see how much had fallen, but when he stirred the hands tightened around his neck and he fell back to the pillow.

Some time later, he didn't know how long, a figure appeared in the door and spoke his name. It was Max.

You got it too, Max croaked.

Grant managed to get up on his elbows. It felt like the thing that had him had died and stiffened, and he would have to drag it along with him forever. He spoke and his voice sounded like somebody else's.

Yep.

You got to get up, Max said. It's heavy out, Murray might need us.

The window had rimed over inside with the moist heat of illness. Snow was falling on the bed. Outside he could see absolutely nothing. Then the shapes of the buildings and grounds rose up out of the white. Already eight inches or more were on the ground.

Sophia got it? Grant said.

I'll get breakfast. Or maybe Cotter's down there already. Max coughed and pain raced across his face. She's in bed still.

When he was gone Grant got himself on his feet and inched across the hallway. She lay tangled in her nightgown, blankeyed and lovely. She frowned when she saw him, as if trying to figure out what he meant.

Max . . . she protested.

He's downstairs.

Go, she said.

What can I get you? His vision blurred and he slumped against the doorframe. You want a hot drink?

Nothing, she said weeping silently. Go, go.

Downstairs he tried to make himself eat the food Cotter had cooked. Kittredge was still in his room, they no longer bothered him with work. He did it when he could. He shook badly almost always, ever since the air turned cold, and his obvious embarrassment moved them to ignore the shaking and to ignore Kittredge, which seemed to make him shake harder still.

Cotter wasn't sick but exhaustion played at the rims of his eyes. He kept glancing at Max and Grant and then out the window. Max pushed his eggs around on the plate with a fork, rubbing his forehead with the other hand.

Cotter said, I think we ought to get out there.

Hard to limber up with this flu, Grant said.

Who brung it?

Max managed a laugh. No more shaking nobody's hand in town. Just nod, he said. Then the telephone rang.

They all turned and looked at it. It rang again. Cotter picked it up. The static was audible from where Grant was sitting and he could hear a woman's voice shouting through it.

Okay, Cotter said. I know the place. He hung up.

Let's go, he said reaching for his coat on the hook.

What! Max said. Grant's flesh was baking with fever, he could smell the sour air coming up off him.

That was Nannie Mott. Dan spotted our ewes piling up in a coulee out by their place. He's up there now.

Max dropped his fork. Can't be ours.

Got our mark on them.

Where's Murray! Where's the goddam dogs! The shouts crumbled into faint coughs.

Hell if I know, Cotter said and shrugged on his coat and plunged out into the weather. Max leapt up cursing. He flung back his chair and made for the door. As he followed, Grant thought of Sophia, her words to him as he watched her suffering. Kittredge would have to take care of her.

•

They rode through the storm navigating the trails by feel. Here and there was an outcrop overhanging sheltered ground the snow hadn't reached, and the bare brown patch hovered in the air like an omen. Grant followed Cotter with Max close behind. It was not too cold, but a wind rose up now and then and the snow flew straight and heavy against them, and the horses shied. They came to drifts between hills they had to scramble up around and creeks not entirely frozen that the horses broke through, the jagged ice cutting their fetlocks and freezing the wounds. Grant felt like a stone statue moored to the saddle. He'd lost his sense of balance and seemed to stay upright by luck alone. He clamped his knees around the horse's ribs in spite of the ache, and ignored the mucus flowing out of his nose, leaving it to freeze on his scarf and the lining of his coat. This wasn't like his fever in spring. He wasn't hallucinating. Everything appeared brutally real, Cotter's back and the snow and his horse's head, a shuddering plow through the mass of gray light, all of it impressing itself painfully upon him like a brand. He closed his eyes to dispel it but it appeared in reverse, the horses and Cotter and the drifting rocks all bright lights in a blackness. He may even have slept, because when he turned to see if Max was with them it was the dead man riding his horse, his face a vegetable pink in the blizzard like a toxic winter blossom. And then it was Max again, shouting Keep up.

Cotter knew the spot, a blind coulee that admitted water in spring. He led them there easily, navigating the false paths the drifts made as if by second sight. When they arrived a break came in the storm, the snow still heavy but suddenly reluctant to reach the ground, and Grant heard voices from above and saw men on horses peering down at them from the ridge. He knew what had happened. In the night the ewes must have got cold and antsy and went for cover, finding it in the lee of this sidehill. At the start of the storm it would have looked good to them, rocks and trees with no snow behind. The wind would have shifted and the drifts fallen over them. They panicked. One bolted and bumped another and climbed up onto her, and the next climbed on them both, the hooves digging and the snowcaked wool pressing down, and the heat of their bodies melted the snow and ice, and the weight and the water crushed and suffocated. The fickle wind was pulling the snow now like a curtain open-and-closing. He could glimpse through this curtain the piled sheep, dirt gray against the white snow, the hill of them writhing and tumbling and scrabbling against the backs of the dead, so many that the top ones were nearly up out of the coulee, where men were roping them and pulling them to safety.

Cotter crashed ahead through a low section of drift that had blocked off the exit. Of course the ewes wouldn't have made their way out through it, thinking it part of the hill. Max came from behind, startling Grant's horse, and they trailed Cotter side by side through the opening he made in the drift.

There were a lot of half-buried sheep that hadn't yet pushed up onto the pile. These stood bleating in the low part of the coulee, charging forward in confusion and terror a few feet then retreating, frightened by the cries of the dying. Cotter began driving them out through the gap. He pointed to Grant and shouted above the noise. Keep them together!

Grant did what he was told. He was joined by two more men coming off the ridge. One of them was Dan Mott, a cattleman they'd lived next to all their lives but rarely saw except along the fenceline. The other man was his son Tom. The two broke apart and formed a perimeter for the sheep to gather in, and soon their hooves had trampled the area flat. Grant counted as he guided them in. They came to about a hundred. The pileup was bad but it couldn't have killed all the rest of them. When the flow of animals had slowed he called out to Mott, the words gouging his throat like broken glass.

Where's Murray at?

Mott pointed south-southwest. Flock broke up in the snow! he shouted. He went chasing them down, my other boy's with him! Mott's face, blurred by cold, was a stranger's.

Grant thanked him, though by then Mott was looking off over the snowdrift and may not have heard.

•

He rode where Mott had pointed, toward the lowlands between hills where he knew Murray liked to bed down the sheep in winter. The fever was still running hot under his coat and he begged it not to stop now lest the wind freeze the sweat on his skin. It was getting easier to stay on his horse. The pain in his joints and throat was bad but had been eclipsed by the urgency of the moment. For now he could bear it.

The snow was still heavy but the wind had died, leaving the illusion of safety. There was no trail to follow. Through his fever Grant struggled to remember where the creeks were, and where to cross them. Beneath him the horse heaved, panting, the work beginning to tax. He wiped his face and spat into the snow. He was hungry.

Then for a moment, though he knew where he was and could have got back even if the horse dropped dead where it stood, he began to believe he would perish here. The snow would fall over him and in a few days the coyotes would dig him out. Though Mott knew exactly where he'd gone, though Murray would have to pass this way to meet up with the rest of the flock, death seemed a real possibility. Every direction showed him the same face, thick and cryptic and empty. And then he saw the herder on a hillside, and the Mott boy with him and the flock below, with the horses by the flock and the dogs tied to the wagon, their ropes taut. The dogs were barking wildly.

Grant drew closer and managed a shout. Murray looked up. Like the younger Mott he was holding a long denuded branch and had been driving it over and over into a snowdrift. Now he waved it in the air hollering for Grant to come help him.

He dismounted near Murray's horse where the snow was already tramped flat, and he ran up the hill. Suddenly the ground seemed to give way. He found himself up to his waist in snow. He said, What in the hell—, and the herder lunged toward him.

It's holes! Murray said, his face black against the drift like a hollowed-out walnut, his eyes rough and spent as old coals. The sheep's down in 'em! He thrust another branch at Grant and resumed jabbing at the snow.

Grant remembered. This used to be prospecting territory. Men with picks came thinking they would get rich. His mother had fed a few of them. They wandered the federal land digging holes, thinking there'd be no one to hold them responsible. They were right. The holes had probably looked good to the spooked ewes, and when the drifts blew over they would have been afraid to come out.

He gripped his stick and started poking. There was something comical about the three of them, as if it was treasure they were looking for, a buried treasure of childhood. All around him Grant struck rock. He inched forward to the edge of the hole he was in, climbed out, and poked again. In ten minutes he found a sheep, and with the others' help pulled it out. It was dead. He found another dead one, then a live one which Murray carried down the treacherous hillside like it was an infant. The snow was slowing, the hour uncertain. They moved across the hill carving channels through the drifts, and the snow stopped entirely and sheep kept turning up below them, most dead. When Grant thought to look back he saw a cluster of dead sheep lying on their sides next to the living flock, laid out straight and true as felled timber. He turned to Murray in awe of his passion, in the absurd fervor of this search, which surely would produce no further living sheep. He wondered how Murray had let them get away.

When they had discovered five living and sixteen dead altogether, the last ten all dead, Grant again stood straight to look down the hill. He felt the world bow around him, flexing. He could not go on. He sat down in the deep snow and it walled up around him, a silent fortress, and he closed his eyes with relief.

•

He woke in darkness on Murray's bunk, his feet unshod and wrapped in rags before the roaring cookstove. He couldn't figure out what was going on. When he wiggled his toes a pain raced up through him and he gasped with the force of it. His hands flew to his thighs and he scratched until the skin was ready to give up blood.

There were voices outside. He wanted to see who it was but feared what moving his legs might do to him, so he shouted out hello. His throat ached. The smell of Murray's bunk was all around.

Cotter came in, pulling the elkskin aside to reveal a clear cold starry night. The wagon creaked and tilted under his weight. He sat down on Murray's stool and lit the lampwick with a twig shoved into the stove.

You're gonna lose a couple of toes, on the right, he said. Left might be okay.

Grant looked down at his swathed feet. I didn't feel a thing, he said. After a silence he asked, What happened? How many'd he lose?

About half. Murray's gone.

Gone?

Left the wagon but took the horse and dogs, Cotter said. He shifted on his stool. Ask me, I think he was sleeping drunk and didn't hear the dogs barking.

Was that our horse or his?

Hell, I don't know.

That was that, Grant thought. Murray wouldn't be back.

They stared at the open door of the cookstove, at the deep orange corpses of the burning logs. Cotter said, almost shyly, What do you think about selling now?

Don't know. And later: Who's out there?

Jess Mott. Max went home. For the girl.

For the girl. A reason to go home, Grant's only reason. His fingers remembered her ribs. And then, easy as letting out breath, he pushed her from his mind. I can herd 'em, he said. It seemed not only possible but correct, inevitable.

Cotter met his eyes. He looked down and took to smoothing his dungarees over his knees.

I don't know, he said.

It won't be trouble for me.

About this outfit, I mean, Cotter said. He shook his head. Mott'd buy if you was selling.

After some consideration Grant said, Go work for Mott if that's what you want to do.

I ain't saying that.

Grant looked at him levelly until finally Cotter stood, keeping bent over because he was too tall to stand straight, and pushed the elkskin aside. I'll bring you in something to eat. We'll go back first light.

All right, Grant said and realized the fever was gone, he had starved or frozen it out. The stink of the mattress had stopped bothering him too. He was comfortable so long as he didn't move his feet or swallow or speak. It wasn't bad being here alone, with food coming and nothing at all in his head worth saying, not bad at all.

·

In the morning Cotter tied wool sacks over Grant's feet and led him home slowly on his horse. The day was stunning bright by the time they returned. Above the house woodsmoke massed, unmoved by wind. Cotter and Max helped him through the kitchen, where Kittredge sat sniffling and drinking coffee, and into his bed. Then they left him alone.

On his way out Max stopped in Sophia's room and asked if she needed anything. Grant heard her whisper a reply. After awhile Max came back and set something on her bedside table, a glass of water by the sound of it. Grant heard her lift the water glass and sip from it and put it back. Or was it Max's hand that brought it to her lips?

He appeared in Grant's doorway, watching him with a kind of practical pity.

Anything for you? Max said.

No.

When he was gone, the house empty of sound but for her breathing and the occasional scrape or footstep from Kittredge, he called out quietly to her. Her name came out roughened though he'd meant it tender. Are you all right?

No, came the barely audible answer.

To hell with Kittredge, he thought. With all of them. He said to Sophia, Can you come here? To me. Come on.

For a long time she said nothing. Then, No— My head—

I'll come to you, he said.

Grant, no—

But what she wanted was unimportant. He slid himself off the bed headfirst, supporting his weight on one hand and then the other, and slowly he lowered his legs, mustering his strength to bring each heel gently to the floor. His feet throbbed in unison. Now he began to move backwards toward the door, one hand, one foot, one hand one foot, looking over his shoulder to see where he was going. The motion ignited new pains all over him, in his calves and thighs where he'd clenched the horse and his shoulders and back from hoisting the lifeless ewes out of the snow. He left his room and entered hers. When she saw him she closed her eyes. She said No, Grant, no, but he dragged himself to her side and up onto the bed and pulled her, weightless and hot, into his sweat-damp shaking arms.

Please, Sophia.

You're hurting me, she said barely.

Tell me. That's all I want. Tell me.

She pushed him away, moaning. He thought, I could squeeze it out of her. I could pull the words right out of her mouth. I could.

But when he let go, when he'd lain there for ten minutes listening to her gasp herself to sleep, he got down off the bed and made his way back to his room.

·

Lafitte took off four toes, three from the right foot and one from the left. The rest would heal, he said. He gave Grant a jar of salve and pills for pain and told him that Sophia had got pneumonia. She would recover, though she might easily have died, it was bad enough. For a week he heard her whistling throat, her coughing. When she was out of bed for good she didn't come see him. Max had nursed her and when she was well enough to go outside he let her back into the studio.

Cotter would watch the ewes until Grant could walk. Until then there was Kittredge to keep him company. His trembling was worse than ever, his guilt over Neeler all-consuming without work to occupy him. He came to Grant while he lay in bed, or when he sat drinking nights at the kitchen table. He said he'd let the boy go bad, he ought to have raised him up right in a regular household where they could've lived year-round. Once, Grant suggested to Kittredge that by the time he'd got hold of Neeler, the boy was already who he was going to be, by blood or experience, and there was no reason to worry himself over it. But Kittredge paid no attention. He wanted to be to blame. He'd convinced himself he caused Neeler's mother's cancer as well, maybe it was something he fed her that didn't agree with her, maybe there was something about him personally that rotted a woman out from inside. He talked without end and didn't seem to want Grant to respond.

After a week of it Grant began to think like Kittredge. The flaws of the world seemed to be his own fault. He could feel Kittredge's words weakening his body, arresting the healing in his feet. The voice lived in his dreams, it kept him awake nights. His mind reshaped itself to its cadences; everything he heard sounded like Kittredge. Chairs were tainted by Kittredge's plaintive huddle in them, and Grant could feel his own hands beginning to shake.

At last Lafitte took the stitches out. Walking felt good, though it was hard to keep his balance on the strangely shaped feet. He packed his horse with dried and canned food and two giant sacks of potatoes. Not a lot to eat, but he figured if he kept still most of the time he wouldn't need to eat so much. He brought salt for the sheep and a dog Cotter had gotten from somebody. It was a good dog, reeking and old and cooperative.

When it was time to leave, Max helped him outfit the horse and gave him a stack of paperbacks he'd been hoarding in the shed. Grant had already read them but he'd forgotten most of the plots. He managed to fit the books into an already bulging pannier. When he was ready he let his brother help him into the saddle.

You're going to need to do that by yourself, Max said.

I'll manage.

You ought to know, she told me she's been in your bed.

Grant ignored him. He buttoned up his coat and tied his hat tight around his chin. It was cold and windy and the sky was clear blue.

I ain't going to hold it against her, Max said. I know I was hard to bear after we buried Daddy. He coughed. I ain't got feelings against you for it either.

There was no possible response. Grant took the reins in hand and set out instead with the dog behind him. He didn't look back. All the way out he imagined the two of them killed together by some act of God, a swollen river or rockslide or storm, which he, with his wits about him, unfettered by emotion, alone survived. In the wreckage their bodies would look so slight and pale, almost imaginary.

11

The first week was hard. Snowed in, alone with his thoughts, sometimes he believed he might go mad. It helped to talk to the dog: a good companion, possessed of a certain authority, the dog seemed interested in what Grant had to say. He talked about his travels mostly, things he'd seen, people he had met or observed. From time to time he looked at his compass, the one Luc had given him. It was correct, but knowing the direction was little comfort. Only when the sun shined, when he brought his folding stool outside and sat with his face bared to the light, did he think the work might be possible to endure.

After two weeks he no longer spoke. There seemed nothing much worth saying. The dog kept to itself, rarely demanding any attention. The sun began to feel like an interruption. He came to long for the snow, for those days when the sky and all but the most conspicuous natural features were erased, and his existence became more hypothesis than fact: those days seemed of almost incalculable value. In the world of things there was nothing more precious, he came to believe, than absence.

It was into this state of near-grace that the dead man arrived. He stood on a far hill watching. Grant could barely make him out across the dazzling expanse of snow but he was there nonetheless, unmistakable as a landmark. For days the dead man kept his distance, wandering in the hills or sitting motionless on a boulder, impervious to the wind. After awhile this reticence bothered Grant more than his appearance in the first place. They were already acquainted, after all. One clear morning the dead man appeared shaded by a distant stand of scrub pines, and Grant stood on the buckboard of the wagon and shouted to him to come say his piece or else go away.

You hear me? he cried. A hawk's call distracted him and he looked away. When his eyes returned to the spot, the dead man had gone, effaced by shifting light and shadow.

For a few days there was no sign of him. Grant slept dreamlessly or else forgot his dreams. His waking hours were flat and calm and flawless. He felt as healthy in mind and body as he ever had in his life, though he'd got thinner in the weeks he'd been here and had to gouge a new hole in his belt with a knife. The extra hole pleased him, his rationing plan was working. He ate the food he brought and occasionally part of a deer he'd shot and dried in strips over the stove, and that was enough.

Then the dead man reappeared. Grant woke knowing he was there and took his time going outside. He lit the stove and heated a pot of water for coffee and to wash himself. When he was done he stepped out and looked around. The dead man was closer this time, walking in among the ewes. The ewes took no notice of him; he looked up at Grant over their snow-mounded backs. Grant thought to scold the dog for not barking, but then again the barking wouldn't have told him anything he didn't already know.

What do you want? Grant called out. The dead man was wearing his gangster's jacket and pants. The now-familiar bare cracked skin was rimy and purpled at the cuts from cold. A smile was on his face but somehow not part of it. He looked up when Grant called but he made no reply.

Well, then get out, Grant said. I'm fine here all by myself. After a moment he added, You're making the ewes nervous.

It wasn't true. The dead man stayed. All right then, there was work to do. Grant went back in for his colored glasses and hat and rifle. He came out and circled the flock, scanning the perimeter for coyote sign. Finding none he returned to the wagon and made himself breakfast and ate it. He brought out one of the paperbacks, a mystery story, and read the first couple of pages in the light of the lantern. None of it sank in. For a short while he worked on scraping the deerskin, intending to make something out of it, maybe a vest or part of a cloak. But the work in the close air fatigued him and he went back outside.

The dead man was right in the little bed-down place where the dog slept in daytime. The dog was nowhere in sight. Grant said, I got to move soon, you know. Sheep can't eat the same grass twice.

The dead man turned and looked south to where Grant would be moving. In response Grant went into the wagon and brought out the folding stool and his cup of coffee, near cold now. He gave the stool to the dead man and lowered himself onto the buckboard. The dead man unfolded the stool, planted it in the packed snow and sat.

You want a cup of coffee? Grant said, and remembered his dream, and laughed. He sipped his coffee. It was not blood. Smirking, he raised it to the dead man in a kind of salute. Some time later the dog returned from whatever he was doing and lay in a sunny spot beside the wagon. Steam came up off him.

Grant said, When you live in a house, you can't wait for winter to end. But when you're out in it you wish it'll just go on forever. The ewes are carrying, though. Can't well birth 'em out here, can I?

The dead man nodded but he was looking out past Grant, out north where a dark shape was moving in the snow. The dog stood and shook himself and ran up to meet the rider. Grant watched, drinking his cold coffee right to the bottom. He flung the grit out over the ground. The dog came back and stood by him and waited.

It was Cotter. How's it going? he said to Grant.

Fine.

Getting along on that foot, are you?

Yep.

Okay, Cotter said, his eyes half closed against the light, or maybe in thought.

You gonna get down off that horse? Grant asked.

Cotter dismounted in the fresh snow and took a bottle and some mail out of his pannier. There were a couple of sacks too, feed for the dog and horse. More salt as well. Cotter shouldered the sacks and leaned them up against a wagon wheel, then came around and sat on the empty stool, first studying it as if he didn't understand why it was there.

You look different, he said.

How so?

Them glasses, I reckon. And you're skinny. Cotter raised the bottle and Grant held out his empty cup.

The liquor looked venomous to Grant, so he didn't drink it, only held it up like he was going to. Cotter drank straight from the bottle. He said, Bills due. Max wants to know should he pay 'em.

He can sign the checks. I'm the herder now.

You don't want me to take over for you?

Nope.

Cotter nodded. He pulled an envelope out of the pile and put the rest into his coat. He handed the envelope to Grant. I don't know where he went to, Cotter said. I would of figured he went home to her but I guess not.

It was a letter to Murray from his wife. The flap was smudged with fingerprints, hers or Cotter's he couldn't tell. He set it on the wagon seat beside him and told Cotter he'd take care of it. After that they didn't have much to say. The dog stood up and went off somewhere. To the west clouds were massing with the color and sharp edges of slate. The sun moved slowly toward them, gradually dimming. The sheep began to simmer, their breaths audible. They moved against one another, the icy wool scraping, a sound like a whispered secret. Cotter stood up and Grant stepped down and the dog reappeared, looking from one to the other and sneezing.

Got to move, Grant said.

All right, said Cotter. He looked at the coming weather and back at Grant. His breath hovered around his head, gathering light like a halo.

It seemed like there was something Cotter wanted to say. Instead he turned and went back the way he came.

·

Grant hooked up the horse and led the ewes south-southeast, where the land was flat and the shrubs stood clear above the snow. It was a seabed here before men were living and there was plenty of salt to the soil. When they'd got to where the grass was thickest between the shrubs, he stopped. Here, away from the hills, the wind had claimed some snow, leaving a patch of nearly bare ground to bed down on. He unhooked the horse and made his rounds with the dog, hoping to catch sight of a pheasant, as he had the taste for meat in him suddenly. But there was nothing to shoot, so he got back in the wagon and ate what he normally did. He made the fire small, trying to conserve wood until he came to the hills again, and fried up a potato and ate it with coffee and jerky. Then he opened up the letter from Murray's wife and read it out loud to the dead man.

Thomas, he read, the girls are good but a goat died today, please send something.

He looked up to see if the dead man was paying attention. I don't know what kind of fool would raise up a family on the goddam plains, do you? he asked.

The dead man was sitting on Grant's bunk. The air, thick and warmed by the fire, was full of sea-smell. Grant remembered his first catch on the *Rose Adams*. He was stationed in the hold where the cod were dumped. In a quirk of the ship's manufacture the fish collected in the shallow end of the hold where the hatch was, and somebody had to stand down in it and rake the cod into the other side. He wore rubber boots too big for him and he slid across the mucus-slicked floor, sometimes falling flat so that the fish closed over him like an oil. For hours the scales abraded his skin where it was exposed. His clothes were heavy with blood and bile and slipped off him from their weight, his trousers hanging low on his hips and his sweater pulling down over his shoulders and hands. He imagined this was what death was like: closeness, heaviness, panic; the light only bright enough to inspire fear, showing the barest outline of the unknown. That was the quality of light in this wagon, with the sun behind the hills and a new moon absent from the sky. The fire was out and cold closed in. He was tired.

Is that what it's like to be dead? he asked. Am I right about that? But the dead man wasn't there, only the mussed bunk with its gnarl of dirty blankets and the stained pillow with the ticking pressed flat.

Grant got under the blankets. He reached beneath the cot and pulled out his pannier, then rummaged in it until he found a pencil and a wrinkled sheet of paper. In the lanternlight he set about composing a letter to Murray's wife.

> Dear Love,
> Im so sorry I was no good to you. Working all alone its easy to forget what it means to be with people. I am leaving here and will be home soon. Tell the girls that I love them. It will be hard to make up for lost time but I have to try.
> Your Thomas

He read the letter over a few times, crossing out and substituting words until they satisfied him. When he was finished he folded the two letters together. He got out of bed and put them in the stove, where they brushed against a grayhot crumb and caught fire. When the letters were burned Grant got back under the blankets. He covered himself up, leaving a space for his nose and mouth to draw air. He wondered what had become of the dead man's killer. Probably he'd been killed by somebody else in revenge.

I won't be the first man to spend his life barely alive, he told himself. Men did it. It was no great feat. He would live—he'd live a few scant miles from the heart of life, on its chill periphery. That suited him after all.

Again he slept uninterrupted by dreams.

•

February passed and in March he led the ewes back for lambing. With the bitterest cold gone and a chinook wind impending he had begun to miss the company of men. He'd talked to the dead man of course, but there was no satisfaction in it. He wanted to be talked back to. Now he moved toward a destination and could anticipate the work that needed doing, tagging the ewes and readying the shelters. Maybe it was possible to build the flock back up. They could take out a loan. Wool prices could rise. It was possible.

But the sight of the home buildings puzzled him. Their familiarity was somehow foreign, his memory of them unclear: he regarded them as a snake might regard the empty skin it has lived in and left behind. Exposed and graying in the fist of the hills, the buildings looked abandoned. Even the barn, newly repaired and painted, had been dulled by winter.

They must have seen him coming, for the doors stood open at the back of the sheep shed. The ewes shouldered ahead, their bellies swaying, and their hooves on the hard earth made a sound like heavy rain. They poured in seeming to remember, needing little encouragement from the dog. Grant shut the doors behind him and dropped the bar, then he led his horse to the barn, leaving the wagon parked behind the shed where it couldn't be seen from the house. Standing in the trampled grass it looked like it had grown there.

He hayed the horse and brushed him out and the horse rested, breathing loudly with one leg cocked up. It was cold in the barn, but a sheltered cold, one you could get to like. When he was done he stood very still listening to the wind buffet the walls. Then in a temporary calm he heard her behind him. He started and spun, and boiled up in anger and shouted an oath. She shied. She was as white from the winter months as if she'd never spent a day outdoors in her life.

You look sick, he said.

I was. You look crazy.

He tossed the brush in the bucket it came from and busied himself about the barn, rearranging things the way they were before he left. He missed the range and wagon already. Here, there was too much to keep track of.

She said, I want to apologize.

You don't have nothing to be sorry for.

She watched him work. He felt her watching. You won't accept it, she said, is that it?

You got my answer.

He was good to me when I was sick, she went on. Grant felt itchy and hot and began banging the implements into their places. His back was aching. Things changed, she said. It isn't that—

I'm done with you! he screamed at the wall he faced, Get out! He stamped his booted foot and pain shot up from the place the toes had been. Get out!

He waited gasping until he heard the door slide closed behind him, then he fell sobbing to his knees, the months of scabbed and weathered callus cracking in an instant, all the dread of death and madness slashed in this silly fit, all over a girl. He was home.

•

This time there were no hired men to help them. They hadn't the money, nor enough sheep to make it worthwhile. When the first ewes began labor a cold descended, and though the patched barn kept the worst out, it was hard to keep the chill off the newborns. Some of them were so weak they died before their eyes opened. Some of the ewes bled to death. It was not as bad as it could have been but the operation had a sparseness about it, with stretches when nothing was happening and they had to talk about or do something to fill the time. They nursed their fingers split from the freeze and thaw. Grant sat listening to Kittredge. He was used to it. There was no talk of Neeler, obviously Kittredge had forced himself to stop. But the effort seemed to have killed something in him. He spent long minutes nodding in response to nothing, like an old man. After these silences he turned to details of his ailment, how he felt the shaking coming on when he woke or when he was hungry or faced with some task the shaking would keep him from doing. He wondered aloud if it was a bacteria that had got in him that made him sick, or some defect that was there all along. Lafitte had told him to sleep when he was tired and not to tax himself, but a little bit of the bottle helped, Kittredge said, in fact he was drinking a lot more than he used to. He had bought it himself, mind you—it wasn't costing the ranch a nickel. There was no evidence that Kittredge cared about or even noticed the words he was using. Listening to him was like standing in a rainstorm.

It was possible to ignore Sophia. She tended suckling lambs, moved the warming lamps from pen to pen, kept the fire going, and said nothing at all. Max worked alongside Cotter and Grant, leading the ewes in when their time came and ushering the lambs dead or alive into the cold world. Grant thought it must be a shock, living for months in that dark soundless summer, then emerging into winter and light. For some time the lambs would associate the two and maybe for that time they would live only reluctantly.

When it was done they had little more than before. There would not be much money made from spring lambs unless they wanted to cull the flock. Late one night while Sophia slept the men sat around the table waiting for someone to come out and say what they all were thinking.

I want out, Max finally said. His eyes were on his glass but the words were aimed at Grant. Me and her are going to move down to Denver. I can get work and paint besides.

Grant said, So go then.

Max looked up. It'd be nice to have a little spending money.

What you telling me for?

I want out.

Now that he was thinner Grant had found he couldn't hold his liquor too well. Max's figure tilted and smeared.

You want money, let her get it from her daddy, he said, knowing full well she couldn't get her daddy's signature on a birthday card if that was what she wanted.

A rattling on the table. It was Kittredge tightly clutching his empty glass.

You know what I'm saying, Max said. His reasonable tone of voice was a put-on. I want my half. Either you go in with somebody else or we sell and split it. We ain't never been any good at this like Edwin would of been. We never cared about the place. Let's get out.

He was right. There was nothing here for them. The thought of dumping the outfit sent a gush of warm blood out of Grant's heart, and it churned through him making him feel nearly human. And yet. And yet, goddam if he was going to write their ticket to Denver. He said, You do what you want with your half. I ain't buying you out.

He looked up and was pleased to discover that Max was stunned. Well, what had he thought? Did he think Grant was going to say Go, go, brother, take her away to Colorado? Like hell. When Grant opened his mouth he found himself talking a little louder.

You'll just have to find some sucker who'll buy you out. I got your interests to protect up on the spring range and I ain't got time to cut a deal for you. Run an ad in the paper.

There was a silence from which not a single breath was drawn.

Well, hell, said Max.

Hell, nothing. I don't know what you expected.

It ain't like I sneaked off with your girl, Max muttered, his face bent and working. It ain't like it was me who broke my mama.

Max, said Cotter.

Wasn't me who sent my poor idiot brother off to war, it was you. So the least you could do is let me have a piece of the life you wrecked. The way I see it, that wouldn't set nothing right, but it's the least goddam thing you could do.

Cotter's hand had made its way to Max's wrist, pinning the arm to the table. The arm had a fist at the end of it and tried to shake Cotter off. But Cotter held it.

Max, he said.

Some kind of reaction was called for, Grant thought. He was supposed to stand up knocking the chair over behind him. Something.

But Max had said nothing that could be disputed. For a moment he considered giving up. Why not let them go, and begin his new still-born life? He could buy a shack somewhere and squat in it and never think about these people again. But he could neither relinquish this final claim nor muster up the desire to defend it. He sat there.

Max seemed awfully far away. The house groaned, giving up its week of stored warmth from the false spring. Max shook his head.

Look at you, he said. You look like a rock. Two months out in it and you can't even feel nothing.

Max tried getting up but Cotter held him. Cotter! he shouted. Let go of my goddam arm!

Cotter let him go. Max stood, opening and closing his fingers. Then he went to the door and opened it, letting the cold air in. As if to say something he turned on the threshold and faced Grant. But in the end there appeared to be nothing he could say, having exhausted all the unthinkable things, and he went out shutting the door quietly and carefully behind him.

·

Grant expected that once he left for spring range he'd never see Max or Sophia again. They would borrow money from Kittredge, who was certain not to turn them down. Whatever the case they would be gone soon and he could get himself into the hills and forget about them. The prospect warmed him. He spent the next day in preparation, gathering supplies, the dog close behind him, its eyes alert inside rings of white fur.

That afternoon Cotter came to him. He stood watching Grant in silence awhile, his hands in his pockets. At last Grant stopped what he was doing and faced him.

Okay, what is it.

Looks like we'll be here another year then?

Grant sighed. At least through shearing, I reckon. Then I'll think about it.

In that case we're gonna need ice.

Ice, Grant said. Cotter nodded.

It was true that ice would have to be cut and hauled to the house. They did it every year, fifteen miles northeast on the springfed lake this side of Eleven. Usually it was done by now, before the first warm day. Grant said, Nobody did it already?

My back ain't what it was, Cotter said. And Max wouldn't do it by himself.

They were standing behind the sheep shed, by the wagon. The sheep knew it was time and milled at the gate like men, the wanderlust in them. Grant looked at Cotter a long while.

Okay, you're telling me I got to do it with Max.

Ain't nobody else.

He had to laugh. He said, You want us to make nice, do you.

I don't care about that, said Cotter. But I ain't gonna spend the summer eating rotten meat and warm iced tea. Unless you want to go to Ashton and get us an electric freezer.

With what money?

Well, then, Cotter said and stiffened his stance in the weeds.

He wondered if Max had put him up to it. Or if Sophia had put Max up to putting him up. Well, all right—if Max was going to try and talk him into selling, so be it. Let him beg. Grant said, Your back's no good, is it?

I'm old.

He shook his head. All right, let's get it done then. Another day of feed for the ewes, it's hardly worth it, but let's get it done.

Cotter nodded. Okay. I'll tell your brother.

Grant watched as he went, stepping delicate as if to favor his back. He thought about the ice, as much as could be got in a day, shrinking under sawdust behind the barn. Maybe they could get their differences worked out before they put in too much effort. Maybe before they'd finished the drive to Church Lake. He would see. It depended what Max said and how he said it. He would see.

·

They set out in the truck next morning, the ax and saw and tongs clattering in the bed behind them, the day cold, the sky crowded with clouds. Church Lake used to have a church overlooking it, some missionary's folly, that blew down one year and floated off in pieces. You could still find clapboards and planks in the mud when the water was low. People usually got their ice in midwinter, soon as it was thick enough, and in April they fished, lining up on the bank where the spring was and where the browns spawned. For about two weeks you could pull a giant fish out of that water practically with your bare hands.

Max drove. Neither spoke. It wasn't the same silence that was customary between them—a silence of preference—but a prideful silence, a silence of will. The landscape rolled past stunned by cold, the road pocked and rutted, no snow except smooth plats on the low grassed humps. They turned off at a mud track frozen into peaks and troughs and rumbled over it.

There was a beach here where the mud was cut with sand someone had dumped once. Tire tracks led all along it, stopping at the water's edge. Max turned around where the ice looked thickest and backed up. They got out and walked onto the surface, testing with their weight. It became necessary to speak.

Good enough.

Looks it.

Grant let himself grin. You got something you want to say to me?

Max looked up. Sounds like you want something said.

Nope.

Okay then, Max said, and he climbed back into the truck and backed it out onto the surface. Grant listened. The ice was silent. He went to the truck and pulled the ax out of the bed, Max the crowbar, and they walked out in opposite directions. Grant had brought the welding glasses with him to keep the ice from his eyes. He put them on and slung the ax up over his head, then drove it into the ice, gouging out chips that skittered across the bare surface.

It was better without snow. It'd be easy to slide the big chunks to the truck and they could lift them on without much effort.

The ax broke through quickly. He returned to the truck. Twenty yards off Max stood barefaced, gouging a line of holes with repeated drops of the crowbar. He took his time and seemed to enjoy being alone. Grant brought the saw and tongs to his cut and knelt before it. The blade fit snugly. He worked counterclockwise, making as tight a circle as the saw would allow. The cold came right up through the thick glove and he had to sit up every few minutes to rub and clap his hands together. After awhile he had cut a block the weight of a man which dropped into the water and bobbed. Grant sunk the ax into the ice beside it for a foothold. Then he wedged the tongs into the crack and pulled the block onto the surface. The rough underside froze to it. He threw his full weight against the block and broke it free, and it skated toward the truck. He followed along behind, pushing it with his boot until it lay behind the truckbed. Max was already there, smoking a cigarette. Grant went back for the ax and tongs, then they lifted the block onto the truck and shoved it up against the cab wall. Max took the ax and tongs and Grant took the crowbar and they returned to their stations and resumed work.

By midafternoon the truck was nearly full. Grant knew they could go further. The ice would freeze up against itself in the bed and could bear the ride back heaped higher. But he was sick of the work, and it was only for Kittredge and Cotter. It was enough.

He had the tools and was sawing out his last piece, closer to the truck. Max was also nearby throwing the crowbar harder, letting out grunts with every throw. When Grant was nearly finished Max came over and took the tongs back to where he was working. Grant watched. Max had managed to gouge out a small piece with the crowbar alone, and he was hauling it from the hole.

Grant turned back to his sawing. Though his arm and shoulder ached the sawing seemed easier now, and when the block detached and he pried up the edge with the saw, he understood why: half the circle had been cut from thinner ice. Someone had cut here before and the water had refrozen flat over the cuts, but neither as deeply nor as sturdily. He stood. Now he could see the line where the cutting had stopped, a barely perceptible division of dark and light that snaked across the water, running nearer the beach and passing under the truck.

Max lifted his block and humped it to the truckbed. The bed was over the thinner side, where the ice was dark. But it was thick enough, wasn't it, or they wouldn't have parked there in the first place.

Max! he called out.

Max was nearly to the truck. He leaned forward with his block and hoisted it up over the tailgate and dropped it—dropped it hard on the ice pile.

Then he slipped. His feet lost their hold and as his legs slid under the fender he grabbed the tailgate with both gloved hands and the ice split.

First the tires went through, and Max was pinned beneath the bed and its burden of ice. There was no sound on the lake but his groan and the slap of his palms against the tailgate.

That sound: Grant was entranced by it, by Max's labor. By his helplessness. He watched his brother struggle and the saw dropped from his fingers and clanked on the surface. He stood still. Max turned his head, the face flushed and the eyes black with despair.

Then the ice cracked again and the falling truck pushed him down, through the breaking ice and out of sight under the water. The chassis rang out against the surface, the truck tipped farther back and the weight of its load slammed the tailgate open, snapping the latches. The cut ice tumbled into the hole after Max and the truckbed after the ice. A couple of pieces broke free and bobbed up around the edges of the hole and stuck there. Now the surface was solid again, except for the empty tipped-back pickup jutting out of the lake like a gravestone.

A second passed. Grant perceived that he was alone on the ice. Then he ran for the truck.

He crouched on the surface pulling at the cut blocks fused together in the hole. They wouldn't move. He crawled around to peer under the bed, in the lean-to the tipped truck made, and could see an irregular strip of open water no more than six inches wide running along the edge of the thicker ice. Once under the truck he plunged his arm down in the bitter water, feeling back and forth for something he could lay a hand on. But nothing was there. He kept his arm in the water until the cold was too painful, then he got out from under the truck and ran to get the tongs. They were frozen to the surface but at last gave, and Grant stumbled and came down hard on his elbow. He ran back slipping and falling, and he got up and gripped the fused blocks with the tongs but none would budge. He flung off the welding glasses and brought his face down to the surface trying to see through the ice.

Max!

He stood on the floe of cut blocks, pounded it with his boots. He climbed into the truckbed and jumped and kicked in the freezing water that had welled there, and the water ran into his boots and flowed around his feet. The ghost toes cried out. He grew dizzy.

Max!

All along the edge of the lake was no one, not a cabin or horse or truck or tree. He stumbled to the front of the pickup where the fender was hanging four feet above the surface, and he pushed down on it using all his weight and strength. He threw himself onto the hood and felt his heart pressing at its cage.

He jumped down and grabbed the ax and chopped wildly all around the frozen hole. Chips flew and clattered against the truck and slid whispering over the smooth ice. Again he called out his brother's name.

Only then did he run to the beach, to the road, shouting for help to the empty dead land. His waterlogged boots thudded against the frozen gumbo and the pits and troughs twisted his ankles. His elbow throbbed. The sky lit up. It was nearly half an hour before the first driver came upon him, nearly running him down in the glare.

12

It took six men two days to find him: Grant, Cotter, Mott and his boy
Jess and a couple of icemen from Ashton. They managed to cut free
the jam the blocks had made and somebody pulled out the truck with
a winch. But nothing surfaced in the hole that was opened. They'd
been cutting near the spring when Max was pushed under; the lake
current had likely carried him toward the creek on the opposite side.
So the men cut in the direction of the flow, careful not to further
weaken the ice. In the daytime hours people from the towns came out
and watched them. Pictures were taken for the paper. A horse-faced
kid in a big suit came stumping out to get an interview. He came up to
Grant and asked him how he felt.

Go talk to the police, Grant told him.

Among the first day's watchers was Sophia. She stood for hours on
the beach wrapped in blankets. When he had called home from the
sheriff's in Ashton it was Kittredge he gave the news to. He still hadn't
spoken to Sophia, not on the telephone nor when Mott showed up
with her on the beach. She stood there all day and at nightfall was
brought home to sleep. The men worked through the night in the
headlights of an idling truck and continued past sunrise.

The police brought them food, which they ate standing.

It was Jess Mott who found him. He had cut a hole and was plunging into it with a hooked pole the icemen had rigged, a broomstick with a clothes hanger wired to the end. The hook caught and Jess shouted. When they came to him there was joy in his face, of being the one. He was nineteen. He reeled in the pole and there was Max's collar snagged on it, and now came his shoulder and his face, the nose pressed flat and frozen in place and the cheeks and forehead scraped and gouged from the irregular belly of the ice.

Grant laughed aloud, recognizing the dead man's face. He took a single step back and crumpled to the surface: it was him all right, fat and colorless as Grant had first found him. The other men pulled the body up and laid it out on its back, and Grant felt a warming as if from memory, thawing him from the heart out to his extremities, and he crouched on the ground before the body and touched its face with his bare burning fingers.

You gonna say something? he said.

He covered the crystalline eyes with his palms and lowered the lids. When he took his hand away its image was left behind, superimposed over the face like a silken glove. Then he was struck in the shoulders and thrown backwards onto the ice and his head cracked against it.

It was Sophia. She knelt at the edge of the hole and grabbed at the body and tried to pull it to her own. But the wet clothes had stuck fast.

The men stared at Sophia and at Grant lying prostrate beside her. Sophia cried out senselessly, tearing at the body with her fingers and thumping its chest. Then she flung herself at Grant, covering his face first with blows and then tears. She pressed herself to him, and the scent of her hair and her hot neck at last tore open the skin that had kept him from grief. He recognized Max's body and ruined face now and wailed for her loss, for his brother gone, for her love.

When later they took up the body, hair remained where his head had lain, frozen to the surface like glacier's tracks on an old stone.

•

Before he would sleep he dug the grave. In the first hours it seemed that the earth had sprouted rocks, like tumors, to thwart him, but then they stopped seeming unfair and he prised them out of the ground the way a sinner would drag the beads across his fingers. He refused help. If the task could occupy him for the rest of his life he believed he would let it: a labor clear and true as a wound. It took all of daylight and much of the night, and afterward he lay in bed until dawn, unable to sleep from the complaint of his muscles and toes and cracked elbow.

But she was asleep, exhausted by anguish. He listened to her breathe.

A few people from town spoke over the casket, later he wouldn't remember who. Rocks and all, the dirt was shoveled into the grave, erasing Grant's work. Then the graveyard, full but for one, was emptied of the living.

Days passed in which he slept when tired, ate when hungry. The sun rose and set. From time to time Grant would look up from where he walked or sat and find himself in a different place from the one he remembered, or in darkness when he thought it was daytime, or alone when he thought other people were around. The only thing that told him time was passing was an inner increase, a stretching and thinning of his skin, a sense that whatever was in him could not be contained. Simple remorse was growing into anger, unease into fear.

He slept and dreamed. It was noon, the sun hot and high, the snow rising into the air as steam, the distant hills shuddering. He was afoot on the flats, his ears attuned to the rustle and strain of the heat-mad grasses. Far away was the figure of a man beside a horse. The man pulled himself onto the horse, first fumbling and falling and at last rolling astride. His body spread across the horse's back, his legs dangling like panniers at its flanks. The horse began to move, stumbling then steadying under the rider's weight.

Grant understood that he was powerless to call back or pursue the rider, yet he struggled to open his throat and lift his feet. Still there was relief in his paralysis. The possibility of action and response fell

234 · J. ROBERT LENNON

away and he stood rooted in a world stripped of its moral component, as he imagined a man would stand on a field of battle, ruled only by fear and command.

Then he woke free and tore his bedclothes away in a moonlit night, his hands groping for the bureau drawer where the flensing knife was hid.

He paused before her door, then leaned in. His vision, tinged by blood, held her in a haze of ebbing life. He could see the vein jump in her neck. If he was to climb in bed beside her she might take him in her arms.

Instead he went down the stairs and across the yard to the back gate. There was time enough to walk. Cotter had taken the ewes to range and Grant knew right where he would go: the gentle nearby hills where the grass was thick and the stock lambs could find their footing. The ground released the day's heat and it rose all around him.

The moon was at his back. Soon it was overhead, the noon of night. He wasn't tired. The kinks had worked themselves out in sleep. When he was close the dog ran out to meet him and fell in stride in a companionable way, yet kept a distance, wary of the moonlit knife.

Grant found them bedded down in the low place between hills. He climbed up on a boulder shaded by a spruce tree where he could watch the flock. Cotter was sleeping outdoors on a tarp. The knife was warm in Grant's hand.

The dog whined and Grant put out a hand to quiet him. Below, Cotter turned over.

Dog, came Cotter's voice, roughened by sleep. The dog pricked up its ears.

Go, Grant whispered.

The dog took off running down the hill and around the bedded flock. Sheep on the edges woke and stood and settled themselves in his wake. The dog went to Cotter then circled the camp. Cotter spoke to the dog and the dog looked up to where Grant was sitting. But the tree kept Grant from sight.

Hey! Cotter said.

Grant thought, Lie down. The dog obeyed.

Lie down, he thought, looking at Cotter. But instead Cotter stood up and lit a cigarette and smoked it leaning against the wagon. Then he lay down again. A long time later he seemed to be asleep.

Grant crept down the hill and into the flock until he was surrounded on all sides by sheep. They were stirring, his presence moving through them, and they began to creep away. The dog stood up. Grant showed him his palm, white and empty. The dog lay down.

He reached out and took a handful of wool between his fingers. He straddled the ewe's back and worked the knife down to the flesh at its throat. The animal was calm. He drew breath and plunged in with the knifepoint, then pulled the blade hard through the windpipe and across the large vein. The ewe jerked, air whistled in its throat and his hand was washed with blood. He clamped his knees tight around the ewe and held its head up by the wool. Blood splashed on the ground. The dog heard and smelled it and stood barking. The sheep moved away from him, pressing into one another.

Grant let the ewe drop and lunged at another, catching it by the hock. He got on top of it and jabbed at its throat but the stroke was hasty and failed to penetrate the wool. The ewe screamed out and the others began to bolt and bleat.

A rifle discharged. The dog continued to bark. He stabbed again and the blade sunk.

What in the hell are you doing? Cotter shouted, and Grant swelled with panic and rage, the cowardly ewes crushing away from him, and he ran after them stabbing blindly.

Grant! Grant!

The knife found backs and bellies and rasped against bones. He stumbled, his throat suddenly aching. Dawn was about to break. Blood covered his arms and his knees and the air tasted of it. He sneezed again and again and couldn't stop. Cotter came down on top of him and his ribs cracked against a rock half buried in the ground.

Pain bloomed and spread through him. The dog, invigorated by blood, clamped its old jaws around his ankle. Grant felt sorry for betraying him, a good dog.

Cotter was heavy and his voice was in Grant's ear. Easy, he was saying. Grant could feel the knife lying flat on the ground beneath him. He struggled to reach it but his arms were pinned.

His ribs were killing him. It was hard to breathe. He could hear the flock racing away in all directions.

He'd wanted them all.

◆

When he came back, she was gone.

13

Here was an afternoon so clear you could almost see the future. Aspens on the creek a mile away snagged the wind and their leaves turned on and off like electric lights. Hawks lifted and circled and dove. Cars leaving the highway raised dust all across the flats; from his stoop Grant saw the clouds rise and disperse. If he could lose himself, forget the time and place he was in, he might believe they were camp-fires from homesteaders' roofless squats, or even Indian fires. But they were cars. It was a car he was waiting for.

It was too hot for him here. He went in the screen door and busied himself around the place. The floor was swept. Still he did it again, to be sure. He'd put cookies on the table but now he put them away: she might be watching her weight. He got out glasses for cold tea and then put them away, too. Best to wait and see. She might not even want to sit down. He went to the front room and lowered himself into his chair and dozed, his half-dreams punctuated by insect and bird songs. The sound of a car slowing on the highway woke him. He went to the door and watched through the screen.

It was a big black car made for rich men, not good out here for much at all. The windows were shut tight against the heat. He could see the woman's head, the hair shorn close, framed in the wide wind-shield. She parked it in the weeds and got out.

She wasn't like he pictured: so young, practically a girl. Stout and pretty but for the hair, strong masculine arms. She'd put on a smile as if she knew he was watching, though he was invisible in the shadows. Her steps were wide and fast as if to compensate for the shortness of her legs. For all that, she seemed all right. He opened the screen door before she had a chance to knock.

Mr. Person?

Come on in, he said.

She carried a leather satchel and looked frankly around his house. Grew up in New York, she'd told him on the phone. A city girl. She'd had an uncle who used to play tenor sax when he was young, and the uncle had pen and ink drawings hanging in his apartment, drawings of himself and others playing in jazz clubs, back in the days after the war. He'd told her the artist's name and where he had come from, and when the uncle died and the drawings were left to her, she remembered that Max Person had come from here. An unlikely place. And now she lived nearby, she worked at a museum in the state capital, and she thought she'd try to track Max Person down. Just find out what had become of him.

Now they stood inside the door, blinking as their eyes adjusted to the dim. She let out breath, straightened herself, then looked up at him, expectant.

Well, he said. It's a long drive for you.

All in a day's work.

They sat in the kitchen. He offered her the iced tea and she accepted. She refused an offer of sugar. For a little while she sat quiet, still smiling, as if waiting for him to speak. He cleared his throat. She said, You're all alone out here?

Coming on fifteen years.

Bet it gets a little scary in the winter.

He said, I get by fine. She shifted in her chair and took a sip of the drink. Her eyes went to the window.

Were you married, Mr. Person?

Was. She's dead now.

I'm sorry. She reached out suddenly for her drink and nearly knocked it over. She sipped, then gulped it.

Wasn't your fault, he said, letting her see that he was smiling. Maybe, he said, you want to go out and have a look.

She seemed relieved. Yes, let's do that, she said.

They stood up together. He led her out the back door, around the little pasture where he kept his sheep and goats, and past the chicken coop. They used to have a couple of horses, but it hurt him to ride now and they weren't worth the trouble besides, not to him. Somehow she'd got ahead and he trailed close behind, smelling the town cleanness of her.

The padlock on the barn door was rusted but from time to time he sprayed a solvent in there to keep it smooth. He fished the key out of his pocket. The lock opened easily. For a moment he paused, his hand on the hasp. Then he rolled the door open and switched on the lights.

A while ago he'd sold an old tractor so he could fix things up right. He'd had a solid cement floor poured and was always pleased to note there were still no cracks. The canvases were stood up in bins he'd made out of scrap lumber, the drawings sorted and laid flat in oak drawers. He'd made the drawers too. When he noticed that bugs and mice were getting in, he decided to go down to the state university to see how you were supposed to take care of art. They gave him a few pointers and he came back and did the work.

There were about a thousand paintings and drawings all told. He couldn't believe it when he found them. All those late nights Max must have been in a kind of fever. He had painted and drawn on anything that was lying around—canvas tarps, an old tee shirt, grocery bags, shirt cardboards. These days people'd call it a compulsion. Then again, you don't get good at something by doing it half-cocked. Grant didn't know if Max was any good; that is, if other people would think he was good. Some of the paintings had begun to rot. The man he talked to at State thought he was some kind of crackpot but told him there'd have to be machines controlling the temperature and humidity. Of course there was no money for that.

The girl opened up the drawers first, coming upon the nudes. The subject was Sophia. He'd looked at them enough times to know from across the room exactly which she was looking at. For years he had just picked them up without thinking until his hands began to darken the edges. Then he bought white gloves, which he washed in bleach.

Some of the pictures were too intimate to show the girl, and these he had taken out.

She said, This model.

Yes?

Did you know her? She knew your brother?

She lived out here, he said. Not here, out near Eleven. With us, when we had the ranch. She was from New York too. When Max died she moved away.

The girl nodded, then turned back to the drawings. Soon she had moved on through the landscapes and the few jazz pictures Max had brought from New York, every few minutes sliding one off the pile and holding it up and giving it a long thoughtful look.

Where'd you say he studied? she said.

I don't know that he studied at any school. He knew some painters but I couldn't tell you which ones.

This model. Do you know her name?

He paused. No harm in telling her. But he only said, Used to.

I wonder if she's still alive.

I don't know, he said. I don't know what became of her.

In due time she turned to the paintings. Again there were portraits, mostly of Sophia, some of Max himself reflected in a cracked mirror, his face halved and skewed or staring blankly out of the frame. The painted landscapes varied. A few were realistic. Most were blurred by some intuition, the colors wrong but according to some plan Grant didn't quite grasp. Then there were interiors, mostly the barn criss-crossed by slatted light, and then the light itself without the barn around it, a lattice of color with edges undefined, the occasional band of color leaving the composition and reaching to the edge of the picture. The last ones were the largest, five or six feet to a side, the paint thick and sloppy. They were painted on cloth nailed to boards from the burnt-down quarters or sometimes done directly on the boards themselves. The lines had a fragmentary quality, as if they'd been chipped off of something with a hatchet. At first Grant never gave these paintings much thought, but they had managed to get under his skin. He regarded them as hostile and grew to fear and despise them. Even today he didn't care for them. They seemed to reject the world that had created them. They were too much like Max.

The girl lingered on these the longest, taking each one out and leaning it against the wall, standing back, mumbling to herself. Time passed, maybe half an hour.

It was what he'd done himself when he put the ranch on the market, he looked at and touched each one, trying to figure out what Max had been thinking. He was glad that he discovered the pictures later, when he was getting ready to leave the valley, and not months before that, just after Max drowned. He might have burned the lot of them then.

Before he left, the mail had brought him an apology. He'd never noticed Sophia's handwriting but looking at it he knew it was hers. The return address was written neatly on the upper left corner of the envelope. She was in Chicago, living with her brother and his wife. She had decided to enroll in a college. He began writing to her and eventually he begged her to come back to him. Her response was a long time in coming. I'm sorry, she wrote.

The following year he came upon a woman whose truck had broken down at the side of the road. Her name was Helen, she was a horse trainer. He gave her a ride into town. Six months later they got married. They lived in Ashton and had three children. One was dead of a cancer. The others lived far off, one in Seattle and the other in Eugene. His son had got married and his wife was expecting a daughter, which would make Grant a grandfather at seventy-seven.

The girl had turned and was staring at him, a hungry gaze that reminded him of Sophia, when she looked at him and seemed to see Max there. He'd hated to be looked at like that, hated when Sophia did it, but now he felt a strange, prideful power. He felt his brother coming to life inside him.

How old was he when he made these? she said.

Twenty-three.

Do you have slides?

Slides?

Of these paintings. I want to show them to the curators. I think I'd like to mount an exhibition but other people need to see the paintings.

No, no slides. Take some back if you want.

This seemed to startle her. She looked at the paintings and back at Grant. Yes, all right, she said. I can take some of the small ones. And some drawings. A few of those.

Whatever you want.

I think they're very good, she said. All of them. I think we can mount a very nice show. Not a large one, mind you, we don't have much space.

She turned again to the paintings, arrayed against the back wall in a crooked row. She said, He evolved so quickly. His line, the materials he was using. Almost as if he knew he didn't have much time.

She looked at Grant, her head cocked, inquiring.

That may be so, Grant said.

◆

Fifteen years ago she had been sitting in the kitchen, wearing jeans despite the heat and a loose cotton shirt. Her hat lay on the table next to her glass of water and pills. He sat across from her covered in sweat from haying. It was a day much like this one, hot and clear. He planned to go into town and hoped she would come and have lunch. He'd left the pills and water out for her, she was sometimes forgetful of them. She looked sick, her skin splotched and sallow, but she often looked that way. She was always pale, heat brought the blood to her face. Her face was much like it had been when they met: full and round, the ears and nose small, the eyes set far apart. The impression was one of kindness, and of fearlessness, and she was both kind and fearless. But it had been awhile since her doctor had let her work full-time. She still went daily out to the horse farm to put in a few hours. She loved the horses and missed them when she was at home.

Going back to the garden? he said.

If I feel any better.

I've got errands. You ought to ride along.

Maybe, she said.

He should have looked more closely. He would recall better today what her mouth had been like, her eyes. She moved her trembling fingers through her hair, still blond but now brittle. It made a faint sound, like falling leaves.

Your pills, he said.

She sighed, stood up with her palms flat on the table. I don't know what it is with me. I'd better take a rest. She headed for the stairs.

Helen—

I'll take them later, when I can keep them down.

Would it have made a difference? Now he doubted it, but for years afterward he blamed himself for failing to press the point. At the time he hadn't wanted to make her angry. She was not much over fifty and it was hard to believe in the danger.

He heard her get settled upstairs. After awhile he went to town alone. He ate his lunch then went back home and put on the radio. Though her hat lay on the table, though the pills and water had not been touched, he thought she must have gone out.

Where to? A neighbor's? What for? And she would have worn the hat, it was hot out. He didn't think about that, though. Not until later.

A good twenty minutes passed. He switched off the radio and listened to the house. He went to the sink and looked out over the backyard, the rose hedge she had cultivated, the animals crowded into the shade of their shelter, the trail of a passing plane, needle-sharp at one end and at the other barely distinguishable from sky. His chest tightened and he hung his head and saw the breakfast dishes lying in the sink.

Helen, he whispered. Then he turned to the stairs and began the long walk to where she lay.

.

Afterward his daughter bought him an air conditioner, as if it was the heat that had killed her. A man delivered it and installed it in the bedroom, then turned it on and went around the house shutting all the windows and doors. Grant watched the man drive off in his van, and when he was out of sight turned off the air conditioner and opened up the house again. The air conditioner was still in the bedroom window, where it shut out the light and air. He slept downstairs on the sofa now.

The girl sat where Helen had sat, her notepad where Helen's pills had lain. She asked him questions about Max's life and he answered the ones he knew the answers to. He didn't know what certain paintings meant or if the images in them were symbols for anything else, or what events in Max's life made him paint the way he did. He told her she could make up a theory if she wanted, it was all right with him. He had a feeling that was what she was planning to do.

The girl coughed and sipped from her glass, but the glass was empty, and she put it down and coughed again.

It's a shame he died so young.

Grant couldn't reply to that. He had a thought he often had, which was that he himself wouldn't have had much of a life at all, had Max lived. He might have longed for her forever. But of course he wouldn't have. He would have had some kind of life, somewhere. It was hard at his age to believe otherwise, despite all that had happened to him.

She was still looking at him, in the wake of what she said. That gaze again, seeking, apprehending. Her eyes darted side to side, taking in the parts of his face. Instead of speaking he reached across the table and took her hand. Gently, barely touching it at all. The girl seemed shocked but did not pull away. Instead her fingers closed around his. He remembered. Then he stood up and she stood up. She picked up the notebook and put it in her satchel. He saw her to the door.

Later on he climbed the steps to the upstairs hallway. He paused at the top to catch his breath. In the rooms he opened drawers and closets and looked into them, finding nothing. At last he reached the bedroom, their bedroom, his and Helen's. He opened the door and walked in. Nothing here had been disturbed. Light leaked in between the curtains over the air conditioner. Photos of their children hung above the bed, their bed. Suddenly tired he lay down on the blankets and closed his eyes. Could it be that she made this bed, fitted and tucked these very sheets? He felt he ought to remember, but he couldn't. It was too long ago.

He remembered why he was here and got up. In the closet, on the floor, were the letters, wrapped with a rubber band and buried in a cardboard box. He slipped one out of the pile at random. The return address was an apartment, she would never be there now. He opened the envelope and looked inside. Folded into the letter was a small black-and-white photograph. It was a tiny portrait of Max and Sophia, both smiling, both impossibly young. A thin beard darkened Max's face. Behind them hung a painted backdrop of a roller coaster alongside the ocean. He unfolded the note.

> Grant,
>
> I thought you might want to have this; I found it with some of my old things. It was taken at Coney Island, in New York, when M. and I first met. You can keep it, I have more.
> I will write you a proper letter soon.
>
> S.

Probably she was alive, he thought. She might not yet be seventy: not old at all, these days.

Maybe he could find her, track her down. But no: she was lost to him now.

He tucked the photo and letter back into the envelope and the envelope into the bundle. He put the letters away and closed the closet door, the bedroom door. Then he went down to the kitchen. Empty glasses, his and the girl's, stood on the table; he washed them, then washed the table and scoured the inside of the sink. For a time he stood listening to the radio: pop songs and bad news. Then he lay down on the sofa to sleep. A long while later he still had not, so he got up and went outside. He could hear the animals moving and saw the backs of the sheep over the hedge.

Some time before, his electric clippers had given out, and rather than buy new ones he'd found an old pair of hand shears and learned how to use them. They were slower and less precise but he liked them better. It was possible to tell from the feel of the cut if it had landed right, from the way the fleece lay on the hand. Now he went to the barn and found the shears. He'd oiled them last season but the rust had crept in, so he scoured them clean and wiped them with a cloth. Then he went out and got the first ewe.

It was quiet in the barn, with light spilling in from the high windows and the smell of hay and rust and mouse. The ewe stood bored and still in front of his stool. He worked the blades into the wool and began to cut, keeping a good level just above the flesh. After a few cuts his hand began to ache, but the ache felt good. The fleece loosened. When he was done he lifted it off and folded it twice and set it down on a spread-out sack. The ewe shook itself.

Thanks, he said to the ewe.

Outside the sky'd begun to purple and the night bugs took flight. He brought the ewe back to its pen and led out the next. In the barn he settled himself and took up the shears. Their sound prophesied, then joined, cricket song. The work was slow. He thought, with pleasure, that it might take half the night.

Acknowledgments

I'd like to thank the following people and institutions for their assistance during the writing and editing of this novel: Lisa Bankoff, Rhian Ellis, Steve Glueckert, Brian Hall, Katy Hope, Bill Kittredge, my uncle James Lennon and parents Eugene and Pauline Lennon, Jack Macrae, Ben Metcalf, Ed Skoog, Robert Turgeon; the Oak (R.I.P.), the Art Museum of Missoula, and the Mann Library at Cornell University, particularly librarian Jim Morris-Knower. Though I read many books and articles while researching *On the Night Plain*, I'd like to single out James Ensminger's excellent *Stockman's Handbook* and *Sheep Husbandry*, and Hughie Call's ranch memoir *Golden Fleece*, which describes some of the dangers (dramatized here) that sheep and their herders are susceptible to in winter. Some, not all, of Max Person's paintings were inspired by those of Henry Meloy, a Montana artist active during the 1930s and 40s. However, Max Person's life is entirely invented. Likewise, the towns of Eleven and Ashton are imaginary, and are not intended to resemble real places. The title is taken from Terry Riley's string quartet "Cadenza on the Night Plain," which, in a recording by the Kronos Quartet, provided a backdrop for my work on the book. I am grateful to the composer for this evocative music.

About the Author

J. ROBERT LENNON is the author of *The Light of Falling Stars* and *The Funnies*. He lives with his wife and sons in Ithaca, New York.

About the Type

This book has been set in Simoncini Garamond, a member of one of the most popular families of typefaces in history. Claude Garamond, a sixteenth-century printer, publisher, and type designer, used the types of Venetian printers from the previous century as his models. The Italian foundry Simoncini created their version of Garamond, designed by Francesco Simoncini and W. Bilz, between 1958 and 1961. Versatile for text and display situations, Simoncini Garamond is more delicate in line and lighter in color than other Garamond versions.

Simoncini Garamond is a registered trademark of Bauer Types, S.A.

Composed by NK Graphics
Printed and bound by RR Donnelley & Sons

GET USED TO IT...

Jackboots walked over the kitchen floor above Jeffrey and Lucretzia, making the planking creak and sending little trickles of dust down into the cellar. To Jeffrey, the dark basement slowly took on a flat, silvery tone as Center boosted his perceptions.

The voice of Raj echoed in Jeffrey's mind: *to the right of the door.*

Jeffrey's hand reached out to the knob, moving with an automatic precision that seemed detached and slow. He jerked it backward, and the Land soldier stumbled through. A grid dropped down over his sight, outlining the enemy. A green dot appeared right under the angle of the man's jaw. His finger stroked the trigger, squeezing.

Crack. The soldier's head snapped sideways as if he'd been kicked by a horse. Jeffrey was turning, turning, the pistol coming up. The second soldier was leveling her rifle, but the green dot settled on her throat.

Crack. The woman fell back and writhed, blood spraying. The soldier behind her was jumping back, out of sight, almost, but the green dot settled on his leg.

Crack. A scream, as the third soldier tumbled out of sight. The grid outlined a prone figure against the planks of the entranceway, and an aiming point strobed. Jeffrey squeezed the trigger four times. But there was one more soldier, and the bark of the rifle was much deeper than Jeffrey's pistol. The nickel-jacketed bullet ricocheted, whining around the stones of the cellar like a giant lethal wasp.

Jeffrey tumbled back down the stairs, snapping open the cylinder of his re~~~~~~~~~~~~~~~~~~~~~~~ass.

"Christ," Jeffrey ~~~~~~~~~~~~~~~~~~~~~~ *four human beings.*

this is what the ~~~~~~~~~~~~~~~~~~~ **ife,** Center said.

THE GENERAL SERIES

The Forge
The Hammer
The Anvil
The Steel
The Sword

S.M. STIRLING
THE CHOSEN
DAVID DRAKE

To Jan, with love.
And to Steve's dad, who did a good job.

THE CHOSEN

A Baen Books Original

Baen Publishing Enterprises
P.O. Box 1403
Riverdale, NY 10471

ISBN: 0-671-87724-0

Cover art by Stephen Hickman

First printing, June 1996

Distributed by Simon & Schuster
1230 Avenue of the Americas
New York, NY 10020

Typeset by Windhaven Press: Editorial Services, Auburn, NH
Printed in the United States of America

Visager
Southern Hemisphere

← Equator
← to the Western Isles

N

LAND OF THE CHOSEN

Konugsburg
Westhavn
Oathtaking
Copenik
Hanver
Pillars
Dorst

The Passage

Artheusa

NORTHERN OCEAN

UNIVERSAL EMPIRE

Corona

Sircusa

Veron   Milana   Ciano

Pada *River*

Collini Penani

WESTERN OCEAN
←

Napoli

Charsson
Noyk
Bosson

Salini

REPUBLIC OF SANTANDER

Dubuk   The Gut

Borreaux   Nanes

SIERRA DEMOCRATICA Y POPULARA

Trois   Rio Arena
Barlon

Fursten   Pokips   Ensburg   **UNION DEL EST**   Nuevo Madrid

Santander City   Alaì   Isivert

Santander   *River*   Rally

Nawlin   Iway   Unionvil

Sanmere

Karlton   Tomsville

border

Desmines   • Bassin du fud

Marsai

Line of furthest
Chosen advance

500 M

SOUTH SEA

to Errif and the
Southern Isles

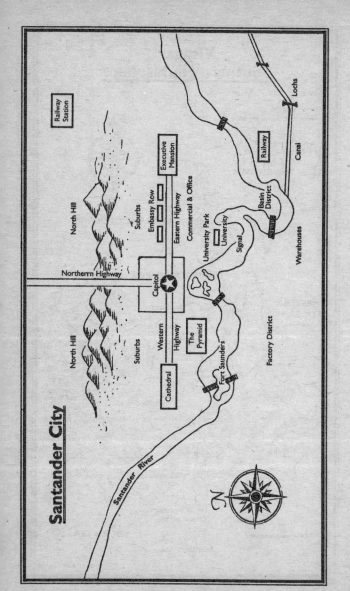

Santander City

Railway Station

North Hill

North Hill

Suburbs

Suburbs

Northern Highway

Cathedral

Capitol

Western Highway

The Pyramid

Fort Saunders

Embassy Row

Executive Mansion

Eastern Highway

Commercial & Office

University Park

University

Signal

Basin District

Railway

Canal

Lochs

Warehouses

Factory District

Santander River

E. KOSTYA

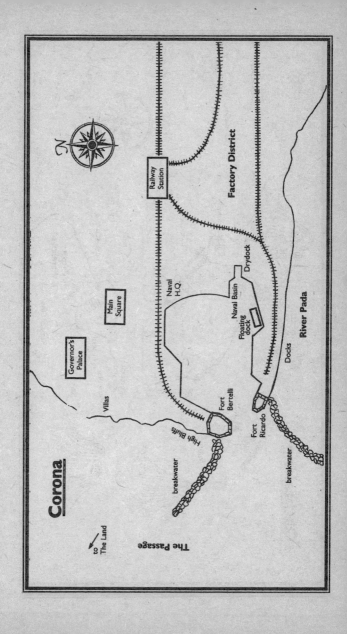

Corona

to The Land

The Passage

breakwater

breakwater

High Bluffs

Fort Bertelli

Fort Ricardo

Docks

River Pada

Naval Basin

Floating dock

Drydock

Naval H.Q.

Main Square

Governor's Palace

Villas

Railway Station

Factory District

N

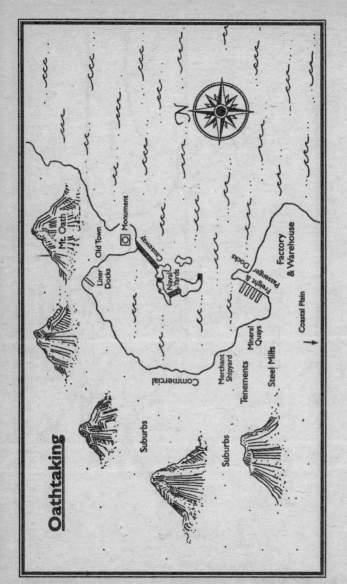

Oathtaking

CHAPTER ONE

Visager
1221 A.F. (After the Fall)
305 Y.O. (Year of the Oath)

Commodore Maurice Farr lifted the uniform cap from his head and wiped at the sweat on his forehead with a handkerchief. He was standing on the liner docks on the north shore of Oathtaking's superb C-shaped harbor. Behind him were the broad quiet streets of Old Town, running out from Monument Square behind his back. There the bronze figures of the Founders stood, raised weapons in their hands—the cutlasses and flintlocks common three centuries ago. The Empire-Alliance war had ended an overwhelming Imperial victory. The first thing the Alliance refugees had done was swear a solemn oath of vengeance against those who'd broken their ambitions and slaughtered everyone of their fellows who hadn't fled the mainland.

After three years in the Land of the Chosen as a naval attaché, Farr was certain of two things: their descendants still meant it, and they'd extended the future field of attack from the Empire to everyone else on the planet Visager. Perhaps to the entire universe.

West and south around the bay ran the modern city of Oathtaking, built of black basalt and gray tufa from the quarries nearby. Rail sidings, shipyards, steel mills, factories, warehouses, the endless tenement blocks that housed the Protégé laborers. A cluster of huge buildings marked the commercial center; six and even eight

stories tall, their girder frames sheathed in granite carved
in the severe columnar style of Chosen architecture. A
pall of coal smoke lay over most of the town below the
leafy suburbs on the hill slopes, giving the hot tropical
air a sulfurous taste. A racket of shod hooves sounded
on stone-block pavement, the squeal of iron on iron and
a hiss of steam, the hoot of factory sirens. Ships thronged
the docks and harbor, everything from old-fashioned
windjammers in with cargoes of grain from the Empire
to modern steel-hulled steamers of Land or Republic
build.

Out in the middle of the harbor a circle of islands
linked by causeways marked the site of an ancient caldera
and the modern navy basin. Near it moved the low hulking gray shape of a battlewagon, spewing black smoke
from its stacks. His mind categorized it automatically:
Ezerherzog Grukin, name-ship of her class, launched last
year. Twelve thousand tons displacement, four 250-mm
rifles in twin turrets fore and aft, eight 175mm in four
twin-tube wing turrets, eight 155mm in barbette mounts
on either side, 200mm main belt, face-hardened alloy
steel. Four-stacker with triple expansion engines, eighteen thousand horsepower, eighteen knots.

The biggest, baddest thing on the water, or at least
it would be until the Republic launched its first of the
Democrat-class in eighteen months.

Farr shook his head. *Enough. You're going home.* He
raised his eyes.

Snow-capped volcanoes ringed the port city of Oathtaking on three sides. They reared into the hazy tropical air
like perfect cones, their bases overlapping in a tangle of
valleys and folds coated with rain forest like dark-green
velvet. Below the forest were terraced fields; Farr
remembered riding among them. Dusty gravel-surfaced
lanes between rows of eucalyptus and flamboyants. A
little cooler than down here on the docks; a little less
humid. Certainly better smelling than the oily waters of
the harbor. Pretty, in a way, the glossy green of the coffee

bushes and the orange orchards. He'd gone up there a couple of times, invited up to the manors of family estates by Chosen navy types eager to get to know the Republic's naval attaché. Not bad oscos, some of them; good sailors, terrible spies, and given to asking questions that revealed much more than they intended.

Also, that meant he got a travel pass for the Oathtaking District. There were some spots where a good pair of binoculars could get you a glimpse at the base if you were quick and discreet. Nothing earthshaking, just what was in port and what was in drydock and what was building on the slipways. Confirming what Intelligence got out of its contacts among the Protégé workers in the shipyard. That was how you built up a picture of capabilities, bit by bit. He'd been here three years now, he'd done a pretty good job—gotten the specs on the steam-turbine experiments—and it was time to go home.

For more reasons than one. He dropped his eyes to the man and woman talking not far away.

What did I ever see in him? Sally Hosten thought.

Her husband—soon to be ex-husband—stood at parade rest, hands clasped behind his back. Karl Hosten was a tall man even for one of the Chosen, broad-shouldered and narrow-waisted, as trim at thirty-five as he had been twelve years ago when they married. His face was square and so deeply tanned that the turquoise-blue eyes glowed like jewels by contrast; his cropped hair was white-blond. He wore undress uniform: gray shorts and short-sleeved tunic and gunbelt.

"This parting is not of my will," he said in crisp Chosen-accented Landisch.

"No, it's mine," Sally agreed, in English.

She'd spoken Landisch for a long time, her voice had been a little rusty when she went to the Santander embassy to see about getting her Republican citizenship back. She'd met Maurice there. And she didn't intend to speak Karl's language again, if she could help it.

"Will you not reconsider?" he said.

Twelve years together had made it easy for her to read the emotions behind a Chosen mask-face. The sorrow she sensed put a bubble of anger at the back of her mouth, hard and bitter.

"Will you give John back his children?" she said.

A brief glance aside showed that her son John wasn't nearby anymore. Where . . . twenty feet or so, bending over a cargo net with another boy of about the same twelve years. Jeffrey Farr, Maurice's son.

Karl Hosten stiffened and ran a hand over his stubbled scalp. "The law is the law; genetic defects must be—"

"A clubfoot is not a genetic defect!" Sally said with quiet deadliness. "It's a result of carriage during pregnancy"—a spear of guilt stabbed her—"which can be, was, corrected surgically. And you didn't even *tell* me you were having him sterilized in the delivery room. I didn't find out until he was eleven years old!"

"Would you have been happier if you knew? Would he?"

"How happy would he be when he found out he couldn't be Chosen?"

Karl swallowed and looked very slightly away. *He is my son too,* he didn't say. Aloud: "There are many fine careers open to Probationers-Emeritus. Johan is an intelligent boy. The University—"

"As a *Washout*," Sally said, using the cruel slang term for those who failed the exacting Trial of Life at eighteen after being born to or selected for the training system. It was far better than Protégé status, anything was, but in the Land of the Chosen . . .

"We've had this conversation too many times," she said.

Karl sighed. "Correct. Let us get this over with."

She looked around. "John!"

John Hosten felt prickly, as if his own skin were too tight and belonged to somebody else. Everyone had been too quiet in the steamcar, after they picked him up at the school. He'd already said good-bye to his friends— he didn't have many—and packed. Vulf, his dog, was already on board the ship.

I don't want to listen to them fight, he thought, and began drifting away from his mother and father.

That put him near another boy about his own age. John's eyes slid back to him, curiosity driving his misery away a little. The stranger was skinny and tall, red-haired and freckled. His hair was oddly cut, short at the sides and floppy on top, combed—a foreigner's style, different from both the Chosen crop and the bowl-cut of a Proti. He wore a thin fabric pullover printed in bizarre colorful patterns, baggy shorts, laced shoes with rubber soles, and a ridiculous looking billed cap.

"Hi," he said, holding out a hand. Then: "Ah, *guddag*."

"I speak English," John said, shaking with the brief hard clamp of the Land. English and Imperial were compulsory subjects at school, and he'd practiced with his mother.

The other boy flexed his fingers. "Better'n I speak Landisch," he said, grinning. "I'm Jeffrey Farr. That's my dad over there."

He nodded towards a tall slender man in a white uniform who was standing a careful twenty meters from the Hosten party. John recognized the uniform from familiarization lectures and slides: Republic of Santander Navy, officer's lightweight summer garrison version. It must be Captain Farr, the officer Mom had been seeing at the consulate about the citizenship stuff.

I wish she'd tell me the truth. I'm not a little kid or an idiot, he thought. That wasn't the only reason she was talking to Maurice Farr so much. "John Hosten, Probationer-hereditary," he replied aloud.

A Probationer-hereditary was born to the Chosen and automatically entitled to the training and the Test of Life; only a few children of Protégés were adopted into the course. Then he flushed. He wasn't going to be a

Probationer long, and he could never have passed the
Test, not the genetic portions. Not with his foot. He
couldn't be anything but a Washout, second-class citizen.

"You don't have to worry about all that crap any more,"
Jeffrey said cheerfully, jerking a thumb over his shoulder at the liner *Pride of Bosson*. "We're all going back
to civilization."

The flag that fluttered from her signal mast had a blue
triangle in the left field with fifteen white stars, and two
broad stripes of red and white to the right. The Republic
of Santander's banner.

John opened his mouth in automatic reflex to defend
the Land, then closed it again. He was going to Santander himself. To live.

"*Ya*, we're going," he said. They both looked over
towards their parents. "Your mother?"

"She died when I was a baby," Jeffrey said.

There was a crash behind them. The boys turned, both
relieved at the distraction. One of the steam cranes on
the *Bosson*'s deck had slipped a gear while unloading
a final cargo net on the dock. The Protégé foreman of
the docker gang went white under his tan—he'd be held
responsible—and turned to yell insults and complaints
up at the liner's deck, shaking his fist. Then he turned
and whipped his lead-weighted truncheon across the side
of one docker's head. There was a sound like a melon
dropping on pavement; the docker's face seemed to dis-
tort like a rubber mask. He fell to the cracked uneven
pavement with a limp finality, as if someone had cut all
his tendons.

"Shit," Jeffrey whispered.

The foreman made an angry gesture with his baton,
and two of the dockers took their injured fellow by the
arms and dragged him off towards a warehouse. His head
was rolled back, eyes disappeared in the whites, bubbles of blood whistling out of his nose. The foreman
turned back to the ship and called up to the seamen
on the railing, calling for an officer. They looked back

at him for a moment, then one silently turned away and walked towards the nearest hatch . . . slowly.

The gang instantly squatted on their heels when the foreman's attention went elsewhere. A few lit up stubs of cigarette; John could smell the musky scent of hemp mingled with the tobacco. A few smirked at the foreman's back, but most were expressionless in a different way from Chosen, their faces blank and doughy under sweat and stubble. They were wearing cotton overalls with broad arrows on them, labor-camp inmates' clothing.

"Hey, that crate's busted," Jeffrey said.

John looked. One wood-and-iron box about three meters on a side had sprung along its top. The stencils on the side read *Museum of History and Nature/ Copernik*. He felt a stir of curiosity. Copernik was capital of the Land, and the Museum was more than a storehouse; it was the primary research center of the most advanced nation on Visager. He'd had daydreams of working there himself, of finally figuring out some of the mysterious artifacts of the Ancestors, the star-spanning colonizers from Earth. The Federation had fallen over a thousand years ago—it was 1221 A.F. right now—and nobody could understand the enigmatic constructs of ceramic and unknown metals. Not even now, despite the way technology had been advancing in the past hundred years. They were as incomprehensible as a steam engine or a dirigible would be to one of the arctic savages.

"What's inside?" he said eagerly.

"C'mon, let's take a look."

The laborers ignored them; John was in a Probationer's school uniform, and Jeffrey was an obvious foreigner— an upper-class boy could go where he pleased, and the Fourth Bureau would be lethally interested if they heard of Protégés talking to an *auzlander*. Even in the camps, there was always someplace worse. The foreman was still trading cusswords with the liner's petty officer.

John grabbed at the heavy Abaca hemp of the net and climbed; it was easy, compared to the obstacle courses

at school. Jeffrey followed in an awkward scramble, all
elbows and knees.

"It's just a rock," he said in disappointment, peering
through the sprung panels.

"No, it's a meteorite," John said.

The lumpy rock was about a meter across, suspended
in an elastic cradle in the center of the crate. It hadn't
taken any damage when the net dropped—unlike a keg
of brandy, which they could smell leaking—but then,
from the slagged and pitted appearance, it had survived
an incandescent journey through the atmosphere. John
was surprised that it was being sent to the museum;
meteorites were common. You saw dozens in the sky,
any night. There must be something unusual about this
one, maybe its chemical composition. He reached
through and touched it.

"Sort of cold," he said. Not quite icy, but not natural, either. "Feel it."

Jeffrey stretched a long thin arm through the crack.
"Yeah, like—"

The universe vanished.

Sally looked over her shoulder. Where *was* John?
Then she saw him, scrambling over the cargo net with
another boy. With Maurice's son. She opened her mouth
to call them back, then closed it. *It's important that they
get along.* Maurice hadn't made a formal proposal yet,
but . . . She turned back.

Karl had his witnesses to either side: his legal children, Heinrich and Gerta, adopted in the fashion of the
Chosen. Heinrich was the son of a friend who'd died
in an expedition to the Far West Islands; they were dangerous, and the seas between, with their abundant and
vicious native life, even more so. The other had been
born to Protégé laborers on the Hosten estates and chris-
tened Gitana. Karl had sponsored her; she was a bright
active youngster and her parents were John's nurse and
attendant valet/bodyguard, respectively.

Maria and Angelo stood at a respectful distance; their daughter ignored them. Ex-daughter; no Chosen were as strict as those Chosen from Protégé ranks. She was Gerta Hosten now, not Gitana Pesalozi.

A Chosen attorney exchanged papers with the plump little Santander consul, then turned to Sarah.

"Sarah Hosten, née Kingman, do you hereby irrevocably renounce connubial ties with Karl Hosten, Chosen of the Land?"

"I do."

"Karl Hosten, do you acknowledge this renunciation?"

"I do."

"Do you also acknowledge Sarah Hosten as bearing full parental rights to John Hosten, issue of this union?"

"Excepting that John Hosten may continue to claim my name if he wishes, I do." Karl swallowed, but his face might have been carved from the basalt of the volcanoes.

"Heinrich Hosten, Gerta Hosten, Probationers-adoptee of the line of Hosten, do you witness?"

"We do."

"All parties will now sign, fingerprint and list their *geburtsnumero* on this document."

Sally complied, although unlike anyone born in the Land of the Chosen she didn't have a birth-number tattooed on her right shoulderblade and memorized like her name. The ink from the fingerprinting stained her handkerchief as she wiped her hands.

The consul stepped forward. "Sarah Jennings Kingman, as representative of the Republic of Santander, I hereby officially certify that your lapsed citizenship in the Republic is fully restored with all rights and duties appertaining thereunto; and that your son John Hosten as issue of your body is accordingly entitled to Santander citizenship also. . . . Where is the boy?"

The universe vanished. John found himself in a . . . place. It seemed to be the inside of a perfectly reflective

sphere, like being inside a bubble made of mirror glass.
He tried to scream.

Nothing happened. That was when he realized that
he had no throat, and no mouth. No body.

No body no body nobodynobody—

The hysteria damped down suddenly, as if he'd been
slipped a tranquilizer. Then he became conscious of
weight, breath, *himself.* For a moment he wanted to
weep with relief.

"Excuse me," a voice said behind him.

He turned, and the mirrored sphere had vanished.
Instead he saw a room. The furnishings were familiar,
and *wrong.* A fireplace, rugs, deep armchairs, books,
table, decanters, but none of them quite as he remembered. A man was standing by a table, in uniform, but
none he knew: baggy maroon pants, a blue swallowtail
jacket, a belt with a saber; a pistol was thrown on the
table beside the glasses. He was dark, darker than a tan
could be, with short very black hair and gray eyes. A
tall man, standing like a soldier.

"Where . . . what . . ." John began.

"Attention!" the man said.

"Sir!" John barked, bracing. Six years of Probationer
schooling had made that a reflex.

"At ease, son," the dark man said, and smiled. "Just
helping you get a grip on yourself. First, don't worry.
This is real"—he gestured around at the room—"but it
isn't physical. You're still touching the meteorite in the
crate. Virtually no time is passing in the . . . the outside world. When we've finished talking, you'll be back
on the dock and none the worse for wear."

"Am I crazy?" John blurted.

"No. You've just had something very strange happen."
The smile grew wry. "Pretty much the same thing happened to me, lad. A long time ago, when I wasn't all
that much older than you are now. Sit."

John sank gingerly into one of the chairs. It was comfortable, old leather that sighed under his weight. He

sat with his feet on the floor and his hands on the arms of the chair.

"My name's Raj Whitehall, by the way. And this"— he waved a hand at the room—"is Center. A computer."

Despite the terror that boiled somewhere at the back of his mind, John shaped a silent whistle. "A *computer?* Like the Ancestors had, the Federation? I've read a *lot* about them, sir."

Raj Whitehall chuckled. "Well, that's a good start. My people thought they were angels. Yes, Center's a hold-over from the First Federation. Military computer, Command and Control type. Don't ask me any of the details. Where I was brought up, experts understood steam engines, a little. Look there."

John turned his head to look at the mirrored surface. Instead, he was staring out into a landscape. It wasn't a picture; there was depth and texture to it. Subtly different from anything he'd ever seen, the moons in the faded blue sky were the wrong size and number, the sunlight was a different shade. It cast black shadows across eroded gullies in cream-white silt. Out of the badlands came a column of men in uniforms like Raj's. They were riding, but not on horses. On *dogs*, giant dogs five feet high at the shoulder. They looked a lot like Vulf, except their legs were thicker in proportion. John whistled again, this time aloud.

The column of men went by, and a clumsy-looking field gun pulled by six more of the giant dogs. Then Raj Whitehall pulled up his . . . well, his giant hound. A woman rode beside him, not in uniform. Her face was dusty and streaked with sweat, and beautiful. Slanted green eyes glowed out of it.

The vision faded, back to the absolutely perfect mirror. John looked back to Raj. "Where was that?" he said. Then, slowly: "When was that?"

Raj nodded, leaning his hips back against the table and crossing his arms. "That was Bellevue, the planet where I was born. About a hundred and fifty years ago."

"You're . . . a ghost?"

"A ghost in a machine. A recording that thinks it's a man. It's a convincing illusion, even to me."

John sat silently for what felt like a minute. "Why are you talking to me?"

"Good lad," Raj said. John felt an obscure jolt of pride at the praise. Raj went on. "Now, listen carefully. You know how the Federation collapsed?"

John nodded. Visager had preserved the records; he'd seen them in school. Expansion from Earth, then rivalries and civil war. Civil war that continued until the Tanaki Nets were destroyed and interstellar travel cut off, and then on Visager itself until civilization was thoroughly smashed. After that a long process of rebirth, slow and painful.

"That happened all over the human-settled galaxy. On Bellevue, the collapse was even worse than here. Center was left in the rubble underneath the planetary governor's mansion. Center waited a long, long time for the time to be right. More than a thousand years; then it found me. Bellevue's problem was internal division. We were set to slag ourselves down again, this time right back to stone hatchets, all the more surely because we were doing it with rifles and not nukes. I was a soldier, an officer. With Center's help—and some very brave men—I reunited the planet. Bellevue's the capital of the Second Federation, now."

"You want me to *unite Visager?*" John felt his mouth drop open. "*Me?*" His voice broke embarrassingly, the way it had taken to doing lately, and he flushed.

Raj shook his head. "Not exactly. More to *prevent* it being unified, at least by the wrong people." He leaned forward slightly. "Tell me honestly, John. What do you think of the Chosen?"

John opened his mouth, then closed it. Memories flickered through his mind; ending with the blank, caved-in faces of the dockers as the unconscious man was carried away.

"Honestly, sir—not much. Mom doesn't, either. I tried talking to Dad about it once, but . . ." He shrugged and looked away.

Raj nodded. "Center can foresee things. Not *the* future always, but what will probably happen, and how probable it is. Don't ask me to explain it—I've had three lifetimes, and I still can't understand it. But I know it works."

maintenance of your personality matrix is incompatible with the modifications necessary to comprehend stochastic analysis.

John started and put his hands to his ears. The voice had come from everywhere and nowhere. It felt *heavy*, somehow, as if the words held a greater freight of meaning than any he'd ever heard. The sound of them in his head had been entirely flat and even, but there were undertones that resonated like a guitar's strings after the player's fingers left them. The voice felt . . . sad.

"Center means that if I was changed that much, I wouldn't be me," Raj said.

john hosten, the ancient, impersonal voice said. **in the absence of exterior intervention, there is a 51% probability ±6%, that the chosen will establish complete dominance of visager within 34 years. observe.**

John looked toward the mirrored wall.

An endless line of men in tattered green uniforms marched past a machine-gun nest manned by Land troops, Protégé infantry, and a Chosen officer. Two plainclothes police agents stood by, in long leather coats and wide-brimmed hats, heavy pistols in their hands. Every now and then they would flick their hands, and the soldiers would drag a man out of the line of prisoners, force him down to his knees. The Fourth Bureau men would step up and put the muzzles of their guns to the back of the kneeling man's head . . .

conquest of the empire, Center said. **observe:**

A montage followed: cities burning, with their names

and locations somehow in his mind. Ships crowded with slave laborers arriving in Oathtaking and Pillars and Dorst. A group of Chosen engineers talking over papers and plans, while a line of laborers that stretched beyond sight worked on a railway embankment.

consolidation. further expansion.

A burning warship sank, in an ocean littered with oily guttering flames, wreckage, bodies, and men who still tried to move. Hundreds of them were sucked backwards and down as the ship upended and sank like a lead pencil dropped into a pool, its huge bronze propellers still whirling as it took the final plunge. Through the smoke came a line of battlewagons, with the black-and-gold banner of the Chosen at their masts. Their main batteries were scorched and blistered with heavy firing, but silent; their secondary guns and quick-firers stabbed out into the waters.

destruction of santander.

Even without Center's information, he recognized the next scene. It was Republic Hall in Santander City. The great red-granite dome was shattered; a man in the black frock coat and tall hat of Republican formality stood before a Chosen general and handed over the Constitution of the Republic in its glass-cased box. The general threw it down and ground the heel of his boot into it while the troops behind him cheered.

consequences.

A shabby tenement street in a Chosen city. Figures clustered about the steps, talking, falling silent as a strange-looking steamcar bristling with weapons hummed by.

"But those are *Chosen*," John exclaimed.

Raj spoke: "What do carnivores do when they've finished off the game?"

metaphorical but correct, Center's passionless non-voice said. **once consolidation is complete, the chosen lines would fall out with each other. the planet cannot support so large a ruling class in**

conditions of intense competition, not indefinitely; and the social system resulting from conquest and slavery cannot be rationally adjusted to maximize productivity. internal reorganization would lead to the creation of a noble caste and the exclusion of most chosen lines.

Armies clashed, armed with strange, powerful weapons. Machines swarmed through the air, ran in sleek low-slung deadliness over the earth. Men died, Protégé soldiers, civilians.

the new nobility would fight among themselves. first with protégé armies. rivalry would build.

A long sleek shape dropped on a pillar of white fire into a desert landscape. Landing legs extended, and a hatchway opened.

technological progress would continue to an interplanetary-transport level, then fossilize. none of the contending factions on visager could afford to divert sufficient resources to reestablish stardrive.

A huge city, buildings reaching for the sun. It took a moment for John to recognize it as Oathtaking, and then only by the shape of the circular harbor and the volcanoes that ringed it. Suddenly one of the giant towers vanished in an eye-searing flash.

one party among the nobility attempts to use the fallen chosen lines against the other. instead they rise against the nobility planet-wide, attempting to restore the old system. the protégés revolt. maximum entropy results.

Rings of violet fire expanded over the sites of cities, rising until the fireballs spread out against the top of the atmosphere.

probability 87%, ±6%, Center added.

John sat, shaken. *I'm just a kid*, he thought. Not even good enough to make the Test of Life, a gimp. *What'm I supposed to do about all this?*

"Why can't you do something?" he asked. "You came

from the stars, you've got another Federation—land a starship and *tell* people what to do!"

"We can't," Raj said. "First, we don't have the resources. There are only four worlds in the Federation, so far. There are *thousands* needing attention. And even if we could, that would just set us up for another cycle of empire, decline and war like the First Federation. The new worlds have to climb out on their own with minimal interference, and do so in the right way."

correct, Center said. **a true federation may achieve stability in an dynamic and mobile sense. a hegemony imposed from without could not.**

"You want me to . . . somehow to stop the Chosen from taking things over," John said.

He felt a flush of excitement. It was a little like what he'd felt last week, when the housemaid looked back over her shoulder at him as she plumped the pillows and smiled, and he knew he *could* right there and then if he wanted to. But it was stronger, deeper. *He* could affect the destiny of a whole planet. *Save* the whole world. He, John Hosten with a pimple on his nose and a foot that still ached when he used it too hard, despite all the surgeons could do.

specifically, you will act to strengthen the republic of santander, Center said. **with my advice and that of raj whitehall, you will rise quickly and be in a position to influence policy. such intervention will drastically increase the probability of the republic emerging as the dominant factor in the cycle of wars which will begin in the next two decades.**

"The Republic will conquer . . . unite the world?"

no. that probability is less than 12%, ±3. observe: Troops in the brown uniforms and round hats of the Republic marched out of a city: Arena, in the Sierra. Crowds lined the streets, hooting and whistling. Sometimes they threw things.

santander lacks the organizational infrastructure to forcefully integrate foreign territories.

"No staying power," Raj amplified. "They can get into wars, and if you push them to the wall they can mobilize like hell, but when it's less vital than that, they don't like paying the butcher's bill or the money either. They'll get into wars occasionally, and piss away men and equipment and then decide it's no fun and go home."

correct. santander will exercise a general hegemony, increasingly cultural and economic rather than military. this will inaugurate a period of intense competition within a framework of minimal government. such episodes are unstable but tend to rapid technological innovation.

"The Republic will go into space because it gives you as much glory as war and it's less frustrating," Raj explained.

observe:

A cylinder taller than a building lifted into the air in a blue-white discharge. The next view was strange: a white-streaked blue disk floating in utter blackness, ringed by unwinking stars. It wasn't until John saw the outline of a continent that he realized he was seeing Visager from space.

From space! he thought. A construct of girders floated across the vision. Men in spacesuits flitted around it and incomprehensible machines with arms like crabs.

a tanaki displacement net, Center said. **in this scenario, visager would enter the second federation without prior political unification. an unusual development.**

The visions ceased, leaving only a mirrored wall at the end of a strange study.

Raj handed him a glass and sat in the chair facing him. John took a cautious sip of the sweet wine.

"Lad, you can leave here with no memories of what you've seen and heard," he said calmly. "Or you can leave here as Center's agent—as I was Center's agent—to help get this planet out of the dead-end it's trapped in and set its people free."

"I'll do it," John blurted, then flushed again.

The words seemed to have come directly from his mouth without passing through his brain.

Raj shook his head. "This isn't a game, John. You could die. You quite probably *will* die."

The mirrored wall dissolved into its impossibly real pictures. This time they were much more personal. John—an older John—lay beside a hedgerow. His face was slack, eyes unblinking in the thin gray mist of rain. One hand lay on his stomach, a blue bulge of intestine showing around the fingers.

John sat stripped to the waist in a metal chair, waist and limbs and neck held by padded clamps; another device of levers and screws held his mouth open. A single bulb shone down from the ceiling. A Fourth Bureau specialist dressed in a shiny bib apron stepped up to him with a curved tool in his hands.

"Shame, Hosten, shame," he said. "You have neglected your teeth. Still, I think this nerve is still sensitive."

The curved shape of stainless steel probed and then thrust. The body in the chair convulsed and screamed a fine mist of blood into the cellar's dark air.

Another John stood in the dock of a courtroom. The Republic's flag stood on the wall behind the panel of judges. They whispered together, and then one of them raised his head:

"John Hosten, this court finds you guilty as charged of treason and espionage. You will be taken from this place to the National Prison, and there hung by the neck until dead. May God have mercy on your soul."

The visions died. John touched his tongue to his lips. "I'm not afraid to die," he whispered. Then aloud: "I'm not afraid, and I know my duty. I'll do what you ask, no matter how long it takes, no matter what the risks."

"Good lad," Raj said quietly, and gripped his shoulder. "You and your brother will both do your best."

*   *   *

Jeffrey Farr looked at the mirrored sphere. "Seems like I'm going to be in action a lot," he said.

He tried to sound calm, but the quaver was in his voice again. Those scenes of himself dying—gut-shot, burned, drowned, the Chosen executioners with whips made of steel-hook chains—they were more real than anything he'd ever seen. He could *feel* it. . . .

"If you say yes," Raj said. "I'm not going to lie to you, son. Soldiering isn't a safe profession; and if you refuse, the final war between the Land and your country may not be for a generation or more, possibly two."

"Yeah, and the horse might learn to sing," Jeffrey said. He was a little surprised at Raj's chuckle. "And if I had kids, they'd be around when it happened, anyway. I'll do it. Somebody's got to. A Farr does what has to be done."

Unconsciously, his voice took on another tone with the last words; Raj nodded approvingly and handed him the balloon snifter.

"Good lad."

"There's just one thing," Jeffrey said. He looked up; the . . . computer . . . wasn't there—wasn't anywhere, specifically, while he was in its mind—but that helped.

"Just one thing. If, ah, Center can predict things, and manipulate them the way you're saying, couldn't you change the Chosen? You showed me what would happen if the Chosen took over by *themselves*, didn't you? Left to themselves, on their own."

correct. Raj nodded.

"So, you could help *them,* and sort of twist things around so that *they* built a star-transport system? It'd be easy enough, with you showing all the technical stuff they had to do every step of the way, not like reinventing it, not really. And you could get whoever you picked to the top in Chosen politics, couldn't you? Make 'em next thing to a living god."

Raj leaned back in his chair. "Smart lad," he said

admiringly. "But then, you've got a different perspective on it than your brother—your brother to be, I mean."

probability of medium-term success with such a course of action is 62%, ±10, Center said. **unusually high degree of uncertainty due to stochastic factors. we cannot be certain of coming into contact with a suitable chosen representative. this course of action is contraindicated by other factors, however.**

Raj nodded, his hard dark face bleak. "It might be possible to get Visager back into interstellar space with the Chosen running things," he said. "But you couldn't change them into something we'd *want* in interstellar space—not without redesigning their society from the ground up, and that would be impossibly difficult."

impressionistic but correct. observe:

The blank hemisphere cleared. Once again Jeffrey saw the blue-white shape of a planet from space, but this time it was not Visager. A shimmering appeared, and spots blinked into existence in the darkness above the planet, tiny until the perspective snapped closer. That showed huge metal shapes—spaceships, he supposed—with the sunburst of the Land on their flanks. Doors opened in their sides, and smaller shapes fell towards the cloud-streaked blue world, shapes with wings and a sleek shark-shape to them. The viewpoint followed them down in a dizzying plunge, through atmosphere and cherry heat, down to the ground. They landed amid flames and rubble, burning vegetation, and shattered buildings. Ramps slid down, and gun-tubs in the assault transports fired bolts that cut paths of thunderous vacuum through the air to clear the perimeter of the landing zone. War machines slid down the ramps on cushions of air, their massive armor bristling with weapons and sensors.

A head appeared in the turret of one of the war machines as it slid to earth and nosed up, dirt howling from around its skirts. The man's helmet visor was flipped up, and his grin was like something out of the deep oceans.

"Let's do it, people," he said. "Let's *go.*"

probability of successful redesign of chosen culture is 12%, ±6, Center said.

"We could put them on top; we could even get them out to the stars," Raj said. "But they'd still attack anything that moved—it's their basic imperative."

"Yeah, I can see that," Jeffrey said, linking and cracking his fingers—then looking down suddenly, conscious that his *real* hands weren't moving at all, somewhere he couldn't see. Raj nodded wryly. *And for him, it's like this all the time.* It *felt* real, but . . .

"Yeah," he went on. "They've got to be stopped, here and now."

"You and your brother will do it," Raj said. "With our help."

—and the meteorite was smooth under his fingers.

John Hosten half fell to the dock. *Raj?* he thought. *Center?* Was this some sort of crazy dream? Maybe he was really back in his bunk at school, waiting for reveille.

The dockers were looking at him, dull curiosity, or simply noting that he was something moving. Jeffrey Farr three-quarters fell down the net after him, his face stunned and slack. John caught him automatically, pushing the limp form against the cargo net so that he could cling and support himself. *You too?*

do not show distress, the machine-voice said in his mind.

Pull yourselves together, lads, Raj continued. The voice was equally silent, but it had the modulation of human speech, without the sense of cold bottomless depth that Center's carried.

"John! Jeffrey!"

There was anger in the adult's voices. Jeffrey's face was pale enough that the freckles stood out like birthmarks, but he smiled his gap-toothed grin.

"Hey, we're in some shit now, man."

"Let's go."

"Say good-bye to your father," Sally Hosten said.

John stepped forward. "Sir."

Karl gave a tiny forward jerk of his head. *"Min sohn."*

He extended his hand; John stared at it in surprise for an instant. That was the greeting among equals. Then he bowed and took it. The impersonal power clamped briefly on his. A servant came forward at Karl's signal.

"Here," Karl said. He handed John a cloth-wrapped bundle. Within was a gunbelt and revolver. "This was my father's. You should have it. This and my name are all that Fate allows me to leave you."

"Thh . . . thank you, sir," John said.

His eyes prickled, but he fought the feeling down. *Why now?* Even by Chosen standards, Karl had never been a demonstrative man.

"You are a boy of good character," Karl said. "If I have ever been less than a father to you, the fault is mine. Your mother and I have parted but for reasons each thinks honorable. Obey your mother; work hard, be disciplined, be brave."

"Yes sir," John said.

Karl hesitated for an instant, began to turn away. Then he swallowed and continued: "You will always be welcome among the Chosen, boy, while I live."

He saluted, fist outstretched. John answered it for the first time—*for the last time,* he realized, as his father strode away with the same stiff-backed carriage.

"Good-bye, sib," Gerta Hosten said. She drew him into a brief hug, leaving him speechless at the display of emotion. "Watch your back among the Santies."

Heinrich clasped hands and thumped him on the shoulder. "The Land's loss but maybe your gain," he said. "Come visit sometime, sprout, when you're rich and famous."

John watched them leave and took a deep breath. "Good-bye, Maria," he said to the Protégé nursemaid.

She folded him to her broad bosom. "Good-bye, little master. Call Maria if you ever need her," she said in her slurred lower-class Landisch.

Her husband bowed and touched John's hand to his forehead. He was a bear-broad man with grizzled black hair. "I, too, young master. Now, go. Your mother waits for you."

John did an about-face and began walking towards the gangplank, his face rigid. His mother's hand took his; he squeezed it for a moment, then freed himself.

No more tears, he thought. *That's for kids. I have to be a man, now.*

CHAPTER TWO

1227 A.F.
310 Y.O.

"People are going to think we're weird," Jeffrey said, panting.

"Hell, we *are* weird, Jeff," John replied.

They fell silent as they raced up the slopes of Signal Hill, past picnicking families and students—it was part of the University Park. The switchbacks were rough enough, but John cut between them whenever there weren't any flowerbeds on the slopes. At last they stood on the paved summit, amid planters and trees in big pots and sightseers paying twenty-five centimes apiece to look through pivot-mounted binoculars at the famous view over Santander City. Jeffrey threw his hand-weights to a bench and groaned, ducking his head into a fountain and blowing like a grampus before he drank.

John stood, concentrating on ignoring the ache in his right foot, drinking slowly from a water bottle he carried at his waist. Signal Hill was two hundred meters, the highest land in the city and right above a bend in the Santander River. From here he could see most of the capital of the Republic: Capitol Square to the northwest, and the cathedral beyond it; the executive mansion with its pillars and green copper roof off to the east, at the end of embassy row. The Basin District, the ancient beginnings of Santander City, was below the hill in an oxbow curve of the river, and the canal basin was on the south bank, amid the factories and working-class

24

districts. Southward the urban sprawl vanished in haze; northward you could just make out the wooded hills that carried the elite suburbs.

The roar of traffic was muted here, the hissing-spark clatter of streetcars, the underground rumble of the subway, the sound of horses and the increasing number of steamcars, even the burbling roar of the odd gas-engine vehicle. He could smell nothing but hot stone and the cool green smells of the park, also a welcome change from most of the city. The sun was red on the western horizon, still bright up here, but as he watched the streetlights came on. They traced fairy-lantern patterns of light over the rolling cityscape, amidst the mellow golden glow of gaslights and the harsher electric glare along the main streets.

He grew conscious of someone watching him: a girl about his own age, but not a student—her calf-length dress was too stylish, and the little hat perched on one side of her head held a quetzal plume. She smiled as he met her eyes, then turned to talk to her matronly companion.

"Looking you over, stud," Jeff said.

John half-grinned. Objectively, he knew he was good-looking enough; tall like his father, with yellow-blond hair and a square-chinned face. And he kept himself in good enough shape . . . *but they don't know.* His foot twinged.

He punched his brother on the arm. "Like Doreen down in the canteen?" he said. They sat on the grass and passed a towel back and forth. "Thank me for it, bro. If I hadn't gotten you into this weird Chosen stuff you'd still be a weed and skinny. She's eating you with her eyes, my man."

Jeffrey Farr had filled out, although he'd always be slimmer than the son of his foster-mother. Only a trace of adolescent awkwardness remained, and his long bony face was firming towards adulthood.

"Doreen? *All* she'll do is look. Her folks are Reformed

Baptist, you know; I've got about as much chance of seeing her skirt up as I do of getting the Archbishop flat. I tried pinching her butt and she mashed my toe so hard I dropped my tray."

John clucked his tongue. "The Archbishop's butt? Hell, I didn't know you had a taste for older women. . . . Pax, pax!"

Jeffrey lit a slightly sweat-dampened cigarette. "Those things will kill you," John said, refusing the offered pack.

"And the other Officer's Training Corps cadets will think I'm a pansy if I don't smoke," Jeffrey said, leaning his elbow on his knee and looking out over the city. "I'll admit, the phys ed side of it is easier because of all this exercise shit you talked me into."

"How's Maurice taking you going into the army?"

Jeffrey shrugged. "Dad's just surprised, is all. Every Farr for five generations has been navy."

"Since the days of wooden ships and iron men," John agreed.

The Republic hadn't had a major land war in nearly seventy years, and the army was tiny and ill-funded. The navy was another matter, since it had always been policy not to let the Empire gain too big an edge.

"More like iron cannon and wooden heads. When do you hear from the diplomatic service?"

"Next week," John said. "But I'm pretty confident."

"You've got the marks for it."

Thanks to Center, he said silently.

Jeffrey's green eyes narrowed and he shook his head. *Even Center can't make a silk purse out of a sow's udder,* he replied, through the relay that the ancient computer provided.

correct, Center said. **i have merely shortened the period of instruction and made possible a broader-based course of study.**

Think we'll have enough time before the Chosen take on the Empire? Jeff thought.

chosen-imperial war within the next two years

is a 17% ±3 probability. within the next four, 53% ±5. within the next six, 92% ±7.

"I should have my commission in a year," Jeff said. "You'll be a member in good standing of the striped-pants-and-spooks brigade."

"Much good it'll do the Empire," John said gloomily, splitting a grass stem between his thumbs.

North lay the rest of the Republic, and the Gut—the narrow waterway that divided the mainland along most of its width. North of the Gut was the Universal Empire, largest of Visager's nations, potentially the richest, and for centuries the most powerful. Those centuries were generations gone.

"And we're doing fuck-all!" Jeff said. "I know politicians are supposed to be dimwits, but the staff over at the Pyramid are even worse, and the admiralty isn't much better, apart from Dad."

"*We're* doing all we can," John said calmly. "The *Republic* isn't doing much yet, but some people see what's coming—Maurice, for example. And he's a rear admiral, now. We ought to have some time after they attack the Empire."

"I suppose so," Jeff sighed. "Hey, you keep me on an even keel, did I ever tell you that? Yeah, even the Chosen aren't crazy enough to take on us and the Empire at once. When that starts, people will sit up and take notice—even *them.*" He nodded towards the capitol building's dome.

"Maurice sometimes doubts they'd notice if the Fleet of the Chosen steamed up the river and began shelling them," John said lightly.

"Dad's a pessimist. C'mon, let's get back to the dorm, shower, and grab a hamburger. Maybe Doreen will take pity on me."

"Teamwork, teamwork, you morons!" Gerta Hosten gasped, hearing the others stumble. "Johan, your turn on point."

The jungle trail was narrow and slick with mud. The improvised stretcher of poles and vines was awkward, would have been awkward even without the mumbling, tossing form of the boy strapped to it. His leg was splinted with branches; the lianas that bound it to the wood were half-buried in swollen-purple flesh.

Gerta dug her heels in and waited until the stretcher came level, then sheathed her knife and took the left front pole. The man she was relieving worked his fingers for a moment, drew his bowie and plunged forward to slash a way for his comrades. She took the left from pole, Heinrich carried both rear poles, and Elke Tirnwitz was on the right front. Johan Kloster moved farther ahead, chopping his way through the vines. Etkar Summeldorf was getting the free ride; *he'd* broken a leg spearing a crocodile that tried to snack on them while they forded a river yesterday.

They'd eaten a fair bit of the croc. You got nothing supplied in the team-endurance event that concluded the Test of Life. Well, almost nothing: a pair of shorts, a pair of sandals, a cloth halter if you were a girl, and a bowie knife. Then they dropped you and four teammates down a sliderope from a dirigible into the Kopenrung Mountains along the north side of the Land, and you made the best time you could to the pickup station. Nobody told you exactly where that was, either. The Chosen of the Land didn't need to have their hands held. If you couldn't make it, the Chosen didn't need you—and you had better *all* make it. The Chosen didn't need selfish grandstanders, either.

"Leave me," Etkar mumbled. "Leave me. Go."

"We *can't* leave you, you stupid git," Elke said in a voice hoarse with worry and fatigue—they were an item, and besides, Etkar had probably saved their lives at the river. "This is a team event. We'd all drop a hundred points if we left you behind."

They'd *all* saved each other's lives.

It was hot: thirty-eight degrees, at least, and steambath

humid. Bad even by the Land's standards. The Kopenrungs were in the far north, nearest to the equator. That was one reason they'd never been intensively developed, that and the constant steep slopes and the lateritic soils. And the leeches, the mosquitoes, the wild boar and wild buffalo and leopards and constant thunderstorms and tornadoes.

Sweat trickled down her skin, adding to the greasy film already there and stinging in the insect bites and budding jungle sores. The rough wood pulled at her arm and abraded the calluses on her palm. Muscles in her lower back complained as she leaned back against the weight of the stretcher and the slope. Branches and leaves swatted at her face.

"Heinrich, *min brueder*," Gerta said, pacing the words to the muscular effort. "Tell me again how wonderful it is to be Chosen."

Elke made a sharp hissing sound with her teeth. The Fourth Bureau was unlikely to be listening, but you never knew. Heinrich grunted a chuckle.

"*Shays*," Johan swore. "Shit." There was wonder in his tone.

"What is it?" Gerta asked. She couldn't see more than a few paces through the undergrowth; this section of hillside had burned off a while ago, and the second growth was rank.

"We made it."

"*What?*" in three strong young voices.

"We made it! That *was* the clearing we saw back on the crest!"

None of them spoke; they didn't slow down, either. Gerta managed a sweat-blurred glimpse at the mist-shrouded, jungle-covered mountains ahead. They looked precisely like the mist-shrouded, jungle-clad mountains she'd been staring at for the entire past week.

When they broke out of the cover onto the little bench-plateau they broke into a trot by sheer reflex. There were pavilions ahead, and a crowd of people—

officers, officials, Protégé servants. A doctor ran forward at the sight of the stretcher.

"How is he?" Elke said.

The doctor looked up and frowned. "The leg doesn't look too bad. Now. He'd have lost it in another twenty hours."

Protégés held out trays. Gerta grabbed at a ceramic tumbler and drank, long and carefully. It was orange juice, slightly salted. She shut her eyes for an instant of pure bliss.

A man cleared his throat. She opened her eyes and snapped to attention with the other members of her team; all but Ektar, who was out with a syringe of morphine in his arm.

The man was elderly, bald, stringy-muscular. He had colonel's pips on the shoulders of his summer-weight uniform, and a smile like Death in a good mood on his wrinkled, bony face. She was acutely conscious of the ring on the third finger of his left hand, an intertwined circlet of iron and gold. The Chosen ring.

"Gerta Hosten, Heinrich Hosten, Johan Kloster, Elke Tirnwitz, Etkar Summeldorf. The ceremony will come later, of course, but it is my honor to inform you that each of you has achieved at least the minimum necessary score in the Test of Life. Accordingly, at the age of eighteen years and six months, you will be enrolled among the Chosen of the Land. Congratulations."

One of the others whooped. Gerta couldn't tell which; she was too busy keeping herself erect. Six months of examinations, tests, psychological tests, tests of nerve, tests of intelligence, tests of ability to endure stress; all topped off with seven hellish days in the Kopenrung jungles—and it was *over.*

I'm not going to be a Washout. She'd decided long ago to kill herself rather than endure that; a large proportion of Washouts did. *Born in a Protégé cottage, and I'm* Chosen *of the Land.*

She snapped off a salute, arm outstretched and fist

clenched. A blood-boil burst and left red running down her mouth as she grinned; the pain was a sharp stab, but she didn't give a damn.

"You are a very wealthy young man," the River Electric Company executive said, looking down at the statement in surprise.

"I had some seed money from my stepfather," John explained. "The rest of it comes from commodities deals, mainly." Courtesy of Center's analysis; that made things childishly easy. "And investment in Western Petroleum."

His formal neckcloth felt a little tight; he suppressed an impulse to fiddle with it. The room was on the seventh story of one of the new office buildings between the Eastern Highway and the river, with an overhead fan and shuttered windows that made it cool even on the hot summer's day. The River Electric exec had very little on the broad ebony expanse of his desk, just a blotter and a telephone with a sea-ivory handset. And the plans John had sent in.

"This . . ."

"Mercury-arc rectifier," John supplied helpfully.

"Rectifier, yes, seems to be very ingenious," the executive said.

He was a plump little man with bifocals, wearing a rather dandified cream-colored jacket and blue neckcloth. There was a parrot's feather in the band of his trilby where it hung on the rack by the door.

"However," he went on, "at present the River Electric Company is engaged in an extensive, a very extensive, investment program in primary generating capacity. Why should we undertake a risky new venture which will require tying up capital in new manufacturing plant?"

John leaned forward. "That's just it, Mr. Henforth. The rectifier will *save* capital by reducing transmission losses. The expense of installing them will be considerably less than the savings in raw generating capacity. *And* the construction can be subcontracted. There are a lot of firms here in the capital, or anywhere in the Eastern Provinces—Tonsville, say, or Ensburg—who could handle this. River Electric's primary focus on hydraulic turbines and turbogenerators wouldn't be affected."

Henforth steepled his fingers and waited.

"And," John went on after the silence stretched, "I'd be willing to buy say, five hundred thousand shares of River Electric at par. Also licensing fees from the patent would be assigned."

"It's definitely an interesting proposition," Henforth said, smiling. "Come, we'll go up to the executive lounge on the roof and discuss this further with some of our technical people." He shook his head. "A young man of your capacities is wasted in the diplomatic service, Mr. Hosten. Wasted."

"Skirmish order!"

The infantry platoon fanned out, three meters between each man, in two long lines. The first line jogged forward across the rocky pasture, their fixed bayonets glittering in the chilly upland air. Fifty meters forward they went to ground, taking cover behind ridges and boulders. The second line moved up and leapfrogged forward in turn.

Ensign Jeffrey Farr watched carefully through his field-glasses. The movement was carried out with precision. *Good men*, he thought. The Republic's army wasn't large, only seventy thousand men. It wasn't particularly well-paid or equipped, either; the men mostly enlisted because it was the employer of last resort. Bottle troubles, wife troubles, farm kids bored beyond endurance with watching the south end of a northbound plowhorse, sheer inability to cope with the chaotic demands of civilian life in the Republic's fast-growing cities. They could still make good soldiers if you gave them the right training, and trained men would be invaluable when the balloon went up. The provincial militias were supposed to be federalized in time of war, but as they stood he had little confidence in them.

He raised his hand in a signal. The platoon sergeant
blew a sharp blast on his whistle and the men rose from
the field, slapping at the dust on their brown tunic jackets. Their stubbled faces looked impassive and tired after
the month of field exercises through the mountains.

"Good work, Ensign," his company commander
nodded. Captain Daniels was a thickset man of forty—
promotion was slow in the peacetime army—with a scar
across one cheek where a Union bullet had just missed
taking off his face in a skirmish twenty years ago.

"Very good work," the staff observer said. "I notice
you're spreading the skirmish line thinner."

"Yes, sir," Jeff said. He nodded at an infantryman jog-
ging by with his weapon at the trail. It was a bolt-action
model with six cartridges in a tube magazine below the
barrel. "Everyone's getting magazine rifles these days,
except the Imperials, and new designs are coming fast
and furious. We've got to disperse formations more."

Although to hear some of the fogies talk, they expected
to fight in shoulder-to-shoulder ranks like Civil War
troops equipped with rifle-muskets.

"Yes, I read that article of yours in the *Armed Forces
Quarterly*," the staff type said. "You think nitro powders
will be adopted for small arms?"

major belmody, Center said. A list of biographical
data followed.

The major looked pretty sharp, if a little elegant for
the field in his greatcoat and red throat-tabs and polished Sam Browne. And being a younger son of the
Belmody Mills Bemodys probably hadn't hurt his rise
through the officer corps either; thirty-two was damned
young to get that high.

"I'm certain of it, sir," Jeff said. The Belmodys were
big in chemicals and mining explosives. "No smoke, less
fouling, and much higher muzzle velocities, flatter trajectories, smaller calibers so the troops can carry more
ammo."

Captain Daniels spoke unexpectedly. "I don't trust

jacketed bullets," he said. "They have a tendency to strip and then tumble when the barrel's hot."

"Sir, that's just a development problem. Gilding metal can't take the temperatures of high-velocity rounds. Cupronickel, or straight copper, that's what needed."

The older officer smiled. "Ensign, I wish I was half as confident about anything as you are about everything."

"God knows we could use some young firebrands in this man's army," Major Belmody said. "In any case, you and Ensign Farr must dine with me tonight."

"After I see the men settled in, sir," Jeff said. The major raised an eyebrow and nodded, returning his juniors' salutes.

"You'll do, Farr," Captain Daniels said, grinning, when the staff officer's car had bounced away over the pasture with an occasional *chuff* of waste steam. "You'll go far, too, if you can learn to be a little more diplomatic about who you deliver lectures to."

Lieutenant Gerta Hosten leaned back against the upholstery of the seat and watched out the half-open window as the train clacked its way across the central plateau. The air coming in was clean; this close to Copernik the line had been electrified, and the lack of coal smoke and the pounding, chuffing sound of a steam locomotive was a little eerie. There was plenty of traffic on the broad concrete-surfaced road that flanked the railway, too, steam or animal-drawn. This was the most pleasant part of the Land, a rolling volcanic upland at a thousand meters above sea level, cooler and a little drier. The capital had been moved here from Oathtaking only a generation after the first wave of Alliance refugees arrived. Copernik's beginnings went back before the coming of the Chosen, right back to the initial settlement of Visager, but nothing remained of the pre-conquest city. Over the past generation as geothermal steam and then hydropower supplemented coal, it had also become a major manufacturing center.

Gerta watched with interest as rolling contour-plowed fields of sugar cane, rice, soya, and maize gave way to huge factory compounds. One of them held an airship assembly shed, a hundred-meter skeletal structure like a Brobdingnagian barn. The cigar-shaped hull was still a framework of girders, with only patches of hull-cladding where aluminum sheet was being riveted to the structure.

She buttoned the collar of her field-gray walking-out uniform, buckled on her gunbelt with the shoulder-strap, and took up her attaché case. Normally she'd have let her batman carry that, but there were eyes-only documents in it. Nothing ultra-secret, or she wouldn't be carrying them on a train, but procedure was procedure.

Behfel ist Behfel, she recited to herself: orders are orders. She also had a letter from John Hosten in there. Evidently he was doing well down in the Republic; he'd gotten some sort of posting in their diplomatic service.

It was a pity about John.

"Wake up, *feldwebel,*" she said.

Her batman blinked open his eyes and stood, taking down the two bags from the overhead rack. Pedro was a thickset muscular man in his thirties, strong and quick and apparently loyal as a Doberman guard dog. Also about as bright; in fact, she'd owned dogs with more mother-wit and larger vocabularies. It was policy to exclude the upper two-thirds of the intelligence gradient when recruiting soldiers and gendarmes from the Protégé caste. She had her doubts about that, and she'd always preferred bright ones as personal servants. More risk, but greater potential gain.

Behfel ist behfel.

The train lurched slightly as it slowed. The pantograph on the locomotive clicked amid a shower of sparks as they pulled into the Northwest Station. There were many tall blond young men in uniform there, but not the one she instinctively sought. Heinrich wouldn't be waiting

for her; that wouldn't be seemly, and anyway she had
to report to Intelligence HQ for debriefing.

My lovely Heinrich, she thought. *I'd fuck you even
if you were my birth-brother.* An exaggeration, but he
was a dear, and of course incest taboos didn't apply to
adoptee-kin. *And this time when you ask me to marry
you, I'm going to say yes.*

The implications of the documents in her attaché case
were clear, if you could read between the paragraphs.
It was time to do her eugenic duty to the Chosen; even
with servants, infants took up a lot of time and effort.
Best do it while there was time.

In a couple of years, they were all going to be very,
very busy.

CHAPTER THREE

1233 A.F.
317 Y.O.

Looks different from a Protégé's point of view, John Hosten thought, carefully slumping his shoulders.

He was walking the streets of Oathtaking in the drab cotton coat and breeches of some middling Protégé worker. He could have been a warehouse clerk, or a store-checker; his hair had been dyed brown, but the best protection was sheer swarming numbers and the fact that nobody *looked* at an average Proti.

He'd forgotten how *hot* the damned place was, too. Hot, the air thick and wet and saturated with coal smoke and smells. Bigger than he remembered from his childhood; the villas went further up the slopes of the volcanoes, the factories were larger and the smokestacks higher, there were more overhead power lines, workers hanging out the sides of the overburdened trolley cars. And many, many more powered vehicles on the streets. Most of them were in army gray, steam-powered trucks and haulers built to half a dozen standard models. A fair number of luxury cars, too, some of them imported models from the Republic. Half a dozen Protégés went by on a gang-bicycle, which was a very clever invention, when you thought about it.

Too heavy for one to pedal—it takes six. Factory workers can use them to commute, but they don't get personal mobility.

Cleverness wasn't a wholly positive quality. . . .

37

He ducked into the brothel's front door; it wasn't hard to find, having BROTHEL #22A7-B, PROTÉGÉ, CLASS 6-b printed on the front door, with a graphic symbol for illiterates. Inside was a depressingly bare waiting room with a brick floor and girls sitting around the walls on wood-slat benches, naked save for cotton briefs, folded towels beside them, and a number on the wall above each head below a lightbulb. They didn't look as run-down as you'd expect, but then few of them were professionals. Temporary service in a place like this was a standard penalty for minor infractions of workplace regulations. A staircase led to cubicles above, and a clerk sat behind an iron grille just inside the door; the place smelled of sweat, harsh disinfectant, and spilled beer.

A hulk stood nearby, an iron-bound club thonged to his massive wrist, picking at his teeth with the thumbnail of his other hand. Probably a retired policeman; he looked John over once, and tapped the head of the club warningly against the stucco. John cringed realistically, turning and ducking his head.

"Prices are posted," the clerk said in a monotone; she was in her fifties, flabby with a starchy diet and lack of exercise. "You want I should read 'em? Booze is extra."

John pushed iron counters across the table and through the scoop trough beneath the iron grille. Fingers arranged them in a pattern; they were from Zeizin Shipbuilding AG, one of the bigger firms.

recognition, Center said. Pointers dropped across the clerk's pasty face indicating pupil dilation and temperature differentials. **97%, ±2.**

That was about as definite as it got; now the question was whether this was his real contact, or whether the Fourth Bureau had penetrated the ring and was waiting for him. His palms were damp, and he swallowed sour bile, eyes flickering to the doors. He wasn't carrying a weapon; it would have been insanely risky, here—a Protégé caught armed would be *lucky* to be executed on the spot. And when they found his *geburtsnumero* . . .

subject is contact, Center reassured him. **anxiety levels are compatible. 73%, ±5.**

A whole *hell* of a lot less certain than the first projection, but still reassuring. A little.

The clerk nodded and pressed a button on her side of the counter. A light went on with a *tick* over the girl closest to the stair; she stood with a mechanical smile and picked up her towel.

The upper corridor was fairly quiet, in midafternoon; a row of cubicles stood on either side, with curtains hung before them on rings and a shower at one end. John's guide pulled aside a numbered curtain and ducked through.

He followed. Within was a single cot, a washstand and tap, and a jar of antiseptic soap . . . and crouched in a corner, the burly form of Angelo Pesalozi. He stood, bear-burly, more gray than John remembered.

"Young Master Johan," he rumbled.

John extended his hand. "No man's master now, Angelo," he said, smiling.

The hand of Karl Hosten's driver and personal factotum closed on his with controlled strength. John matched it, and Angelo grinned.

"You have not grown soft," he said. "Come, we should do our business quickly."

The girl put her foot on the cot and began to push on it, irregularly at first and then rhythmically; with vocal accompaniment, it was a remarkably convincing chorus of squeaks and groans.

"A minute," John said. "My life is at risk here, too, and will be again, and I must understand. Karl Hosten is a good master, and your own daughter is one of the Chosen. Why are you ready to work against them?"

Brown eyes met his somberly. "He is a good master, but I would have no master at all, and be my own man. I have four children; because one is a lord, should the others be slaves, and my grandchildren? There are more bad masters than good."

He jerked his head towards the girl. "She dropped a tray of insulator parts, and so she must whore here for a month—is this justice? If a man speaks against the masters when they send his wife to another plantation, or take his children for soldiers, his brother for the mines, he is hung in an iron cage at the crossroads to die—is this justice? No, the rule of the Chosen is an offense against God. It must cease, even if I die for it."

John met his eyes for a long moment. **subject is sincere; probability—** He silenced the computer with a thought. *I know.*

And Angelo had always been kind to a boy with a crippled foot . . .

"Yes," John said. "That is so, Angelo."

The Protégé nodded and produced folded papers from inside his jacket; they were damp with sweat, but legible.

"These I took from the wastebasket, before the daily burning," he said. "Here is an order, concerning five airships—"

"I worry about that boy," Sally Farr said.

"I don't," Maurice Farr replied.

They were sitting on the terrace of the naval commandant's quarters, overlooking Charsson and its port. This was the northernmost part of the Republic of Santander, hence the hottest; the shores of the Gut were warmer still, protected from continental breezes by mountains on both sides. The hot, dry summer had just begun; flowers gleamed about the big whitewashed house, and the tessellated brick pavement of the terrace was dappled by the shade of the royal palms and evergreen oak planted around it. The road ran down the mountainside in dramatic switchbacks; there were villas on either side, officers' quarters and middle-class suburbs up out of the heat of the old city around the J-shaped harbor.

The roofs down there were mostly low-pitched and

of reddish clay tile; it looked more like an Imperial city from the lands just north of the Gut than like the rest of Santander. Much of the population was Imperial, too—there had been a steady drift of migrant laborers in the past couple of generations, looking for better-paid work in the growing mines and factories and irrigation farms.

Farr's eyes went to the dockyards. One of his armored cruisers was in the graving dock, with a cracked shaft on her central screw. The other four ships of the squadron were refitting as well; when everything was ready he'd take them up the Gut on a show-the-flag cruise.

"John," he continued, "is on his way to becoming a very wealthy young man. *And* he's doing well in the diplomatic service.

"Thank you," he went on to the steward bringing him his afternoon gin and tonic. Sally rattled the ice in hers.

"He has no social life," she said. "I keep introducing him to nice girls, and nothing happens. All he does is study and work. The doctors say he should be . . . umm, functional . . . but I worry."

Maurice turned his head to hide a quick smile. From what Jeffrey told him, John had been seen occasionally with girls who *weren't* particularly nice. Enough to prove that the infant vasectomy the Chosen doctors had done *hadn't* caused any irreparable harm in that respect, at least.

"Do you know something I don't?" Sally said sharply.

"Let's put it this way, my dear: there are certain things that a young man does not generally discuss with his mother."

"Oh."

Smart, Maurice thought fondly. *Pretty, too.*

Sally was looking remarkably cool and elegant in her white and cream linen outfit and broad straw hat, the pleated skirt daringly an inch above the ankle. Only a little gray in the long brown hair, no more than in his. You'd never know she'd had four children.

"Besides," he went on, "he's been assigned to the embassy in Ciano. From what I know of the tailcoat squadron there, social life is about all he'll have time for—it's a diplomat's main function. Count on it, he'll meet *plenty* of nice girls there."

"Oh." Sally's tone wavered a little at the thought. "Nice *Imperial* girls. Well, I suppose . . ." She shrugged.

She looked downslope in her turn. There were fortifications there, everything from the bastion-and-ravelin systems set up centuries ago to defend against roundshot to modern concrete-and-steel bunkers with heavy naval guns.

"John seems to think that there's going to be war," she said. "Jeffrey, too."

Maurice nodded somberly. "I wouldn't be surprised. War between the Chosen and the Empire, at least."

"But surely we wouldn't be involved!" Sally protested.

"Not at first," Maurice said slowly. "Not for a while."

"Thank goodness Jeffrey's in the army, then," she said. The Republic of Santander had no land border with either of the two contending powers. "And John's safe in the diplomatic corps."

"You dance divinely, Giovanni," Pia del'Cuomo said. "It is not fair. You are tall, you are handsome, you are clever, you are rich, and you dance so well. Beware, lest God send you a misfortune."

"I've already had a few from Him," John Hosten said, keeping his tone light and whirling the girl through the waltz. The ballroom was full of graceful swirling movement, gowns and uniforms and black formal suits, jewels and flowers and fans. "But He brought me to Ciano to meet you, so he can't be really angry with me."

Pia was just twenty, old for an Imperial woman of noble birth to be unmarried, and four years younger than him. Also unlike most Imperials of her sex and station, she didn't think giggles and inanities were the only way to talk to a man. She was very pretty indeed, besides, something he was acutely conscious of with their hands linked and one arm around her narrow waist.

No, not pretty—beautiful, he thought.

Big russet-colored eyes, heart-shaped face, creamy skin showing to advantage in the glittering low-cut, long-skirted white ballgown, and glossy brown hair piled up under a diamond tiara. Best of all, she seemed to like *him.*

The music came to a stop, and they stood for a moment smiling at each other while the crowd applauded the orchestra.

"If jealous eyes were daggers, I would be stabbed to death," Pia said with a trace of satisfaction. "It is entertaining, after being an old maid for years. My father has been muttering that if I wished to do nothing but read books and live single, I should have found a vocation before I left the convent school."

John snorted. "Not likely."

"I would have made a *very* poor nun, it is true," Pia said demurely. "And then I could not have gone on to so many picnics and balls and to the opera with a handsome young officer of the Santander embassy. . . ."

"A glass of punch?" he said.

Pia put her hand on his arm as he led her to the punch table. The white-coated steward handed them glasses; it was a fruit punch with white wine, cool and tart.

"You are worried, John," she said in English. Hers was nearly as good as his Imperial, and her voice had turned serious.

"Yes," he sighed.

"Your conversations with my father, they have not gone well?"

Even for an Imperial commander, Count Benito del'Cuomo was a blinkered, hidebound. . . . With an effort, John pushed the image of the white muttonchop whiskers out of his mind.

"No," he said. "He doesn't take the Chosen seriously."

Pia sipped at her punch and nodded to her chaperone where she sat with the other matrons against one wall. The older woman—some sort of poor-relation hanger-on of the del'Cuomos—frowned when she saw that Pia was still talking with the Republic's young chargé d'affaires. They began walking slowly towards the balcony.

"Father does not think the Land will dare to attack us," she said thoughtfully. "We have so many more soldiers, so many more ships of war. Their island is tiny next to the Empire."

"Pia—" He didn't really want to talk politics, but she had reason to be concerned. "Pia, their note demanded extraterritorial rights in Corona and half a dozen other ports, control of grain exports, and exclusive investment rights in Imperial railroads."

Pia checked half a step. She *was* the daughter of the Minister of War. "That . . . that is an ultimatum!" she said. "And an impossible one."

John nodded grimly. "An excuse for war. Even if your emperor and senatorial council were to agree to it, and you're right, they couldn't, then the Chosen would find some new demand."

"Why do they warn us, then? Surely they are not so scrupulous that they hesitate at a surprise attack."

"Scarcely. I have a horrible suspicion that they *want* the Empire to be prepared, so you'll have more forces in big concentrations where they can get at them," John said.

They walked out into the cooler air and half-darkness of the great veranda. Little Adele and huge Mira were both up and full, flooding the black-and-white checkerwork marble with pale blue light, turning the giant vases filled with oleander and jessamine and bougainvillea into a pastel wonderland. The terrace ended in a fretted granite balustrade and broad steps leading down to gardens whose graveled paths glowed white amid the flowerbanks and trees. Beyond the estate wall, widely spaced lights showed where the townhouses of the nobility stood amid their walled acres, with an occasional pair of yellow kerosene-lamp headlights marking a carriage or steam-car. Westward reached a denser web of lights, mostly irregular—Ciano had a street plan originally laid out by cows, except for a few avenues driven through in recent generations. Those centered on the Imperial palace complex, a tumble of floodlit white and gilded domes.

From here they could just make out the glittering surface of the broad Pada River; the dockyards and warehouses and slums about it were jagged black shapes, no gaslights *there*. Above them two lights moved through the sky, with a low throbbing of propellers. An airship, making for the west and the great ocean port of Corona at the mouth of the Pada.

"Chosen-made," John said, nodding towards it. "Pia, your soldiers are brave, but they have no conception of what they face."

Pia leaned one hip against the balustrade, turning her fan in her fingers. "My father . . . my father is an intelligent man. But he . . . he thinks often that because things were as they were when he was young, so they must remain."

"I'm not surprised. My own government tends to think the same way." *If not to quite the same degree,* he added to himself.

They were silent for a few minutes. John felt the tension building, mostly in his stomach, it seemed. Pia was looking at him out of the corner of her eyes, the beginning of a frown of disappointment marking her brows.

"Ah . . . that is . . ." John said. "Ah, I was thinking of calling on your father again."

Pia turned to face him. "Concerning political matters?" she asked, her face calm.

An excuse trembled on his lips. *Yes. Of course.* That would be all he needed, to add cowardice to his list of failings. A crippled soul to join the foot.

"No," he said. "About something personal . . . if you would like me to."

The smile lit up her eyes before it reached her mouth. "I would like that very much," she said, and leaned forward slightly to brush her lips against his.

probability of sincerity is 92% ±3, with motivations breakdown as follows—Center began.

Shut the fuck up! John thought.

He could hear Raj's amusement at the back of his mind. ***Damned right, lad.***

Jeff's voice: *God, but that one's a looker, isn't she?* He must be getting visual feed from Center, through John's eyes.

Will you all kindly get the hell out of my love life?

"Giovanni, there are times when I think you are talking to God, or the saints, or anyone but the person you are with!"

John mumbled an apology. Pia's eyes were still glowing. "The only question is, will he consent?"

"He'd better," John said. Pia blinked in surprise and slight alarm at the expression his face took for a moment. He forced relaxation and smiled.

"Why shouldn't he?" he said. "He knows I'm not a fortune hunter"—the del'Cuomos were fabulously wealthy, but he'd managed to discreetly let the Count know the size of his own portfolio—"and if he didn't like me personally, he'd have forbidden me to see you."

Pia nodded. "Well, I do have three younger sisters," she said with sudden hard-headed shrewdness. "It isn't seemly for them to marry before me—and also, my love, I think Father thinks he can beat you down on the dowry by pretending that the marriage is impossible because you are not of the Imperial Church."

John grinned. "He's right. He *can* beat me down."

Some cold part of his mind added that Imperial properties weren't likely to be worth much in a little while.

He took a deep breath. It was like diving off a high board: once you were committed, there was no point in thinking about the drop.

"Pia, there is something I must tell you." She met his

eyes steadily. "I am . . . I was born with a deformity."
He averted his eyes slightly. "A clubfoot."

She let out her breath sharply. His glance snapped
back to her face. She was smiling.

"Is it nothing more than that? The surgeons must have
done well, then—you dance, you ride, you play the . . .
what is the name? Tennis?" She flicked a hand. "It is nothing."

Breath he hadn't been conscious of holding sighed out
of him. "It's why my father never accepted me," he said
quietly.

She put a hand up along his face. "And if he had, you
would be in the Land, preparing to attack the Empire,"
she said. "Also, you would not be the man I love. I have
met Chosen from their embassy here, and beneath their
stiff manners they are pigs. They look at me like a piece
of kebab. You are not such a man."

He took the hand and kissed it. "There is more." John
closed his eyes. "I cannot have children."

Pia's fingers clenched over his. He looked up and
found her eyes brimming, the unshed tears bright in the
starlight—and realized, with a shock like cold water, that
they were for *him*.

"But—"

He nodded jerkily. "Oh, I'm . . . functional. Sterile,
though, and there's nothing that can be done about it."
He turned his head aside. "It was done, ah, when I was
very young."

"Then you too have reason to hate the Chosen," Pia
said softly. "Look at me, Giovanni."

He did. "You are the man for whom I have waited.
That is all I have to say."

Jeffrey Farr smiled.
"You find our ships amusing?" the Imperial officer
asked sharply.

The steam launch chuffed rhythmically along the line
of anchored battlewagons. He'd noticed the same

attitude often in Imperial naval officers. Unlike the Army—or the squabbling committees in Ciano who set policy and budgets—they had to have *some* idea of what was going on abroad. Not that they'd admit the state their service was in, of course. It came out in a prickly defensiveness.

"Quite the contrary," Farr said smoothly. "I smiled because I recently received news that my brother, my foster-brother, is going to be married. To a lady by the name of Pia del'Cuomo."

And I don't think your ships are funny. I think they're pathetic, he added to himself.

The Imperial officer nodded, mollified and impressed. "The eldest daughter of the Minister of War? Your brother is a lucky man." He pointed. "And there they are, the pride of the Passage Fleet."

Ten of the battleships floated in the millpond-quiet bay of the military harbor, flanked by the great fortresses. Lighters were carrying out supplies, much of it coal that had to be laboriously shoveled into crane-borne buckets and hoisted again to the decks for transfer to the fuel bunkers. The ships were medium-sized, about eleven thousand tons burden, with long ram bows and a pronounced tumblehome that made them much narrower at the deck than the waterline. They each carried a heavy, stubby single 350mm gun in a round cheesebox-style turret fore and aft, and their secondary batteries in a string of smaller one-gun turrets that rose pulpit-style from the sides. Each had a string of four short smokestacks, and a wilderness upperworks of flying bridges, cranes, and signal masts.

They'd been perfectly good ships in their day. The problem was that the Empire was still building them about twenty years after their day had passed.

correct, Center observed. **roughly equivalent to british battleships of the 1880s period.**

Eighteen . . . ah. Center used the Christian calendar, which nobody on Visager did except for religious purposes. For one thing, it was based on Earth's twelve-month year, nearly thirty days shorter than this planet's rotation around its sun. For another, the numbers were inconveniently high.

Jeffrey shivered slightly. The period Center named was two thousand years past. Interstellar civilization had been born, spread, and fallen in the interim, and a new cycle was beginning.

"You're loading coal, I see," he said to the Imperial officer . . . Commodore Bragati, that was his name. "Steam up yet?"

"No, we expect to be ready in about a week," Bragati said. "Then we'll cruise down the Passage, and show those upstarts in the Land who rules those waters."

Two weeks to get ready for a show-the-flag cruise? Raj thought with disgust. *I'd say these imbeciles deserve what's probably going to happen to them, if so many civilians weren't going to be caught in it.*

"The main guns are larger than anything the Land has built," Bragati said.

low-velocity weapons with black-powder propellant, Center noted with its usual clinical detachment. **the chosen weapons are long-barreled, high-velocity rifles using nitrocellulose powders.**

He thought he detected a trace of interest, though, as well. Jeffrey smiled inwardly; the sentient computer wasn't all that much different from his grandfather and the cronies who hung around him—military history buffs and weapons fanciers to a man. Center was a hobbyist, in its way.

"And the main armor belt is twelve inches thick!"

laminated wrought iron and cast steel plate, Center went on. **radically inferior to face-hardened alloy.** Which both the Land and the Republic were using for their major warships.

None of the battleships looked ready for sea. Less excusably, neither did the scout cruisers tied up three-deep at the naval wharves, or the torpedo-boat destroyers. Or even the harbor's own torpedo boats, turtle-backed little craft.

On the other hand . . . "Well, the fleet certainly looks in good fettle," Jeffrey said diplomatically.

So they were, painted in black and dark blue with cream trim. Sailors were scrubbing coal dust off the latter even as he watched. He shuddered to think of the amount of labor it must take to repair the paintwork after a practice firing. If they did have practice firings; he had a strong suspicion that some Imperial captains might simply throw their quota of practice ammunition overboard to spare the trouble.

"Thank you for your courtesy," he said formally to the Imperial commodore.

At least he'd learned one thing. Bragati wasn't the sort of man he wanted to recruit into the stay-behind cells he and John were setting up. Too brittle to survive, given his high rank.

"Damn, I hate dying," John said as the scene blinked back to normalcy.

Or Center's idea of normalcy, which in this scenario was a street in a Chosen city—Copernik, to be specific—during the rainy season. There was no way to tell it from the real thing; every sensation was there, down to the smell of the wet rubberized rain cape over his shoulders and the slight roughness of the checked grip of the pistol he held underneath it. Watery rainy-season light probed through the dull clouds overhead, giving a pearly sheen to the granite paving blocks of the street. Buildings of brick and stone reached to the walkways on either side, shuttered and dark, frames of iron bars over their windows.

John looked down for a second at his unmarked stomach. There hadn't been any way to tell the impact of the hollowpoint rifle bullet from the real thing, either— Center's neural input gave an *exact* duplicate of the sensation of having your spleen punched out and an exit wound the size of a woman's fist in your lower back.

The machine had let the scenario play through to the final blackout. His mouth still felt sour and dry. . . .

"Do you have to make it quite that realistic?" he muttered, sidling down the street, eyes scanning.

"For your own good, lad." Raj's voice was "audible" here. "Priceless training, really. You can't get more rigorous than this; and outside, you won't be able to get up and start again."

"I still—"

A sound alerted him. He whirled, drawing the pistol from the holster on his right hip and firing under his own left arm, into the planks of the door. His weight crashed into it before the ringing of the shots had died, smashing it back into the room and knocking the collapsing corpse of the Fourth Bureau agent into his companions. That gave John just enough time to snapshoot, and the secret policeman's weapon flew out of a nerveless hand as the bullet smashed his collarbone . . .

. . . blackness.

The street reformed. "I still really hate dying. One behind me?"

correct. Center did not bother with amenities like speaking aloud. **scanning to your right as you entered the room was the optimum alternative.**

"I hated it, too," Raj said unexpectedly.

The street scene faded to the study where they'd first . . . John supposed "met" was as good a word as any. Raj puffed alight a cheroot and poured them both brandies.

"Hunting accident—broke my neck putting my mount over a fence," he said. "Quick, at least. I was an old, old man by that time, and the bones get brittle. Still, I had enough time to know I'd screwed the pooch in a major way. The real surprise was waking up—" He indicated the construct. "I was expecting the afterlife, the *real* afterlife." He frowned. "Although this isn't precisely my soul, come to think of it. Maybe I'm in two heavens . . . or hells."

"At least you got to see your own funeral," John said.

His body-image still carried the revolver. He opened the cylinder and worked the ejector to remove the spent brass, then reloaded and clicked the weapon closed with his thumb. The action was wholly automatic, after thousands of hours of Center's instruction—and Raj's, too. The personality of the general gave the training an immediacy that the machine intelligence could never quite match, one that remembered the flesh and the unpleasant realities to which it was subject.

"My grandchildren were touchingly grief-stricken," Raj said, his grin white in the dark face. "And now, back to work."

"This is play?" John asked.

His own bedroom in the embassy complex snapped back into view; it was private, with the door locked, and big enough for his body to leap and move in puppet-obedience to what his mind perceived in Center's training program. Experience had to be ground into the nerves and muscles, as well as the mind and memory. The rest of the staff thought he had an eccentric taste for calisthenics performed in solitude.

The phone rang, the distinctive two long and three short that meant it was from the ambassador.

John sighed silently as he picked it up. There were times when it was easier to deal with the Chosen; they were more straightforward.

Gerta found the embassy of the Land of the Chosen in the Imperial capital of Ciano reassuringly familiar, down to the turtle helmets and gray uniforms and brand-new magazine rifles of the guards at the gate. They snapped to present as her car halted; an officer checked her papers and waved her through, past two outward-bound trucks. In the main courtyard, staff were setting up fuel drums and shoveling in a mixture of file folders and kerosene distillate. The smoke was rank and black, towering up into the sky over the pollarded trees and the slate-roofed buildings. The guards at the entrance gave her a more detailed going-over.

"Captain Gerta Hosten, Intelligence Section, General Staff Office, *geburtsnumero* 77-A-II-44221," she said.

"Sir," the embassy clerk said, after a moment's check of the tallysheet before him. "Colonel von Kleuron will see you immediately."

I should hope so, Gerta thought with perfectly controlled anger as she walked through the basalt-paved lobby of the main embassy building. *After dragging me out here for Fate-knows-what when the balloon's about to go up*.

It was busy enough that several times she had to dodge wheeled carts full of documents being taken down to the incinerators. Not so busy that several passersby in civilian dress didn't to a slight check and double-take at her Intelligence flashes; probably the Fourth Bureau spooks were about as happy to see her here as they would be to invite Santander Intelligence Bureau operatives in. The air was scented with the smell of paper and cardboard burning, and with fear-sweat.

She repeated the identification procedure at the Intelligence chief's office. This time it was a Chosen NCO who checked her against a list.

"Welcome to Ciano, Captain," he said. "No problems at the airship port?"

"Walked straight through, barely looked at my passport," she said. "The colonel?"

The NCO hopped up from his desk—it was covered with files being sorted—opened the door and spoke through it, then opened it fully and stepped aside.

Gerta marched through, tucked her peaked cap precisely under her left arm. Her heels clicked, and her right arm shot out at shoulder-height with fist clenched.

"Sir!"

Colonel von Kleuron turned out to be a middle-aged woman with a long face and pouches under her eyes.

Her office, with its metal filing cabinets, table with a keyboard-style coding machine, and plain wooden desk, seemed to still be in full operation. All in military gray, nothing personal except a photograph of several teenage children on the desk.

"At ease, Captain." She looked at Gerta with a slight raise of her eyebrow. "You seem to be throttling a considerable head of steam, Hosten."

"Sir, Operation Overfall is scheduled to commence shortly. My unit is tasked with an important objective, and we've been training for nearly a year. Nobody's indispensable, but I'll be missed."

"We should have you back shortly, Captain," von Kleuron said. "Not to waste time: give me your appraisal of Johan—John—Hosten, your foster-brother."

Gerta blinked in surprise. That she had *not* expected. Von Kleuron tapped the folder open before her; a picture of John was clipped to the front sheet. Gerta recognized it; it was a duplicate of one she'd gotten from him. She also recognized the correspondence tucked into the inner jacket of the file; of course, she'd submitted all her letters for approval before sending, and turned over copies of all his immediately. Plus, the Fourth Bureau would have their own from the censors in the postal system, but that was another department.

"As in my reports, Colonel. Intelligent and resourceful, and, as I remember him as a boy, with considerable nerve and determination. Certainly he overcame his handicap well. From what he's accomplished in the Republic over the last twelve years, he's become a formidable man."

"His attitude towards the Chosen?"

"I think he had reservations even as a boy. Now?" She shrugged. "Impossible to say. We don't discuss politics, only family matters."

"Weaknesses?"

"Sentimentality." The Landisch word she used could also mean "squeamishness."

"Are you aware that Johan Hosten has become an operative for the Republic's Foreign Intelligence Service? As well as a diplomat." The last was a little pedantic; in Landisch, diplomat and spy were related words.

Gerta's eyebrows went up slightly. "No, sir, I wasn't aware of that. I'm not surprised."

"It has been decided at a high level to attempt to enlist the subject as a double agent. We are authorized to waive Testing and offer Chosen status, and appropriate rank."

Gerta frowned. It smacked of an improvisation, not a good idea on the eve of a major war. On the other hand, John *would* be an asset if he could be turned . . . and it would be pleasant to have him on-side. If possible. It was obvious why she'd been brought in; she was the only Chosen intelligence operative with a personal link to John. Heinrich had known him as well, but he was a straight-leg, an infantry officer. *And* far more conspicuous in Ciano; her height and physical type was far more common in the Empire than his.

On the other hand, women who could bench-press twice their own weight were *not* common here, and she hoped very much she wouldn't have to try looking like an Imperial belle in a low-cut dress. She didn't even know how to walk in a skirt.

Behfel ist Behfel. "How am I tasked, sir?"

John tapped his walking stick against the front of the cab. "Driver, pull up."

The horses clattered to a halt, and the driver set the brake and jumped to the cobblestones to open the door.

"Signore?" he said, looking around.

They were in a district of upper-middle-class homes, about halfway between the theater district north of the main railway station and the apartment John kept near the Santander embassy.

"I've changed my mind, I'm going to walk home," he said.

Shameless self-indulgence, he thought. He *should* make up for taking an evening off at the opera with Pia by going straight home and reading files. On the other hand, he had his cover as a effete diplomat to maintain. The Santander diplomatic service was supposed to be a harmless dumping ground for well-connected upper-class playboys. Many of them were, and the rest found it useful camouflage.

He paid the cabbie the full value of his intended trip, and the horses clattered off through the dark.

Ciano was a pleasant city to walk through, this part at least, on a warm spring night. The sidewalk was brick, with trees at four-meter intervals—oaks, he thought—and cast-iron lampstands rather less frequently. Most of the houses on either side had wrought-iron railings separating them from the street, often overgrown with climbing roses or honeysuckle. The gaslights gave a diffuse glow to the scene, soft yellow light on the undersides of the trees; the street had a melancholy feel, like most of the Imperial capital, a dreamy sense of past glories and a long sleep filled with reverie.

John twirled the walking stick and strolled, unclasping his opera cloak and throwing it over his left arm. It was very quiet, the air smelling of dew and roses. Quiet enough that he heard the footsteps not long after Center's warning.

four following, the computer said. **there are two more at the junction ahead.**

John was suddenly, acutely conscious of the feel of the brick beneath his feet, the slight touch of the wind on his face beneath the glossy black topper. Twelve years of Center's scenarios and Raj's drill had given him a training nobody on the planet could match, but he'd never had anyone try to kill him before. *Odd, I'm not really frightened.* More like being extremely alert and irritated at the same time.

There was a double-edged steel blade inside his walking stick, the gold head made a very effective bludgeon, and a small six-shot revolver nestled under one armpit. It didn't seem like much, right now, but it would probably be enough if these were street toughs out to roll a toff.

The wall by his side was brick. John turned casually and set his back against it, like a man pausing to admire the view toward the north and the Imperial Palace.

Four men came up the sidewalk behind him. They were dressed in double-breasted jackets and bag-hats, peg-leg trousers and ankle-boots; middle-class streetwear for Ciano. Their faces were unremarkably Imperial as well, rather swarthy and blue-stubbled for the most part. There was something about the way they moved, though, the expressions on the faces—or rather the lack of them. Big men, thick-shouldered. With flat bulges under their left armpits; one of them was holding his right hand down by his side, as if something was resting in the loosely curled fingertips The hilt of a knife, perhaps, or a lead-weighted cosh.

Protégés, he thought. Tough ones, at that. Operatives. Fourth Bureau, or Military Intelligence.

correct, Center said. **97%, ±2.**

Well, it was some comfort to know his judgment was good.

The men halted and spread out, waiting with a tense wariness. One spoke:

"Excuse, sir. You will please to come with us." A guttural accent in the Imperial, one natural to someone who'd grown up speaking Landisch.

Four of them, and two more waiting close by. *Not good odds.* And if they'd wanted him dead, he'd be dead. A steamcar and a couple of shotguns, no problem and no fuss. Or someone waiting in his apartment, the Chosen could certainly find a good shooter when they needed one. This was a snatch team, not hitters.

"All right," he said, turning and walking ahead of them.

Two closed in on either side. One quietly relieved him of the walking stick. Another leaned over, put a hand

under his jacket and took his revolver, dropping it into
his own coat pocket. A few seconds later, fingers plucked
the little punch-dagger out of the collar of his dress coat.
There was a sound at that, something like a very quiet
chuckle smothered before it began. The men closed in
on either side of him—nobody in front, of course. This
lot had been fairly well-trained.

They all halted under the streetlight at the T-shaped
intersection. The two men waiting there both threw their
cigarettes into the center of the road. Seconds later a
quiet hum of rubber tires sounded as a steamcar came
down the road and halted—a big Santander-made four-
door Wilkens in plain blue paint, with wire-spoke wheels
and two sofa-style seats facing each other in the rear
compartment. The head of the snatch team signaled John
to enter.

There was a woman sitting in the front seat, with her
back to the driver's compartment. The interior of the
Wilkens was fairly dark, only the reflected light of the
streetlamps. That was enough to show the oily blued
sheen of a weapon in her hand; it gestured him back
to the rear of the vehicle. He obeyed silently. Two of
the Protégé gunmen sat on either side of him, wedg-
ing him into position. The front door *chunk*ed closed.
Just for insurance, the Protégé beside John had a short
double-edged blade in his hand, under the limp hat. That
put the point not more than a couple of millimeters from
his short ribs. John's lips quirked. They certainly weren't
taking any chances with him; but then, the preferred
Chosen method of dealing with ants was to drop an anvil
on them.

The woman leaned out the window and spoke to the
other members of the team. "Report to the safe house,"
she said. Gray uniform tunic, Captain's rank-tabs, red
General Staff flashes, Military Intelligence insignia.

The motion left the light on her face for a second.
She was in her late twenties, not much older than he;
a dark brunette, black hair cropped to a plush sable cap,

black eyes, high cheekbones, and a rather full mouth. An Imperial face or Sierran, except for the hardness to it, the body beneath close-coupled and muscular but full-bosomed. He blinked, surprise tugging at his mind.

"Gerta!" he blurted.

probability subject identity not gerta hosten is too low to be meaningfully calculated, Center noted, overlaying the woman's face with a series of regressions that took it back to the teenager who'd said good-bye to him on the docks of Oathtaking twelve years ago.

She sat back and let the pistol rest on her knee; it was a massive, chunky, squared-off thing, not a revolver. **recoil-operated automatic, magazine in the grip,** Center said. **11mm caliber, six to eight rounds.**

"Hi, Johnnie," she said in Landisch. "Nice to see you again."

John took a deep breath. "If you wanted to talk, you could have invited me more politely," he said in a neutral tone.

"Behfel ist behfel, Johnnie."

"I'm not under Chosen orders."

She smiled and waggled the automatic.

"All right, I grant that. I presume you're not going to kill me?"

"I'd really regret having to do that, John," she said. **veracity 95% ±3,** Center observed. A brief flash showed pupil dilation and heat patterns on Gerta's face.

Of course, the way she phrased it implied that she might have to kill him anyway. Looking at her, he didn't have the least doubt she'd do it—regrets or no.

"How're the children?" he asked after a moment.

"Erika's just starting school, and Johan's at the stage where his favorite word is *no,"* she said. "We've adopted two more, as well. Protégé kids, a boy and a girl. The boy's a byblow, probably one of Heinrich's."

"Two?" John said, raising his eyebrows.

"Policy."

Which was information, of a sort. The Chosen Council

must be anticipating casualties . . . and not just in the upcoming war with the Empire, either.

He didn't try to look out the windows as the wheels hammered over the cobblestones, then hummed on smoother main street pavement of asphalt or stone blocks. Gerta uncorked a silver flask. John took it and sipped: banana brandy, something he hadn't tasted in a long time.

"*Danke*," he said. "Anything you can tell me?"

"The colonel will brief you, Johnnie. Just . . . be reasonable, eh?"

"Reasonable depends on where you're sitting," he said, returning the flask.

"No it doesn't. When someone else holds all the cards, reasonable is whatever they say it is."

He looked at the pistol. She shook her head.

"Not just this. The Chosen hold all the cards on Visager; it'd be smart to keep that in mind."

He was almost relieved when they pulled into a side entrance to the Chosen embassy compound. The Wilkens was as inconspicuous as a steamcar in Ciano could be— powered vehciles weren't all that common here, even now—and the rear windows were tinted. The embassy itself was fairly large, a severe block of dark granite from the outside, the only ornamentation a gilded-bronze sunburst above the ironwork gates. The area within was larger than the Santander legation, mainly because all the Land's diplomatic personnel lived on the delegation's own extraterritorial ground. It might have been something out of Copernik or Oathtaking inside, boxlike buildings with tall windows and smooth columns, low-relief cataryids beside the doors. Fires were burning in iron drums in the open spaces between, while clerks dumped in more documents and stirred the ashes with pokers and broomsticks.

Christ, he thought. The sight hit him in the belly like a fist, more than the danger to himself had. War was *close* if the embassy was torching their classified papers.

He was hustled through a doorway, down corridors, finally into a windowless room with a single overhead light. It shone into his eyes as he sat in the steel-frame chair beneath it, obscuring the two figures at a table in front of him. One of them spoke in Landisch:

"Let's dispose with the tricks, shall we, Colonel?" Gerta said. "This isn't an interrogation."

The overhead light dimmed. He blinked and looked at the two Chosen officers. Both women—nothing unusual with that, in the Land's forces—in gray Army uniforms. Intelligence Section badges. A middle-aged colonel with gray in her blond brushcut and a face like a starved hound.

"Johan Hosten," the senior officer said. "We have arranged to speak with you on a matter of some importance."

John nodded. He could guess what was coming.

"The Land of the Chosen has need of your services, Johan Hosten."

"The Land of the Chosen rejected me rather thoroughly when I was twelve," he pointed out. "I'm a citizen of the Republic of Santander."

"The Republic is a democracy with universal suffrage," the colonel said. "Hence, weak and corrupt, with no real claim on your allegiance." She spoke in a flat, matter-of-fact tone, as if commenting on the law of gravity. "Your father is second assistant of the general staff of the Land and a member of the Council. The implications are, I think, plain."

They certainly were. "I'm not Chosen and not qualified to be so," he said. *Think, think.* If he rolled over too quickly, they'd be suspicious.

"The regulations governing admittance have been waived or modified before," the intelligence officer said. "I am authorized to inform you that they will be again, in your case. Full Chosen status, and appropriate rank."

"You want me to defect?" he said slowly.

"Of course not. You will remain as an agent in place

within the Santander intelligence apparat—of course, we know that your diplomatic status is a cover—and provide us with information, and your nominal superiors with disinformation which will be furnished. We can feed you genuine data of sufficient importance so that you will rise rapidly in rank. At the appropriate moment, we will bring you in from the cold."

She nodded towards Gerta. *Ah. They sent Gerta along as an earnest of good faith.* The offer probably *was* genuine. And to the Chosen's way of looking at it, perfectly natural. Perhaps if he'd never been contacted by Center, it might even have been tempting.

There were times he woke up at night sweating, from dreams of the man he might have become in the Land.

"Let me think," he said.

"Agreed. But not for long."

He dropped his head into his hands. *Jeff, you following this?*

You bet, brother. You going to ask them for something in writing?

Out of character, he answered. *A Chosen officer's word is supposed to be good. I don't have much time.*

Although surely *they* knew that *he* knew he'd never leave the room alive if he refused. The embassy could be relied upon to have a way of disposing of bodies.

He raised his head again. No problem in showing a little worry, and he could smell his own sweat, heavy with the peculiar rankness of stress.

"I'm engaged to be married to an Imperial," he said.

The colonel shrugged. "Marriage is out of the question, of course, but after the conquest, you can have your pick for pleasure. Take the bitch as you please, or a dozen others."

Gerta winced and touched her superior on the sleeve, whispering in her ear.

John shook his head. "Anything that applies to me, applies to Pia. Or no deal."

The colonel's eyes narrowed. "You have already been offered more than is customary," she warned.

"No. Pia, or nothing."

Gerta touched the colonel's sleeve again. "We should discuss this, sir," she said.

"Agreed. Hosten, retire to the end of the room, please."

He obeyed, facing away from the table. The two Chosen leaned together, speaking in whispers. Far too softly for anyone to overhear . . . anyone without Center's processing power, that was. The computer was limited to the input of John's senses, but it could do far more with them than his unaided brain.

"What do you make of it, captain?" the colonel asked.

"I'm not sure, sir. If he'd agreed without insisting on the woman, I'd have said we should kill him immediately—that would be an obvious fake. The woman . . . that makes it possible he's sincere . . . but he'd also know that *I* know him well."

Thanks a lot, Gerta.

"As it is, I still suspect he's lying. Immediate termination would be the low-risk option here."

"I was under the impression that you thought highly of this Johan Hosten."

"I do. Heinrich and I named a son after him. I respect his courage and intelligence; which is why he's too dangerous to live unless he's on our side."

"He seems inclined to agree to the proposition."

"He'd have to anyway, wouldn't he?"

"What evidence do you have to suppose he lies?"

"Gestalt. I lived with him until he was twelve and we've corresponded since. He's committed to the Republic, absurd though that may sound. He *believes*. And John Hosten would never betray a cause in which he believed."

A long silence. "As you say, the Republic's ideology is absurd—and he is, from the records, not a stupid or irrational man. Termination is always an option, but it is irrevocable once exercised. We will test him; his position is potentially a priceless asset. And we are offering him the ultimate reward, after all."

"Colonel, please record my objection and recommendation."

"Captain, this is noted." Aloud: "Johan Hosten, attend."

When he was standing beside the chair, she continued: "We will concede this woman Probationer-Emeritus status."

Second-class citizenship, but if married to one of the Chosen her children would be automatically entitled to take the Test of Life. Although they'd know he could sire no children. He blinked, keeping his face carefully neutral. Pia had wept when he told her that, and he'd been afraid, really afraid.

"This is . . ." He stopped and began again. "You understand, I've been growing more and more frustrated with Santander. You must know that, if your sources inside the Foreign Office are as good as I suspect. I keep *telling* them the risks, and they ignore them." He shrugged. "As you said, it makes no sense to fight for those who won't fight for themselves." He stood, and gave the Chosen salute. "I agree. Command me, colonel!"

The colonel returned the gesture. Gerta stared at him with cold appraisal, biting at her lip thoughtfully. Then she shook her head and made a small gesture to the senior officer, a thumb-pull, much the same as one would make to cock a pistol before shooting someone in the back of the head.

Colonel von Kleuron looked at them both and then shook her head.

John fought back an impulse to let out a long sigh of relief. *They aren't going to kill me now.* Thanks, Gerta, *thanks a lot.*

Although he should have expected it. He'd always known his foster-sister was smart, and she *did* know him well.

"Johan Hosten."

The basset-hound face of the colonel allowed itself a slight smile.

"You have made a wise decision. You will be dropped at some distance, and contacted when appropriate. May your service to the Chosen be long and successful."

"Welcome back, Johnnie," Gerta said. "I'm sure you'll make a first-class operative. You've got natural talent."

Lucky bastard, Jeffrey said silently.

No, it's Chosen arrogance, John replied from half a continent away. A faint overlay of the controls of a road steamer came through the link, beyond it a long dusty country road.

Jeffrey smiled, imagining serious expression and the slight frown on his stepbrother's face.

Have they contacted you since? he said/thought.

No. It's only been three days, and they're very busy. The whole Land embassy staff left on the last dirigible.

Jeffrey lifted his coffee cup. It was morning, but some of the other patrons in the streetside cafe had already made a start on something stronger. Many of them were settling in with piles of newspapers or books, or just enjoying the perennial Imperial sport of people-watching. The coffee was excellent, and the platter of pastries extremely tempting; you had to admit, there were some things the Imperials did very well. His contact should be showing up any minute.

Give me a look at the activity in the harbor, John requested. Jeffrey turned slightly in his seat and looked downhill; Center would be supplying the visual input to John.

Awful lot of Chosen shipping still there, his stepbrother commented.

They're still delivering coal, Jeffrey replied. *To the naval stockpiles, no less.*

My esteemed prospective father-in-law, John thought

dryly, *assures me that the Imperial armed forces are ready down to the last gaiter button. Quote unquote.*

Is the man a natural-born damned fool?

No, he just can't afford to face the truth. I think he wishes he'd died before this . . . and he's glad Pia will be safe in Santander.

Speaking of which, we should— Jeffrey began. Then: *Wait.*

A dirigible was showing over the horizon, just barely. Jeffrey was in officer's garrison dress, which included a case for a small pair of binoculars as well as a service revolver. He drew the glasses and stood, looking down the long street leading to the harbor. The airship wasn't in Land Air Service colors, just a neutral silvery shade with a *Landisch Luftanza* company logo on the big sharkfin control surfaces at the rear. A large model, two hundred meters in length and a quarter that in maximum diameter. One of the latest types, with the gondola built into the hull and six engines in streamlined pods held out from the sides by struts covered in winglike farings.

"That isn't a scheduled carrier," he said to himself.

correct. vessel is land air service heavy military transport design. A brief flash of a report he'd read several months ago. **sharkwhale class.**

"I have a bad feeling about this," he said. "John, I'm going to be busy for a while."

I suspect we all are, his brother answered. *Better try and make it to the legation.*

CHAPTER FOUR

"Coming up on Ciano. Airspeed one hundred and four kilometers per hour, altitude one thousand four hundred. Windspeed ten KPH, north-northwest. Fifteen kilometers to target."

The bridge of the war dirigible *Sieg* was a semicircle under the bows, with slanting windows that gave a 180-degree view forward and down. Gerta Hosten was the only one present not in the blue-trimmed gray of the Landisch Air Service; she was in army combat kit, stone-gray tunic and pants, webbing gear and steel helmet. Her boots felt a little insecure on the stamped aluminum panels of the airship's decking, unlike the rubber-soled shoes the crew wore. The commanding officer, Horst Raske, stood by the crewman who held the tall wheel that controlled the vertical rudders. Another wheel at right-angles turned the horizontal control surfaces. Ballast, gas, and engines all had their own stations, although each engine pod also held two crewmen for repairs or emergencies.

"Off superheat," Raske said.

A muted *whump* went through the huge but lightly built hull of the airship. Vents on the upper surface of the ship were opening, releasing hot air from the ballonets that hung in the center of the hydrogen cells. The dirigible felt slower and heavier under her feet, and the surface of the water began to grow closer. Land was a thick line of surf ahead, studded with tiny doll-like buildings. The broad estuary of the Pada River lay southward, to the right; just inside it were the deep dredged-out harbors of Corona, swarming with shipping.

"All engines three-quarter, come about to one-two-five." Ranke's voice was as calm and crisp as it had been on the practice runs on the mockup. Nobody had ever flown a dirigible into a real combat situation like this before; airships had only existed for about forty years. "Commencing final run."

He turned to Gerta. "Thirty minutes to target," he said. "The observer"—in a bubble on top of the airship—"reports the rest of the air-landing force is following on schedule. Good luck."

Gerta returned his salute. "And to you, Major."

You'll need it, she thought. *She* was getting off this floating bomb; into a firefight, granted, but at least she wouldn't have a million cubic meters of hydrogen wrapped around her while she did it.

The catwalk behind the bridge led down through crew quarters, past the radio shack, and into the hold. That was a huge darkened box across the belly of the *Sieg,* spanned with girders higher up; the only vertical members were several dozen ropes fastened to the roof supports and ending in coils on segments of floor planking. Crouched on the framework floor were her troops, three hundred of the Intelligence Service Commando, special forces, reporting directly to the general staff and tasked with the very first assault. Most of the dirigibles and surface ships following were crowded with line troops, Protégé slave-soldiers under Chosen officers. The Protégé infantrymen were getting four ounces of raw cane spirit each about now. The IS Commando were all-Chosen, only one candidate in ten making the grade.

The sergeant of the headquarters section handed her a Koegelmann machine-carbine. Half the commando was armed with them or pump-action shotguns rather than rifles, for close-in firepower. She slapped a flat disk drum on top of the weapon and ran the sling through the epaulet strap on her right shoulder so that it would hang with the pistol grip ready to hand.

"Right," she said in a voice just loud enough to carry. "This is what we've all been training for. We're the first in, because we're the *best*. It looks like the Imperials are sitting with their thumbs up their butts . . . but once we land, even they'll realize what's going on. Remember the training: hit hard, hold hard, and by this time tomorrow Corona will belong to the Chosen. Corona, and then the Empire. Then the *world*. And for a thousand years, they'll remember that *we* struck the first blow."

A short growl rippled over the watching faces, not quite a cheer; the sort of sound a pack of dires would make, closing in on a eland herd. The company and platoon leaders grouped around her as she knelt.

"No clouds, not much wind, unlimited visibility," she told them. "And no last-minute screwups from Intelligence, either."

"Meaning either everything's as per, or the reports were totally fucked in the first place and nobody's found out better," Fedrika Blummer said.

"Exactly. Fedrika, remember, *don't* get tied up in the scrimmage. Get those Haagens set up on the perimeter, or the Imperials will swamp us before the main force arrives. Kurt, Mikel, Wilhelm, all of you remember this—we're going to be heavily outnumbered. The only way we can pull this off is if we hit so hard and so fast they never suspect what's coming down. Go through them like grass through a goose and don't leave anyone standing."

"*Ya*," Wilhelm Termot said. The others nodded.

"Let's do it, then."

Jeffrey Farr dumped the papers in the cast-iron bathtub and sprinkled them with lamp oil. He flicked a match on his thumb and dropped it onto the surface. The mass of documents flared up in a gout of orange flame and black smoke and a coarse acrid smell. He retreated from the bathroom into the bedroom.

Jeffrey began throwing things into a satchel—his camera, spare ammunition for his revolver—and checked the bathroom. It was full of smoke, but the papers were burning nicely. They held the details of the network he'd been setting up here in Corona—but Center was the perfect recording device, and one that couldn't be tapped. For that matter, he'd carefully refrained from memorizing them himself. What he didn't know he couldn't tell, and Center could always furnish him with the details. It put need-to-know in a whole different category. He waited until the tub held nothing but flaky ash, then quenched it with a jug of water from the basin before he jogged up to the flat roof of the apartment building. It was four stories tall, and the roof was set with chairs and planters; nothing but the best in this neighborhood.

He got out the heavier pair of binoculars and focused on the dirigible. It was close now, slowing. Heading for Fort Calucci at the outer arm of the military harbor, from the looks of it.

What in the hell are they going to try there? he thought. That was HQ for the whole Corona Military District.

an assault with air-transported troops, Center said. **probability 78%, ±3. observe:**

—and troops in gray Land uniforms slid down ropes on to the roof of the HQ complex—

Looks like it, Raj said. *The bastardos have nerve, I'll grant them that.*

"Oh, shit," he whispered a moment later.

What's the matter? John's voice.

"Lucretzia," he said.

Well—

"I know, I know, she's not the girl you bring home to mother—but she's down by the portside."

the legation would be the lowest-risk area for temporary relocation, Center hinted.

"Yeah, but I've got to do something about her," Jeffrey said. "It's personal, and besides, she's a good contact."

Good luck, John said.

And watch your back, lad, Raj added.

The fabric of the *Sieg* groaned and shivered with a low-toned roar.

Valving gas, Gerta thought. *Negative buoyancy.*

As if to confirm it, the falling-elevator sensation grew stronger. The nose of the dirigible tilted upwards and the engines roared as the captain controlled the rate of fall with the dynamic lift of air rushing under the great hull. She tasted salt from the sweat running down her face. Any second now.

"Ready for it!"

The commandos were bracing themselves with loops set into the aluminum deck planking. Gerta snugged the carrying strap of the carbine tight and ran both arms and a foot through the braces. The engine roar died suddenly, down to idle. Into the moment of silence that followed came a grinding, tearing clangor. The ship wrenched brutally, struck, bounced, struck, flinging her body back and forth. Then it came to a queasy, rocking halt with the floor at an angle. The bellow of valving gas continued.

"Now! Go, go, go!"

Booted feet slammed against quick-release catches. Two dozen segments of floor plating fell out of the belly carrying the coils of rope with them; light broke into the gloom of the hold, blinding. Men and women moved despite it, in motions trained so long that they were reflex. Twenty-four jumped, wrapped arms and legs around the sisal cables, and dropped out of sight. Others followed them with the regular precision of a metronome. Gerta and the headquarters section went in the third wave, precisely thirty-five seconds after the first.

Noise hit her as she slid out of the hold, into the giant

shadow of the huge structure overhead. The *Sieg* was shifting, beginning to bob up a little as the weight left it. The pavement of the tower's flat roof was only eight meters down, less than a third the distance the teams sliding down into the fortress courtyard had to cover. There were half a dozen Imperials below her, gaping and pointing at the dirigible overhead. They didn't start to move until shots and screams broke out below. There was a moment of controlled fall and she struck the ground, rolling off the segment of decking and reaching under the horizontal drum magazine of the Koegelmann to jack the slide back. The blowback weapon was new; it had a grip safety that was supposed to keep the bolt from racking forward.

She'd found that the safety wasn't completely reliable. A really sharp jar could send it forward, chambering and firing a round. *Not* a good idea to arm it just before you jumped down a rope.

Gerta came down in a perfect four-point prone position and stroked the carbine's trigger. It roared and hammered backward into her shoulder, spent brass tinkling on the painted metal surface of the tower's top. The bullets were pistol-caliber but heavy, 11mm, and they were H-section wadcutters. They punched into the Imperials with the impact of so many soggy medicine balls, blasting out exit wounds the size of teaplates. The rest of the section was firing as well. Seconds later, the area was clear of living enemies.

Something whirled by overhead, towards the heavy disk-shaped metal hatch that led from the rooftop down into the main section of the tower. A man was standing on the ladder below. His face was gray with shock, but he was struggling with the massive covering. The stick grenade struck his hands where they rested on the locking wheel of the hatch. He screamed and sprang backwards off the ladder, falling out of sight. The grenade hit the lip of the entryway, spun twice and then toppled out of sight down the shaft after the Imperial soldier.

The hatch fell, too, pulled past its balance point before the Imperial noticed the grenade. Gerta came off the ground like a spring-launched missile, diving forward to try and jam the butt of her carbine into the gap. Halfway through the movement the grenade went off below, but though dust and grit billowed out, the pressure wasn't enough to slow the several hundred kilos of mass. It whumped down into the locking collar and the buttplate of her carbine rang against it with a dull clank. She flipped up to her knees and reached for the small close-set wheel in the top of the mushroom-cap hatch. Three others joined her, but the wheel turned irresistibly under her fingers, and she could hear the holding bars sinking into their sheaths. The locking wheel on the inside was much larger than the topside equivalent, with greater leverage.

Damn, she thought, coming erect and looking around. *Somebody down there must be able to find his dick without a directory.*

Water pattered down, thick as a Land thunderstorm in the rainy season. The great bulk of the *Sieg* was rising and turning, dumping ballast as she went for extra lift. The dirigible seemed to bounce upward, the shadow falling away from the fortress, turning southward for the river estuary with a roar of engines. Ropes fell away from it like writhing snakes to lie draped across walls and pavement.

The tower roof held only live Chosen and dead Imperials; mostly dead, one with a chunk of skull missing was still sprattling like a pithed frog. She duckwalked quickly to the edge of the roof, avoiding the spreading pools of blood—the last thing she needed was slippery boots— and looked down. There were a few bodies in the courtyard. Gunfire came from the buildings that ringed it: shotgun blasts, rifle fire, the distinctive burping chatter of machine carbines. Then a long ripping burst; that could only be one of the tripod-mounted, water-cooled machine guns the heavy-weapons platoon had brought in.

Good. Fedrika must have gotten out to the perimeter.

"Right, Elke, Johan, pop it."

They'd come prepared. Two years after Gerta was born, construction started on a complete duplicate of this fortress in the jungles of the Kopenrungs. The Chosen believed in planning ahead. Fort Calucci had been built back when bronze smoothbore cannon were the most formidable weapons available, but it had been updated continuously since. The last building program had been fifteen years ago, after some sea skirmishes between the Empire and the Republic of Santander. The whole complex had been girdled with five- to fifteen-meter thick ferroconcrete, and the tower clad with the armor of several scrapped battleships. Even modern high-velocity naval rifles would have problems with it.

Fortunately, every fortress had its weaknesses.

The two Chosen trotted over to the hatchway with the charge between them. It was a cone, broadside down, supported on stubby iron legs to give an exact distance from the target. She didn't know precisely how it worked—the principle was suicide-before-reading secret—but she'd seen models tested. The bomb clanged as it dropped to the center of the hatch.

"Fire in the hole!" the two commandos shouted as they triggered the fuse and dove away.

All the force of the explosion went straight down, like a welding-torch jet. Or *almost* all. The sheathing was thin metal and would disintegrate with an *almost* complete lack of shrapnel. Almost was not a very comforting word, when you were on a flat steel pie plate with no cover at all. She pressed her back against the bulwark around the rim, curled her knees up against her chest, tucked her chin down to her throat and held the Koegelmann over her body.

BWAAMP. Shock picked her up and slammed her down on the decking. A spatter of hot steel dropped across her; she cursed and scrabbled with a gloved hand to get the gobbets off her clothing. The smell of scorched hair, uniforms, and wood added its bit to the stink; someone yelled as a droplet struck a spot too tender for self-control.

Metal pinged and scattered. Before the noise died, the explosives experts were on their feet and racing towards it. Smoke was pouring out of a round melted-looking hole in the middle of the metal hatch. The wheel was frozen, either still locked from below or warped by the blast. The sappers stuffed rods of blasting explosive into the gap; it would have been futile to try it against the unbroken surface, since the force of the explosion would dissipate along the line of least resistance, into the open air.

"Fire in the hole!"

A flare soared up into the air from the courtyard below and popped green. Gerta looked at her watch. *Five minutes.* The company tasked with taking the gates and powerplant had succeeded. Good fast work. . . .

The blasting sticks made the whole top of the tower flex like a giant tympanum. This time a *lot* of metal went flying. Trapped inside the pierced hatchway the fast-moving gasses of the explosion had plenty of leverage and no place else to go. Bits and pieces went *ting* against the armored rooftop, or the bulwark around her. Somebody screamed once and then fell silent. The force picked her up and slammed her down painfully, items of equipment ramming themselves into her with bruising force. She blinked watering eyes.

A few bent and twisted remnants of the hatch stood up, like the lid of a badly opened tin can.

Two grenades arched into the gap. Three seconds later they exploded, and the Chosen commandos began dropping through the way the blasting charges had opened.

"Shit," Jeffrey Farr whispered again.

He ducked into the little Shcrrinford and stamped repeatedly on the foot-pump, building pressure for the fuel and water feeds. When the bell rang, he flicked the switch for the spark-starter. A muted *whump* sounded as the flash boiler lit, sounding a bit breathy without the force-pump draft that ran off the flywheel. Red fluid began rising in the glass columns set into the dashboard that showed steam temperature, boiler pressure, water, fuel, battery condition, and air resevoir. Plenty of fuel and the battery was new, thank God. Thirty seconds later another bell rang and the steam temperature and pressure gauges rose over the operating minimum level. He eased the engine into reverse with the engaging lever beside the wheel, backed out cautiously into traffic and headed south.

There were *dozens* of big dirigibles coming in from the southwest, huge elongated teardrop shapes moving like clouds to a grating roar of engines. No attempt at disguise with these; they had the Land sunburst on their flanks. The first wave passed overhead at two thousand meters, heading east. The second slowed and began turning in formation over the harbor and defenses. Slots opened in the bottoms of the hulls. Dark objects tumbled out. Oblong shapes rained down, like torpedoes with fins.

aerial bombs, Center said. **not aerodynamically optimum, but functional.**

"I'll say," Jeffrey muttered.

A large dirigible could carry *tons* of cargo; some of the latest models had forty or fifty tons useful lift.

Crump. Crumpcrumpcrumpcrump—

They probably sailed empty from the Land, then took on their loads from ships over the horizon, Raj observed.

probability 76%±4, Center said.

"Damn. I'd better get to the—"

A long whistling roar. Jeffrey jerked at the wheel, going up on the sidewalk with two wheels and scattering yelling pedestrians. Dust fountained over him through the open windows of the canvas-topped car, and the road seemed to drop out from under him for a second. Coughing, he saw the apartment block three buildings down fall into the street in a slow-motion avalanche. That was bad aiming, they were probably trying for the gasworks about a kilometer away, but he supposed it didn't matter if you had *enough* bombs. He spat dust-colored saliva and watched as the shark-shape of the dirigible slid away overhead, explosions following it like a trail of monstrous eggs. A dozen of them, and then a huge globe of fire rising over the rooftops; they *had* gotten the gas-storage tanks.

Time to go, lad.

"No argument."

He let the throttle out, up to fifty kilometers an hour—well over the speed limit, but that was purely theoretical in Corona at the best of times. There were a few people milling around, but not many. The crowds were standing and pointing, open-mouthed; a few were crowding towards the broken apartment building, but there was fire in the rubble—broken gas mains, and water spurting from severed pipes. A horse-drawn fire engine went by with clanking bells and sparks flying from its hooves. An Imperial officer with gold epaulets and a spiked wax mustache rode by in the other direction. He had his pistol in his hand and he was riding towards the harbor, although what he planned to do there was a mystery. The naval dockyards three kilometers away were a mass of fire and smoke, with columns of fire from the secondary explosions showing red through the black clouds.

One mother was holding her child up to see the explosions, apparently under the impression they were some kind of fireworks.

Not many seemed to be panicking as yet—which showed ignorance, not steady nerves. He could catch glances in between dodging trolley cars and pedestrians. Half a dozen Land merchantmen had beached themselves by the harbor forts on either side of the

entrance from the Pada estuary. It was too far away to
see men, but the hulls were darkened in a spiderweb
pattern, boarding nets dropped over the side so that
embarked troops could climb down to the corniche road.
Sections of their hull sides dropped open, revealing ped-
estal-mounted guns. The flat *whump* of the cannon
joined the rising chorus of small-arms fire.

Something else was firing, a little like a gatling gun
but not much. *Trotting out all the novelties for the party,*
he thought. *But they'll have to do better than this.*

The streets grew narrower as he got down onto the
flats where there were older buildings, sometimes leaning
out over the cobbles. The rough street hammered at the
car's suspension, and he had to squeeze the bulb of the
horn—and keep his speed up—to get through the
crowds. When he stopped, it was beneath a leaning tenement where laundry flapped from lines strung across
the street. The balconies were crowded with chattering
tenants pointing southward.

Jeffrey leaned out the window and flourished a coin.
"*Eh, bambino!*" he called.

A barefoot urchin with pants held up by a single sus-
pender elbowed through to him. "Tell Lucretzia Col-
lossi that Jeffrey is here to see her," he said. "And tell
her to bring her jewels. Another one of these if she's
here in five minutes."

The boy—he was about nine—grinned, showing gaps
in his teeth, and disappeared in a flash of bare heels.
Jeffrey got out of the car and waited tensely, one hand
on the butt of his revolver. He didn't expect trouble;
there were few Imperials his size, people in this neighborhood avoided uniforms, even unfamiliar ones, and
it wasn't really all that rough anyway. Still, no sense in
taking chances.

The spectators were disappearing from the balconies.
Finally showing some sense, he thought. A trickle of traffic appeared, heading north and uphill away from the
harbor. Then a woman hurried out of the tenement's

front doors. She was a year or two younger than him, dressed much better than the neighborhood standard, and extremely pretty in a dark full-figured way. She smiled at him, but there was a nervous wariness in her eyes; she carried her jewel box, and a small suitcase, moving like a dancer even now. Of course, she *was* a dancer, and quite a good one. Nice girl, even if she wasn't a nice girl, so to speak. And very useful. To recruit agents, he had to have respect; and to an Imperial, if Jeffrey didn't have a woman, he wasn't manly enough to take seriously. It generally paid to talk to people in their own language, he'd found.

Jeffrey flicked another coin to the boy and slid behind the wheel. Lucretzia kissed him as she took the passenger's seat.

"Is it the war?" she said.

"It is," Jeffrey replied. "With a vengeance."

"Where are we going?" Her voice rose.

Jeffrey did a sharp right and headed south down the alleyway. "The corniche. It's likely to be the quickest way to the consulate, and short of getting out of town, that's the safest place right now."

The growing crowd parted before the bow of the Sherrinford. The bumper rapped sharply against the wheel of a pushcart full of fruit; it spun away, showering oranges and melons into the crowd, and the owner screamed curses after the car. Jeffrey slid his revolver free and held it in his lap.

"Why . . ." Lucretzia licked her lips. "Why don't we do that, leave town?"

"Because a big flotilla of those dirigibles went right over when this all started," Jeffrey said grimly. "One gets you nine they dropped troops right on the main roads and the railway to Ciano."

probability 88%, ±2, Center said.

"But that would mean . . . that would mean a real *war*," she said.

Her voice rose a little again; Lucretzia was nobody's

fool. She had her career path planned out, down to the dressmaking shop she intended to buy, and her previous "friend" had been a post-captain in the Imperial Navy. The Imperials had been expecting a few skirmishes in the Passage, perhaps a raid or two, followed by some diplomatic chair-polishing. That had happened before.

The scenario had changed.

A new series of *thud* sounds punctuated the thought.

They came out of the narrow alleyway and onto the broad paved esplanade, and Lucretzia crossed herself. Battleship Row was plainly visible from here. Or would have been, if the warships between here and the naval docks hadn't been spewing so much black coal smoke from their sharply raked funnels.

"Damn," he said mildly. "Must be two dozen of them."

twenty-six, Center said. **including two which are damaged beyond minimal functionality.**

They were all the same type, slim little craft throwing plumes of water back from their sharply raked bows. Built for speed, with smooth turtlebacks over their forward decks to shed water; a light gun-turret behind that, and a multibarreled weapon of some sort aft. Alongside the funnels were pivot-mounted torpedo launchers, each with four U-shaped guide tubes fastened together.

None of the battlewagons had managed to get their main or secondary batteries into action. The heavy guns wouldn't have done much good, anyway, since they took so much time to train and reload. Several of them *had* gotten their quick-firers working; four-barreled cannon firing little two-pound shells at one per second per barrel, worked by lever-actions and fed from hoppers. The light weapons were a continuous crackle of noise and red tongues of flame along the sides of the big warships, with a pall of dirty gray smoke rising to the sky. Two of the Land vessels were dead in the water, burning and listing, with quick-firer shells sending up spurts of water all around them. The others bored in like wolves slashing at aurochos. Their speed was amazing, almost impossible.

thirty-one knots, Center said.

They must be turbine-powered, Jeffrey thought. He was vaguely conscious of driving, and of Lucretzia's nails digging into his shoulder. The Chosen had been experimenting with steam turbines for more than a decade now. Santander was doing the same, as a possible way to generate electric power. It was obvious that the Land had had other applications in mind.

Another Chosen destroyer was hit. This one staggered in the water, then vanished in a globe of fire that sent water and steel scrap and probably—undoubtedly—body parts up in a plume hundreds of meters high. The quick-firers must have hit the torpedo warheads. When the spray and smoke cleared the bow and stern of the light craft were already disappearing under the water.

Now the first flotilla of destroyers was within a thousand meters of the battleships. They peeled off, turning, heeling far over with the momentum of their charge. As each came to a quarter off their original course the torpedoes lanced overside in a hiss of steam from the launching cylinders. The long shapes splashed home into the still waters of the harbor and streaked towards their targets. The muzzles of the quick-firers depressed, trying to detonate the torpedoes before they struck, but they were only a few hundred meters away, and the destroyers' own weapons were raking the open firing positions. Jeffrey saw four tin fish strike the *Empress Imelda* from stern to three-quarters of the way to her bow.

Each of the warheads held over a hundred kilos of guncotton. Confined by the water, the explosions would punch holes big enough for two or three men to walk in abreast . . . and Imperial warships had lousy internal compartmentalization. For that matter, safe at anchor the watertight doors would be dogged open for convenience sake while they made ready for sea. He let out the throttle lever and braked to a stop.

"What are you *doing?*" Lucretzia asked.

"Taking a better look. Shut up for a second."

He pulled back the fabric top of the car and stood with his binoculars, bracing his elbows against the metal rim of the frame holding the windscreen. The *Empress* rolled over as he watched, shedding ant-tiny men. A few managed to run up onto the bottom as the weed- and barnacle-encrusted plates came into view, but the ship was settling fast as well as capsizing. Most of the rest of the heavy warships were listing or sinking. As he watched the *Emperor Umberto* blew up with a violence that was stunning even at this distance. Jeffrey shook his head and ignored the ringing in his ears, letting the binoculars thump down on his chest and sliding behind the wheel.

There were Land merchantmen heading in towards the docks, with uniformed figures crowding out from the holds onto the decks. He didn't want to be here when they arrived. His watch read 10:00. Barely an hour after the first dirigibles arrived overhead.

The Republic's legation in Corona was not far from the liner docks; most of its business was linked to the maritime trade. The highway up from the corniche was mostly empty now, except for a couple of craters and gasfires. Unfortunately, one of the craters occupied the site of the legation. From the looks of it, at least two or three six-hundred-kilo bombs had landed around it in a tight group. Nothing was left but shattered pieces of the limestone blocks which had made up the walls.

Christ.

His mind felt numb. Everyone he'd worked with for the past year was probably in there—most of them at least. The consul lived there, with his family. Captain Suthers. Andy Milson . . .

The instructors were right. Masonry doesn't have much resistance to blast damage.

"Christ," he said aloud.

He looked over at Lucretzia. She was looking at *him.*

CHAPTER FIVE

"Telegraph center under control, Captain," the runner said.

Gerta nodded. The troops assigned to that task included several who could duplicate the "fist" of the Imperial Navy signalmen.

She dabbed at the wound on her cheek with the back of her hand. Not serious, just a slice from a grenade fragment—you had to follow on quickly, to catch the opposition while they were still stunned from the blast. She'd been a little *too* quick, that was all. It just stung a little, no real damage, not worth taking time to bandage.

A deep breath. The Imperial commandant's office—he was an admiral, technically—was a segment of a wedge, one level down from the top of the tower. A window was dogged shut; the shutter was a half-meter of armorplate, but it was still a silly thing to do, weakening the structural integrity of the building that way. There was a fine Union rug, an ornate desk with several telephones—Imperial technology didn't run to efficient exchanges yet—and a smaller desk for the admiral's aide. He sprawled backward over it, most of his face missing and his brains leaking over the edge in a gelatinous puddle. The thin harsh smell of the new nitro powder was heavy in the room, under the stink of death.

Two signalers were working at the locking wheel of the window. They got it open, sliding it back like a pie-wedge of steel, and set up a heliograph.

"Send *phases one and two completed on schedule*," Gerta said.

A telephone rang, three sharp clatters. She picked it up.

"Yes, Vice-Admiral del'Gaspari," she said, holding a neckerchief over the pickup and pitching her voice low. With luck, her soprano would come across as a bad connection. "Admiral del'Fanfani will be here shortly. Speak louder, please, I cannot—" She pushed the receiver down. It began to ring again immediately.

Her Imperial was good enough, at least, complete with Ciano upper-class accent. But she hoped—ah.

The admiral came through the door, hands bound behind him; he was a tall thin man, balding, with white walrus mustaches. His eyes were fixed and blank, the stare of a man who is rejecting all the input his senses deliver. Behind him was a short fat woman, and a dark slim girl in her mid-teens. His wife and daughter; she recognized them from the files. Half a dozen troopers followed them.

"Sir. Commandant's quarters are secure."

Gerta nodded. The whole complex was in Chosen hands now. She looked at her watch. Twenty-seven minutes from start to finish. Amazing; it had actually gone *better* than planned. She'd expected it to take an hour at least.

"Good work, Sergeant." Then, more sharply: "Admiral del'Fanfani."

The old man straightened and blinked. "What is the meaning of this?" he said. "I demand—"

Gerta gestured. A trooper slammed the butt of his rifle home over the Imperial officer's kidneys; not too hard, but the man collapsed forward, his mouth working. The Chosen commandos hauled him upward. She stepped closer.

"It is necessary that you cooperate with us," she said. *Or at least be useful.* Nothing vital depended on it, but it would be handy. "You will speak as I direct."

The admiral drew himself up. "Never!" he said hoarsely.

Gerta shrugged. One of the ones holding the Imperial drew her knife and raise her eyebrows.

"No, I don't think a shank will make him sufficiently cooperative," she said. "We'll stick with the plan."

Intelligence had very complete dossiers on the Imperial command staff, and a fair grasp of their psychology. Imperials were odd about certain bodily functions.

One of her troopers swept a table clear of documents and oddments; they crashed to the floor with a tinkle of glass. Two more picked the daughter up and slammed her down on it, on her back.

"Papa!" she screamed, flailing and kicking her legs.

Then just screamed, as the troopers each grabbed a leg and bent them back until the knees nearly touched her shoulders. Another stepped up and grabbed the collar of her dress, running his dagger under it and slitting the heavy fabric down until it peeled off her. A few more strokes and the undergarments were cut. The soldier grinned, sliding the knife back into its sheath and unbuttoning his fly. He spat into one hand. Gerta spared them a glance—the girl was quite pretty, but female bodies did nothing for her erotically, and besides, this was business—and then turned back to the Imperial officer.

The girl's mother hit the ground with a heavy thud, her eyes rolling up in her head in a dead faint. The admiral was quivering like a racehorse in the starting gate, opening and closing his mouth.

"I will—" he began.

The girl gave a shrill cry. "Stop," Gerta said. The soldier did, which said a good deal for Chosen discipline.

"I will speak! Leave her alone!"

Gerta made a gesture, and the commandos released his daughter. The girl jackknifed into a fetal shrimp-curl on her side, face to knees, whimpering quietly. Gerta put a hand on the telephone.

"As long as you cooperate," she said. "You will speak as follows . . ."

"Damn!" Jeffrey said.

There was a barricade ahead, wagons and furniture and ripped-up paving blocks. Behind it were fifty or so Imperial soldiers and some sailors in their striped jerseys and berets. They all had rifles, and there was a six-barrel gatling on a field-gun mount. He looked up at the buildings on either side. More men there. *Somebody* around here had some faint conception of what he was supposed to be doing, but it was probably a junior officer. He braked and began to turn the car around.

"*Alto!*"

Men ran out from either side, pointing rifles. Single-shot rifles, but it only took one, and there were half a dozen pointing at him.

"Here's one of the Chosen dog-suckers now!"

The Imperial seaman who shouted that and poked his bayonet close had probably never seen a Land military uniform. On the other hand, he'd probably never seen one from the Republic of Santander, either.

"Take me to your officer!" Jeffrey said, loudly and clearly. "Immediately."

Reflex warred with hysteria in the young man's face. Jeffrey stepped down from the car, keeping his movements brisk but not threatening, and handed Lucretzia down to the pavement. She was a little pale, but she adjusted her hat and laid her hand on his arm in fine style. That probably pulled the soldiers out of their combination of funk and bloodlust; their mental picture of an invader didn't include a young Imperial woman dressed like a lady—not quite like a lady, but they wouldn't have the social skills to pick that up. They walked behind the pair up to the barricade, not quite hustling them.

The Imperial in charge was a naval lieutenant, about nineteen, with *INS Emperor Umberto* on his cuff. He also had acne, a pathetic attempt at a mustache, and the fixed look of a man doing his damndest in a situation he knew was utterly beyond him.

Lucky fellow, Jeffrey thought. *For now.*

"Lieutenant," he said. "Captain Jeffrey Farr, Republic of Santander Army."

"Captain," the young man said, saluting. "You will excuse me, but—"

"I understand," Jeffrey said smoothly. "Now, if you'll excuse *me*, I'm responsible for this young lady's safety and the consulate has been destroyed."

"The consulate? The Chosen have declared war on the Republic?"

The young Imperial lieutenant looked hopeful for a moment. Jeffrey felt slightly guilty.

"No, I'm afraid not—accident of war, but the rest of the consular staff are dead enough for all that. My government will doubtless lodge a complaint, but in the meantime, I'm a neutral."

"Then I will not detain you, sir," the lieutenant said.

Jeffrey hesitated for an instant. "Lieutenant . . . as one fighting man to another, are you in contact with your superiors?"

The lieutenant swallowed. "No, sir, I am not. The city telegraph and telephone lines appear to be inoperable or under enemy control."

"The Chosen are landing in force at the docks." That was less than half a kilometer away. "Lieutenant, without support, you haven't a prayer. I'd strongly advise you withdraw until you *do* get in contact with your chain of command."

It would be an even better idea to ditch the uniforms and weapons and hide in a cellar, then pretend to be harmless laborers, but he didn't think the young Imperial would take that sort of advice.

"If I have no orders, I have my duty; but thank you, Captain Farr. There are better than thirty thousand Imperial military personnel in Corona. If we all do something, the situation may yet be salvaged. You'd better go, this isn't your fight."

The hell it isn't. It wasn't his *battle*, though. If every Imperial officer had this one's aggression and instincts, Corona could have been saved. That was very unlikely.

He looked over his shoulder. Two of the Imperial soldiers were driving the car up to the barricade, and others were pushing aside a cart to give it room to pass.

"You understand, of course," the lieutenant went on, "I must commandeer your vehicle."

Jeffrey hadn't understood anything of the sort— although it would be invaluable, particularly with the communications network down. Cars weren't common in Corona. And it didn't make much sense to object, not when the Imperial had fifty or sixty armed men at his back. Lucretzia seemed more inclined to argue; Jeffrey took her by the arm and hurried her past.

"Where can we go without the car?" she hissed.

"Where could we go *with* it? The main roads are blocked. I'm trying to get to a safe house. Now *move*."

They walked quickly up the street. The crowds were thicker here, but milling around as if they weren't sure where to go. That included numbers in Imperial military uniforms. Columns of smoke were rising to the air from dozens of points in the city now. He looked at his watch. 11:00 hours.

BAAAAMM. A volley from the barricade a hundred meters behind them. The gatling there cut loose with a slow *braaaap . . . braaaap* as the operators turned its crank. Jeffrey half-turned, then recognized the next sound.

"Down!" he shouted, and pancaked, carrying the woman with him.

The whistling screech ended in a sharp *crack* about twenty meters back. Someone fell thrashing across Jeffrey's legs. He pushed at them with his feet, but the body resisted with the boneless slackness of a sack of rice; he had to roll onto his back and push with one boot to get the twitching weight free. That gave him an excellent view of what was coming up the roadway. Even at several hundred meters it looked huge, a rhomboid shape of riveted steel armor leaking steam along its flanks, with the Land's sunburst on its bow. Endless belts of linked metal plates supported it on either side. Between the top and bottom track each flank held a sponson-mounted cannon; 50mm by the look, light naval quick-firers. On the top of the boxy hull was a round turret mounting two thick shapes that must be the new water-cooled automatic machine-guns Intelligence had been reporting.

They were. The turret swiveled and the muzzles of the automatics flashed, with a sound like endless ripping canvas. Bullets chewed into the Imperial's barricade in a continuous stream, ripping wood into splinters and silencing the ineffectual rifles. Men turned and ran; the lieutenant waved his sword in their faces, trying to rally them. Then the other side-mounted cannon in the Chosen tank cut loose. The shell landed nearly at the Imperial officer's feet, exploding in a puff of smoke with a malignant red snap at its core. One of the lieutenant's boots was left, toppling over slowly. The rest of him was splashed across the paving blocks. In the silence that followed they could hear the tooth-grating squeal of steel on stone as the Chosen fighting vehicle ground up the slope towards them.

For a long moment, he was paralyzed. Instinct tugged at the small hairs along his spine. He'd seen war machines far worse in Center's scenarios, but this was *here*, lurching and grinding its way towards him. He didn't blame the Imperials for bugging out at all.

"Come on!" Lucretzia was tugging at his sleeve.

Good idea. Jeffrey took her hand and ran.

The basement room was hot and close, stuffy with their breath and sweat. Jeffrey put a cautious eye to the slat-covered cellar window, looking out. The firing had stopped, the slow banging of the Imperial rifles and the fast flat cracks of the Land repeaters. He could see one Imperial soldier trying to crawl away in the kitchen-garden outside, dragging his limp legs. Boots stepped up behind him, jackboots with gray uniform trousers tucked into them. A rifle with a knife-bayonet attached followed, pointed to the back of the wounded man's head. It barked, and the body slumped forward, hidden by the thigh-high corn.

Damn. It was pure bad luck, to get right to the edge of town—they were in a straggling suburb of market-gardens and villas—and then get caught up in a skirmish.

The Land soldier kneeled and went through his victim's pockets; then he paused to reload his rifle, pulling the bolt back and up, then thumbing in two stripper-clips of five rounds from the pouches on his webbing. He was a dark-tanned man of medium height, the helmet clipped to his belt revealing a shaven skull. The face below it was beetle-browed and hard; he looked to be exactly what he was, a highly-trained human pit bull. Savage, not too bright, but abundantly deadly. He smacked the bolt forward, chambering a round, and turned to shout a question over his shoulder. Someone answered in the same Protégé-accented Landisch, and three more joined him. Unseen others pounded away in lockstep, a platoon column by the sound of it.

Lucretzia had her hands locked over her mouth, eyes wide. *Been a hard day for her. Hell, for both of us.* He sincerely hoped she wouldn't scream.

They heard a door burst open above. Things smashed, crockery, glass. There was a sudden overpowering smell of wine. *Bad.* The Protégé soldiers must be so wrought up they weren't even stopping to loot more booze. He eased the revolver out of his holster and slowly, quietly thumbed back the hammer. It was a double-action, but saving a fraction of a second on the pull might be worthwhile. Jeffrey swallowed through a mouth gone cotton-dry. When they didn't find anything upstairs, they might just move along, probably they had a lot of territory to cover . . . they might not shoot at someone in the uniform of a neutral third country . . .

probability 8%, ±2.

Thanks. Just about his own calculation of the odds on Protégés understanding what "neutral" meant, or caring if they did.

Jackboots walked over the kitchen floor above them, making the planking creak and sending little trickles of dust down into the cellar. Slowly, the light in the basement took on a flat, silvery tone. Jeffrey set his teeth; he'd experienced what Center could do with his perceptions before, but he'd never liked it.

Neither did I, but you use what's to hand, Raj said. *To the right of the door.*

That stood at the top of a flight of stairs. It was thin pine boards; if there had been only one Land soldier, Jeffrey would have fired through them when the knob began to turn. But there were at least four.

The catch clicked, but the door didn't open immediately. Instead there was a slight *shink* sound . . . exactly what the point of a bayonet would sound like, touching on dry planking. Jeffrey's hand reached out to the knob, moving with an automatic precision that seemed detached and slow. He jerked it backward, and the Land soldier stumbled through. A grid dropped down over his sight, outlining the enemy. A green dot appeared right under the angle of the man's jaw. His finger stroked the trigger, squeezing.

Crack.

The soldier's head snapped sideways as if he'd been kicked by a horse. His helmet went flying off into the dimness of the cellar, dimness that made the muzzle flash strobe like a spear of reddish fire. It hid the flow of brain and bone that followed, but blood spattered back into Jeffrey's face. He was turning, turning, the pistol coming up. The second Land soldier was levelling her rifle, but the green dot settled on her throat.

Crack.

The woman fell back and writhed for an instant, blood spraying over everything, him, the stairs, the ceiling . . . The soldier behind her was jumping back, face slack with alarm. Out of sight, almost, but the green dot settled on his leg.

Crack.

A scream as the Land soldier tumbled out of sight. The grid outlined a prone figure against the planks of the entranceway and an aiming-point strobed. Jeffrey squeezed the trigger four times.

Oh shit. There was another one—

The bark of the rifle was much deeper than his pistol. The nickel-jacketed bullet was also much heavier and faster; it punched through the thin planking and ricochetted, whining around the stones of the cellar like a giant lethal wasp. Jeffrey tumbled back down the stairs, snapping open the cylinder of his revolver and shaking out the spent brass. He snapped the three-round speedloaders into the cylinder and flipped it closed— bad practice normally, but he was in a hurry—and skipped back two steps before firing again through the overhead planks. The soldier fired back the same way, three rounds rapid, and Jeffrey threw himself down again as the ricochettes spun through the cramped confines of the basement before thumping home into the piled-up firewood and potatoes.

Lucretzia was scrambling at the belt of the fallen Land soldier. *Damn, what's she doing?* Then: *Damnation, I should have taken his rifle!*

He scrabbled over to the corpse, ignoring what he was crawling through. Just before he reached it, Lucretzia figured out how to pull the tab on one of the potato-masher grenades the dead soldier had been carrying in loops at his belt. Her toss was underhand and rather weak; the grenade landed spinning on the top step of the cellar stairs and hung for a moment before it tumbled over the lip of the doorsill into the kitchen.

. . . three, four, five—

The confined space of the room upstairs magnified the blast, not nearly as much as having it go off in the cellar would have, of course. Jeffrey pounded up the stairs on the heels of the sound, caromed off the doorway and into the kitchen. The Land soldier was just staggering to her feet, blood running from her nose and ears. The green spot settled on the bridge of her nose, and Jeffrey's finger tightened.

Crack.

The flat brightness faded from his eyes. "Christ," he muttered, staggering. *I just killed five human beings.* He'd been in skirmishes before, minor stuff, but this . . .

this is what the world will be, for the rest of your life, Center said.

"You sure?" Jeffrey said.

Lucretzia nodded, looking down the street. "I am a danger to you. And you to me. Alone, I can fade into the city. Alone, you can move quickly—or find an enemy officer who will respect your neutrality."

The Imperial woman leaned forward and kissed him lightly. "I have the code. I will be in touch, Jeffrey. And thank you."

"You're welcome," he muttered, shaking his head.

a prudent decision, Center observed. **chances of survival are optimized for both individuals.**

"I still don't like it," Jeffrey said.

You'll like what comes next even less, lad, Raj said at the back of his mind. *You'd better find an officer and turn yourself in.*

chances of personal survival roughly equivalent to attempted flight in that scenario, Center said. **mission parameters—**

"I know, I know, mission first," he said. "Let's do it."

Reluctantly, he laid down the rifle he'd taken from the body of the Protégé trooper. Logically, he should already be inside the Chosen unit's skirmisher screen.

Depending on how closely they were following Land doctrine, and how screwed up things had gotten . . .

He began ghosting down the street, staying close to the buildings and pausing to listen. It was late afternoon, the sun cruelly beautiful as it slanted through the hazy air. He could hear the heavy *crump*ing of explosions from the south, down towards the river basin and the factory district. And closer, a rhythmic tramping.

He ducked into a doorway, the carved jamb and edge providing a little cover. A platoon of Land infantry were coming down the street, on alternate sides by eight-trooper squads; jog-trotting effortlessly with their bay-onetted rifles across their chests at the port. And yes, an officer with them.

"Gestan!" he called out in Landisch. "Wait! *Nie shessn!* Don't shoot!"

A whisle blew, and the platoon went to earth in trained unison, weapons bristling outward. He stepped forward, hands in the air and uneasily conscious of how his tes-ticles were trying to crawl up into his stomach.

"Attention!" he barked at the two Protégé riflemen who came running up at a crouch.

They stiffened instinctively at the bark in upper-class Landisch.

"Take me to your officer immediately," he went on, walking past them at a brisk stride and tucking his swag-ger stick under his left arm. He could hear the silence of hesitation behind him, and then the clack of hobnails on the brick pathway as they followed. Doubtless the points of the bayonets were hovering an inch or so from his kidneys. *Got to maintain the momentum.*

The officer was waiting with a folded map in her hand and a bulky automatic pistol in the other. Blue eyes nar-rowed as they recognized his brown Santander uniform, and he could sense thoughts moving behind them. *She's in the middle of a mission and doesn't need complica-tions,* Jeffrey thought. The hand holding the pistol gave a slight unconscious twitch. *One bullet in the head, and there's no complication at all*. If anyone found his body, it would be an unfortunate accident.

"Captain, Jeffrey Farr, Army of the Republic," he said, staluting casually with a touch of the swagger stick to the brim of his peaked cap. "Congratulations, *fahnrich*, on a soldierly job of work—taking a city this size by storm is quite an accomplishment!"

He extended his hand. The Chosen officer took it automatically; at close range he could see that she wasn't more than twenty, under the cropped hair and hard muscularity. There was a trace of baffled hesitation at this glib stranger who spoke the tongue of the Chosen like a native. He gave a firm squeeze and pumped the hand up and down once.

Good work, Raj said. ***Personal contact always makes it a little more difficult to shoot someone.***

"Most impressive. Now, since you've got the situation well in hand, if I could trouble you for an escort to your colonel?"

"Jeffrey Farr?" the Chosen colonel said. His square, blond-stubbled face split in an unexpected smile. "Well, I'll be cursed. We're relatives, of a sort—Colonel Heinrich Hosten, at your service, Captain."

The command post was set up in a small park, a few officers grouped around tables carried out from nearby houses. Heinrich Hosten was a big man, easily an inch or two over Jeffrey's six feet, and broad-shouldered, slab-built. A pair of field glasses were hanging around his neck, and there was a square of surgical gauze lightly spotted with blood taped to the side of his bull neck.

He spoke fairly loudly; a battery of mule-drawn field guns was trotting by on the stone-block pavement beyond the park; Jeffrey's mind catalogued them automatically, M–298's, the new standard piece—75mm calibre, split trail, shield, hydropneumatic recuperators that returned the tube to battery position after every round. Behind them came a brace of field ambulances, also

mule-drawn—the animals looked as if they'd been commandeered locally—that pulled aside to let stretcher-
bearers take their contents to a church being used as
an aid station. More troops were marching up from the
harbor, passing the banner and waiting motorcycle cou-
riers of the regimental HQ.

Jeffrey smiled back at the Chosen colonel. *Damned
dangerous man,* he thought, remembering John's descrip-
tion. *Not at all the guileless bruiser he looked. Smart.
Dedicated.*

Bet he's glad of an audience, Raj said. *These john-
nies haven't fought a war in a long time. They're
good, but they want to show off, too.*

"Looks like you caught the dagoes asleep at the tiller,"
Jeffrey said, turning and shading his eyes with his hand.
He touched the cased glasses at his side with his hand.
"If you don't mind?"

"*Klim-bim,*" Heinrich said; a useful Chosen expression which could mean anything from *affirmative* to *all's
right with the world.*

Jeffrey focused the glasses. Nothing was left of the
Imperial fleet that he could see; black stains on the surface, the protruding masts of a couple of battlewagons.
Fire and billowing columns of dark smoke marked the
naval basin; warships and merchantmen were burning,
sinking, or listing all over the harbor. Black flags with
golden sunbursts marked both the great fortresses at the
entrance to the harbor, although Fort Ricardo on the
south had the burnt-out skeleton of a dirigible draped
over it. The Land's flag also flew over the governor's
palace off to the west, and the city hall and railway station directly south. Fires were burning out of control
in a dozen places, vivid against the dusk of evening, and
there was a continuous staccato crackle of small-arms
fire over the mass of tile rooftops.

"Looks like you've cut them up into pockets," Jeffrey
said.

"*Ja.* Easier than we anticipated. Speed and planning

and impact. There were a lot of them, but we had the jump from the beginning. Light casualties."

"And you had those . . . what are they called, those moving fortresses?"

"*Tanks*." Heinrich snorted, and a few of the other officers smiled sourly. "Terrifying when they work, which is less than half the time. We're supposed to have one here."

Jeffrey turned his glasses northward; the city suburbs thinned out from here, although it was harder to see since there wasn't a slope over the intervening ground.

"You're preparing for counterattack?" he said.

Heinrich laughed again and jerked a thumb at the dirigible passing overhead. "I love those things," he said. "We dropped battalion-sized task forces with lots of automatic weapons at the road-rail junctions halfway to Veron. The wops have something like six divisions concentrating there, but there's no way they can do a damned thing for a week—and by then we'll have linked up with the airborne forces, plus we'll have landed the better part of an army corps."

Jeffrey nodded, pasting a smile on his face. That seemed like a very good analysis. But there were times when you wanted so *badly* to be wrong.

"Impressive," he said.

Heinrich laughed heartily. "Stay with us for a while," he said. "And we'll show you impressive."

CHAPTER SIX

"In the sight of Almighty God, God the Parent, God the Child, God the Spirit, I pronounce these two as one. What God has joined, let none dare put asunder."

John Hosten gripped Pia's hand, conscious that his own was slightly damp and sweaty. The long embroidered cord was bound around their joined hands and wrists in the ritual knot. Incense rose towards the tall vaulted ceiling of the cathedral. The wedding party was small and sparse, old Count del'Cuomo in his dress outfit, a few other men in Imperial field uniform, some friends from the embassy. They rattled like a handful of peas in the huge, dim, scented stone bulk of the place, lost in the patterns of light from the stained-glass windows that occupied most of its walls.

He raised her veil and kissed her, soft contact and a scent of verbena.

The priest raised his staff for the blessing, then halted, listening.

They all did, and looked upward. A dull *crump . . . crump . . .* came in the distance; everyone in Ciano knew that sound now. Hundred-kilo bombs from a Chosen dirigible bomber, working its way across the sky at two thousand meters.

"Down by the docks," John whispered to himself, "trying for the gasworks."

probability 93%, ±2, Center said.

"John!"

He looked down at Pia. Her lips were fixed in

98

determination. "This is my wedding day. I will not let those *tedeschi* pigs interfere with it."

Pia's tone was conversational, but it carried in the stillness of the cathedral. A murmur of approval went through the watchers. John could feel Raj smiling at the back of his mind.

You're a lucky man.

"I *am* a lucky man," John murmured aloud.

count no man lucky until he is dead, Center observed.

The open-topped car hummed down the roadway, gravel crunching under the hard rubber of its wire-spoked wheels, throwing a rooster-tail of dust behind it. Shade flicked welcome across John's face from the plane trees planted beside it, each one whitewashed to the height of a man's chest. Through the gaps he could see the fields, mostly wheat in this district, with the harvest just finishing. Stooks of shocked grain drew a lacy pattern across the level fields; here and there peasants were finishing off a corner of a poplar-lined field with flashing sickles. Ox-drawn carts were in the field, piled high with yellow grain, hauling the harvest to the barns and threshing floors; the laborers would spend the rainy winter beating out the grain with flails.

Damn, but that's backward, John thought, holding the map across his knees with his hands to keep the wind from fluttering it. At home in Santander, all the bigger farms had horse-drawn reapers these days, and portable steam threshing machines had been around for a generation.

Downright homelike for me, Raj said. *Except that there weren't many places on Bellevue as fertile as this. Fattest peasants I've ever seen.*

The road climbed slightly, through fields planted to alfalfa, and then into hilly vineyards around a white-painted village. He scrubbed at his driving goggles with the tail-end of his silk scarf and squinted. The guidebooks said the village had a "notable square bell tower" and a minor *palazzo*.

"Castello Formaso," John called ahead to the driver. "This ought to be it."

It was; most of an Imperial cavalry brigade were camped in and around the town. Cavalry wore tight scarlet pants and bottle-green jackets, with a high-combed brass helmet topped with plumes, and they were armed with sabers, revolvers, and short single-shot carbines. You could follow those polished brass helmets a long way; there were patrols out all across the plain to the west of town, riding down laneways and across fields and pastures, disappearing into the shade of orchards and coming out again on the other side. The troopers closer to hand were watering their horses or working on tack or doing the other thousand and one chores a mounted unit needed.

The road was thick with mounted men, parting reluctantly to the insistent *squeeee-beep!* of the car's horn. Animals shied or kicked at the unfamiliar sound; one connected with the bodywork in an expensive and tooth-grating crunch of varnished ashwood.

Then the car swerved under a brutal wrench at the wheel. John looked up from his map in the back seat as it flung him against the sidewall; his broad-brimmed hat went over into the roadside dust. A dirigible was passing overhead, nosing out of a patch of cloud at about six thousand feet. A six-hundred-footer, *Eagle*-class, reconaissance model. Some of the Imperial cavalry were popping away at the airship with their carbines, and in the village square ahead they had an improvised anti-aircraft mounting for a gatling gun—a U-shaped iron framework on a set of gears and cams. The carbines were merely a nuisance, but letting off six hundred rounds a minute straight up was a *menace*.

"You there!" John barked, tapping the shoulder of his driver. The car came to a halt with a tail-wagging emphasis as the man stood on the brakes. John vaulted out over the rear door and strode towards the gatling.

"You there!" John continued, rapping at the frame with his cane for emphasis. The Imperial NCO in charge looked up. "That thing is out of range, and you'd be dropping spent rounds all over town. Do *not* open fire."

The soldier braced to attention at a gentleman's voice. John nodded curtly and turned to where the cavalry brigade's command group were sitting under a vine-grown pergola in the courtyard of the village *taverna*.

Nothing wrong with their nerves, John thought. The portly brigadier had his uniform jacket unbuttoned, his half-cloak across the back of his chair, and a huge plate of pasta and breaded veal in front of him. Several straw-wrapped bottles of the local vintage kept the food company. He looked up as John rapped out his orders at the gatling crew, his face purpling with rage as the stranger strode over to his table.

"And who the hell are you? *Teniente*, get this civilian out of here!"

John bowed with a quick jerk of his head, supressing an impulse to click heels. Showing Chosen habits was *not* the way to make yourself popular around here right now.

"I am John Hosten, accredited charge d'affaires with the Embassy of the Republic of Santander," he said crisply. He pulled out a sheaf of documents. "Here are my credentials."

"I don't care shit for—" The Imperial officer stopped, paling slightly under his five o'clock shadow. "The signore John Hosten who married Pia del'Cuomo?"

Who is the favorite daughter of the Minister of War, yes, John thought. "The same, sir," he continued aloud. "Here to observe the course of the war."

"Excellent!" the brigadier said, a little too heartily, mopping his mouth on a checkered linen napkin. "We drove these pig-grunting beasts into the sea once before centuries ago, and you can watch it done again!"

A murmur of agreement came from the other officers around the table, in a wave of wineglasses and elegant cigarette holders. Polished boots struck the flagstones in emphasis. John inclined his head.

Considering that we're four hundred kilometers west of Corona and he doesn't know fuck-all about where the enemy's main force is, I'd say that was just a little over-optimistic, Raj commented dryly.

"Brigadier Count Damiano del'Ostro," the portly cavalryman said, extending a hand. "At your service, *signore.*"

John shook the plump, beautifully manicured hand extended to him in a waft of cologne and garlic, and looked up. The Land dirigible was gliding away on a curving pathway that would take it miles to the east, down the road to the capital and then back towards the Pada River near Veron. According to the newspapers, a strong Imperial garrison was holding out in that river port, preventing the Land's forces from using it to supply their forward elements.

You could believe as much of that as you wanted to. John did know that at least ten Imperial infantry divisions and two of cavalry were concentrating—slowly—at a rail junction about fifty miles east; he'd driven through them that morning. The dirigible was doing about seventy-five miles an hour. It would be there in three-quarters of an hour, and reporting back in two. John looked back at the cavalry commander, who was supposed to be locating the Land's armies and screening the Imperial forces from observation.

"You've located the enemy force, Brigadier del'Ostro?" he said.

The brigadier twirled at one of his waxed mustachios. "Soon, soon—our cavalry screen is bound to make contact soon. The cowards refuse to engage our cavalry under any circumstances. Why, *their* cavalry are mounted on *mules,* if you can believe it."

"The Land doesn't have any cavalry, strictly speaking,"

John pointed out gently. "They have some mounted infantry units on mules, yes. One mule to two men; they take turns riding. They march very quickly."

Del'Ostro laughed heartily and slapped a hand to his saber. "Without cavalry, they will be blind and helpless. Desperate they must already be; do you know, they let *women* into their army?"

John smiled politely with the chorus of laughter. *I hope you never meet my foster-sister,* he thought. *Then again, considering that you're partly responsible for this, I hope you do meet Gerta.*

"Come, I'll show you how my men scout!" del'Ostro said.

He threw the napkin to the table and strode out, buckling his tunic and calling orders. He and his staff headed towards four Santander-made touring cars, evidently the mechanized element of this outfit. Guards crashed to attention, a drum rolled, a bugle sounded, and Brigadier Count del'Ostro mounted to the backseat, standing and holding the pole of a standard mounted in a bracket at the side of the car.

"Hate to think what those spurs are doing to the upholstery," John murmured to himself—in Santander English, which the driver did not speak. "Follow," he added in Imperial. "But not too close."

"*Si, signore,*" the driver said.

John opened a wicker container bolted to the rear of the front seat and brought out his field glasses; big bulky things, Sierra-made, the best on the market.

"Halt," he said after a moment.

Steam chuffed, and the engine hissed to a stop. The car coasted and then braked to one side of the road, under the shade of a plane tree. John pushed up his driving goggles again and leaned his elbows on the padded leather of the chauffeur's seat.

Brigadier del'Ostro had forgotten his foreign audience in his enthusiasm. His party swept down the long straight road in a plume of dust and a chorus of loyal cries; the mounted units using the road scattered into the ditches, not a few troopers losing their seats. One light field gun went over on its side, taking half its team with it, and lay with the upper wheel spinning in the cars' wake. John ignored them, scanning to the west over the rolling patchwork of grainfields and pasture. There weren't any peasants in that direction; he supposed they were too sensible to linger when the Imperial cavalry screen arrived.

There *were* spots of smoke on the skyline: burning grain-ricks, perhaps, or buildings. He didn't think that the Land's forces would be burning as they came, too wasteful and conspicuous, but fires followed combat as surely as vultures did.

Ah. A dull thudding noise, like a very large door being slammed some distance away. It repeated again and again, at slow intervals. Artillery.

Over a rise a mile away came a bright spray of Imperial cavalry; some of them were turning to fire behind them with their carbines. Little white puffs of smoke rose from their position. Then came a long rattling crackle. A shape lurched over the rise, and two more behind it. John focused his glasses; it was a big touring car, with a carapace of bolted steel plate on its chassis, and a hatbox-shaped turret on top. Two fat barrels sprouted from the turret's face: water-cooled machine guns. They fired again, a long ripping sound, faint with distance. Men and horses fell in a tangled, kicking mass, and the screaming of the wounded animals carried clearly. The Sierra binoculars were excellent; he could see carbine slugs ricochetting off the gray-painted metal in sparking impacts, leaving smears of soft lead and bright patches where bare metal was exposed.

"Driver, reverse," John said calmly. *Because this is no longer near the front. I think it's just become a salient about to be pinched off.*

Nothing happened. He looked down; the driver was staring westward, too, hands white-knuckled on the wheel of the car.

"Driver!"

He rapped a shoulder, and the chauffeur came out of his funk like a man broaching deep water, shaking his head.

"Get us out of here, man. *Now.*"

"*Si, signore!*"

He wrenched at the wheel and reversing lever, got the long touring car around without putting it into either of the roadside ditches although one wheel hung on the edge for a heart-stopping moment. John reversed himself, kneeling and looking back along the road.

More and more of the Imperial cavalry were pouring back towards the village of Castello Formaso; the ones there were streaming out of town heading east, or dismounting and deploying around the town. The party with Brigadier del'Ostro were trying to backtrack as well, but two of the cars had collided and blocked the road. As he watched, machine-gun fire raked the tangle, punching through the wood and thin sheet metal of the vehicles as easily as it did the brightly uniformed bodies that flopped and tumbled around them. Brigadier del'Ostro was still standing on the seat, waving his sword when his car exploded in a shower of parts and burning gasoline. The wreckage settled back, rocking on the bare rims of the wheels, and men ran flaming from the mass.

And over the hill where the armored cars had appeared came a column. John focused on it: Land troops, half mounted on mules, the other half trotting alongside, each soldier holding on to a stirrup leather. As he watched they halted, the mounted half dismounted, handlers took the mules by the reins, and the whole column shook itself out into a line advancing in extended order. Behind them, teams were unloading machine guns with their tripods and boxes of ammunition belts from pack mules.

He could imagine the *clink-clank-snap* sounds as the heavy weapons with their fat water-filled jackets were dropped onto the fastenings and clamped home; the operators raising the slides, feeding the tab at the end of the belt through, snapping the slide back down, jerking back the cocking lever and settling in with their hands on the spade grips and thumbs on the butterfly trigger while the officer looked through his split-view range finder . . .

"Faster," he said to the driver, licking salt off his upper lip.

His hand went to check the revolver under his left armpit; there was a pump-action shotgun in a scabbard on the back of the driver's seat. Nothing much, but it might come in handy if worst came to worst.

"Uh-oh," he mumbled involuntarily, looking ahead. Castello Formoso was a solid jammed mass of riders, horses, carriages and carts and field guns and ambulances.

Shoomp. His head came up and looked eastward, beyond the village. *Whonk!* An explosion on the road; nothing dramatic, not nearly as large as a field-gun shell, but definitely something exploding. John tracked left and right with the binoculars. More armored cars.

Those things couldn't mount a cannon! he thought.

examine them again, please. Center thought.

The war machines were insectile dots, even with the powerful glasses. A square appeared before John's eyes, and the image of the car leaped into it, magnified until it seemed only a few yards away. The picture was grainy, fuzzy, but grew clearer as if waves of precision were washing across it several times a second.

maximum enhancement, Center said. The round cheesebox turrets of these held only one machine gun; beside it was a tube, canted up at a forty-five degree angle.

mortar, Center said. **probable design—**

A schematic replaced the picture of the armored car. A simple smoothbore tube, breaking open at the breech like a shotgun, with a brass cup to seal it, firing a finned bomb with rings of propellant clipped on around the base.

Shoomp. Whonk! They were dropping mortar shells on the main road, stopping the outflow of men and carts from the village. The mounted troopers were spilling out into the vineyards on either side in a great disorderly bulge, but the trellised vines were a substantial obstacle even to horses. A few officers were trying to organize, and a field gun was being wheeled out to return fire at the war-cars.

And as sure as death, there's a flanking force ready to put in an attack to follow up those armored cars, Raj thought.

It all happened so quickly! John thought.

It always does, when somebody fucks the dog bigtime, Raj thought grimly. *I knew officers like del'Ostro well. Mostly because I broke so many of them out of the service; and whoever's running the show on the enemy side is a professional. Those aren't bad troops, but they're dogmeat now. Get out while you can, son.*

Good advice, but it looked easier said than done. John took two deep breaths, then stood in the base of the car and held onto one of the hoops that held the canvas top when it was up.

"Driver," he said. "Take that laneway." It was narrow and rutted, but it led east—and at at an angle, southeast, away from where the Land war-cars had appeared.

"*Signore*—"

"Do it."

It would *not* be a good thing to be captured, particularly given what was strapped up in the luggage in the rear boot of the car. He doubted, somehow, that diplomatic immunity would extend to not searching him, and Land Military Intelligence would be *very interested* to find out what he had planned.

"Jeffrey, I hope you're doing better than I am," he muttered.

CHAPTER SEVEN

"Watch this," Heinrich said. "This is going to be funny, the first bit."

Jeffrey Farr took a swig from his canteen—four-fifths water and one-fifth wine, just enough to kill most of the bacteria. The machine gunner ahead of them made a final adjustment to her weapon by thumping it with the heel of her hand, then stroked the bright brass belt of ammunition running down to the tin box on the right of the weapon.

The command staff of the Fifteenth Light Infantry (Protégé) was set up not far behind the firing line, on a small knoll covered in long grass and scrub evergreen oak. The infantry companies of the regiment were fanning out on either side, taking open-order-prone positions; many were unlimbering the folding entrenching tool from their harnesses, mounding earth in front of themselves, as protection and to give good firing rests.

He looked behind. An aid station was setting up, a heavy weapons company was putting their 82mm mortars in place, a reserve company was waiting spread out and prone, ammunition was coming down off the packmules and being carried forward. . . .

"Very professional," he said.

Heinrich nodded, beaming, as pleased as a child with an intricate toy. "*Ja*. Although this hasn't been much of a challenge so far. I do wish we still had those armored cars assigned to us, though."

Jeffrey took another swig at the canteen. He was parched, and his feet hurt like blazes, even worse than the muscles in his calves and thighs. The weather was hot and dry, and the spearhead of the Land forces had been moving *fast*. Everyone was supposed to be able to do thirty miles a day, day in and day out, with full load, and the Chosen officers were supposed to do *better* than their Protégé enlisted soldiers. After four weeks with them, he was starting to believe some of the things the Chosen said about themselves. Company-grade officers and up were entitled to a riding animal—mules, in this outfit—but he'd rarely seen one using a saddle except to get around more quickly during an engagement. Heinrich's light-infantry regiment moved even faster than the rest, and they treated the dry, dusty heat of a mainland summer as a holiday from the steambath mugginess of the Land.

Through his field glasses, the approaching Imperial force looked professional too, in its way. The cavalry were maintaining their alignment neatly, despite the losses they'd had in the last few engagements, in blocks a hundred wide and three ranks deep, with a pennant at the center of each, advancing at a trot. Light field guns and gatlings bounced and rattled forward between each regiment of horse; the whole Imperial line covered better than two kilometers, and infantry were deployed behind it, coming forward at the double in a loose swarm.

"How many would you say?" Jeffrey asked.

"Oh, four thousand mounted," Heinrich said. "The foot—"

He turned to another officer, one stooping to look through a tripod-mounted optical instrument.

"Better part of two brigades, from the standards, sir," she said. "Say seven to nine thousand, depending on whether they were part of the bunch that tried to force the line of the Volturno."

Jeffrey looked left and right; three battalions, less losses; say fifteen hundred rifles, with one machine gun to a company and a dozen mortars.

"Rather long odds, wouldn't you say?" he said.

"Oh, it'll do," Heinrich replied. He began stuffing tobacco into a long curved pipe with a flared lip and a hinged pewter cover. "Mind you"—he struck a match with his thumbnail and puffed the pipe alight, speaking around the stem—"I wouldn't mind if the rest of the brigade came up, or at least that *ferdammt* artillery we're supposed to have, but it'll do."

The Chosen colonel turned his head slightly. "*Fahnrich* Klinghoffer; mortars to concentrate on enemy crew-served weapons, commencing at two thousand meters. Automatic weapons at fifteen hundred, infantry at eight hundred; flank companies to be ready to swing back. Runner to General Summelworden, and we're engaged to our front; attempted enemy break-out. Dispositions as follows—"

Messengers trotted off on foot; one stamped a motorcycle into braying life and went rearward in a spray of dust and gravel. That would be the message to rear HQ—there were only three of the little machines attached to the regiment and they were saved for the most important communications.

"Wouldn't a wireless set be useful?" Jeffrey asked.

Heinrich gestured with his pipe. "Not really. Too heavy and temperamental to be worth the trouble; telegraphs are bad enough—the last thing any competent field commander wants is to have an elecric wire from Supreme HQ stuck up his arse. Let them do their jobs, and we'll do ours."

I wouldn't have minded having this fellow working for me, Raj thought.

chosen staff training ensures uniformity of method, Center noted. **this reduces the need for communications.**

"Twenty-two hundred," the officer at the optical said. "Picking up the pace."

"Still, twelve thousand to two . . ." Jeffrey said.

Heinrich grinned disarmingly. "We're holding the neck of the bag. All we have to do is delay them long enough for the rest of the corps to come up, and they've lost better than two hundred thousand men. Worth a risk."

Jeffrey nodded. Down below the riflemen finished digging and were snuggling the stocks of their weapons into their shoulders; a few pessimists were setting out grenades close to hand. The machine gunners sat behind their weapons, elbows on knees, bending to look through the sights: all Chosen, he noticed—one Chosen NCO as gunner, five Protégé privates to fetch and carry and keep the weapon supplied with ammunition and water.

The Imperial field gunners halted their teams, wheeling the guns and running them off the limbers. The clang of the breechblocks was lost under the growing, drumming thunder of thousands of hooves. Elevating wheels spun. The Imperial guns were simple black-powder models with no recoil gear; they'd have to be pushed back into battery after every shot, but there were a lot of them.

Behind Jeffrey, hands poised mortar bombs over the muzzles. The Chosen officer at the optical raised her hand, then chopped it downward.

Schoonk. Schoonk. Schoonk. Twelve times repeated.

The mortar shells began dropping. Each threw up a minor shower of dirt, like a gigantic raindrop hitting silt. The first rounds dropped all across the axis of the Imperial advance, some ahead of it, some behind; four or five plowed into the mass of cantering horsemen, sending animals and men to the ground. The ranks expanded around the casualties, then closed up again with a long ripple.

The observers called corrections. *Schoonk. Schoonk . . .* This bracket landed much closer to the Imperial field guns. One landed on a limber, which went up in a giant globe of orange fire, shells whistling across the sky like fireworks. The noise was loud even at this distance. Another went up a second later.

"Tsk, tsk," Heinrich said. "Sympathetic detonation— too close together. Careless."

In Landisch, saying someone was sloppy was a serious moral criticism, worse than theft, although not quite as bad as eating your children. The Chosen assumed courage; what they really respected was an infinite capacity for taking pains.

An Imperial gun cut loose in an enormous puff of off-white smoke. Something went overhead in a tearing rising-pitch whistle and exploded behind them, sending a poplar tree shape of dirt into the air. The next shell hammered short, just beyond the Land infantry line. One over, one under, which meant . . .

Heinrich made a small gesture with one hand; everyone whose job permitted it went to ground, including Jeffrey Farr. He wished he had one of the Land helmets; even a thin layer of stamped manganese-nickel steel was a comforting thing to have between you and an airburst.

Crack. The next shell *was* an airburst, a little off-center and a bit high up. Imperial fuses weren't very modern, either, so that was good shooting with what they had available. Somebody screamed nearby, and a call went up for stretcher-bearers. Guns were firing all along the Imperial line now, but the hooves were louder.

Much louder. The cavalry were swinging into a gallop, and as he watched the sabers came out, a thousandfold twinkling in the hot sunlight, like slivers of mirrored glass. The troopers swung the swords down, holding them forward along the horses' necks with the blades parallel to the ground. On his belly, Jeffrey could feel the thunder of thousands of tons of horseflesh thudding into the ground on metal-shod hooves.

"Steady now, steady," Heinrich murmured to himself, glancing left and right at his regiment.

Jeffrey stared at the approching Imperials with a complex mixture of emotions. If they overran this position, he'd probably die . . . and he'd like nothing better than to see the Chosen stamped into the earth by the hooves, cut apart by those sabers, pistoled, annihilated. But he didn't want to share the experience, if possible.

Beneath that his mind was calculating, measuring distances by the old trick of how much you could see—so many yards when a man was a dot, so many when you could make out his arms, his legs, the belts of his equipment. The Land soldiers were doing the same. Behind them the mortars kept up a steady *schoonk . . . schoonk . . .* stopping now and then to adjust their aim.

The machine gun cut loose with a stuttering rattle, faster and more rhythmic than the gatlings he was familiar with. Every fourth round was tracer, and they arched out pale in the bright sunlight. More of the automatics opened up along the regiment's line. The closest gunner traversed smoothly, tapping off four-second bursts, smiling broadly to herself.

Jam, Jeffrey prayed. *Jam, damn you, jam tight!*

But they didn't jam. The cavalry charge disintegrated instead, hundreds of horses and men falling in a few seconds. At the gallop there was no time to halt, no chance to pull aside. The first rank went down as if a giant scythe had cut their legs from beneath them, and the succeeding ones piled into them in a kicking, rolling, tumbling wave of thousand-pound bodies that reached three layers high in places. He could see men thrown twenty feet and more as their mounts ran into that long hillock of living flesh, saw them crushed under tons of thrashing horse. The sound was indescribable, the shrill womanish shrieking of the horses and the desperate wailing of men.

Tacktacktacktacktacktacktack—

A shell landed near one of the machine guns, probably by sheer chance, leaving a tangle of flesh and twisted metal. The others continued, concentrating on the main mass of stalled horsemen; individual riders came forward, and dismounted men—horses were bigger targets than humans. Some of them were firing their carbines as they came. Far beyond their range, but not that of the

Landisch magazine-rifles, with high-velocity jacketed slugs and smokeless powder. Land riflemen opened up, the slower *crack . . . crack . . .* of their weapons contrasting with the rapid chatter of the machine guns.

Imperials fell; the Land infantry could fire ten or twelve aimed rounds a minute, and they were all good shots. More green-uniformed soldiers crowded forward, some crawling, others running in short dashes. There were infantry in peaked caps among them now, as well as the dismounted cavalry. One of the big soft-lead slugs whipcracked by Jeffrey, uncomfortably close; he hugged the dirt tighter. Not far away a Land soldier sprawled backwards kicking and blowing a froth of air and blood through his smashed jaw. Others crawled forward to drag the wounded back to where the stretcher-bearers could get at them, then crawled back to their firing positions.

"Hot work," Heinrich said, propping himself up on his elbows. "Ah, I expected that."

More and more Imperials were filtering up, taking cover behind the piles of dead horses and men, working around the edges of the Land regiment. Steam hissed from the safety cap on the top of the jacket of the machine gun in front of the knoll; a Protégé soldier rose to fetch more water and pitched back with a grunt like a man belly-punched, curling around the wound in his stomach. He sprawled open-eyed after a second's heel-drumming spasm, and another rose to take his place. The Chosen gunner wrapped her hand in a cloth and unscrewed the cap. Boiling water heaved upward and pattered down on the thirsty soil, disappearing instantly and leaving only a stain that looked exactly like that left by the soldier's blood. Soldiers poured their canteens into the weapon's thirsty maw, and the gunner took the opportunity to switch barrels.

"Sir! *Hauptman* Fedrof reports enemy moving to our left in force—several thousand of them. Infantry, with guns in support."

Jeffrey saw Heinrich frown, then unconsciously look

behind to where the supports would be coming from . . . if they came.

"Move one company of the reserve to the left. Refuse the flank, pull back a little to that irrigation ditch and laneway. Tell the mortars to fire in support on request. And *Fahnrich* Klinghoffer, get me a report on our ammunition reserves."

"Hot work," Jeffrey said.

"*Watch* it!" John barked involuntarily as the left wheels of his car nearly went into the ditch.

The refugees were swarming on both sides of the road, trampling through the maize fields on both sides and gardens. Every once and a while they surged uncontrollably back onto the roadway, blocking the westbound troops in an inextricable snarl of handcarts, two- and four-wheeled oxcarts, mule-drawn military supply wagons, guns, limbers . . .

"Take the turnoff up ahead," he said, as the vehicle inched by a stalled sixteen-pounder field gun.

The gun had a six-horse hitch, with a trooper riding on the off horse of every pair. They looked at him with incurious eyes, glazed with fatigue, bloodshot in stubbled, dirt-caked faces. The horses' heads drooped likewise, lips blowing out in weary resignation. From the looks of them, the men had already been in action, and somebody had gotten this column organized and heading back towards the fight. For that matter, there were plenty of Imperial soldiers in the vast shapeless mob of refugees heading eastward away from the fighting—some in uniform and carrying their weapons, others shambling along in bits and pieces of battledress, a few bandaged, most not.

The car crept along the column, the driver squeezing the bulb of the horn every few feet, heading west and towards the blood-red clouds of sunset. It was risky—the chances of meeting an officer who wasn't particularly impressed with the son-in-law of the war minister increased with every day, and a car was valuable, even one with hoof-marks in the bodywork.

Better than going the other way. When he was heading away from the fighting, the refugees kept trying to get aboard. It was really bad when the mothers held up their children; a few had even tried to toss the infants into the car.

They turned up a farm lane, over a low hill that hid them from the road, past the encampments of the refugees; some were lighting fires, others simply collapsing where they stood. The sun was dropping below the horizon, light turning purple, throwing long shadows from the grain-ricks across the stubblefields. The lane turned down by a shallow streambed, into a hollow fringed with trees. An old farmhouse stood there, the sort of thing a very well-to-do peasant farmer would have, built of ashlar limestone blocks, with four rooms and a kitchen. Outbuildings stood around a walled courtyard at the back; a big dog came up barking and snarling as the car pulled into the stretch of graveled dirt in front of the house.

Two men followed it, both carrying shotguns. One shone a bull's-eye lantern in John's face.

"You are?" the man behind the lantern said.

"John Hosten," he said.

"Arturo Bianci," the man with the lantern said. His hand was firm and callused, a workingman's grip. "Come."

They went into the farmhouse, through a hallway and into the kitchen; there was a big fireplace in one end, with a tile stove built into the side, and a kerosene lantern hanging from a rafter. Strings of garlic and onions and chilies hung also; hams in sacks, slabs of dried fish scenting the air; there were copper pans on the walls. Four men and a woman greeted him.

"No more names," John said, sitting at the plank table. "This group is big enough as it is, by the way."

Silence fell as the woman put a plate before him:

sliced tomatoes, cured ham, bread, cheese, a mug of watered wine. John picked up a slab of the bread and folded it around some ham; it was an important rite of hospitality, and besides that, meals had been irregular this last week or so.

"We wondered if you could get through, with the refugees," Arturo said slowly, obviously thinking over the implications of John's remark.

"Fools." Unexpectedly, that was the woman; she had Arturo's looks in a feminine version, earthy and strong, but much younger. "Do they think they can run faster than the *tedeschi*? All they do is block the roads and hamper the army."

John nodded; it was a good point. "They're afraid," he said. "Rightly afraid, although they're doing the wrong thing."

"Not only them," Arturo said. "Our lords and masters have—" he used a local dialect phrase; John thought he identified "sodomy" and "pig," but he wasn't sure. "You think we will lose this war, *signore*?"

"Yes," John confirmed. "The chances are about—"

92%, ±3, Center said helpfully.

"—nine to one against you, barring a miracle."

The other men looked at each other, some of them a little pale.

"I don't understand it—we are so many, compared to them. It must be treason!" one said.

"Never attribute to treason or conspiracy what can be accounted for by incompetence and stupidity," John said.

Arturo rubbed a hand over his five o'clock shadow, blue-black and bristly. The sound was like sandpaper.

"I knew we had fallen behind other countries," he said. "I have relatives who moved to Santander, to Chasson City, to work in the factories there. I might have myself, if I had not inherited this land from my father. That was why I joined the Reform party"—somewhat illegal, but not persecuted very stringently—"so that we might have what others do, and not spend every year as our grandfathers did. I did not know we had become so primitive. These devil-machines the Chosen have . . ."

"Their organization is more important, their training, their attitude," John said. "They've been planning for this for a long time. Your leadership has what it desires, and just wants to keep things the way they are. The Chosen . . . the Chosen are *hungry*, and eating the whole world wouldn't satisfy them."

Arturo nodded. "All that remains is to decide whether we submit, or fight from the shadows," he said. "We fight. Are we agreed?"

"We are agreed," one of the men said; he was older, and his breeches and floppy jacket were patched. "But I don't know how many others we can convince. They will say, what does it matter who the master is, if you must pay your rent and taxes anyway?"

The woman spoke again. "The Chosen will convince them, better than we."

The men looked at her; she scowled and banged a coffe pot down on one of the metal plates set into the top of the stove.

"It is true," Arturo said. "If half of what I have heard is so, that is true."

"It's probably worse than what you've heard," John said grimly. "The Chosen don't look on you as social inferiors; they look on you as animals, to be milked and sheared as convenient, then slaughtered."

Arturo slapped his hand on the plank. "It is agreed. And now, come and see how we have cared for what you sent us!"

He took up the bull's-eye and clicked the shutter open. They went out the back door, into a farmyard with a strong smell of chickens and ducks, past a muddy pond and into a barn. Several milch-cows mooed from their stalls, and a pair of big white-coated oxen with brass balls on the tips of their horns. Their huge mild eyes blinked at the light, and then went back to meditatively chewing their cuds. The cart they hauled was pushed just inside the door, its pole pointing at the rafters; tendrils of loose hay stuck down through the wide-spaced boards of the loft. Towards the rear of the barn were stacked pyramids of crates, one type long and thin, the other square and rectangular.

Arturo opened one whose nails had been pulled. "Enough of us know how to use these," he said, throwing John a rifle.

It was the standard Imperial issue, but factory-new, still a little greasy from the preservative oil. A single-shot breechloader, with a tilting block action and a spring-driven ejector that automatically tipped the block down and shot the spent cartridge out to the rear when the trigger was pulled all the way back. Not a bad weapon at all, in its day, and it could still kill a man just as dead as the latest magazine rifle. The smaller crates were marked AMMUNITION 10MM STANDARD 1000 ROUNDS.

"Two hundred rifles, and revolvers, blasting powder, a small printing press," Arturo said.

"Where were you planning on hiding them?" John said, looking around at the set peasant faces, underlit by the lamp Arturo had set down on the packed earth floor of the barn.

"The sheep pen. Under hard dung, six inches thick."

"Good idea, for some of them," John said, easing back the hammer of the rifle. The action went *click*. "But you shouldn't put more than a dozen in one place. Nor should any one of you *know* where the rest are. You understand me?"

Arturo seemed to, and his daughter, possibly a few of the others. John went on.

"You know what the Chosen penalty is for unauthorized possession of weapons—so much as one cartridge, or a knife with a blade longer than the regulations allow?"

"A bullet?" one of the peasants asked.

"Not unless they're in a real hurry. Generally, they hang you up by the thumbs and then flog you to death with jointed steel whips made out of chain links with hooks on them. Small hooks, about the size of a fish-hook, and barbed. I've seen it done; it can take hours, with an expert." Silence fell again.

"You want to frighten us?" one of the men asked.

"Damned right," John replied. "You'll stay alive longer, that way; and hurt the Chosen more."

Watch out, lad—you want to get them thinking, not terrorize them, Raj said. *Time enough for realism when they're committed.*

Arturo nodded thoughtfully. "We will have to organize . . . differently. Nothing in writing. Small groups, with only one knowing anyone else, and that as little as possible."

Good. We don't have to explain the cell system to him, at least, John thought.

Although the idea of the Fourth Bureau getting its hands on these amateurs . . . needs must. If nobody fought the Chosen, they'd *win.* That meant you had to accept the consequences.

"And then," Arturo said, "when we are ready—when enough are ready to follow us—we can start to hurt them. Blowing up bridges, picking off patrols, perhaps their clerks and tallymen, sabotage. We will have *some* advantages: we know the ground, the people will hide us."

"You'll have to strike fairly far from your homes, though," John said.

"Why?"

"Because the Chosen reprisals will fall hardest on the location where guerilla activity flares up. You strike away from where you live, and it kills two birds with one stone; you get the people who suffer the reprisals hating the Chosen, and you protect your base."

Arturo tilted the lantern to shine the light on John's face. That emphasized the structure of it, the slabs and angles.

"You are a hard man, *signore*," he said. "As hard as

the Chosen themselves, perhaps."

John nodded. "As we all will need to be, before this is over," he said. *Those of us still alive.*

The Chosen officer's blue eyes stared unblinking up at the moonlit night sky. It was bright, full moon, the disk nearly as large as the sun to the naked eye and almost too bright to look at, so Jeffrey could see them clearly. Her helmet had rolled away when the bullet went in through the angle of her jaw and out the top of her head; fortunately the shadow hid most of what the soft lead slug had done when it lifted off the top of her skull. Jeffrey was glad of that, and the bit of extra cover the body provided. Bullets thudded into the loam of the little hillock, or keened off stones with a *wicka-wicka* sound like miniature lead Frisbees.

Every minute or so a shell would burst along the Chosen gunline, stretched back now into a U-shape with the blunt end towards the enemy. The shellbursts were malignant red snaps in the night, a flash of light and the crack on its heels. Every few minutes a Land hand-grenade would explode where the Imperials had gotten close, but the invaders were running short on them. Short on everything.

The night air was colder, damper, and it carried the smell of cordite, gunpowder and the feces-and-copper scent of violent death. Bodies lay scattered out from the line, sometimes two-thick where automatic weapons or concentrated riflefire had caught groups charging forward—the Imperials' training kept betraying them, making them clump together. The field of the dead seemed to move and heave as wounded men screamed or whimpered or wept, calling for water or their mothers or simply moaned in wordless pain. Through it darted the living, more and more of them filtering in. Their firepower was diffuse compared to the Land's rapid-fire weapons, but it was huge, and the sheer weight of it was beating down resistance.

Goddamn ironic if I die here, Jeffrey thought. He'd devoted his whole life to the defeat of the Chosen. . . .

"I think the next push may make it this far," Heinrich said. "You can't claim our hospitality's been dull."

He was chewing the stem of his long-dead pipe as he unbuckled the flap of his sidearm. Most of the surviving command group had armed themselves with the rifles and bayonets of dead Protégé soldiers, those who hadn't gone out to take charge of units with no officers left alive.

"Damn," Heinrich went on. "We must have killed or crippled a good third of them. Didn't think they'd keep it up this long."

"Here they come again," someone said quietly.

The forward Imperial postions were no more than a hundred yards away. The firefly twinkling of muzzle flashes sparkled harder, concentrating on the surviving machine guns, and men rose to charge. A bugle sounded, thin and reedy. The machine guns were fewer now, firing in short tapping bursts to conserve ammunition. Jeffrey could feel something shift, a balance in his gut. This time they would make it to close quarters.

Listen, Raj said. *Is that—*

airship engines, Center said. **probability approaching unity. approaching from the southwest, throttled down for concealment; the wind is from that direction. four kilometers and closing.**

Heinrich turned his head. A light flashed in the darkness above the ground, a powerful signal-lamp clicking a sequence of four dots and dashes.

"Damn," Gerta Hosten said mildly.

The muzzle flashes down below and ahead outlined the Land position as clearly as a map in a war-college *kriegspiel* session; you could even tell the players, because the Imperials' black-powder discharges were duller and redder. It was fortunate that dirigibles had proven to be more resistant to fire than expected; punctures in the gas cells tended to leak up, rather than lingering and mixing with oxygen . . . usually.

A night drop—another first. Well, orders were orders, and it *was* Heinrich down there. She'd really regret losing Heinrich.

"We could do better with a bombing run," the commander of the dirigible muttered. "And parachuting in the ammunition they need."

"With a four-thousand-meter error radius, Horst?" Gerta asked absently, tightening a buckle on her harness.

"That's only an average," he said defensively. "The *Sieg* usually does better than that."

Airdrops of supplies to cut off forces had proven invaluable; unfortunately, an embarassing percentage had dropped into enemy positions.

"*Befehl ist befehl,*" she said, which was an unanswerable argument among the Chosen.

"Coming up on drop," the helm said. "Five minutes."

The *Sieg* was drifting with the wind and would come right in over the position, if the wind stayed cooperative.

This is going to be tricky, she thought as she ducked back down the corridor and into the hold. The lights cast a faint greenish glow over it; there was little spare space, even though her unit had taken heavy casualties—the problem with being a fire brigade was that you got sent to a lot of hot places. A good deal of the crowding was the cargo load: rifle ammunition, boxes of machine-gun belts, mortar shells, grenades. *Just* what you wanted to drop with you into the darkness and a firefight.

"Ready for it. On the dropmaster's signal," she said.

The waiting . . . she'd expected it to get better, after the first time. It didn't; you didn't ever get used to it.

"*Now!*"

A brief roar of propellors as the engines backed to

kill the *Sieg's* drift. They all swayed, and the pallets of
crates creaked dangerously. Then the hatchways in the
floor of the gondola snapped open.

The ground was *close* below, even in the gloom. Crates
strapped to cushioned pallets slid out the gaping holes
in the decking, to crash down and set the airship surging
upward. Gas valved with a hollow booming roar as she
leaped for the dangling line and slid downward, the
ridged sisal of the cable biting into gloved hands and
the composition soles of her boots.

"Oh, *shays*," she muttered.

It was a good thing that Land military doctrine called
for decentralized command, particularly in all-Chosen
units, because unless her eyes deceived her she was sliding right down on top of an Imperial gatling-gun crew.
An alert one, because they were turning the muzzle of
their weapon towards her, the line of flashes strobing
as it turned . . .

Thump. She hit the ground and rolled reflexively, then
rolled again, trying for dead ground where the gatling
could not bear. Chosen died behind her, seconds too
slow. The gatling ceased fire for an instant as another
group hit the ground and opened up with rifles and
machine carbines. Gerta unslung her own weapon and
jacked the slide.

"Hell!"

Jeffrey Farr rolled frantically as a one-ton pallet of
cargo crashed out of the sky towards him. It landed,
slithered downslope, and pitched on its side, resting
against a gnarled dead grapevine. The outline of the dirigible was suddenly clear against the stars, the diesels
bellowing and the exhausts red spikes in the night. For
an instant the heavy oily stink of the exhaust overrode
the other smells of the night battle, the fireworks scent
of black powder and death.

He rolled again as a dark figure lunged out of the
shadows at him behind the point of an eighteen-inch

THE CHOSEN 125

socket bayonet, an Imperial infantryman. Jeffrey's pistol came free in his hand as the bayonet went *shunk* into the rocky clay next to him, and his finger tightened on the trigger. In the red light of the muzzle blast he could see the contorted face of the Imperial soldier for a flickering second, before the man dropped away, folding around his belly. Jeffrey froze for an instant; he'd just killed a man, an ally . . .

Happens more often than you'd think, Raj thought/said crisply. *Get moving, lad. Time enough for night-mares later.*

Something went *pop* overhead. Actinic blue-white light flooded the field.

The man behind the gatling pitched forward; his face jammed the mechanism as the cranker kept grinding for an instant. Several of the crew turned, snatching up their carbines. Gerta went down on one knee, snuggled the butt of the machine-carbine into her shoulder, and began shooting. The range was less than thirty meters, point-blank if you knew the weapon. Someone was shooting at the crew from the other side, a rifle by the sound of it. That distracted them the few seconds necessary to cut down half of them with four short bursts. Muzzle flare from the Koegelman was blinding in the darkness, enough to make her eyes water and leave afterimages of a bar of fire dancing before them.

The drum of the machine-carbine clicked empty just as the parachute flare went off overhead; whoever had been supporting her wasn't anymore, and the Imperials stopped trying to get their jammed gatling going again. Six of them charged her; no time to reload one of the cumbersome drums. She blinked her eyes frantically in the jerky shadows, waiting tensely.

They were trying for her with cold steel, probably out of ammunition or saving their last shots for point-blank range in this uncertain light. The first lunged, almost throwing himself forward behind the point, eyes wild.

Gerta buttstroked aside the bayonet and slammed the steel plate into his throat. Cartilage crunched in and he fell backward, choking, knocked off his feet by the combined impetus of her blow and his own rush. She dropped the carbine and drew the long fighting knife slung at the small of her back with one hand and her automatic with the other.

One. Coming at her with his carbine clubbed, grasped by the barrel. Wait, wait. She went in under the blow, felt it fan the air inches from her forehead, and ripped the long blade upward. It slid in under the left ribs, sawing upward until the point was through lung and heart. Weight slumped onto her right hand.

Gerta pivoted with the body before her, and the man behind hesitated an instant. She shot over the shoulder of the twitching corpse. The bullet hit the bridge of the Imperial's nose and snapped his head backward as if it had been kicked by a mule. A bullet thumped into her meat-shield; she fired again, again, until the twelve rounds in her automatic were exhausted.

I'm alive, she thought, staggering and letting the dead weight slip off the end of her knife. She took a step and stumbled; something had gouged a groove across her left thigh and she hadn't even noticed. Gerta pushed away the pain while her hands automatically ejected the spent clip and reloaded the pistol. She moved forward, limping, up the slope to where the bulk of her unit should—should—be. Another parachute flare burst, and she threw herself down and crawled as machine-gun bullets whipcracked through the air where she had been. Spurts of sand and rock flicked into her face, and the wound was starting to *hurt*. The Land position ought to be just ahead . . . assuming there was anyone left alive besides that trigger-happy gunner who'd just come within a hair of sawing her in half.

"What a ratfuck."

*   *   *

Boots nearly landed on him as the dirigible turned

away. Something whipped across his body, hard enough to hurt: a sisal cable. Dozens of others were dropping down out of the night, and human forms were sliding down them. Two more nearly trampled on him, ignoring Jeffrey and the corpse in their rush; they *did* use the body of the man he'd just killed as a springboard. A half-dozen grappled with the big pallet that had nearly crushed him. Seconds later they were stripping out a heavy water-cooled machine gun with its tripod and ammunition, slapping it down and opening up on the masses of Imperial infantry caught charging to finish off the Land blocking force. Tracers whipped out through the darkness, irridescent green, like bars of St. Elmo's fire. Infantry shook themselves out into their units and swept down the Land line, winkling out Imperials who'd made it that far.

Damn, I've never seen troops move that fast, he thought. They were in full marching kit, and they moved like leopards.

an all-chosen unit, Center observed. Jeffrey's vision took on a flat brightness. **identifying markers—** The brightness strobed over unit badges.

They've been culling out the weakest ten percent of their own breed every generation for four hundred years, Raj said. *And skimming off the top one or two percent of their Protégés at the same time. You'd expect it to show.*

Jeffrey shuddered, even with rounds still splitting the air above him. *It's a good thing there aren't more of them,* he thought. *There'd be no stopping them.*

if there were more, Center observed, **it would be impossible to support so large and so specialized a nonproductive class.**

Always a lot fewer carnosauroids than grazers, Raj amplified.

The image that came with the thought made him shudder a moment even then: something man-sized and whip-slender, leaping to slash a bloody gouge in an ox's side with a sickle-shaped claw on its hind foot, like a fighting cock grown big enough to scythe his belly open.

Heinrich was back on his feet, bellowing orders. Protégé troopers broke open boxes of ammunition, dashing back to their positions with cotton bandoliers around their necks and boxes of machine-gun belts in their hands.

Jeffrey did a three-point spin at a sound behind him, landing on hip and one hand. He froze as he found himself looking down the use-pitted muzzle of a Land automatic. A Chosen woman with captain's insignia on her field-gray rose; short for one of that race, and dark, he could tell that even in the moonlight. Blood was runneling black down one thigh, where the unform had been ripped open by a grazing shot.

"What the hell is a Santy doing here?" she said, standing, favoring the wounded leg a little.

"You!" Heinrich said, turning, a broad grin on his square face. "I might have known."

"I was the closest—the marching reliefs ought to get here about dawn," the woman said. "What the hell is a Santy officer doing with you, Heinrich?"

Closer, he could see the General Staff Intelligence Commando flashes on cuff and collar. *Must be—*

gerta hosten, captain, intelligence branch, Center supplied helpfully.

A dangerous one, son, Raj said. *Be very careful.*
Jeffrey could have told that. The eyes fastened on him were the coldest he'd ever seen, colder than the far side of the moon.

"Oh, we picked him up in Corona," Heinrich said.

"You should have turned him over to us, or the Fourth Bureau."

"Well, he's a neutral—and a relative of sorts, Johan's foster-brother. At loose ends, the Santy legation in Corona stopped a couple of thousand-kilo bombs with its roof."

"Jeffrey Farr," Gerta said; she seemed to be filing and

sorting information behind her eyes. "He's a *spook*, Heinrich. You ought to shoot him."

"I haven't been showing him the plans for the new torpedo," Heinrich said, a slight exasperation in his voice.

Gerta shrugged, and holstered her automatic. Jeffrey felt a slight prickle of relief. Unlikely that she'd just shoot him down as he stood—

probability 27%, ±7, Center said.

—but it was still a relief. She shrugged.

"It's your command. Let's get this ratfuck organized, shall we?"

"*Ya.*" Heinrich turned his head slightly, towards Jeffrey: "My wife, Captain Gerta Hosten." Back to her: "What's the theater situation?"

"FUBAR, but we're winning—not exactly the way we expected to, but we are. Once this position's blocked, General Summelworden's got them in the kettle and we can turn up the heat; Ciano next. Where do you want my machine guns? And get me something to stop this leak, would you? I can't keel over just yet."

"Automatics over by—"

The conversation slid into technicalities. Heinrich waved at a passing medic who then knelt to put a pressure bandage on Gerta's thigh.

Ciano next, Jeffrey thought. *That's going to be ugly.*

CHAPTER EIGHT

Everything was calm and unhurried in the Imperial situation room. There was a huge map of the Empire on one wall, stuck with black pins to represent Land forces and green ones for Imperial. A relief map of the same territory stood in a sunken area in the center of the floor, with a polished mahogany rail around it, and enlisted men pushed unit counters with long-handled wooden rakes. One wall of the big room was all telephones and telegraphs, their operators scribbling on pads and handing them to decoders.

Aides in polished boots and neat, colorful uniforms strode back and forth; generals frowned at the maps; the Emperor tugged at his white whiskers and blinked sleepy, pouched eyes. Behind him stood guards in ceremonial uniform, and several civilians . . .

No, John Hosten thought, appraising them. Their eyes flickered ceaselessly over the room, appraising, watching. Waiting. *The real guards. And by their looks, the only people in this room who're doing their jobs.*

John Hosten approached, flanked by two ushers, and made his bow. Behind the surface of his mind he could feel Raj and Center examining the maps, the computer's passionless appraisal and Raj's cold scorn.

Systematic lying, Raj thought. *All the way up the chain of command. It's always the commander's fault when that happens. Once you let people start telling you what you want to hear, you're fucked—and everyone else with you.*

130

"Rise, *Signore* Hosten," the Emperor said.

He was an old man, but John was slightly shocked at his appearance; there was a perceptible tremble to his hands now, and a faint smell of sickness. Count del'Cuomo beside him looked even worse, if possible— but then, he probably had better information available, as Minister of War.

"Your Majesty," John said.

He handed over the folder of documents, neatly tied with a green-and-red ribbon.

"My credentials, Your Majesty. And my regrets, but my government requires my services at home. I will be returning to Santander City."

The Emperor smiled absently. "And taking one of our fairest flowers with you . . . where is young Pia?"

"Currently, she's working as a volunteer nurse," John said. *Against my advice.*

The Emperor frowned. "Not . . . not really *suitable*, I'd have thought," he murmured.

Count del'Cuomo shrugged. "She was always too much for me, your Majesty," he said. He looked up at John. "But my son-in-law will take good care of her, and return in happier times, when we have driven the *tedeschi* back to their island, as we did before."

John bowed again, more deeply, and took the required four paces backward. That nearly ran him into an aide with a stack of telegrams, but he ignored the man. Ignored everything, until a turn down the corridor gave him a view down over the city. Then he took in a sharp breath.

It was early morning, still almost dark. The news of the fall of Milana must have reached the people in the hour or so he'd spent waiting. Not from a courier or coded message, surely; the Imperial armies hadn't fallen apart quite that drastically . . . yet. More probably from a refugee on a fast riverboat. As for official statements, by this time they just confirmed what they denied. Even when they were sincere, and he'd bet it just meant that the lower-level functionaries writing them had been suckered by their own propaganda.

John Hosten stood for a moment looking down at the rioting and the fires, past the gardens of the palace and the cordon of Guard troops stationed along the perimeter. A man of thirty, tall and a hard-faced, in a diplomat's black morning coat, wing collar and dark-striped trousers. A servant almost walked into him, saw his face and silently stood aside.

"Back to the embassy," John said to himself; then aloud, to the driver of his car.

"Don't know if we can, sir," the driver said. He was an embassy man himself, diplomatic service, and quite capable. *Harry. Harry Smith,* John reminded himself. It was too easy to forget about people, when you spent time looking at the world through Center's eyes.

Too true, son, Raj said. *And if you think it's a problem for you . . .*

"Lot of the streets looked to be blocked," Smith went on. He shrugged. "Kin find m' way through, maybe."

"Mr. Smith," John said.

The driver twisted around to look at him; he was a slight, grizzled man, with blue eyes and wrinkles beside them. There was a slight eastern twang in his Santander. John recognized it, and the manner.

"My wife is down near the train station, working in the emergency hospital," he said. "I have to get to the embassy to get some help so I can get through to her. If you don't think you can make it through, I'll drive."

The blue eyes squinted at him. "Nossir. You watch our back, I'll drive." He reached under the front seat and pulled out a pump-action shotgun. "You know how to use one of these, sir?"

Smiling, John took it and racked the action. A shell popped out; he caught it one-handed and fed it back into the gate in front of the trigger. A wary respect came into Smith's eyes; it increased when John tucked the weapon under a traveling rug on the seat beside him.

"I'll bring it out if we need to use it, or show it to somebody," he said. "Now let's get going."

"I need some volunteers," John said. "To get someone out of the city."

He nearly had to shout over the clamor of the crowd outside the gilded wrought-iron gates of the embassy compound. There were thousands of them, more crowded down the street, surging and screaming. Marine guards in blue dress uniforms were stationed inside the gate and along the walls, carrying rifles with fixed bayonets. A little ceremonial saluting cannon had been wheeled out and faced the main entranceway, just as a hint in case the crowd decided to try and batter the metal down. That was unlikely; under the gilding the bars were as thick as a woman's wrist. The Marines were discouraging those trying to break through with the butts of their rifles, or short jabs with their bayonets. Nothing more was needed, not yet.

A slow trickle was getting in, through the postern gate beside the main ones; people with valid Santander papers, or spouses, or embassy personnel who'd gotten trapped out in the city.

"Sir?" The Marine captain looked around incredulously.

"Captain, my wife is out there, and I need some volunteers to help me get through the crowd."

The captain opened his mouth; John could see the snap of refusal forming. He looked the man in the eye.

"This is *very important* duty," he said meaningfully.

It wasn't much of a secret in the compound that John was with the Secret Service. Nor that he was immensely rich, or that he had connections at the highest levels, military and civilian.

"I'm not sending any of my men out into that," the officer said bluntly, jerking a hand towards the near-riot beyond the gate. Just then was a barked order, and the dozen troopers by the gate fired a volley into the air.

The crowd surged back with screams of panic, then ran forward again when nobody fell.

"I wouldn't ask you to," John said. "I'm going, whether anyone wants to come with me or not. I'd appreciate some help, but I don't expect you to *order* anyone out."

The Marine officer hesitated. "My responsibility is to guard the perimeter."

"And to assist the staff in their functions."

Decision crystallized. "All right, sir. You can *ask*. Sergeant!"

A thickset man with a shaven head covered in a network of scars looked up. The Santander Marines saw a lot of travel, mostly to places where the locals didn't like them.

"Sir!"

"Mr. Hosten needs some volunteers to accompany him into the city and pull someone out. See if anybody feels like it."

What was left of the sergeant's eyebrows—they'd evidently been burned off his face at some point—rose. He looked appraisingly at John and smiled like a dog worrying a bone.

"Hey, Sarge."

John looked around; it was the driver.

"Yeah, Harry?"

"It's righteous, Sarge. I'm going."

The noncom looked down at the driver's legs, and the graying man shrugged.

"Hey, we're driving—I don't have to sprint."

"You always were a natural-born damned fool, Harry," the sergeant said. He looked back at John. "I'll pass the word, sir."

John stripped off the morning coat as he waited, switching to the four-pocket hunting jacket his valet brought and gratefully throwing aside the starched collar of his dress shirt. Smith glanced at the shoulder rig that lay exposed.

"Guess I shouldn't have asked about the scattergun, sir," he said.

"How could you know?" John pointed out. "Look, am I likely to get anyone?"

"Besides me?" Harry shrugged. "I've been out of the corps a while now, but Berker knows me—hell, Berker carried me out when I got a slug through both legs. He'll—"

The bald sergeant returned, with five men behind him. They were all armed, and several of them were stuffing gear into field packs.

"Sir!" he said. "Corporal Wilton, privates Goms, Barrjen, Sinders, and Maken." In a whisper: "Ah, sir, I sort of hinted there'd be some sort of reward, you know?"

"There certainly will be," John said. To the men: "All right, here's the drill. We're heading for the main train station and the emergency hospital that's been set up there. We're going to pick up Mrs. Hosten—Lady Pia Hosten—and then we're either coming back here, or getting out the city to the east, depending on which looks most practical. I expect anyone who comes with me to follow orders and not be nervous about risks. Understood?"

A chorus of *yessirs*, a couple of grins. None of the men looked like angels, but then they were Marines, and assignment to the embassy guard in Ciano had been something of a plum, reserved for men with something on their records besides a decade of well-polished boots.

He looked up. Something was flying through the pillars of smoke that reached up into the sky over Ciano. A huge shark-shape, three hundred meters long, a shining teardrop droning through the air to the sound of motors. Dozens more followed it, a loose wedge coming in from the west like the thrust of a spearpoint.

"Let's do it, then."

Wounded men screamed in fear as the building shook. Pia Hosten grabbed a pillar and held on as the stick of bombs rattled the iron girders of the roof. The fitted stone swayed slightly under her touch, a queasy feeling. Half the nursing sisters were gone, and there were wounded everywhere—hundreds in this room, thousands in the building, the heat mounting under the tall arches and the smell of puss and gangrene mounting, and more still coming in. The gas was off, and the mains.

"Water . . . water . . ."

I should have done as John said, she thought, hurrying over with a dipper.

She raised the man's head and put the rim to his lips. He drank, then choked and began to thrash.

"Sister Maria!" Pia called.

The man arched, then slumped; his eyes rolled up and went still.

The nun arrived, then scowled. "He is dead."

"He wasn't when I called you!" Pia snapped, then leaped up to hold the older woman as she sagged. "I am sorry, Sister."

"There are so many," the nun whispered. "My God, my God, why have you forsaken us?"

"Where is Doctor Chicurso?"

"Gone—most of them are gone. The guards at the entrances, they are gone also. Only the ambulances keep arriving."

"The guards are gone?" Pia asked sharply.

"Yes, yes. An officer came, and said they were needed. But many had just left, I think, taken off their uniforms and . . ."

She made a weary gesture towards the rest of the city.

Pia swallowed and stood, walking quickly towards her work station, taking off the hideously stained apron that covered her plain gray dress. If the guards were gone, it would be very bad.

John was right. I should have left for the embassy yesterday. There was no more she could do here. But it was hard, very hard, to leave the Sister standing slumped amid the impossible need of the hurt.

She walked quickly along the aisle that separated the rows of men lying on the floor, through to the cubicle that had served her and a dozen other volunteers and nurses. She heard a scream and a crash before she arrived, and men's voices.

The door was half-open; she slammed it back. The sharp reek of medical alcohol hit her like a wave; the three army hospital orderlies had been drinking it. The scream had come from Lola Chiavri, one of the volunteers; two of them had her pressed down on a table, her dress ripped open to the waist. The third was wrestling with her thrashing legs, trying to rip down her underdrawers, laughing and staggering. They turned to stare at her, open-mouthed. One sniggered.

"Hey, Gio', somebody new for d'party."

Pia drew herself up. "Release that lady at once! Where is your officer?"

The one at the foot of the table was a little less drunk than the others. He released the other woman's legs and turned, grinning like a dog worrying a bone.

"Officers all run away, missy, 'fore the *tedeschi* gets here. Why shou' the *tedeschi* get all the liker an' cooze? C'mere!"

He turned towards her, his pants obscenely unbuttoned, laughing and fondling himself with one hand and reaching for her with the other. Pia drew the four-barrel derringer from her pocket and pointed it.

"Y'gonna *hurt* me with that little thing?" the man laughed. "Oh, don' *hurt* me, missy!"

Snap. The sound was like a piece of glass breaking in the tiny room. A black dot appeared between the would-be rapist's eyes, precisely 5.6mm in diameter, turning red as she watched. The expression slid off his face like rancid gelatin, and he toppled forward to lie at her feet. His skull struck the stone floor with a final-sounding *thock.*

Pia hid her surprise. She'd been aiming at his stomach, and he was only four feet away. The other two orderlies were backing towards the far wall, their hands held out palm-up, making incoherent sounds.

"There are three more bullets in this gun," she said crisply, backing up two paces and standing aside. "Go!" They hesistated, unwilling to approach any closer. "Go now, or I will shoot."

The two men sidled past her and ran blundering down the corridor, eyes fixed on the four muzzles of the little gun. Pia waited until they were out of sight before letting the hand that held the derringer drop. Acrid-tasting bile forced itself up her throat as she looked down at the man she'd killed.

"It was so *quick*," she whispered, and forced herself to swallow.

Just then Lola struck her, clinging and whimpering. Pia shook her sharply. "Get dressed! We have to get out of here!"

Back to the palace district; the embassy was there, or at least there wouldn't be total anarchy.

Pia remembered John pleading with her not to go to the hospital today. *I should have listened.*

"Sweet Jesus on a crutch," Harry Smith muttered.

A thousand yards down the hill a crowd was tipping a car over. It was an aristocrat's vehicle—few others could afford them, in the Empire, and this was a huge six-wheeler—strapped all over with luggage. The owners were still inside; a woman tried to crawl out one of the rear windows and was met with sticks, fists, pieces of cobblestone. She screamed and slumped, and hands dragged her limp and bleeding body back inside. A gun spoke; the noise covered the report, but John could see the puff of smoke.

"Stupid," he whispered.

Half a dozen rifles answered the shot; there were scores of Imperial army deserters in the crowd, many with their weapons. John could see sparks flying as bullets hit the metalwork of the car. Some ricochetted into the densely packed ranks of the rioters. One must have punctured the fuel tanks, because a deep soft *whump* and billow of orange flame drove the mob back, some of them on fire. Both the figures that tried to crawl out of the burning automobile were on fire, and probably would have died even without the hail of rocks that beat them back.

"All right, Harry," he went on. "What's your plan?"

"Well, sir, there's a side route," the driver said thoughtfully. "But it's a bit narrow."

"You're the expert," John said.

For once, he was glad that diplomatic corps conservatism stuck the embassy with steamers; they had less pickup than the latest petrol-engine jobs, but they were *quiet*. Smith spun the wheel away from the main avenue, down a side-street, and into a maze of alleyways. Some of them were old enough to date back to the founding of Ciano, to the centuries right after the Collapse, when men first started building again in stone. The wheels drummed on cobbles and splashed through refuse and waste, throwing him lurching into the four Marines packed into the rear of the touring car. Normally the district would have been crowded, but most of the people were missing.

Probably out rioting. Not that it would do them any good when the Chosen showed up, but he supposed it was more tolerable than sitting and waiting. The ones who were left were mostly children, or old. They slammed shutters and ducked aside at the sight of an automobile filled with uniforms and armed men.

"*Uh*-oh."

The hill was steeper here, and it gave them an excellent view south over the river to the industrial section—the prevailing winds in the central Empire were always from the north, which meant that residential properties were on the north bank of the Pada. They could see the Land airships coming in over the flatter southern shore at two thousand feet, only a thousand feet above their own position.

Probably aligning on landmarks, Raj thought at the back of his mind.

probability near unity, Center confirmed.

John felt a spurt of anger. *God damn it, that's my wife down there,* he thought coldly.

I could never keep mine out of it, either, Raj thought. **And she was a lot less of a romantic than yours.**

The dirigibles were coming in fast, seventy miles an hour or better; the lead craft seemed to be aimed straight at him. The bomb bay doors were open, but nothing was coming out. John looked out of the corners of his eyes; the Marines looked a little tense, but not visibly upset. They kept their eyes on the buildings around them, only occasionally flicking to the approaching bombers.

"Smith, pull in here. We'll wait it out and then continue."

Here was a nook between two walls, both solid. *Bad if the buildings come down, good otherwise. You paid your money and you took your chances. . . .*

"Anyone who wants to can get out and take cover," John said in a conversational tone.

Nobody did, although they squatted down. The dirigibles were over the river now, moving into the railyards and the residential sections of Ciano. Their shadows ghosted ahead of them, black whale-shapes over the whitewashed buildings and tile roofs.

"Hey," one of the Marines said. "Why aren't they bombing south? That's where the factories and stuff are."

Smith's hands were tight on the wheel. "Because, asshole, they don't want to damage their own stuff—they'll have it all in couple of days. *Shit!*"

Crump. Crump. Crump . . .

The bombs were falling in steady streams from the airships; the massive craft bounced higher as the weight was removed.

"Fifty tons load," John whispered, bracing his hand on the roof-strut of the car and looking up. "Fifty tons each, thirty-five ships . . . seventeen hundred tons all up."

"Mother," someone said.

"Won't kill y'any deader here than back at the embassy."

"They wouldn't bomb the embassy."

"Yeah, sure. They're gonna be *real* careful about that."

"Can it," the corporal said. "For what we are about to receive . . ."

The sound grew louder, the drone of the engines rasping down through the air. John could see the Land sunburst flag painted on their sides, and then the horseshoe-shaped glass windows of the control gondolas. A few black puffs of smoke appeared beneath and around the airships; some Imperial gunners were still sticking to their improvised antiairship weapons, showing more courage than sense. The pavement beneath the car shook with the impact of the explosions. Dust began to smoke out of the trembling walls of the tenements on either side. The crashing continued, an endless roar of impacts and falling masonry.

"Here—" someone began.

The shadow of a dirigible passed over them, throwing a chill that rippled down his spine. There was a moment of white light—

—and someone was screaming.

John tried to turn, and realized he was lying prone. Prone on rubble that was digging into his chest and belly and face. He pushed at the stone with his hands, spitting out dust and blood in a thick reddish-brown clot; more blood was running into his left eye from a cut on his forehead, but everything else seemed to be functional. And someone was still shouting.

One of the Marines, lying and clutching his arm. John came erect and staggered over to the car, which was lying canted at a three-quarter angle. The

intersecting walls of the nook they'd stopped in still
stood, but the buildings they'd been attached to were
gone, spread in a pile of broken blocks across what
had been the street.

the angle of the walls acted to deflect the blast,
Center said. **chaotic effect, and not predictable.**

Good thing for the plan it did what it did, John
thought as he rummaged for the first-aid kit.

**your death at this point would decrease the probability of an optimum outcome from 57% ±3 to
41% ±4,** Center said obligingly.

"Nice to know you're needed," John said.

The ringing in his ears was less, and he could see
properly. Good, no severe concussion; he squatted beside
the wounded Marine.

"Hold him," he said to the others. "Let's take a look
at this."

Two men held the shoulders down. The arm was not
broken, but it was bleeding freely, a steady drip rather
than an arterial pulse. He slipped the punch-dagger out
of his collar and used it to cut off the sleeve of the uniform jacket; not the ideal tool—it was designed as a
weapon—but it would do. The flesh of the man's forearm was torn, and something was sticking out if it. John
closed his fingers on it. A splinter of wood, probably
oak, from a structural beam. Longer than a handspan,
and driven in deep.

"This is going to hurt," John said.

"Do it," the Marine gasped, gray-faced.

One of the others put a rifle sling between his teeth.
John gripped firmly, put his weight on the hand that held
the man's wrist to the ground, and pulled. The Marine
convulsed, arching, his teeth sinking into the tough
leather.

The finger-thick dagger of oak slid free. John held it
up; no ragged edges, so there probably wasn't much left
in the wound—hopefully not too much dirty cloth, either,
since there was no time to debride it.

"Let it bleed for a second," he said. "It'll wash it clean."

There was medicinal alcohol and iodine powder in the kit. John waited, then swabbed the wound clear with cotton wool and poured in both. This time the Marine simply swore, and John grinned.

"You must be recovering." He packed the wound, bandaged it, and rigged a sling. "Try not to put too much strain on this, trooper."

"Yessir. Ah . . . what the hell do we do now, sir?"

They all looked at him, battered, bruised, a few bleeding from superficial cuts, but all functional. He looked down the street; there was a breastwork of stones four feet high in front of them, and more behind, but the road downslope looked fairly clear. Smoke was mounting up rapidly, though; the fires were out of control; the waterworks were probably hit and the mains out of operation. It lay thick on the air, thick between him and Pia.

"First we'll get this road cleared," he said briskly, spitting again. "Goms"—who looked worst injured—"there's some water in the boot of the car, see to it. Smith, check the car and see what it needs. Wilton, Sinders, Barrjen, Maken, you come with me."

He studied the way the rocks interlocked in the barrier ahead of them. "We'll shift this one first."

"Sir? Prybar?" corporal Wilton said. The crusted block probably weighed twice what John did, and he was the heaviest man there.

"No *time*. Barrjen, you on the other side, there's room for two."

Barrjen was three inches shorter than John, but just as broad across the shoulders, and thick through the belly and hips as well; his arms were massive, and the backs of his hands covered in reddish hair. He grinned, showing broad square teeth.

"If'n you say so, sor," he said, and bent his knees, working his fingers under the edges of the block.

John did likewise and took a deep, careful breath.
"*Now*."

He lifted, taking the strain on back and legs, exhaling
with the effort until red lights swam before his eyes and
something in his gut was just on the edge of tearing.
His coat *did* tear across the back, the tough seam parting
with a long ripping sound. The stone resisted, and then
he felt it shift. Shift again, his feet straining to keep their
balance in the loose rubble, and then it was tumbling
away down the other side like a dice from the box of
a god, hammering into the pavement and falling into
the gutter with a final *tock* sound.

Barrjen staggered backward, still grinning as he
panted. "You diplomats is tougher'n you looks, sor," he
said, in a thick eastern accent.

John spat on his hands. Center traced a glowing network of stress lines across the rockfall, showing the path
of least resistance for clearing it.

"Let's get to work."

"I want to go home," Lola said—whimpered, really.

Pia fought an urge to slap her. The other woman's eyes
were still round with shock; understandable, and she was
less than twenty, but . . .

"Up here."

The staircase was empty; it filled the interior of the
square tower, with a switchback every story and narrow
windows in the cream-colored limestone. Smoke was
drifting through them, enough to haze the air a little.
The light poured in, scattering on the dust and smoke,
incongrously beautiful shafts of gold bringing out the
highlights and fossil shells in the stone. Pia labored
upward, feeling the sweat running down her face and
soaking the nurse's headress she wore, thanking God that
skirts had gone so high this year—barely ankle-length.

"Come on," she said. "We'll be safe up here."

"Safe for a little while," Lola said. Then: "Mother of
God," as they came out onto the flat roof of the tower.

Ciano was burning. The pillars of fire had merged into columns that covered half the area they could see. Heavy and black, smoke drifted down from the hillsides, covering the highways that wound through the valleys running down to the Pada. The warehouse districts along the river were fully involved, the great storage tanks of olive oil and brandy bellowing upward in ruddy flame like so many giant torches.

"Nobody's fighting the fires at all," Pia whispered to herself. The waterworks must have been finally destroyed. And the streets by the docks, they were stuffed with timber, coal, cotton, so much tinder. She could feel the heat on her face, worse even in the few moments since they had come out onto the flat rooftop.

Lola looked around. "What can we do?"

"Wait," Pia said. "Wait and pray."

Thunder rumbled from the eastward. Pia's head came around slowly. The sky was summer blue, save for the great pillars of black smoke. Rain would be a mercy, but God had withheld His mercy from the people of the Empire. The sound rumbled again, then again—too regularly spaced for thunder, in any case.

The rain was not coming. The Chosen were, and those were their guns. She slipped to her knees and crossed herself, bringing the rosary to her lips.

Come to me, John, she thought. *Come quickly, my love.*

Then she began to plan.

CHAPTER NINE

"Ciano's burning," Jeffrey Farr said, opening his eyes.
Get out of there, he added silently to his brother. After-images of buildings sliding into streets in sheets of fiery rubble washed across his vision as the link through Center faded.

"*Ya,*" Heinrich Hosten said cheerfully. "Maybe we shouldn't have bombed it quite so heavy."

He looked eastward, toward the smoke that hazed the horizon. The distant *thump . . . thump . . .* of artillery sounded, slow and regular.

"Street fighting," the Chosen officer went on. "We may have trapped them too well—there are a quarter of a million troops in there, less what's getting out, the net's not watertight."

"Why not just let it burn?" Jeffrey asked.

"The High Command may do that for a while. Praise the Powers That Be, *we* won't be pitchforked into it right away."

The survivors of Heinrich's regiment had been pulled into reserve, not completely out of action, but things would have to take a decided turn for the worse before they were put back into the line any time soon. More than a third of the roster had died blocking the Imperial breakout for those crucial hours, and as many again were wounded. The survivors were billeted now in the grounds of a nobleman's country estate; they could see the smoke-shadowed buildings of Ciano in the distance to the east. Heinrich had spent the last couple of days rounding up supplies for the celebration that bellowed and sprawled across the gardens: oxen and whole pigs roasted on spits, barrels stood at the ends of tables heaped with food. A roar went up from the troops—the male majority, at least—as a crowd of women were herded through the gates.

Jeffrey averted his eyes and ignored the screams. Nothing he could do, nothing at all . . . for now. Heinrich beamed indulgently down at the scene below the terrace and bit the last meat off the turkey drumstick in his hand.

"They've earned a little rest," he said, idly stroking the hip of the naked girl who poured his glass full again. "Did damned well."

The rest of the surviving officers were grouped around the tables on the balustraded terrace, paying serious attention to the feast the villa's staff had prepared for the new overlords. Most Chosen ate rather sparingly at home; in the food-poor Land red meat was a luxury except for the wealthiest among the upper caste. Jeffrey remembered John telling him how the Friday pork roast was the high point of the week, and that was for an up-and-coming general's family. Now that they had the biggest area of rich farmland on Visager under their control, the Chosen were making up for lost time.

The thought made the food taste a little better. *Maybe they'll get soft.*

probability 87% ±3, defining "soft" as significantly reduced militechnic functionality, Center supplied.

After more than a decade, Jeffrey could sense overtones of meaning in the words, even though they seemed machined out of thought the way engine parts were lathed from bar stock.

But? he supplied.

significant reduction would require 7 generations, plus or minus—

Never mind.

Heinrich tore off another drumstick and pulled the girl into his lap. "Victory, it is wonderful!" he said.

"Yeah," Jeffrey Farr replied. *It will be.*

"Are you sure this is a good idea?" Lola asked, ripping up the last of her petticoat.

"No," Pia said. "But the only other thing I can think of is to wait here for the Chosen. My Giovanni will come—but *look* at that out thére!"

Ciano was the largest city in the world; for centuries, it had been the *capital* of the world, when the Universal Empire had been what its name claimed for it, leading humanity on Visager back from the Fall. Now it was dying, and mostly by its own hand.

"We've gotta find some broad in *this*?" Goms said.

Probably more crowded a couple of hours ago, John thought.

"Jesus," the marine finished, coughing in the thick air, a compound of smoke and explosion-powdered brick and stone.

"Back! Back!" the driver shouted, as half a dozen men in Imperial uniforms rushed towards the car.

They ignored him, if they heard at all; their faces had the fixed, carved-wood look of utter desperation sighting a chance of survival. A marine raised his rifle, cursed, lowered it again.

"If they get to the car, we're all dead," John said.

"He's right," Harry said. "Shit . . ."

The rifle blasted uncomfortably close to John's ear. He stood motionless, his hand resting on the top of the windscreen. It had been a warning shot; he could hear the sick whine of the ricochet, see the bright momentary spark where jacketed metal hit the cobblestones. The Imperials ignored it. More from the milling crowd were following; none of them looked to be armed—the Imperial army had regarded this as the ultimate rear area until a day or two ago—but there were a lot of them, all convinced that the car represented their chance to get *out*. They probably weren't thinking much beyond that.

"Damn," the marine said softly, and worked the bolt.

"Five rounds rapid!" Corporal Wilton said.

The marines had been waiting with their second finger on the trigger and their index lying under the bolt. *BAM* and five rounds blasted out. *Click* and the index finger flipped up the rear-mounted bolt handle of the rifles. Spring tension shot the bolt back halfway through its cycle as soon as the turning bolt released the locking lugs; a quick pull back and the shell was ejected; a slap with the palm of the hand and *chick-Chack!* the next round was in. Well-trained men could fire twelve aimed rounds a minute that way, and all the marines had "marksman" flashes on their shoulders.

Face frozen, John watched the first Imperial double over like a man punched in the belly—even at point-blank range the marines were aiming for the center of mass, as they'd been taught. The Imperial slumped forward and slid facedown, blood flowing over the cobbles. The shots cracked, quick careful firing with a half-second pause to aim. He didn't have to order *cease-fire* when the survivors turned and ran.

Wilton pulled the bolt of his rifle back and pushed a five-round stripper clip into the magazine with his thumb. The zinc strip that had held the cartridges tinkled against the side of the car. The crowd surged away from the car, milling aimlessly.

John didn't think anyone else would try to steal it for a while. It stood in one of the narrower laneways leading into the big plaza that stood before the train station; the station building itself wasn't burning . . . yet . . . but a stick of bombs had left a series of craters across the plaza, leading towards the twenty-meter high columns of the facade like an arrow on a map. The plaza had been crowded with mule- and horse-drawn wagons and ambulances, supply vehicles, even a few powered staff cars.

Most of the vehicles were abandoned, some burning or overturned. Wounded animals screamed, their voices shrill over the calling of hundreds—thousands—from within the great building, adding the last touch of hell. Wounded men were pouring out of the tall blushwood portals and out into the square, all of them who could move. Or could stagger along grasping at the walls, or support each other, or crawl. The stink of death and gangrene came with them in waves, strong enough that even a few of the marines gagged at it.

"Sir," Henry said, "we'd never have made it down if we'd left half an hour later. And there's no way in hell we're going to drive back to the embassy."

"No," John said, smiling slightly as he checked his pistol and then slid it back into the shoulder-holster under his frock coat. "But I don't think we'll have much of a problem finding my wife."

He nodded towards the left-hand tower. Someone on top had strung two strips of brightly colored cloth from corner windows to the middle of the front facing, and another straight down from the point at which they met. Together they formed an arrow —>, pointing upward at the tower-top. He took his binoculars out of the dashboard compartment and focused on the tiny figure waving at the apex of the signal.

"Let's go," he said.

The driver cleared his throat. John released Pia and stepped back; even then, in that charnel house of a place, the Marines were grinning. Pia blushed and tucked strands of hair back under her snood.

"Sir," Harry said. "We're not going to get back to the embassy."

"No, we have to get out of the city entirely," John said thoughtfully.

They were in one of the loading bays of the station; fewer bodies here, fewer of the moaning, fevered wounded. None of the Marines was what you'd call squeamish—they'd all seen action in the Southern Islands—but several of them were looking pale. So did Pia's friend; a couple of the troopers were courteously handing her safety pins to help fasten up her ripped dress.

"Sure you're all right?" John asked again.

"As right as can be," Pia said stoutly. "We cannot go to the embassy?"

John shook his head. "The fires are out of control, and there's fighting in the streets. The Chosen are close to the western end of the city, too."

Pia shivered and nodded. John turned his head slightly.

"Sinders," he said, "didn't you say you worked for the North Central Rail before you joined the corps?"

Sinders blinked at him. "Lord love you, sir, so I did," he said. "Locomotive driver. Had a bit of a falling out with the section foreman, like."

Someone spoke sotto voce: "Had a bit of a falling down with his daughter, you mean."

"Follow me," John said. He hopped down from the platform; cinders crunched under his boots. They handed down the women and walked over the tracks to the other side of the vast shed. "There, that one. Could you drive it?"

A steam engine and its fuel car stood pointing eastward; vapor leaked from several places, hiding the green-and-gold livery of the Imperial Pada Valley Line.

"Sure, sir. It's Santander made, anyway—standard 4–4–2, rebuilt for the Imperial broad gauge. That's if we got time to raise steam, that could take a while."

"It has steam up," John said. Center drew a thermal schematic over his sight.

"But where would we go on it, sir?"

"East a ways, at least."

The Marines looked uncertain. "Ah, beggin' yer pardon, sir," the corporal said. "But ain't those Land buggers all around?"

"Maybe not to the east. And if we do run into them,

we've got a better chance of standing on diplomatic immunity when they're in the field and under control by their officers than when they're turned loose on the city. I can speak Landisch and I've got the necessary papers."

And code words to prove he was a double agent working for Land Military Intelligence, if it came to that. Useful with the army, although the Fourth Bureau would probably kill him. Military Intelligence was as much the Fourth Bureau's enemy as anything in Santander was.

"Let's go," he finished.

They jogged over to the engine, grateful when its clean smell of hot iron, oil and soot overcame the slaughterhouse stink of the abandoned dying. John lifted Pia up with both hands on her waist, then her friend. Three of the Marines scrambled up onto the heap of broken coal that filled the fuel car; the rest of the party jammed themselves into the cab.

"Going to be a bit crowded," Sinders said, tapping at gauges and studying the swing of dials and the level of fluid in segmented glass tubes. "She's hot, though— plenty of steam. Could use a little coal . . . not that way, ye daft pennyworth!"

One of the marines jerked his hand back from the handle of the firebox set into the forward arch of the cab's surface.

"Use the shovel!" Sinders said. "Lay me down some, and I'll get this bitch movin'—beggin' your pardon, ma'am," he said to Pia.

John took the worn, long-handled tool down from the rack, sliding through the press of men and women. The ashwood was silky-smooth under his hands; he flicked the handle of the firedoor up and to the side, swinging the tray-sized oblong of cast iron open until it caught on the hook opposite. Hot dry air blasted back into the cab of the locomotive, with a smell of sulfur and scorched metal.

"Wilton, you get back with the others on the fuel car,

I'm going to need some room here. Darling, could you and—"

"Lola. Lola Chiavri," the other woman said.

"Miss Chiavri get on those benches." Short iron seats were bolted under the angled windows at the rear sides of the cab, so that an off-duty fireman or stoker could sit and watch the track ahead.

John spat on his hands and dug the shovel into the coal that puddled out of the transfer chute at the very rear of the cab.

"Spread it around, like, sir," Sinders said, turning valve wheels and laying a hand on one of the long levers. "Not too much. Kind of bounce it off that-there arch of firebrick at the front of the furnace, you know?"

John grunted in reply. The second and third shovelfuls showed him the trick of it, a flicking turn of the wrists. *Have to get someone to spell me,* he thought. He was amply strong and fit for the task, but his hands didn't have the inch-thick crust of callus that anyone who did this for a living would develop.

WHUFF. WHUFF. Steam billowed out from the driving cylinders at the front of the locomotive.

"Keep it comin', sir. She's about ready." Sinders braced a foot and hauled back on another of the levers. "Damn, they shoulda greased this fresh days ago. Goddam wop maintenance."

There was a tooth-grating squeal of metal on metal as the driving wheels spun once against the rails, the smell of ozone, a quick shower of sparks. Then the engine lurched forward, slowed, lurched again and gathered speed with a regular *chuff . . . chuff . . .* of escaping steam. Pia grinned at John as he turned for another shovelful of coal; he found himself grinning back.

"Did it, by God," he said, then rapped his knuckles against the haft of the shovel in propitiation.

Sunlight fell bright across them as they pulled out of the train station; he flipped the firedoor shut and slapped Sinders on the shoulder.

"Halt just before that signal tower and let me down for a moment," he half-shouted over the noise into the Marine's ear. "I'll switch us onto the mainline."

The trooper looked dubiously at the complex web of rail. "Sure you . . . yessir."

John leaped down with the prybar in hand. The gravel crunched under his feet, pungent with tar and ash. A film of it settled across the filthy surface of what had once been dress shoes; he found himself smiling wryly at that. He looked up for an instant and met Pia's eyes. She was smiling too, and he knew it was at the same jape.

That's some woman, he told himself, as he turned and let Center's glowing map settle over his vision. She recovered fast.

connections are here . . . and here.

Thanks, he thought absently.

you are welcome.

He drove the steel into the gap between the rails and heaved. *After all these years, I'm still not sure if Center has a sense of humor.*

Neither am I, if it's any consolation, Raj replied.

Chunk. The points slid into contact. He sprinted down the line a hundred yards and repeated the process, then waved. The locomotive responded with a puff of steam and a screech of steel on steel as Sinders let out the throttle. At his wave, it kept going; he sprinted alongside and grabbed at the bracket, grunted, took two more steps and swung himself up into the crowded cabin.

He looked ahead, southeastward. The track was clear. "Let's go home," he said.

"Home," Pia whispered. She buried her head against John's chest, and his arm went around her shoulders.

Pia went pale as she slid down from the saddle, biting her lip against the pain. Lola was weeping, but silently, and he was feeling the effects of days of hard riding himself. The Marines were in worse condition than John; they were fit men, but they were footsoldiers, not accustomed to spending much time in the saddle.

"See to the horses," John said, looking upslope to the copse of evergreen oaks.

They were only a hundred miles from the Gut, and the landscape was getting hillier; the deep-soiled plain of the central lowlands was behind them, and they were in a harder, drier land. Thyme and arbutus scented the air as he climbed quickly to the crest of the hill; the other side showed rolling hills, mostly covered in scrub with an occasional olive grove or terraced vineyard or hollow filled with pale barley stubble. Occasional stands of spike grass waved ten meters in the air. The rhizome-spread native plant was almost impossible to eradicate, but individual clumps never expanded beyond pockets where the moisture level and soil minerals were precisely correct. And a dusty gray-white road, winding a couple of thousand yards below them. On it, coming down from the north . . .

John relaxed. That was no Chosen column. A shapeless clot of humanity grouped around half a dozen two-wheeled ox carts, a few men on horseback, mostly civilians on foot, some pulling handcarts heaped with their possessions.

"Refugees," he said, as Pia and several of the Marines came up. "We can cut—wait."

He pressed himself flat again and raised his field glasses. There was no need to say more to the others; four weeks struggling south through the dying Empire had been education enough for all of them. The troops pouring over the hills on the other side of the road were ant-tiny, but there was no mistaking the smooth efficiency with which they shook themselves out from column into line. Half were mounted—on mules—the other half trotting on foot beside, holding on to a stirrup iron with one hand.

Chosen mobile-force unit, Raj said. *You can move*

fast that way, about a third again as fast as march-
ing infantry.

The Land troops were all dismounting now, mule-
holders to the rear, riflemen deploying into extended
line. There was a bright blinking ripple as they fixed bayonets. Others were lifting something from panniers on
the backs of supply mules, bending over the shapes they
lifted down.

machine guns, Center commented.

"Christ on a crutch," Smith whispered. "They're
gonna—"

The refugees had finally noticed the Chosen troops.
A spray of them began to run eastward off the road
about the same time that the Land soldiers opened fire.
The machine guns played on the ones running at first;
the tiny figures jerked and tumbled and fell. The rest
of the refugees milled in place, or threw themselves into
the ditches. Two mounted men made it halfway to where
John lay, one with a woman sitting on the saddlebow
before him. The bullets kicked up dust all around them,
sparking on rocks. The single man went down, and his
horse rolled across him, kicking. The second horse crumpled more slowly. A group of soldiers loped out toward
it, and the male rider stood and fired a pistol.

The long jet of black-powder smoke drifted away.
Before it did the man staggered backward; three Land
rifles had cracked, and John saw two strike. He dropped
limply. The woman tried to run, holding something that
slowed her, but the Protégé troopers caught her before
she went a dozen strides. She seemed to stumble, then
fell forward with a limp finality. There was a small *snap*
sound. One of the troopers slammed his bayonet through
her back and wrenched it free with a twist; the body
jerked and kicked its heels. Another kicked something
out of her outstretched hand, picked it up, then flung
it away with an irritable gesture. It landed close enough
to the ridge for him to see what it was—a pocket derringer, a lady's toy in gilt steel and ivory.

John turned his head aside, shutting his ears to the screams from the road, and to the whispered curses of Smith and the Marines. That showed him Pia's face. It might have been carved from ivory, and for a moment he knew what she would look like as an old woman—with the face sunk in on the strong bones, one of those black-clad matriarchs he'd met so often at Imperial soirées, and as often thought would do better at running the Empire than their bemedalled spouses.

The Land soldiers kept enough of the refugees alive to help drag the bodies and wrecked vehicles off the roadway. Then they lined them up with the compulsive neatness of the Chosen and a final volley rang out. The column formed up on the gravel as the slow *crack* . . . *crack* . . . of an officer's automatic sounded, finishing the wounded. Then they moved off to the Santander party's left, heading north up the winding road through the dun-colored hills.

John waited, motioning the others down with an extended palm. Five minutes passed, then ten. The sun was hot; sweat dripped from his chin, stinging in a scrape, and dripped dark spots into the dust inches below his face with dull *plop* sounds. Then . . .

"Right," he muttered.

Two squads of Land soldiers rose from where they'd hidden among the tumbled dead and wagons, fell into line with their rifles over their shoulders and moved off after their comrades at the quickstep.

"Tricky," Smith said. "What'll we do now, sir?"

"We go down there," John said, standing and extending a hand to help Pia up. "Pick up supplies and head south along that road toward Salini just as fast as the horses can stand."

Pia looked down towards the road and quickly away. Smith hesitated. "Ah, sir . . . if it's all the same . . ."

"Do it," John said. Smith shrugged and turned to call out to the others.

No harm in explaining, as long as it isn't a question of discipline, Raj prompted him.

John nodded; to Raj, but Smith caught the gesture and paused.

"We can move faster on the road," John said. "Also if we don't have to stop for food, including oats for the horses. That detachment was clearing the way for a regimental combat team. With our remounts, we can outrun them."

Smith blinked in thought, then drew himself up. "Yessir," he said, with a small difficult smile. "Just didn't like the idea of, well—"

Pia's hand tightened in John's. "That was what happens to the weak," she said unexpectedly. "We're all going to have to become . . . very strong, Mr. Smith. Very strong, indeed."

The Santander party moved forward over the crest and down the slope towards the road, leading their horses over the rough uneven surface speckled with thorny bushes. The shod hoofs thumped on dirt, clattered against rocks with an occasional spark. None of the humans spoke. Then John's head came up.

What's that noise? he thought.

A thin piping. Pia stopped. "Quiet!" she said.

John put up his hand and the party halted. That made the sound clearer, but it had that odd property some noises did, of seeming to come from all directions.

the sound is— Center began.

Pia released John's hand and walked over to the body of the woman who'd shot herself rather than be captured by the Land soldiers. John opened his mouth to call her back, then shut it; Pia had probably—certainly—seen worse than this in the emergency hospital back in Ciano.

The Imperial girl rolled the woman's body back. John could see her pale; the soft-nosed slug from the derringer had gone up under the dead woman's chin and exited through the bridge of her nose, taking most of the center of her face with it. Not instantly fatal, although it would have been a toss-up whether she bled out from that first or from the bayonet wound through the kidneys.

—**an infant,** Center concluded, as Pia picked up a cloth-wrapped bundle from where the woman's body had concealed it. She knelt and unbound the swaddlings. John came closer, close enough to see that it was a healthy, uninjured boychild of about three months—and reassured enough by the contact to let out an unmistakable wail. Also badly in need of a change; Pia ripped a square from the outer covering and improvised.

"There's a carrying cradle on the saddle of that horse, I think," she said, without looking up. "Why doesn't someone get it for me and save the time?"

Don't even try, lad, Raj said at the back of John's mind.

Nightmare images of himself trying to convince Pia that it was impossible to carry a suckling infant on a forced-march journey through the disintegrating Empire flitted through John's mind. He smiled wryly, even then.

Besides, he thought, looking down at the road, *there's been enough death here.*

"Sinders, do that," he said aloud. "Let's get moving. And if there's a live nanny goat down there, somebody truss it and put it over one of the spare horses."

CHAPTER TEN

The throng filling the Salini waterfront had the voice of surf on a gravel beach: harsh, sometimes louder or softer, but never silent. A mindless, inhuman snarl.

The bridge of the protected cruiser *McCormick City* was crowded as well. Many of those present were civilians whose only business was to speak with Commodore Maurice Farr, Officer Commanding the First Scouting Squadron. The situation didn't please Farr. Captain Dundonald, the flagship's captain, was coldly livid, though openly he'd merely pointed out that the admiral's bridge and cabin in the aft superstructure would provide the commodore with more space.

Farr sympathized with his subordinate, but "subordinate" was the key word here. He had no intention of removing himself to relative isolation while trying to untangle a mare's nest like the evacuation of Santander citizens and their dependents from Salini. Farr was sleeping in the captain's sea cabin off the bridge, forcing Dundonald to set up a cot in the officers' library on the deck below.

"Commodore Farr," said Cooley, spokesman for the captains of the five Santander freighters anchored in the jaws of the shallow bay that served Salini for a harbor, "I want you to know that if you don't help us citizens like your orders say to, you'll answer to some damned important people! Senator Beemody is a partner in Morgan Trading, and there's other folk involved who talk just as loud, though they may do it in private."

Three of the other civilian captains nodded

meaningfully, though grizzled old Fitzwilliams had the decency to look embarrassed. Fitz had left the navy after twelve years as a lieutenant who knew he'd never rise higher in peacetime. That was a long time ago, but listening to a civilian threaten a naval officer with political consequences still affected Fitzwilliams in much the way it did Farr himself.

"Thank you, Captain Cooley," Farr said. "I'll give your warning all the consideration it deserves. As for the specifics of your request . . ."

He turned to face the shore, drawing the civilians' attention to the obvious. The Salini waterfront crawled with ragged, desperate people for as far as the eye could see. The *McCormick City* and two civilian ferries hired by the Santander government were tied up at the West Pier. A hundred Santander Marines and armed sailors guarded the pierhead with fixed bayonets.

Behind them, the six staff members of the Santander consulate in Salini sat at tables made from boards laid on trestles. The vice-consuls poured over huge ledgers, trying to match the names of applicants to the register of Santander citizens within the Empire.

The job was next to hopeless. No more than half the citizens visiting the Union had bothered to register. The consulate staff was reduced to making decisions on the basis of gut instinct and how swarthy the applicant looked.

Every human being in Salini—and there must have been thirty thousand of them as refugees poured south as the shockwave ahead of unstoppable Chosen columns—wanted to board those two ferries. Farr's guard detachment had used its bayonets already to keep back the crowd. Very soon they would have to fire over the heads of a mob, and even that wouldn't restrain desperation for long.

"Gentlemen," Farr said, "the warehouses on Pier Street might as well be on Old Earth for all the chance you'd have of retrieving their contents for your employers. If I landed every man in my squadron, I still couldn't clear the waterfront for you. And even then what would you do? Wish the merchandise into your holds? There aren't any stevedores in Salini now. There's nothing but panic."

Farr's guard detachment daubed the forelocks of applicants with paint as they were admitted to the pier. It was the only way in the confusion to prevent refugees from coming through the line again and again, clogging still further an already cumbersome process.

A middle-aged woman with a forehead of superstructure gray leaped atop a table with unexpected agility, then jumped down on the other side despite the attempt of a weary vice-consul to grab her. She sprinted along the pier. Two sailors at the gangway of the nearer ferry stepped out to block her.

With an inarticulate cry, the woman flung herself into the harbor. Oily water spurted. One of the Santander cutters patrolling to intercept swimmers stroked to the spot, but Farr didn't see her come up again.

"There's a cool two hundred thousand in tobacco aging in the Pax and Morgan Warehouse," Cooley said. "Christ knows what all else. Senator Beemody ain't going to be pleased to hear he waited too long to fetch it over."

This time he was making an observation, not offering a threat.

Salini's Long Pier was empty. The two vessels along the East Pier, itself staggeringly rotten, had sunk at their moorings a decade ago.

The wooden-hulled cruiser *Imperatora Giulia Moro* still floated beside the Navy Pier across the harbor, but she was noticeably down by the stern. The *Moro* had put out a week before along with the rest of the Imperial Second Fleet under orders from the Ministry in Ciano. The Second Fleet was a motley assortment. Besides poor maintenance and inadequate crewing levels, all the vessels had in common was their relatively shallow draft. That made operation in the Gut less of a risk than it would have been for heavier ships, since the Imperial Navy's standard of navigation was no higher than that of its gunnery.

The *Moro* had limped back to her dock six hours later. She hadn't been out of sight of the harbor before her stern seams had worked so badly that she was in imminent danger of sinking. Now her decks were packed with refugees to whom the illusion of being on shipboard was preferable to waiting on land for Chosen bayonets.

The *Moro*'s crew had vanished in the ship's boats, headed across the Gut to Dubuk in Santander. Farr couldn't really blame them. Those men were likely to be the fleet's only survivors—unless the other vessels had cut and run also.

A steam launch chuffed toward the *McCormick City*'s port quarter, opposite the pier. A Sierra flag hung from the jackstaff. Diplomats? At any rate, another complication on a day that had its share already. For the moment, Captain Dundonald's crew could deal with the matter.

The remaining civilian present on the bridge was the one Farr had sent armed guards to summon: Henry Cargill, Santander's consul in Salini and the official whose operations Farr was tasked to support. Turning from the bridge railing—brass at a high polish, warmly comforting in the midst of such chaos—Farr fixed his glare on the haggard-looking consul.

"Mr. Cargill," Farr said, "if we don't evacuate this port shortly there will be a riot followed by a massacre. I have no desire to shoot unfortunate Imperial citizens, and I have even less desire to watch those citizens trample naval personnel. When can we be out of here?"

"I don't know," the consul said. He shook his head, then repeated angrily, "I'm damned if I know, Commodore, but I know it'll be sooner if you let me get back to the tables. I'm supposed to be spelling Hoxley now—for an hour. Which is all the sleep he'll get till midnight tomorrow!"

Cargill waved at the waterfront. The refugees stood as dynamically motionless as water behind a dam—and as ready to roar through if a crack appeared in the line of Santander personnel.

"They're coming from the north faster than we can process the ones already here," he continued. "Formally, I have orders to aid the return of Santander citizens to the Republic. *Off* the record, I have an expression of the government's deep concern lest large numbers of penniless refugees flood Santander."

A party of armed men had pushed their way through the crowd to the pierhead. Farr tensed for a confrontation, then relaxed as the guard detachment passed the new arrivals without even painting their foreheads. There were women among them, and unless the distance was tricking Farr's eyes, some of the men wore portions of Santander Marine *dress* uniforms.

Cargill bitterly quoted, " 'The Ministry trusts you will use your judgment to prevent a situation that might tend to embarrass the government and draw the Republic into quarrels that are none of our proper affair.' The courier who brought that destroyed the note in front of me after I'd read it, but I'm sure the minister remembers what he wrote. And the president does, too, I shouldn't wonder!"

Farr looked at the consul with a flush of sympathy he hadn't expected to feel for the man who was delaying the squadron's departure. Consular officials weren't the only people who were expected to carry the can for their superiors in event an action had negative political repercussions. "I see," he said. "I appreciate your candor, sir. I'll leave you to get back to your—"

Ensign Tillingast, the *McCormick City*'s deck officer, stepped onto the bridge with a look of agitation. Behind him were a pair of armed marines and a bareheaded civilian wearing an oilskin slicker.

Tillingast looked from Farr to Captain Dundonald, who curtly nodded him back to the commodore. Farr commanded the squadron, but he *didn't* directly control the crew of the flagship. He tried to be scrupulous in going through Dundonald when he gave orders, but the natural instinct of the men themselves was to deal directly with the highest authority present in a crisis.

"Sir, he came on the launch," Tillingast said, "I thought I should bring him right up."

The stranger took off his slicker and folded it neatly over his left forearm. Under it he wore the black-and-silver dress uniform of a lieutenant in the Land military service, with the navy's dark blue collar flashes and fourragere dangling from his right epaulet. To complete his transformation he donned the saucer hat he'd carried beneath the raingear.

"I am not of course a spy," the Land officer said with a crisp smile to his surprised audience. He was a small, fair man, and as hard as a marble statue. "The ruse was necessary as we could not be sure the animals out there—"

He gestured toward the crawling waterfront.

"—would recognize a flag of truce."

Drawing himself to attention, he continued, "Commodore Farr, I am *Leutnant der See* Helmut Weiss, flag lieutenant to *Unterkapitan der See* Elise Eberdorf, commander of the Third Cruiser Squadron."

He saluted. Farr returned the salute, feeling his soul return to the stony chill that had gripped it every day of his duty as military attache in the Land.

"I am directed to convey *Unterkapitan* Eberdorf's compliments," Weiss said, "and to inform you that she is allowing one hour for neutral shipping to leave the port of Salini before we attack."

"I see," Farr said without inflection.

The ships of Farr's squadron were almost as heterogeneous a group as the Imperial Second Fleet. The *McCormick City* was a lovely vessel—6,000 tons, twenty knots, and only five years old. She mounted eight-inch guns in twin turrets fore and aft, with a secondary

battery of five-inch quick-firers in ten individual sponsons on the superstructure. The *Randall* was five years
older, slower, and carried her four single eight-inch guns
behind thin gunshields at bow and stern. Farr was of
the school that believed armor which wasn't at least
three inches thick only served to detonate shells that
might otherwise have passed through doing only minor
damage.

At least the *Randall*'s secondary battery had been
replaced with five-inch quick-firers during the past year.
Guns that used bagged charges instead of metallic cartridges loaded too slowly to fend off torpedo attack.

The *Lumberton* was older yet, with short-barrelled
eight-inch guns and a secondary battery of six-inch
slow-firers that had been next to useless when they were
designed—at about the time Farr was a midshipman.
Last and least, the *Waccachee Township* wore iron armor
over a wooden hull much like the poor *Imperatora
Giulia Moro* across the harbor. She'd never in her career
been able to make thirteen knots.

"Attack what?" Captain Dundonald said. "Good God,
man! Does this look like a military installation to you?"

Lieutenant Weiss chuckled. "Yes, well," he said. "You
must understand, gentlemen, that though it will doubtless
take a year or two to reduce the animals to a condition
of proper docility, we must first close the cage door.
Besides, the squadron needs target practice. We were
escorting the transports at Corona."

He eyed the *Moro*. The brightly clad refugees gave
the impression that the ship was dressed in bunting for
a gala naval review of the sort the Empire had so dearly
loved. "From what those who were present at Corona
say, the Imperial main fleet wasn't much more of a
danger than that hulk will be."

Farr tried to blank his mind. The image of shells slamming home among the mass of humanity on the *Moro*
was too clear; it would show on his face. And if he spoke,
something unprofessional would come out of his mouth.

"Commodore—" said a breathless Ensign Tillingast, bursting onto the bridge again.

"Ensign!" Farr shouted. "What the *hell* do you think you're doing, breaking in on—"

"Your son, sir," Tillingast said.

"Jeffrey?" Farr blurted. He wished he could have the word back as it came out, even before John Hosten stepped through the companionway hatch.

John was limping slightly. He'd lost twenty pounds since Farr last saw him; and, Farr thought, the boy had lost his innocence as well.

"Sir, I'm sorry," John said. "I became separated from Jeffrey in Ciano. He was in Corona when—"

John appeared to be choosing his words with as much care as fatigue and sleeplessness allowed him. Farr had seen his son's eyes flick without lighting across Weiss' uniform.

"When we last spoke," John resumed, "Jeffrey intended to present himself to a Chosen command group. He felt association with Land forces was of more benefit to his professional development and that of the Republic's army than remaining with the Imperials would be."

Lieutenant Weiss allowed himself a tight smile. Captain Dundonald ostentatiously turned his back.

"I'm confident that so long as my sons live, they'll do their duty as citizens of the Republic of the Santander," Farr said, his voice as calm as a wave rising on deep water. "As will their father."

If at full strength—probable since Weiss said they hadn't seen action—the Land's Third Cruiser Squadron would be four nearly identical modern vessels. They were excellent sea boats and faster than even the *McCormick City*—unless their hulls were foul; don't assume the enemy is ten feet tall, though be prepared in case he is.

On the other hand, the cruisers were small ships, less than 3,000 tons standard displacement. The ten ten-centimeter quick-firers each carried in hull sponsons were no serious gunnery threat to Farr's squadron . . . but the three torpedo tubes were another matter. Corona had proved how effective Chosen torpedoes could be.

"Lieutenant Weiss," Farr said. "I have orders to give to my command before I reply to your message. I'd like you to remain present so that you can provide your superior with a full accounting."

Weiss clicked his heels to emphasize his nod.

"Commander Grisson," Farr said to his staff secretary, "Signal the squadron, 'Under way in ten minutes.' "

That was a bluff. His ships had one or at most two boilers lighted to conserve coal at anchor. Peacetime regulations. . . . Still, Eberdorf had kept her cruisers over the horizon, so by the time Weiss returned with Farr's reply more than the "hour's deadline" would have passed.

"Make it so, Ryan!" Dundonald snapped to his own signals officer, staring wide-eyed from the wheelhouse. The *McCormick City*'s captain had no intention of standing on ceremony now.

"Gentlemen," Farr continued to the freighter captains watching from the starboard wing of the bridge, "as senior military officer present, I'm asserting federal control over your vessels. You will dock—"

"You can't do that!" Captain Cooley said.

"I *have* done it, Captain," Farr said without raising his voice. "And if you want to return to Santander in the brig of this vessel, just open your mouth once more."

Cooley started to speak, took a good look at the commodore's face, and nodded apology.

Bells rang through the *McCormick City*'s compartments. A gun fired a blank charge as an attention signal; yeomen tugged at the flag halyards, relaying the commodore's orders to the rest of the squadron.

"You will take on board as many civilians as possible," Farr resumed. "By that I mean as many as you can cram on board with a shoehorn. I don't care if you've only got a foot of freeboard showing—it's just eighty miles to Dubuk and the forecast is for calm. Mr. Cargill—"

"Yes." There was a trace of a smile on the consul's worn visage.

"Your personnel will direct civilians onto the transports. Any processing can be done after we dock in Dubuk. I'll leave you forty men for traffic control, which I trust will be sufficient."

"Giving those poor Wops their lives back should be sufficient in itself, sir," Cargill said. "Thank you."

"The remainder of the shore party will be broken down into five twelve-man detachments, Grisson," Farr said. "They will board the federalized transports in order to aid the civilian crews in recognizing naval signals."

"In view of the need for haste, sir," Grisson said, "I assume the signal detachments will proceed directly to their new assignments rather than returning to their home vessels to deposit their sidearms?"

"That's correct," Farr said. Grisson was a nephew of Farr's first wife; a very able boy.

"Commodore," Captain Fitzwilliam said, "I don't guess I've forgotten the signal book in the twenty years I been out. Don't short your gun crews for the sake of the *Holyoke*. We'll be where you put us."

Farr returned his attention to Lieutenant Weiss. The Land officer's face had somehow managed to become even harder and more pale than it had been when he arrived.

"Lieutenant," Farr said, "I regret that I will be unable to comply with Commander Eberdorf's request because it conflicts with my orders to aid the consular authorities to repatriate Santander citizens from Salini. As you've heard, I've taken measures to streamline the process. I'm afraid the loading will nonetheless continue until after nightfall."

Weiss' eyes were filled with cold hatred. Farr suppressed a wry smile. His own feeling toward the Chosen officer were loathing, not hatred.

"Until the process is complete, I must request that Land military forces treat Salini as an extension of the

Republic of the Santander," Farr continued. With age had come the ability to sound calm when the world was very possibly coming apart. "I regret any inconvenience this causes Commander Eberdorf or her superiors. Do you have any questions?"

"I have no questions of a man who doesn't know his duty to his country, *Kommodore*," Weiss said.

"When I have questions about my duty, Lieutenant Weiss," Farr said in a voice that trembled only in his own mind, "it will not be a foreigner I ask for clarification."

Weiss began to put on his oilskins methodically. His eyes were focused a thousand miles beyond the bulkhead toward which he stared.

The freighter captains had been exchanging looks and whispers. Now Captain Cooley spat over the railing and said, "Commodore? The rest of us reckon we can figure out naval signals, too, until this business gets sorted out back home."

He nodded toward the waterfront and added, "Only don't count on that lot being on board by nightfall. If we're not still at the dock at daybreak, then my mother's a virgin."

The Land officer strode for the companionway without saluting or being dismissed.

"Lieutenant Weiss?" Farr called. Weiss stopped and nodded curtly, but he didn't turn around.

"Please inform your superior that if she's dead set on having a battle," Farr said, "we can offer her a better one than her colleagues appear to have found at Corona."

Weiss trembled, then stepped down the companionway.

Farr had never felt so tired before in his life. "Commander Grisson," he said, "Signal the squadron, 'Clear for action.' "

"This is the first time I've seen Corona, Jeffrey," Heinrich said. "The regiment dropped north of town and we never had occasion to work back." He chuckled. "Not such a tourist attraction as I'd been told."

A tang of smoke still hung in the air ten weeks after Land forces overran the city. Work gangs had cleared the streets, using rubble from collapsed structures to fill bomb craters, but there'd been no attempt to rebuild.

There was no need for reconstruction. The port city's surviving civilian population had been removed from what was now a military reservation closed to former citizens of the Empire.

Corona was the node which connected the conquering armies to their logistics bases in the Land. Protégés from the Land performed all tasks. Labor here was too sensitive to be entrusted to slaves who hadn't been completely broken to the yoke. Convoys of vehicles were pouring up from the docks: steam trucks, Land military-issue mule wagons, and a medley of impressed Imperial civilian transport pulled by everything from oxen to commandeered race horses. There was little disorder; military police were out in force directing traffic, wands in their hands and polished metal brassards on chains around their necks. Troops marched by the side of the road, giving way to Heinrich and Jeffrey on their horses. The Chosen officer exchanged salutes with his counterparts as they passed, running a critical eye over the Protégé infantry.

It wasn't the smoke that made Jeffrey Farr's nose wrinkle as he dismounted and handed the reins to the Protégé groom who'd run at his stirrup from the remount corral at the edge of town. Nobody'd made an effort to find all the bodies in the wreckage either. Some of them must be liquescent by now. Well, he'd smelled plenty of other dead bodies in the past weeks. Humans weren't as bad as horses, and nothing was as bad as a ripe mule.

"So," the Chosen colonel said with a grin, "I hope our honored guest found his tour of our new territories to have been an interesting one?"

"Rather a change from the round of embassy parties

I expected when I was posted to Ciano, that's true, Heinrich," Jeffrey said. Part of him wanted to bolt for the gangplank of the *City of Dubuk*, the three-stack liner chartered by the Santander government to repatriate its citizens through Corona. There was no need to do that. Heinrich liked him.

And, God help him, he liked Heinrich. The blond colonel epitomized the virtues the Land inculcated in its Chosen citizens: courage, steadfastness, self-reliance, and self-sacrifice.

You don't have to hate them, lad, said Raj Whitehall in Jeffrey's mind. *Just crush them the way you would a scorpion.*

Though Jeffrey'd seen plenty to hate as well.

Jeffrey lifted the rucksacks paired to either side of his saddlehorn and threw them over his left shoulder. He'd picked up his kit on the move. Clothing, mostly; all of it Land-issue. Life with Heinrich's fire brigade was dangerous enough without being mistaken for an Imperial infiltrator. He'd replace it on board if possible. Already late arrivals boarding the *Dubuk* were giving him hard looks.

"Very luxurious, no doubt," Heinrich said, eyeing the liner critically. "Well, I don't begrudge you that. I'm looking forward to a transient officers' hostel with clean sheets tonight myself. And a few someones to warm them with me, not so?"

The *City of Dubuk*'s whistle blew a two-note warning: a minute till the gangplank rose. Crewmen were already taking aboard lines preparatory to undocking. If Jeffrey had missed this ship, he would have had to take a freighter to the Land and there transship to Santander. At least for the present the Chosen had embargoed all regular trade between their newly conquered territories and the rest of Visager.

a pity, that, said Center. **but clandestine supply routes into the area will be sufficient to support our low-intensity guerrilla operations.**

Jeffrey was very glad he was here to board the *Dubuk*. After the campaign he'd just watched, he didn't want to be around the Chosen any longer than necessary.

"Thank you for your hospitality, Heinrich," he said. "And your help in getting me here in time to save a long swim home."

Heinrich laughed and leaned from his saddle to clasp Jeffrey Chosen-fashion, forearm-to-forearm with hands gripping beneath one another's elbow. "An excuse to take my troops out of the field," he said as he straightened. "I'm not the only one who appreciates a little rest and recreation."

The *Dubuk's* whistle blew its full three-note call. Heinrich kicked his horse forward so that its forehooves rested on the gangplank. The animal whickered nervously at the hollow sound. A sailor on the deck above shouted a curse.

"Go then, my friend," Heinrich said. He smiled. "And tell the person who just spoke that if his tongue wags again, I will ride aboard and add it to my other trophies."

Jeffrey started up before someone on shipboard said the wrong thing in trying to clear the gangplank. He knew Heinrich too well to take the threat as a joke.

Nor would I count on the fact he likes you making much difference in the way Heinrich carries out his duties, lad, Raj said. *Nor should it, of course.*

A middle-aged civilian and the *Dubuk's* purser waited for Jeffrey at the head of the ramp. Their grim expressions faded to guarded question when they viewed the diplomatic passport he offered them.

Jeffrey tugged the sleeve of his Land uniform tunic. "I was in the wrong place when the fighting broke out," he said in a low voice. "If you can help me find the sort of clothes human beings wear, I'd be more than grateful."

"Jeffrey, my friend?" Heinrich called as he let his nervous horse step back. A hydraulic winch immediately began to haul the gangplank aboard. "When you have rested, come visit me again. These animals will be providing sport for years, no matter what the Council says!"

Jeffrey waved cheerfully, then moved away from the railing. If Heinrich could no longer see him, he was less likely to shout something that would put Jeffrey even more on the wrong side of an us-and-them divide with everyone else aboard the *City of Dubuk*. "Needs must when the Devil drives," he murmured to the men beside him.

"You're related to John Hosten, I believe, sir?" the civilian asked in a neutral voice.

his name is beemer, Center said. **he is deputy director of the ministry's research desk, though his cover is consular affairs.**

"John's my brother," Jeffrey said thankfully. "Stepbrother, really, but we're very close."

Beemer nodded. "I'll see about replacing your clothes, sir," he said. To the purser he added, "Ferrington? I only need one of the rooms in my suite. I suggest we put Captain Farr in the other one. I know his brother."

The purser still looked puzzled, but he shrugged and said, "Certainly, Mr. Beemer. Captain Farr? That'll be Suite F on the Boat Deck. Would you like a steward to take your luggage there?"

The *City of Dubuk* blew a deep blast. The pair of tugboats on the vessel's harbor side shrilled an answer. Their propellers churned water, taking up the slack in the hawsers binding them to the liner.

Jeffrey hefted his saddlebags with a wan smile. "Thank you, I think I'll be able to manage on my own," he said. "If you gentlemen don't mind, I'll watch the undocking from the bow."

"Of course," said Beemer equably. "I hope you'll have time during the trip to chat with me about your recent experiences."

"Whatever you'd care to do, captain," the purser said. "So far as the crew of the *City of Dubuk* is concerned, this is an ordinary commercial voyage. We're here to assist you."

Jeffrey paused. "For a while there," he said, "I didn't think I'd ever see home alive."

And *that* was the truth if he'd ever told it. He bowed to the two men and walked forward. The deck shivered with the vibration of the tugs' engines.

Center? he asked. *Did Dad think Eberdorf would attack the harbor while he was there?*

There was no chance of that, lad, Raj said. **Commander Eberdorf spent the past three years at a desk in the navy's central offices in Oathtaking. She's too politically savvy to start a second major war while the first one's going on.**

The *City of Dubuk* swayed as she came away from the dock. The lead tug signaled with three quick chirps.

But did Dad *know that?* Jeffrey demanded.

your father does not have access to the database that informs your decisions—and those of raj, Center replied after a pause that could only be deliberate. **nor does he have my capacity for analysis available to him. he viewed the chance of combat as not greater than one in ten, and the risk of all-out war resulting from such combat as in the same order of probability.**

Jeffrey put his hand on the wooden railing. It had the sticky roughness of salt deposited since a deckhand had wiped it down this morning.

Dad thought the risk was better than living with the alternative.

At the time Jeffrey's link through Center had showed him the scene on the bridge of the *McCormick City*, his own eyes had been watching Heinrich and two aides torturing a twelve-year-old boy to learn where his father, the town's mayor, had concealed the arms from the police station.

The ship swayed again, this time from the torque of her central propeller as she started ahead dead slow.

I was so frightened . . . but I'd never have spoken to Dad again if he'd permitted a massacre like the ones I watched.

I had men like your father serving under me, Raj said. *They could only guess at the things Center would have known, but they still managed to act the way I'd have done.*

The *City of Dubuk* whistled again, long and raucously, as all three propellers began to churn water in the direction of home.

I've always thought those people were the greatest good fortune of my career, Raj added.

CHAPTER ELEVEN

Gerta Hosten spat in the dry dust of the village street.

"*Leutnant*, just what the *fik* do you think you're doing?" she asked.

"Setting the animals an example!" the young officer said.

"An example of what—how to show courage and resistance?" she asked.

The subject of their dispute hung head-down from a rope tied around his ankles and looped over a stout limb of the live oak that shaded the village well. He spat, too, in her direction, then returned to a cracked, tuneless rendition of "Imperial Glory," the former Empire's national anthem. Two hundred or so peasants and artisans stood and watched behind a screen of Protégé infantry; the town's gentry, priests, and other potential troublemakers had already been swept up. The packed villagers smelled of sweat and hatred, their eyes furtive except for a few with the courage to glare. The sun beat down, hot even by Land standards on this late-summer day, but dry enough to make her throat feel gritty.

Gerta sighed, drew her Lauter automatic, jacked the slide, and fired one round into the hanging man's head from less than a meter distance. The flat elastic *crack* echoed back from the whitewashed stone houses surrounding the village square and from the church that dominated it. The civilians jerked back with a rippling murmur; the Protégé troopers watched her with incurious ox-eyed calm. Blood and bone fragments and

glistening bits of brain spattered across the feet of the
Protégé who had been waiting with a barbed whip. He
gaped in surprise, lifting one foot and then another in
slow bewilderment.

"*Hauptman*—"

"Shut up." Gerta ejected the magazine, returned it
to the pouch on her belt beside the holster, and snapped
a fresh one into the well of the pistol. "Come."

She put her hand on the lieutenant's shoulder and
guided him aside a few steps, leaning toward him
confidentially. Young as he was, she didn't think he
mistook the smile on her face for an expression of
friendliness; on the other hand, she was a full captain
and attached to General Staff Intelligence, so he'd
probably listen at least a little.

"What exactly did you have planned?" she said.

"Why . . . ammunition was found in the animal's
dwelling. I was to execute him, shoot five others taken
at random, and then burn the village."

Gerta sighed again. "*Leutnant*, the logic of our
communication with the animals is simple." She clenched
one hand and held it before his nose. "It goes like this:
'Dog, here is my fist. Do what I want, or I will *hit* you
with it.'"

"*Ya, Hauptman*—"

"Shut up. Now, there is an inherent limitation to this
form of communication. You can only burn their houses
down *once*—thereby reducing agricultural production in
this vicinity by one hundred percent. You can only kill
them *once*. Whereupon they cease to be potentially useful
units of labor and become so much dead meat . . . and
pork is much cheaper. Do you grasp my meaning, boy?"

"*Nein, Hauptman.*"

This time Gerta repressed the sigh. "Terror is an
effective tool of control, but only if it is applied
selectively. There is nothing in the universe more
dangerous than someone with nothing to lose. If you
flog a man to death for having two shotgun shells—

loaded with birdshot, he probably simply forgot them—then *what incentive is left to prevent them from active resistance?*"

"Oh."

The junior officer looked as if he was thinking, which was profoundly reassuring. No Chosen was actually *stupid*; the Test of Life screened out low IQs quite thoroughly, and had for many generations. That didn't mean that Chosen couldn't be willfully stupid, though—over-rigid, ossified.

"So. You must apply a *graduated* scale of punishment. Remember, we are not here to exterminate these animals, tempting though the prospect is."

Gerta looked over at the villagers. It was *extremely* tempting, the thought of simply herding them all into the church and setting it on fire. Perhaps that would be the best policy: just kill off the Empire's population and fill up the waste space with the natural increase of the Land's Protégés. *But no. Behfel ist behfel.* That would be far too slow, no telling what the other powers would get up to in the meantime. Besides, it was the destiny of the Chosen to rule all the rest of humankind; first here on Visager, ultimately throughout the universe, for all time. Genocide would be a confession of failure, in that sense.

"No doubt the ancestors of our Protégés were just as unruly," the infantry lieutenant said thoughtfully. "However, we domesticated them quite successfully."

"Indeed." *Although we had three centuries of isolation for that, and even so I sometimes have my doubts.* "Carry on, then."

"What would you suggest, *Hauptmann?*"

Gerta blinked against the harsh sunlight. "Have you been in garrison here long?"

"Just arrived—the area was lightly swept six months ago, but nobody's been here since."

She nodded; the Empire was so damned *big*, after the strait confines of the Land. Maps just didn't convey the reality of it, not the way marching or flying across it did.

"Well, then . . . let your troopers make a selection of the females and have a few hours recreation. Have the rest of the herd watch. From reports, this is an effective punishment of intermediate severity."

"It is?" The lieutenant's brows rose in puzzlement.

"Animal psychology," Gerta said, drawing herself up and saluting.

"*Jawohl. Zum behfel, Hauptman*. I will see to it."

Gerta watched him stride off and then vaulted into her waiting steamcar, one hand on the rollbar.

"West," she said to the driver.

The long dusty road stretched out before her, monotonous with rolling hills. Fields of wheat and barley and maize—the corn was tasseling out, the small grains long cut to stubble—and pasture, with every so often a woodlot or orchard, every so often a white-walled village beside a small stream. Dust began to plume up as the driver let out the throttle, and she pulled her neckerchief up over her nose and mouth. The car was coated with the dust and smelled of the peppery-earthy stuff, along with the strong horse-sweat odor of the two Protégé riflemen she had along for escort.

Wealth, I suppose, she thought, looking at the countryside she was surveying for her preliminary report. Warm and fertile and sufficiently well-watered, without the Land's problems of leached soil and erosion and tropical insects and blights. Room for the Chosen to grow.

"We're in the situation of the python that swallowed the pig," she muttered to herself. "Just a matter of time, but uncomfortable in the interval." That was the optimistic interpretation.

Sometimes she thought it was more like the flies who'd conquered the flypaper.

"Mama!"

Young Maurice Hosten stumped across the grass of the lawn on uncertain eighteen-month legs. Pia Hosten waited, crouching and smiling, the long gauzy white skirts spread about her, and a floppy, flower-crowned hat held down with one hand.

"Mama!"

Pia scooped the child up, laughing. John smiled and turned away, back toward the view over the terrace and gardens. Beyond the fence was what *had* been a sheep pasture, when this house near Ensburg was the headquarters for a ranch. Ensburg had grown since the Civil War, grown into a manufacturing city of half a million souls; most of the ranch had been split up into market gardens and dairy farms as the outskirts approached, and the old manor had become an industrialist's weekend retreat. It still was, the main change being that the owner was John Hosten . . . and that he used it for more than recreation.

"Come on, everybody," he said.

The party picked up their drinks and walked down toward the fence. It was a mild spring afternoon, just warm enough for shirtsleeves but not enough to make the tailcoats and cravats some of the guests wore uncomfortable. They found places along the white-painted boards, in clumps and groups between the beech trees planted along it. Out in the close-cropped meadow stood a contraption built of wire and canvas and wood, two wings and a canard ahead of them, all resting on a tricycle undercarriage of spoked wheels. A man sat between the wings, his hands and feet on the controls, while two more stood behind on the ground with their hands on the pusher-prop attached to the little radial engine.

"For your sake I hope this works, son," Maurice Farr said sotto voce, as he came up beside John. He took a sip at his wine seltzer and smoothed back his graying mustache with his forefinger.

"You don't think this is *actually* the first trial, do you, Dad?" John said with a quiet smile.

The ex-commodore—he had an admiral's stars and anchors on his epaulets now—laughed and slapped John on the shoulder. "I'm no longer puzzled at how you became that rich that quickly," he said.

If you only knew, Dad, John thought.

wind currents are now optimum, Center hinted.

"Go!" John called.

"Contact!" Jeffrey said from the pilot's seat, lowering the goggles from the brow of his leather helmet to his eyes. The long silk scarf around his neck fluttered in the breeze.

The two workers spun the prop. The engine cracked, sputtered, and settled to a buzzing roar. Prop-wash fluttered the clothes of the spectators, and a few of the ladies lost their hats. Men leaped after them, and everyone shaded their eyes against flung grit. Jeffrey shouted again, inaudible at this distance over the noise of the engine, and the two helpers pulled blocks from in front of the undercarriage wheels. The little craft began to accelerate into the wind, slowly at first, with the two men holding on to each wing and trotting alongside, then spurting ahead as they released it. The wheels flexed and bounced over slight irregularities in the ground.

Despite everything, John found himself holding his breath as they hit one last bump and stayed up . . . six inches over the turf . . . eight . . . five feet and rising. He let the breath out with a sigh. The plane soared, banking slowly and gracefully and climbing in a wide spiral until it was five hundred feet over the crowd. Voices and arms were raised, a murmured *ahhhh.*

The two men who'd assisted at the takeoff came over to the fence. John blinked away the vision overlaid on his own of the earth opening out below and people and buildings dwindling to doll-size.

"Father, Edgar and William Wong, the inventors," he said. "Fellows, my father—Admiral Farr."

"Sir," Edgar said, as they shook his hand. "Your son's far too kind. Half the ideas were his, at least, as well as all the money."

His brother shook his head. "We'd still be fiddling

around with warping the wing for control if John hadn't suggested moveable ailerons," he said. "*And* gotten a better chord ratio on the wings. He's quite a head for math, sir."

Maurice Farr smiled acknowledgment without taking his eyes from where his son flew above their heads. The steady droning of the engine buzzed down, like a giant bee.

"It works," he said softly. "Well, well."

"Damned toy," a new voice said.

John turned with a diplomatic bow. General McWriter probably wouldn't have come except for John's wealth and political influence. He stared at the machine and tugged at a white walrus mustache that cut across the boiled-lobster complexion . . . or that might be the tight collar of his brown uniform tunic.

"Damned toy," he said again. "Another thing for the bloody politicians"—there were ladies present, and you could hear the slight hesitation before the mild expletive as the general remembered it—"to waste money on, when we need every penny for *real* weapons."

"The Chosen found aerial reconnaissance extremely useful in the Empire," he said mildly, turning the uniform cap in his fingers.

McWriter grunted. "Perhaps. According to young Farr's reports."

"According to *all* reports, General. Including those of my own service, and the Ministry."

The general's grunt showed what he thought of reports from sailors, or the Ministry of Foreign Affairs' Research Bureau.

"They used dirigibles, you'll note," McWriter said, turning to John. "What's the range and speed? How reliable is it?"

"Eighty miles an hour, sir," John said with soft politeness. "Range is about an hour, so far. Engine time to failure is about three hours, give or take."

The general's face went even more purple. "Then what

bloody f . . . bloody *use* is it?" he said, nodding abruptly
to the admiral and walking away calling for his aide-de-
camp.

"What use is a baby?" John said.

"You're sure it can be improved?" the elder Farr said.

"As sure as if I had a vision from God"—*or Center*—
"about it," John said. "Within a decade, they're going
to be flying ten times as far and three times as fast, I'll
stake everything I own on it."

"I hope so," Farr said. "Because we are going to need
it, very badly. The navy most of all."

"You think so, Admiral?" another man said. Farr
started slightly; he hadn't seen the civilian in the brown
tailcoat come up.

"Senator Beemody," he said cautiously.

The politician-financier nodded affably. "Admiral.
Good to see you again." He held out a hand. "No hard
feelings, eh?"

Farr returned the gesture. "Not on my side, sir."

"Well, you're not the one who lost half a million,"
Beemody said genially. He was a slight dapper man, his
mustache trimmed to a black thread over his upper lip.
"On the other hand, Jesus Christ with an order from
the President couldn't have saved those warehouses, from
my skipper's reports . . . and you're quite the golden
boy these days, after facing down that Chosen bitch at
Salini. 'We can offer her a better one than her colleagues
appear to have found at Corona,'" he quoted with relish.
The senator's grin was disarming. "What with one thing
and another, grudges would be pretty futile. And I have
no time for unproductive gestures, Admiral. You think
we'll need these?"

"Damned right we will. Knowing your enemy's location
is half the battle in naval warfare. Knowing where he
is while he doesn't know where you are is the other half.
We've relied on fast cruisers and torpedo-boat destroyers
to scout and screen for us, but the Chosen dirigibles
are four times faster than the fastest hulls afloat. *Plus*

they can scout from several thousand feet. We need an equivalent and we need it very badly, or we'll be defeated at sea in the event of war."

"Which some think is inevitable," Beemody said thoughtfully. "I'm not entirely sure—but the news out of the Empire certainly seems to support the hypothesis. Admiral. John."

"People can surprise you," Farr said reflectively as the senator moved through the crowd, shaking hands and dropping smiles.

"Beemody knows when to jump on a bandwagon," John said. "And he's big in steel mills, heavy engineering—a naval buildup will be like a license to print money, to him. And he's no fool; I've done enough business with him to know that."

"Darling," Pia's voice broke in. She hugged his arm; the nursemaid was behind her with the child. "Father." Her eyes went up to the aircraft that was circling downward above them. "I would *love* to do that someday."

John put an arm around her shoulders. "Maybe in a few years," he said. "Here comes Jeffrey."

The plane ghosted down, seemed to float for an instant, then touched with a lurching sway. The Wong brothers ran out to grip the wingtips and keep its head into the wind; other workers brought cords and tarpaulins to stake it down. Jeffrey Farr swung down from the controls, pulling off his helmet and waving to the cheers of the crowd. He vaulted the fence easily with one hand on a post, then walked towards his father and stepbrother. One arm was around the waist of a pretty dark girl who clung and looked up at him, laughing.

"I see you've already found a way to profit from the glamour of flight, Jeff," John said, bending over her hand.

"Too late," Jeffrey replied. "Meant to tell you, you're going to be best man."

John looked up quickly, to find Pia laughing at him.

"Some things even the wife of your bosom doesn't tell you," he said resignedly.

And I told Center not to tell you, either, Raj said. There was a smile in the disembodied voice.

"Well, I haven't told Mother yet, either," Jeffrey said. "There are limits to even *my* courage."

"I'm sure your mother will be delighted," the elder Farr said, bending over Lola's hand in his turn. "But not surprised, after the last year. The Empire has conquered both her sons, it seems."

Pia's face went rigid for an instant, and then she forced gaiety back to it. "A fall wedding, perhaps?"

Jeffrey nodded. "And John won't escape mine—although I should bar him from the church, the way he got hitched without me there, the inconsiderate bastard."

John chuckled. "I'm sure you could see it as vividly as if you'd really been there," he said dryly. "How does she fly?"

"Too businesslike, that's your problem." Jeffrey shrugged. "Sweet, for a machine that underpowered. Very maneuverable, now that the movement of the flaps is extended. The canard keeps the stalling speed low, but I think it'll have to go when you move to an enclosed cockpit; the eddy currents around it close to the ground are tricky. Apart from that, she needs a better engine and something to cut the wind."

"And you must make a speech about it," Pia said, putting her hand through John's elbow.

"Damn," he muttered, looking at the assembly.

About fifty people. Important people, high-ranking military officers, industrialists, reporters for the major papers and wire services, politicians on the military committees.

"It is part of your job," Pia said relentlessly.

John sighed and straightened his lapels. Nobody had ever said the job would be agreeable.

*   *   *

"So much for reports that it could not be done," Karl Hosten said, looking down at the summaries.

Gerta Hosten closed her own file folder with a snap. "Well, sir, it was scarcely a secret that powered heavier-than-air flight was possible. We are here, and not on ancient Terra, after all."

"But our ancestors did not arrive in winged vehicles with propellers," the Chosen general said with a sigh.

Gerta looked up with concern. There was more white than gray in her foster-father's face now, and his face looked tired even at ten in the morning. *Duty is duty,* she reminded herself. Not all the work of conquest was done out on the battlefield.

She was back in Corpenik for a while herself. There wasn't much in the way of fighting left in the Empire—*former Empire, now the New Territories*—for one thing, and for another she was pregnant again, enough months along to rate desk duty for a while. The whitewashed office in the General Staff HQ building was on the third floor; she could see out over the courtyard wall from here, to a vast construction site where gangs of slave labor from the New Territories dug at the red volcanic earth of the central plateau, filling the warm damp air with the scent of mud. Some office building, she supposed; bureaucrats were a growth industry these days. The Land's government had always been tightly centralized and omnicompetent, and there was a lot more for it to do. Or it might be factories. A lot of those were going up, too.

She looked down at the folder. "According to John's report, the Santies are going to push these heavier-than-air craft mainly because their experiments with dirigibles have been such a disaster."

General Hosten nodded and pushed a finger at a photograph. It was a grainy newspaper print, showing the ghost outline of a wrecked and burned airship strewn across a bare grassy hillside with mountains in the distance.

"I am not surprised. Success or failure in airship design is mostly a matter of details, and an infinite capacity for taking pains is our great strength."

Whereas our great weakness is obsession with details at the expense of the larger picture, Gerta thought, silently. There were things you didn't say to a General Staff panjandrum, even if he was your father.

"Still, we'll have to follow suit," Gerta said. "Dirigibles are potentially very vulnerable to aircraft of this type, and they could be very useful in themselves."

Karl nodded thoughtfully, running a finger along his heavy jawline. "I will raise the matter in the next staff meeting," he said. "The Air Council must be informed, of course." Looking down at the folder: "Johan has done good service here."

He was frowning, nonetheless. Gerta noted the expression and looked quickly away. *Not completely comfortable with it*, she thought. *Didn't expect Johnny ever to be false to a cause, even for the Chosen.* She agreed, for completely different reasons, but again, it wasn't the time to mention it.

"Sir, the next item is the Far Western Islands appropriation."

Karl nodded and opened the file. "It seems clearcut," he said. "The islands have a climate that is, if anything, more difficult than the Land; the distance is extreme"— over eight thousand miles—"and the value of the minerals barely more than the cost of extraction."

Gerta licked her lips. "Sir, with respect, I would strongly advise against abandoning the base there at present."

Karl's eyebrows rose. "Why? It scarcely seems cost-effective, now that the Empire is ours."

"Sir, the Empire is poor in minerals, particularly energy sources. Our processing industries here in the Land will be expanding dramatically and the petroleum in the Islands may come in very useful. Besides, I just don't like giving up territory we've spent lives in taking."

He nodded slowly. "Perhaps. I will take the matter under advisement. Next, we the report on our agents in the Union del Est." He smiled bleakly. "The Republic of Santander is not the only party who can play the game of stirring up trouble on the borders."

"*Fuck* it!"

Jeffrey Farr swore into the sudden ringing silence within the tank. The only sound was a dying clatter as something beat itself into oblivion against something equally metallic and unyielding.

He pushed up the greasy goggles and stuck his head out of the top deck. Black oily smoke was pouring up out of the grillwork over the rear deck; luckily there was a stiff breeze from the east, carrying most of it away. The rest of the four-man crew bailed out with a haste bred of several months experience with Dirty Gerty and her foibles, standing at a respectful distance with their football-style leather helmets in their hands.

Jeffrey climbed down himself, conscious that he was thirty-one years old, not the late teens of the other crewmen. Not that he wasn't as agile, it just hurt a little more; and he was tired, mortally tired.

"Filter again?" said the head mechanic of Pokips Motors, the civilian contractors.

"I think," Jeffrey replied, spitting the smell of burning gasoline and lubricating oil out of his mouth and taking a swig from the canteen someone offered. "Then that tore a fuel line or broke the oil reservoir."

The military reservation they were using was on the southern edge of the Santander River valley, two hundred miles west of the capital. A stretch of flatland, then some tree-covered loess hills leading down to the floodplain, ten thousand acres or so. A holdover from days before land prices rose so high; this was prime corn-and-hog country—cattle, too—all around. Most of *this* section was now torn up by the jointed-metal tracks of

Gerty and her kindred, and by the huge wheels of the steam traction engines that winched them home when they broke down, which was incessantly. Gerty was the latest model: a riveted steel box on tracks, about twenty feet long and eight wide, with a stationary round pillbox on top meant to represent a turret. The engineers were still working on the turret ring and traversing mechanism, and hopefully close to finishing them.

"Th' prollem is," the mechanic said, "yer overstrainin' the engines somethin' fierce. Got enough *horsepower*, right enough—two seventy-five-horsepower saloon-car engines, right enough. But the torque load's more'n they wuz designed to stand."

"Well, we'll have to *redesign* them, won't we?"

Jeffrey kept his voice neutral. The man was trying his best to do his job; it wasn't his fault that engineering talent was so much thinner on the ground here in the western provinces of Santander. It was yeoman-and-squire country here, and always had been. Outside the eastern uplands, manufacturing was mostly limited to the port cities and focused on maritime trade and textiles. The problem was that this was prime tank country; the provincial militias here were actually *interested* in the prospect of armored warfare. Nobody but a few dinosaurs like General McWriter thought much of the prospects of horsed cavalry anymore, not after what had happened in the Empire.

Jeffrey felt his skin roughen. The machine guns flickered in his mind, and the long rows of horsemen collapsed in kicking, screaming chaos . . .

"Transmission," he said. "We need a more robust transmission."

"What've yer got in mind?"

Jeffrey pulled out a diagram. "Friction plate," he said. "It's not elegant, but I think it won't keep breaking like this chain drive setup. Like you say, these tanks just have too much inertia for a system designed for three-ton touring cars."

"Hmmmm." The mechanic studied the diagram. "Interestin'."

He looked up at Gerty. A couple of his men had gotten the engine grille up and were spraying water on the flames flickering there.

"How'd them Chosen bastids keep theirs going?" he asked. "Heavier'n this, I hears."

"They use steam engines and mostly they *don't* keep going," Jeffrey said. "We need something reliable enough to do exploitation as well as breakthrough."

The mechanic looked down at the diagram again. "Need some fancy machinin' fer this."

"Hosten Engineering can do you up a model, and jigs," Jeffrey said. "They've got the plans."

John Hosten leaned back in the chair and sipped his lemonade. Oathtaking was hot, as usual, and sticky-humid, as usual, and the air was thick with coal smoke. The hotel was close by the docks; they'd extended hugely since his last visit, new berths extending further into what had been coastal forest reserve and farmland. In fact, he could see one freighter unloading now from this fourth-floor veranda. It was a smallish ship of fifteen hundred tons, swinging sacks of grain ashore with its own booms and steam winches. As he watched the net fell the last four feet to the granite paving blocks of the wharf. Half the bottom layer split, spraying wheat across the stone and into the harbor. Screams and curses rang faintly as the cable paid out limply on top of the heap. Stevedores scurried about, overseers lashing with their rubber truncheons. Eventually a line formed, trotting off with the undamaged sacks on their backs. Others started sweeping up the remainder with brooms and dumping it in a collection of boxes and barrels.

God, I'm glad I don't have to eat that, he thought silently. In this heat and humidity, they'd be lucky not to get ergot all over it.

He nodded towards the dock. "You'd get less spoilage

if you moved to bulk-handling facilities," he said mildly. "Elevators, screw-tube systems, that sort of thing."

Gerta Hosten raised her eyes from the diagrams before her. "We're not short of labor," she said, with a smile that didn't reach the cold, dark eyes.

Meaning they are short of the type of labor that bulk transport would need, Raj said thoughtfully.

An image drew itself at the back of John's consciousness: short, dark-skinned men with iron collars around their necks loading a train—an unbelievably primitive train, with an engine like something out of a museum, an open platform and a tall, thin smokestack topped with sheet-metal petals. Each staggered sweating under a bundle of dried fish secured in netting, heaving it painfully onto the flatcars. Other men watched them, soldiers with single-shot rifles mounted on giant dogs. Occasionally a dog would snap its great jaws with a door-slamming sound and the laborers would shuffle a little faster.

Who needs wheelbarrows when you've got enough slaves? Raj said with ironic distaste. *We got over that, eventually. Thanks to Center.*

and to you, raj whitehall, Center replied.

John reached into the inner pocket of his light cotton jacket and took out his cigarette case. From what he'd described, the centralized god-king autocracy Raj Whitehall had been born into had been almost as nasty as the Chosen—more desirable only because Center and Raj could put their own man on the throne and use that as the fulcrum to move society off dead center. *There seem to be more wrong paths than right,* he thought.

correct. high-coercion societies locked in stasis alternating with barbarism are the maximum probability for postneolithic humanity, Center observed dispassionately. **the original breakthrough to modernity on earth was the result of multiple low-probability historical accidents. observe—**

Later we may have time for lectures, Raj observed. *Meanwhile, John has a job of work to do.*

Gerta looked up again, stacking the reports neatly on the hotel room's table, and took a long drink of water.

"This . . . Whippet?"

"It's a type of racing dog," John said helpfully.

"This Whippet looks like a very useful *panzer*, if you . . . if the Santies can get it working," she observed.

"True enough," John said. "There's a lot of controversy. The western provinces are pushing it, but the easterners want more effort to go into aircraft. And they have most of the internal-combustion manufacturing capacity."

"Yes, I read the speech of this . . . Senator Darman? The representative from Ensburg, in any case—you thoughtfully supplied it with the latest reports. 'I put my faith in our mountains'; a very colorful phrase."

Her strong, calloused fingers turned the sheaf of papers over. "Now, this, this *Land-Cruiser*, it's going to give the Army Council's engineers hives."

The blueprints on the table showed a massive boxy machine, mounting a six-inch gun on its centerline, a two-inch quick-firer in a turret above, and six machine-guns in sponsons on either side.

"What a monstrosity," she went on. "If the Santies are having trouble making the Whippet go, how do they expect this . . . this *thing* to move?"

John leaned forward. A lot of work, mostly Center's, had gone into the Land-Cruiser. It was no easy task to design something beyond Visager's current technological level, but *just* beyond, close enough that competent engineers would be kept busy on the tantalizing quest for this particular Holy Grail. Disinformation was much more than simple lying.

"Each bogie has its own engine," he pointed out.

The huge machine rested on four bogies on either side, each riding on a pivot with bell-crank springs. "See, there's a drive train run through this flexible shaft coupling, and then through meshed gears to the toothed sprocket here between the load-bearing wheels."

"Porschmidt will love this. Unfortunately."

At John's glance she went on: "The new head of Technical Development. He's brilliant, but he keeps trying to make bad designs good instead of junking them—he'd rather design three force pumps and an auxiliary circulation system into an engine rather than just turn a part over to keep it from leaking. You should see what he did to the heavy field gun. It's enough to make a Test of Life examiner cry. He's the sort who gives engineering a bad name; convinced that just because it's his, his shit doesn't stink."

"Well, if the Republic's wasting its time, so much the better," John said with a smile.

"*Ya.* Only, is the Republic wasting its time, or are you wasting ours?"

John kept the expression on his face genial, as his testicles tried to climb back into his abdomen. It was impossible to have a cold sweat in Oathtaking's climate, but you could feel clammy-nauseated.

"Gerta, *min soester,* do you think so little of me?"

"Johan, *min brueder,* I think very highly of you. I think somehow you're fucking Military Intelligence up the butt and making them like it." She grinned, and this time the expression went all the way through. "But you're giving us so much real information to sweeten the pot that I can't convince anyone of it . . . yet."

She sighed, relaxed, and put the documents away in her attaché case, spinning the combination lock. Then she poured some banana gin from the carafe into her water, and a dollop into his lemonade. "Now I'm officially off-duty."

He sipped; the oily-sweet kick of the distillate seemed to match the surroundings, somehow. And one wouldn't affect his judgement noticeably.

"So, I hear you've adopted a child," Gerta said.

"Yes. See, I *am* practicing Chosen custom, as far as I can." They both laughed. "How's your youngest?"

"A shapeless lump of protoplasm, the way they all are at that age," Gerta said.

She pulled a picture from her uniform tunic. A baby looked out, with one chubby hand stuffed in its mouth; the fuzzy background was probably a Protégé wetnurse, from the linen bodice.

"Young Sigvard. That's four, now; I think I've done my duty by the Chosen, don't you? It's an interesting experience, pregnancy, but I wouldn't want to overindulge."

"And the adoptees?"

"Good children, every one," Gerta said. "The one good thing about desk duty is that I get to see more of them; they've been practically living in Father's house most of the time, the last two years, what with the war."

John produced a snapshot of Pia and Maurice junior; Gerta looked at it critically. "Sound enough stock," she said . . . which was a high compliment, by the standards of the Land.

"I hear Heinrich made brigadier?"

"*Ya*, same dispatch-and-notice list that bumped me to full colonel," Gerta said, leaning back and stretching. "They added another six divisions to the regular roster, lots of new hats to go around. Especially with all the demotions and such after the Campaign Study."

John nodded. The General Staff had high standards; there had been a lot of shaking up after the campaign in the Empire. Mere success wasn't good enough . . .

Mark of a good army, lad, Raj said. *Anyone can learn from his mistakes. It takes sound doctrine to be able to learn from winning.*

"Enough other compensations to go around, I suppose," he said aloud.

Gerta chuckled. "Well, the Council *has* been handing out estates fairly liberally. Mostly in the west, around Corona, to start with. Too much unrest for it to be safe for us to scatter ourselves around widely, just yet." A shrug. "We'll deal with that in due course."

CHAPTER TWELVE

"Christ, how do I git myself inta these things?" one of the Marines behind him in the longboat muttered.

John smiled in the darkness. That was Barrjen. The stocky Marine had managed to volunteer—unofficially, the whole mission was highly off the record—despite his loud relief at making it home last time. In fact, the ones who'd been with him from Ciano to Salini had *all* volunteered, even Smith with his gimp foot. Some of them had been pretty shamefaced about it, as if they were mentally kicking themselves, but they'd all done it.

It was a moonless night and overcast, typical weather for winter in the Gut. The whaleboat glided silently over the dark water; they might as well have been rowing in a closet, for all that he could see. Water purled under the muffled oars, breath smoked. Only the radium dial of his compass guided them, that and . . .

"Down!" he hissed quietly.

The dozen men in the boat shipped oars and turned their cork-blackened faces downward in the same motion. A few seconds later the quiet thumping of a marine steam engine came over the water. A searchlight stabbed out into the darkness, blinding bright, the arc light flicking over the waves. Behind it was a gaggle of other boats. Fishing boats; the Chosen couldn't shut down the Gut fishery, it was too important to the economy, and too many of the important pelagic species were best caught in darkness. They *did* send out a gunboat to make sure nobody tried to make a break for the Santander or Union shores, and probably kept the families of the fishermen hostage, too.

The light flicked past them. Weaker lights were breaking out among the fishing boats, lure lanterns strung out over bows and sides. John waited tensely until they were surrounded by the other boats, several dozen of them spread out widely.

"Wait for it . . ."

A thrashing of whitewater as something big broached and snapped for the dangling lantern of a boat, something with a long head full of white teeth. Yells drifted over the water, and he could see a man poised with a harpoon, backlit against the oil lamp. He struck, and a monstrous three-lobed tail came up out of the water. Other boats were closing in, to help with the first catch and wait for the others that would be drawn by the commotion and the blood in the waters.

"Now! Stroke, stroke!"

The Land gunboat was out further in the Gut, hooting its steam whistle and scanning with the searchlight . . . but it was guarding against attempts to get *away*, not looking for boats making for the ex-Imperial shore. John kept his right hand on the whaleboat's tiller, flicking an occasional glance down at the compass in his left. That was mostly for show; Center kept a ghostly vector arrow floating before his gaze.

there are now echoes from cliffs of the configuration indicated, the machine said. **distance one thousand meters and closing.**

Thump. John's head whipped around. That was the gunboat's cannon . . . ah. "Just a big 'un," he whispered to the crew.

You got an occasional one of those, even in the shallow waters of the Gut. Nothing like the monsters that made sailing the outer seas hazardous, but too much for a harpooner to handle. There had been very little life on land when humans arrived on Visager, but the oceans more than made up for it. The Chosen officer on the gunboat probably thought of it as sport, something to break the dull routine of night escort work. And very good cover for John.

"We'll be coming up on the cliffs soon," he said quietly. "Half-stroke . . . half-stroke . . ."

The oars shortened their pace, scarcely dipping into the water. He could hear the slow boom of surf now, thudding and hissing on rock. John held up his signal lantern and carefully pressed the shutter: two long, two short, one long.

A flicker answered him, two shorts, repeated—all that they dared use, with the light pointing out to the Gut.

"Yarely now," the lead Marine in the head of the boat said. There was a quiet *plop* as he swung the lead. "By the mark, six. Six. Five. Six. Four. Four."

Rock loomed up on either hand, just visible as the waves broke and snake-hissed over it. A river broke the cliff near here, cutting a pathway that men or goats could use.

"By the mark, seven. Ten. No bottom at ten."

The pitching of the boat changed, calmer as they moved into the sheltered waters. John felt sweat matting his hair under the black knit stocking cap. The guerrillas would be waiting; the guerrillas, or a Fourth Bureau reaction squad.

"Rest oars," he said.

The poles came in, noiseless. The boat coasted, slowing . . . and the keel crunched on shingle. Four men leapt overboard into thigh-deep water, fanning out with their weapons ready. The rest followed them a second later, putting their shoulders to the whaleboat's sides and running it forward. John drew the revolver from his shoulder rig and ran forward to leap off the bow.

there, Center said, reading input from his ears too faint for his conscious mind to follow.

He walked forward, sliding his feet to avoid tripping on the uneven surface. A match glowed, cupped in a hand, just long enough for him to recognize the face.

Arturo Bianci, the *cotadini* he'd shipped the arms to, back when the war began. Two years looked to have aged the man ten, which wasn't all that surprising.

A hand gripped his. "No lights," John warned.

Bianci made a sound that was half chuckle. "We have learned, *signore*. Those of us who live, have learned much."

They had; there were ropes strung from sticks to guide up the steep rocky path. Guerrillas joined the Marines in unloading the crates and lashing them to their shoulders with rope slings. John swung crates down from the boat, pleased with the silence and speed . . . and waiting for the moment when lights would spear down from the clifftop and voices sound in Landisch. At last the boat road high and empty, rocking against the shingle.

"This way," John said.

Harry Smith nodded, and together they pushed it upstream, under an overhang of wild olive and trailing vines. Smith reached in, rocking it to one side with his weight, and pulled the stopper. Water gurgled into the whaleboat, and it sank rapidly in the chest-deep stream.

"I'll put a few rocks in her," Smith said. "She'll be here when y'all get back. So'll I be. Good luck, sir." He racked a shell into the breech of his pump shotgun.

"Thanks. To you, too—we're all going to need it."

Heinrich Hosten looked at the thing that twitched and mewled on the table. The Fourth Bureau specialist smiled and patted it on what was left of its scalp.

"Yes, I'd say they're definitely planning on something to do with the train," she said. "Can't tell you exactly where, though—the subject didn't know, that's for certain."

Heinrich nodded thanks as he left. Outside he stood thoughtfully beside his horse for a while, looking around at the buildings of the little town, then pulling a map from the case at his side and tilting it so that the lantern outside the Fourth Bureau regional HQ shone on the paper. When he mounted, he turned towards the barracks, his escort of riflemen clattering behind him through the chill night.

"No, don't wake Major van Pelt," he said to the sentry outside the main door. It had been a monastery before the conquest, perfect for its new use; a series of courtyards with small rooms leading off, and large common kitchens, refectories for mess halls. "Who's the officer of the day?"

That turned out to be a very young captain. Heinrich returned her salute, then smiled as he stuffed tobacco into his big curved pipe.

"*Hauptman* Neumann, what's a junior officer's worst nightmare?"

"Ah . . ." Captain Neumann knotted her brow in thought. "Surprise attack by overwhelming numbers?" she said hopefully.

"Tsk, tsk. That would be an *opportunity* for an able young officer," Heinrich said genially. "No, a nightmare is what you are about to undergo; an operation conducted with a senior officer along to look over your shoulder and jog your elbow. What forces are stationed here in Campo Fiero?"

"One battalion of the Third Protégé Infantry, currently at ninety-eight percent of full strength, and a squadron of armored cars—five currently ready, three undergoing serious maintenance. That is not counting," she added with an unconscious sniff, "police troops. Plus the usual support elements."

"Troops so-called," Heinrich said, nodding agreement. He turned to the map table that filled one corner of the ready room. "Ah, yes. Now, find me a train schedule. While you're at it—I presume your company is on reaction status? Good. While you're at it, get your troops ready to move, full field kit, but no noise. Nobody to enter or leave the barracks area."

He stared at the map, puffing with the pewter lid of

the pipe turned back. *Now,* he thought happily, *if I were a rebellious animal, where would I be?*

"Good choice," John said.

Bianci grunted beside him. "The bridge would have been better, but there are blockhouses there now—a section of infantry and a couple of their accursed machine guns at each end. With signal rockets always at the ready."

John nodded. Oto was up; the smallest of Visager's three moons also moved the fastest, and although it was little more than a bright spark across the sky, it did give *some* light. Enough to see how the railway track curved around a steep rocky hill here, falling away to a stretch of marsh and then a small creek on the other side. The guerrillas numbered about sixty; Bianci hadn't offered to introduce anyone else, which was exactly as it should be.

"We got quite a few trains at first," Bianci said. "But then the *tedeschi* began making villagers from along the lines ride in carriages at front."

"You can't allow that to stop you," John said.

Bianci glanced his way, a shadowed gleam of eyeball in the faint moonlight, the smell of garlic and sweat.

"We didn't," he said. "But the villagers began to patrol the rail line themselves . . . to protect their families, you understand. So now we pick locations far from any habitation. Like this."

"Good ground, too," John said.

One of the Marines came up the hill, trailing a spool of thin wire. Another squatted next to John, placing a box next to him. It had a plunger with an handbar coming out of the top, and a crank on the side. Bianci leaned close to watch as the Marine cut the wire and split it into two strands, stripping the insulation with his belt knife. The raw copper of the wire matched the hairs on the backs of his huge freckled hands, incongruously delicate as they handled the difficult task in near darkness.

"Ahh, *bellissimo*," the Imperial said. "We've been using black powder with friction primers—and since they started putting a car in front of the locomotive, that doesn't work so well."

"We can get detonator sets to you," John said. "But you'll have to come up with the wire—telegraph wire will do well enough."

Bianci nodded again. "That we can do." He looked down at the track hungrily. "Every slave in the rail yards tells us what goes on the cars. This one has military stores, arms and ammunition, medical supplies, and machine parts for a new repair depot north of Salini; the *tedeschi* have been talking of double-tracking the line from the Pada to the coast . . . why, do you think?"

"They'll be reopening the trade with the Republic and the other countries on the Gut, soon," John replied. "And to be able to move supplies and troops faster. They have—"

Far away to the northwest, the mournful hoot of a locomotive's steam whistle echoed off the hills. Bianci laughed, an unpleasant sound. "Right on time. The trains run on time, since the *tedeschi* came . . . except when we arrange some delays."

John burrowed a little deeper behind a scree of rock. *I have to be here, dammit,* he thought. The guerrillas had to see that they were getting some support, however minimal. The problem was that the Santander government wasn't ready to really give that support, not yet. It was surprising what you could do with some contacts and a great deal of money, though.

Silence stretched. Bianci raised himself on an elbow. "Odd," he said. "They should be on the flat before this stretch of hills by now."

"Glad you stopped," Heinrich said, shining his new electric torch up at the escort car.

"Yessir."

The vehicle was a standard armored car, fitted with

outriggers so that it could ride the rails, and a belt-drive from the wheels to propel it. Doctrine said that fighting vehicles had to have a Chosen in command; in this case, a nervous young private, showing it by bracing to attention in the turret and staring straight ahead, rigid as the twin machine guns prodding the air ahead of him.

"At ease," the Chosen brigadier said. "Now, we want to do this quickly," he added to Captain Neumann. "Unload boxcars four through six."

Greatly daring, the commander of the armored car spoke: "Sir, those are—"

"Military supplies. I'm aware of that, Private." The rigid brace became even tighter. He turned back to Neumann. "Then get the I-beams rigged and we'll load the cars."

Luck had been with him; there had been a stack of steel forms, the type used to frame the concrete of coast-artillery bunkers, in Campo Fiero. Used as ramps, they could get an armored car onto the train . . . with ropes, pulleys, winches, and a lot of pushing. Getting down would be easier, he hoped.

Orders barked sotto voce had the hundred-odd troopers of Neumann's company slinging crates out of boxcars, the Chosen officers pitching in beside their subordinates. Others were unstrapping the steel planks from the armored cars waiting where the little dirt road crossed the rail line. Heinrich moved forward as the crew of sweating Protégé infantry staggered; they were still panting from the five-mile forced march to intercept the train.

But nobody saw us get on, the Chosen officer thought a little smugly, catching the corner of the heavy metal shape. Muscle bulged in his arms and neck as he braced himself and heaved it around, teeth clenched around the stem of his pipe.

"Dominate that piece of equipment!" he barked as the Protégés took up the strain.

They obeyed, looking at him out of the corners of their

eyes. A slightly awed look; he'd taken two strong men's load for half a minute. The steel clanged down on the side of the flatcar, and the armored vehicle's driver started to back and fill, aligning his wheels with the ramp.

Heinrich stepped back, dusting his palms. Somewhere south of here waited a pack of animals with delusions of grandeur. Somehow that reminded him of Jeffrey Farr, Johan's foster-brother. A good man: sound soldier, a bit soft, but sound. A great pity they'd probably have to kill him someday.

"And I was right," he muttered to himself. "There *is* going to be good sport here for years."

"The sun sets, but it also rises," Bianci whispered, putting his hand to the pushbar of the detonator set.

"Hmmm?" John said, startled out of reverie.

"An old saying, *signore*."

The train whistle hooted again, louder. *Always a melancholy sound*, John thought, taking a swig from his canteen. Oto was nearly down, but Adele was up, brighter and slower as it rose over the horizon. An armored car running on the rails came first, buzzing along with the belt from its rear wheels slapping and snarling. The turret moved restlessly, probing the darkness. A light fixed above the machine guns swept across the slope. John tensed.

Nothing, he thought, breathing in the scent of the dew-damp thyme crushed beneath his body. *Good fire discipline*. Not one of the men on the slope had been detected, and not one moved.

"Now," Arturo breathed, spinning the crank on the side of the detonator. Then he pushed down on the plunger.

WHUMP. WHUMP. WHUMP.

Three globes of magenta fire blossomed along the curving stretch of rail. One before the escort car; it braked desperately, throwing roostertails of sparks from its outrigger wheels. Not quite fast enough. The front wheels tumbled into the mass of churned earth and twisted iron that the dynamite had left, and the hull toppled slowly sideways, accelerating to fall on its side and skid down the gravel and earth of the embankment. The locomotive was a little more successful, braking in a squeal of steel on steel that sent fingers of pain into John's ears even half a thousand yards away. The front bogie dropped into the crater the explosive mine left, tipping the nose of the locomotive down. That jacknifed the coal car and first boxcar upward off the tracks, leaving them dangling by the couplings that held them to the engine. The rest of the boxcars jolted to a crashing halt. Most of them partially derailed, lunging to the right or left until brought up by the inertia of the car ahead, leaving the whole train of two dozen cars lying in a zigzag. But none were thrown on their sides. . . .

"Going too slow," Arturo said, puzzled.

Realization crystallized, like a lump in John's gut. *"Trap!"* he shouted. "Get—"

Schoonk. A mortar threw a starshell high into the sky above them. Blue-white light washed over the stretch of hill and swamp, acintic and harsh to their dark-adapted eyes. *Schoonk. Schoonk.*

A rippling crackle of small-arms fire broke out across the hillside and from guerillas concealed in the swamp across the embankment; they'd learned that an ambush worked best with two sides. A captured machine gun was in place there, too, its brighter muzzle flashes contrasting with the duller, redder light of the ex-Imperial black-powder rifles most of the partisans carried.

"Pull back!" John shouted into Arturo's ear. "Get out, leave a rearguard and *get out now.*"

The guerilla leader hesitated. With a sound like a giant ripping canvas across the sky, more than a dozen belt-fed Haagen machine guns cut lose from the train. The guerillas' rifle fire was punching through the thin pine boards of the boxcars, but John could see it sparking and ricochetting from steel within. Gunshields; the machine guns were fortress models, with an angled steel plate to protect the gunner. Their fire beat across the hillside like flails of green tracer, intersecting hoses of arched light through the night. Sparks scattered as the high-velocity jacketed bullets spanged off stone; little red glows showed where rounds had cut reeds in the swamp, like the mark of a cigarette touched to thin paper. Scores of Protégé infantry were tumbling out of the cars, too, some falling, more going to ground along the train and returning fire.

And the doors of the rear boxcars were thrown open from within. Steel planks clanged down, and the dark lurching shape of armored cars showed within. The first skidded down the ramp, landing three-quarters on, almost going over, then steadying. Its engine chuffed loudly as the wheels spun and spattered gravel against the side of the train, and then the turret traversed to send more machine-gun fire against the hillside. Squads of infantry rose and scurried into its shelter, advancing behind it as the car nosed towards the lower slopes of the hill. A grenade crunched with a malignant snap of light. Three more of the war-cars thudded to the ground, crunching through the trackside gravel.

John grabbed Arturo's shoulder. "*Get the fuck out of here!*" he screamed in the partisan's ear. Then to Barrjen: "Collect the rest. Time to bug out."

"Yes *sir.*"

With a long dragon hiss, a rocket rose from the wrecked train. It kept rising, a thousand yards or more, then burst in a shower of gold—the colors of the Chosen flag, yellow on black.

"Sound the *halt in place*," Heinrich Hosten said, standing with his hands on his hips. "And remember, live prisoners."

Troopers were moving down the hillside under the

glare of the arc light, prodding at bundles of rags with their bayonets. Occasionally that would bring a response, and the soldiers would pick up the wounded guerilla; cautiously, after the first one who'd stuffed a live grenade under his body was found.

The trumpet sounded, four urgent rising notes. A slow crackle of skirmish fire in the hill country to the west died down. In the comparative silence that followed he could hear the relief train that the signal rocket was intended for, with the rest of the battalion and its equipment. Plus the equipment and workers to repair the track, of course. It was surprisingly difficult to do lasting damage to a railway track without time or plenty of equipment.

"Shall we pursue when the rest of the battalion comes up, Brigadier?" Captain Neumann said.

"*Nein*," he said. "Too much chance of ambushes in the dark." He got out his map case. "But it would be advisable to push blocking forces *here* and *here*. Then in a few hours, we can sweep and see how many of these little birds we can bag."

Captain Neumann looked at the emergency aid station where her wounded were being looked after. There were four bodies with their groundsheets drawn over their faces.

"We only killed twenty or so of them," she said. "This is a bad exchange rate."

"The operation is not over," Heinrich said. "And we have taught them a little lesson, I think."

"That is the problem—when we teach them a lesson, they *learn*," Neumann said unexpectedly.

Heinrich shrugged. "We must see that we learn more than they," he added, knocking the dottle out of his pipe.

The cave smelled bad: damp rock, and the wastes of the survivors, since they hadn't dared go outside for the last three days. Weak daylight was leaking through, enough penetrating this far into the cave to turn the absolute blackness into a gray wash of light.

"We failed," Arturo said bitterly.

"We survived," John replied. "Enough of us. Next time we'll do better."

"So will they!" the guerilla said.

"We'll just have to learn faster," John said. "Besides, there are more of us than of them."

He looked toward the light. "Now we'd better check if their patrols are still looking," he said. "It's a fair hike back to the cove."

John Hosten's wasn't the biggest steam yacht under Santander registry, by a considerable margin; they were a common status symbol among the rising industrial magnates of the Republic. The *Windstrider* was only about twelve hundred tons displacement. It *was* the most modern, with some refinements that Center had suggested and John had made in the engineering works he owned. One of them was a wet-well entrance on the side that could be flooded or pumped dry in less than a minute, as well as turbine engines, something no vessel in the Republic's Navy had yet. The little ship lay long and sleek against the morning sun, a black silhouette outlined in crimson.

"Row! Bend yer *backs* to it, y'scuts!"

Smith's voice had a hard edge from the bows. John knew why; he could hear it without turning from his position at the tiller. A deep chuffing, the hollow sound steam made when exhausted into the stack of a light ship, and the soft continual surf noise of a bow wave curving away from the prow, just on the edge of hearing. The gunboat had picked them up twenty minutes ago, and it had grown from a dot on the horizon to a tiny model boat that grew as he watched, shedding a long plume of black coal smoke behind from its single cylindrical funnel.

"Stroke!" he barked, willing strength to flow from his

voice through the crew to the oars. "Stroke! Almost home! Stroke!"

Sweat glistened on their faces, mouths gasping for air. A new sound came through the air, a muffled droning.

"Smith!"

One-handed, John tossed the binoculars to the ex-Marine. He took them and looked upward. "Oh, shit, sir. One of them gasbag things. Just comin' into sight, like."

"How many engine pods?"

"Four. No, four at the sides an' one sort of at the back."

"Skytiger. Patrol class," John said. Center helpfully offered schematics and performance specifications. "They've got a squadron of them operating out of Salini now."

The *Windstrider* was very close. John felt himself leaning forward in a static wave of tension, and grinned tautly at himself. If things went badly, the yacht was no protection at all, merely a way to get a lot of other people killed with him. And his subconscious *still* felt as if he was racing for absolute safety. A ghost-memory plucked at him, something not his own. Raj Whitehall spurring his riding dog for a barge, with enemies at his heels. . . .

Damn, he thought. *You seem to have had a much more picturesque life than me.*

Adventure is somebody else in deep shit, far, far away, Raj said. **And I think you're about to be that somebody. Focus, lad, focus.**

The long hull loomed up. John threw his weight on the tiller and the whaleboat heeled sharply, turning in its own length to curve around the bow and come down the side away from the Land gunboat. The narrow black slit of the loading door came up fast, perhaps too fast.

. . .

"Ship oars!" he called.

The long ashwood shafts came inboard with a toss;

Marines were well-trained in small-boat operations. One caught the edge of the steel slit nonetheless, snapping off and punching a rower in the ribs with enough force to bring an agonized grunt. The whaleboat shot into the gloom of the inner well; the overhead arc light seemed to grow brighter as the metal door slid shut. The air was humid, hot, with a smell of machine oil and sweat.

The crew collapsed over their oars, wheezing, faces red and dripping. John vaulted onto the sisal mats that covered the decking—an irony there, since the fiber had probably been imported from the Land—nodded in return to the crew's salutes, and took the staircase three rungs at a time. The hatchway to the boat chamber clanged shut below him; someone dogged it shut below, and a crewman threw matting over the hatch, leaving it looking identical to the rest of the corridor. He stepped through a doorway, and suddenly he was in the passenger section of the yacht. Soft colorful Sierran carpets underfoot, walnut panelling . . . by the time he reached his cabin, his valet was already towelling down his torso. He changed with rapid, precise movements, stuck a cigarette into a sea-ivory holder, and strolled out on deck.

"About bloody time," Jeffrey observed, making a show of looking at the approaching Chosen gunboat with his binoculars. "How'd it go?"

"You saw it—a damned ratfu— er, walking disaster."

Pia came up and took John's arm. "*Tedeschi* pigs," she muttered under her breath. Her eyes were fixed on the Chosen vessel, as well.

Good thing she's not on the guns, John thought.

There were four guns on the yacht, port and starboard forward and aft of the mid-hull superstructure. Nothing too remarkable about that; any vessel on Visager's seas had to have some armament, given the size and disposition of the marine life. The two-and-a-half-inch naval quick-firers on pedestal mounts were not entirely typical, however—nor was the fact that they could elevate to ninety degrees. Two were, their muzzles tracking the leisurely approach of the Chosen dirigible; the other two followed the gunboat. *That* had a three-inch gun behind a shield on the forecastle, another at the stern, and pom-poms—scaled-up machine guns firing a one-pound shell—bristling from either flank. The Chosen captain wouldn't be worried about the purely *physical* aspects of any confrontation, even without the airship. Although that confidence was possibly overstated, since the yacht had an underwater torpedo tube on either side.

"Try to look like a man on his honeymoon," John told his stepbrother.

"I'm trying," Jeffrey replied through clenched teeth. "He's signaling . . ." A bright light flickered from the Chosen gunboat. "*Heave to and prepare to be boarded,*" he read. "Arrogant bastards, aren't they?"

"Jeffrey?" Lola Farr, *née* Chiavri, came up the companionway to the bridge, holding on to her hat. "Is there—" She caught sight of the Chosen vessels. "Oh!"

"Don't worry," Jeffrey said. He nodded his head upward towards the pole mast in front of the yacht's funnel. The flag of the Republic of the Santander snapped in the breeze. "They're not going to start a war."

Although they might be quite willing to endure an embarassing diplomatic accident, John thought morbidly. He wished Pia and Lola weren't along, but then, it would look odd if they weren't, given the cover story. *And Pia wouldn't stay if I nailed her feet to the kitchen floor.*

"Captain," John said quietly to the grizzle-bearded man who stood beside the wheel with his hands clasped behind his back. "Signal *Santander ship, International Waters,* and *sheer off.*"

"Sir." He passed along the orders. "Shall I make speed?"

"No, just maintain your course," John said. The *Windstrider* could probably outrun the Chosen gunboat, but not the airship—or a cannon shell, for that matter. "Act naturally, everyone."

Jeffrey grinned. "*Natural*, under the circumstances, would be scared s— spitless."

"Act arrogant, then; the Chosen understand that."

John looked around at the bridge of the yacht. It was horseshoe-shaped, with another horseshoe within it; the inner one was enclosed, a curved waist-high wall of white-painted steel with windows above that, meeting the roof above. That held the wheel, binnacle, engine-room tele-graph, and chart table. The outer semicircle was open save for a railing of teak and brass and empty save for the two couples and a few stewards. They were in cream-colored livery; Jeffrey wore a summer-weight brown colonel's uniform, and John white ducks, the sort of outfit a wealthy man might wear for playing tennis . . . or yacht-ing. Pia and Lola were in gauzy warm-weather dresses of peach and lavender, looking expensive and haughty.

Perfect, John thought.

The gunboat was running on a converging course, white water foaming back from its bow. As he watched, it swung parallel to the yacht, almost alongside, and slowed to match speed. John smiled tightly and touched Pia's hand where it rested in the crook of his arm. She gave his arm a squeeze and released it. He took a drag on the cigarette, supressing a cough, and strolled in a jaunty fashion to the starboard wing of the open space. His hand rested on the railing, casually touching a certain bronze fitting.

The vessels were less than a dozen yards apart—showing good handling on the part of both crews. That meant that the gunboat was less than a dozen yards from the sixteen-inch midships torpedo tube, armed and flooded. The fitting under his hand was connected to a simple bell-telegraph and light; if he pressed it twice, the men crouched behind the little circular door would pull levers . . . and a slug of high-pressure compressed air would shove the tin fish out of the tube. A few seconds and the Chosen gunboat would be a broken-backed hulk sliding under the waters.

Of course, that would ruin his cover; the airship would report back, or someone in the yacht's crew would talk even if they got lucky . . .

"Ahoy there!" a voice bellowed through a speaking trumpet from the low bridge of the gunboat. Its Santander English was accented but fluent. "'Tis iz *Leutnant der See* Annika Tirnwitz. Prepare to be boarded."

Cannon and pom-poms and machine guns were trained with unnerving steadiness on him, ready to rake the *Windstrider* into burning wreckage in seconds— about as many seconds as the torpedo would take to do its work. The gray-uniformed crew waited in motionless tension, all except for a dozen who were shouldering rifles and making ready to swing a launch from its davits. John pitched his voice to carry.

"This is sovereign territory of the Republic of the Santander. You have no authority here and any act of aggression will be resisted."

"That iz un private vessel! You do not diplomatic immunity haff!"

John pointed up to the flag. "*Leutnant*, you may come aboard with no more than one other member of your crew. Otherwise, I must ask you to get out of my way."

Half-heard orders carried from the gunboat to the yacht. Most of the boarding party who'd been preparing the launch grounded arms and stood easy; the little boat slid down into the water, and several figures in Land uniform slid down ropes from the gunboat's deck to man it. Smuts of black smoke broke from the slender funnel at its stern, a small steam engine chugged, and the launch angled in towards the Santander ship.

"Captain," John called over his shoulder. "Party to greet the *Leutnant*. And a rope ladder, if you please."

Whistles fluted as the Chosen officer came over the side. The escort for her and the Protégé seaman who followed behind were distantly polite; the rest of the crew glared. Everyone was wearing a cutlass and revolver, and carbines stood ready to hand.

Aren't you laying it on a bit thick? Jeffrey thought, the familiar mental voice relayed by Center. *You're supposed to be secretly on their side, after all.*

That's exactly it, John replied. *A good double agent plays his part well—and my part is a wealthy playboy who dabbles in diplomacy, but who is secretly a Foreign Office spook and violently anti-Chosen.*

The irony of it was that the best way to convince his Chosen handlers that he was a competent double agent was to act the way he would if he *wasn't* a double agent, except for his reports to them—he was an information conduit, not an agent of influence. Which meant, of course, that they could never be sure he wasn't a *triple* agent, but that was par for the course.

Espionage could make your head hurt.

Annika Tirnwitz was a tall lanky woman of about thirty, with a brush of close-cropped brown hair and a face tanned and weatherbeaten to the color of oiled wood. Her blue eyes were like gunsights, tracking methodically across the yacht, missing nothing. John thought he saw a little surprise at the quality of the crew and the arms, but . . .

correct, Center thought. **subject tirnwitz is surprised.** A holograph appeared over her face, showing temperature patterns and pupil dilation. A sidebar showed pulse rate and blood pressure. **subject is also experiencing well-controlled apprehension.**

"*Leutnant der See* Annika Tirnwitz," the Chosen said, with a slight stiff nod. "Who is in command here?"

John replied in kind. In accentless Landisch he replied: "Johan Hosten, owner-aboard. What can I do for you, *Leutnant?*"

subject's apprehension level has increased markedly.

Nice to know that he wasn't the only one feeling nervous here, and even nicer that he had Center to reveal what was behind that poker face. Of course, only a fool *wouldn't* be a little fearful of the possible consequences of a fight here. Not the physical ones—

cowards didn't make it through the Test of Life—but the political repercussions. Relations between the Land and Santander had never been all that good, and since the fall of the Empire they'd gone straight down the toilet. The press back home was having a field day with the atrocity stories the refugees were bringing in; the Chosen were too insular to even try countermeasures, they didn't understand the impact that sort of thing had on public opinion in the Republic. John's own papers were leading the charge . . . and the stories were mostly true, at that.

The Chosen *did* understand status and territory and pissing matches, though. Sinking the yacht of a wealthy, powerful man related to a Santander Navy admiral . . .

"*Herr* Hosten?" Tirnwitz said. She cleared her throat. "My vessel was pursuing a small boat. Carrying subversive terrorist elements."

John made a sweeping wave of his hand. "As you can see, *Leutnant*, there's no boat here except our ship's lifeboats, all of which are secured and lashed down . . . and dry."

His eyes lifted slightly to the dirigible. It was much closer now, but when he'd come aboard it had been too far to the north to see what actually happened.

Tirnwitz's lips thinned in frustration. The *Windstrider*'s boats *were* lashed down and tight in their davits; nobody could have hoisted one aboard in the time they'd had. Nor could a whaleboat have made it over the horizon in the yacht's shelter . . . although possibly the men on one could have scrambled aboard and pulled the plug on their boat.

He could see that thought going through Tirnwitz's head. "I must make inspection and question your crew," she said after a moment.

"Impossible," John replied.

Jeffrey moved up to his side. "And to paraphrase what my father said in Salini last year, if you want to start a war, this is as good a place as any."

Pia waved a steward forward with a tray; it looked rather incogruous when combined with the cutlass and revolver at his waist, and the short rifle slung over his shoulder.

"Perhaps the *Leutnant* would like some refreshments?" she said with silky malice. "Before she returns to her ship."

The sailor behind the Chosen captain growled and half moved, then sank back quivering with rage at a fingermotion from her. She stared at Pia for a moment.

"An Imperial. The animals are less insolent in the New Territories these days," she said. "Teaching them manners can be diverting." She nodded to John. "Someday we may serve Santander refreshments, a drink you'll find unpleasant. *Guten tag.*"

CHAPTER THIRTEEN

The blast furnace shrieked like a woman in childbirth, magnified ten thousand times. A long tongue of flame reached upward into the night, throwing reddish-orange light across the new steelworks. John nodded thoughtfully as the bell-cap was lowered down onto the great cylinder, like a cork into a bottle taller than a six-story building. The flames died down as the cap intercepted the uprush of superheated gases from the throat of the furnace, channeling them through pipes where they were cleaned and distributed to heat ovens and boilers. A stink of cinders and sulfur filled the air, and the acrid nose-crackling smell of heated metal. Gravel crunched under his feet as he turned away, the small party of engineers and managers trailing at his heels.

A train of railcarts rumbled by, full of reddish iron ore, limestone, and black-brown coke in careful proportions. The carts slowed, then jerked and picked up a little speed as the hooks beneath them caught the endless chain belt that would haul them up the steep slope to the lip of the furnace.

"Nice counterweight system you've installed, sir," the chief engineer said. "Saves time on feeding the furnace."

John nodded. *Courtesy of Center,* he thought.

"Saves labor, too," the engineer said. "God knows we're short."

"How are those refugees shaping up?" John said.

"Better'n I'd have thought, sir, for Wop hayseeds. They're not afraid of shedding some sweat, that's for sure."

"Pay's better than stoop work in the fields," John said.

A lot of the Imperial refugees who'd left the camps outside the cities on the south shore of the Gut ended up as migrant workers following the crops across Santander. They'd jumped at the chance of mill work. A couple of them snatched off their hats and bowed as he passed, teeth gleaming white against their soot-darkened olive skins. John touched the gold head of his cane to his own silk topper; luckily white spats were out of fashion, or Pia would be even more upset than she was likely to be with him anyway.

"No damned strikes, either," the plant's manager said.

"Shouldn't be, with the wages we pay," John said.

Off to the left a huge cradle of molten iron was moving, slung under a trackway that ran down the center of the shed. It dropped fat white sparks, bright even against the arc lights, then halted and tipped a stream of white-hot incandescence into the waiting maw of the open-hearth furnace. Further back, beyond the soaking pits for the ingots, the machinery of the rolling mill slammed and hummed, long shafts of hot steel stretching and forming.

The engineer nodded towards them. "We're fully up to speed on the rail mill," he said. "If you can keep the orders coming in, we can keep the steel going out."

John nodded. "Don't worry about the orders," he said. "Plenty of new lines going in, what with the double-tracking program. And the Chosen are buying for their new lines in the Empire."

That brought the conversation behind him to a halt. He looked back at the expressions of clenched disapproval and grinned; it was not a pleasant thing to see.

"You're selling to the Chosen?" the engineer said.

"I prefer to think of it as getting the Chosen to finance our expansion program," John replied.

What's more, it's good cover. Several times over. It gave him a good excuse for traveling to the Land, which helped with his ostensible work as a double agent in the employ of the Chosen. The shipments were also splendid cover for agents and arms to the underground resistance.

"And besides the sheet-steel rolls, you'll be getting heavy boring and turning lathes soon. From the Armory Mills in Santander City."

That rocked the man back on his heels. "Ordnance?" he said. "That'll *cost*, sir. We'll have to learn by doing, and it's specialist work."

John nodded. "Don't worry about the orders," he said again. "Let's say a voice whispered in my ear that demand is going to increase."

He touched the cane to his hat brim again and shook hands all around. His senior employees had learned to respect John Hosten's "hunches," even if they didn't understand them. Then walked across the vacant yard to where his car was waiting by the plant gate under a floodlight.

"Back home, sir?" Harry Smith said, looking up from polishing the headlamps with a chamois cloth.

"Home," he said. "For a few days."

"Ah," the ex-Marine in the chauffeur's uniform said. "We're going somewhere, then, sir?"

John nodded and stepped into the passenger compartment of the car as Smith opened it for him, tossing hat and cane to one of the seats. There were six, facing each other at front and rear. One held Maurice Hosten, sleeping with his head in Maurice Farr's lap; the older man looked down at his five-year-old namesake fondly, stroking the silky black hair that spilled across the dark blue of his uniform coat. Pia glanced up, with a welcoming smile that held a bit of a frown.

"Even on your son's birthday, you cannot keep from business?" she said.

"Only a little bit of business, darling," he said, settling back against the padded leather of the seat; it sighed for him. "Quietly, or you'll wake him."

Maurice Farr chuckled. "After the amount of cake this

young man put away, not to mention the lemonade, the spun candy, the pony rides, the carousel, and the Ferris wheel, a guncotton charge couldn't wake him—you should know that by now."

"He does; he's just using that as an excuse." Pia's hand took John's and squeezed away the sting of the words. "This one, you wave the word 'duty' in front of him, and he reacts like a fish leaping for a worm."

"And the hook's barbed," John said ruefully, nodding to Smith through the window that joined the passenger compartment and the driver's position up ahead. The car moved forward with a hiss of vented steam.

"Your lady's been running an interesting notion past me," Admiral Farr said.

"This Ladies'—"

"Women's," Pia corrected.

"Women's Auxiliary?" John finished.

"Yes. *If* we get into an all-out war with the Land, we could use it. Though I'm not sure how the public would react; there was a lot of bad feeling during the agitation over the franchise, a decade or so ago. People claiming it was the first step to Chosen corruption and so forth."

"I don't think that'll be much of a problem," John said thoughtfully. Center provided the probable breakdown of public sentiment in various combinations of circumstance. "After all, Pia's idea is to have women take jobs that *release* men to fight. There are already plenty of women in the nursing corps—have been since the last war with the Union, you know, whatshername with the lantern and all that."

"And if the big war happens, we'll need every fighting man we can get," the admiral said thoughtfully. "We'll not win that one without a damned big army, and the fleet'll have to expand, too. We won't be able to spare men for typing and filing and whatnot."

"And factory work," Pia said. "First, we must have a committee—women of consequence, to be respectable, but also of . . . energy."

"If it's energy you want, what about your sisters-in-law?" Maurice said. "If it's one thing my daughters have, it's energy . . . oh."

Pia nodded. "Them I talk to first," she said. "They are young, but there is time."

"It'll be a while," John said. Pia nodded; his foster-father looked at him a little strangely, struck by the certainty of the tone. "But it's not too early to get started laying the groundwork."

"Son, for a man of thirty, sometimes you sound pretty damned old," Maurice said. He touched his graying temples. "Maybe I'd better retire, and leave the field to you younger bucks."

"I don't think you can be spared, Father," John said. "And . . . it isn't all *that* long until the balloon goes up."

"Is it indeed?" Maurice Farr said.

"The situation in the Union's getting pretty tense," John said. "The People's Front may win the next election there."

"The Chosen certainly won't like that," Maurice said. "I'm not too certain I do either. The Union's not going to solve its problems by an attack on property . . . although the way the wealthy act there is a standing invitation to that sort of thing."

John nodded. "The Chosen have a lot of influence in certain circles there," he said. "And I don't think those circles are going to lie down and die just because they lose an election. It'll take a couple of years for things to boil over, but the Land is certainly heating up the pot."

Maurice Farr blinked slowly, his face slowly losing the shape of a grandfather's and becoming an admiral's. "They can't get supplies into the Union except by sea," he said thoughtfully.

John shook his head. "We can't fight them over aiding one faction in the Union," he said. "Western provinces wouldn't go for it."

"All that good soil softens the brain, I think," Farr said.

"Amazing what being a couple of hundred miles from the action will do. And they've always resisted the easterners' attempts to get the Republic as a whole involved in Union affairs; it'll take a while for them to realize this is different."

Pia looked up at him. "This is why you must travel to the Union, my love?" she said.

John sighed unhappily. "Jeffrey and I will be in and out of there for years now," he said. "Until the crisis comes. But don't worry, it shouldn't be particularly risky. We're only advising and playing politics, after all."

Jeffrey Farr had never liked the Union del Est very much. For one thing, the waiters, innkeepers, clerks, and such made it a point of pride to be surly, and he'd never liked seeing a job done badly. For another, the women didn't wash or change their underclothes often enough to suit him; he supposed that that was an academic point now that he was a married man with a nine-year-old daughter and another child on the way, but the memory rankled . . . *and she looked so good, before and after she took off her drawers. But phew!*

The men didn't wash much, either, but that was less personal.

Still, the coastal city of Borreaux looked well enough; the terrain was less mountainous than most of the southern shore of the Gut, a long narrow plain flanking a river between low mountains. The plain was covered with vineyards, mostly; the foothills of the mountains were gray-green with olives, and the upper slopes still heavily forested with oak and silver fir despite centuries of cutting for buildings and ship timber and barrels. The town itself sprawled along the river in a tangle of docks and basins, backed by broad, straight streets lined with trees and handsome three-story blocks of buildings in a uniform cream limestone. The slums weren't quite as bad as in most Union cities and were kept decently out of sight. The rooftop terrace of this restaurant was quite pleasant—sun shining through the striped awnings, servers in white aprons bearing food and drink on trays . . .

. . . and just to spoil it, three Chosen officers in gray were at a table nearby, two men and a woman, and two local ladies. The Land aristocrats were plowing their way through a five-course meal, and punishing a couple of bottles of the local wine fairly hard. Or rather, the two men were, and laughing occasionally with their local companions, who were either extremely high-priced talent or the minor gentlewomen they appeared to be. The Chosen woman was sipping at a single glass of the wine and looking around. Medium-height, dark hair and eyes . . .

Christ, it's Gerta! Jeffrey thought, with a jolt of alarm that turned the hunger in his stomach to sour churning. *Why didn't you tell me?*

Would have, lad, if it'd been an emergency. Don't want you to lose your alertness, though. We can't always notice things for you.

He tried to keep a poker face, but Gerta must have seen some change. She raised the wineglass slightly, and an eyebrow with it. The mannerism reminded him of John a little—but then, they'd been raised together. It startled him sometimes to remember that John had been born among the Chosen. If it wasn't for that clubfoot . . .

observe:

A man's looks were more than muscle and bone; the personality within shaped them, everything from the set of his mouth to the way he walked. It took a moment for Jeffrey to realize that the tall man in the uniform of a Land general was John. The face was the same, but full of a quiet, grim deadliness. The city behind him was familiar, too: Borreaux, but in ruins. A dirigible floated overhead, and columns of Land troops were marching up from the docks.

john hosten is in the upper 0.3% of the human ability curve, Center said. **in the absence of his disability, and assuming no intervention on our**

part, the probability of his achieving general rank
by this date in his timeline is 87%, ±4. probability
of becoming chief of general staff, 73%, ±6.
probability of becoming head of chosen council of
state, 61%, ±8. probability of chosen conquest of
visager increases by 17% ±5 in that eventuality.

Jeffrey gave a slight internal shudder. With no
clubfoot—and no Center—he and John would probably
have spent their lives fighting each other.

correct. probability—

Shut up, Raj and Jeffrey thought simultaneously.

The waiter arrived at last, and laid a bowl of the
famous Borreaux fish stew before him; trivalves in their
shells, chunks of lizard tail, pieces of fish, all in a broth
rich with garlic, tomatoes, and spices. It smelled
wonderful; it would have been even more wonderful if
the waiter hadn't had a rim of grime under his thumbnail, and the thumb hadn't been dipping into the stew.
Jeffrey forced himself to ignore that, and what the
kitchen was probably like; he poured himself a glass of
white wine and tore a chunk of bread off the end of a
long narrow loaf. Say what you liked about the Unionaise,
they did know how to cook.

And it was a damned unlucky chance that Chosen
officers, and Gerta of all people, happened to be right
here when he was expecting—

A small, slight man came up to Jeffrey's table and sat,
taking off his beret and stubbing out a villainous-smelling
cigarette in an ashtray. His eyes flicked sideways toward
the Chosen three tables away.

"They can't hear us," Jeffrey said. "And we're facing
away."

So that they couldn't lip-read. Offhand, he thought
that the two male Chosen were straight-legs; Gerta
certainly wasn't, though, and might well have been
trained in that particular skill. As to what they were doing
here . . .

"And we have business," Jeffrey went on, spooning

up some of the fish stew. "Damn, but that's good," he said mildly.

"Vincen Deshambre," the thin man said. Jeffrey took his hand for a moment. "Delegate of the *Parti Uniste Travailleur*." He slid a small flat envelope out of his jacket and across the table.

"Colonel Jeffrey Farr," Jeffrey replied, reading it.

He spoke fair Fransay, and read it well; the Union del Est had been the Republic's main foreign enemy until a generation or so ago, with skirmishes even more recently. Santander military men were expected to learn the language, for interrogations and captured documents, if nothing else.

Vincen looked over again at the table with the Chosen. "Bitches," he said, his voice suddenly like something that spent most of its time curled up on warm rocks.

Jeffrey looked up, raising his eyebrow. Only one of the Chosen could possibly qualify.

"Not the foreigners," Vincen said. A light sheen broke out across his high forehead, up to the edge of the thinning hair. "They're just pirates. If we were united, we could laugh at them."

I don't think so, Jeffrey thought. Alone, the Union against the Land of the Chosen would be a match between the hammer and the egg. Not *quite* as easy a victim as the Empire had been, of course. For one thing the terrain was worse, for another it was farther away, and for a third the country wasn't quite so backward. *Still, I see his point.* And the Land wasn't about to simply invade the Union. That would mean war with Santander, and the Chosen weren't ready . . . yet.

Neither was Santander.

"Those *whores* are what's wrong, them and those like them."

Jeffrey did a quick scan across the other table, then turned and let Center freeze the picture in front of him, magnifying until they all seemed to be at arm's length. "I don't think they're professionals," he said.

Vincen flushed more deeply; it was a little disconcerting to see a man actually sweating with hate.

"Elite," he said, using the Fransay term for the upper classes. "*Merdechiennes* are losing their power, so they call in foreigners to prop it up for them."

"Well, two can play at that game," Jeffrey said.

The Unionaise gave him a sharp look. Santander had taken several substantial bites out of the western border of the Union, in the old wars. Jeffrey smiled warmly.

"We're not territorially expansive . . . not anymore, at least."

Of course, much of the western Union was an economic satellite of the Republic these days, and the *Travailleur*—Worker—party didn't like it one little bit. Despite the fact that without that investment, its members would still be scratching out a living farming rocks as *metayers*, paying half the crop to a landlord.

Vincen grunted. "As you say. We have the evidence now. General Libert is definitely in correspondence with Land agents. They offer transport for his Legion troops back to the mainland."

Center called up a map for Jeffrey. The Union del Est covered a big chunk of the southern lobe of Visager's main continent, between Santander and the sort-of-republic of Sierra. South of it wasn't much but ocean right down to the south polar ice cap, but there were a series of fairly substantial islands, some independent, some held by the Republic or the Union.

"Libert's on Errif, isn't he? That's quite a ways out, seven hundred kilometers or so. Can't your navy squadron in Bassin du Sud keep him bottled up?"

The Legion were the best troops the Union had, and mostly foreigners at that. They were the ones who'd finally beaten the natives on Errif, after a war where the Union regulars nearly got thrown back into the sea. And there were large units of Errifan natives under Union officers on the islands too, now. They'd probably be about as tough fighting against the Union government as they had been in the initial war.

"The navy is loyal to the government, yes," Vincen said. "But the Land, they offer air transport if there is a matching military uprising on the mainland."

Jeffrey whistled silently, remembering the air assault on Corona in the opening stages of the Imperial war. *Can't fault the Chosen on audacity,* he thought. Errif was a lot further from their bases. *Overfly the Union,* he thought, calculating distances. They could at that; the *Landisch Luftanza* had a concession to run a route that way. Refuel at sea, from ships brought round the continent in international waters. *Yes, it's possible. Just.* You had to be ready to take chances in war; otherwise it turned into a series of slugging matches. Big risks could have big payoffs . . . or disaster, if things went into the pot.

"Why don't you recall him and jail him?" Jeffrey asked. "Before he has a chance to rebel."

Vincen clenched his fists. "Because this coalition so-called government has even less balls than it has brains!" His half-howl brought stares from the tables around them, and he lowered his voice. "Us, the damned syndicalists, the regional autonomists—everyone but the twice-damned anarchists and separatists, and name of a dog! We have to keep them sweet, too, because we need their votes in the *Chambre du Delegats*."

He made a disgusted sound through his teeth, hands waving. Unionaise were like Imperials that way: tie their hands and they were struck dumb as a fish.

"Last year, we could have arrested him. Arrested all the traitors in uniform. What did our so-called government do? Pensioned half of them off! Gave them pensions wrung out of the workers' sweat, so that they could plot at their leisure."

"'Never do an enemy a small injury,'" Jeffrey quoted. "Old Imperial saying." Very old, from what Center said.

Vincen's small eyes were hot with agreement. "We

should have executed the lot of them," he said. "Now it's too late. The government is holding off on General"— he virtually spat the word—"Libert in the hopes that if they don't *provoke* him, he'll do nothing."

"Stupid," Jeffrey said in agreement. "They're also probably afraid that if they send troops to arrest him, they'll go over to him instead."

Vincen nodded jerkily. "There are loyal troops—the Assault Guards, for instance—but yes, the ministry is concerned with that."

"Which brings us down to practicalities," Jeffrey said. "If there *is* a military uprising with Land support, what exactly do you plan to do about it?"

"We will fight!"

"Yes, but what will you fight *with*?"

The little Unionaise linked his fingers on the table. "We have confidence that part of the army at least will remain loyal. Beyond that, there are the regional militias."

Jeffrey nodded. He had no confidence in them; for one thing, they had even less in the way of real training than the provincial militias back home. Some of the states of the Union were run by the conservative opposition parties, and thereby pro-Chosen. Even in the ones that weren't, too many of the militias were under the influence of local magnates, almost all of whom supported the conservative opposition parties, as did the Church here. The Church here *was* a great landed magnate, come to that.

"And we'll hand out arms to the party militias of the coalition, and to the workers in the streets—let's see how the Regulars like being drowned in a *sea* of armed workers."

"It's good to see you're in earnest," Jeffrey said. It all sounded like a prescription for a bloodbath, but that was preferable to another swift Chosen triumph, he supposed. "For my part, I can assure you that my government will declare any outright intervention in internal Union affairs an unfriendly act."

That meant less than it should; semi-clandestine intervention wouldn't provoke Santander retaliation. The Republic simply wasn't ready for war, either physically or psychologically.

"And I think we can guarantee that you'll be allowed to purchase weapons. Speaking in my private capacity, you'll also find some of our banks sympathetic in the matter of loans. Provided your government is equally reasonable."

"I suppose you'll want concessions. . . ."

They settled down to dicker; when Vincen left, the expression on his face was marginally less sour. Fortunately, the Chosen officers left a little later. The men went with their local companions; one of them stopped to say a final word with Gerta Hosten. She laughed and shook her head. The man shrugged, and the girl with him pouted. When they had left, Gerta picked up her wineglass and came over to Jeffrey's table.

"You're welcome," he said as she seated herself without asking permission.

The hard dark face showed a slight smile. "We meet again. A pleasure. It would have been an even bigger one if Heinrich had had the sense to shoot you four years ago. I *told* him you were a spook."

"I'm here on vacation," Jeffrey said, smiling back despite himself. "Besides, Heinrich doesn't have your suspicious mind."

"Which is why he's a straight-leg. Too damned good-natured for his own good." Gerta raised her wineglass. "These Unionaise make some pretty things," she said as the cut crystal sparkled in the evening sun. "And they make good wine. But they couldn't organize sailors into a whorehouse."

"Well, that's your problem," Jeffrey said. "You're the ones with the training mission here."

"Purely as private contractors, on leave from our regular duties," Gerta said piously.

"And I'm a tourist," Jeffrey said.

Unwillingly, he joined in Gerta's chuckle.

"You know the best thing about competing with you Santies?" Gerta asked. When he shook his head, she continued: "It's not that you're short of guts, because you aren't, or because you're stupid, because you aren't that, either. It's that you're never, ever *ready*." She finished her wine and rose.

"And we're going to win this round," she said.

"Why's that, the invincible destiny of the Chosen race?"

"Invincible muleshit," she said cheerfully, with a grin that might have come out of deep water, rolling over for the killing bite. "The reason that we're going to win this one is that we're trying to help fuck this place up—and the Unionaise are positive geniuses at that, anyway."

CHAPTER FOURTEEN

Everyone in Bassin du Sud was afraid. John Hosten could taste it, even without Center's quick flickering scans of the people passing by. The narrow crooked streets were less full of people than he'd seen on previous business visits, and the storekeepers stood at the ends of their long narrow shops, ready to drop the rolling metal curtain-doors. Windows were locked behind the scrolled ironwork of their balconies, and similar ironwork doors had been pulled across most of the narrow entranceways that led to interior courtyards. He could still get glimpses down them, the sight of a fountain or a statue in old green bronze, or a line of washing above plain flagstones.

Gerta's smile haunted him, seen through Jeffrey's eyes.

Every time he'd seen her smile like that, people started dying in job lots.

There was something else about the streets, he decided. *I hope Jean-Claude is still there.* Something very odd about the streets, but he couldn't quite put his finger on it.

few military personnel, Center said.

Bassin du Sud had a fair-sized Union garrison, plus a navy base. In fact, if he turned, he could see part of it downslope from the rise he was on. His stepfather would have gone into a cold rage at the knots hanging from the rigging of the three hermaphrodite cruisers at the dock, and the state of their upperworks, but . . .

The sound hit a huge soft pillow of air, knocking him backward. Down by the naval docks a hemisphere of fire blossomed upwards, with bits and pieces of iron and

231

wood and crewmen from the three cruisers. A stunned silence followed the explosion, then a great screaming roar like nothing he had ever heard in his life.

A mob, Raj's mental voice said softly. *That's the sound of a hunting mob.*

Over it came sounds he had no problem recognizing. First a series of dull soft thuds in the distance, like very large doors slamming. Then a burbling, popping sound that went on and on, rising and falling. Artillery and small arms.

"I'm *late,* God damn it," he said, and began to run. Perhaps too late. The rough pavement was slippery and uncertain under his boots; he kept his right hand near the front of his jacket, ready to go for a weapon.

Careful, lad, Raj cautioned. *I don't think foreigners are going to be all that popular around here right now.*

The narrow street widened a little, into a small cobbled plaza the shape of an irregular polygon, with a fountain in the middle spilling water into granite horse troughs around it. A bullet spanged through the air. He dove forward and rolled into the cover of the troughs, ignoring the stone gouging at his back, and came up with the automatic ready in his hand.

A man in a monk's brown robe was staggering away from the little church on the other side of the plaza. He was a thick-bodied man, with a kettle belly and a round, plump face. A few hours earlier it might have been a good-natured face, the jolly monk too fond of the table and bottle of the stories. Now it was a mask of blood from a long cut across the tonsured scalp. Dozens of men and women in the rough blue clothing of city laborers were following the monk, jeering and poking him with sticks, spitting and kicking. The cleric's heavy body jerked to the blows, but his wide fixed eyes looked out of blood-wet skin with a desperate fixed expression, as if his mind had convinced itself that the exit to the plaza represented safety.

There was no safety for him. One of the mob tired of the fun. The pried-up cobblestone he swung must have weighed ten pounds; the monk's head burst with a sound much like a watermellon falling six stories onto pavement. He collapsed, his body still twitching beneath the brown robe. John swore softly to himself and rose, letting the pistol fall down by his side. The black crackle finish of the weapon's steel probably wouldn't show much against his frock coat . . . and while the ten rounds in the magazine also wouldn't be much good against a charging mob, he didn't intend to die alone if it came to that.

"Hey, there's one of the Chosen dog-suckers who're in bed with the elite and the Christ-suckers!" someone bawled.

"Santander!" John shouted, in a controlled roar. It cut through the murmur of this little outlier of the mob. "I'm from Santander"—*though I was born in Oathtaking and my father's a general on the Council, but there's no need to complicate matters*—"on diplomatic business."

He pulled out his passport with his left hand and held it up. Half the crowd probably couldn't read, much less recognize official stamps, but his accentless Fransay and his manner made them hesitate.

"I'm on my way to the Santander consulate right now," he went on, and pointed to the northward where the sound of fighting was heaviest. "Don't you people have business up there?"

The crowd milled, people talking to their neighbors; individuals once more, rather than a beast with a single mind and will. John holstered his weapon and trotted past them, past the church where flame was beginning to lick out the shattered stained-glass windows. A quick glance inside showed the chaos of swift incompetent looting and the body of a nun lying spread-eagled in a huge pool of blood from her gashed-open throat.

What lovely allies, he thought dryly, and mentally waved aside Center's comments. *I know, I know.*

The streets broadened as he climbed the slope above

the harbor and gained the more-or-less level plateau that
held the newer part of the city. The press of people
grew too, crowds of them pouring in from the dock
areas behind him and from the factory-worker suburbs.
He dodged around an electric tram standing frozen in
the middle of the street, past another burning church—
from the columns of smoke, there were fires all over
town—and past cars, lying abandoned or passing
crammed past capacity. Those held armed men, in civilian clothes or green Assault Guard *gendarmerie* uniforms with black leather hats, or army and navy gear.
All the men in them had red armbands, though, and
some had miniature red or black flags flying from their
long sword-bayonets. John cursed, kicked, and pushed
his way through the crowds, but the press grew closer
and closer; it was like being caught in heavy surf, or
a strong river current.

Suddenly the crowd surged around him, an eddy this
time. He barely cleared the corner onto the Avenue
d'Armes when the shooting broke out ahead, louder this
time. He was enough taller than the Unionaise crowd
to see why. A dozen military steam cars had pulled up
and blocked the road fifty yards ahead. They weren't
armored vehicles, but they each had a couple of pintle-
mounted machine guns. Infantry followed, rushing up
and deploying on and around the cars. Their rifles came
up in a bristle, and the crews of the machine guns were
slapping the covers down and jacking the cocking levers.
The fat water jackets of the automatic weapons jerked
and quivered with their fearful haste.

John felt a cold rippling sensation over his belly and
loins. Everything seemed to move very slowly, giving him
plenty of time to consider. A man in front of him was
pushing a wheelbarrow full of stones and half-bricks,
ammunition for the riot which this no longer was. He
squatted—there was no room to bend—gripped the man
by waist and ankle, and heaved. The Unionaise pitched
forward, flying over the toppling wheelbarrow and into

the three men ahead of it, staggering them. They fell
backward against the wood and iron in the same instant
that John dove forward and down onto the bricks it
spilled, into the space it had made, the only open space
in the whole vast crowd.

A giant gripped a sheet of canvas in metal gauntlets
and *ripped*. John curled himself into a ball behind the
wheelbarrow and barred his teeth at the picture his mind
supplied of what was happening ahead. The crowd
couldn't retreat, not really, not with so many thousands
behind them still pressing forward and the high blank
walls on either side.

Twenty machine guns fired continuously, and several
hundred magazine rifles as fast as the soldiers could work
their bolts and reload. Bodies fell over the wheelbarrow,
over John, turning his position into a mount that kicked
and twitched and bled. He heaved his back against the
sliding, thrashing mass; if he let it grow he'd suffocate
here, trapped beneath a half-ton of flesh. The barricade
of bodies shuddered as bullets smacked home. John was
blind in a hot darkness that stank with the iron-copper
of blood and slimy feces and body fluids. They ran down
over him, matting his clothing, running into his mouth
and eyes. He heaved again, feeling his frock coat rip
with the strain. Bodies slid, and a draft of fresher air
brought him back to conscious thought.

Can't attract attention . . .

Through a gap he could see the rooftops beyond the
barricade of war-cars. Something moved there, and
something smaller flew though the air.

Crump. The dynamite bomb landed between two cars
and rolled under the front wheels of one. It backflip-
ped onto the vehicle next to it with a rending crash of
glass and metal; superheated steam flayed men for yards
around as the flash-boiler coils in both ruptured. Some
officer with strong presence of mind was redirecting fire
to the rooftops on either hand, but more dynamite
bombs rained down. *Crump. Crump. Crump.*

There hadn't been time for panic to infect the whole
mob, even though hundreds—thousands—had been
killed or wounded. Not even Center could have predicted
their reaction. The survivors ran forward, and John ran
with them. One machine gun snarled back into action
briefly, and then the forefront of the mob was scrambling
over the ramp of dead and dying that stood four and five
bodies deep in front of the wrecked war-cars. He dove
over it headfirst, while the surviving soldiers shot down
the rioters silhouetted upright on the edge. The automatic
was in his hand as he knelt. A green grid of lines settled
over his vision, and the aim strobed red as he swung from
one target to the next. *Crack.* A soldier pitched backward
from the spade grips of his machine gun with a round
blue hole between his eyes and the back blown out of
his head by the wadcutter bullet. *Crack.* An officer folded
in the middle as if he'd been gut-punched, then slid
foreward to lie limply among the other dead. *Crack.*
Crack. The slide locked back and his hands automatically
ejected the empty magazine and replaced it with one from
the clips attached to the shoulder-holster rig.

John blinked, breathing hoarsely. His hand shook
slightly as he holstered the automatic and he blinked
again and again, trying to shed the glassy sensation that
made him feel like an abandoned hand-puppet.

I never liked it either, Raj said. There was the
momentary image of a room in a tower, with half a dozen
men sprawled in death across tables and benches. *It's*
necessary, sometimes. Brace up, lad. Work to be
done.

John nodded and wiped at the congealing blood on
his face. *Well, that didn't work.* He stripped off his
businessman's frock coat and used the relatively dry lining
instead, cleaning away enough so that his eyes didn't stick
shut and spitting to clear the taste out of his mouth.
Then he bent to pick up a soldier's fallen rifle and bandolier; the weapon was Land-made or a copy. *No,*
Oathtaking armory marks. He thumbed two stripper

clips into the magazine and slapped the bolt home before working his way to the edge of the crowd. Not much chance his contact would be at home, but it wasn't far and he had to check.

Snipers were firing from the towers of the Bassin du Sud cathedral. The *Maison Municipal* was directly across from it, with improvised barricades of furniture and planter boxes full of flowers in front of the entrances and people shooting back from behind them, and from the windows above. John went down on his belly and leopard-crawled along the sidewalk from one piece of cover to the next. When he was halfway across an explosion lifted him and slammed him against the wall of the building, leaving him half-stunned as the cathedral facade slid into the square in a slow-motion collapse, falling almost vertically. Quarter-ton limestone building blocks mixed with gargoyles and fretwork and fragments of glass avalanched across the pavement. John pressed his face into the sidewalk and hoped that the plane trees and benches to his right would stop anything that bounced this far. There was a pattering of rubble, and something grazed his buttocks hard enough to sting; then a cloud of choking dust swept across him, making him sneeze repeatedly. The earthquake rumble died down, and he doggedly resumed his crawl.

Willing hands pulled him over the barricade; the crowd behind it included everyone from Assault Guards to female file clerks, armed with everything conceivable, including fireplace pokers and Y-fork kid's catapults. Many of the people there were standing on the piled furniture and cheering the ruin of the cathedral, despite the fact that hostile fire was coming from other buildings around the plaza as well. John prudently rolled to one side before coming erect, grunting slightly as his bruises twinged. An Assault Guard looked at him, unconsciously fingering the pistol at his side.

"Who are you?" he said.

"I'm here to see Jean-Claude Deschines," John replied.

"Just like that?" The *gendarme* had narrow eyes and a heavy black stubble. "I asked who you are."

"And I asked to see Jean-Claude. Tell him John is here with the package he was expecting."

The other man's eyes narrowed; he nodded and trotted off. John set his back against a twisting granite column and wrestled his breath and heartbeat back under control, ignoring the sporadic shooting and cheering and trying to ignore the deadly whine of the occasional ricochet making it through the barricaded windows. Ten years ago he wouldn't have been breathing hard. . . . The entrance hall was dark because of those barricades, just enough light to see the big curving staircase at its rear, and the usual allegorical murals depicting Progress and Harmony and Industry, the sort of thing the *Syndicat d'Initative* put up in any Unionaise town hall. One did catch his eye, a mosaic piece showing Bassin du Sud as it had looked a couple of centuries ago, with only the grim bulk of the castle on its hill, and a small walled village at its feet. That castle had been built as a base to stop Errife corsairs, back when the island pirates had virtually owned the coast, setting up bases and raiding far inland for slaves and loot.

The castle was still there. And it was the garrison HQ for the Bassin du Sud military district. The curtain walls and moats and arrowslits weren't all that relevant anymore, but there were heavy shore-defense mortars in the courtyards, Land-made breechloaders, capable of commanding the harbor if the plotters consolidated their hold on the garrison.

A tall man with a swag belly clattered down the staircase; he had a police carbine over his shoulder and a pistol thrust through the sash around his waist.

"Jean!" he roared genially, and came toward John with open arms for the hug and kiss on both cheeks that was the standard friendly greeting in the Union. At the last moment he recoiled.

John looked down briefly at his shirt. "Most of it's other people's blood," he said helpfully.

"Name of a dog! You were caught in the street fighting?"

John nodded. "Nearly got massacred by some soldiers with car-mounted machine guns, but somebody dropped dynamite on them. There seem to be a lot of explosions going on today." He jerked his head towards the doors leading out onto the plaza.

"My faith, yes," the mayor of Bassin du Sud said happily. "Copper miners. I . . . ah . . . arranged for a special train to bring in a few hundred of them from up in the hills. Ingenious fellows, aren't they?"

John nodded. They were also anarchists almost to a man, those that weren't members of the radical wing of the *Travailleur* party. A few years ago, when the Conservatives had been in power, they'd taken up arms in a revolt halfway between a damned violent strike and outright revolution. The government had turned General Libert's Legionnaires and Errife loose on them when the regular army couldn't put the insurrection down.

"You're going to need more than dynamite and hunting shotguns to get the garrison out of the castle. Especially if you want to do it before Libert arrives. What've you got in the way of ships to stop him crossing?"

"Three cruisers were lost."

"I saw it. Sabotage?"

The mayor nodded. "Time bombs in the magazines, we think. But there's one corsair-class commerce raider, and some torpedo boats. There were nothing but merchantmen in Errif harbor at last report."

"That's last report. He may shuttle men over by air. Chosen 'volunteers' under 'private contract.' In fact, I wouldn't put it past the Chosen to escort his troopships in with a squadron of cruisers."

"That would mean war!" The mayor's natural olive changed to a pasty gray. "War with the Republic."

"Not if they could claim a local government invited them in."

"Nobody could—"

"*Mon ami,* you don't know what Santander lawyers are like. They could argue the devil into the Throne of God—or at least tie everything up on the question for a year or better. Which is why you have to get some transport down to my ship; she's stuffed to the gills with rifles, machine guns, ammunition, explosives, mortars, and field-guns."

Jean-Claude nodded decisively. "*Bon.*" He turned and began to shout orders.

Gerta Hosten put her eye to a crack in the worn planks of the boathouse. It was crowded, with the half-dozen Chosen commandos and the fishing boat pulled up on the ways, and the stink of old fish was soaked into the oak and pine timbers. The rubber skinsuit she was wearing was hot and clammy out of the water; she shrugged back the weight of the air tank on her back and peered down the docks.

"Still burning nicely," she said, looking over to the naval dockyards. "The storehouses and wharfs are burning, too. Considerate of the enemy to use wooden hulls."

Obsolete, but this was a complete backwater in military terms. All the Union's few modern warships were up in the Gut, and it would take weeks to bring any down here. By then this action would be settled, one way or another. Her companions were too well disciplined to cheer, but a low mutter of satisfaction went through them. Then someone spoke softly:

"Native coming." They wheeled and crouched, hands reaching for weapons. "It's ours."

The Unionaise knocked at the door, three quick and then two at longer intervals. One of the commandos opened it enough for him to sidle in; he looked around at the hard-set faces and swallowed uneasily.

"What news, Louis?" Gerta said, in his language. She spoke all four of Visager's major tongues with accentless fluency.

"Our men are pinned in the garrison and the seafront

batteries," he said. "The *syndicistes* are slaughtering everyone they can catch—everyone wearing a gentleman's cravat, even, priests, nuns . . ."

The Chosen shrugged. What else would you do, when you had the upper hand in a situation like this? Louis swallowed and went on:

"And they are handing out arms to all the rabble of the city."

"Where are they getting them?" Gerta asked. According to the last reports, most of the weapons in Bassin du Sud were in the castle or the fortified gun emplacements that guarded the harbor mouth.

"There is a Santander ship in dock, one that came in a few days ago but did not unload. The cargo is weapons, all types—fine modern weapons. They are handing them out at the dock and sending wagons and trucks full of others all around the city."

"Damn," Gerta swore mildly. That *would* put a spanner in the gears. "Show me."

She unfolded a waterproof map of the harbor and spread it on the gunwale of the fishing boat. Louis bent over it, squinting in the half darkness until she moved it to a spot where a sliver of sunlight fell through the boards.

"Here," he said, tapping a finger down. "Quay Seven, Western Dock."

"Hmmm." Gerta measured the distance between her index and little fingers and then moved them down to the scale at the bottom of the map. "About half a mile, say three-quarters, as we'll swim."

Bassin du Sud had a harbor net, but like all harbors the filth and garbage in the water attracted marine life. And on Visager, marine life meant death more often than not. They'd already lost two members of the team.

"Nothing for it," she said. "Hans, Erika, Otto, you'll come with me. The rest of you, launch the boat and bring it *here*." She tapped a finger on the map; the others crowded around to memorize their positions. "Function check now."

Everyone went over everyone else's air tanks, regulators, and other gear. Hard hat suits with air pumped down a hose had been in use for fifty or sixty years, but this equipment was barely out of the experimental stage.

"Air pressure."

"Check."

"Regulator and hose."

"Check."

"Spear-bomb gun."

"Check."

"Mines."

"Check and ready."

The last of the foot-thick disks went into the teardrop-shaped container, and the man in charge of it adjusted the internal weights that kept it at neutral buoyancy Gerta pulled the goggles down over her face and put the rubber-tasting mouthpiece between her lips. She checked her watch: 18:00 hours, two hours until sunset. Ideal, if nothing held them up seriously. Lifting her feet carefully to avoid tripping on her fins, she waded into the water.

The *Merchant Venture* had her deck-guns manned and ready when John leapt off the running board of the truck and down onto the dock at the foot of the gangway. She also had full steam up and her deck-cranes rigged to unload cargo.

"Go!" John said, trotting towards the deck.

"Is that *you*, sir?" Barrjen blurted.

The blood on his face must look even more ghastly now that it had a chance to dry.

"Not mine," he said again. "Get the first load down on the dock," he went on. "Get some crewmen up here and form a chain to hand rifles and bandoliers down to anyone who comes up and asks for one."

The ex-Marine blinked at that, but slung his own weapon and began barking orders. It was a relief sometimes, having someone who didn't *argue* with you all the time.

Stevedores were pushing rail flats onto the tracks alongside the Santander merchant ship; Jean-Claude had gotten them out of the fighting and moving fast enough. Steam chugged and a winch whirred with a smell of scorched castor oil on the deck ahead of the ship's central island bridge. The crates coming out of the hold were the heavier stuff: field-guns and mortars and their ammunition. More trucks were arriving, honking their air-bulb horns, and growing crowds of people with Assault Guards to shove them into some sort of line.

"Damndest fucking way—begging your pardon, sir— I've ever seen of unloading a ship," Adams, the vessel's first mate, said unhappily.

"No alternative at present," John said.

He lifted his eyes to the hills. *Chateau du Sud* was invisible from here, all but the pepperpot roof of one of the towers. That gave them direct observation for the fall of shot, though; and those 240mm *Schlenki Emma* up there could drop their shells right through the deck. When the stored ammunition and explosives went off, it would make the destruction of the Unionaise cruisers earlier in the day look like a fart in a teacup.

Long narrow crates full of rifles and short square ones full of ammunition began going down the gangways hand to hand, then out into the eager crowd. John restrained an impulse to get into the chain and swing some weight, and another to look up at the castle again. Nothing he could do now but wait. At least there was also nothing the rebels or their Chosen backers could do to him either, except fire those guns . . . and they didn't seem to suspect what was going on. Yet.

The harbor water was murky and dark, tasting of oil and rot. Gerta felt the reach of the tentacle before she saw it, flicking up from the mud and scattered debris of the bottom, thick as a big man's arm and coated on one side with oval suckers and barbed bone hooks. The back of it buffeted her aside, tumbling her through the water like a stick. It wrapped itself around Hans Dieter with the snapping quickness of a frog's tongue closing around a fly. Then it jerked him downward, screaming through the muffling water. Blood and gouting air bubbles trailed behind him; so did the streamlined container of limpet mines, anchored by a stout cord to his waistbelt.

Scheisse, Gerta thought.

Her body reacted automatically, stabilizing her spin, jacknifing and plunging downward as fast as her fins could drive her. The darkness grew swiftly, but the creature was moving upward with its strike. Ten meters long, a torpedo shape with a three-lobed tail; the mouth had three flaps as well, fringed with teeth like ivory spikes around a rasping sucker tongue, with a huge reddish eye above each. The tentacles were threefold. A second had closed around Hans' legs, pulling his legs loose from his torso and guiding them into the sausage-machine maw. The third lashed out at her.

She whirled, poising the speargun, and fired. A slug of compressed air sent the bulbous-headed spear flashing down and kicked her back; she could feel the *schunnnk* as the mechanism cycled in her hands. The spear slammed into the base of the tentacle just as the hooks slashed through her skinsuit and tore at her flesh. She shouted into the rubber of the mouthpiece, tasting water around it, and curled herself into a ball. The shock of the explosion thumped at her, sending her spinning off into the murky water.

It had been muffled by flesh. There was inky-looking blood all around her. She extended arms and legs frantically to kill the spin. That saved her life; the long shape of the killer piscoid floundered by where she would have been, flailing the water with its two intact tentacles, mouth gaping. Gerta fought to control her speargun while the creature bent itself double to attack again. There was a crater in the rubbery flesh where its third tentacle had been, gouting blood into the water, but that didn't seem to be fazing it much. The mouth opened as broad as the reach of her arms, the other two tentacles trailing back in its wake and still holding bits of Hans. Some crazed corner of her mind wondered if it was coming *at* her or *up* at her or *down* . . .

No matter. One last chance . . . she fired.

The mouth closed in reflex as something entered it. Swallowing was equally automatic. This time she had a perfect view of the consequences. The smooth body behind the eyes was as thick as her own torso. Now it belled out like a gun barrel fired when the weapon's muzzle was stuffed with dirt. The mouth flew open the way a flower did in stop-motion photography, with bits and pieces of internal organ and of Hans Dieter shooting out at her. The predator fish drifted downward, quivering and jerking as its nervous system fired at random.

Got to get out *of here,* she thought. The blood and vibrations would attract scavengers from all over the harbor. And then: *Where are the mines?*

Otto swam up pulling the container. Gerta felt her shoulders unknot in relief, enough that she was dizzy and nauseous for an instant before control clamped down. It had been so *quick* . . . and Hans had been a good troop. She grabbed a handhold on the other side of the container and signaled to Elke with her free hand, telling her to take over the watch. It would be faster with two pulling, and they'd lost time.

The additional risk was something they'd just have to take.

"About half done," John said to himself.

He half turned to speak to Adams when the deck surged under his feet. Water spouted up between the dock and the hull, a fountain surge that drenched the whole front of the ship. Seconds later the hull shuddered again, and another mass of water fell across her midships; and a third, this time at the stern. Dead sea-things bobbed to the surface.

John looked up reflexively. But there had been no sound of a heavy shell dropping across the sky. *Torpedo?* his mind gibbered. There wasn't more than a yard or two between dock and hull . . .

a mine, Center said. **attached to the hull by strong magnets. put in place by divers with artificial breathing apparatus. probability approaches unity.**

Crewmen vomited out of the hatches, screaming. A second wave came a few seconds later, dripping and sodden with seawater, some of them dragging wounded crewmates. John stood staring blankly, fists squeezing at either side of his head. Then the deck began to tilt towards the quayside, scores of tons of water dragging the port rail down. His ears rang, so loudly that for a moment he couldn't hear Barrjen's shouted questions.

John shook his head like a wet dog and grabbed Adams' shoulder. "Where are the starboard stopcocks?" he said, then screamed it into the man's ear until the expression of stunned incredulity faded.

"What?"

"The stopcocks! We've got to counterflood or she'll capsize!"

"But if we flood, she'll fookin' *sink.*"

"There's only ten feet of water under her keel; we can salvage the cargo and float her later, but if we don't flood she'll capsize, man. *Now!*"

He could feel the force of his will penetrate the seaman's mental fog. "Right," the mate said, wiping a hand across his face. "This way."

"I'll come, sir," Barrjen said.

"Good man. Let's go."

The companionway down from the bridge was steep and slippery with oily soot from the funnels at the best of times. Now it was canted over at thirty degres, and John went down it in a controlled fall. The hatchway below flapped open, abandoned in the rush to get away from the waters pouring through the rent hull. He dropped through it into water already ankle-deep, bracing himself against the wall with one hand to keep erect on the tilting deck.

"Don't tell me," he said as Adams staggered beside him. "The stopcocks are on the other side of the ship."

"Yessir."

"No time like the present," John said grimly, and gave him a boost forward. The trip across the beam of the ship became steadily more like a climb. Adams staggered ahead, pushed from behind by John and the ex-Marine. At last they came to a complex of wheels and pipes.

"That one!" Adams shouted, pointing. Then he looked down the side of the ship. "Oh, Jesus, the barnacles are showing—Jesus Son of God, Mary Mother, she's going to go over."

"No she isn't," John said, fighting off a moment's image of drowning in the dark with air only a few unreachable feet away through the hull. He spat on his hands. "Let's do it."

The spoked steel wheel was about a yard in diameter, locked by a chain and pin. Adams snatched it out, and John locked his hands on the wheel. It moved a quarter of an inch, stopped, moved again, halted. John braced a foot against the wall and heaved until his muscles crackled and threatened to tear loose from his pelvis.

"Jammed," Adams said. "Must've jammed—shaft torqued by the explosion."

"Then we'll unjam it."

John looked around. Resting in brackets on the side of the central island of the ship were an ax, sledgehammer, and prybar.

"Jam these through the spokes," he said briskly. "Here and here. Now both of you together, *heave*."

They strained; there was silence except for grunts of effort and the distant shouts on the dock. Then the ax handle snapped across with a gunshot crack. Barrjen skipped aside with a curse as the axhead whipped past him and bounced off the wall, leaving a streak of shiny metal scraped free of paint on the wall.

"Fuck *this*," John shouted.

He snatched the sledgehammer from Adam's hands, jammed the crowbar firmly in place, and braced himself to strike. That was difficult; the ship was well past its center of gravity now. A few more minutes, and the intakes for the flood valves would be above the surface. That would happen seconds before she went over.

Clung. The vibrating jolt shivered painfully back up his arms, into his shoulders, starting a pain in the small of his back. He took a deep breath as the sledge swung up again, focused, exhaled in a grunt of total concentration as the hammer came down. *Clung. Clung. Clung.*

Adams' nerve broke and he fled back up the ladder. Two strikes later Barrjen spoke, at first a breathy whisper as he stared at the wheel with sweat running down his face.

"She's moving." Then a shout: "The hoor's moving!"

It was; John had to reposition himself as it turned a quarter revolution. Easier now. He flung the sledgehammer aside and pulled the crowbar free, grabbing at the wheel with his hands. Barrjen did likewise on the other side. Both men strained at the reluctant metal, faces red and gasping with the effort, bodies knotted into straining statue-shapes. The wheel jerked, moved, jerked. Then spun, faster and faster.

A new sound came from beneath their feet, a vibrating rumble.

"Either that works, or she's already too far gone," John gasped. "Let's see from the dock."

There was a crowd waiting. They cheered as John and the stocky ex-Marine jumped from the tilted deck to the wharfside, a score of hands reaching to steady them. John ignored the babbled questions. He did take a proffered flask of brandy, sipping once or twice before handing it back and never taking his eyes from the ship.

"She's not tilting any further," Barrjen said.

"And she's settling fast."

Four minutes and the decks were awash. Another and they heard a deep rumbling *bong*, a sound felt through the soles of their feet more than through the ears. The funnels, central island and crane-masts of the merchantman trembled through a thirty-degree arc to a position that was nearly vertical as the relatively flat bottom of the ship rolled it nearly upright on the mud of the harbor bottom.

John flexed his hands and took a deep breath. "Right," he said, when the cheers died down. "Get some small explosive charges here, we'll want to kill off any sea life." Scavengers were swarming in. "We'll need diving suits, air pumps, more ropes. Get moving!"

He looked up into the darkening evening sky, then over towards the castle. He was just in time to see the great bottle-shaped spearhead of flame show over the courtyard walls. The siege howitzers were in action at last. His shoulders tensed as he listened to the whirring, ripping sound of the shell's passage, toning lower and lower as it approached. The three-hundred-pound projectile came closer, closer . . . then went by overhead. John pivoted on one heel, part of a mass-movement that turned the crowd like sunflowers following the sun across the sky. A red gout of flame billowed up from the gun batteries holding the approaches to the harbor. Seconds later the other heavy howitzer in the castle fired, and the high-velocity guns in the batteries were in fixed revetments. They couldn't be turned to face the castle, and wouldn't be able to elevate that high if they did. . . .

"I'll be damned," John said softly. "The garrison went over to the government side."

Probably after killing all their officers. The Unionaise regular army was short-service conscript.

Barrjen pounded him on the back. "We won, eh, sir? Goddam."

John shook his head. "We won some time." He looked at the celebrating crowd. "Let's see if we can get the snail-eaters to make some use of it."

CHAPTER FIFTEEN

There were no Land dirigibles in the air over the city of Skinrit. Commander Horst Raske felt a little uneasy without the quiver of stamped-aluminum deckplates beneath his feet. Several of the other Air Service captains around him looked as if they felt the same, and everyone in the Chosen party looked unnatural out of uniform—still more as they were in something resembling Unionaise civil dress. Raske kept his horse to a quick walk and spent the time looking around.

"Bad air currents here," he muttered.

Several of his companions nodded. Skinrit itself was nothing remarkable, a little port about three steps up from a fishing village, smelling of stale water inside the breakwater, and strong stinks from the packing and canning plants that were its main industries—the cold currents down here below the main continent were heavy with sea life. Hundreds of trawlers crowded the quays, and battered-looking tramp steamers to take their cargoes of salted and frozen and canned fish to the north. The area around the town was hilly farmland and pasture; most of the buildings were in the whitewashed Unionaise style and quite new—built since their predecessors were burnt in the Errifean Revolt ten years ago. Around them reared real mountains, ten thousand feet and more, their peaks gleaming salt-white with year-round snow, their sides dark with forests of oak, maple, birch, and pine.

Vicious, he thought. Convection currents, crosswinds, unpredictable gusts. *Oathtaking is bad, but this will be worse.*

None of the crowds in the street seemed to be taking much notice of them, which was all to the good. Most were Unionaise themselves, sailors or settlers here; the remainder Errife in long robes, striped or checked or splotched in the patterns of their clans. Occasionally soldiers would come through, usually walking in pairs with their rifles slung, and always surrounded by an empty bubble of fear-inspired space. They wore the khaki battledress of the Union Legion, and its fore-and-aft peaked cap with a tassle. Raske thought that last a little silly, but there was nothing laughable about the troops themselves; quite respectable, about as tough-looking as Protégé infantry, looking straight ahead as they swung through the crowd.

They moved out of the street into the main plaza of Skinrit, past the legion HQ with its motto in black stone above the door: *Vive le Mort*—Long Live Death. A couple of Errife skulls were nailed to the lintel, with scraps of weathered flesh and their long braided hair still clinging to them. It was a reassuring sight, rather homelike, in fact. . . .

The governor's palace was large and lumpy, in a Unionaise style long obsolete. Errif had been a Unionaise possession in theory for some time, although they'd held little of the ten thousand square miles of rock, mountain, and forest until a few decades ago. Just enough to stop the pirate raids that had once been the terror of the whole southern coast of the continent; a few Errife corsairs had gotten as far north as the Land, although they'd seldom returned to the islands alive.

Servants showed them into a square room with benches, probably some sort of guard chamber.

"Masquerade's over," Raske said.

"Good!" one of his officers said.

She stripped off the Unionaise clothing with venom; back in the Land, only Protégé women wore skirts. They switched into the plain gray uniforms in their packs and holstered their weapons. The lack of those had made them feel considerably more unnatural than the foreign clothing. Gerta Hosten gave him a bland smile.

"You do the talking, Horst," she said.

He nodded stiffly. It wasn't his specialty, airships were. On the other hand, a Unionaise general would probably be more comfortable talking to a man, and they needed this Libert . . . for the moment.

"Why on earth didn't they send an infantry officer?" he asked plaintively.

"*Behfel ist Behfel*, Horst. This is the transport phase. They are going to send an infantry officer, once Libert's on the ground and we start sending in our own people. 'Volunteers,' you know . . .

"Who's the lucky man?"

"Heinrich Hosten."

Horst Raske smiled blandly at the Unionaise officer. General Libert was a short, swarthy, tubby little man with a big nose. He looked slightly ridiculous in the khaki battledress of the Union Legion, down to the scarlet sash around his ample waist under the leather belt and the little tassel on his peaked cap.

The Chosen airman reminded himself that the same tubby little man had restored Union rule here when the Errife war-bands were burning and killing in the outskirts of Skingest itself, and then taken the war into their own mountains and pacified the whole island for the first time. The way he'd put down the miners' revolt on the mainland had been almost Chosen-like.

Libert abruptly sat behind the broad polished table, signaling to the staff officers and aides behind him. Raske saluted and took the seat opposite; Errife servants in white kaftans laid out coffee. He recognized the taste: Kotenberg blend, relatives of his owned land there.

"We agree," Libert said after a moment's silence.

Raske raised an eyebrow. "That simple?"

"You charge a high price, but after the fiasco at Bassin du Sud, time is pressing." He frowned. "You would have done better to be more generous; the Land's interests are not served by an unfriendly government in Unionvil."

"Nor by a premature war with Santander, which is a distinct risk if we back you fully," Raske pointed out. "That requires compensation, besides your gratitude."

Libert allowed himself a small frosty smile, an echo of Raske's own. They both knew what gratitude was worth in the affairs of nations.

"Very well," Libert said. He held a hand up, and one of the aides put a pen in it. "Here." He signed the documents before him.

Raske did likewise when they'd been pushed across the mahogany to him.

"When can we begin loading?" Libert said. "And how quickly?"

"I have twenty-seven *Tiger*-class transports waiting," Raske said. "One fully equipped infantry battalion each; say, seven hundred infantry with their personal weapons and the organic crew-served machine guns and mortars. Ten hours to Bassin du Sud or vicinity, an hour at each end for turnaround, and an hour for fueling. Say, just under two flights a day; minus the freightage for artillery, ammunition, immediate rations, and ten percent for downtime—which there *will* be. Call it four days to land the thirty thousand troops."

Libert nodded in satisfaction. "Good. This is crucial; my Legionnaires and Errife regulars are the only reliable force we have in the southern Union. We should be able to get the first flight underway by sundown, don't you think?"

Raske blinked slightly. Beside him, Gerta Hosten was smiling. It looked as if they'd picked the right mule for this particular journey.

Jeffrey Farr closed his eyes. Everyone else in the room might think it was fatigue—he'd been working for ten hours straight—and he *was* tired. What he wanted, though, was reconnaissance.

As always, the view through his brother's eyes was a little disconcerting, even after nearly twenty years of practice. The colors were all a little off, from the difference in perceptions. And the way the view moved under someone else's control was difficult, too. Your own kept trying to linger, or to focus on something different.

At least most of the time. Right now they both had their eyes glued to the view of the dirigible through the binoculars John was holding. A few sprays of pine bough hid a little of it, but the rest was all too plain. Hundreds of soldiers in Union Legion khaki were clinging to ropes that ran to loops along its lower sides, holding it a few yards from the stretch of country road ten miles west of Bassin du Sud. It bobbled and jerked against their hold; he could see the valves on the top centerline opening and closing as it vented hydrogen. The men leaping out of the cargo doors were not in khaki. They wore the long striped and hooded kaftans of Errife warriors. Over each robe was Unionaise standard field harness and pack with canteen, entrenching tool, bayonet and cartridge pouches, but the barbarian mercenaries also tucked the sheaths of their long curved knives through the waistbelts. John swung the glasses to catch a grinning brown hawk-face as one stumbled on landing and picked himself up.

The Errife were happy; their officers had given them orders to do something they'd longed to do for generations: invade the mainland, slaughter the *faranj*, kill, rape, and loot.

How many? Jeffrey asked.

I think they've landed at least three thousand since dawn, maybe five. Hard to tell, they were deploying a perimeter by the time I got here.

Jeffrey thought for a moment. *What chance of getting the Unionaise in Bassin du Sud to mount a counterattack on the landing zone?*

Somewhere between zip and fucking none, John

thought; the overtones of bitterness came through well in the mental link. *They all took two days off to party when the forts in the city surrendered. Plus having a celebratory massacre of anyone they could even imagine having supported the coup.*

Don't worry, Jeffrey said. *If Libert's men take the town, there'll be a slaughter to make that look like a Staff College bun fight. What chance do you have of getting the locals to hold them outside the port?*

Somewhere between . . . no, that's not fair. We've finally gotten the ship unloaded, and there's bad terrain between here and there. Maybe we can make them break their teeth.

Slow them down, Jeffrey said. *I need time, brother. Buy me time.*

He opened his eyes. The space around the map table was crowded and stinging blue with the smoke of the vile tobacco Unionaise preferred. Some of the people there were Unionaise military, both the red armbands on their sleeves and the rank tabs on their collars new. Their predecessors were being tumbled into mass graves outside Unionvil's suburbs even now. The rest were politicians of various types; there were even a few women. About the only thing everyone had in common was the suspicion with which they looked at each other, and a tendency to shout and wave their fists.

"Gentlemen," he said. A bit more sharply: "Gentlemen!"

Relative silence fell, and the eyes swung to him. *Christ,* he thought. *I'm a goddamned foreigner, for God's sake.*

That's the point, lad. You're outside their factions, or most of them. Use it.

"Gentlemen, the situation is grave. We have defeated the uprising here in Unionvil, Borreaux, and Nanes."

His finger traced from the northwestern coast to the high plateau of the central Union and the provinces to the east along the Santander border.

"But the rebels hold Islvert, Sanmere, Marsai on the southeast coast, and are landing troops from Errife near Bassin du Sud."

"Are you sure?" His little friend Vincen Deshambres had ended up as a senior member of the Emergency Committee of Public Safety, which wasn't surprising at all.

"Citizen Comrade Deshambres, I'm dead certain. Troops of the Legion and Errife regulars are being shuttled across from Errif by Land dirigibles. Over ten thousand are ashore now, and they'll have the equivalent of two divisions by the end of the week."

The shouting started again; this time it was Vincen who quieted it. "Go on, General Farr."

Colonel, Jeffrey thought; but then, Vincen was probably trying to impress the rest of the people around the table. He knew the politics better.

"We hold the center of the country. The enemy hold a block in the northeast and portions of the south coast. They also hold an excellent port, Marsai, situated in a stretch of country that's strongly clerical and antigovernment, yet instead of shipping their troops from Errif to Marsai, the rebel generals are bringing them in by air to Bassin du Sud. That indicates—"

He traced a line north from Bassin du Sud. There was a railway, and what passed in the Union for a main road, up from the coastal plain and through the Monts du Diable to the central plateau.

"Name of a dog," Vincen said. "An attack on the capital?"

"It's the logical move," Jeffery said. "They've got Libert, who's a competent tactician and a better than competent organizer—"

"A traitor swine!" someone burst out. The anarchist . . . well, not really leader, but something close. De Villers, that was his name.

Jeffrey held up a hand. "I'm describing his abilities, not his morals," he said. "As I said, they've got Libert,

Land help with supplies and transport, and thirty to forty thousand first-rate, well-equipped troops in formed units. Which is more than anyone else has at the moment."

There were glum looks. The Unionaise regular army had never been large, the government's purge-by-retirement policy had deprived it of most of its senior officers, and most of the remainder had gone over to the rebels in the week since the uprising started. The army as a whole had shattered like a clay crock heated too high.

"What can we do?" Vincen asked.

"Stop them." Jeffrey's finger stabbed down on the rough country north of Bassin du Sud. "Get everything we can out here and stop them. If we can keep their pockets from linking up, we buy time to organize. With time, we can win. But we have to stop Libert from linking up with the rebel pocket around Islvert."

"An excellent analysis," Vincen said. "I'm sure the Committee of Public Safety will agree."

That produced more nervous glances. The Committee was more selective than the mobs who'd been running down rebels, rebel sympathizers, and anyone else they didn't like. But not much. De Villers glared at him, mouth working like a hound that had just had its bone snatched away.

"And I'm sure there's only one man to take charge of such a vital task."

Everyone looked at Jeffrey. *Oh, shit,* he thought.

"What now, mercenary?" De Villers asked, coming up to the staff car and climbing onto the running board.

"Volunteer," Jeffrey said, standing up in the open-topped car.

It was obvious now why the train was held up. A solid flow of men, carts, mules, and the odd motor vehicle had been moving south down the double-lane gravel road. *You certainly couldn't call it a march,* he thought. Armies moved with wheeled transport in the center and infantry marching on either verge in column. This bunch sprawled and bunched and straggled, leaving the road to squat behind a bush, to drink water out of ditches—which meant they'd have an epidemic of dysentery within a couple of days—to take a snooze under a tree, to steal chickens and pick half-ripe cherries from the orchards that covered many of the hills. . . .

That wasn't the worst of it, nor the fact that every third village they passed was empty, meaning that the villagers had decided they liked the priest and squire better than the local *travailleur* or anarchist school-teacher or cobbler-organizer. Those villages had the school burnt rather than the church, and the people were undoubtedly hiding in the hills getting ready to ambush the government supply lines, such as they were.

What was *really* bad was the solid column of refugees pouring north up the road and tying everything up in an inextricable tangle. Only the pressure from both sides kept up as those behind tried to push through, so the whole thing was bulging the way two hoses would if you joined them together and pumped in water from both ends. *And* they'd blocked the train, which held his artillery and supplies, and the men on the train were starting to get off and mingle with the shouting, milling, pushing crowd as well. A haze of reddish-yellow dust hung over the cross-roads village, mingling with the stink of coal smoke, unwashed humanity, and human and animal wastes.

"We've got to get some order here," Jeffrey muttered.

The anarchist political officer looked at him sharply. "True order emerges spontaneously from the people, not from an authoritarian hierarchy which crushes their spirit!" De Villers began heatedly.

"The only thing emerging spontaneously from this bunch is shit and noise," Jeffrey said, leaving the man staring at him open-mouthed.

Not used to being cut off in midspeech.

"Brigadier Gerard," Jeffrey went on, to the Unionaise Loyalist officer in the car. "If you would come with me for a moment?"

Gerard stepped out of the car. The anarchist made to follow, but stopped at a look from Jeffrey. They walked a few paces into the crowd, more than enough for the ambient sound to make their voices indaudible.

"Brigadier Gerard," Jeffrey began.

"That's Citizen Comrade Brigadier Gerard," the officer said deadpan. He was a short man, broad-shouldered and muscular, with a horseman's walk—light cavalry, originally, Jeffrey remembered. About thirty-five or a little more, a few gray hairs in his neatly trimmed mustache, a wary look in his brown eyes.

"Horseshit. Look, Gerard, you should have this job. You're the senior Loyalist officer here."

"But they do not trust me," Gerard said.

"No, they don't. Better than half the professional officers went over to the rebels, I was available, and they *do* trust me . . . a little. So I'm stuck with it. The question is, are you going to help me do what we were sent to do, or not? I'm going to do my job, whether you help or not. But if you don't, it goes from being nearly impossible to completely impossible. If I get killed, I'd like it to be in aid of something."

Gerard stared at him impassively for a moment, then inclined his head slightly. *"Bon,"* he said, holding out his hand. *"Because appearances to the contrary, *mon ami*"—he indicated the milling mob around them—"this *is* the better side."

Jeffrey returned the handshake and took a map out of the case hanging from his webbing belt. "All right, here's what I want done," he said. "First, I'm going to leave you the Assault Guards—"

"You're putting me in command here?" Gerard said, surprised.

"You're now my chief of staff, and yes, you'll command this position, for what it's worth. The Assault Guards are organized, at least, and they're used to keeping civilians in line. Use them to clear the roads. Offload the artillery and send the train back north for more of everything. Meanwhile, use your . . . well, troops, I suppose . . . to dig in here."

He waved to either side. The narrow valley wound through a region of tumbled low hills, mostly covered in olive orchards. On either side reached sheer fault mountains, with near-vertical sides covered in scrub at the lower altitudes, cork-oak, and then pine forest higher up.

"Don't neglect the high ground. The Errife are half mountain goat themselves, and Libert knows how to use them."

"And what will you do, Citiz—General Farr?"

"I'm going to take . . . what's his name?" He jerked a thumb towards the car.

"Antoine De Villers."

"Citizen Comrade De Villers and his anarchist militia down the valley and buy you the time you need to dig in."

Gerard stared, then slowly drew himself up and saluted. "I can use all the time you can find," he said sincerely.

Jeffrey smiled bleakly. "That's usually the case," he said. "Oh, and while you're at it—start preparing fallback positions up the valley as well."

Gerard nodded. De Villers finally vaulted out of the car and strode over to them, hitching at the rifle on his shoulder, his eyes darting from one soldier to the other.

"What are you *gentlemen* discussing?" he said. "Gentleman" was not a compliment in the government-held zone, not anymore. In some places it was a sentence of death.

"How to stop Libert," Jeffrey said. "The main force will entrench here. Your militia brigade, Citizen Comrade De Villers, will move forward to"—he looked at the map—"Vincennes."

De Villers' eyes narrowed. "You'll send us ahead as the sacrificial lambs?"

"No, I'll *lead* you ahead," Jeffrey said, meeting his gaze

steadily. "The Committee of Public Safety has given me the command, and I lead from the front. Any questions?"

After a moment, De Villers shook his head.

"Then go see that your men have three days rations; there's hardtack and jerked beef on the last cars of that train. Then we'll get them moving south."

When De Villers had left, Gerard leaned a little closer. "My friend, I admire your choice . . . but there are unlikely to be many survivors from the anarchists."

He flinched a little at Jeffrey's smile. "I'm fully aware of that, Brigadier Gerard. My strategy is intended to improve the government's chances in this war, after all."

"So."

General Libert walked around the aircraft, hands clenched behind his back. It was a biplane, a wood-framed oval fuselage covered in doped fabric, with similar wings joined by wires and struts. The Land sunburst had been hastily painted over on the wings and showed faintly through the overlay, which was the double-headed ax symbol of Libert's Nationalists. A single engine at the front drove a two-bladed wooden prop, and there was a light machine gun mounted on the upper wing over the cockpit. It smelled strongly of gasoline and the castor oil lubricant that shone on the cylinders of the little rotary engine where they protruded through the foreward body. Two more like it stood nearby, swarming with technicians as the Chosen "volunteers" gave their equipment a final going-over.

"So," Libert said again. "What is the advantage over your airships?"

Gerta Hosten paused in working on her gloves. She was sweating heavily in the summer heat, her glazed leather jacket and trousers far too warm for the sea-level summer heat. Soon she'd be out of it.

"General, it's a smaller target—and much faster, about a hundred and forty miles an hour. Also more maneuverable; one of these can skim along at treetop level. Both have their uses."

"I see," Libert said thoughtfully. "Very useful for reconnaissance, if they function as specified."

"Oh, they will," Gerta said cheerfully.

The Unionaise general gave her a curt nod and strode away. She vaulted onto the lower wing and then into the cockpit, fastening the straps across her chest and checking that the goggles pushed up on her leather helmet were clean. Two Protégé crewmen gripped the propellor. She checked the simple control panel, fighting down an un-Chosen gleeful grin, and worked the pedals and stick to give a final visual on the ailerons and rudder. *I love these things,* she thought. One good mark on John's ledger; he'd delivered the plans on request. And the Technical Research Council had improved them considerably.

"Check!" she shouted.

"Check!"

"Contact!"

"Contact!"

The Protégés spun the prop. The engine coughed, sputtered, spat acrid blue smoke, then caught with a droning roar. Gerta looked up at the wind streamer on its pole at a corner of the field and made hand signals to the ground crew. They turned the aircraft into the wind; she looked behind to check that the other two were ready. Then she swung her left hand in a circle over her head, while her right eased the throttle forward. The engine's buzz went higher, and she could feel the light fabric of the machine straining against the blocks before its wheels and the hands of the crew hanging on to tail and wing.

Now. She chopped the hand forward. The airplane bounced forward as the crew's grip released, then bounced again as the hard unsprung wheels met the uneven surface of the cow pasture. The speed built, and the jouncing ride became softer, mushy. When the tailwheel lifted off the ground she eased back on the stick, and the biplane slid free into the sky. It nearly slid sideways as well; this model had a bad torque problem. She corrected with a foot on the rudder pedals and banked to gain altitude, the other two planes following her to either side. Her scarf streamed behind her in the slipstream, and the wind sang through the wires and stays, counterpoint to the steady drone of the engines.

Bassin du Sud opened beneath her; scattered houses here in the suburbs, clustering around the electric trolley lines; a tangle of taller stone buildings and tenements closer to the harbor. Pillars of smoke still rose from the city center and the harbor; she could hear the occasional popping of small-arms fire. Mopping up, or execution squads. There were Chosen ships in the harbor, merchantmen with the golden sunburst on their funnels, unloading into lighters. Gangs of laborers were transfering the cargo from the lighters to the docks, or working on clearing the obstacles and wreckage that prevented full-sized ships from coming up to the quays; she was low enough to see a guard smash his rifle butt into the head of one who worked too slowly, and then boot the body into the water.

The engines labored, and the Land aircraft gained another thousand feet of altitude. From this height she could see the big soccer stadium at the edge of town, and the huge crowd of prisoners squatting around it. Every few minutes another few hundred would be pushed in through the big entrance gates, and the machine guns would rattle. General Libert didn't believe in wasting time; anyone with a bruise on their shoulder from a rifle butt went straight to the stadium, plus anyone on their list of suspects, or who had a trade union membership card in his wallet. *Anyone who still has one of those is too stupid to live,* Gerta thought cheerfully, banking the plane north.

There were more columns of smoke from the rolling coastal plain, places where the wheat wasn't fully harvested and the fields had caught, or more concentrated where a farmhouse or village burned. Dust marked the main road, a long winding serpent of it from Libert's Legionnaires and Errife as they marched north. The wheeled transport was mostly animal-drawn, horses and mules, and strings of packmules too. That would change when the harbor was functional again; the Land ships waiting to unload included a fair number of steam trucks, and even some armored cars. The infantry was marching on either side of the road in ordered columns of fours; heads turned up to watch the aircraft swoop overhead, but thankfully, nobody shot at her.

The mountains ahead grew closer, jagged shapes of Prussian-blue looming higher than her three thousand feet. There was a godlike feeling to this soaring flight; to Gerta's way of thinking, it was utterly different from airship travel. On a dirigible you might as well be on a train running through the sky. This was more like driving a fast car, but with the added freedom of three dimensions and no road to follow; alone in the cockpit she allowed herself a chuckle of delight. You could go *anywhere* up here.

Right now she was supposed to go where the action was. A faint *pop-pop-popping* came from the north. *Ah, some of the enemy are still putting up a fight.* The resistance in Bassin du Sud and on the road north had been incompetently handled, but more determined than she'd have expected.

Gerta waggled her wings. The other two airplanes closed in; she waited until they were close enough to see her signals clearly, then slowly pointed left and right, swooped her hand, and circled it again before pointing back southward. Her flankers each banked away. *Funny how fast you can lose sight of things up here,* she thought. They dwindled to dots in a few seconds, almost invisible against the background of earth and sky. Then she put one wing over and dove.

Time to check things out, she thought as the falling-elevator sensation lifted her stomach into her ribs.

*   *   *

Somebody screamed and pointed upwards. John Hosten craned his neck to look through the narrow leaves of the cork-oak, squinting against the noon sun. The roar of the engine whined in his ears as the wings of the biplane drew a rectangle of shadow across the woods. It came low enough to almost brush the top branches of the scrubby trees, trailing a scent of burnt gasoline and hot oil strong enough to overpower the smells of hot dry earth and sunscorched vegetation. He could see the leather-helmeted head of the pilot turning back and forth, insectile behind its goggles.

Everyone in the grove had frozen like rabbits under a hawk while the airplane went by, doing the best possible thing for the worst possible reason.

"It's a new type of flying machine," John said. "They build them in Santander, too; that one was from the Land, working for Libert."

The *chink* of picks, knives, and sticks digging improvised rifle pits and sangars resumed; everyone still alive had acquired a healthy knowledge of how important it was to dig in. John still had an actual shovel. He worked the edge under a rock and strained it free, lifting the rough limestone to the edge of his hole.

"Sir," one of his ex-Marines said. "They're coming."

He tossed the shovel to another man and crawled forward, sheltering behind a knotted, twisted tree trunk, blushing pink since the cork had been stripped off, and trained his binoculars. Downslope were rocky fields of yellow stubble, with an occasional carob tree. In the middle distance was a farmstead, probably a landlord's from the size and blank whitewashed outer walls. A defiant black anarchist flag showed that the present occupants had different ideas, and mortar shells were falling on it. Beyond it, Errife infantry were advancing, small groups dashing forward while their comrades fired in support, then repeating the process. John shaped a silent whistle of reluctant admiration at their bounding agility, and the way they disappeared from his sight as soon as they went to earth, the brown-on-brown stripes of their kaftans vanishing against the stony earth.

Good fieldcraft, Raj said. *Damned good. You'd better get this bunch of amateurs out of their way, son.*

"Easier said than done," John muttered to himself.

"Ah, sir?" Barrjen said, lowering his voice. "You know, it might be a good idea to sort of move north?"

There were about three hundred people in the stretch of woodland, mostly men, all armed. There had been a couple of thousand yesterday, when he began back-peddling from the ruins of Bassin du Sud. He was still alive, and so were most of the Santander citizens he'd brought with him, the crew of the *Merchant Venture*, and all the ex-Marines from the Ciano embassy guard. *Not so surprising, they're the ones who know what the hell they're doing*, he thought. He doubted he'd be alive without them.

"All right, we've got to break contact with them," he said aloud. "The only way to do that is to move out quickly while they're occupied with that hamlet."

Most of the Unionaise stood. About a third continued to dig themselves in. One of them looked up at John:

"*Va.* We will hold them."

"You'll die."

The man shrugged. "My family is dead, my friends are dead—I think some of those *merdechiennes* should follow them."

John closed his mouth. *Nothing to say to that,* he thought. "Leave all your spare ammunition," he said to the others. Men began rummaging in pockets, knapsacks and improvised bandoliers. "Come on. Let's make it worthwhile."

"Damn, but I'm glad to see you."

Jeffrey was a little shocked at how John looked; almost

as bad has he had when he got back from the Empire. Thinner, limping—limping more badly than Smith beside him—and with a look around the eyes that Jeffrey recognized. He'd seen it in a mirror lately. There was a bandage on his arm soaked in old dried blood, too, and a feverish glitter in his eyes.

"You, too, brother," Jeffrey said.

He glanced around. The comandeered farmhouse was full of recently appointed, elected, or self-selected officers (or *coordinateurs*, to use their own slang) of the anarchist militia down from Unionvil and the industrial towns around it. Most of them were grouped around the map tables; thanks to John and Center, the counters marking the enemy forces were quite accurate. He was much less certain of his own. It wasn't only lack of cooperation; although there was enough of that, despite the ever-present threat of the Committee of Public Safety. Most of the *coordinateurs* didn't have much idea of the size or location of their forces either.

"C'mon over here," he said, putting a hand under John's arm. "Things as bad as you've been saying?"

"Worse. Those aeroplanes they've got, they caught us crossing open country yesterday."

observe, Center said.

—and John's eyes showed uprushing ground as he clawed himself into the dirt. It was thin pastureland scattered with sheep dung and showing limestone rock here and there.

"Sod this for a game of soldiers," someone muttered not far away.

A buzzing drone grew louder. John rolled on his back; being facedown would be only psychological comfort. Two of the Land aircraft were slanting down towards the Bassin du Sud refugees and the Santander party. They swelled as he watched, the translucent circle of the propellor before the angular circle of pistons, and wings like some great flying predator. Then the machine gun over the upper wing began to wink, and the *tat-tat-tat-tat* of a Koegelman punctuated the engine roar. A line of dust-spurting craters flicked towards him . . . and then past, leaving him shaking and sweating. A dot fell from one of the planes, exploding with a sharp *crack* fifty feet up.

Grenade, he realized. Not a very efficient way of dropping explosives, but they'd do better soon. Voices were screaming; in panic, or in pain. A few of the refugees stood and shot at the vanishing aircraft with their rifles, also a form of psychological comfort, not to feel totally helpless like a bug under a boot. The aircraft banked to the north and came back for another run. Most of the riflemen dove for cover. Barrjen stood, firing slowly and carefully, as the lines of machine-gun bullets traversed the refugees' position. Both swerved towards him, moving in a scissors that would meet in his body.

"Get down, you fool!" John shouted. *Dammit, I need you!* Loyal men of his ability weren't that common.

Then one of the machines wavered in the air, heeled, banked towards the earth. John started to cheer, then felt it trail off as the airplane steadied and began to climb. He was still grinning broadly as he rose and slapped Barrjen on the shoulder; both the Land planes were heading south, one wavering in the air, the other anxiously flying beside it like a mother goose beside a chick.

"Good shooting," he said.

Barrjen pulled the bolt of his rifle back and carefully thumbed in three loose rounds. "Just have t'estimate the speed, sir," he said.

Smith used his rifle to lever himself erect. "Here," he said, tossing over three stripper clips of ammunition. "You'll use 'em better than me."

—and John shook his head. "There I was, thinking how fucking ironic it would be if I got killed by something designed to plans I'd shipped to the Chosen," he said.

Jeffrey closed his eyes for an instant to look at a still close-up of Center's record of the attack. "Nope, they've made some improvements. That was moving faster than anything we've got so far."

correct, Center said to them both. **a somewhat more powerful engine, and improvements in the chord of the wing.**

"I still sent them the basics," John said.

"Considering that your companies have been doing the work on 'em, and they know they have, it would look damned odd if their prize double agent *didn't* send them the specs, wouldn't it?" Jeffrey said. "You know how it is. If disinformation is going to be credible, you have to send a lot of good stuff along with it."

John nodded reluctantly. "I'm getting sick of disastrous retreats," he said.

Jeffrey smiled crookedly. "Well, this isn't as bad as the Imperial War," he said. "We're not fighting the Land directly, for one thing."

He looked over his shoulder and called names. "Come on, you need a doctor and some food and sleep. The food's pretty bad, but we've got some decent doctors. Barrjen, Smith, take care of him."

"Do our best, sir," Smith said. "But you might tell him not to get shot at so often."

The two Santanders helped John away. Jeffrey turned back to the map, looking down at the narrow line of hilly lowland that snaked through the mountains.

"We'll continue to dig in along this line," he said, tracing it with his finger.

"Why here? Why not further south? Why do we have to give up ground to Libert and his hired killers?" De Villers wasn't even trying to hide his hostility anymore.

Jeffrey hid his sigh. "Because this is right behind a dogleg and the narrowest point around," he said. "That means he can't use his artillery as well—we have virtually none, you'll have noticed, gentle . . . ah, Citizen Comrades. And the mountains make it difficult for him to flank us. Hopefully, he'll break his teeth advancing straight into our positions."

"We should attack. The enemy's mercenaries have no reason to fight, and our troops' political consciousness is high. The Legionnaires will run away, and the Errife will turn on their officers and join us to restore their independence."

A few of the others around the table were nodding.

"Citizen Comrades," Jeffrey said gently. "Have any of you seen the refugees coming through? Or listened to them?"

That stopped the chorus of agreement. "Well, do you get the impression that the Legion or the Errife refused to fight in Bassin du Sud? Is there any reason to believe that they'll be any weaker here? No? Good."

He traced lines on the map. "Their lead elements will be in contact by sunset, and I expect them to be able to put in a full attack by tomorrow. We need maximum alertness."

He went on, outlining his plan. In theory it ought to be effective enough; he had fewer men than Libert in total, but the terrain favored him, and holding a secure defensive position with no flanks was the easiest thing for green troops to do.

The problem was that Libert knew that too, and so did his Chosen advisors.

CHAPTER SIXTEEN

"What news from the academy?"

Libert's aide smiled. "The report from *Commandant* Soubirous is *nothing to report*, my general."

The pudgy little man nodded seriously and tapped his map. There was enough sunlight through the western entrance of the tent to show clearly what he meant; the Union Military Academy was located at Foret du Loup, out on the rolling plateau country, between the mountains and Unionvil.

"When we have cleared the passes through the Monts du Diable, we must send a column—a strong column— to the relief of the academy. The Reds must not be allowed to crush Commandant Soubirous and the gallant cadets."

Heinrich Hosten coughed discreetly. "My general," he said, in fluent but accented Fransay. "Surely we should be careful not to disperse our forces away from the main *schwerepunkt*? Ah, the point of primary effort, that is."

"I am familiar with the concept," Libert said.

He looked at the Chosen officer; the foreigner was discreetly dressed in the uniform of a Union Legion officer, without rank tabs but with a tiny gold-on-black sunburst pin on the collar of his tunic.

"Yes, my general," Heinrich said.

"However, this will probably be a long war—and it is perhaps better that way," Libert said. The Chosen in the room reacted with a uniform calm that hid identical surprise. The Unionaise commander smiled thinly.

"This is a political as well as a military struggle. A swift victory would leave us with all the elements that brought on the crisis intact. A steady, methodical advance means that we do not simply defeat but annihilate all the un-Unionist elements. And it gives us time and opportunity to thoroughly *cleanse* the zones behind our lines, in wartime conditions."

"As you say, sir," Heinrich said. "That presupposes, however, that we succeed in getting out of this damned valley to begin with."

"I have confidence in the plan you and my staff have worked out," Libert said, turning back to the map.

Heinrich ducked his head and left the tent. "Damned odd way of looking at it," he said to Gerta.

"Sensible, actually," Gerta said, smiling and shaking her head, "when you look at it from his point of view. We could stand being a little more methodical ourselves; this whole operation here has the flavor of an improvisation, to me."

They stopped for a moment to watch Protégé workmen and Chosen engineers assembling armored cars from crated parts sent up by rail.

"It's an opportunity," Heinrich said after a while.

"It's a temptation," Gerta said. "We've had less than a decade to consolidate our hold on the Empire—"

"Nine years, six months, two days, counting from the attack on Corona," Heinrich said with a smile of fond reminiscence.

"Quibbler." She punched him lightly on his shoulder. "We should wait for a generation at least before taking on Santander. And this is probably going to mean war with the Republic eventually, if our little friend"—she jerked her head back at the tent—"wins."

"They're getting stronger, too," Heinrich pointed out. "You know the production problems we're having with labor from the New Territories."

"Yes, but we've got the staying power. *We* don't have an underlying need to believe the world is a warm, fuzzy-pink playground where everyone's nice down deep except for a few villains who'll be defeated at the end of the story. We can get the animals working well enough, given enough time—and the Santies will go to sleep and let down their guard if we don't make obvious threats."

"We're not threatening them, strictly speaking."

"Land forces on their border? Even a *Santy* can't convince himself that's not a threat. We're waking a sleeping giant, and stiffening his backbone."

Heinrich shrugged. "But if we beat the Santies, everything else is mopping up. Anyway, it's a matter for the Council, *nein?*"

"*Jawohl.* Orders are orders. Let's get this battle done."

Heinrich smiled more broadly. "Actually, you've got a different job."

"Oh?"

"Libert's pretty taken with this academy thing. He'd probably spend six months avenging the place and the gallant cadets if it fell, which would be an even worse diversion of effort than marching to relieve it. So we'd better make sure it doesn't fall. . . ."

"*Shays.*"

"And how are you, sir?" the train steward asked.

"Not so great," John mumbled. "Drink, please—water, something like that."

"Sir."

The steward bowed silently as he left the compartment. The revolution hadn't reached this part of the Union yet, evidently. Or perhaps it was just that this was a Santander-owned railway, and close to the border, and John was evidently rich enough to command a whole first-class compartment for himself, and another for half a dozen tough-looking armed men.

The view out the window was much like the eastern provinces of the Republic outside the cities. An upland basin surrounded by mountains with snow gleaming at their tops, the peaks to the west turning crimson with sunset. Grass, tawny with summer, speckled with walking cactus and an occasional clubroot, smelling warm and dusty but fresher than the lowlands to the east. Herds of red-coated cattle and shaggy buffalo and sheep, with herdsmen mounted and armed guarding them. Occasionally a ranch house, with its outbuildings and white-washed adobe walls; more rarely a stretch of orchards and cultivated fields around a stream channeled for irrigation, very rarely a village or mine with its cottages and church spire.

It looked intensely peaceful. A hawk stooped at a rabbit flushed by the *chufchufchuf* of the locomotive, and the carriage swayed with the clacking passage of the rails. John wiped sweat from his forehead and touched the arm in its sling with gingerly fingers, wincing a little. Better, definitely better—he'd thought he was going to lose it, for a while—but still bad. Thank God the doctor had believed what he said about debriding wounds, but then, a massive bribe never hurt.

Home soon, he thought.

The door to the compartment opened again: the steward, immaculate in white jacket and gloves, with a tray of iced lemonade. Behind him were the worried faces of Smith and Barrjen.

"You all right, sir?"

"I would be if people stopped bothering me!" John snapped, then waved a hand. "Sorry. I'm recovering, but I need rest. Thank you for asking."

The two men withdrew with mumbled apologies as the steward unlatched the folding table between the seats and put the tray on it. John took a glass of the lemonade and drank thirstily, then put the cold tumbler to his forehead.

"Shall I put down the bunk, sir?"

John shook his head. "In a little while. Come back in an hour."

"Will you be using the dining car, sir?"

His stomach heaved slightly at the thought. "No. A

bowl of broth and a little dry toast in here, if you would."
He slipped across a Santander banknote. "In a while."

The steward smiled. "Glad to be of assistance, Your
Excellency."

John closed his eyes. When he opened them again
with a jerk it was full night outside, with only an occasional lantern-light to compete with the frosted arch of
stars and the moons. The collar of his shirt and jacket
were soaked with sweat, but he felt much better . . .
and very thirsty. He drank more of the lemonade, and
pushed the bell for the steward to bring his soup.

*I must be reaching second childhood, and I'm not even
thirty-five,* he thought. *Making all this fuss over a superficial wound and a little fever.*

Nothing little about a wound turning nasty, Raj
said in his mind. **I've seen too much of that.**

There was a brief flash of hands holding a man down
to blood-stained boards. He thrashed and screamed as
the bone-saw grated through his thigh, and there was
a tub full of severed limbs at the end of the makeshift
operating table. Unlike Center's scenarios, Raj's memories carried smell as well; the sickly-sweet oily rot of
gas gangrene, this time.

You even had Center worried for a while.

**calculations indicate a 23% reduction in the
probability of a favorable outcome if john hosten
is removed from the equation at this point,** Center
said. **such analysis does not constitute "worry."**

How's Jeff doing? he asked.

observe:

—and he was looking through his foster-brother's eyes.

Evidently Jeffrey was out making a hands-on inspection, riding a horse along behind the Loyalist lines. *Scattered clumps might be a better way to put it than "lines,"*
John thought.

Oh, hi, Jeffrey replied. *How's it going?*

He pulled up the horse behind a large bonfire. Militiamen and some women were lying around it; a few

hardy souls were asleep, others toasting bits of pungent sausage on sticks over the fire, eating stale bread, drinking from clay bottles of wine and water, or just engaging in the universal Unionaise sport of argument. The rifle pits they'd dug were a little further south, and their weapons were scattered about. Perhaps three-quarters were armed, with everything from modern Union-made copies of Santander magazine rifles to black-powder muzzle loaders like something from the Civil War three generations back. One anarchist chieftain had a bandanna around his head, two bandoliers of ammunition across the heavy gut that strained his horizontally striped shirt, three knives, a rifle, and two pistols in his sash.

There was even a machine gun, well dug in behind a loopholed breastwork of sandbags.

Well, somebody *knows what they're doing,* John observed.

Jeffrey nodded. The Union had compulsory military service; in theory the unlucky men were selected by lot, but you could buy your way out. Any odd collection of working-class individuals like this would have some men with regular army training.

He looked up at the stars; John opened his own eyes, and there was an odd moment of double sight—the same constellations stationary here, and through the window of the moving train four hundred miles northwest. That put Jeffrey in a perfect position to see the starshell go off.

Pop. The actinic blue-white light froze everything in place for an instant, just long enough to hear the whistle of shells turn to a descending ripping-canvas roar.

. Jeffrey reacted, diving off the horse into the empty pit behind the machine gun. The guns were light, from the sound of the crumping explosions of the shells, but that wouldn't matter at *all* if he was in the path of a piece of high-velocity casing.

Somebody else slid in with him, in the same hug-the-bottom-of-the hole posture. They waited through seconds that seemed much longer, then lifted their head in the muffled silence of stunned ears. More starshells burst overhead. . . .

"Five-round stonk," Jeffrey said. A short burst at the maximum rate of fire the gunners could manage. Which meant . . .

An instant later he collided with the other occupant of the hole as they both leapt for the spade grips of the machine gun. "Feed me!" Jeffrey snarled, using his weight and height to lever the Unionaise soldier—it must be the veteran, the one who'd dug the weapon in—aside.

There was light enough to see, thanks to the rebel starshell. The nameless Unionaise ripped open the lid of a stamped-metal rectangular box. Inside were folds of canvas belt with loops holding shiny brass cartridges; he plucked out the end of the belt with its metal tab. Jeffrey had the cover of the feed-guide open and their hands cooperated to guide the belt through as if they had practiced for years. The Unionaise yanked his hand aside as Jeffrey slapped the cover down and jerked the cocking lever back twice, until the shiny tab of the belt hung down on the right side of the weapon.

"Feed me!" he snapped again—it was important for the loader to keep the belt moving evenly, or the gun might jam.

The whole process had taken perhaps twenty seconds. When he looked up to acquire a target, figures in stripped kaftans were sprinting forward all across his front, horribly close. Close enough to see the white snarl of teeth in swarthy, bearded faces and hear individual voices in their shrieking falsetto war cry.

Must've crawled up, his mind gibbered as his thumbs clamped down on the butterfly trigger.

The thick water jacket of the gun swept back and forth, firing a spearhead of flame into the darkness; the starshells were falling to earth under their parachutes, none replacing them. Errife mercenaries fell, some scythed down by the hose of glowing green tracer, some

going to ground and returning fire. Muzzle flashes spat
at him, and he heard the flat *crack* of rounds going overhead. Other rifles were firing, too, where militiamen had
made it back to their foxholes or started firing from
wherever they lay. One jumped up out of the blankets
he'd been sleeping in and ran out into the beaten
ground, making it a hundred yards southward before his
blind panic met a bullet.

"Jesus, there are too *many* of them!" Jeffrey said,
swinging the barrel to try and break up concentrations.
The Errife came forward like water through a dam built
of branches, flowing around anything hard, probing for
empty spots. He fired again and again, clamping down
the trigger for short three-second bursts, spent brass tinkling down to roll underfoot and be trodden into the
dirt.

A dim figure tumbled into the slit trench with them.
The Unionaise soldier dropped the ammunition belt and
snatched up an entrenching tool stuck into the soft earth
of the trench side and began a chopping stroke that
would have buried it in the newcomer's head.

"It's me! Francois!"

With a grunt of effort the first man turned the shovel
aside, burying it again in the earth.

"You're late," he panted, turning back to the box. "Get
your rifle and make yourself useful."

There was nothing but moonlight and starlight to shoot
by now. Just enough to see the stirring of movement
to his front.

"What's your name?" Jeffrey said, between bursts.

"Henri," the loader said. "Henri Trudeau." Then:
"Watch it!"

Something whirred through the air. They both ducked;
behind them Francois stood for a few fatal seconds, still
fumbling with the bolt of his rifle. The grenade thumped
not far above the lip of the machine gun nest. There
was a wet sound from behind them, and Francois' body
slumped down. Jeffrey didn't bother to look; he knew

what the spray of moisture across the back of his neck came from. Instead, he pushed himself back up while the dust was still stinging his eyes, drawing the automatic pistol at his waist.

An Errife was pointing his rifle at Jeffrey's head from no more than three feet away. He froze for an instant, so close to the enemy trooper that he could hear the tiny *click* of the firing pin. The rifle did not fire. *Bad primer,* Jeffrey thought, while his hand brought up the pistol. *Crack.* The barbarian flopped backwards. *Crack.* A miss, and the next one was on him, long curved knife flashing upward at his belly. Jeffrey yelled and twisted aside, clubbing at the Errife's head with his automatic. It thumped on bone, muffled by the headcloth twisted around the mercenary's skull. Jeffrey grabbed for his knife wrist and struck twice more with frantic strength, until the robed man slumped back against the rear wall of the trench and Jeffrey jammed the muzzle of his pistol into his stomach and pulled the trigger twice.

Out of the corner of his eye, Jeffrey saw Henri's entrenching tool flashing again and again, used like an ax. The impacts were soft blubbery sounds, underlain by crunching.

"*Cochon,*" the Unionaise wheezed. "*Morri, batard—*"

"He *is* dead," Jeffrey said. Henri wheeled, shovel raised, then let it fall. "Now let's get out of here."

The volume of fire was slackening, but the ullulating screech of the Errife rose over it—and other voices, screaming in simple agony. The islanders liked to collect souvenirs.

"You go get things in order," Henri said. "I'll man this gun. You do your job and I'll do—"

"Jesus Christ in a starship couldn't get any order here," Jeffrey said. "Let's get moving. This isn't going to be the last battle."

Henri stared at him for an instant, his face unreadable in the dark. "*Bon,*" he said at last. "*Voyons.*"

CHAPTER SEVENTEEN

"Nothing to report, nothing to report, nothing to *fucking* report—you had me stuck there for three damned months."

Gerta knocked back a shot of banana gin and followed it with a draught of beer, savoring the hot-cold *wham* contrast of flavors. The place had been a nobleman's townhouse before the Chosen took Ciano and the Empire with it, and an officer's transit station-cum-club since. Gerta and her husband were sitting on the outdoor terrace, separated from the street by a stretch of clipped grass and a low wall of whitewashed brick. It was hot with late summer, but nothing beside the sticky humidity of this time of year in the Land, and there was an awning overhead. She reached moodily for another chicken, lettuce, and tomato sandwich. At least it wasn't rotten horsemeat, and she'd gotten rid of the body lice.

"And there wouldn't have been anything but a bloody hole in the ground to report at Libert's precious Academy, if I hadn't been there," she said. "The froggie imbecile supposedly in command didn't even remember elementary tricks like putting out plates of water in the basement to detect the vibrations of sappers trying to dig under the walls. *And* I had to practically stick a knife in his buttocks to get him to listen."

"Still, I hear that got exciting," Heinrich said. "The countermining."

"Too exciting," Gerta said dryly, remembering.

—cold wet darkness, water seeping through the belly of her uniform. Squirming down like birth in reverse, and

280

then the dirt crumbling away ahead of her, falling through into the enemy tunnel, slamming against a timber prop, the man's mouth making an O in the dim light of the lanterns as she brough her automatic up . . .

"What took you so long?" she asked again.

"Well, you were the one who thought there was something to Libert's 'methodical' approach," Heinrich said reasonably. He lit his pipe and blew a smoke ring skyward, watching as the shapes of dirigibles heading for the landing field passed across it. "We took so long because every time we took a village we'd stop to shoot everyone suspicious, then everyone Libert's police could winkle out, then waited while Libert appointed everyone from the mayor down to the sewer inspector and checked that things were working smoothly."

"Got stopped butt-cold outside Unionvil, too," Gerta said. "By *Imperials*, of all things."

"By the Freedom Brigades," Heinrich corrected. He closed the worked pewter lid of his S-shaped pipe and reached for a sandwich. "Imperial refugees, Santies, some Sierrans, Santy officers, damned good equipment and so-so training. But plenty of enthusiasm."

"Well, what are we going to do about it?" Gerta demanded. "I've been working internal-security liaison since I got back."

"Two can play at that game," Heinrich said with satisfaction. "That's why I'm back here. We're going to 'volunteer'—"

Pop.

The small spiteful crack on the sidewalk outside was almost inaudible under the traffic noise. Gerta was out of her chair and halfway across the lawn with a single raking stride; Heinrich was too big a man to be quite as graceful, but he was less than two paces behind her at the start and they vaulted the wall in tandem, landing facing each way with their automatics out.

A woman ran into Gerta, looking back over her shoulder. She bounced off the Chosen as if she had run into a wall; Gerta grabbed and struck twice, punching with clinical precision. Something tinkled metallically, and the Imperial Protégé collapsed to the brick sidewalk, her face turning scarlet as she struggled to suck breath through a paralyzed diaphram. Behind her the dense crowd had scattered like mercury on dry ice, leaving a Chosen officer lying facedown. He was doggedly trying to crawl forward when Heinrich stooped over him.

"Lie still," he said. The bark of command penetrated the fog of pain; Heinrich cut cloth and wadded it into a pressure bandage. "Bullet wound, left of the spine, just south of the ribs. Looks nasty."

Gerta came up, nostrils flaring slightly at the iron scent of blood. There was no fecal smell, so the intestine hadn't been perforated, but there were too many essential organs and big blood vessels in that part of the body for comfort. She was dragging the Protégé woman by one ankle, and holding something in the other.

Heinrich looked at it and almost laughed. It was like a child's sketch of a pistol; a short tube, a wire outline for a grip and another piece of wire to act as a spring and drive a striker home on the single cartridge within.

"What sort of weapon is that?" he asked.

"It's not a weapon, it's an assasination tool. One shot and you throw it away; just the thing for killing a straw boss, or one of *us* on a crowded street."

Heinrich's features clamped down to a mask. After a moment he said: "Wouldn't have thought the Santies would come up with that."

"They're nasty when they get going," Gerta said. "We've been finding more and more of these. The problem is tracing back the chain of contacts. This animal will tell us something, perhaps."

"Indeed."

They looked up; a medic had arrived, with two Landborn Protégé assistants, and a man in civilian clothes. The long leather coat might as well have been a uniform: Fourth Bureau.

"That was quick," Gerta said neutrally. *Not the time for another intercouncil pissing match,* she told herself. This *was* their turf.

"Not quick enough. We had some information, but clearly it was insufficient."

The woman had recovered enough breath to recognize what was standing over her. She tried to crawl away, then screamed when he stamped on her hand.

It died away to a whimper when he knelt beside her and held up something: a jointed metal like a gynecologist's speculum, but with a toothed clamp on the end. Gerta recognized it, an interrogation instrument designed to be inserted in the subject's vagina, clamped on the uterus and tear it out with one strong pull.

"Now, my dear, I would like to ask you some questions," the secret policeman said. "And you would like to avoid pain . . . and there is so *much* pain you can feel." His hand clamped on her jaw. "No, no, you cannot bite off your tongue. Not yet."

Heinrich stood as the specialists staunched the bleeding of the wounded man, set up a saline drip, and began to ease him onto the stretcher. An unmarked police car drew up as well; the woman was drugged with a swift injection and thrown into the wire cage at the back.

"My oath, but going back into combat down in the Union looks better and better," he said.

Gerta looked morosely at the bloodstain on the deserted sidewalk. "Better and better, but where's it leading?"

"We'll win, of course."

"We won here."

Heinrich hesitated. "You know, you've got a point." He shrugged. "It's the Santies behind all this. If we finish them off, we can pacify successfully."

"Come on baby, you can do it," Jeffrey crooned.

The dogfight had swirled away into patchy cloud to the west; all he could see were two plumes of smoke rising from the ground where planes had augered in. The engine coughed again, a skip in its regular beat that produced a sympathetic lurch in his own heart. He banked gently over the zigzag trenches that scarred the land below, breaking into knots of strongpoints and bunkers in the ruined buildings of the university complex just south of Unionvil. Even now he shivered slightly at the sight of them; the winter fighting there had been ghastly, stopping the last Nationalist offensive in the very outskirts of the capital city.

"Come on," he said again.

Bits of fabric were streaming back from the cowling and upper wing of his Liberty Hawk II, ripping off as the slipstream worried at the bullet holes. That wasn't his main concern; the Mark I had sometimes had the whole wing cover peel off in circumstances like this, giving the remaining fuselage the aerodynamics of a brick in free-fall, but the new model was sturdier. He *really* didn't like the sound the engine made, though. Slowly, carefully, he brought the little fighter around and began to descend towards the landing field. Only a mile or two now . . .

And the engine coughed again and died. "Shit," he said with resignation, and yanked at the tab to cut the fuel supply. Then: "*Shit!*" as he looked down and saw a thickening film of gasoline in the bottom of the cockpit. "I *hate* it when things like that happen!"

Make a note to write to the design team, Raj prompted. If it had been Center, he would have taken that literally. . . .

A few black puffs of antiaircraft fire blossomed around him. Friendly fire, which was just as dangerous as the opposition's. It petered out; someone must have noticed the red-white-and-blue rondels on his wings, the mark of the Freedom Brigades' Air Service. Then the X shape of the field came into view over a low ridge, a ridge uncomfortably close to the fixed undercarriage. He concentrated on the white line of lime down the center of the graded dirt runway, ignoring the crash-truck that was speeding out to meet him with men clinging to its sides and standing on the running boards. A pom-pom in a circular pit near the edge of the runway tracked him, its twin six-foot barrels looking bloated in their water jackets, but at least that bunch seemed to keep their eyes open—a single fighter of Santander design with its prop stationary was hard to mistake for a Chosen or Nationalist raiding group, but every now and then a gun crew with active imaginations managed it.

Lower. Lower. Wind whistling through the wires and struts, flapping his scarf behind him. Lower . . . *touch*. The hard rims of the wheels ticked at the ground in a scurf of dry dirt and gravel, ticked again, settled with a rattling thud. The unpowered aircraft slowed rapidly to a halt. Jeffrey snapped open his belts and swung out to the lower wing, then to the ground, and lumbered away as fast as the weight of the parachute and the fleece-lined leather flight suit would let him.

"Motherfucking son of a *bitch*!" he shouted, throwing the leather helmet and goggles to the ground, followed by the parachute.

"You all right?"

That was one of the Wong brothers. Jeffery rounded on him. "The interruptor gear still isn't working right," he said as the crew from the crash truck swarmed over the Hawk, fire extinguishers at the ready.

"My guns *both* jammed. Which left me a sitting duck. And the fuel lines are still leaking into the pilot's compartment when the integral tank gets cut—do you have any fucking *idea* how good that is for pilot morale?"

Wong made soothing motions with his hands. "As soon as we can get more rubber, we can make the tanks self-sealing," he said.

Jeffrey snorted. The Land had all the natural rubber on Visager—the only places that could grow it were the Land itself and the northernmost peninsula of what had once been the Empire. John's factories were just beginning to produce a trickle of synthetic rubber from oil, but it was fiendishly expensive and the Land would cut off the natural type the minute their extremely efficient spies caught Santander using it for military purposes.

Crazy war, he thought. *We're fighting here in the Union, but it's all "volunteers" and normal trade goes on.*

"And the latest Land fighter is still better than ours."

"The triplane?" Wong said with interest.

"Yes, the Skyshark. It's almost as fast as our Mark II and it's got a better turning radius in starboard turns."

Wong took out a notepad and began to scribble as they walked back towards the squadron HQ; behind them the crew hitched up the plane and pulled it away towards the hangar and revetments, half a dozen walking behind with a grip on its wings to steady it. A group was waiting for Jeffrey.

"You should not risk yourself so, General Farr," General Pierre Gerard said.

"You must be really pissed, Pierre; you never call me that otherwise."

The loyalist officer shrugged, a very Unionaise gesture. "Still, it is true. And someone must tell you."

You, John, my wife, and my two invisible friends, Jeffrey thought. *And I can never get away from those two.*

"I have to have hands-on experience to work effectively with the designers," he said, looking over his shoulder for Wong. The little engineer and ex-bicycle manufacturer was trotting off to take a look at the shot-up Mark II. "Also to help refine our tactics for the pilot schools. We're sending them up with less than thirty hours flight time, so at least we should be teaching them the *right* things."

They walked into the HQ, a spare temporary structure of boards and two-by-fours. John stripped out of the flight suit, shivering slightly as the chill spring air of the central plateau hit the sweat-damp fabric of his summer-weight uniform.

"What *is* your appraisal?" Gerard said.

"The enemy have more and better planes than we do," Jeffrey said, sitting down and accepting the coffee an orderly brought. Coffee was another thing they were going to miss if—when—all trade with the Land was cut off. "And better pilots, more experienced. If it's any consolation, we're improving faster than they are, but we're starting from a lower base."

Gerard frowned, looking down at his hands on the rough table. "My friend, this is bad news. Although perhaps the government will listen now when I tell them the offensive on the eastern front is a bad idea."

Jeffrey halted the coffee cup halfway to his mouth. "They're still going ahead with that?" he asked incredulously.

"And they will strip men, guns, aircraft from every other front for it," he said. "The Committee talks of recapturing Marsai and splitting the rebel zone in half."

"The Committee has its head up its collective butt," Jeffrey said.

Gerard's head swiveled around. *Unfair,* Jeffrey chided himself. *He* could say that; the Committee of Public Safety had no jurisdiction over Brigade members, they'd insisted on that from the beginning. Gerard was in high favor after helping to stop Libert's thrust for the capital in the opening months of the war, but even so the Committee's name was nothing to take in vain. Chairman Vincen seemed to think that if he made himself into a worse mad bastard than Libert and the Chosen, he could *beat* Libert and the Chosen. It didn't necessarily work that way, but desperate men weren't the best logicians.

Gerard cleared his throat. "And it will be even more difficult if they can continue to use Land dirigibles to shift troops and supplies at will behind their lines."

"They can as long as they can keep our planes from punching through," Jeffrey said. "Those gasbags are sitting targets for fighters, but we don't have the numbers or the range to penetrate their own fighter screens.

Gerard's bulldog face grew longer. "Then they will be able to shift faster than I can—what is that expression you used?"

Jeffrey sighed. "They can get inside your decision curve. I just hope things are going better back home."

Admiral Arthur Cunningham was a big, thickset man, with graying blond hair. Right now his face and bull neck were turning red with throttled rage, and he pulled at his walrus mustache as he stared at the ship model in the center of the glossy ebony table.

The hull was a large merchant variety, an eight-thousand-ton bulk carrier of the type used to ferry manganese ore from the Southern Islands under Santander protectorate. The top had been sliced off and replaced with a long flat rectangular surface; the funnels ran up into an island on the port side, and a section had lowered like an elevator to show rows of biplanes in the huge hold below the flight deck.

"It's an abortion," Cunningham said.

"It's what we need for scouting," Maurice Farr corrected.

The rings on his sleeves and the epaulets on his shoulders marked him as a rear admiral, and kept Cunningham superficially respectful. Nobody could mistake his expression, or the meaning in the look he shot John Hosten where he sat beside his father.

"Farr, I'm surprised. I expect *politicians* to act this way." From his tone, he also expected them to have sexual intercourse with sheep. "You're a navy man and the son of a navy man. Why are you doing this?"

"We *work* for politicians, Cunningham—there's a little thing called the Constitution that more or less tells us to. And in this instance, the politicians are right. We need aerial scouting if we're going to match the Land's fleet; otherwise they'll be able to lead us around like a bull with a ring in its nose."

"We need airships with decent open-sea range, not

flying toys on this abortion of a so-called ship!" Cunningham said, his voice rising toward a bellow and his fist making the coffee cups rattle.

John spoke: "We've tried, Admiral Cunningham. Here."

He pulled glossy photographs from an envelope and slid them across the table. "You see the results."

The frame spread across a hillside was just recognizable as a dirigible's, after the fire.

"The Land is too far ahead of us on the learning curve with lighter-than-air craft. They've got the diesels, the hull design, and most of all, plenty of experienced construction teams and crews. We can't match them, not at acceptable cost, not with everything else we're trying to do. And land-based aircraft just don't have the range to give cover and reconaissance to a fleet at sea. Hence, we need the . . . aircraft carriers, we're calling them."

"Your shipyards need the contracts, you mean," Cunningham said bluntly. "Farr, this is diverting effort from capital ships."

Farr shook his head. "Look, Arthur, you know very well the bottleneck there is the heavy guns and the armor-rolling capacity."

Cunningham rose and settled his gold-crusted cap. "If you will excuse, me, sir—" he began.

"Admiral Cunningham, *sit down!*" Farr barked.

After a moment's glaring test of wills, the other man obeyed. "Admiral Cunningham, your objections are noted. You will now cooperate fully in carrying out the decisions of the Minister of Marine and the Naval Staff, or you will tender your resignation immediately. *Is that clear?*"

Twenty minutes later John Hosten sank back in his chair, shaking his head as he looked at the door that Cunningham had carefully *not* slammed behind him.

"I hope there aren't too many more like him, Dad," he said.

Maurice Farr sighed. His close-cut hair and mustache

were gray now, but he looked as trim as he had when he stood on the docks of Oathtaking nearly two decades before.

"I'm afraid there are quite a few," he said. "A lot of the officers are convinced that this is being forced on the navy by politicians—and highlander politicians from the east, at that, with their industrialist friends." He smiled. "They're right, aren't they?"

"But—" John began, then caught the look in his stepfather's eye. "You can still get me going, can't you?"

Farr laughed. "You take everything a bit too seriously, son," he said. "Don't worry; Artie Cunningham would rather eat his young than resign just before the first big naval war in a generation. If he has to swallow that"— he nodded at the model of the aircraft carrier that filled the center of the big table—"he'll swallow it, for the sake of the battlewagons."

Farr lit a cigarette. "He's not stupid, just rather specialized," he went on. "I can understand him; I'm a cannon-and-armorplate sailor myself. But I don't like operating blind." He stared at the model. "I *do* hope this concept's as workable as you and Jeffrey say. It looks good on paper, certainly, but I don't like ordering straight from the drawing board."

"Dad, I'm as sure as if I'd seen them fight battles myself."

pearl harbor, Center said helpfully. **the pursuit of the bismark. taranto. midway—**

Great, and how do I tell Dad that? John replied. Hastily: *That was a rhetorical question.*

Maurice Farr rose and began stacking papers in his briefcase. "No rest for the wicked—I've got to get back to HQ and deal with more bumpf. God, for a fleet command."

"Not long, I think, Dad," John said.

A long moment after his stepfather had left John heard the door behind him open.

"Touching," a voice said in Landisch.

"English," John said sharply. "Tradecraft."

"Oh, indeed."

The man—he was dressed in Santander civilian clothes, with a well-known yachting club's pattern of cravat—came and sat not far from John. He looked at a duplicate set of the airshipwreck photos.

"What caused this?"

"The design was overweight and underpowered; they took out a section in the center and enlarged it to take an extra gasbag. The bag chafed against the bolts internally, and they had a terrible problem with leaks. Probably they nosed in on that hill in the dark, or there was a fire from static discharge, or both."

"Sloppy," the Chosen officer said, tucking the pictures away. He nodded to the model of the aircraft carrier. "Will this work?"

"Probably, after a fashion. I can't turn down *all* the good ideas, you know—not and keep my standing with the military and defense industries."

"Indeed."

"I suppose we'll have to build them, too. Dirigibles are so vulnerable to heavier-than-air pursuit planes."

"Perhaps," the intelligence officer said. "And perhaps not."

"Straight and level, straight and level, damn your eyes," Horst Raske said, in a tone that was as close to a prayer as one of the Chosen was likely to get.

The bridge of the *Grey Tiger* was vibrating itself, very slightly, despite the skilled hands on the wheels and controls set about the U-shaped space. Through the vast semicircle of clear window they could see the teardrop shape of the experimental airship carrier *Orca* as she quivered in the clear air over the Land's central plateau, a hundred miles north of Copernik. The craft was huge, nearly a thousand feet from nose to stern, with beautiful swept control fins in an X at the rear, its smooth sheet-aluminum hull showing it to be one of the new metalclads.

Underneath it a small biplane fighter was making another run, first matching speeds with the dirigible, then edging upwards. A strong metal loop was fastened to the biplane's upper wing, and a long trapezoidal hook mechanism dangled below the airship's belly. The fighter swayed and dipped as it rose into the buffeting wake of the huge dirigible, then again as it hit the prop-wash of the six bellowing high-speed diesels. It rose sharply, and the observers on the *Grey Tiger*'s bridge sucked in their breaths, certain it would crash into the thin structure of the airship's belly.

Instead it pulled nose-up, almost stalling, then slipped into contact with the hook. A cable locked the mechanism shut, and it moved smoothly backwards with the aircraft pivoting and jerking on the hook-and-ring connection. The rise stopped with the biplane just below the entrance hatch intended for it.

"What?" Professor Director Gunter Porschmidt spoke with his usual quick, slightly angry tone. Some of the white-coated assistants around him moved away a little. "What? Why do they wait?"

Gerta Hosten replied. "Because, *Herr Professor*, the plane will only fit into the entrance hatch if aligned precisely with the airship's keel . . . and it is difficult to get it to point that way traveling at ninety miles per hour."

Porschmidt blinked at her. "Oh. Yes, yes, make a note." One of the assistants scribbled busily.

Tiny human figures on ropes dropped out of the airship's belly. Laboriously, they fixed rope tackle to the biplane's wings and body, and the trapeze swung it up once more. On the second try—the first crumpled a wing against the side of the hatch—they got it through. Porschmidt beamed, and there was a discreet murmur of applause from the Research Council officials with him.

"Good, good," the chief scientist said. "But perhaps

we should assign a better pilot to the next series of tests?"

"The pilot is Eva Sommers," Gerta said. "Her reflexes were among the ten best ever recorded in the Test of Life; she has fifteen kills to her credit from the war down in the Union and is currently the Air Council's best test pilot."

"Oh." Porschmidt shrugged. "Well, the purpose of operational testing is to improve the product."

"*Herr Professor?*"

"Yes?"

"While this is undoubtedly a great technical achievement," Gerta said, "given our current quality control problems, don't you think—"

He made a dismissive gesture. "The Chosen Council told me to design a device which would give us greater heavier-than-air scouting capacity than the enemy's new ship-borne aeroplanes. Production is not my department."

Horst Raske waited until they had left his bridge before putting a hand to his forehead and sighing.

"Well, this proves one thing conclusively," Gerta said, watching the *Orca* turn away.

"What?"

"That the Chosen are still Visager's supreme toymakers," she added.

"Brigadier, I do not think that is funny."

"It isn't. Porschmidt falling out a hatchway without a parachute at six thousand feet, *that* would be funny."

"If only the man were an incompetent!"

"If he were an incompetent, he wouldn't have passed the Test of Life," Gerta said. "Unfortunately, that is no guarantee that he will not be wrong—just that he'll be plausibly, brilliantly wrong with ideas that sound wonderful and are just a tantalizing inch beyond realization."

Raske shuddered. "I hope some of his ideas work out better than *that*." He nodded towards the disappearing airship. "When I think of the conventional models we

could have made for the same expenditure of money
and skilled manpower . . . and you're right, quality control has fallen off appallingly."

"A complete waste of—" Gerta stopped, struck. "Wait
a minute. The problem there is hull turbulence, right?"

Raske looked at her. "Yes. No way to eliminate it, that
I can see. An airship pushes aside a lot of air, and that's
all there is to it."

"But fifty, sixty feet down there's less problem?"

"Of course—but you can't put the hook gear *that* far
down. The leverage would snap it off at the first strain."

"Yes, but why do we want to hoist the plane aboard
the airship's cargo bay?"

She began to talk. Raske listened, his face gradually
losing its hangdog expression.

"Now why can't Porschmidt come up with ideas like
that?" he asked.

"Oh, some of Porschmidt's brainchildren work well
enough, better than I expected." Gerta said. She smiled.
"As our friends to the south will soon find out."

CHAPTER EIGHTEEN

"A great difference from the beginning of the war, *n'est pas?*" General Gerard said with melancholy pride.

Many of the soldiers trudging along the sides of the dusty road cheered as the car carrying Gerard and Jeffrey went by. They were almost all Unionaise on this front, not Freedom Brigades, so they were probably cheering the local officer—although Jeffrey was popular enough.

And they do shape a lot better, Jeffrey thought. For one thing, they were all in uniform and almost all had plain bowl-shaped steel helmets, and they all had the Table of Organization and Equipment gear besides. More importantly, they were moving in coherent groups and not getting tangled up or scattering across the countryside. Infantry marching on either side, horse-drawn guns and mule-drawn wagons and ambulances towards the middle, and a fair number of Santander-made trucks, Ferrins, and big squarish Appelthwaits. Occasionally an airplane would pass by overhead, drawing no more than a few curious stares; the men were accustomed to the notion that they had their own air service, these days.

The air was thick with dust and the animal-dung-and-gasoline stink of troops on the move. Around them the central plateau stretched in rolling immensity, with the snowpeaks of the Monts du Nord growing ever closer on the northeast horizon. The grainfields were long since reaped, sere yellow stubble against reddish-yellow earth, with dust smoking off it now and then. Widely spaced vineyards of trained vines looking like bushy cups covered many of the hillsides, and there was an occasional

296

S.M. Stirling & David Drake

grove of fruit trees or cork oaks. The people all lived in the big clumped villages, looking like heaps of spilled sugar cubes with their flat-roofed houses of whitewashed adobe. The peasants came out to cheer the Loyalist armies; Jeffrey suspected that prudence would make them cheer the Nationalists almost as loudly. Not that the government wasn't more popular than the rebel generals, who brought the landlords back in their train wherever they conquered, but Unionvil's anticlerical policies weren't very popular outside the cities, either.

"Everyone seems to be expecting a military picnic," Jeffrey said, leaning back in the rear seat of the big staff car.

It was Santander-made, of course; a model that wealthy men bought, or wealthy private schools. Six-wheeled, with a collapsible top, and two rows of leather-cushioned seats in the rear. Gerard had had the original seats replaced with narrower, harder models, plus communications gear and maps, with a pintle-mounted twin machine gun set between the driver's compartment and the passengers. Henri Trudeau stood behind the grips of the weapons, carefully scanning the sky.

"Morale is good," Gerard acknowledged. "The men know they've gotten a lot better, these past two years."

"You've done a good job," Jeffrey said.

"And you, my friend. Those suggestions for an accelerated officer-training system helped very much."

Ninety-day wonders, courtesy of Raj and Center, Jeffrey thought. Center had a *lot* of records of sudden mobilizations for large-scale warfare.

"Well, combat is the best way to identify potential leaders," Jeffrey said. "It's sort of expensive as a sorting process, but it works."

Henri spoke unexpectedly. "Things wouldn't be going this well if you hadn't got those anarchist *batards* killed off right at the start, sir."

Gerard looked up with a smile; the Loyalist Army was still informal in some respects. Jeffrey shook his head.

"The rebels inflicted heavy casualties on the anarchist militia, that's true," he said judiciously. *I'm becoming a politician like John*, he thought. "But that's scarcely my fault. They wanted to fight, and I put them where they could fight. Besides, you were with them, Henri."

The Unionaise solider grinned. "I wanted to *win*, sir. Which is why I've stuck with you since. And they were a wonderful example, in their way—everyone could see what came of their notions."

Then his head came up. "Watch it!" The machine gun swiveled around on its pivot.

"Listen up, people."

The selection of Chosen officers who would be supporting the offensive braced to attention inside the green dimness of the tent.

"Colonel Hosten is Military Intelligence for this operation and also our liaison with the Union Nationalist forces. She will conclude the briefing."

Gerta stepped up in front of the map easle. "At ease. The situation is as follows . . ."

She talked for ten crisp minutes, answering the occasional question. *What a relief*, she thought. Liaison work was a strain; foreigners chattered, they didn't know how to concentrate on the business at hand, they wandered off into irrelevancies. At last she finished.

"Now, let's go out there and *kill*."

"Inspiring and informative," Heinrich said. The double stars of a general rested easy on his shoulders, standing out from the hybrid uniform of the Eagle Legion, the Land "volunteer" force fighting with the Nationalists. "I suppose you'll go collate some reports?"

Gerta smiled. "Well, actually, Copernik wants detailed reports on the performance of the Von Nelsing twoseater," she said.

Heinrich shrugged his shoulders ruefully. "There are times when I think this whole war is nothing but a laboratory experiment," he said.

"It is," Gerta said. "Good on-the-job training, too."

"True." He frowned. "The problem is, the enemy learns as well—and they needed it more than we. So they improve more for an equal amount of experience. If you play chess with good chess players, you get good."

My darling Heinrich, you are extremely perceptive at times, Gerta thought as she ducked out of the tent and headed for the landing field.

The squadron looked squeaky-clean and factory-new, even the untattered wind sock and the raw pine boards of the messhall. Everything but the pilots. They'd all been transferred from Albatros army-cooperation planes to the new Von Nelsings; Gerta walked around hers admiringly. The fuselage was light plywood, a monocoque hull factory-made in two pieces and then fastened together along a central seam, much stronger than the old fabric models and extremely simple to make, which was crucial these days. There were two engines in cowlings on the lower wings, giving the craft a higher power-to-weight ratio than a fighter; it was heavier than the pursuit planes, but not twice as heavy. Six air-cooled machine guns bristled from the pointed nose, and there was a twin-barreled mount facing backwards from the observer's seat. Protégé groundcrew were fastening four fifty-pound bombs under each wing, and then a one-armed Chosen supervisor came along to inspect. Gerta gave the plane a careful going-over herself. They'd set up a multiple checking system, but with all the new camps full of Imperial deportees making components, it paid to be careful.

"All in readiness, sir," the squadron commander said expressionlessly, saluting.

And it would be even more ready if a hot-dogger from HQ wasn't pushing her way in, Gerta finished for him silently. She didn't mind; she *was* a hot-dogger from HQ, and she *was* pushing her way in shamelessly.

She was also a better pilot than any of the youngsters here; she'd been flying since the Land first put heavier-than-air craft into the sky.

"Let's show what these birds can do, then," she said.

The Protégé gunner made a stirrup of her hands and Gerta used it to vault up and climb into the cockpit. Then she stuck a hand down and helped the other woman into the plane. More than half the aircrew were female; they had lower averages on body weight and higher on reflexes, both of which counted on the screening test. This one seemed quite competent, if not a mental giant, and what you needed in an observer-gunner was good eyes and quick hands.

The first planes were already taxiing when she completed her checklist and signaled to the groundcrew to pull the chocks from before the spat-streamlined wheels. This production model seemed very much like the prototypes she'd flown back home, but the airfield was at three thousand feet rather than sea level. She pulled her goggles down over her eyes and followed the crewman with the flags; four more seized the tail of her plane and lifted it around to the proper angle. They held the plane against the growing tug of the motors until she chopped her hand skyward and it leapt forward.

Good acceleration, she noted. There'd been a bit of a tussle between the three aircraft companies over the scarce high-performance engines, with some claiming they were wasted on a cooperation airplane. *Smoother on the ground, too.* The new oleo shock-absorbers on the wheel struts were reducing the pounding a plane normally took on takeoff. The fabric coverings of the wing rippled slightly, as they always did. *Have to see how those experiments with rigid surface wings are going.* No reason in theory why the wings shouldn't be load-bearing plywood on internal frames like the body. That would *really* speed up production.

Up. She pushed the throttles forward and waggled her wings to test the balance of the engines, then banked upward and started glancing down at the ground, smiling to herself with the familiar exhilaration of flight. And there was *nothing* more fun than strafing missions. There

was the Eboreaux River, the town of Selandrons . . .
and the irregular line of the trenches. Not a solid maze
of redoubts and communications lines like some sections
of the front, just field entrenchments. Enemy artillery
sparkled along it and through it—their offensive was getting off to a good start, penetrating the thin defenses
and thrusting for the river.

Ground crawled beneath her, like a map itself from
six thousand feet. The cold, thin air slapped at her face,
making her cheeks tingle. An occasional puff of black
followed the squadron as the converted naval quick-firers
the Santies had supplied to the Reds opened up, but
there were a *lot* of targets up here today; aircraft were
rising from all along the front, swarming up from the
front-line airfields by the hundreds. There were planes
on either side as far as she could see, black dots against
the blue and white of the sky, the drone of engines filling
her ears.

Magnificent, she thought. Even better, the fighter
squadron assigned to give them top cover was in place.

Ahead, the squadron commander waggled his wings
three times and then banked into a dive. At precise ten-
second intervals the others followed. Gerta grinned
sharklike as she flipped up the cover on the joystick and
put her thumb lightly on the firing button.

"Those aren't ours," Gerard said sharply, standing.

No, they aren't, Jeffrey thought with sharp alarm. The
Loyalists and Brigades didn't use that double-arrowhead
formation.

"Get me some reports," Gerard said sharply to the
communications technician.

She—the Union forces had a Women's Auxiliary now,
too—fiddled with the big crackle-finished Santander
wireless set that occupied one side of the great car. There
weren't many other sets for the tech to talk to; wireless small enough to get into a land vehicle was a recent
development . . . courtesy of Center. Jeffrey kept his

eyes on the growing swarm of dots along the western horizon, but he could hear the pattern of dots and dashes through the tech's headphones. Center translated them for him effortlessly, but he waited until the tech finished scribbling on a pad and handed the result to Gerard.

"Sir. Enemy planes in strength attacking the following positions."

Gerard took it and flipped through the maps on the table. "Artillery parks and shell storage areas and fuel dumps behind our lines."

Another series of dots and dashes. "And our airfields. Fortunate that most of our planes are already up."

Jeffrey whistled, leaning against one of the overhead bars and bracing his binoculars. "I make that over two hundred," he said. "Fighters . . . and there are two-engined craft as well."

"The new Von Nelsings we've heard about. That puts a stake through the heart of this offensive."

"I'd say we've run right into a rebel offensive," Jeffrey said.

"Exactly. And I will advance no further into the jaws of a trap. Driver! Pull over!"

The big car nosed over to the side of the road. Several smaller ones full of aides and staff officers drew up around it.

"No clumping!" Gerard ordered sharply. "You, you, you, come here—the rest of you spread out, hundred-yard intervals." He began to rap out orders.

A fighter cut through the Land formation, the red-white-and-blue spandrels on its wings marking it as a Freedom Brigades craft. The twin machine guns sparkled, and a series of holes punctured the wing to her right; one bullet spanged off the steel-plate cowling of the engine. Behind Gerta, the Protégé gunner screamed with rage as she wrestled the twin-gun mount around, tracer hammering out in the enemy fighter's wake. The Von Nelsing next to her dove after it, but the more nimble pursuit plane turned in a beautifully tight circle, far tighter than the twin-engine craft could manage.

However, Gerta thought, and dove.

That cut across the cord of the Brigades fighter's circle; the heavier Von Nelsing dove *fast*. For a moment the wire circle gunsight behind her windscreen slid just enough ahead of the Santy Mark II. Her thumb stabbed on the button, and the six machine guns ahead of her hammered. Over a hundred rounds struck the little biplane fighter in the second that her burst lasted, ripping it open from nose to tail like a knife through wrapping paper. It staggered in the air, collapsed in the middle, and exploded into flame all in the same instant. The burning debris fluttered groundward in pieces, the dense mass of the engine falling fastest.

"And fuck you very much!" Gerta shouted, banking sharply to the right and heading groundward.

The Brigader had interrupted her mission. *There* was the road, still crowded with troops and transport. The men were running out into the fields on either side, or taking cover in the ditches, but the vehicles were less mobile. She lined up carefully, coming down to less than two hundred feet, ignoring the rifles and machine guns spitting at her. You'd have to be dead lucky to hit a target like this from the ground, plus being a very good shot, and the engines were protected.

Now. She yanked at the bomb release and fought to hold the plane steady as the fifty pounders dropped from beneath each wing. The explosions in her wake were heavier than shells of the same weight; less had to go into a strong casing, leaving more room for explosives. They straddled the roadway, raising poplar shapes of dirt and rock, also wood and metal and flesh. The guns in the nose of her airplane stammered, drawing a cone of fire up the center of the road.

Jeffrey dove for the floor of the car, pulling Gerard after him. Hot brass from the twin mounting fountained over them both. Bullets cracked by and pinged from the metal of the car. There was a fountain of sparks from the wireless and the operator gave a choked cry and slumped down on them with a boneless finality that Jeffrey recognized all too well, even before the blood confirmed it. It was amazing how *much* blood even a small human body contained. A second later there was another explosion, huge but somehow soft and followed by a pillow of hot air; a wagon of galvanized iron gasoline cans had gone up.

The two men heaved themselves erect; Gerard paused for an instant to close the staring eyes of the wireless operator. Henri was still swinging the twin-barrel mount, hoping for another target. The driver slumped in the front seat, lying backward with the top clipped off his head and his brains spattered back through the comparment. Other vehicles were burning up and down the road, and some of the roadside trees as well. A riderless horse ran by, its eyes staring in terror. Other animals were screaming in uncomprehending pain. The officers who'd gathered around Gerard were bandaging their wounded and counting their dead.

"You all right?" Jeffrey asked.

Gerard daubed at his spattered uniform tunic and then abandoned the effort. *"Bien, suffisient.* Yourself?"

"None of it's mine."

"Then let us see what we can do to remedy this—what is it, your expression?"

"Ratfuck."

"This ratfuck, then."

"Damn, they actually got them to work," Jeffrey said, scratching. *Damn. Lice again. I may be a lousy general, but I'd rather it wasn't literal.*

Two weeks into the latest offensive, and the Loyalists were already back nearly a hundred miles from their start-lines. One of the reasons was parked in the valley below them. It was a rhomboid shape more than forty feet long and twenty wide, thick plates of cast steel massively bolted together. The top held a boxy turret with a naval four-inch gun mounted in it, and each corner of the machine had a smaller turret with two machine guns; a field mortar's stubby barrel showed from the top as well, to deal with targets out of direct line of sight. There were drive sprockets in four places along the top of each tread, and steam leaked from half a dozen apertures. The long shadows of evening made it look even larger than it was, gave a hulking, prehistoric menace to the outline.

A Loyalist field-gun lay tilted on one wheel in front of the Land tank, its horses and men dead around it. Three lighter tanks had clanked on by up the valley towards the tableland, and only a few infantry and crew stood around the monster, the crew pulling maintenance through open panels, inspecting the tracks, or just enjoying spring air that must be like wine from heaven after the black, dank heat of the interior. A thick hose extended from its rear deck to the village well, jerking and bulging occasionally as the pump filled its tanks with water.

"That thing must weight fifty tons." *And we gave them the idea. Some disinformation.* You had to hand it to the Chosen engineers; they were perennially overoptimistic, but their hubris brought some amazing tour-de-force technical feats at times.

the vehicle weighs sixty one point four three tons, Center said. **maximum armor thickness is four inches at thirty degrees slope. estimated range eighty miles under optimum conditions. mechanical reliability and ergonomics are poor. cost effectiveness is low.**

Beside him on the ridge Henri was staring at the Land tank, his mouth making small chewing motions. Jeffrey had a hundred-odd men with him, Brigade troops and Loyalists, whatever had been left when the front broke. Many of them were taking a look and beginning to sidle backwards. There was a phrase for it now: "tank panic."

The ordinary ones were bad enough, but these new monsters were worse.

"No movement," he snapped.

Discipline held enough to keep his makeshift battle group from dissolving right there. Then again, the ones who'd felt like quitting had mostly gone in the days since the rebel counterattack and its Land spearheads had broken through the Loyalist front. These were the ones with some stick to them.

"Gather around, everyone but the scouts." He waited while the quiet movement went on; the men had good fieldcraft, at least. "All right, there's a heavy tank down there. They're dangerous, but they're also slow and clumsy, and the enemy doesn't have very many of them. We're behind their lines now, and they feel fairly safe. As soon as it's dark, I'm leading a forlorn hope down there to take it out with explosives. I need some volunteers. The rest will cover our retreat, and we'll break out to our own front. Who's with me?"

He waited a moment, then blinked in surprise as more than half lifted their hands. A nod of thanks; there was nothing much to say at a time like this.

"Ten men, no more. Henri, Duquesne, Smith, Woolstone, McAndrews—"

Night fell swiftly, and the highland air chilled. The commandos spent the time checking over their weapons, and making up grenade bundles—taking one stick grenade and tying the heads of a dozen more around it. Those who thought several days stubble and grime insufficient blacked their faces and hands with mud; a few prayed.

"How does a general keep getting himself into this *merde*, sir?" Henri asked, grinning.

"Going up to the front to see what's going on," Jeffrey said. "It's a fault, but then so are women and wine."

He looked up; it was full dark, and still early enough in spring to be overcast.

Rain? he asked.

chance of precipitation is 53%, ±5, Center replied. "We'll go with it," he said aloud. "Spread out. Avoid the sentries if you can; if you can't, keep it quiet."

The commandos moved down from the ridge, through the aromatic scrub and into the stubblefields of the valley bottom. There was little noise; the men with him had all been at the front for long enough to learn night-patrol work. *I'd have had more posts and a roving patrol here,* he thought.

Whoever was in charge wanted to keep pursuing as fast as he could, Raj said. **He left the minimum possible with the tank when it broke down. Sound thinking. The chances of a Loyalist band big enough to cause trouble being bypassed are low. But even low probabilities happen sometimes.**

There was a low choked cry from off to the left in the darkness, and a wet thudding sound. *We're going to—*

A rifle cracked, the muzzle flash bright in the darkness. Jeffrey could see the crew around the tank scrambling up out of their blankets and heading for their machine; half or better of them would be Chosen and deadly dangerous even surprised in their sleep. He tossed his pistol into his left hand and drew the bundle of grenades out of the cloth satchel at his side, running forward, stumbling and cursing as clods and brush caught at his feet. Abruptly the landscape went brighter, to something like twilight level. *Thanks,* he thought; Center was reprocessing the input of his eyes and feeding it back to his visual cortex. It no longer felt eerie after more than twenty-five years with Center in his brain.

A red aiming dot settled on a panicked Protégé soldier staring wildly about him in the near-complete darkness. Jeffrey fired, then dove and rolled to avoid the bullets that cracked out at the muzzle flash of his weapon. He didn't need to check on the enemy soldier. The dot had been resting right above one ear. A series of viscious blindsided firefights was crackling around the rebel encampment, men firing at sounds and movement glimpsed in split seconds. Or firing at what they *thought* was sound or movement.

Chooonk. The mortar in the turret of the Land heavy tank fired. Jeffrey dove to the ground again, squeezing his eyes shut. Reflected light from the ground still dazzled him for an instant as the starshell went off.

What was really frightening was a high-pitched *chuff* and squeal of steel on steel. The tank was live; they must have kept the flash-boilers warm for quick readiness. He'd counted on the half hour it took to bring the huge machine on-line.

One of the corner turrets cut loose, beating the ground with a twin flail of lead and green tracer. Then the four-inch gun in the main turret fired. That must be more for intimidation than anything else, since they didn't have a target worth a heavy shell. It *was* intimidating, a huge leaf-shaped blade of flame, the ripping crash and the *crump* of high explosive from the hillside where the load struck.

He couldn't fault the men he'd left behind on the ridge. They opened fire on the camp and the Chosen tank, dozens of winking fireflies showing from their rifles. Sparks danced over the heavy armor of the panzer as it shed the small-arms bullets like so many hailstones . . . but it *did* force the commander to stay buttoned up, vision limited to whatever showed through the narrow vision blocks that ringed the cupola on top of the tank.

Schoonk. Another starshell. The machine-gun turrets were beating at the ridge, trying to supress the riflemen there, and doing a good job of it. The enemy infantry were taking cover behind the tank, firing around it. Then it began to move, grinding across the little valley towards the ridge. Towards him.

Stupid, Jeffrey thought as he hugged the dusty earth, blinking it out of his eyes. The Loyalist force didn't have anything that could threaten the four-inch armor plate of the Land war machine. *That's the Chosen for you.* Aggressive to a fault, ready to attack whether it was necessary or not.

Of course, if he was unlucky they'd reduce his own personal ass to a grease spot in this stubblefield.

The earth shook as the massive weight ground slowly, slowly towards him. The machine gun bursts from the four turrets and the coaxial weapon blended together into a continuous chattering punctuated by the occasional chugging of the mortar, firing illuminating rounds or high explosive to probe the dead ground behind the ridge. Closer. Closer.

Now it was looming over him. *Good.* No one had noticed him in the dark and the flickering shadows of the descending starshells as they wobbled on their parachutes. Steel screamed in protest and the earth groaned with a creaking sound as the walking fortress rolled towards him, lurching as the driver tried to keep the treads working at equal speeds. His stomach felt watery, and his testicles were trying to crawl up into it for comfort: "tank panic" felt a lot more understandable, even sensible, right now.

Black shadow passed over him as the prow moved by. There should be more than two feet of clearance between the tank's belly and the dirt. More than enough for him, if this was one of the ones without hinged blades fitted to the bottom. He rolled on his back, despite the voice at the back of his head screaming that he should bury his face in the dirt. The pitted, rusty surface of the hull was moving only inches from his face, closer when a bolthead went by. And there were the big eyebolt rings near the rear, fitted for use with a towing line.

He dropped his pistol on his stomach and reached out with both hands. *There.* He pushed the handle of the stick grenade through the bolt. His cap stuffed in beside it snugged it close enough not to move for a few seconds. He scooped up the pistol again with his right hand, and kept hold of the pull-tab at the base of the stick grenade with his left, letting the motion of the tank pull it loose, arming the weapon.

Don't stop now, baby, please, he thought.

It didn't. The commander must have been waiting until he was closer to use the main gun again, and the automatic weapons were reasonably effective on the move. The weight rolled from overhead, like freedom from the grave. Jeffrey began to crawl frantically, then rose and ran two dozen paces.

The first explosion was muffled by the bulk of the tank. It seemed absurdly small beneath the huge bulk of the Land vehicle, but even on something weighing sixty tons the armor couldn't be thick *everywhere*. The tank came to a lurching halt, although one machine-gun turret continued to fire for fifteen seconds. Then there was a second explosion, this one *inside* the tank. Steam jetted from the back deck, then a few seconds later from every opening and crack in the hull, squealing into the night like so many locomotive whistles. Jeffrey could feel his skin crawl slightly at the thought of what it must have been like inside, the sudden wash of superheated vapor flaying the crew alive.

That did not stop his pumping run. A low wall of crumbling stone and adobe showed ahead of him; he hurdled it and went to the ground with his face pressed to the dirt. Hot metal was in contact with ruptured shell casings and vaporized gasoline, and right about—

Whump. The fuel and ammunition went off together, and the Land panzer came apart along the lines where the sheets of cast and rolled armor were riveted together. Chunks plowed into the wall a few feet from him, showering powdered dirt and small stones with painful force. He raised his head cautiously; he could see nothing moving near the twisted wreckage of the tank, although the light from the burning remnants was bright enough to read by. The turret lay on its side a few yards distant; further out still were bodies that lay still. Mostly still.

"I hope none of them were mine," he muttered. His voice sounded faint and faraway in his ringing ears. Louder: "Rally here! Rally here!"

CHAPTER NINETEEN

"Those are their final orders?" Jeffrey asked.

"*Oui*. Unionvil is to be held at all costs. No troops may be diverted; instead we are to committ our strategic reserve. Chairman Deschambre assures me that the political consequences of losing the capital would be 'disastrous,' quote unquote. Minister of Public Education and Security Lebars tells me that they shall not pass."

"Quote unquote," Jeffrey supplied. "What strategic reserve, by the way?"

"The one we pissed away with that misbegotten offensive towards the Eboreaux last year and have never been able to replace," Gerard said.

Jeffrey nodded. His eyes felt sandy from lack of sleep, and his ears rang from too many cups of strong black coffee, the taste sour on his tongue. Outside the tent light flickered and stuttered along the horizon; it might have been thunder and heat lightning, but it wasn't. It was heavy artillery, firing all along the buckling front south and east of Unionvil. The traffic on the road outside was heavy, troops and supply wagons moving up to the front, wounded men coming back—some in ambulances, more hobbling along supporting each other, their bandages glistening in the light of the portable floods outside the HQ tents. A convoy of trucks came through, flatbeds crowded with reinforcements whose faces seemed pathetically young under their helmets. At least the mud wasn't too bad, despite spring rains heavier than usual. They'd had three years to improve the roads around here, three years with the front running through what had been the outermost satellite villages of Unionvil. That didn't look like being true much longer.

"*Baaaaaa.*"

Gerard's head came up, trying to find the man who'd bleated like a sheep. It was fifty yards to the road, and dark.

"*Baa. Baaaa. Baaaa.*" More and more of the wounded along the sides of the road were bleating at the reinforcements, mocking the lambs going to the slaughter. Gerard walked to the door of the big tent.

"Captain Labushange. This is to stop."

Whistles blew and feet pounded; there was always a company of Assault Guards and another of military police attached to the regional headquarters.

"And now I must use the *Assaulteaux* against wounded men for telling the truth," Gerard said. "By the way, my friend, Minister Lebars also assures me that it is better to die on your feet rather than live on your knees."

"Does the woman always talk like that?"

"Invariably. It's not just the speeches." Gerard looked down at the map table. "Leave us," he said to the other officers.

"So I have no choice," he went on, touching a red plaque with a fingertip. It fell on its side, lying behind an arrowhead of black markers. "And how am I different from Libert, now?"

"Libert started it," Jeffrey said, putting a hand on the other man's shoulders. "You couldn't be like him if you tried. We'll do what's necessary."

"I will," Gerard said. "Keep the Freedom Brigade troops in the line. This is a Union matter."

Jeffrey nodded. "Don't hesitate," he warned.

It was probably wise to keep the Brigade troops out of Gerard's coup, although they were just as rabid about the Committee of Public Safety as the native Union soldiers of the Loyalist army. Still, they were foreigners.

"Hesitate? My friend, I have been hesitating for six months. Now I will act."

He strode out of the room, calling for aides and staff officers. Jeffrey remained, looking down at the map. Unionvil was a bulge set into the rebel line, a bulge joined to the rest of the Loyalist sector by a narrow bridge of secure territory.

"I hope you're not acting too late," he said, reaching for his greatcoat.

Heinrich Hosten was in charge on the other side, looking at the same map. Jeffrey knew Heinrich, and he also knew exactly what he'd do in Heinrich's boots at this moment.

Jeffrey ducked out into the chilly night.

"Senator McRuther?"

The meeting was relatively informal. At least, John wasn't being grilled in front of the Foreign Affairs Committee in full, in the House of Assembly, with a dozen reporters following every word. This oak-paneled meeting room was much quieter, redolent of polish and old cigars, not even a stenographer taking notes. Most of the faces across the mahogany table were formidable enough, age and power sitting on them like invisible cloaks.

Senator McRuther was nearing seventy, and he still wore the ruffled white shirts and black clawhammer jackets that had been modish when he was a young man. He represented the Pokips Provincial District in the western lowlands, and he'd done that since he was a young man, too.

"Mr. Hosten," he said—turning the "s" sound almost into a "z" with malice aforethought, the Chosen pronunciation. "What exactly have you accomplished with your policy of 'constructive engagement,' except to get us into a war?"

John nodded. "You're right, Senator. We *are* in a war, although not a declared one. However, I might point out that the Land of the Chosen has over forty thousand of its regular army troops in the Union del Est. They're backing General Libert, and they're *winning*. I suggest that this is not in the national interests of the Republic of the Santander."

"Hear, hear," Senator Beemody said.

A few others nodded or murmured agreement; not all of them were from the eastern highlands, either. John's eyes took tally of them. Beemody's eastern Progressive bloc; a number from the western seacoast cities, which were growing fat on new naval contracts. And a scattering from the rural districts of the western lowlands, some of them McRuther's own Conservatives. The elderly senator hadn't kept office for fifty years by being stupid, even if he was set in his ways.

"As you say, they're winning. Never do an enemy a small injury; you've succeeded in antagonizing the Land without stopping them. If Libert and his Nationalists win we'll have a close ally of the Land on our eastern frontier, a powerful garrison of Land troops keeping him loyal, and we'll have to support this grossly inflated standing army *forever*. I realize that you and the rest of the highlander industrialists would love that, but *my* constituents pay the taxes to keep soldiers in idleness."

"Senator," John said quietly, "the Land is not antagonistic to Santander because we've backed the Loyalist side in the Union civil war. It's antagonistic to us because we're the only thing that keeps the Land from overruning the whole of Visager. And I hope I don't have to go into further detail about what rule by the Chosen means."

More murmurs of agreement. John's newspapers had been publicizing exactly what that meant for years. Refugees from the Empire, and now from the Union, had been driving home the same message. Militia had had to be called out to put down anti-Chosen rioting when the pictures of the Bassin du Sud massacre came out.

Senator Beemody coughed discreetly. "General Farr"—the high command had confirmed his promotion as soon as he'd stepped back on Santander soil—"I gather you do not recommend an immediate declaration of war."

"No," Jeffrey said. McRuther blinked in surprise, his eyes narrowing warily.

"We're not ready," the younger Farr went on.

Beside him in his rear admiral's uniform, his father nodded. The family resemblance was much closer now that there was gray at Jeffrey's temples and streaking his mustache. The lines scoring down from either side of his nose added to it as well.

"We're much stronger now than we were four or five years ago," Jeffrey went on. "Military production of all types is up sharply, and now we've got field-tested models. Our latest aircraft are as good as the Land models, and we're gradually getting production organized. The Freedom Brigades've given us a *lot* of men with combat experience, including a lot of officers; besides that, they're thirty-five thousand veterans as formed troops, and if the Union falls they'll retreat over the border. So will a lot of the Loyalist Army. But we're still not mobilized, a lot of the new Regular Army formations are weak, and the Provincial militias need to be better integrated. Admiral Farr can speak to the naval situation."

Jeffrey's father nodded.

"We have a tonnage advantage of three to two," he said. "More in battleships. The Land Navy has more experience, particularly in cruiser and torpedo-boat operations in the Gut, which could be crucial. Still, I'm fairly confident we could dominate the Gut. The problem is that operating further north, in the Passage, we'd be sticking our . . . ah, necks into a potential meatgrinder, with strong Land bases on either side and a long way from our own. If we lose our fleet, we'd be a long way towards losing the war itself. Furthermore, nobody knows what aircraft will mean to naval war. The Chosen have more experience, but only with dirigibles. We need time to finish the aircraft carriers and to train the fleet in their use."

"Senators," Beemody said, "the Republic of the Santander cannot tolerate a Union which is satellite to the Land. Are we agreed?"

One by one the men on the other side of the table lifted their hands. McRuther sighed and followed suit, last and most reluctant.

"Then that is the sense of the Foreign Affairs Committee," Beemody said. "On the other hand, we are not yet ready for full-scale conflict. I therefore suggest that we recommend to the Premier that in the event of the fall of the Loyalist government in the Union, the Republic should declare a naval blockade of all Union ports pending the removal of foreign forces from Union soil."

"But that *means* war!" McRuther burst out.

"Not necessarily. As Admiral Farr has pointed out, we *do* have more heavy warships than the Land. The Gut is closer to our bases than theirs; we can blockade the Union and they'd be in no position to retaliate without risking their seaborne communications across the Passage. And while losing command of the sea *might* be disaster for us, it would *certainly* be a disaster for them. They can lose a war in an afternoon, in a fleet action. With the Union blockaded, they'd be forced to pull in their horns. They can't afford to isolate the expeditionary force they've committed to the Union. It's our hostage."

McRuther pointed to the map on the easel at the end of the table. "They can supply through the Sierra—and the Sierra is neutral."

Senator Beemody looked to the three men sitting across the table, in naval blue, army brown, and the diplomatic service's formal black tailcoat.

"Sirs, there's only a single track line from north to south through the Sierra," Jeffrey said. "Besides that, it's narrow gage, so you'd have to break bulk at both ends, the old Imperial net and the Union's."

"General?" Beemody prompted.

"Assuming that the Union was fully under Libert's control, and that the Chosen went along with a naval

blockade?" Beemody nodded. "Supplying their forces
would be just possible. Daily demand would go down
and they could supply more from Union resources. It
would certainly take some time for a squeeze to be effective, in terms of logistics."

"We *can* interdict the Gut," Admiral Farr said. "That
I can assure you gentlemen."

"But the role of the Sierra will be crucial," Beemody
said. "Senators, I move that the Foreign Ministry be
directed to dispach a special envoy with sealed plenipotentiary powers to secure the assistance of the Sierra
Democratica y Populara in a preemptive blockade of the
Union to enforce the neutralization and removal of all
foreign troops. It's risky," he said to their grave looks, "but
I sincerely believe it's our only chance. Otherwise in six
months time we'll be confronted with a choice between
a war that might destroy us and accepting a Land protectorate on our border, which is intolerable. A show of
hands, please, Senators."

This time the vote was less than unanimous. McRuther
kept his hand obstinately down, switching his pouched
and hooded blue eyes between Beemody and the Farrs.

"Fifteen ayes. Five nays. The ayes have it. The recommendation will be made. I remind the honorable senators that this meeting of the Foreign Affairs Committee
is strictly confidential."

"Agreed," McRuther said sourly. "It's no time for a
war of leaks."

"Then if that's all, Senators?"

The big room seemed larger and more shadowy when
only Beemody, Farr, and his sons were left. The faces
of past premiers looked down somberly from oil paintings on the walls; the old-fashioned small-paned windows were streaked with rain. Branches from the oaks
around the building tapped against the glass like skeletal fingers. John Hosten had a sudden image of men—
men not yet dead, the dead of the greater war to come—
rising from their graves and traveling back to this

moment, *tap-tap-tapping* at the windows, pleading for their lives. Tens of thousands, hundreds of thousands, millions.

observe:

Center showed him a vision he'd seen times beyond number, since that year on the docks of Oathtaking. Visager from space, the globes of fire expanding over cities, rising in shells of cracked white until they flattened against the upper edge of the atmosphere and the whole globe turned dirty white with the clouds. . . .

His stepfather cleared his throat. "You don't really think the Chosen will swallow a blockade of the Union?" he said to the head of the Foreign Affairs Committee.

Beemody shook his head. "About as likely as a hyena giving up a bone," he said frankly. "But it's as good a *casus belli* as any, the Senate will swallow it because they're desperate and desperate men believe what they want to, and the public will go along, too. Even McRuther will go along; he knows we can't dodge this much longer. But we *do* need more time, and we *do* need the Sierrans to come in on our side. They should; if we fall, they're next."

"But it's easier to see that when you don't have someone ahead of you in the lineup to the abbatoir," Jeffrey said with brutal frankness. "Hope springs eternal—and the Sierrans aren't just decentralized, they've got the political nervous system of an amoeba. Getting them to agree where the sun comes up is an accomplishment."

"Perhaps," John said slowly, "we could get the Chosen to do our arguing for us."

His foster-father frowned in puzzlement. Jeffrey shot him a glance, then tilted his head slightly towards the older men.

There comes a time when you have to use an asset, John said. *If you won't risk it, what bloody use is it?*

Center? Jeffrey asked.

probability of success is in the fifty percent

range, the machine voice said. **chaotic factors render closer analysis futile at this point. success would increase the probability of a favorable outcome to the struggle as a whole by 10%, ±3.**

John nodded mentally. "Here's what I propose," he said. "First, sir"—he nodded to Admiral Farr—"Senator, you should be aware that we have a very highly placed double agent who the Chosen—Land Military Intelligence, to be precise—think is their mole and who they rely on implicitly for analysis of the Republic's intentions. I can't be more specific, of course. And this is entirely confidential."

The Admiral and Senator Beemody nodded in unison. There was no telling where the real moles were, of course.

"Here's what I think we should do—"

Gerta Hosten was walking stiffly when she entered the room. John stood.

"Are you all right?" he asked, surprised to find the concern genuine, even after all these years.

"Flying accident," she said, looking around.

The little house was a gem, in its own way; patterned silk wallpaper, Errife rugs, inlaid furniture, all discreetly tucked away in a leafy suburb north of the embassy section of Santander City. Just what a millionaire industrialist would use for assignations he wanted to keep thoroughly secret from his wife, which was the cover John was using. *Good tradecraft,* she thought grudgingly; John could read that on her face, even without Center's supremely educated guesses.

"Not serious, I hope." John sat and poured the coffee and brandy.

"Just a wrenched back for me. Thankfully, the plane totaled itself in front of half the Chosen Council. That damned bomber is a flying—just barely flying—abortion. If it'd had a full fuel load, much less bombs, I'd be in bits just large enough to plug a rat's ass."

"The Air Council's finally given up on using airships as strategic bombers?"

"I should hope so, after we lost a dozen trying to hit Unionvil in the last offensive," she said. "But those eight-engine monsters Porschmidt came up with, they're no better. Only marginally faster, the bomb load is a joke, they're unbelievably expensive to build and maintain, and landing them's more dangerous than combat. The bugger's got the Council's ear, though, him and his backers. Now he's throwing good money after bad, trying to *improve* the fuckers." She sighed. "To business."

"Here," John said, sliding the folder across the ivory-and-tortoise-shell of the table.

It had three separate sets of "Top Secret" and "Eyes Only" stamps on it, Army General Staff, Naval Staff, and Premier's Office, the latter a miniature of the Great Seal that only he and his chief aide could use. Gerta whistled silently as she picked it up. Her face went totally unreadable as she finally looked up at him. "This is serious?"

"Totally. Note the Premier's sign-off."

She flipped to the end. *To be implemented, as soon as possible.* "I'll be damned," she said. "I wouldn't have thought the Santies could get their shit together like this."

"Jeff advised it, strongly," John said. "He's quite the fair-haired boy right now, and not just with the general public."

"He deserves it," Gerta said, refilling her cup. "Heinrich was extremely impressed with the way he got most of the Brigades out of Unionvil before we pinched off the pocket there. Excuse me, before General Libert pinched off the pocket with the assistance of volunteer contractors from the Land operating without the approval of the Chosen Council."

She grinned like a wolf. "Heinrich picked up some very pretty things there when we sacked the city."

John matched her expression, although in his case it wasn't a smile. "What'll you recommend?"

"Me? I'm just MilInt's messenger girl," Gerta said. "You're also the daughter of the Chief of the General

Staff," John pointed out. "And you've been carrying the hatchet for them for fifteen years now."

"That's between me and the *vater*, Johnnie," Gerta said, taking out a camera the size of a palm from the street purse resting beside her chair. She opened it, checked the ambient light, and began photographing each page of the folder with swift, methodical care. "Besides, all doing a good job gets you is more jobs— you know how it works.

"I'll tell you, though," she said as she worked, "that I told him we shouldn't get involved in the Union, and that if we had to make another grab so soon it should be the Sierra instead."

"Tougher nut," John observed.

"True, but not one we had to swim to get to," she replied. "Frankly I think the navy flatters its chances when the balloon goes up. The Union thing could leave our tits in the wringer if things go wrong. This"—she nodded to the papers between snaps—"is exactly what the Santies *should* do, after all. But the Union was just too tempting, the political situation. I wish there were more women on the Chosen Council."

John looked up at the irrelevancy. The Chosen had equality of the sexes, but males did predominate slightly at the higher ranks.

"Men never can resist the chance to stick it in an inviting orifice," Gerta said, and finished her pictures. "Heinrich's as smart as a whip, for example, but he spends an unbelievable amount of time and effort improving the Union's genetic material. It's the same with politics. No patience."

"Do I detect a certain note of complaint?"

They both laughed. "Plenty left over," Gerta said. She rose and saluted. "Thanks, Johnnie . . . if it's genuine."

CHAPTER TWENTY

"It's like something out of th' Bible," Harry Smith blurted, looking down from where the car rested on a high track beside a customs station.

Belton Pass was the main overland route between the Union and the Republic of the Santander. The saddle was only seven thousand feet high, and hilly rather than mountainous; on either side the Border Range reared up to twenty thousand feet or better, capped by glaciers and eternal snow above the treeline. There were enigmatic Federation ruins on the slopes, built of substances no scientist could even identify, and tunnels where strange machines crouched like trolls in an ancient tale—some as pristine as the day they were last used, some crumbling like salt when exposed to air or sunlight. In the centuries after the Fall mule trains had used the pass, and border barons had built stone keeps whose tumbled stone had supplied material for shepherd's huts in later years. Wars between the two countries had left their legacy of forts, the more recent sunken deep in the rock and covered in ferroconcrete and steel. There was a motorable road now, too, and a double-tracked railway built with immense labor and expense all the way from Alai in the western foothills.

Trains had been coming out of the Union for weeks now. The first had carried the last gold reserves of the Loyalist government, and the most precious records. Later ones had carried everything that could be salvaged from the factories of the Union's western provinces, some with the labor forces sitting on the machine tools. More and more carried people, shuttling back and forth with crowds riding packed so tightly that smothered bodies were unloaded at every stop, and the roofs of the freight cars black with refugees. Even more poured by cart and horse and ox-wagon, scores of thousands more on foot carrying their few possessions on their backs or in handcarts and wheelbarrows. They packed the lowlands in a moving mass of black and dun-brown, dust hanging over them like an eternal cloud. Only behind the Santander border posts with their tall flagpoles did they begin to fray out, as soldiers and volunteers directed them.

Pia Hosten leaned against her husband's long limousine, dark circles of fatigue under her eyes. She pulled off the kerchief that covered her hair and shuddered.

"It will be like a plague out of the Bible if we do not get more of the delousing stations set up. Typhus and cholera, those people are all half-starved and filthy and they have had no chance to wash in weeks."

"We'll do it," John said. "The government's sending in more troops to set up the camps and keep order, and we're shipping in food and medical supplies as fast as the roads and rail net will bear." He looked at his wife, and brushed back a strand of hair that fell down her forehead. "There would be thousands dead, if it weren't for your Auxiliaries," he said. "Nobody else was ready."

She turned and buried her face in his shoulder. "I feel as if I am trying to bail the ocean with a spoon," she said.

"You're exhausted. You've done an enormous job of work, and I'm proud of you."

"Dad!"

Maurice Farr came bounding up the slope, handsome young olive face alight, trim and slender in the sky-blue uniform of the Air Cadets.

"Dad—I mean, sir—Uncle Jeff, I mean General Farr, is coming. With General Gerard!" He stopped. "Mom, are you all right?"

She straightened. "Of course." Then she looked down at her plain dress, stained with sweat and her work. "My God, I can't—"

"It's not a diplomatic reception, darling," John said soothingly. "And I don't think Jeff or Pierre will care much about appearances. Not after what you've been doing."

The car that drew a trail of dust up the gravel road was much less elegant than John's, although it was the same big six-wheeled model. It had patched bullet holes in several places, a few fresh ones, and three whip antennae waving overhead. Rock crunched under the wheels as it drew to a stop and stood, the engine pinging and wheezing as metal cooled and contracted. The men who climbed down were ragged and smelled strongly of stale sweat, and there was dust caked in the stubble on their faces.

Pierre, Gerard drew himself up, saluted, and held out his pistol butt-first. "As representative of the Union del Est—" he began.

John took the weapon and reversed it, handing it back to the Union general. *And head of state, don't forget that,* he reminded himself.

"General Gerard, as representative of the Republic of the Santander, it is my privilege to welcome you, your government, your armed forces and your people to our territory. I am instructed to assure you that you will all be welcome until the day when you can return to restore your country's independence, and in the interim the government and people of the Republic will extend every aid, and every courtesy, within their power."

He smiled and held out his hand. "That goes for me, too, of course, Pierre."

The other man took his hand in a strong dry grip for an instant. Then he clicked heels and bent over Pia's. "We've heard what you and your ladies have done for my people," he said quietly. "We are in your debt, forever."

"We're in your debt," John said. "You've been fighting the common enemy for five years. And you'll see more fighting before long, if I'm any judge of events."

Jeffrey Farr nodded. "Damned right."

Both men twisted sharply at the sound of aircraft engine. The planes coming up the valley from the west were Hawk III's, over a dozen of them. They relaxed.

"Most of the aircraft will be crossing further north," Gerard said. "All the troops that are going to make it out here will be across by tomorrow. Except for the rearguard."

John nodded with silent grimness. Those would have to fight where they were until overrun, to let the civilians and what was left of the Brigades and the Loyalist armies break contact and retreat over the border.

"The perimeter around Borreaux's holding for now," he said. "We've got ships shuttling continuously from there to Dubuk with refugees. Navy ships, too. My father created a precedent for that at Salini."

Gerard smiled wryly. "Wars are not won by evacuations, however heroic," he said.

John nodded. "I assume Jeffrey's filled you in on the deployments for your troops?"

"*Oui.* Rather far forward."

Jeffrey spread his hands in embarassment. "If—when—the enemy attack, we'll need men who can be relied on not to break," he said. "The Brigades won't, and neither will your men."

Gerard nodded. "The civilians, though?"

"We're setting up temporary camps around Alai, Ensburg, and Dubuk," John said. "From there we'll try to move people where there's housing and jobs."

Gerard looked down on the mass of humanity filling the great pass below and the roads to the east. "We come as beggars, but we can fight, and work. Everyone but the children and cripples will. We have a debt to collect, from Libert and his *allies.*" He spat the last word. "Does Libert know he's a puppet, yet?"

John shook his head. "There's an old saying," he replied. "If you owe the bank a thousand and can't pay, you're in trouble. If you owe a million and can't pay, the *bank* is in trouble. Libert and his army are saving the Chosen a great deal of trouble and expense, just by existing. I'm sure he'll use that leverage."

Jeffrey nodded. "I think that's why the pursuit hasn't been pressed more vigorously," he said thoughtfully. "Libert *wants* us to get enough men over the border to be a standing menace. That means that the Chosen have to keep him on, or risk having the whole population go over to the Loyalist side who're waiting to return. They don't have enough troops in the Union to hold it down by themselves, not and keep an offensive capacity. Not yet, at least."

Gerard shrugged and saluted. "I must get back to my men."

John shook his head again. "Visit my home soon," he said. "You won't do your people any good by collapsing."

The shrewd brown eyes studied him. "You will not be there?" he said.

"No. There's . . . trouble brewing. Exactly what I can't say, but I can say that the board's going to be reshuffled thoroughly, and soon."

"Citizens!"

The sixth of the twelve-man Executive Council of the Sierra Democratica y Populara stood to address the seven hundred members of the Board of Cantonal Delegates. One of his colleagues passed him a ceremonial spear, the mark of the speaker, and pushed the button on top of a very modern timer clock.

I do not believe this, Gerta Hosten thought to herself. She and the Land delegation were sitting in the visitors' seats to one side of the Executive Council. An extremely ancient oak in the middle of the beaten dirt of the circle hid many of the delegates from her, and from each other. This was where the first representatives of the people-in-arms had met four hundred years ago to proclaim the Sierra, probably under the parent of this very tree, and so here they *still* met, where the city of Nueva Madrid had grown up. And met, and met, and met; the speeches had been going on for a week and looked good for another two.

Every one of them carried a rifle and wore a bandolier. That was about the only uniformity. Dress ranged from fringed leather to Santander-style business suits, with a predominance of berets and ferocious waxed mustaches. There were no women, since females didn't have the vote in any of the Sierran cantons, although they weren't badly treated otherwise.

Every adult male *did* have the vote, and every delegate here could be recalled at any time by the cantonal voters meeting in open assembly. Any hundred men could call an assembly. The delegates chose the twelve-man executive, but the voters could recall them at any time, and often did.

I do not believe anything this absurd has survived this long, she thought. *Whenever I think our councils are cumbersome, I should remind myself of this.*

The speaker shouted in an untrained bellow, with a strong up-country peasant accent to his Ispanyol: "Citizens! For four hundred years, no enemy has gotten anything but disaster from attacking us. We drove out the Imperials!"

Well, that's no particular accomplishment, she thought. Then: *To be fair, that was when the Empire was a real power. They drove us into the ocean back then.*

"We drove out the Union! We threw the Errife back into the sea when their ships ranged every coast! We made the Republic withdraw from our island of Trois! In the Sierra, every one of us is a fighting man, every one!"

Funny, in most places half the population are women, Gerta thought as the delegates cheered wildly.

"So let the cunt-whipped Chosen perverts fuck

themselves!" The speaker's mountain-peasant accent grew thicker. "Let the dirty money-grubbing Santanders fuck themselves! The Sierra pisses on all of them!"

Eventually the timer rang, loud and insistent. The president pro tem of the Executive Council—each member held the office in rotation for a week—cleared his throat as he took back the spear.

"We must, in courtesy, listen to the arguments of the honorable Thomas Beemer, Ambassador Plenipotentiary to the Sierra from the Republic of the Santander."

Assistant head of the Research Department of the Foreign Ministry, Gerta reminded herself. That made him the equivalent of the second-in-command of the Fourth Bureau back home, although the Research Department didn't have the internal security functions the Fourth Bureau did. A very high-powered spook. A rabbity-looking little man, bald and peering out through thick glasses. Important not to underestimate him because of that.

"Honorable delegates," Beemer said. "The Chosen took the Empire fifteen years ago. Over the last five they have conquered the Union. Only you Sierrans and we in the Republic remain independent.

"The Republic does not intend to let the Chosen eat the world, not all in one gulp or one nibble at a time. I am here to announce that from this midnight, the Republic of the Santander declares a total naval blockade of the Union. This blockade will be maintained until all foreign troops are withdrawn and a legitimate government chosen by free elections under Santander supervision. The Republic will regard it as a grave breach of friendly relations if the Democratic and Popular Sierra allows overland transit to evade this blockade."

Johnny was telling the truth, Gerta thought, still mildly suprised. First a blockade, and then the seizure of the Sierra in cooperation with pro-Santander and anti-Chosen factions among the cantons. Those slightly outnumbered the neutralists, which wasn't surprising considering the position the Sierra found itself in. Nobody here was actually pro-Chosen, of course. That would be like expecting a pig to be pro-leopard.

This time the roar went on for twenty minutes. Delegates milled, shouted into each other's faces, shook their fists or used them and were clubbed down by their neighbors. Occasionally someone would fire his rifle, into the air, thankfully, although the bullet had to come down *somewhere*. The Chosen embassy sat in stolid silence, upright and expressionless, their round uniform caps resting on their knees. When the noise eventually died down, Ebert Meitzerhagen stood, walked forward three precise steps and stood at parade rest.

He was a vivid contrast to Beemer, one reason he'd been chosen for the role. His cropped pale hair and light eyes stood out the more vividly for the deep mahogany tan of his skin; his face and bull-neck were seamed with scar tissue, and the massive shoulders strained at his uniform jacket. The great hands dangling at his sides were equally worn and battered, huge spatulate things that looked capable of ripping apart oxen without bothering with tools. All in all, he looked to be exactly what he was: a brutal, methodical, merciless killer. The Sierrans wouldn't necessarily be intimidated, but they weren't fools enough to believe all their own bombast, either.

"Sierrans," Meitzerhagen said. "We wish no war with you. We have no territorial demands on you."

Yet, Gerta thought. General Meitzerhagen was being truthful enough: the Chosen Council wanted a decade of peace now. If they could get it on their own terms, which did *not* include giving up the fruits of victory in the Union.

"If you join with Santander in attacking us and our allies, do not expect us to meekly endure it. When someone strikes us a blow, we do not just strike back— we crush them."

He held out a hand palm up and slowly closed it into

a fist, letting the delegates look at the knuckles, scarred and enlarged.

Gerta called up a mental map of the Sierra. Mountains north and south, high ones—too high for dirigibles, except in a few passes, and they'd have to come uncomfortably close to the ground even there. A spine of lower mountains down the center, joining the two transverse ranges and separating two wedges of fertile lowland on the west and east coasts. The eastern wedge was drained by the Rio Arena, from here at Nueva Madrid to Barclon at the river's mouth. The Arena valley was the heartland of the Sierra, where most of the agriculture and population and trade lay, although the national mythology centered on the shepherds and hill farmers of the mountain forests.

This is going to be very tricky, she thought. *And we don't have much time.*

Fortunately, good staff work was a Chosen specialty.

Admiral Maurice Farr tapped the end of the polished oak pointer he'd been using on the map into his free hand. "Gentlemen, that concludes the briefing. The blockade begins as of midnight tonight." He looked out over the assembled captains of the Northern Fleet. "Any questions?"

"Admiral Farr." Commodore Jenkins, commander of the Scout Squadron of torpedo-boat destroyers spoke. A thickset, capable-looking man, missing one ear from a skirmish in the Southern Islands. "Could you clarify the rules of engagement?"

"Certainly, Commodore. No ships, except Unionaise fishing vessels, are to be allowed within four miles of any of the Union ports on the list, or to within five miles of the coast, or to offload or load any cargo. You will issue warnings; if the warning is ignored you will fire over the vessel's bow. If the warning shot is disregarded, you may either board or sink the vessel in question at your discretion."

"And if the violator is a warship?"

"You will proceed as I have outlined."

There was a slight rustle among the blue-uniformed men in the flagship's conference room.

"Yes, gentlemen, I am aware that this may very well mean war. So is the Premier."

And not a moment too soon, if there's going to be a war, he thought. The Republic's lead in capital ships was shrinking, as the Chosen finally got their building program under way. At a fairly leisurely pace, since they'd been planning on war a decade hence, but they had some first-rate designs on their drawing boards. One in particular had struck his eye, a huge all-big-gun ship with twelve twelve-inch rifles in four superimposed triple turrets fore and aft of the central island, and a daunting turn of speed. If it worked the way John's intelligence report said it would, nothing else on Visager's oceans could go near it and live. Fortunately, they hadn't even laid down the keel, and this conflict would be fought with existing fleets.

Santander's fleet was as ready as he could make it. That left only the personal question. *Am I too old?* Fleet command in wartime needed a man who could make quick decisions under fatigue and stress. Maurice Farr was within a year of the mandatory retirement age. Should he be at a desk in Charsson, or at home working on the book? *I'm a grandfather with teenage grandchildren.* He took stock of himself. He'd kept himself in trim, and he didn't need to shovel coal or heave propellant charges into a breech. No failure of memory and will that he could detect. *No. I can do it.* He spoke again, into the hush his words had made.

"You will accordingly keep your ships on full alert at all times, with steam raised and ready to weigh anchor at one hour's notice. All leaves are cancelled, and naval and other reservists have been notified to report to their duty stations."

Jenkins nodded. "If I may, Admiral, how are we

going to maintain a blocking squadron along the Union's south coast? Bassin du Sud and Marsai are the only good harbors or fully equipped ports between Fursten and Sircusa."

"The Southern Fleet"—a grand name for a collection of candidates for the knacker's yard and armed civilian vessels, with only two modern cruisers—"will blockade Bassin du Sud and Marsai. At need, they can be reinforced from the Northern Fleet. Any more questions? No?"

Mess stewards entered, with trays of the traditional watered rum, one for each of the officers. The toast offered by the senior officer present was equally a matter of tradition.

"Gentlemen—the Republic and Liberty!"

"The Republic!"

CHAPTER TWENTY-ONE

"Dammit!"

Commodore Peter Grisson raised his binoculars again. The dawn light was painting the Chosen dirigible an attractive pink, a tiny toy airship at the limit of visibility to the north. Far out of range of anything the ships below it could do. They all had the new high-angle anti-aircraft guns, but the distance was far too great.

I hate that bloody thing, he thought, wishing for a storm. You could get some monsters down here south of the main continent, with nothing but the islands between here and the antarctic ice and nothing at all all the way around the planet east or west to break the winds. His ships, some of them at least, could keep station better than that floating gasbag.

But the ocean was like a millpond, only a trace of white at the tops of the long dark blue waves. The *McCormick City* and the *Randall* steamed on, heading east-northeast for their blockade stations off the southern Union coast. They were making eight knots, well below their best cruising speed, because most of the gunboats and naval reserve yachts and whatnot around them couldn't do any better. Certainly the pathetic hermaphrodite—wood-hulled and iron-armored—relics that made up the other six cruisers couldn't. Neither of his two best ships were new, but at least they were steel-hulled and armored, and they'd both had extensive refits recently, virtual rebuilding.

Then a light began to flicker on the nose of the Land dirigible. Grisson smoothed his mustache with a nervous gesture. *What would Uncle Maurice do?* he thought, and looked at the captain of the *McCormick City*.

The captain lowered his own binoculars. "Coded, of course," he said neutrally.

"Of course. But Land scout dirigibles carry wireless." The Land's armed forces didn't make as much use of that on land as the Republic's did, but they had plenty for sea service. "So whoever he's signaling is *close*."

Grisson thought for a moment. The rules of engagement and his own orders from the Admiralty gave him virtually complete discretion. One thing Uncle Maurice wouldn't do was sit with his thumb up his ass waiting for things to happen to him.

I can't run, he knew. Intelligence on the Land naval forces in the area and their Unionaise allies was scanty, but whatever they had was likely to have the legs on his motley squadron. *Therefore . . .*

"Squadron to come about," he said, giving the new heading. "Signal *battle stations* and sound *general quarters*. My compliments to Commander Huskinson, and the torpedo-boat destroyers are to deploy. Tell him I have full confidence in his ships' scouting ability. No ship is to fire unless fired upon or on my order."

Bells rang, signal guns fired, yeomen hoisted signals to the tripod mast of the *McCormick City*. "Oh, and general signal: *The Republic expects every man to do his duty*."

Armored panels winched up across the horseshoe shape of the fighting bridge, leaving slits for viewing all around. A signals yeoman bent over his pad near the wireless station, decoding a message.

"Sir. From the destroyers."

Grisson took the yellow flimsy.

Am under attack by Land heavier-than-air twin engine models stop more than a dozen stop smoke plumes detected to northeast eight ships minimum approaching fast stop.

For a moment Grisson's mind gibbered at him. The

distance to shore was more than twice the maximum range of any Land-made airplane. *Stop that*, he told himself. *It's happening. Deal with it.*

"Signal: Wait for me stop am proceeding your position best speed stop."

The key of the wireless clicked as the operator rattled it off. Eyes were fixed on him from all over the bridge; he could taste salt sweat on his upper lip. He'd known this moment had to come all his professional life—ever since he was a snot-nosed teenage ensign on this very ship, when Maurice Farr faced down the Chosen at Salini and saved fifty thousand lives. *I expected this, but not so soon.*

"Signal to the fleet. Maximum speed." All of ten knots, if they were to keep together. "Add: We are at war. Expect hostile aircraft before we engage enemy surface forces. Plan alpha. Acknowledge. Stop. Repeat signal until all units have acknowledged receipt."

Some of the reservists would probably be a little slow on signals, and he didn't want anyone haring off on his own.

There was a collective sigh, half of relief. "Yeoman," he went on to the wireless operator, "do you have contact with Karlton?"

"Yessir."

"Then send: Commodore Grisson to Naval HQ. Southern Fleet in contact with Land and Libertist-Unionaise naval forces. Have received unprovoked attack in international waters. Am engaging enemy. Enemy twin engine heavier-than-air attack aircraft sighted at distances exceeding two hundred nautical miles from shore. Long live the Republic. Grisson, Commander, Southern Fleet. Stop. Repeat until you have acknowledgment."

"Yessir."

The rhythm of the engines hammered more swiftly under his feet. The black gang would probably be cursing his name. *Insubordinate bastards*, Grisson thought, the irrelevancy breaking through the tension that gripped his gut. It'd be a relief when the fleet all finally converted to oil-firing and turbine engines. A few score stokers could contribute more disciplinary offenses and Captain's Mast hearings than the entire crew of a battlewagon.

Neither side was going to have heavy ships here . . . at least, that was what the reports said. The Chosen had a complete squadron of modern protected cruisers in Bassin du Sud: six ships, *von Spee*-class, the name ship and five consorts. Seventy-five hundred tons, turbine engines—coal-fired though, the Land was short of petroleum—four eight-inch guns in twin turrets fore and aft, each with a triple six-inch turret behind it superimposed on a pedestal mount. They carried pom-poms and quickfirers as well, of course. There would be a squadron of twelve torpedo-boat destroyers as well, and the cruisers carried torpedo tubes, too. Land torpedos were excellent.

"Captain," he said. "All right; we're going to be at a disadvantage in weight of gun metal and torpedoes both, but less so in gunpower. We'll try to maintain optimum firing distance with the heavier ships and slug it out, while the lighter craft with torpedo capacity close in. Gunboats and others are to engage their destroyers."

"What about our destroyers, sir?"

"I'm going to send them in at the cruisers. They're outnumbered by their equivalents; we'll just have to hope one of them gets lucky. A couple of hits could decide the action, one way or another."

And thank God the practice ammunition allowance was raised last year. Somebody at Navy HQ had insisted on not putting *all* the increased appropriation into new building.

The *McCormick City* began to pitch more heavily as the northward turn put the sea on her beam. In less than fifteen minutes he could see the smoke from his quartet of three-stacker destroyers, and beyond them a gray-black smudge that must be the enemy. Black dots were circling in the sky over the destroyers, stooping and diving in turn. The little scout ships were curving and twisting to avoid them, their wakes drawing circles of white froth against the dark blue of the ocean. Their pompoms and high-elevation quick-firers were probing skyward, scattering puffs of black smoke against the cerulean blue of the sky.

"Signal to the destroyers," Grisson said. "Ignore those planes and go for the cruisers."

Aircraft couldn't carry enough bombs to be really dangerous, and their chance of hitting a moving target wasn't big enough to be worth worrying about.

The Land cruisers were hull-up now, their own screen of turtleback destroyers lunging ahead. The smaller Santander craft swarmed forward, disorderly but as willing as a terrier facing a mastiff.

"The signal," Grisson said quietly, "is *fire as you bear*."

If you only knew how I begged and pleaded to save your sorry ass, Gerta thought, smiling at the dictator of the Union.

At least General Libert had learned to ignore her gender—she suspected he thought of Chosen as belonging to a different species, in any event. He was being polite, today, here in Unionvil. No reason not to; he'd achieved his objectives.

"In short, the Council of the Land expects me to declare war on Santander," he said dryly. "What incentives do you offer?"

Not shooting you and taking this place over directly, Gerta thought. *I used every debt and favor owed me to help convince the General Staff that it wasn't cost-effective. Don't prove me wrong.*

"General Libert, if you *don't*, and we lose this war, the Santies have a certain General Gerard waiting in the wings to replace you. With his army, now deployed along the Santander-Union frontier. I very much doubt that the Republic is going to distinguish you from us in *its* formal declaration of war, which should get through the House of Assembly any hour now."

Libert nodded. He looked an insignificant little lump againt the splendors of carved and gilded wood in the presidential palace, beneath the high ceilings painted in allegorical frescos. The place had the air of a church, the more so since Libert had had endless processions of thanksgiving going through with incense and swarming priests; most of his popular support came from the more devout areas of the Union.

His eyes were cold and infinitely shrewd. "And if you *win*, Brigadier, what bargaining power or leverage do I retain?"

"You have your army," Gerta pointed out. "Expensively equipped and armed by us."

Libert stayed silent.

"And you'll have additional territory. I am authorized to offer you the entire area formerly known as the Sierra Democratica y Populara. Provided you assist to the limit of your powers in its pacification, and subject to rights of military transit, mining concessions, investment, and naval bases during and after the war. We get Santander. It's a fair exchange, considering the relative degrees of military effort."

Libert's eyebrows rose. "You offer to turn over a territory you will have conquered yourselves? Generous."

"Quid pro quo," Gerta said. *Now, the question is, does Libert realize that we'd turn on him as soon as the Santies are disposed of?* He was more than realistic enough, but he might not understand the absoluteness of Chosen ambition.

Libert sipped from the glass of water before him. "The Sierrans have a reputation for . . . stubborness," he said. "I have studied the histories of the old Union-Sierran wars. This may be comparable to the gift of a honeycomb, without first removing the bees and their stings."

"We intend to smoke out the bees," Gerta said. "Or

to put it less poetically, we intend to depopulate the Sierra, with your assistance. Your people aren't fond of the Sierrans"—that was an understatment, if she'd ever made one—"and after the war, you can colonize with your own subjects. There will be land grants for your soldiers, estates for your officers, a virgin field for your business supporters—including intact factories, mines and buildings. We'll leave enough Sierrans for the labor camps."

"Ah." Libert's face was expressionless. "But in the meantime, the Union would need considerable support in order to undertake a foreign war so soon after our civil conflict."

"Could you be more specific?" Gerta said wearily.

"As a matter of fact, Brigadier . . ."

He slid a folder across the table to her, frictionless on the polished mahogany. She opened it and fought not to choke. Oil, wheat, beef, steel, chemicals, machine tools, trucks, weapons—including tanks and aircraft.

"I'm . . ." Gerta ground her teeth and fought to keep her voice normal. "I'm sure something can be arranged. But as you must appeciate, General, we need to strike *now*."

"That would indeed be the optimum military course," Libert said. *And so you must give me what I ask, or risk unacceptable delay,* followed unspoken.

"I will consult with my superiors," she said. "We must, however, have a definite answer by dawn."

Or we'll kill you and take this place over ourselves, equally unspoken and equally well understood.

Gerta rose, saluted, and walked out.

"Why do we tolerate this animal's insolence?" young Johan Hosten hissed to her as their boot heels echoed in step through the rococo elegance of the palace's halls.

"Because with Libert cooperating, we gain an additional two hundred thousand troops," she said. "Most of them are fit only for line-of-communication work, but that's still nine divisional equivalents we *don't* have to detach for garrison work. Plus another hundred thousand that we *don't* have to use to hold down the Union in our rear while we fight the Santies."

Her aide subsided into disciplined silence—disciplined, but sullen.

I'm going to enjoy our final reckoning with Libert myself, she thought. Aloud: "I'd rather have three teeth drilled than go through another negotiating session with him, that's true," she said.

"Sir . . ."

Gerta looked aside. "Speak. You can't learn if you don't ask."

"Sir, you were against opening our war with Santander this early. Have you changed your mind?"

"That's irrelevant," she said. "We're committed now. Conquer or die." She sighed. "At least my next job is a straightforward combat assignment."

Air assault was no longer a radical new idea. Most of the troops filing into the dirigibles nestled in the landing cradles of the base were ordinary Protégé infantry, moving with stolid patience in the cool predawn air. A few of the most important targets still rated a visit from the General Staff Commando, and she'd ended up on overall command. Gerta looked around at the faces of the officers; they seemed obscenely young. No younger than she'd been at Corona, mostly.

It's déjà vu all over again, she thought to herself.

"That concludes the briefing. Are there any questions?"

"Sir, no sir!" they chorused.

Confident. That was good, as long as you didn't overdo it. Most of them had more experience than she'd had, her first trip to see the elephant. Policy had been to rotate officers through the war in the Union, as many as possible without doing too much damage to unit cohesion.

"One final thing. The Sierrans have much the same line of bluster that the animals did here, before we conquered the Empire. They have a word for it in their language . . . *machismo*, I think it is. There's one crucial difference between the two, though."

She looked around, meeting their eyes. "The Sierrans actually *mean* it. They couldn't organize an orgy in a whorehouse, but they're not going to roll over at the first tap of the whip either. Don't fuck up because you expect them to run."

"Sir, yes Sir!"

As they scattered to their units she wondered briefly if they'd take the warning seriously. Probably. Most of them had enough experience not to take the legends about Chosen invincibility too literally.

"All over again," she murmured aloud.

"Sir?" her aide said.

Fairly formal considering that they were alone and that Johan Hosten was her eldest son, but they were in a military situation, not a social one. And Johan was still stiffly conscious of being an adult, just past the Test of Life. She remembered that feeling, too.

"It reminds me of the drop on Corona," she said.

Half my lifetime ago. Why do I get this feeling that I keep doing the same things over and over again, only every time it's more difficult and the results are less? All the same, down to the smell of burnt diesel oil. The tension was worse; now she knew what they were heading into. She buckled on her helmet, slung the machine-carbine and began drawing on thin, black leather gloves as they walked through the loading zone. Wood boomed under their boots as they climbed the mobile ramp to a side-door of the gondola built into the hull beneath the great gasbags. Crew dodged around them as she walked back to the main cargo bay; Horst Raske wasn't in charge this time, he was with the new aircraft carrier working-up with the Home Fleet based out of Oathtaking.

What a ratfuck, she thought. *The Santies build aircraft carriers, and we waste six months in a pissing match over who gets to build ours.* The Councils had finally decided, in truly Solomonic wisdom—she'd read the Christian Bible as part of her Intelligence training—to split the whole operation. Building the hull was to be Navy; the airplanes and the personnel, plus logistics, training and operations, were done by the Air Council. The Navy would command when the fleet was at sea. *How truly good that's going to be for operational efficiency,* she thought. At least she'd managed to persuade Father to appoint Raske, who didn't confuse territorial spats and service loyalties with duty to the Chosen.

There were a company of the General Staff Commando in the cargo bay, plus a light armored car on a padded cradle that rested on a specially strengthened section of hull. It was one of the new internal-combustion models, and someone had the starter's crank ready in its socket at the front, below the slotted louvers of the armored radiator. Somehow it looked out of place in the hold of an airship, a brutal block of steel in a craft at once massive and gossamer-fragile. They were tasked with taking out the Sierran central command, such as it was. Although she frankly doubted whether that would help or hinder the resistance.

"Make safe," she said. "Lift in five minutes."

They squatted, resting by the packsacks and gripping brackets in the walls and floor. Gerta's station was by an emergency exit; that gave her a view out a narrow slit window. Booming and popping sounds came from above, as hot air from the engine exhausts was vented into the ballonets in the gasbags. More rumbling from below as water poured out of the ballast tanks. The long teardrop shape of the airship quivered and shook, then bounced upwards as the grapnels in the loading cradles released.

The dirigibles were out in force this time; she could see them rising in ordered flocks, one after another turning and rising into the lighter upper sky. The air was calm, giving the airship the motion of a boat on millpond-still water, no more than a slight heeling as it circled for altitude. Down below the airbase was a pattern of harsh arc lights across the flat coastal plain on the Gut's northern shore. The surface fleet with the main army wasn't in sight. They'd left port nearly a day before, to synchronize the attacks. There were biplane fighters and twin-engine support aircraft escorting the airships; as she peered through the small square window in the side of the hull she could see a flight of them dropping back to refuel from the tankers at the rear of the fleet.

You put on a safety line and climbed out on the upper wing with the wind trying to pitch you off—sometimes you did, and had to haul yourself back on. In a single-seater, someone from the airship had to slide on a body-hoop down the flexing, whipping hose. Then you had to fasten the valves, dog them tight, and keep the tiny airplane and huge airship at precisely matching speeds, because if you didn't the hose broke, or the valve tore out of the wing by the roots. If that happened the entire aircraft was likely to be drenched in half-vaporized gasoline and turn into an exploding fireball when it hit the red-hot metal surfaces of the engine. . . .

She raised her voice: "Listen up!

They were over the surface fleet now; hundreds of transports from ports all along the northern shore of the Gut, escorted by squadrons of cruisers and destroyers. The ships cut white arrowheads on the green-blue water six thousand feet below.

"Magnificent," Johan Hosten whispered.

This time Gerta nodded. It *was* a magnificent accomplishment, throwing a hundred thousand troops and supporting arms into action, fully equipped and briefed, at such short notice.

But we were supposed to fight Santander in another five to eight years. With our new battleship fleet ready, and another fifty divisions and a thousand tanks. Now . . . we're reacting, not initiating. The enemy should be responding to our moves, not us to theirs.

"Thirty minutes to drop!"

*   *   *

"This is a new one," Jeffrey shouted over the explosions.

"Too damned familiar, if you ask me," John said grimly, checking his rifle.

It was a Sierran-made copy of the Chosen weapon. They'd managed a few improvements, mostly because everything was expensively machined. No cost-cutting use of stampings *here*, by God—which meant that only about half of the Sierrans had them. The rest were making do with a tube-magazine black-powder weapon, also a fine example of its type.

"I've been caught in far too many goddamned Land invasions."

"Yes, but it's the first time we've been in one *together*," Jeffrey pointed out. There was gray in his rust-colored hair, but the grin took years off him.

"Let's go make ourselves useful."

"Yup. No hiding in embassies this time." Jeffrey sobered. "Damned bad news about Grisson. He was a good man; Dad thought a lot of him."

"Going to be a lot of good men die before this one's over," John said.

"Hopefully not us. . . . Watch it!"

The room shook from a near-miss. Dust and bits of plaster fell around them. The Santander embassy was in coastal Barclon, where most of the business was done, rather than in inland Nueva Madrid, the ceremonial capital. Right now that meant it was within range of the eight-inch guns of the offshore Land cruisers, as well as the aircraft. The Sierran antiaircraft militia was putting a lot of metal into the air; too much for dirigibles to sail calmly overhead and drop their enormous bombloads, which was something to be thankful for.

An embassy staffer ran down the stairs. Her face was paler than the plaster dust that spattered her face and dress, and she waved a notepad.

"They're dropping troops on Nueva Madrid," she

said, her voice rising a little. "And they're attacking from north and south over the mountains, too. Sanlucar has fallen—the last message said shells were bursting inside the fortress."

John's eyebrows went up. That was the main fortress-city guarding the passes from the old Empire south into the Sierra.

The staffer went on: "And the Chosen Council has issued a statement, demanding that we declare ourselves strictly neutral in the Sierran-Land war, and 'cease all hostile and unfriendly actions.'"

Ambassador Beemer nodded, checking the old-fashioned revolver in the shoulder holster beneath his formal morning coat.

"Not a chance," he said. He looked up at John and Jeffrey. "Admiral Farr is never going to forgive me. I should have sent you home yesterday."

"We both thought the Chosen would wait until the Sierrans voted," John said.

"Why? It was obvious which way it was going to go." He hesitated. "They'll be landing troops here?"

"Sure as they grow corn in Pokips," Jeffrey said. "Coordination is a strong point of theirs. In fact, I'd give you odds they're landing on both sides of the city right now."

Nobody was going to fall for the "merchantmen" full of soldiers, not after the attack on Corona. There wasn't any way to prevent ships loitering offshore, though.

"Then I suppose . . . well, according to diplomatic practice, the Chosen should intern us and exchange us for their own embassy personnel in Santander City."

Beemer didn't sound very confident. John nodded. "Sir, I'd recommend suicide before falling into Chosen hands—and that's assuming you get past the kill-crazy Protégés in the first wave. If the Chosen win, international law won't exist anymore, because there will be only one nation. And if they lose, they don't expect to be around to take the blame."

Beemer's head turned, as if calculating their chances.

North and south the armies of the Land were pouring over the mountain passes into the Sierra. West was the Chosen . . .

"Sir, I made arrangements, just in case. If we can get to the docks . . ."

Beemer started to object, then nodded. "You're a resourceful young man," he said mildly. "I'll get our people together."

Luckily there were only about half a dozen Santander citizen staff on hand; most of them had been sent home last week, when the crisis began. None of the Sierran employees were here; they'd all headed for their militia stations and the fighting half an hour ago. Two of the embassy limousines could hold them all, with a little crowding. John took his seat beside Harry Smith, sitting up on one knee with the rifle ready.

"Just like old times, eh?" he said.

Smith grinned tautly. "Barrjen is going to be mad as hell," he said. "I talked him into staying home for this one."

Another salvo of heavy shells went by overhead just as the limousines cleared the gates of the embassy compound. They struck upslope, and blast and debris rattled off the thin metal of the cars' roofs. John had a panoramic view of Barclon burning, pillars of familiar greasy black smoke rising into the air. He could also see the Land naval gunline out in the harbor, cruising slowly along the riverside town. There weren't any battleships, but there *were* a couple of extremely odd-looking ships, more like huge armored barges than conventional warships. Each had a barbette with a raised edge in the center and the stubby muzzle of a heavy fortress howitzer protruding from it.

Well, I guess that explains what happened to the harbor forts, John thought. Coastal forts were designed to shoot it out with high-velocity naval rifles, weapons with flat trajectories. They'd be extremely vulerable to plunging fire. *We'd better move fast.*

estimated time to chosen landing in barclon itself is less than thirty minutes, Center said.

Land aircraft were circling the city, spotting for the naval guns. John looked up at them with a silent snarl of hatred.

I'd have sworn that dirigible aircraft carrier idea was completely worthless, he thought.

It was, lad, Raj said quietly. **At a guess, I'd say they retreated to something less ambitious—using the dirigibles to carry fuel and arranging some sort of midair hookup.**

correct. probability approaches unity.

The streets were surprisingly free of crowds; what there were seemed to be moving to some purpose: armed men heading for the docks or the suburbs to the south, women with first-aid armbands or the civil-defense blue dot. Smith kept his foot on the throttle and made good use of the air horn. More barges were appearing from behind the Land fleet, coastal craft hastily converted to military use. They were black with men. Behind them lighter ships, gunboats and destroyers, moved in to give point-blank support to the landing parties with their quick-firers and pom-poms.

"Here!" John shouted.

The limousines lurched to a stop and the Santander citizens tumbled out, white-faced but moving quickly. Jeffrey and Henri brought up the rear; John stopped to drop grenades down the fuel tanks of both. Their pins were pulled, but the spoons were wrapped in tape. John hoped some Land patrol was using the cars by the time the gasoline dissolved the adhesive tape.

They had stopped in front of a boathouse in the fishing section of the port, a typical long shed with doors opening onto the water where a boat could be hauled out on rollers. This one was more substantial than most but just as rundown.

"Do you think a boat can make it out past the Land Navy?" Beemer asked dubiously.

John unlocked the doors. "No, I don't, sir," he said. "Therefore—"

Even with the sound of the bombardment in their ears, a few of the embassy staff paused to gawk. Within the dim barnlike space of the shed was a large biplane; each lower wing bore two engines back to back, with props at the leading and trailing edge. The body of the craft was a smooth oval of stressed plywood, broken by circular windows; the cockpit was separate, with only a windscreen ahead of it. Two air-cooled machine guns were mounted on a scarf ring in the center of the fuselage, where the upper wing merged with it. Bearing the plane's weight were two long floats, like decked-over canoes.

"Fueled and ready to go," John said. "Prototype—the navy's ordering a dozen. Jeff! Get some hands on the props!"

Bright sunlight made him blink as the big sliding doors were thrown back. The body of the airplane began to quiver as men spun the props and the engines coughed into life in puffs of blue smoke. He looked back into the body of the aircraft; Jeff's Unionaise bodyguard was stepping up into the firing rest beneath the machine guns. His foster-brother slid into the other seat in front of the controls, while Smith showed frightened embassy staff how to snap their seatbelts shut as they took their places along either side of the big biplane.

"Good thinking," Jeffrey said.

"I like gadgets," John said. He looked ahead. "I didn't think the Chosen could get aircraft here to support a landing, though."

"Neither did I." He ran his hands over the controls. "Shall I?"

"You're the expert, Jeff."

Jeffrey Farr had run up quite a score in the aerial fighting over the Union. It was partly innate talent, but also because Center could put an absolutely accurate

gunsight in front of his eyes, one that effortlessly calculated the complex ballistics of firing from one fast-
moving plane and hitting an equally elusive target.

The engines bellowed, and the biplane wallowed out
onto the surface of Barclon's harbor. The sun was behind them, still low in the east, but the wind was coming directly down the Gut; the corsair's wind, they'd
called it in the old days. Right now it meant charging straight into the line of muzzle flashes from the
heavy guns of the Land fleet. One landed not three
hundred yards away; the undershot produced a
momentary tower of white water and black mud, and
a wave that rocked the seaplane on its floats.

"Time's a-wasting," Jeffrey said, and opened the
throttles.

The line of gray-painted warships grew with terrifying speed, closer and closer. *Nice spacing*, Jeffrey
thought absently. *Dad would approve*. It wasn't easy
to get warships moving so precisely and keeping such
good station in the midst of action. He supposed this
was action, although he couldn't see much in the way
of shooting back—just an occasional burst from a field-
gun shell, militia firing from the harbor mouth streets.

The floatplane skipped across the slight harbor swell,
throwing roostertails of spray from the prows of the
floats. It was odd and a little unsettling to taxi in a plane
that was horizonal and not down at the rear where the
tail wheel rested. The craft felt a little sluggish; probably loaded to capacity with all these people, and the fuel
tanks were full, too. But it *was* feeling lighter, the salt
spray on his lips less as the floats began to flick across
the surface of the waves rather than resting fully in the
water. The controls bucked a little in his hands, and
he drew back on the yoke.

Bounce. Bounce. Bounce, and *up*. He climbed slowly,
not trying to avoid the Chosen ships. *Let 'em think
we're one of theirs*. There certainly weren't any Sierran aircraft in the air today. For that matter there

hadn't been more than a couple of dozen of them to begin with, and he'd bet the Chosen had taken them all out in the first few minutes of the strike, somehow. Infiltrated a strike commando days ago and activated them at a predetermined time, at a guess.

correct. probability 87%, ±5.

The sheer numbers of ships behind the gunline was stunning, and their upperworks were all gray-black with troops.

"Must be a hundred thousand of them," he said. "That's a big gamble; over fifteen percent of their total strength."

John had worries more immediate than strategy. "Fighter coming down to look us over," he shouted back over the thundering roar of the airsteam.

The biplane swooping towards them had the rounded cowling of a von Nelsing, but the wings looked a little different, plywood covered and with teardrop-section struts instead of the old bracing wires and angle-iron.

"How fast is this thing?" he asked.

one hundred fourteen miles an hour in level flight at three thousand feet, Center said. **the latest mark of von nelsing pursuit plane has a maximum speed of one hundred forty miles an hour.**

"Thank you so much," Jeffrey said.

No chance of outrunning it. He looked down; they were over the tail end of the Chosen fleet, the last straggle of commandeered trawlers rigged for minesweeping or laying, and a screen of four-stacker destroyers. Ahead he could just make out a line of dirigibles, keeping watch up the Gut. Another thirty miles or so and he'd be in sight of the Isle of Trois, the big island that filled most of the eastern end of the narrow sea.

"How long do you think it'll take—"

"For the pilot to twig that we aren't Land Air Service?" John said. "About three minutes."

Land pilots were all Chosen, trained to use their initiative. Not much doubt about what this one would chose to do.

"You tell Henri," Jeffrey said. "We'd better be quick about this."

He pushed the stick forward, putting the big plane on a downward slope. Its weight made it faster thus, and reducing the dimensions the nimble enemy fighter could use also improved the situation. The higher buzz of the von Nelsing's engine grew stronger. He could almost hear the *chick-chack* sound as the pilot armed the twin machine guns in the nose.

The water came closer, until he could see the thick white lines along the tops of the waves, running west to east as they almost always did in the Gut this time of year. The wind was more variable here, gusting and falling away. His hands were busy on stick and rudder pedals, keeping the big aircraft level. In the rearview mirror the machine-gun position was empty, with the guns pointing backward as if locked in their rest positions.

John came back. "He's ready," he said. Reaching down the side of the cockpit, he came up with a pump-action shotgun and held it across his lap. "Whenever you signal."

Jeffrey wished he could spit to clear the gummy texture out of his mouth. This was like trying to fight while stuck neck-deep down a whale's blowhole. The fighter crept up from behind them, a hundred feet or so above. He could see the goggled face craning and bending to get a glimpse of them, and waved cheerfully up at him. *Or her.* Who knew, that might even be Gerta Hosten. . . .

probability 3%, ±1, Center said.

Shut up.

The aircraft grew closer. The Chosen pilot waggled his wings and pointed backward with an exaggerated gesture; he was getting impatient. So—

"Now!"

He banked the plane sideways, towards the enemy. The Chosen pilot acted the way pilots did, on instinct, pulling up sharply for height. Henri erupted out of the open gun mount, slamming the guns up to their maximum ninety degrees. For a moment the bigger biplane seemed joined to the fighter above it by twin bars of tracer, then the von Nelsing staggered in the air and peeled away trailing smoke. John stood in the open cockpit, shielding his eyes with one hand and grabbing at the edge of the cowling to brace the blocky strength of his upper torso against the savage pull of the slipstream.

"Pilot's dead or unconscious," he said aloud as he dropped back. Seconds later the fighter plowed into the surface of the water at full diving speed and a seventy-degree angle. It disintegrated, the engine continuing its plunge towards the shallow bottom of the Gut and the fuselage and wings scattering in fragments of wood, some burning.

Henri shouted in triumph, and the passengers cheered. John continued to crane his head backward and around. "Hope nobody saw that," he said.

Jeffrey nodded. "By the way, brother of mine, where the hell are we headed?"

"I've got a couple of trawlers spotted up the Gut with fuel under the hatches," John said. "All just in case. If they're not there, there's an inflatable dinghy in the baggage compartment."

"And if that doesn't work, we'll swim," Jeffrey said, flying one-handed while he felt in the pockets of his tunic for his cigarettes.

"No, actually, I've got a motor launch hidden in a cove on the east coast of Trois," John said seriously.

Jeffrey laughed. "And a slingshot in your underwear," he said. More soberly: "I hate like hell being cut off like this. What's going on, and who's doing what?"

"I suspect the Chosen are doing most of the doing right now," John replied. "I just hope we're not the only ones keeping our heads while all about are losing theirs."

"If we are, they'll blame it on us," Jeffrey said. "I'll bet Dad's doing something constructive, though."

CHAPTER TWENTY-TWO

Maurice Farr stood at the head of the table in the admiral's quarters of the *Great Republic*, pride of the Northern Fleet, and stared at the messenger.

The captains and commodores along either side looked up from their turtle soup, some of them spilling drops on their ceremonial summer-white uniforms. The overhead electrics blazed on the polished silver, the gold epaulets, the snowy linen of the tablecloth, and the starched jackets of the stewards serving the dinner. It would take news of real importance to interrupt this occasion.

"Gentlemen," Farr said, quickly scanning the message, "Land forces have attacked the Sierra. Preliminary reports are sketchy, but it looks like they caught them completely flat-footed. Hundreds of transports escorted by squadrons of cruisers and destroyers have landed troops around Barclon in the Rio Arena estuary, and up and down the coast. Air assault troops are landing in Nueva Madrid, and the mountain passes on the northern and southern borders are under simultaneous attack."

Another messenger came in and passed a flimsy to the admiral. He opened it and read: *Brothers Katzenjammer have flown the coop. Stop. Never again. Stop. Love, J&J.*

Farr's shoulders kept their habitual stiffness, but he sighed imperceptibly. One less thing to worry about personally . . . and the Republic was going to need both his sons in the time ahead.

A babble of conversation had broken out around the

table. "Gentlemen!" Silence fell. "Gentlemen, we knew we were at war yesterday."

When the news of Grisson's disaster had come through. *And the politicians will blame it on him.* Two modern ships and a score of relics and converted yachts against a dozen first-rate cruisers with full support. One of the Land craft had made it back to Bassin du Sud with her pumps running overtime, and several of the others had taken damage. All things considered, it was a miracle the Southern Fleet had been able to inflict that much harm before it was destroyed.

"Now we have a large target. Silence, please."

The tension grew thicker as Maurice Farr sat with his eyes closed, gripping the bridge of his nose between thumb and forefinger.

"All right, gentlemen," he said at last. One or two of the hardier had gone on eating their soup, and now paused with their spoons poised. "Here's what we'll do. I'm assuming that all of you have steam up"—*you'd better* went unspoken—"and we can get under way tonight."

That raised a few brows; a night passage up the Gut would be a definite risk, even after the exercises Farr had put the Northern Fleet through after assuming command six months ago.

"Steaming at fourteen knots, that should place us"— he turned to the map behind him—"*here* by dawn tomorrow. Then . . ."

Admiral der See Elise Eberdorf blinked at the communications technician.

"They report *what*?" she said.

"Sir, the entire Santander Navy Northern Fleet is steaming down the Gut towards us at flank speed, better than fifteen knots. Distance is less than forty miles."

Eberdorf blinked again, staring blindly out the narrow armored windows of the *Grossvolk*.

"Sixteen battleships, twenty-two fast protected cruisers,

auxiliaries in proportion," the man read on. "Approaching—"

That is *the entire Northern Fleet*, she thought. Less the *Constitution*, which was downlined with a warped main drive shaft according to the latest intelligence. They were approaching through the southern strait around Trois; they must have left their base last night and made maximum speed all night, ignoring the chance of grounding or mines. Which meant . . .

She looked out at the chaos that covered the waters before Barclon. The Land's gold sunburst on black was flying over most of the city's higher buildings, those still standing. The fires were still burning out of control in some districts, and the forts guarding the harbor mouth were ruins full of rotting flesh. The water was speckled with half the Land's merchant fleet and about a third of its navy, many of them working shore-support and punching out enemy bunkers for the army.

Two-thirds of the Republic's navy was heading this way, and the Republic had a bigger navy to start with.

Fools, she thought with cold anger. *I told them that we should concentrate on building battleships.*

Enough. Duty was duty; and her duty here was clear.

"Signals," she said crisply. They had waited motionless, but she could sense the slight relief when she began to rap out orders. "To all transports in waves A and B." Those closest to the dock. "Enemy fleet approaching. Beach yourselves upriver."

That way the crews and troops could get off the ships, at least.

"All transports drawing less than five feet are to proceed upriver."

Where they'd be safe from the shells of Santander battlewagons, at least. The animals still held parts of the river not far inland, but that was a lesser risk.

"Waves C through F are to make maximum speed northward." With luck, most of them would have enough time to get under the protection of the guns of the

fortresses that marked the seaward junction of the old
Sierran border. Imperial forts, but adequately manned
and upgunned since the conquest.

"Order to the fleet," she said. Sixty miles . . . just
time enough. "Captains to report on board the flagship, with the following exceptions. Battleships
Adelreich and *Eisenrede* are to make all speed north
and rendezvous at Corona." Sending them out of
harm's way; the navy would need every heavy ship it
had to keep control of the vital passage.

"Mine-laying vessels are to proceed to the harbor
channels and dump their cargos overboard. Maximum
speed; ignore spacing, just do it. End. Oh, and trans-
mit to Naval HQ."

"Sir."

Her chief of staff stepped up beside her, speaking
quietly into her ear. "Sir, the enemy will have seven times
our weight of broadside. What do you intend to do?"

Eberdorf's face was skull-like at the best of times,
thin weathered skin lying right on the harsh bones. It
looked even more like a death's-head as she smiled.

"Do, Helmut?" she said. "We're going to buy some
time. And then we're all going to die, I think."

"*Watch* it!" someone said on the bridge.

Maurice Farr didn't look around. He also didn't flinch
as the Land twin-engine swept overhead, not fifty feet
above the tripod mast of the *Great Republic*. He was
looking through the slide-mounted binoculars of the
combat bridge as the bombs dropped. One hit squarely
on A turret, the forward double twelve-inch gun mount.
The ship groaned and twisted, but when the smoke
cleared he could see only a star-shaped scar on the hardened surface of the thick rolled and cast armor.
Behind him a voice murmured:

"A turret reports one casualty, sir." That was to the
Great Republic's captain. "Turret ready for action."

"Give me the ranges," Farr said.

"Eleven thousand, sir. Closing."

Farr nodded. They were slanting in towards the Land ships, like not-quite-parallel lines, but there was shoal water between the fleets, far too shallow for his heavy ships, or even for most cruisers.

"Admiral," the captain of the *Great Republic* said, "at maximum elevation, I could be making some hits by now with my twelve-inchers."

"As you were, Gridley," Farr said emotionlessly.

"Yes, sir."

Two more Land aircraft were making runs at the Santander flagship, both twin-engine models. One was carrying a torpedo clamped underneath it; the other carried more of the sixty-pound bombs. He stiffened ever so slightly; the torpedo was a real menace, and he hadn't know that aircraft could be rigged for—

The torpedo splashed into the shallow green water. Seconds later it detonated in a huge shower of mud. The Land biplane flew through the column of spray, its engines stuttering. Just then one of the four-barrel pom-poms on the side of the central superstructure cut loose. It was loud even in comparison to the general racket of battle, and the glowing globes of the one-pound shells seemed to flick out and then float, slowing, as they approached it. That was an optical illusion. The explosion when the aircraft flew into a dozen of the little shells was very real; it vanished in a fireball from which bits of smoking debris fell seaward.

The stick of bombs from the next aircraft fell in a neat bracket over the Santander battleship, raising gouts of spray that fell back on the deck. Tentacled things floated limply on the water, or landed on the deck and lashed their barbed organic whips at the riveted steel.

Thud. *Flash*. Thud. *Flash*. The eight-inch guns of the Land cruisers on the other side of the shoal were opening up on him. He smiled thinly, observing the fall of shot. Water gouted up, just short of the leading elements of his seventeen battleships—the eighteenth,

the *President Cummings*, was aground on a mudbank
back half a kilometer and working frantically to it. The
shell splashes were colored, green and orange and
bright blue, dye injected into the bursting charges to
let observers spot the point of impact. All were just
a little short, although the foremost Santander battleship
had probably been splashed. Another flotilla of four-
stacker destroyers was darting out from behind the
Land heavy ships, surging forward over the shoal water
impassable to the deeper keels.

For a moment, he abstractly admired their courage.
Then he spoke:

"Secondary batteries only, if you please."

"Yes, sir. Admiral, there may be mines in the channel ahead."

"I don't think so; we rushed them. In any case, damn
the mines, continue course ahead."

"Yes, sir."

The *Great Republic* had her weapons arranged as most
modern warships did: two heavy turrets fore and aft,
in this case twin twelve-inch rifles, and four turrets for
the secondary armament, two on either side just forward and abaft the central superstructure. That meant
each of the battleships could fire a broadside of four
eight-inch secondaries. They bellowed, the muzzle blasts
enough to rock every man on the bridge and remind
them to keep their mouths open to avoid pressure-
flux damage to the eardrums. Shells fell among the Land
destroyers, sixty-eight at a time. Four destroyers were
hit in the first salvo, disappearing in fire and black smoke
and spray as the heavy armor-piercing shells tore into
their fragile plate structures.

One destroyer came close enough to the *Great
Republic* to begin to heel aside, the center-mounted
three-tube torpedo launcher swinging on its center
pivot. Every pom-pom on the battleship cut loose at
it, hundreds of one-pounder shells striking from stem
to stern of the destroyer's long slender hull. So did

the six five-inch quick-firers in sponson mounts along the armored side. Afterwards, Farr decided that it had probably been a pom-pom shell hitting a torpedo warhead that started the explosions, but it might have been a five-incher penetrating into a magazine. The light was blinding, but when he blinked back his sight and threw up a hand against the radiant heat there was still a crater in the water, shrinking as the liquid rushed back into the giant bubble the shock wave had created. Of the destroyer there was very little to see.

Another salvo of Land eight-inch shells went by, overhead this time.

All along the line of Santander battlewagons the main gun turrets were turning, muzzles fairly low—they were close enough now that the flat trajectories of the high-velocity rifles would strike without much elevation. Farr didn't trust high-angle fire at long range; it was deadly when it hit, but the probabilities were low given the current state of fleet gunnery.

He smiled bleakly. *I've waited a long time for this,* he thought. Aloud:

"You may fire when ready, Gridley."

Sixty-eight twelve-inch guns spoke within two seconds of each other, a line of flame and water rippling away from the muzzle blast all along the two-mile stretch of the Santander gunline. The *Great Republic* shivered and groaned, her eighteen-thousand-ton mass twisting in protest. The massive projectiles slapped out over the furrows the propellant gasses had dug in the water, reaching the height of their trajectory as the sea flowed back.

Then they began to fall towards the Chosen, multiple tons of steel and high explosive avalanching down. When their hardened heads struck armor plate, it would flow aside like a liquid.

Heinrich Hosten looked out over the harbor of Barclon with throttled fury. The surface of the water was burning, floating gasoline and heavier oils from the sunken tankers still drifting in flaming patches. The masts of sunken freighters slanted up out of the filthy water, among the floating debris and bodies. A few hulls protruded above the surface, nose-down with the bronze propellors dripping into the filth below. Other columns of smoke showed low on the western horizon, where the Santander battleships and their consorts were heading for home. The air stank of death and burnt petroleum, with the oily reek of the latter far more unpleasant.

"At least the enemy are withdrawing," the naval attaché said.

Heinrich swallowed bile. "Captain Gruenwald, the enemy are withdrawing because they have accomplished their mission and there are no targets left which warrant risking a capital ship. Now, get down there and see what assets we have left—if any. Or get a rifle and make yourself useful. But in either case, get out of my sight."

"*Jawohl.*"

The naval officer clicked heels, did a perfect about-face, and left. Heinrich's head turned like a gun turret to his chief of staff.

"Report?"

"We got about ninety percent of the troops and support personnel off the transports," he said. "Half the supplies, mostly ammunition. Very little of the food"—it had been in the last convoys—"and only about one-quarter of the motor fuel. We may be able to recover a little more from tankers sunk in shallow water."

So much for the masterpiece of my career, Heinrich thought. An operation going absolutely according to plan, which was a minor miracle—until the Santander fleet showed up. *It could have been worse. A day earlier, and they'd have slaughtered the entire army at sea.*

Aloud: "Well, then. Immediate general order: All motor fuel to be reserved for armored fighting vehicles. The officers can walk or ride horses. Next, the reports from the other elements."

This was a four-pronged invasion: his, down here in the coastal plain; an air assault on Nueva Madrid and points between here and there; and the two overland drives into the mountains on the Sierra's northern and southern flanks.

"Sir. Brigadier Hosten reports successful seizure of the central government complex in Nueva Madrid, most of the personnel on the critical list, of the National Armory, and the refinery. The refinery will be operational within six to ten days. She anticipates no problem holding her perimeter until linkup with the main force. All the other air-landing forces report objectives achieved."

Heinrich grunted with qualified relief. The rhythm of operations would be badly disrupted still, but at least he wouldn't run completely dry of fuel when what he had on hand was gone. When he held the triangle of territory based on the Gut and reaching to Nueva Madrid, the bulk of Sierra's population and industry would be under Chosen control.

The aide went on: "General Meitzerhagen reports that the northern passes are now secured and he is advancing south along the line of the railway. Resistance is disorganized but heavy and consistent. Also, there have already been raids on his line of communication."

Heinrich grunted again, running a thick finger down the line of rail leading towards the central lowlands, with a branch westward along the Rio Arena.

"My compliments to General Meitzerhagen, and his followup elements are to secure the line of rail by liquidating the entire population within two days foot-march of the railways."

The aide blinked; that was a little drastic, even by Chosen standards. Cautiously, he asked, "*Herr General*, will that not distract from our primary mission?"

"No. Santander can interdict the Gut, but they cannot land significant forces here—they don't have enough to spare from the Union border. Hence, the outcome of this campaign is not in doubt, given the forces available here. For reasons you have no need to know, it is now absolutely imperative that we secure the rail passage across the Sierra to our forces in the Union. Guerillas cannot operate without a civilian populace to shelter and feed them. These Sierrans are stubborn animals, and I have no time to tame them by gentle means. Their corpses will give us no trouble except as a public health problem."

"*Zum behfel, Herr General.*"

"And my compliments to Brigadier Hosten: signal *Well done.*"

"Why, thank you, Heinrich," Gerta muttered to herself, tossing the telegraph form onto her desk.

That had belonged to one of the Executive Council of the Sierra until yesterday morning. There was still a spatter of dried blood across it where a submachine-gun burst had ended that particular politician's term of office; it was beginning to smell pretty high, too. The windows were permenantly opened—grenade—which cut it a little; it also let her listen to mop-up squads finishing off the pockets of resistance all across Nueva Madrid.

"Enter," she said; the words were blurred by the bandages across one side of her face, and by the pain of the long gash underneath.

Her son snapped to attention. "Sir. The last fires in the refinery are out. Here are the casualty reports. The technicians say that the water supply can be restarted as soon as we hold the reservoir; Colonel von Seedow asks permission to—"

Colonel von Seedow came in, walking rather stiffly.

"You may go, *Fahnrich*," she said. Johan was young enough to still be entranced by military formality.

Von Seedow saluted more casually. "It's an easy enough target," she said. "My scouts report that the

enemy aren't holding it in force, and I'd rather we
didn't give them time to think of poisoning it."

Gerta considered; she was tasked with taking the
capital and a set surrounding area and holding until
relieved. On the other hand, she had considerable lat-
itude, resistance had been light, and just sitting on
her behind waiting had never been her long suit.

Speaking of which . . . "That a wound, Maxine?" she
said, as the other Chosen officer sat in a gingerly fashion.

"In a manner of speaking, Brigadier. You don't like
girls, do you?"

Gerta blinked; it was a rather odd question at this
point. "No. About as entertaining as a gynecological
exam, for me. Why?"

"Well, in that case my warning is superfluous, but
watch out for the ones here. They *bite*."

They shared a chuckle, and Gerta pulled out the
appropriate map. "Through here?" she said, drawing a
line with her finger to the irregular blue circle of the
reservoir.

"*Ya*. And a couple of companies around here. Can
you spare me some armored cars?"

"That's no problem, we only lost two in action."

Maxine von Seedow ran a hand over the blond stubble
that topped her long, rather boney face. "Good. We did
lose more infantry than I anticipated."

"Stubborn beasts, locally."

Von Seedow rose, wincing slightly. "Tell me about
it, Brigadier. In my opinion, we should exterminate
them. I should have the reservoir by nightfall."

"Good. The last thing I want is an epidemic of dysentry. Or rather, the last thing *you* want is an epidemic
of dysentry."

Maxine raised her pale eyebrows.

"In their infinite wisdom, the General Staff are pulling
me out. They've got another hole and need a cork."

CHAPTER TWENTY-THREE

"War! Extra, extra, read all about it—Republic at war with Chosen! Admiral Farr smashes Chosen fleet!"

"Well, part of it," Jeffrey Farr said, snatching a copy thrust into his hands and flipping a fifty-cent piece back.

The car was moving slowly enough for that; the streets of Santander City were packed. Militiamen were rushing to their mobilization stations, air-raid wardens in their new armbands and helmets were standing on stepladders to tape over the streetlights, and everybody and his Aunt Sally were milling around talking to each other. Smith pulled the car over to the curb for ten minutes while a unit of Regulars—Premier's Guard, but in field kit—headed towards the main railway station. The newspaper was full of screaming headlines three inches high, and so were the mobilization notices being pasted up on every flat surface by members of the Women's Auxiliary, who also wore armbands.

The crowds cheered the soldiers as they marched. John nodded. "Hope they're still as enthusiastic in a year," he said grimly.

"Hope we're alive in a year," Jeffrey replied, scanning the article. His lips shaped a soundless whistle. "Hot *damn*, but it looks like Dad completely cleaned their clocks. Eight cruisers, a battleship, and half their transports. Good way to start the war."

"Improves our chances," John said. "I wonder if Center—"

admiral farr's actions indicate the limit of

stochastic multivarient analysis, Center said. **in your terms: a pleasant surprise. probability of favorable outcome to the struggle as a whole is increased by 7%, ±1.**

Jeffrey nodded. "Wonder what they'll do now," he mused. "What'd you do, in their boots?"

"Stand pat," John said at once. "Fortify the line of the Union-Santander border, concentrate on pacifying the occupied territories, and build ships and aircraft like crazy—taking Chosen personnel out of the armies to do it, if I had to. Absolutely no way we could fight our way through the mountains."

Good lad, Raj said. *That would make their tactics serve their strategy.*

correct, Center replied, dispassionate as always. **the stragety john hosten has outlined would give probability of chosen victory within a decade of over 75%; probability of long-term stalemate 10%; probability of santander victory 15%. in addition, in this scenario there is a distinct possibility of immediate and long-term setback to human civilization on visager, as the effort of prolonged total war and the development of weapons of mass destruction undermines the viability of both parties.**

"Fortunately, they're not likely to do that," Jeffrey said. "The Chosen always did tend to mistake operations for strategy."

probability of full-scale chosen attack on santander border is 85%, ±7, Center confirmed.

"They'll try to roll right over us," John said. "The question is, can we hold them?"

"We'd better," Jeffrey said. "If we don't hold them in the passes, if they break through into the open basin country west of Alai, we're royally fucked. The provincial militias just don't have the experience or cohesion to fight open-field battles of maneuver yet."

"The Regulars will have to hold them, then."

Jeffrey's face was tired and stubbled; now it looked

old. "And Gerard's men," he said softly. "There in the front line."

John looked at him. "That'll be pretty brutal," he warned. "They'll be facing the Land's army—in the civil war, it was mostly Libert's troops with a few Land units as stiffeners."

Jeffrey's lips thinned. "Gerard's men are half the formed, regular units we have," he said. "We need *time*. If we spend all our cadre resisting the first attacks, who's going to teach the rush of volunteers? We've split up the Freedom Brigades people to the training camps, too."

John sighed and nodded. *"Behfel ist behfel."*

"Good God, what *is* that?" the HQ staffer said.

Jeffrey Farr looked up from the table. All across the eastern horizon light flickered and died, flickered and died, bright against the morning. The continuous thudding rumble was a background to everything, not so much loud as all-pervasive.

"That's the Land artillery," he said quietly. "Hurricane bombardment. Start sweating when it stops, because the troops will come in on the heels of it."

He turned back to the other men around the table, most in Santander brown, and many looking uncomfortable in it.

"General Parks, your division was federalized two weeks ago. It should be here by now."

"Sir . . ." Parks had a smooth western accent. "It's corn planting season, as I'm sure you're aware, and—"

"And the Chosen will eat the harvest if we don't stop them," Jeffrey said. "General Parks, get what's at the concentration points here, and do it fast. Or turn your command over to your 2-IC." Who, unlike Parks, was a regular, one of the skeleton cadre that first-line provincial militia units had been ordered to maintain several years ago, when the Union civil war began ratcheting up tensions. "I think that'll be all; you may return to your units, gentlemen."

He looked down at the map, took a cup of coffee from the orderly and scalded his lips slightly, barely noticing. The markers for the units under his command were accurate as of last night. Fifty thousand veterans of the Unionaise civil war; another hundred thousand regulars from the Republic's standing army, and many of the officers and NCO's had experience in that war, too. Two hundred and fifty thousand federalized militia units; they were well equipped, but their training ranging from almost as good as the Regulars to abysmal. More arriving every hour.

Half a million Land troops were going to hit them in a couple of hours, supported by scores of heavy tanks, hundreds of light ones, thousands of aircraft.

"None of Libert's men?" Gerard said quietly, tracing the unit designators for the enemy forces.

"No. They're moving east—east and north, into the Sierra."

"Good," Gerard said quietly. Jeffrey looked up at him. The compact little Unionaise was smiling. "Not pleasant, fighting one's own countrymen."

"Pierre . . ." Jeffrey said.

Gerard picked up his helmet and gloves, saluted. "My friend, we must win this war. To this, everything else is subordinate."

They shook hands. Gerard went on: "Libert thinks he can ride the tiger. It is only a matter of time until he joins the other victims in the meat locker."

"I think he's counting on us breaking the tiger's teeth," Jeffrey said. "God go with you."

"How not? If there was ever anyone who fought with His blessing, it is here and now."

"Damn," Jeffrey said softly, watching the Unionaise walk towards his staff car. "I hate sending men out to die."

If you didn't, you wouldn't be the man you are, Raj said. *But you'll do it, nonetheless.*

*   *   *

Maurice Hosten stamped on the rudder pedal and wrenched the joystick sideways.

His biplane stood on one wing, nose down, and dove into a curve. The Land fighter shot past him with its machine guns stuttering, banking itself to try and follow his turn. He spiraled up into an Immelmann and his plane cartwheeled, cutting the cord of his opponent's circle. His finger clenched down on the firing stud.

"*Fuck!*" The deflection angle wasn't right; he could feel it even before the guns stuttered.

Spent brass spun behind him, sparkling in the sunlight, falling through thin air to the jagged mountain foothills six thousand feet below. Acrid propellant mingled with the smells of exhaust fumes and castor oil blowing back into his face. Land and cloud heeled crazily below him as he pulled the stick back into his stomach, pulled until gravity rippled his face backward on the bone and vision became edged with gray.

Got the bastard, got him—

Something warned him. It was too quick for thought; stick hard right, rudder right . . . and another Land triplane lanced through the space he'd been in, diving out of the sun. His leather-helmeted head jerked back and forth, hard enough to saw his skin if it hadn't been for the silk scarf. The rest of his squadron were gone, not just his wingman—he'd seen the Land fighter bounce Tom—but all the rest as well. The sky was empty, except for his own plane and the two Chosen pilots.

Nothing for it. He pushed the throttles home and dove into cloud, thankful it was close. *Careful, now.* Easy to get turned around in here. Easy even to lose track of which way was up and end up flying upside down into a hillside convinced you were climbing. There was just enough visibility to see his instruments' radium glow: horizon, compass, airspeed indicator. One hundred thirty-eight; the Mark IV was a sweet bird.

When he came out of the cloudbank there was

nobody in sight. He kept twisting backward to check the sun; that was the most dangerous angle, always. The ground below looked strange, but then, it usually did. Check for mountain peaks, check for rivers, roads, the spaces between them.

"That's the Skinder," he decided, looking at the twisting river. "Ensburg's thataway."

Ensburg had been under siege from the Chosen for a month. So that train of wagons on the road was undoubtedly a righteous target. And he still had more than half a tank of fuel.

Maurice pushed the stick forward and put his finger back on the firing button. Every shell and box of hardtack that didn't make it to the lines outside Ensburg counted.

"Damn, that's ugly," Jeffrey said, swinging down from his staff car.

The huge Land tank was burnt out, smelling of human fat melted into the ground and turning rancid in the summer heat. The commander still stood in the main gun turret, turned to a calcined statue of charcoal, roughly human-shaped.

"This way, sir," the major . . . *Carruthers, that's his name* . . . said. "And careful—there are *Lander* snipers on that ridge back there."

The major was young, stubble-chinned and filthy, with a peeling sunburn on his nose. From the way he scratched, he was never alone these days. He'd probably been a small-town lawyer or banker three months ago; he was also fairly cheerful, which was a good sign.

"We caught it with a field-gun back in that farmhouse," he said, waving over one shoulder.

Jeffrey looked back; the building was stone blocks, gutted and roofless, marked with long black streaks above the windows where the fire has risen. There was a barn nearby, reduced to charred stumps of timbers and a big stone water tank. The orchard was ragged stumps.

"Caught it in the side as it went by." He pointed; one of the powered bogies that held the massive war machine up was shattered and twisted. "Then we hit it with teams carrying satchel charges, while the rest of us gave covering fire."

The ex-militia major sobered. "Lost a lot of good men doing it, sir. But I can tell you, we were *relieved*. Those things are so cursed hard to stop!"

"I know," Jeffrey said dryly, looking to his right down the eastward reach of the valley. The Santander positions had been a mile up that way, before the Chosen brought up the tank.

"This is dead ground, sir. You can straighten up."

Jeffrey did so, watching the engineers swarming over the tank, checking for improvements and modifications. "The good news about these monsters, major, comes in threes," he said, tapping its flank. "There aren't very many of them; they break down a lot; and now that the lines aren't moving much, the enemy don't get to recover and repair them very often."

"Well, that's some consolation, sir," Carruthers said dubiously. "They're still a cursed serious problem out here."

"We all have problems, Major Carruthers."

The factory room was long, lit by grimy glass-paned skylights, open now to let in a little air; the air of Oathtaking, heavy and thick at the best of times, and laden with a sour acid smog of coal smoke and chemicals when the wind was from the sea. Right now it also smelled of the man who was hanging on an iron hook driven into the base of his skull. The hook was set over the entrance door, where the workers passed each morning and evening as they were taken from the camp on the city's outskirts. The body had been there for two days now, ever since the shop fell below

quota for an entire week. Sometimes it moved a little
as the maggots did their work.

There was a blackboard beside the door, with
chalked numbers on it. This week's production was
nearly eight percent over quota. A cheerful banner
announced the prizes that the production group would
receive if they could sustain that for another seven
days: a pint of wine for each man, beef and fresh fruit,
tobacco, and two hours each with an inmate from the
women's camp.

Tomaso Guiardini smiled as he looked at the banner.
He smiled again as he looked down at the bearing
race in the clamp before him. It was a metal circle;
the inner surface moved smoothly under his hand,
where it rested on the ball-bearings in the race formed
by the outer U-shaped portion.

Very smoothly. Nothing to tell that there were metal
filings mixed with the lubricating matrix inside. Nothing
except the way the bearing race would seize up and
burn when subjected to heavy use, in about one-tenth
the normal time.

He looked up again at the banner. Perhaps the
woman would be pretty, maybe with long, soft hair.
Mostly the Chosen shaved the inmates' scalps, though.

He glanced around. The foreman was looking over
somebody else's shoulder. Tomaso took two steps and
swept a handful of metal shavings from the lathe across
the aisle, dropping them into the pocket of his grease-
stained overall, and was back at his bench before the
Protégé foreman—he was a one-eyed veteran with a
limp, and a steel-cored rubber truncheon thonged to
his wrist—could turn around.

"Dad!" Maurice Hosten checked his step. "I mean,
sir. Ah, just a second."

He pulled off the leather flyer's helmet and turned
to give some directions to the ground crew; the blue-
black curls of his hair caught the sun, and the strong

line of his jaw showed a faint shadow of dense beard of exactly the same color. His plane had more bullet holes in the upper wing, and part of the tail looked as if it had been chewed. There were a row of markings on the fuselage below the cockpit, too—Chosen sunbursts with a red line drawn through of them. Eight in all, and the outline of an airship.

John Hosten's blond hair was broadly streaked with gray now, and as he watched the young man's springy step he was abruptly conscious that he was no longer anything but unambiguously middle-aged. He still buckled his belt at the same notch, he could do most of what he had been able to—hell, his biological father was running the Land's General Staff with ruthless competence and he was thirty years older—but doing it took a higher price every passing year.

Maurice, though, he certainly isn't a boy any longer.

War doesn't give you much chance at youth, Raj agreed, with an edge of sadness to his mental voice.

The young pilot turned back. "Good to see you, Dad."

"And you, son." He pulled the young man into a brief embrace. "That's from your mother."

"How is she?"

"Still working too hard," John said. "We meet at breakfast, most days."

Maurice chuckled and shook his head. "Doing wonders, though. The food's actually edible since the Auxiliary took over the mess." They began walking back towards the pine-board buildings to one side of the dirt strip.

"I wish *everything* was going as well," he said, with a quick scowl.

"I'm listening," John said.

"You always did, Dad," Maurice said. He ran a hand through his hair. "Look, the war's less than six months old—and there are only three other pilots in this squadron besides me who were in at the start. And one of *them* had experience in the Union civil war."

"Bad, I know."

"Dad, we're losing nearly two-thirds of the new pilots in the first *week* they're assigned to active patrols."

60% in the first ten days, Center said inside his head. **a slight exaggeration.**

"The Chosen pilots, they're *good*. And they've got experience. Our planes are about as good now, but Christ, the new chums, they've got maybe twenty hours flying time when they get here. It's like sending puppies up against Dobermans! I have to force myself to learn their f— sorry, their goddamned names."

"You were almost as green," John pointed out.

"Dad, that's not the same thing, and you know it. I had Uncle Jeff teaching me before the war, and I'm . . . lucky."

He's a natural, Raj said clinically. ***It's the same with any type of combat—swords, pistols, bayonet fighting. Novices do most of the dying, experienced men do most of the killing, and a few learn faster than anyone else. This boy of yours is a fast learner; I know the type.***

"What do you suggest, son?"

"I—" Maurice hesitated, and ran his fingers through his hair again. "What we really need is more instructors—experienced instructors—back at the flying schools."

"You want the job?" John said.

"Christ no! I . . . oh." He trailed off uncertainly.

"Well, that's one reason," John said. "For another, we don't have *time* to stretch the training. The Chosen were getting ready for this war for a long time. Our men have to learn on the job, and they pay for it in blood; not just you pilots, but the ground troops as well. We've lost two hundred and fifty thousand casualties."

Maurice's eyes went wide, and he gave a small grunt of incredulous horror.

"Yes, we don't publicize the overall figures; and that doesn't count the Union Loyalist troops; they were virtually wiped out. The weekly dead-and-missing list in the newspapers is bad enough. In Ensburg, they're eating rats and their own dead. We estimate half the population of the Sierra is gone, and in the Empire, we're supplying guerillas who keep operating even though they know a hundred hostages will be shot for every soldier killed, five hundred for every Chosen. *But we stopped them.* They thought they could run right over us the way they did the Empire, or the Sierra . . . and they didn't. They've nowhere gotten more than a hundred miles in from the old Union border, and our numbers are starting to mount. The Chosen are butchers, and we're paying a high butcher's bill, but we're learning."

Maurice shook his head. "Dad," he said slowly, "I wouldn't have your job for anything."

"Not many of us are doing what we'd really like," John said. "Duty's duty." He clapped his hand on his son's shoulder. "But we're doing our best—and you're doing damned well."

None of the command group was surprised when Gerta Hosten arrived; if they had been, she'd have put in a report that would ensure their next command was of a rifle platoon on the Confrontation Line. The pickets and ambush patrols passed her through after due checks, and she found the brigade commander consulting with his subordinates next to two parked vehicles in what had been Pueblo Vieho before the forces of the Land arrived in the Sierra the previous spring. A lieutenant was talking, pointing out the path her command had taken through the pine woods further up the mountain slopes, above the high pastures.

Gerta vaulted out of her command car—it was a six-wheeled armored car chassis with the turret and top deck removed—and exchanged salutes and clasped wrists with the commander. " *'Tag,* Ektar," she said. "How are things in the quiet sector? Missed you by about an hour at your headquarters."

"Just coming up to see how things are going at the business end," Ektar Feldenkopf said. "Not a bad bag: seventeen men, twenty-four women, and a round dozen of their brats. The yield from these sweeps has been falling off."

The air of the high Sierran valley was cool and crisp even in late summer. Most of it had been pasture, growing rank now. The burnt snags of the village's log houses didn't smell any more, or the bodies underneath them. There were still traces of gingerbread carving around the eaves. Several skeletons lay on the dirt road leading to the lowlands, where the clean-up squad had shot them as they fled into the darkness from their burning houses. The bodies laid out in the overgrown mud of the street had probably run the other way, up into the forests and the mountains, to survive a little longer and steal down to try and raid the conqueror's supply lines. The women and children taken alive knelt in a row beyond the corpses, hands secured behind their backs.

"Which means either they're getting thinner on the ground, or better at hiding, or both."

"Both, I think—the interrogations will tell us something. The males had a rifle each and about twenty rounds, plus some handguns, but no explosives."

Johan was looking at one of the prisoners, a blond who probably looked extremely pretty when she was better fed and didn't have dried blood from a blow to the nose over most of her face. Gerta smiled indulgently; young men had single-track minds, and he'd been doing his work very well. He had some scars of his own now, although nothing like the one that seamed the side of her face since the drop on Nueva Madrid, and drew the left corner of her face up in a permanent slight smile.

"All right," she said. "But don't undo her hands and watch out for the teeth. Remember *Hauptman* von Seedow."

The three Chosen shared a brief chuckle; poor Maxine had been laid up in a field hospital for a month with her infected bite, and the joke was still doing the rounds of every officer's mess in the Land's armed forces. She'd nearly punched one wit who offered her a recipe for a poultice.

She'll never live it down, Gerta thought, as her son walked over to the prisoners. Still chuckling, he hauled the girl—she was about his own age—to her feet by her hair and marched her off behind the ruins of one of the buildings.

"How are they surviving?" Gerta asked. None of them were what you'd call well-fleshed, but they weren't on the verge of starvation either.

"These mountain villages, they store cheese and dried milk and so on up in the caves," the officer said, waving towards the jagged snow-capped mountains to the north. "There are a *lot* of caves up there. And there's game, deer and bison, rabbits and so forth, and a lot of cattle and sheep and pigs gone wild in the woods. Half-wild to begin with. Still, they're getting hungrier, and we're whittling them down. It's good rest and recreation for units pulled out of the line."

"How do the Unionaise shape?" she asked.

There was a brigade of them down the valley a ways, at the crossroads twenty miles west of the railroad, under their own officers, but also under the operational control of the Land regional command.

"Not bad," the officer said, as a shrill scream sounded from behind the wrecked building. It trailed off into sobs. "Not as energetic at their patrolling as I'd like. Good enough for this work, I'd say; I couldn't swear how they'd do in heavy combat. Settling in to that town as if they owned the place."

"They think they do," Gerta replied. "Well, things appear to be under control here. Which is more than I can say about some other places."

The garrison commander frowned and lowered his

voice. "How does the Confrontation Line develop? The official reports seem . . . overly optimistic."

Gerta spoke quietly as well. "Not so well. We're killing the Santies by the shitload, that part of the offical story is true enough. They keep attacking us with more enthusiasm than sense, but it's getting more expensive, and we're not taking much territory. Ensburg's still holding out."

"Still?" The man's brows rose. "They must be starving."

"They are. I was in the siege lines last week; nothing left inside but rubble, and you can smell the stink of their funeral pyres. Starvation, typhus, whatever—but they're not giving up."

She spat into the dirt. "If that monomaniac imbecile Meitzerhagen hadn't killed the garrison of Fort William after they surrendered and bellowed the fact to the world, they might have been more inclined to give up. So would a lot of the other garrisons we cut off in the first push; mopping them up took time the Santies used to get themselves organized. We lost momentum."

The other officer nodded. "Meitzerhagen's a sledge-hammer," he said. "The problem is—"

"—not all problems are nails," she finished.

"Stalemate, for the present, then."

"*Ja*. We can push them, but we outrun our supplies. And even when we beat them, they don't *run*, and there are always more of them. Their equipment's good, too. Now that they're learning how to use it . . ." She shrugged.

"How is our logistical situation, then?"

"It sucks wet dogshit. We can't move dirigibles within a hundred miles of the front in daylight, the road net's terrible, the terrain favors defense . . . and the Santies are right in the middle of their main industrial area, with their best farmlands only a few hundred miles away on first-class rails and roads."

"I presume the staff is evolving a counterstrategy."

"*Ya.* No details of course, but let's just say that we're going to encourage their enthusiasm and prepare to receive it. Also if we can't use the Gut, there's no reason they should be able to either."

The officer sighed and nodded. "Well, you can tell them that my brigade at least is doing its job," he said. "Trying to keep the rail lines through the Sierra working would have been a nightmare if we'd used conventional occupation techniques. Bad enough as it is."

Young Johan returned, pushing the dazed and naked Sierran girl before him. He dropped into parade rest behind Gerta, smiling faintly as the prisoner stumbled back to kneel with the others.

"In a year or two, there won't be any left to speak of. . . . Speaking of which, you said there was a new directive?"

Gerta nodded. "*Ya,* we're running short of labor for the construction gangs, importing from the New Territories is inconvenient, big projects all over, and the local animals might as well give some value before they die," she said. "Send down noncombatant adults fit for heavy work—ones that give up when you catch them. Keep killing all those found in arms or not useful. Except children under about five. As an experiment, we're sending those back to the Land to be raised by senior Protégé-soldier families."

Long-serving Protégé soldiers were allowed to marry, as a special privilege for good service. "They might be useful, that way, in the long term. At your discretion, though; don't tie up transport if you're busy."

The other Chosen nodded. "*Jawohl.* Odd to think of us running short of manual workers, though."

"Well, even the New Territories' population has dropped considerably," she said. "We'll have to be less wasteful after the war."

Gerta returned his salute and turned to her open-topped armored car. When you carried a hatchet for the General Staff, your work was never done.

CHAPTER TWENTY-FOUR

Jeffrey Farr whistled soundlessly. Not that anyone could have heard him in the rear seat of the observation plane; the noise of the engine and the slipstream was too loud. He reached forward and tapped the pilot on the shoulder, circling his hand with the index finger up and pointing it downwards. The pilot nodded and circled, coming down to four thousand feet.

A couple of light pom-poms opened up, winking up at them from the huge piles of turned earth below; then a heavier antiaircraft gun, that stood some chance of reaching them. Black puffs of smoke erupted in the air below, each with a momentary snap of fire at its heart before it lost shape and began to drift away. Anttiny, hordes of laborers dove for the shelter of the trenches they had been digging, leaving their tools among the piles of timber, steel sheet and reinforcing rod.

There was a big camera fastened to brackets ahead of the observer's position, but Jeffrey ignored it. He'd seen pictures; this trip was for a personal look.

All right, he thought. *Nice job of field engineering.* Everything laid out to command the ground to the east, but not just simple positions on ridge tops. Machine-gun bunkers at the base of the ridges, giving maximum fields of fire; heavier bunkers for field guns, revetted positions for heavy mortars on the reverse slopes, with communications trenches and even tunnels to bring reserves forward quickly without leaving them exposed to direct-fire weapons. All-round

fields of fire, so that each position could hold out if
cut off, and heavier redoubts further back, layer upon
layer of them.

They must have half a million men working on this,
Jeffrey thought, impressed.

correct to within ten thousand ±6, Center said.
**assuming an equivalent effort in other sectors of
the front, as intelligence reports indicate.**

"Well, we'll have to take this into account," Jeffrey
said. He tapped the pilot's shoulder again; despite their
two-squadron escort, the man was looking nervously east
and upward, to where Land attackers would come diving
out of the morning sun. The plane banked westward.

"Thank you gentlemen for meeting on such short
notice," Jeffrey said.

They were in the Premier's bunker beneath the hilltop Executive Mansion, nearly a hundred yards underground, as deep as you could get near Santander City
without hitting groundwater. The impact of the bombs,
a dull *crump . . . crump . . .* was felt more through
the soles of their feet than heard through their ears.
Every now and then the overhead electric light flickered, and dust filtered down, making men sneeze at
its acrid scent.

"I thought you'd made it suicidal for dirigibles to
fly over our territory," Maurice Farr said dryly to the
Air Force commander.

The commander flushed and pulled at his mustache.
"In daylight, yes. But the speed and altitude advantage of our fighters is fairly narrow. At night, it's much
harder. Those might be their new long-range eight-
engine bomber planes, too. We're having more of a
problem with those."

At the head of the table, Jeffrey held up a hand.
"In any case, the error radius of night bombing is so
huge that it consumes more of their resources to do
it than it does of ours to endure it."

The Premier tapped a pencil sharply on the table. "General, we're losing hundreds, perhaps thousands of civilian every time one of those raids breaks through."

Jeffrey dipped his head slightly. "With all due respect, sir, there were a hundred and fifty thousand people in Ensburg—and I doubt ten thousand of them are alive now, and those are in Chosen labor camps."

A pall of silence fell around the table. The siege of Ensburg had been a morale-booster for the whole Republic. Its fall had been a correspondingly serious blow. Jeffrey went on:

"So with all due respect, Mr. Premier, *anything* that helps keep the enemy back is a postive factor, and that includes attacks that hurt us but hurt him more."

"There's the effect of bombing on civilian morale," the politician pointed out.

observe:

Scenes floated before Jeffrey's eyes: cities reduced to street patterns amid tumbled scorched brick, air-raid shelters full of unmarked corpses asphyxiated as the firestorms above sucked the oxygen from their lungs, fleets of huge four-engined bombers sleeker and more deadly than anything Visager knew raining down incendiaries on a town of half-timbered buildings crowded with refugees while odd-looking monoplane fighters tried to beat them off.

"Sir, our citizens could take a lot more pain than this and still keep going. In any case, if we could turn to the matter at hand?"

The men around the table—generals, admirals, heads of ministries—opened the folders that lay before them. Heading each bundle of documents were aerial photographs of enormous twisting chains of fortifications. Maps followed, and intelligence summaries.

"Is this reliable?" the Premier asked.

"Sir, I've seen a good deal of it with my own eyes," Jeffrey said. "And we have the labor gangs working on it penetrated to a fare-thee-well. It's genuine, and it's a major effort. Not just the labor, they've got plenty of that, but the transport capacity it's tying up and the materials. Steel, cement, explosives for the minefields."

"So you're right. They're going to withdraw," the Premier said. "We're beating them!"

"Sir." The elected leader of the Republic looked up at Jeffrey's tone. "Sir, we're making them retreat—and that's *not* the same thing. We have to consider the strategic consequences. If you'll all turn to Report Four?"

They did; it started with a map. "That line—they're code-naming it the Gothic Line, for some reason—is cursed well laid-out. When it's finished, they'll make a fighting retreat and then sit and wait for us."

"We've pushed them back once, we can do it again!" the Premier said. "No invader can be left on the Republic's soil, whatever the cost."

Christ. Usually the Premier's aggressive pugnacity was a plus for Jeffrey and the conduct of the war; he'd trampled the political opposition into dust, and the people had rallied around him as a symbol of the national will—they were calling him "the Tiger," now. But if he got the bit between his teeth on this—

observe:

Men in khaki uniforms and odd soup-bowl helmets clambered out of trenches and advanced into a moonscape of craters and bits of trees, ends of twisted barbed wire, mud, rotting fragments of once-human flesh. They walked in long neat lines, precisely spaced. From ahead, beyond the uncut barbed wire, the machine guns began to flicker in steady arcs . . .

. . . and men in different uniforms, blue, helmets with a ridge down the center, huddled in a shell crater. Bulbous masks hid their faces, turning them into snouted insectile shapes. Bodies bobbed in the thick muddy water at the bottom of the shell hole, their flesh stained yellow. Somehow he knew that the air was full

of an invisible drifting death that would burn out lungs
and turn them to bags of thick liquid matter . . .

. . . and a man in neat officer's uniform with a
swagger stick in his hand and the red tabs of the staff
looked out over a sea of mud churned to the consis-
tency of porridge. It was too viscous even to hold the
shape of craters, although it was dimpled like the face
of a smallpox victim. Plank walkways lead off into the
steady gray rain; about them lay discarded equipment,
sunken in the mire. So was a mule, still feebly struggling with only the top quarter of its body showing.

"Good God," the man said, his face gray as the
churned and poisoned soil. "Did we send men out to
fight in *this?*" His face crumpled into tears.

Jeffrey shook his head; the problem with visions like
that was that the implications stayed with you.

"Sir, right now we've managed to turn the war from
one of movement into one of attrition favoring us. This
is the Chosen countermove. If we attack their prepared positions, we'll bleed ourselves white; attrition
will favor them. Believe me, sir, please—if you've ever
trusted my military judgment, trust it now. We'd break
ourselves trying. The ground up there favors defense—
that's how we survived their initial attack—and those
fieldworks of theirs are as impregnable as the mountains. And that's not all."

He stood and took up a pointer, tracing the Gothic
Line with its tip. "This shortens their line, and with
massive artillery support and good communications
from their immediate rear, they can thin out the forces
facing us. Which means they can concentrate a real
strategic reserve, not just rob Peter to pay Paul, pulling
units out of the line to plug in again elsewhere. They
haven't had a genuine reserve. If they get one, it frees
up the whole situation and concedes a lot of the initiative to them."

The Premier looked at John. "Your guerillas were
supposed to tie down their forces," he said.

"They are, Mr. Premier," he said. "They have two hundred thousand men holding their lines of communication in the old Empire, and another hundred thousand in the Sierra, plus most of Libert's Nationalist army. Which, incidentally, is only useful to them as long as Libert's convinced they're going to win. If they had the free use of those forces, we'd have lost the war in their big push last fall."

John looked around the table. "Gentlemen?" There was a murmur of agreement, reluctant in some cases.

"Guerillas can be crucially useful to us," John went on. "But they can't win the war. They *can* make it possible for us to win it, though."

The Premier smoothed a thumb across his slightly tobacco-stained white mustache; that and his great shock of snow-colored hair were his political trademarks, along with the gray silk gloves he affected.

"Neither will sitting and looking at the Chosen forts—Chosen forts on *our* soil," he growled. "Admiral?"

Maurice Farr nodded reluctantly. "We can't risk an attack on the Land Home Fleet in the Passage," he said. "Not at present. It's too far from our bases and too close to theirs. And while our operational efficiency is increasing rapidly, more than theirs—they were already at war readiness—they're building as fast as they can. They've got severe production problems, their labor force doesn't want to work, but they're also experienced at that. If they can complete their latest shipbuilding cycle, our margin of superiority will be severely reduced."

He shrugged. "For the next two years, we have a margin of naval superiority that will remain steady or increase. After that, I can give no assurances."

He looked at his sons and shrugged again. If the Premier requested an analysis within his area of expertise, Maurice Farr would give it.

Jeffrey coughed. "Well, Mr. Premier, the thing is that while the Gothic Line enables the enemy to regain some freedom of action, it does the same for us—and sooner."

The Premier looked at him sharply. Jeffrey went on: "They're not going to come out of those fortifications at us, not after going to that much trouble, and not as long as we maintain a reasonable force facing them. That means we can pull most of our experienced divisions out of the line, recruit them back up to strength, and put the new formations in facing the enemy. That'll give them experience; we don't have to put in full-scale assaults to do that, just patrol aggressively. And so *we* will have a strategic reserve, and sooner than they will. They don't dare thin their force facing us until those works are complete."

The Premier leaned back in his chair. He'd gotten his start in radical politics—and fought several duels with political opponents and what he considered slanderous journalists, back when that was still legal in some of the western provinces. John reminded himself not to underestimate the man; he was not just the pugnacious bull-at-a-gate extremist some made him out. Plenty of brains behind the shrewd little eyes, and plenty of nerve.

"So," he said. "You think that we can *do* something with this strategic reserve of yours, in the two years during which we have . . . what is the military phrase?"

"Window of opportunity, Mr. Premier," the military men said.

"Your *window of opportunity?*" the Premier continued.

"Yes, sir," Jeffrey said. *From our window of opportunity to my window of opportunity?* he thought. *Well, that certainly makes it plain who's to blame if anything goes wrong.*

He is a politician, Jeff, Raj thought. A brief mental image, of Raj lying facedown on a magnificent mosaic floor, while a man stood above him shouting, dressed in magnificent metallic robes that blazed under arc lights. *I know the breed.*

The political leader looked back at Mauric Farr. "What do you say, Admiral?"

"We have to take some action in the next two years," he said with clinical detachment. "As I said, for that period, our strength will increase relative to theirs. But they control three-quarters of the planet's useful land area, resources, and population now; while it'll take time for them to make use of what they've grabbed, eventually they will. Then the balance of forces will start to swing against us. Naval and otherwise."

Most of the military men around the table nodded, reluctantly.

The Premier leaned his elbows on the table, closed one hand into a fist and clasped the other over it, and leaned his chin on his knuckles. The pouched eyes leveled on Jeffrey. "Tell me more," he said.

"Well, sir . . ." he began.

The elevator was still functioning when the meeting broke up. "God damn, but I hope there aren't any leaks in that bunch," John said, waiting with his foster brother while the first loads went up.

"That's why I confined myself to generalities," Jeffrey replied, yawning. "I can remember when these late nights were a pleasure, not something that made your eyes feel as if they'd been boiled, peeled and dredged in cayenne pepper."

John shook his head. "Useful generalities, though," he fretted.

Jeffrey grinned slightly and punched his arm. "Bro, there's no way we can stop the Fourth Bureau or *Militarische Intelligenz* from finding out our *capabilities*, he said. "And from that, deducing our general intentions. What we have to do is keep the precise intentions secret. It'll all depend on that."

John nodded unhappily. "I still don't like it."

"Of course not," Jeffrey said, his voice mock-soothing. "You're a spook. You're not happy unless you know everything about everybody and nobody else knows anything at all."

The elevator rattled to a stop at the bottom of the shaft, and the sliding-mesh doors opened. They stepped in; the little square was decorated in the red plush carpet, mirrors, and carved walnut of the upper part of the Executive Mansion, not like the utilitarian warrens beneath added in the years before the war. The attendant pushed the doors closed and reached for the polished wood and brass of the lever that controlled it.

"Ground floor, I presume, gentlemen?" he said, with a slight Imperial accent.

John nodded, and said in the man's own language, "How is it up top, Mario?"

The elevator operator grinned at the patron who'd found him this job. "Bad, *signore*," he replied. "The *tedeschi* swine are out in force tonight. God and Mary and the Saints keep you safe."

"Amen," John said, and took his cigarette case out of his jacket. The cigarillos within were dark with a gold band; he offered it to the other men, then snapped his lighter.

The smoke was rich and pungent. "Sierran," Jeffrey said. "Punch-punch claros. We won't be seeing any more of those for a while."

The elevator operator nodded somberly. "The *tedeschi* have gone mad there, *signore*," he said. "They act as beasts in the Empire, but now in the Sierra . . ."

"I think they're mad with frustration," John said. "*Ciao*, Mario. My regards to your family."

"*Signore*. And many thanks for Antonio's scholarship."

"He earned it."

"Is there anywhere you *don't* have them stashed?" Jeffrey said, as they walked out to the entrance—the nonceremonial one, for unofficial guests.

"It never hurts to have friends in . . ." John began, as they accepted hat and cane, uniform cap, and swagger stick, from the attendant. Then he paused on the polished marble of the steps. "*Shit.*"

They both stopped on the uppermost stair. The Executive Mansion had an excellent hilltop site. From here they could see for miles: darkened streets, the swift flicker of emergency vehicle headlights with the top halves painted black to make them less visible from above. Fires burned out of control down by the canals and the riverside warehouses, blotches of soft light amid the blackout darkness. Searchlights probed upward like fingers, like hands reaching for the machines that tormented the city below, sliding off the undersides of clouds and vanishing in the gaps between. Every few seconds an antiaircraft gun would fire, a flicker of light and a flat *brraack*, then the shell would burst far above, sometimes lighting a cloud from within for an instant. When they finally fell silent, sirens spoke all over the great city, a rising-falling wail that signaled the "all clear." As they died, the lesser sirens of fire engines could be heard, and the clangor of bells.

"And now they'll sleep for a little while," John said softly. "Those that can. Tomorrow they'll get out of bed and go to work."

Jeffrey nodded. "You're right. Center's right, this is hurting the Chosen more than us . . . but it's got to stop, nevertheless."

Harry Smith was waiting in the car; dozing, actually, with his head resting on his gloved hands. He woke as the two men approached. "Sorry, sir, Mr. Jeffrey."

"Why the hell weren't you in the shelter?" John asked, his voice hovering between resignation and annoyance.

"Wanted to keep an eye on the car," Smith said.

John sighed. "Home."

Home was in the North Hill suburbs, beyond Embassy Row. There was little direct damage there;

no factories, and none of the densely packed working-class housing common further south on the bank of the river, or across it. The streetlights were still blacked out, and so were the houses. The steamcar slid quietly through the darkened streets, passing an occasional Air Raid Precautions patrol, helmeted but with no uniforms beyond armbands—many of them were Women's Auxiliary volunteers. Once, an ambulance went by with its bell clanging, and once, they had to detour around a random hit, a great crater in the middle of the street with water hissing ten feet high from a broken main. There might be gas, too; sawhorse barricades were already up, and Municipal Services trucks were disgorging men in workman's overalls.

"That looks a bit like our place did," Jeffrey said; the younger Farr's household had been the recipient of several Land two hundred and fifty pounders, luckily while everyone was out. "Thanks again for saving us from the horrors of Government Issue Married Quarters, officers for the use of."

John snorted. The car paused for a moment at wrought-iron gates, and then the tires hummed on the brick of a long driveway.

"Get some sleep," John said to Smith. "We're going on a trip in a few days."

Smith grinned. "With some old friends, sir?" John nodded. Smith put on a good imitation of an upper-class drawl. "Just the time of year one *likes* a little vacation on the Gut, eh?"

A sleepy butler opened the front doors of the big, rambling brick house. He stumbled backward as a four-year-old made a dash past his legs and down the stairs, leaping for Jeffrey.

"Daddy!" The girl wound herself around him, clinging to his belt. "Daddy, we all went and sat inna basement and sang!"

"That's good, punkin, but it's past your bedtime," Jeffrey said, hoisting her up.

She wrinkled her nose. "You smell funny, Daddy."

"Blame the Premier and his tobacco—ah, here's Irene."

A nursemaid came out, clutching her sleeping robe around her and clucking anxiously. "*There* she is, Mr. Jeffrey. Honestly, sometimes I think that child is part ape!"

"A born commando. Off to bed, punkin." John was still smiling as he walked up the stairs, fending off the butler's offer to wake the cook. There were advantages to being a very rich man, but a good deal of petty annoyance came with it as well. He might have raided the icebox and made a sandwich himself, if he'd been living in a middle-class apartment, but rousting someone out of bed at one o'clock to slap some chicken between two pieces of bread was more trouble than it was worth and hubristic besides.

The light was still on in the bedroom, but Pia was asleep. Her reading glasses were lying on top of a stack of documents on the carved teak sidetable beside a silver-framed picture of Maurice in his pilot's uniform. John smiled; his wife was living proof that not all Imperial woman got heavy after thirty. *Just magnificent,* he thought, undoing his cravat.

She woke, stirred, and smiled at him. "Hello, darling," she said. "I can smell the Premier's tobacco, so I know you told the truth, it was politicians and not a mistress."

John grinned. "You can have proof positive in a moment, if you'll stay awake."

"Hurry then."

Gerta forced her hands to relax from their white-knuckled grip on the armored side of the car.

"I hope you're getting every moment of this," she muttered to the cameraman beside her.

The Protégé nodded without pulling away from the eyepiece of the big clumsy machine clamped to the side of the vehicle. His hand cranked the handle with metronomic regularity, and geared mechanisms whirred within it. Beside it a small searchlight added to the dawn gloaming, bringing the ambient light up enough to make filming practical.

The huge biplane bombardment aircraft was staggering in towards its landing . . . or crash, whichever. The long fuselage was tublike, with open circular pits for the pilot and copilot, and others for bombadiers and gunners. Between each of the long wings were four engine pods, each pod mounting a puller and pusher set. The undercarriage settled towards the ground, struck dust from the packed earth. Gravel spurted. On the second impact, the splayed legs of the big wheels spread further, the whole plane sinking closer to the ground as it raced across the runway. Then the bottom touched in a shower of sparks and tearing of wood and fabric. Half the lower part of the fuselage abraded away as it gradually came to a halt, spinning around like a top once or twice before it did. Rescue teams raced out, bells ringing, although the props didn't *quite* touch the earth and nothing caught fire . . . this time.

"Got that?"

"Yes, sir," the Protégé replied, and began the complex process of changing a reel of film.

Gerta pulled her uniform cap off, crumpling it in her hand. That was the only outward sign of her rage; she sternly repressed the impulse to throw it down and stamp on it.

The squadron commander came over to her open-topped car. "I understand completely, Brigadier," he said. "Will your film do any good?"

"Well, I can now confirm with visual aids that we lose ten percent of those things in *normal* operations with each mission, not counting enemy action. When I think of how many fighters or ground-attack aircraft we could have for the same resources—"

"Just get them to stop telling us to fly these abortions," the man said. He was very young, not more than twenty-five; turnover in the bomber squadrons was heavy. "It isn't that we mind dying for the Chosen, you understand—"

"—it's just that you'd like it to have some sort of point," Gerta finished for him. "I'll do my best. Porschmidt has a lot of friends in high places."

"I'd like to take them to a high place—over Santander City or Bosson, and dump them off with the rest of the bombload."

Gerta nodded. "If it's any consolation, we're doing some things that are smarter than this."

"It couldn't be worse."

CHAPTER TWENTY-FIVE

John Hosten gripped Arturo Bianci's hand. "You're still alive," he said.

The guerilla leader looked closer to sixty than the forty-five or so John knew him to be. His once-stocky frame was weathered down to bone and sinew and a necessary minimum of muscle, and the dense close-cropped cap of hair that topped his seamed, weathered face was the same silver as the stubble on his jaw.

"Not for want of the *tedeschi* trying," he said. The smile on his face looked unpracticed. "They've had a high price on my head these sixteen years."

He led John back into the cave. It was deep and twisting, opening out into broader caverns within and spreading out into a maze that led miles into the depths of the Collini Paeani. An occasional kerosene lantern cast a puddle of light; now and then an occupied cave showed men sleeping under blankets, working on their weapons, or stacking crates and boxes under waxed tarpaulins. There was even a stable-cavern, where picketed mules drowsed in rows and fodder was stacked ten feet high against one wall. The caves smelled of old smoke, dirt, and damp limestone; there were underground rivers further in, rushing past to who knew where.

"Big operation," John said.

"One of many," Arturo said. "We try not to put too much in one place, in case there is an informer or the *tedeschi* are lucky with a patrol. More and more come to us. The *tedeschi* take more land for plantations, and always there are more labor drafts. If a man is marked down for the camps or the factories in Hell"—he used the slang term for the Land—"he can only escape by coming to us."

"Or by volunteering for the army, or the police," John pointed out.

The guerilla leader's face went tight as a clenched fist. "Some do. And of those, some are *our* men, to be spies, and to wait for the day we call. The enemy do not much trust units they raise here, nor do they dare mix them much with Protégés from the Land."

They came to a medium-sized chamber and pushed through the blankets hung over the entrance. An old woman tended a pot of stew over a small charcoal fire, and a group as ragged and hard-looking as Arturo waited around a rickety table. There was no attempt at introductions, simply a wolfish patience or a slight shifting of the weapons that festooned them. Some of them were tearing at lumps of hard bread, or dunking the chunks in bowls of the stew, eating with the concentration of men who went hungry much of the time. They looked at John expressionlessly, taking in Barrjen and his little squad of middle-aged ex-Marines with wary respect.

John was dressed in high-laced boots and tough tweeds, Santander hunting or hiking clothes. He swung his pack to the table and unbuckled the flap.

"Here," he said, tapping his finger on the map he produced. It was Republic Naval Survey issue, showing a section of the north shore of the Gut a hundred miles east and west of Salini.

The men around the table were mostly ex-peasants, with a scattering of shopkeepers and artisans, but they'd all learned to read maps since the Chosen conquest. The spot he indicated was at the end of a south-trending bulge, a little almost-island at a narrow part of the great strait.

"Fort Causili," one said. "Old fort, but the *tedeschi* have been building there. Two, three thousand laborers, and troops, for most of the past year. And they have put in a spur rail line."

John nodded. He took out photographs, blurred from enlargement and hurried camera work, but clear enough. Some were from the air, others taken with concealed instruments by workers on the base. They showed deep pits, concrete revetments with overhead protection set into the cliffs, and at the last, special flatcars with huge cylindrical objects under heavy tarpaulin cover.

"More than a fort," John said. "Those are special long-range guns, six of them. Twelve-inch naval rifles, sleeved down to eight inches and extended. They range most of the way to shoal water on the southern shore . . . and the enemy hold that, it's Union territory. There's another fort there that commands the only passage, it's got heavy siege mortars. Between them they can close the Gut almost exactly at the old Union-Santander border."

A few of the guerilla commanders shrugged. One muttered: "Bad. But so? There is a infantry brigade in that area, dug in, fully prepared. Those of us who wanted to die have done so long ago."

"Very bad," Arturo said. "If they can close the Gut, they can put their own ships on it and use it to move supplies. That will solve many of their problems. It will free troops to be used elsewhere, and free more labor, locomotives. And your navy will not be able to raid along the coast, or drop off supplies to us. Very bad. But Vincini is right, we cannot do more than harass it."

Vincini drew a long knife; it looked as if it had been honed down from a butcher's tool. He traced a circle with the point.

"A quiet area. Few recruits for us. That would change if we staged some operations there—the *tedeschi* would kill in reply, and that would bring the villagers to our side."

John nodded; the guerillas always struck away from their base areas. The Chosen killed hostages from the areas where the attacks occurred, which merely convinced the locals they might as well be hung for sheep as lambs.

"I'm not asking you to take the base yourselves," he said. "But believe me, we cannot allow the enemy to complete it. If they command the Gut, they have gone far towards winning the war—if Santander falls, your cause is hopeless."

That earned him some glares, but reluctant nods as well. He went on:

"Remember, all the world is at war. We attack the enemy in many places. You cannot take the base alone, but you can *help*. Here is what I propose—"

Angelo Pesalozi grunted as the Santander sailors hauled him over the gunwale of the motor torpedo boat. The Protégé looked around. The little vessel was blacked out, but there was enough starlight and reflected light from the moons to see it. There was an elemental simplicity to the design; a sharp-prowed plywood hull, shallow but exquisitely shaped. The forward deck held a double-barreled pom-pom behind a thin shield, but the real weapons were on either side: a pair of eighteen-inch naval torpedoes in sealed sheet-steel launch tubes. There was a small deckhouse around the wheel amidships, and a wooden coaming over the big aircraft engines at the stern that could hurl the frail concoction through a calm sea at better than thirty knots. Right now it was burbling in a low rumbling purr, like the world's biggest cat, muffled by a tin box full of baffles at the stern that showed the hasty marks of an improvised fitting. The blue exhaust filled the night with its tang and the wind was too calm to disturb it much.

A dozen more like it waited outside the harbor of Bassin du Sud. Not a scrap of metal gleamed, and the faces of the crews were equally dark with burnt cork and black wool stocking-caps. The commander of the little flotilla was the oldest man in the crews, and he was several years short of thirty; most of his subordinates had been fishermen two years ago, or scions of families wealthy enough to own motorboats. Kneally's father was a newspaper magnate with ambitions for his sons. His wasn't the only grin as he extended his hand to the heavyset Protégé.

"Welcome aboard," he said, in fair Landisch. "Commander James Frederick Kneally, at your service. You've got it?"

Silent, Angelo reached inside his jacket and pulled out an oilskin map. The Santander naval officer unwrapped it and spread it on the engine coaming, clicking on a small shaded flashlight.

"Oh, very nice," Kneally breathed. No changes from the ones Intelligence had given them back in Karlton.

A Land Naval Service-issue map, with the minefields marked in red, compass deviations, bearings, the lot; typical Chosen thoroughness. The Santander officer laid his compass on the map and looked up. Two lights flashed from different parts of the hills above Bassin du Sud, and he was busy with straight-edge and slide rule for a moment.

"Right here," Kneally said, marking the map. "All *right*. Thanks again."

The Protégé dipped his head. "I must return; I am on an errand for my master that gives me some freedom from suspicion, but not much. Give me ten minutes."

The flotilla commander shook his hand again, then returned entranced to the map as he was handed back over the side to his little steam launch. He half-noticed that the tiny pennant at the rear was the checked black-and-white of the Land General Staff, then dismissed it.

"Helm," he said. "Prepare to follow a course to my direction, dead slow. Signal to the flotilla, follow in line astern."

A dim blue light just above the waterline snapped on at the very stern of the lead torpedo boat. The man at the wheel spat overside and wiped first one hand, then the other on his duck trousers. The commander ducked his head through a hole in the coaming, into the stuffy darkness of the engine compartment. The petty officer in charge and his two ratings crouched by the big internal-combustion motors like acolytes worshiping some god of iron and brass, tools and oil can at the ready. They'd spent the past week going over every part and link and piece of the motor train as if their lives depended on it. Which, of course, they did.

"Ready?"

"Ready as we'll ever be, sir."

He pulled himself back up and looked at the stars. One moon full, the other half, a little scattered cloud, dead calm with only the inevitable southern ocean swell. Inside the breakwaters of the harbor it would be as calm as a bathtub. He looked at the map again, noting the markings on currents.

"Three knots," he said quietly to the helm. "Come about twelve degrees and maintain for four minutes. Carefully now. It's a tight fit."

"Tight as a cabin boy's bum, sir," the helmsman agreed, and let out the throttle inch by careful inch.

The muffler on the stern burbled a little louder, and the commander winced. The Chosen had beefed up the port defenses considerably, and while he had what looked like perfect intelligence on them, knowing exactly how a 250-pound prizefighter would throw a right hook did you little good if you were a ninety-pound weed with a glass jaw. Kneally's boats were plywood shells over explosives and highly volatile fuel; a heavy machine gun could turn them to burning splinters, much less a pom-pom, much less a 240mm shell from the Emmas in the castle or the harbor forts. *And* there were gunboats constantly patrolling.

The minefields were laid with the clear passages staggered by horizontal lanes, making doglegs nobody could negotiate by luck. It would be difficult enough in daylight, with a pilot conning the helm; the enemy had lost a couple of supply ships to their own mines.

"Gently, gently. Blink the stern light. Now come about to port, ninety degrees. Gently, man, gently."

Sweat soaked his stocking cap and stung in the shaving cuts on his chin. The mines were down there, dull iron balls studded with pressure-sensitive brass horns, floating like malignant flowers on their chain tethers. He wiped his face with the back of his jacket. The lights of Bassin du Sud were coming into view; there were a few of them, mostly low down by the water. *Maybe we* should *have staged an air raid at the same time*, he thought. Get them looking up. *No, the brass were right for once*. It would just get them awake and ready, and a crew could swing a quick-firer from ninety degrees to horizontal a lot faster than they could get out of their racks and on line.

Something bumped against the hull forward. Bump . . . bump . . . bump . . .

His stomach lurched. Every man on board froze, except for the helm's careful twitch at the wheel. Then the crew of MTB 109 shuddered and relaxed as the sound died astern, and the sudden annihilating blast *didn't* lift their craft out of the water broken-backed. Another turn ahead. He looked behind. Barely possible to make out MTB 110. Good. This follow-the-leader put his nerves even more on edge; small errors could accumulate and throw the last boats right into the mines. Although God knew they'd practiced often enough at the mockups back at base in Karlton. The base there had never been much, but it rattled empty

since the Southern Fleet was wiped out in the opening
days of the war.

The ships that slaughtered four thousand Santander sailors were waiting ahead . . . and they'd carefully spent half a day shooting or running down the
survivors in the water, too. His teeth showed white
in his darkened face.

"All right, we're out." If the map was complete.
"Signal to deploy."

He brought up his binoculars and squinted. There
was just enough background scatter to see the line of
Land cruisers silhouetted against the diffuse glow . . .
he hoped. They were a couple of thousand yards away,
smoke visible from one or two stacks on each ship,
keeping some steam up; a boom with antitorpedo netting out, floating low, a line across the dead calm of
the harbor. And the lights of a patrol boat, low-powered searchlights looking for infiltrators or defectors
trying to make it out in rubber dinghies.

The Santander torpedo boats spread out into line
abreast. "Six knots," Kneally said.

The engines burbled a little louder. *How long?* Eventually they were going to notice. . . .

A searchlight speared out at them and an alarm
wailed.

"Goose it, Chief! Goose it!"

The helm slammed the throttles forward. Now the
engines roared, a shattering noise no muffler could
mute. White water peeled back from the bows in two
high roostertails of spray, throwing salt across his lips.
Lights flicked on along the line of Land cruisers, and
starshells blossomed high above.

"Too late, you leather-sucking perverts!" Kneally
yelled.

The boom was less than five hundred yards ahead.
There was just time enough for the torpedo boats to
reach the maximum safe speed. Kneally clamped his
hands on the bracket ahead of him and braced himself.

The smooth strip of reinforcing steel down the torpedo boat's keel slalomed it into the air in an arc that ended in an enormous splash that threw water twice the height of the little vessel's stub signal mast. Then each pair was driving for a cruiser's side, and the big ships loomed like gray steel cliffs. Cliffs speckled with fire, as the first pom-pom crews made it to their stations and began to open fire.

The MTB 109 was skipping forward like a watermelon seed squeezed between thumb and forefinger. One-pound shells pocked the water around it, and the boat's own forward pom-pom was punching out a stream of bright fire-globes itself. They wouldn't harm the cruiser, but they might throw off the crews of the bigger ship's antitorpedo-boat armament. A quick-firer banged from its sponson mount, and a shell threw up a fountain of spray to their left. All the time, Kneally's mind was estimating distances with the skill of endless practice.

"Ready—"

THUD.

MTB 110 blew up in a globe of yellow flame, its breath like the foretaste of hell.

"Hold her steady!" Kneally yelled, helping the CPO wrestle with the wheel as blast knocked the shallow dish-like hull sideways.

They plunged through the flame in a single searing instant, the spray-plumes of their passage helping to keep it from searing them too badly. MTB 109 was travelling as fast as anything on the oceans of Visager now, bounding forward like a porpoise driven by the power of four hundred horses. A thousand yards, maximum range. Nine hundred. The nose of the 109 was trained precisely on the cruiser's stern, lined up on the winking light of the pom-pom tub there. The shells drifted out towards him and then snapped by overhead.

"Fire one! Turn her, Chief!"

With a flat bang the launching charge slammed the first torpedo out of its tube. The frail fabric of the torpedo boat shuddered as the silver cylinder arched into the water, its contrarotating propellors already spinning. The boat was heeling to the right, its bow tracing an arc that carried it along the whole length of the enemy warship.

"Fire two! Fire three! Fire four! *Get us the fuck out of here!*"

The night was a chaos of flickering shapes and blinding lights, tracers and searchlights and explosions. Kneally twisted in the coaming to look over his shoulder. White water cataracted up from the side of the cruiser that had been their target—from others, too. He howled a catamount screech, until his teeth clicked painfully shut. This time they had hit the boom much harder, and there was an ominous crackle from the framework of the MTB 109.

But it only had to hold together a little longer. Another light was blinking to port, the guerilla pickup who would smuggle them out through the mountains, if they could reach shore and then avoid the Land patrols. Kneally's head swiveled, trying to see everything at once. It was still too dark, too tangled with lines and bars of light that bounced across his eyes. If one of the cruiser's magazines had not exploded behind them he would never have seen the destroyer coming. The actinic light showed it all too clearly: the turtleback forward deck and four billowing smokestacks, and the waves curling back from the cruel knife bows looming over his boat.

Kneally threw himself backward with a yell. A huge impact threw him pinwheeling into the air, and the water hit him like concrete. Somehow he pushed the whirling darkness away and fought his way to the surface, aided by the buoyancy of the cork vest he wore. Prop-wash sucked at him, and he bobbed in the destroyer's wake. Oily water slopped into his mouth.

"Jesus," he grunted, almost giggling with incredulous relief at finding himself alive. "And Dad wanted
me to be a hero."

His viewpoint was too low to see much, but several of the cruisers that had been his squadron's targets were burning, and he could see a stern rising
into the sky with its huge twin bronze screws glint-
ing in the light of fires and searchlights.

That sobered him, and he turned towards the beach
and began to swim doggedly. If they didn't kill him,
he'd live . . . and there would be other battles.

He almost missed a stroke. The adrenaline was wearing off, and he was remembering the look on the chief's
face as the destroyer's bows loomed over them. He
might be the only survivor of the dozen crew who'd
manned MTB 109.

Kneally shuddered. *Another battle.*

"About bloody time," Gerta said with satisfaction.

Only the last gunpit was still uncovered, and work
was going on through the night under the harsh light
of the arcs.

It was sunk deep into the cliff face, taking advantage of a natural ravine through the chalky limestone.
Labor gangs and explosives had hollowed out an oblong
chamber, wider at its rear than at the face of the steep
rock. It still smelled of green concrete, but the complex metal mountings of the giant guns were in place,
and the two tubes themselves were being fastened in
their cradles below. The same great cranes—modified
shipbuilding models—that had lowered the guns were
now transferring beams and planks of steel that were
small only by comparison. Down below pneumatic riv-
eters hammered and arc welders stuttered as hundreds
of Protégé laborers and Chosen engineers assembled
the intricate jigsaw puzzle into multiple layers of steel.
Tommorrow other teams would begin burying it under
layer upon layer of concrete laced with rebar and filled

with massive rubble from the original excavation, topped with twenty feet of granite quarried from the old Imperial fort.

Gerta inhaled the scent of ozone and scorched metal, fists on hips, pivoting to take in the bustling scene. The other three gunpits were already in place, spread out in a semicircle along the outer edge of the near-island. Each pit was open only along the narrow slit through which the guns would fire—and they would show their muzzles only slightly, and that only when run out for a shoot. Tunnels ran between the pits, and between the pits and their ammunition bunkers, underground barracks and mess halls, fuel stores, generator rooms; but they were all carefully kinked and equipped with blast doors taken from junked battleships to contain internal damage.

"About bloody time is right," Kurt Wallers said. He was carrying colonel's tabs, with dual artillery and engineering branch-of-service slashes. "We were complete idiots to wait this long. If we'd had this installation in place when we attacked the Sierrans, that ratfuck in Barclon would never have happened. The Santies couldn't have put so much as a harbor barge down the Gut without getting it pounded into scrap."

Gerta shrugged. "My sentiments exactly, Kurt—if that's any consolation."

The other Chosen officer hesitated. Gerta slapped him lightly on the shoulder. "Spit it out—we *did* go through the Test of Life together, after all. You've done a good job here, too, you're three months ahead of schedule."

"Well, then . . . your father is the chief of the General Staff. What the fuck was he thinking of?"

Gerta sighed. "He's chief of the General Staff, not the Chosen Council. They've got a bad case of victory disease, and it's been getting worse since we overran the Empire. That was too easy, and they've been dispersing effort on pet projects and hobbyhorses ever since. Sitting back in Copernik, looking at large-scale maps, it looks like we're conquering the world. The Empire, the Union, now the Sierra."

"We *are* conquering the world. The problem is *holding* the world. We beat the Imperials because we could concentrate our force. Now—" He made a spreading gesture with his hands.

"Tell me, Kurt. I told the general often enough. *He* lobbied the Council often enough, but their pet projects got in the way. They had this scheduled for the beginning of the war with Santander . . . about five to eight years from now."

"Well, better late than never," Kurt said. "This'll be a significant nail holding down what we've conquered. It makes their naval bases at Dubuk and Charsson useless as far as the Gut's concerned. They've been harassing the shit out of us, I can tell you. *And* landing supplies to the animals in the hills virtually at will, since Barclon. That's getting as bad as it was right after the conquest, or worse; they're smarter now."

Gerta nodded. "When can you start test firing?"

"Oh, I wouldn't want to do that for another couple of weeks, even on the first pair. The concrete has to set *hard* before we put that much stress on the mountings."

"How're the secondary works coming?"

"About a third done." She followed as he walked inland. "The usual close-in works, machine guns, bunkered field-guns, mortars, minefields, wire, steel spike obstacles. We've got half the *Schlenke Emmas* in their pits, too, so pretty soon we can drop high-angle fire on anything that gets too close for the big guns to deal with."

"You're getting a lot of work out of these animals," she said, eyeing the swarming construction site.

"You can catch more flies with honey than with vinegar," he said. "I've done a lot of engineering work in the New Territories, and—"

An aide trotted up. "Sir. Message over the wireless."

Kurt took it and read, tilting the yellow flimsy to catch the lights. "Attack on Bassin du Sud," he said. "Considerable damage sustained in beating it off."

Gerta grunted in surprise. That was communique language for *they whipped our arse*.

"*Fuck* it. Damn, damn, if they damage the Southern Squadron badly, there goes our route around the eastern lobe to Marsai."

Kurt nodded. "Still, it won't be too bad even so; they can ship straight south from Corona by rail and then through the Gut, now that we've got this."

"*Ya.*" Gerta's eyes narrowed. "The question is, do the Santies realize that?"

Kurt looked at the flimsy again. "Not many details. I wonder how they got through the minefields? And those howitzers in the fort, they should take care of any ships."

"Should. But—"

Another messenger. "Sir. The Air Service scout airship *Guthavok* reports it is under attack from Santander heavier-than-air pursuit planes."

They both looked south by reflex. "At *night*?" Kurt Wallers said incredulously.

Fire blossomed in the night, five thousand feet up and miles to the south.

Wallers began to bark orders. Gerta turned on her heel and trotted back to her scout car, vaulting up the fixed ladder and then into the open compartment with one hand on the rim. Her son was already peering south through the heavy rail-mounted glasses. Gerta looked around; the wireless was fired up and ready, and the vehicle had pressure and was ready to move.

"Signals," she said. The operator looked up, earphones on and hand poised over the signal key. "To regional HQ in Salini. Fort under heavy attack from Santander seaborne forces, including battleships and amphibious element of unknown strength. Stop. As representative of the General Staff I order repeat order immediate mobilization all available forces and their concentration on this point. Stop. Brigadier Gerta Hosten. Stop. Send until acknowledged."

The signals technician was sending before Gerta had finished the first sentence. Johann turned to her; by now he'd learned enough to merely raise his brows.

"Ya. If that was wrong, I will be lucky to command a one-company garrison post guarding a bridge," she said. "But I'd rather risk being a damned fool."

To the driver: "Get us out of here. Out on the north road, then east towards Salini."

She pulled the machine-carbine out of its clamps over her seat, checked the flat drum magazine, and reached for the helmet that hung beside it. With a chuff of waste steam, the car pulled out through the growing chaos of the half-built fort.

CHAPTER TWENTY-SIX

"Aren't you getting a little senior for commanding from the front?" Admiral Maurice Farr asked quietly.

Jeffrey grinned at his father. "I notice you're here, sir, and not back in Dubuk."

Farr shrugged. "An admiral has to command from a ship."

"And a general has to be where there's some chance of getting useful information in timely fashion," Jeffrey replied reasonably. He drew himself up and saluted. "Admiral."

"General," the elder Farr replied. "Good hunting, and we'll give all the support we can."

Jeffrey turned, swung over the rail, and scrambled down the rope ladder. A young aide tried to assist him as he jumped down into the waiting steam launch.

"I'm not quite decrepit yet, Seimore," Jeffrey said dryly, and took a swig from his canteen. "We're better off than the rest of the force, here."

The men were climbing down netting hung on the sides of the transports and into the waiting flat-bottomed motor barges, or waiting crammed shoulder to shoulder and probably seasick in similar vessels that had sailed with the fleet from Dubuk. The Gut was calm tonight, but the flat-bottomed barges would pitch and sway in a bathtub.

"Let's go," Jeffrey said quietly.

The launch swung in towards the shore; it was low and sandy here, in contrast to the cliffs that marked most of this section of the Gut's northern shore. Low and sandy on either side of the fort that was their objective. The first wave of troops would be going ashore right now, and from the lack of noise, meeting little or no resistance. Well, they'd expected that.

Jeffrey looked at his watch. 0500 hours, nearly dawn. Right about now they should—

BOOM. BOOM. BOOM—

The big guns of the fleet cut loose, firing from west to east in a long, slightly curved line. The great bottle-shaped muzzle flashes lit the scene with a continuous strobing illumination that was brighter than the false dawn. It was still dark enough for the red-glowing dots of the shells to be visible with their own heat, arching up into the sky to fall towards the Chosen.

Dust filtered down onto Kurt Waller's head. The gun position shook as twelve- and eight-inch shells landed on the surface above, or hammered deep into the soft limestone of the cliffs.

I built well, he thought. Aloud: "Well, the enemy has provided us with an aiming point. Return fire."

"But sir!" someone protested. "The mountings—"

"Are not hard-set yet," he replied. "Nevertheless, you have your orders."

With hydraulic smoothness, the muzzle of the great gun began to move downward in its cradle.

Ten miles outside Salini, John Hosten grinned into the low red light of dawn. He washed down a mouthful of half-chewed hardtack with a swig from his canteen and slapped the cork back into it. It was like eating pieces of a clay flowerpot, but it kept you going, and if you were careful it didn't break your teeth. The air smelled of dew-wet rock and aromatic shrub and old sweat from the clothes of the guerillas around him.

"Quick of them," he said. "They're in a hurry."

The road through the low rocky hills was quite good, not exactly a paved highway, but thirty feet wide and cut out of the hillside with generous shoulders and ditches. Right now it was crowded with a convoy. Two light tanks in the front, the Land copy of the Santander Whippet, trucks crammed with infantry, more trucks pulling field-guns and pompoms and supplies, more infantry, some more tanks . . .

. . . and a forty-degree slope on either side of the road.

"That is their mobile reaction force," Arturo said.

John nodded. Not even Santander could afford to give all its infantry and guns motor transport; the Land had roughly the same output of vehicles, but a much bigger army and fewer wheels per head.

The lead tank was near the ferroconcrete bridge. "Now?" John said.

Arturo nodded. "They are in a *great* hurry," he said, smiling like something with tentacles, and pressed the plunger beside him.

The explosions at the bottom of the bridge pylons weren't very spectacular, although the sound echoed off the stony slopes. A puff of dust and smoke—pulverized concrete and plain dirt—and the uprights heaved, twisted, and sank slowly at an increasing tilt. The flat slab roadway crumbled in chunks as its support was removed, falling down towards the bottom of the gorge and the dry-season trickle that ran there. The first tank went with it, sparks flying as its treads worked backwards.

Arturo laughed at the sight. Even then, John had time to be slightly chilled at the sound. Nearly five hundred feet to fall, knowing that when you hit—

The tank cracked open like an eggshell on the boulders, and the dust of its impact was followed seconds later by a fireball as the fuel caught. Shells shot out of the fireball, trailing smoke, as the ammunition cooked off.

As ye sow, so shall ye reap, Raj said relentlessly. *Remember what the Imperials were like before the*

Chosen came. As they are now, the Chosen made them.

Rifles and machine guns opened up on the stalled convoy, and mortars as well. A huge secondary explosion threw trucks tumbling as a shell landed in a truckload of ammunition, or perhaps on the limber of a field-gun. Birds rose in clouds as the racket of battle replaced the early morning calm. Order spread among the chaos below, soldiers taking cover and officers spreading them out. The first were already beginning to work their way upslope. Men died and rolled downward; others took their place. The four-pounder guns of the light tanks coughed and coughed again, and their machine guns beat the slope with an iron hail.

Below John was a guerilla sniper, invisible even at ten yards in his camouflage blanket, a net sewn with strips of cloth in shades of ochre, gray, and brown. The muzzle twitched slightly, and the rifle snapped.

Scratch one Chosen officer, probably, John thought.

Arturo was examining the scene below with his binoculars. "We cannot hold them long," he warned. "If we try, the rear elements of the convoy will work around behind us—there are trails, and their maps are good."

"No, we can't," John said. "But they were in a *great* hurry . . . and this is not the only ambush."

Arturo smiled again. This time John joined him.

"Who the *fuck* does he think he's shooting at?" Johan Hosten said, pulling himself erect in the open-topped armored car and glaring after the two-engine ground attack aircraft that was hedgehopping away.

Gerta grinned at her son's indignation, although that *had* been a bit of a nerve-wracking surprise. There were fresh lead smears on the flanks of her war-car.

"At Santies, of course," she said.

Granted, there was a bloody great Land sunburst painted on the rear deck of the war-car, but she knew from personal experience how hard it was to see anything accurately when you were doing a strafing run in combat conditions.

"Only thing more dangerous than your own artillery is your own air force, boy," she said, slapping him on the shoulder. "Especially in a ratfuck like this where nobody knows where anyone is, including themselves."

It's a relief in a way, having nothing but a fight on my hands.

They turned a bend in the road. "And speaking of Santies—"

The eastbound road wound through rolling ground covered in olive groves. Men in brown uniforms were ahead of them, and two light-wheeled vehicles were on the gravel surface of the road. They had whip antennae bobbing above them. Some sort of command group, then.

"Driver! Floor it!" Gerta barked, pulling a grenade from a box clipped to the inside of the sloping armored side of the war-car.

He did. The five-ton vehicle was too heavy to actually leap ahead, but it accelerated, more slowly than a newer model with an IC engine; on the other hand, the steam was almost silent. The Santies noticed only just before Johan opened up with the forward machine gun, walking bursts across the men grouped around the hood of one of the light cars.

Gerta shouted wordlessly as the prow of the war-car rammed one vehicle aside, crumpling the frame and knocking it into the ditch. She tossed the grenade at the wreckage and followed it with a spray of pistol-calibre bullets from her machine carbine. Jumping with combat-adrenaline, her eyes picked out one face/body/movement gestalt as the man leaped for cover behind a rock. She fired, twisted, cursed as her son at the machine gun blocked her line of sight, grabbed at another grenade and threw it.

Return fire pinged off the riveted armor plates of

the car, making the crew duck, and then they were past.

"Keep going!" she said, raising her head for a look.

"Jesus!"

Jeffrey raised his head, coughing in the plume of dust left behind by the turtle-shaped Chosen vehicle; some sort of six-wheeled armored car. As it turned the corner and zipped out of sight ahead, an arm appeared over the side of the hull with one finger extended from a clenched fist, and pumped in an unmistakable gesture.

Wounded men screamed. For an instant everyone else stayed frozen and flat to the earth, waiting for the follow-up.

"Keep moving!" Jeffrey said aloud. "That was a straggler."

"*Merde,*" Henri muttered beside him, levering himself up with the butt of his rifle.

My sentiments exactly, Jeffrey thought as he took stock. Two regimental commanders out of it, and one of the priceless radios.

"Runner," he said, "tell their seconds what's happened, and that I have full confidence in them. Somebody get that fire out." The wrecked car was sending licking flames and black smoke upward, just the sort of marker a cruising Land Air Service pilot would need. "And let's get back to work," he went on calmly.

His mouth was full of gummy saliva. That had been far too sudden, and far too close. A few of the faces that bent over the map with him were pale beneath their coating of summer dust, but nobody was visibly panicky.

The map showed the bulge of coastline that held the fort they were attacking. "We've just about closed the circle around the landward side," he said. "Now, Colonel McWhirter, you're going to dig in along this line and hold them off us. The partisans are doing a good job of slowing them down, but when they hit, it'll be hard. The rest of us will press on the perimeter."

"Going to cost," someone commented. "They're expecting us, by now."

Jeffrey shrugged. "We'll keep their attention. They don't have much of a garrison there yet, mostly construction battalions. With a little luck, the Resort Brigade will do its job."

Major Steven Durrison, Fifth Mountain Regiment— known familiarly in the Army of the Republic as the Resort Brigade, since so many mountain-climbing hobbyists filled its ranks—looked up the rest of the gully. *Not much of a climb,* he thought. About a sixty-degree slope, the natural rock overlain with rubble. The enemy had evidently been dumping construction fill down it, since it led up to the lip of the plateau. From the way they'd cut footings into the sides, they'd probably planned to build something here. They hadn't had time.

And they were otherwise occupied right now. More shells trundled across the sky to burst on the plateau tops above. The ships out in the Gut looked like toys at this distance, a fleet a child might sail in his bathtub. The earthquake rumble and shudder of the earth under his body showed how out of scale distance made the scene. Rock and concrete fountained over the cliffs, past the firing slits of the heavy guns, to land on the beach below. More shaking through the rock beneath him; he tried to imagine what it was like to be caught in the open up there, and failed. *If that doesn't keep their heads down, nothing will.*

The mountaineer looked back over his shoulder; men were strung out down nearly to the beach, along the line of rope secured by iron stakes driven into the rock by the advance clement. Most were armed with the new submachine guns, for close in work, or with pump-action shotguns, and festooned with bandoliers, satchel charges, coils of rope, and pitons.

"Lieutenant," he called, "we'll start to work our way across from there."

He pointed; no climber could mistake what he meant, a long shadow slanting upward across the cliff-face to their right. "Signaller."

The heliograph squad had set up a little way down the ravine. The sergeant in charge of the squad looked up.

"You've got contact with the flagship?"

"Yessir."

Durrison nodded, hiding his relief. The alternative was colored rockets. That would *work*, but even with dozens of heavy shells landing up above, someone was likely to notice. Heliograph signals—light reflected off mirrors—were effectively line of sight. None of the enemy would see his going out.

"Send: 'Am proceeding with Phase Two.'"

About bloody time, Maurice Farr thought, lowering his binoculars. The signals station were scribbling on their pads, but he could still read code himself.

The *Great Republic* twisted and heeled in the water as her broadside fired. Light flashed in return from the upper third of the cliffs, and three seconds later the whole eighteen-thousand-ton bulk of the battleship shuddered and rang like a giant gong struck with a sledgehammer. Farr blinked at the fountain of sparks as the shell struck her main belt armor.

"Sir!" It was Damage Control, speaking to the flagship's captain. "Flooding in compartment C3. That one hit us below the waterline."

Gridley nodded. "Get them to work on it," he said. "Containment measures."

That meant sealing off the affected area behind the watertight doors, hopefully not before they got the personnel out of it. C3 was unpleasantly close to the A turret magazines as well.

Those guns certainly have punch, he thought. Eight-inch, but fired with a twelve-incher's powder charge, and an extra-long barrel. The velocity was unbelievable. *Much faster and you could fire shells into orbit.*

"Sir." This time to the fleet commander. "Sir, *Templedon City* reports that they've got the fires out and stabilized by counterflooding."

A heavy cruiser. "What speed can they make?"

"Sir, they report no more than six knots."

"They're to withdraw. Detach two destroyers to escort." And to pick up survivors if they didn't make it back to Dubuk.

Farr raised his glasses again. "I'd say it was about time we did something about this fort they were building, wouldn't you, Gridley?" he said calmly.

"Christ yes, Admiral. If they'd got it fully operational . . ." The flagship captain's voice faded off.

A biplane plunged past the bridge, trailing smoke. It smashed into the water and exploded not far from the bow of a destroyer; the whole thing happened too fast for him to see the national insignia. Dozens more were swarming through the air above the cloud of smoke and shellbursts that marked the surface of the fort, like flies around a piece of meat left in the sun.

Good thing we're in range of ground-based air support here, Farr thought.

His sons were inland there, where the fighting was—steadily increasing fighting, as the Land forces battered their way through guerilla harassment and started to bring their weight to bear on the Santander blocking elements. His eldest grandson was in one of those wood-and-canvas powered kites . . . if he hadn't been the one who plunged out of the sky and died just now. Pride came in many flavors; right now it tasted like fear. An old man might not fear for himself, but anyone living still had something hostage to fortune. His family, his country . . .

I think we'd be in a very bad way indeed if it weren't for John and Jeffrey, he thought. *If John hadn't been born with a clubfoot, or if I hadn't gotten that posting as naval attaché in Oathtaking . . .*

"Carry on," he said aloud. "Let's keep them busy. And stand by to fire support missions for the ground forces."

"I don't give a living shit how many partisans there are out there, Colonel," Heinrich Hosten said with quiet venom. His fingers were white on the field telephone. "Ignore them. Ignore your fucking flanks. Hit the Santies, and hit them hard, or by the Oath, you'll be in the Western Islands dodging blowgun darts from the savages next month, if you're unlucky enough to be still alive."

He retuned the handset to its cradle with enormous care, fighting throught the rage that clouded his vision. He looked at the pin-studded map and tried to force himself to be objective. *I'm not justified in going to the front. More information is getting through now. I'm in a better position to coordinate from here.*

He could hear the Santy naval bombardment from here, though, a continuous rumble to the south. Guns were firing closer than that, medium field pieces; Land batteries, shooting obstacles out of the way in the narrow passages of the hills.

One of his staff handed him the field telephone again. "Sir, you'll want to hear this yourself."

He picked it up. "*Ja?*"

Gerta's voice. He closed his eyes; *nothing* should surprise him today.

"You'll never guess which old friend of yours I ran into today," she said. "Ran into literally, but I didn't quite manage to kill him."

There were times when he was tempted to believe in malignant spirits.

Kurt Wallers jammed his palms over his ears and opened his mouth. The gun fired again, and the pressure wave battered at him. No point in going back to the command bunker deeper in the rock; the observation stations weren't operational yet. With those and the calculating machine it would have been possible to direct accurate fire nearly to the southern shore of the Gut. As it was, each tube was firing under independent control—over open sights.

And not doing a bad job. He hated to think what had happened to the construction people up above; he'd spent a long time training them. *All we have to do is hold out until the reinforcements drive off the landing parties.* Then—

"Sir! Movement on the beach below us!"

He blinked. "Get some extra propellant charges." They came in fabric containers the size of small garbage cans. "Strap grenades to them. Pull the tabs and roll them over the edge of the casement. *Move.*"

Suddenly the background rumble of naval shellfire exploding on the plateau overhead ceased. Wallers looked up; that took his eyes away from the slit of light where the embrasure mouth pierced the cliff. Something flew in. His head whipped around, and trained reflex threw him down, not quite in time.

Durrison plastered himself to the lip of concrete above the gun embrasures. Every time the long cannon within fired, the concussion threatened to flip him off the ledge, despite the rope sling fastened to pitons driven firmly into the rock above. A couple of his men *had* been flipped, to dangle scrabbling on their ropes until the hands of their squadmates could haul them back. The enemy hadn't noticed, thank God; the embrasures might be narrow firing slits in comparison to the size of the guns within or the scale of the three-hundred-foot height of the cliffs, but they were still fifteen feet from top to bottom.

The gun fired again. Durrison kept his mouth open to equalize the pressure, but his head still rang as if there were midgets inside with sledgehammers, trying to get out. The rock flexed against his belly; no telling how long the pitons would hold, with that sort of vibration. The wind was building out of the south, with dark clouds along the horizon south of him—perhaps one of the rare summer thunderstorms of the Gut.

Joy. Absolute fucking joy. At last a man came around the curve of the rock to his right, clinging like a spider as he made his cautious way.

"Everyone's in place, sir!" he screamed into Durrison's deafened ear.

The moutaineer officer nodded and pulled the flare gun out of his belt, pointed it up and out.

Fumpf. The trail of smoke reached upward. *Pop.*

Abruptly, the rolling bombardment from the fleet stopped. One last eight-inch shell ripped its way through the air overhead, and relative silence fell as the continuous thunder of explosions overhead ceased.

That was the signal. A half-dozen men swung their satchel charges out on cords for momentum and then inward, to fly through the openings of the gun embrasures. Durrison freed the submachine gun and clamped his right hand on the pistol grip. His left took the rope that held him by the slipknot and he let his weight fall on it, crouching and bending his knees to his chest with the composition soles of his high-laced mountain boots planted firmly against the rock.

Four. *Five.*

Smoke and debris vomited out of the opening below his feet, bits trailing off down the cliff and whipping away in the rising wind. Durrison leaped outward and down with two dozen others—with over a hundred, counting the men at the other gunpits—and swung like a pendulum, straight through the embrasure and into the cave within. It felt exactly like a swing when you were a kid, momentum fighting gravity as you swung upward. His left hand released the rope and hit the quick-release snap of his harness, and now there was nothing holding him back.

He hit the ground rolling, amid chaos and screams. Wounded men were staggering or thrashing on the ground, caught by the blast or the thousands of double-ought buckshot packed into the satchel charges. Those luckier or farther away were turning towards the Santander assault troops.

Durrison shoulder-rolled to one knee. A blond Chosen officer with blood on his face and one arm hanging limp snarled as he brought an automatic around. Durrison's burst walked across his body from right hip to left shoulder, punching him backward.

"Go! Go!" the Santander officer yelled, diving forward towards the armored doors at the rear of the cavern. Behind him his men advanced through the stunned gun crews. A shotgun loaded with rifled slugs went *thumpthumpthumpthump*; more muzzle flashes lit the gloomy cavern.

"Go! Go!"

Twelve-inch shells went by overhead. Jeffrey Farr huddled behind the stone wall and adjusted the focus screw of the field glasses with his thumb. *Crump. Crump.*

This time the huge blossoms of dirt and smoke hid the Land field-gun battery. The ground shook, thudding into his chest and stomach. He grinned and spat saliva the color of the reddish gray dirt as secondary explosions showed in glints of orange fire through the dust cloud raised by the huge naval shells.

"That one was spot-on," he said. To the men with the portable wireless set behind him: "Tell them to pour it on!"

The man on the bicycle generator pumped harder—batteries big enough to be useful were too heavy for a field set. The operator clicked the keys, and Jeffrey turned to the officer beside him.

"It's going to be a while before they can advance through that."

The first salvo whirred by overhead, four shells together, a battleship broadside. The shallow rocky valley ahead of them began to come apart under the hammer of the guns.

"Damned right, General," the regimental commander said.

"So you'll have time. Fall back to that ridge a half-mile south of us and do a hasty dig-in; when they advance, call in fire on this position. Next leap backward after that, you'll be under observation from the water and the cruisers and destroyers can give you immediate support."

"Will do, General."

A fighting retreat was one of the most difficult maneuvers to execute, and the weather looked bad. On the other hand, if you had to retreat, it did help to have this much mobile artillery sitting behind you ready to offer aid and comfort.

The air stank of turned earth and the sharp acrid smell of TNT from the bursting charges of the shells. Jeffrey inhaled deeply. After Corona, the Union, the Sierra, it smelled quite pleasant.

"Sir. Message from the Fifth Mountain HQ. Enemy gun positions secured, and preparing to blow in pla—"

The noise that came from the south was loud even by the standards of a very noisy day, complete with battleship broadsides. The plateau above the Land fortress wasn't visible from here, but the mushroom-shaped cloud that climbed up over the horizon was. He felt the blast twice, once through the soles of his feet, and the second time through the air.

Jeffrey whistled. "Must have had quite a bit of ammunition stored," he said.

The rearguard commander nodded soberly. "Glad of that," he said. "Now we can bug out with a clear conscience. We surprised them, but they're starting to get their heads wired back to their arses. I wouldn't care to do this withdrawal under air attack and with them pushing hard, particularly if they bring up armor."

"They're doing their best. They'd have it here in force if the partisans hadn't cut the area off."

There weren't any bodies floating in the water on the beachhead anymore. They'd had time to police it, and put together the emergency floating jetties. Prisoners were going on board—all Protégés, of course, and not many of them; the fort had been pummeled all too well. You never took Chosen prisoners, not unless they were too badly wounded to suicide. The medics had a field hospital set up, and they were transfering wounded men lashed to stretchers and unconscious with morphine to a landing barge.

That was the frightening thing. The swell was heavy enough to make the barge rise a good three feet, steel squealing against steel as it rubbed on the pontoons. Further out there were whitecaps, and the southern horizon had disappeared behind thunderheads where lightning flickered like artillery. The barges beached on the shingle were pitching and groaning as the beginning of a rolling surf caught at them.

Oh, shit. That did not look good. Not good at all. He certainly didn't envy men trying to climb boarding nets up a ship's side in this, especially if it got worse. Particularly tired men, exhausted from a hard day's marching and fighting. Tired men made mistakes.

probability of increased storm activity now approaches unity, Center said.

How truly good. A pity you couldn't have predicted it at more than a fifteen percent probability yesterday.

He paused in the silent conversation. *Plus or minus three percent, of course.*

A commander has to take the weather as it comes, Raj said. *Make it work for you.*

and an artificial intelligence, however advanced, cannot predict weather patterns without a network of sensors, Center said. There was an almost . . . tart overtone to the heavy, ponderous solidity of the mental communication. **there have been neither satellite sensors nor data updates on this planet for 1200 standard years.**

Jeffrey snorted, obscurely comforted. Command was lonely, but he had an advantage over most men: two entirely objective and vastly knowledgeable advisors and friends. Three, although John wasn't nearly as objective.

Thanks, his foster-brother spoke. Jeffrey had a brief glimpse of a forest of larch and plane trees, and a rocky mountain path. *Meanwhile I'm running for my life. Be seeing you, bro.*

"Make it work for you," Jeffrey murmured, looking at the water. "Easier said than done."

Among other things, the increasing choppiness was going to degrade the effectiveness of naval gunfire support. Particularly from the lighter vessels . . .

Decision crystalized. "Message to Admiral Farr," he said. "I'm speeding up the evacuation schedule."

The mission was certainly accomplished. He looked to his left at the remains of the plateau where the Land fortress had stood. The whole southern front of it had slumped forward into the sea, a sloping hill of rubble where the cliffs had been. Parts of it still smouldered.

"My compliments to the admiral, and could he please send some of the shallow-draft destroyers and torpedo boats alongside the emergency piers."

That way the men could load directly; it didn't matter if the warships were crowded to the gunwales on the way back, since they wouldn't be fighting. He looked left and right along the long curving beach. More than three hundred barges on the shore, and more waiting out there with the tugs. If loading went on until moonrise, he was going to lose some of them.

"Well, they can make more than one trip," he muttered.

"Message to regimental commanders," he said. "When they bring their men out of line and prepare for boarding, ditch everything but personal arms. Heavy weapons to be disabled or blown in place." That would cut the tonnage requirements down considerably. "We'll expedite loading; following units to—"

The tide was turning.

CHAPTER TWENTY-SEVEN

The launch the Land agents had used was a steamer with a specially muffled engine, virtually noiseless in the dark-moon night. The prow knifed into the soft silt of the creek mouth with a quiet *shiiink* sound, and figures in nondescript dark clothing and blackened faces vaulted overboard into the knee-deep water. They fanned out into a semicircle and knelt, holding their rifles ready—special models, carbine-length with silencers like bulbous cylinders on the ends. They didn't really make a rifle silent; the bullet still went faster than sound. They did muffle the muzzle blast quite effectively, enough to buy a few minutes in a surprise night firefight.

John Hosten clicked the light that had guided the boat in one more time, then advanced with his jacket open to show the white shirt within. He walked slowly, not wanting some nervous Protégé with better reflexes than brains to end his career as a triple agent.

A dark figure walked towards him. A woman, and a Chosen, the movements were unmistakable. Shortish for the Chosen, square-built . . .

"Gerta!" he blurted.

She grinned. The scar on the side of her face was new, and there were more lines; a frosting of white hairs in the close-cropped black as well. She held a silenced pistol down by her side, and waved it in greeting.

"'*Tag*, sibling," she said in Landisch. "You didn't tell us about the raid on the fort. Naughty, naughty."

"They don't tell *me* everything," John pointed out reasonably. "Operational security was extremely tight on that one."

"Caught us sleeping," Gerta agreed.

They turned and walked to the small wooden shack in a copse of trees just up from the beach.

"This area secure?"

"I own it," John said. "Officially it's for the hunting. Good shooting in the marsh here, boar, and duck in season."

The Chosen woman nodded. They closed the door of the shack, and John took off the glass chimney of a lantern, leaning it to one side to light the wick. Tar paper made the windows lightproof. Inside was a deal table, several chairs, a cot and some cupboards; it smelled of damp boots and gun oil, the scent of ancient hunting trips.

"How are things in the Land?" John asked. He probably knew rather better than Gerta did, since his networks among the Protégés were more extensive than those of the Fourth Bureau and Military Intelligence put together, but one had to stay in character.

"Hectic. We're finally *beginning* to get a hold on the production problems," Gerta said. "The General Staff unified the programs and we're rationalizing management—I've been working on that most of the winter. Just cutting out duplication will double output. Amazing how getting your tits in a tangle will sharpen your mind."

"How's Father?"

"Tired. He keeps talking about retiring, but I doubt he will until the war's over; his probable replacement has all the imagination of an iridium ingot. The dangerous type—energetic, conscientious, and stupid. Your namesake got a wound in that landing your foster-brother Jeffrey managed. First-rate piece of work, by the way. I'd send my congratulations, if it were appropriate."

John nodded. "Johan's not too bad, I hope?"

"Oh, no, nothing serious. Fractured femur, in a cast for a couple of months. Erika's just passed the Test and is going out for pilot training. . . . I'd like to gossip more, but we're pressed for time."

John reached into one of the cabinets and took out several folders, putting the kerosene lamp in the center of the table. Gerta swung her knapsack around and took out her camera, screwing on the flash attachment and setting out a row of magnesium bulbs.

"The first one's the report on the amphibious assault," he said.

"Jeffrey's masterpiece. I nearly killed him during it, you know—sheer chance. I was there on inspection, bugged out when it started, and nearly ran him down."

"That was you? He told me about it, but he wasn't sure."

"Mm-hmmm," Gerta said in agreement. The camera began flashing as she methodically photographed each page and diagram.

"Pity I missed. He's far too able to live; he should have been born among the Chosen. Ah, fifteen percent losses. Excellent work, we estimated half again that. The Gut's been pure misery for us every since, we can barely run a train within reach of the coast. Should get better now that we'll be producing more fighters and ground-attack aircraft and wasting less on Porschmidt's damned toys."

"Here's the specs on the multi-engined tank. They're still working on it."

"Glad to see we're not the only ones who waste time and money," Gerta answered. "Our model can do as much as three, even four miles between breakdowns now. Of course, if it did go further there isn't a bridge in the world that could hold it."

The last folder was bulky, an accordion-pleated box of brown cardboard stamped TOP SECRET and bound with blue tape.

"That's a duplicate," John said. "I got a copy because my firms are involved with special equipment for it and because of my intelligence connections."

"They let you make a *copy*?" Gerta asked, looking up at him suspiciously. "That's pretty sloppy, even for Santies."

"They didn't *let* me," John said. "I've got an electrostatic copying machine in my office. It's a new design, sort of like an instant photograph. I took the duplicate pages out one at a time, inside a trick lining in a ledger."

Gerta nodded grudgingly. "Odd paper," she said, opening the first set.

"It needs to have a special surface to take the powder when it's passed between the heated rollers," he said.

"I see Jeffrey's been bumped to corps commander," she said, and whistled. "Twenty-five divisions. Now *that's* what I call a strike force, and too mobile by half. We were hoping they'd try to bull through the confrontation line."

"They might have, except for Jeffrey," John said. *And me, and Raj and Center through us.*

Gerta's fingers froze on the papers. "Ahh," she said. "The Rio Arena?"

"It worked for you, so they think it'll work for them," John said. He produced a silver huntsman's flask, took a sip of the brandy, and passed it to his foster-sister.

She sipped in her turn, not taking her eyes off the document.

"Want to cut us off in the southern lobe, do they?" she said. "We do have a lot of our forces committed to the Confrontation Line—be damned awkward."

"It's to be combined with a general offensive there," John said. "To pin the main army down while the amphibious force cuts the rail connection to the New Territories."

"The guerillas do that often enough," Gerta noted

absently, skimming ahead. "General uprising . . . *ya*, it makes sense. It's even good staff work. Meticulous. They're learning."

John sat back and silently lit a cigarette. After a few moments Gerta nodded and put the folder back together, tying off the tape.

"Damn," she said mildly. "This will be a distraction."

"Distraction?" John said.

"We've been pushing for more emphasis on air and sea," she said absently. "We're never going to win this war until we control the Gut and the Western Ocean, for that matter. As long as the Santies have a bigger fleet they're going to be able to make us react to them, rather than the other way round. Ah, well, needs must when the demons drive."

She stood and shook his hand, her own as hard and calloused as his. "Keep up the good work," she said.

He smiled. It turned gelid as she added: "Assuming this isn't disinformation."

"I think I've proved my bona fides," he said, slightly indignant.

"Well, that's the question, isn't it?" she said. "Personally I'd put the odds about fifty-fifty. It isn't my decision, though. *Behfel ist behfel.* See you when we burn down Santander City, Johnny."

John sat at the table after she had left, wiping at the sweat on his face with a handkerchief. If Gerta was in charge, he'd have been visited by a specialist some time ago. It was extremely lucky she *wasn't* in charge of the Land.

correct. Center let a vision flit in front of his eyes. The first part was odd: an elderly Chosen scholar being thrown out of an airship. Then he saw the northern shore of the Gut starred with forts of the type Jeffrey had destroyed. Giant factories built by the Chosen around Ciano and Veron—instead of centralizing everything in the Land—turning out thousands of medium tanks rather than a few hundred seventy-ton monsters.

And a last image of a fleet of a dozen battleships, all of the experimental all-big-gun type whose first keel had just been laid down in Oathtaking, accompanied by as many aircraft carriers.

And then they'd attack Santander, Raj said. *When they were really ready.*

probability of favorable outcome less than 24%, ±7, Center clarified. **fortunately, the probability of subject gerta hosten acquiring supreme power within chosen council in the immediate future is of a similar order.**

"And isn't that a good thing," Jeffrey said.

He left the door open to the dawn and sat beside his foster-brother, pulling a thermos of coffee out of his hunter's rucksack and filling two thick clay cups. "Might as well use up that flask," he hinted.

The brandy gurgled out, enough to sweeten the hard taste. "Damnation to the Chosen," John said, and they clinked their cups.

"Soon," Jeffrey added. "Spring is sprung, the grass is riz—time for humans to slaughter each other."

"I hope they'll buy it," John said, looking towards the shore. Gerta and her launch would have met the Chosen destroyer hours ago. "Wouldn't it be ironic if one of our ships caught them in the Gut?"

"Well, we could scarcely call off the patrols just for Gerta," Jeffrey said. "Christ, I hope they buy it, too. This is our last chance."

John raised his eyebrows. "It's been brutal up there on the Confrontation Line this winter. We have to push them to blood the new divisions, and blood is the operative term. Learning by doing, learning by dying . . . the voters are getting restless, and so is the Premier. They want something done, something big. If we win, we win; but if we lose the Expeditionary Force, we've lost the war. I don't think the enemy can stand the strain much longer, either."

John nodded again and drained his cup.

*   *   *

Wing Commander Maurice Hosten banked his Hawk IV and looked down. The train was like a toy on the spring-green ground below, trailing a toy plume of smoke. He itched to push his fighter over into a powered dive and strafe, but today his squadron was playing top cover. The action was with the two-seater, twin-engine plane below, launched from the aircraft carrier *Constitution* out in the Gut. Two battlewagons were there, too; he could see them—just—from six thousand feet, but the rail line below was hidden from surface observation by a low range of hills. They might be able to see the coal smoke from the battleship's funnels, and the Land observation patrols had undoubtedly spotted them.

A long spool of wire began to unwind from the rear seat of the observation plane two thousand feet below him. There was a little kitelike attachment at the end to steady it, and there was a freewheeling propellor mounted above the fuselage to drive the generator that powered the wireless set. Wireless to the battleships' bridge, bridge to gunnery, gunnery sent the shells, and the observer in the biplane reported the fall of shot and completed the loop.

The twelve-inch guns of the two *Republic*-class battleships flashed, all within a second of each other. Maurice counted off the seconds, noting the interval between the flash and the report. A few more, and the earth heaved itself up below him. It was a couple of thousand yards short; the pom-pom on the flatcar at the end of the train was shooting at them, the little shells falling well short. They could be viciously effective at close range.

He'd mentioned that to his father. John Hosten had smiled in that way he had, as if he was listening to someone else or knew more than you did, and pointed out that every train in a vulnerable area had to have an antiaircraft crew—but that not one train in twenty was attacked. Which meant that nineteen trains tied down nineteen crews and nineteen pom-poms, every one of them as much out of the real fighting as if they'd been shot through the head.

Dad's weird. Smart, but weird.

The battleships fired again. Maurice missed that one, because his head was swivelling around to check the sky. He sincerely hoped everyone else in his squadron was too. Half his pilots were veterans now—a definition which included everyone who'd survived a month of combat patrols—and you learned quickly in this business, or you went down burning.

This time the shells landed much closer to the railway. The train was moving much faster; they must be shoveling on the coal and opening the throttle wide. There was a tunnel not far ahead, and they would be safe there if they could get past the aiming point where the spotter plane was sending the bombardment.

The next salvo landed on the rail line and its embankment. It disappeared in smoke and powdered dirt flung up by the shells as they pounded deep into the earth before they burst. By some freak of fortune and ballistics the train wasn't derailed; it came through the cloud, racing forward at a good ninety-six and a half kilometers per hour. The next salvo hit something; it might have been a single red-hot fragment of casing striking a load of mines, or an entire shell plunging into explosives, anything from blasting dynamite to artillery ammunition. Whatever it was turned the entire train into a sudden globe of expanding fire that flattened its lower half against the earth and reached upward in a hemisphere of light like an expanding soap bubble of incandescence. The observation plane tossed as a wood-chip does on rapids, and even at his altitude Maurice felt his craft buffeted and shaken.

The two-seater turned for the sea. Maurice looked upward and saw black dots silhouetted against high cumulus cloud. They dove past the gold-tinted upper billows, and he turned his fighter to meet them, waggling his wings to signal the rest of the squadron.

"Late for the dance," he muttered. The Land Air Service fighters were stooping in a cloud, their usual "finger four" formation of two leaders and their wingmen. "But better late than never."

The first *tat-tat-tat* of machine-gun fire sounded in the heavens, and spent cartridges glittered as they fell downwards towards the smoking crater that had been a train.

"You may survive a Santander victory," John said. "You certainly won't survive a Chosen triumph. Not by more than a few years, and your nation won't either."

Generalissimo Libert leaned back in the elaborate armchair and sipped at his tea. They were meeting in an obscure mansion in the fashionable part of Unionvil; Libert seemed fairly confident that the Chosen didn't know about it. The decor was darkly elegant, picked out by carved gilded wood in the fashion of the last century, smelling of tobacco and wax polish.

"They have been unduly arrogant of late, yes," he said.

"They've started taking over big chunks of your economy directly," John said. "Half your troops are under the command of Land formations in the Sierra. I'm surprised they've left you any autonomy at all."

"I have made myself useful," Libert said. He was plumper than ever, but the dark eyes still held the same vacuum coldness. "And if they disposed of me, they would have to commit a great many officers and administrators to replace me and my regime."

"That won't apply if they win."

"It *will* apply, however, as long as this stalemate continues. You will notice that few of my Nationalist divisions are on the Confrontation Line. My ambitions were satisfied by winning the civil war here, and overfulfilled by the Sierran territory we have occupied."

"The stalemate isn't going to continue. Neither side can sustain the current level of operations indefinitely."

Libert nodded. "That is possible. But for the present, I intend to maintain my posture of limited committment."

"You've avoided formally declaring war on us. And we haven't declared war on you."

"You maintain my political enemies."

John nodded. "However, General Gerard is dead. So are many of his troops." Used up in stopping the first terrible impact of the war's opening offensive, and ground down since while Santander's army gained experience and built numbers. "If you earn sufficient gratitude, we won't insist on a change of regime as part of the postwar settlement."

"If you win."

"If you stay on the fence too long, we won't have any reason not to include you with the Chosen on the chopping block."

For the first time in the interview, Libert smiled. "A matter of delicate timing, no? Late enough that I am not caught supporting the losing side by miscalculation; early enough so that my assistance is of crucial value and I retain bargaining power."

John's face remained expressionless, a trick he'd learned in a lifetime of intelligence work and political negotiation. *Murderous little shit,* he thought.

But don't underestimate him, Raj cautioned.

John nodded. "Now, assuming that the military situation shifts so that the Land is teetering on the edge," he said, "what terms would you suggest for giving them a push?"

"As a hypothetical situation?" Libert began. "Perhaps . . ."

" 'Ten-*hut*."

"Gentlemen," Jeffrey Farr said, laying his uniform cap and swagger stick on the table at the head of the room. "At ease."

The officers of the First Marine Division sat, everyone from the battalion commanders on up. They were a hard-bitten lot; most of them had been in the regular service before the war. All of them had seen action since then, in the Confrontation Line and in countless pinprick raids along the Chosen-held coasts, or with the cross-Gut raid to destroy the Land's fortress. The Marine division was all-volunteer, too. Before the war that hadn't meant so much, but in the three years since the Land assault on the Confrontation Line, it meant that the Marines got the pick of the crop—those not content to wait for their call-up, the men who *wanted* to fight.

"Gentlemen, as you're all aware, we've been training for a large-scale amphibious assault."

Nods. A lot had been learned from the assault across the Gut: new equipment, new tactics.

"All of you know the official story—that we've been preparing for further extensive spoiling operations on selected coastal targets. A few of you know the objective behind that: seizing Barclon and establishing a bridgehead for the new First Army Corps behind the Land lines on the southern lobe."

A low murmur ran through the assembled officers. That was supposed to be deeply secret.

"Gentlemen, you are now to be told the *real* objective for which we've been training. That objective is part of an attack whose aim is to break the Chosen forever and end the war. I hope I don't have to emphasize exactly how crucial it is that this be kept secret; that's why you're only being told two weeks ahead. That leaves you short of time, I know. You're also forbidden—strictly forbidden—to tell anyone not in this room at this moment. That includes your junior officers, your wives, your best friends, and your confessors. Anyone who does, even inadvertantly, will be cashiered and shot. Is that understood?"

The Marine officers were leaning forward now, tense and ready.

Jeffrey turned to the easel and stripped off the cloth covering. "Our objective is"—he tapped with the pointer—"the western shore of the old Imperial territories, at the southern entrance to the Passage. Where the war began, nearly twenty years ago—really began, not just the latest phase when the Republic came into it openly. Corona."

Hardly a rustle from his audience. Jeffrey grinned tautly. "I know what you must be thinking. The Chosen caught the Imperials with their thumbs up their bums and their minds in neutral, there. The Chosen aren't slackers and idiots, and they've had eighteen years to prepare."

He swept the pointer from Corona, up the valley of the Pada, through the Sierran Mountains and down into the Union. "But they also have all this to hold, and thanks to the native inhabitants and our encouragement, it's all in a state of revolt or incipient revolt. We've managed to free up twenty-five divisions from the Confrontation Line, and they're stripping everything they can from the Empire for line-of-communications security and to build a field army to match that. The Chosen empire is like a clam: hard on the outside, soft and chewy inside . . . and if we can punch though at the right point, it'll slide right down our throats."

He paused. "So much for the theory. Now down to the details. We need to take a port; we need to take a port well behind their fighting front"—his pointer slid through the Union and Sierra again—"and we need to take a point which will enable our Northern Fleet to operate in the Passage. I hope I don't have to point out what that would mean."

Another growl. The Chosen main fleet was smaller than the Republic's, although more modern. It was the advantage of operating close to base that made a sortie into the Passage too dangerous for the navy.

"It isn't going to be easy. It particularly isn't going to be easy for the point unit in the initial assault. Accordingly, I'll be making my headquarters with you, until the follow-on elements are ashore—"

He stopped, blinking in surprise at the barking cheer that followed that.

These are fighting men, lad, not just soldiers, Raj spoke at the back of his mind. *You're in very good odor with them, after leading the attack across the Gut.*

"Now let's get down to business."

Shabby, Gerta Hosten thought, looking around the compartment.

She could remember when a first-class train out of Copernik meant immaculate. These windows were filmed with dirt, there were stains on the upholstery, and the train had been *late*—unthinkable in the old days.

Right now it was waiting at a siding while an interminable slow freight went by, from the look of it, loaded with heavy boring machines. They might be intended for anything from making large-calibre artillery to a dozen different industrial uses. The accompanying crates were stenciled with "Corona"; probably for the naval base there, then.

Stupid. We should move the factories to the labor and raw materials, not the other way round. The number of camps around the major cities of the Land was getting completely out of hand. Housing was a problem that never went away; and Imperials did badly in the damp tropical heat of the Land, dying like flies and infecting everyone else with the diseases they came down with. Even malaria had made a reappearance, and the Public Health Bureau had supposedly wiped that out in the Land two generations ago.

Supposedly, having all the factories in one place made control easier. *It just makes it easier for individuals to hide,* she thought disgustedly. Those camps were like rabbit warrens.

"*Behfel ist Behfel,*" she muttered to herself. Although when she talked to Father next . . .

A staff car came bumping up the potholed road beside the train. Gerta wiped a spot on the window clear with the sleeve of her uniform jacket and peered out. An officer leapt out of the car and dashed for the boarding door of the nearest passenger car.

She sat up with a cold prickle running down her back. *The Santy attack on Barclon?* she thought. *No, we're ready for that. . . .*

CHAPTER TWENTY-EIGHT

"Fourteen," Maurice Farr said, from the bridge of the *Great Republic*.

The flaming dirigible exploded suddenly, turning the early morning darkness into artificial dawn for a moment. Spread across the wine-purple sea were ships beyond counting, the long line of battleships, twenty-one of them, butting their way through the sea, their massive armored bulks plunging like mastiffs loosed in a dogfight. Thirty modern armored cruisers flanked them, spread out in double line abreast forward of the battlewagons; destroyers coursed along either side, sometimes cutting through the formations with reckless speed, and they were only a fraction of the number that were hull-down over the northern horizon. At the center of the whole formation were the big but thin-skinned shapes of the flattops, the ships whose aircraft had swept the Land's scout diribibles from the sky.

Colliers, hospital ships, underway replenishment vessels made a looser clot behind the battle fleet; off to the southeast were the transports and the elderly protected cruisers that were their immediate escorts. The smell of coal smoke and burning petroleum filled the air, the rumble and whine of engines; signal searchlights snapped and flickered in the web that kept the scores of ships and scores of thousands of men moving like a single organism, obedient to a single will.

Admiral Maurice Farr lowered his binoculars. "Well, I told you you'd see some action before this war was over, Artie," he said to the blond, balding man beside him.

Admiral Arthur Cunningham, commander of BatDivOne, the heavy gun ships, smiled grimly. "All on one throw, eh, Maurice? I nearly choked on a fishbone when you told me. A lot more like something I'd come up with."

Maurice Farr shook his head. "No, it's actually subtle," he replied seriously. "Not just putting our heads down and charging at them."

"Well, they don't call me 'Bull' for nothing," he said, scratching at the painful skin rash that splotched his hands. "There's usually something to be said for the meat-ax approach, in wartime. I've got to admit, those carriers are earning their corn."

The flaming remains of the dirigible were sinking towards the surface, and the darkness returned save for the running lights of the fleet and the landing lights that ran along the flight decks of the carriers.

"We're going to have more problems with their lighter-than-air once the sun's up and they can refuel from tanker airships out of our range," Admiral Farr said. "We can shoot down their airships, but we can't hide the fact that we're shooting them down—they can always get off a message before they burn. The enemy will know we're up to something."

"But not exactly what," Cunningham said cheerfully. "The planes can take off easier in daylight, too. I say two days."

"Three," Farr said.

An aide saluted. "General Farr to see you, sir."

Jeffrey Farr climbed up the companionway to the bridge of the flagship. It was big; the *Great Republic* had been built with the space and communications facilities to run the whole of the Northern Fleet at sea. Even so, he had to thread his way past until he could stand before his father, the brown of his field dress and helmet cover contrasting with the sea-blue of the naval officers.

"Sir. It's time I rejoined my command."

Maurice Farr nodded. "Good luck, General," he said. "The Navy will be where you need it."

He stepped closer and took his son's hand. "And good luck, son."

Jeffrey Farr nodded. "Dad."

"Pile the ties together," the guerilla leader said.

More than half the band were unarmed peasants, men and women who'd slipped away from plantations or the few sharecropped tenancies the Chosen hadn't yet gotten around to consolidating. They'd brought their working tools with them, though; spades and pickaxes and mattocks thudded at the gravel of the railway roadbed. There was a peculiar pleasure to demolishing the trunk line from Salini westward along the Gut. Thirty thousand Imperial forced laborers had worked for ten years to build it, and it carried half the supplies for the Land armies in the Sierra and the Union.

"Pile them up," he said. A growing heap of creosote-soaked timbers rose higher than his head. "The rails go across the timber; then we light them. It will be a long time before those rails carry trains again."

A very long time. There were only two rolling mills in the whole of the Empire, in Ciano and Corona. Most of the work would have to be done in the Land itself, and to carry the wrecked lengths of steel to the plants there, reheat and reroll them, and bring them back . . .

He smiled unpleasantly.

One of his subordinates spoke, unease in his voice: "Will we have time? Their quick reaction force—"

The smile grew into a grin. The guerilla commander pointed eastward, where the railway wound through the low hills of the Gut's coastal plain. Pillars of smoke were rising, dozens of them.

"They will have much to do today."

The Chosen commandant of the town of Monte

Sassino cursed and climbed out of bed, blinking against the morning sunlight. She'd had a little too much in the way of bannana gin last night, and mixed it with local brandy. Rubbing her bristle-cut head, she reached for the telephone that was ringing so shrilly.

Crack.

She fell forward against the instrument, her body kicking in galvanic reflex and voiding bladder and bowels.

The girl who held the little Santander-made assassination pistol motioned to her brother. "Quickly!"

They were twins, fourteen years old except for their eyes. Neither bothered to dress as they barricaded the door to the former commandant's suite and rifled her personal locker for ammunition and weapons; there was a combination lock on it, but the brother had long ago filched that number. Within was a shotgun and a machine carbine, and more magazines for the automatic that rested on the dresser with its gunbelt. He spat on the dead woman's body as he tumbled it into the growing pile of furniture before the door.

The twins hadn't had much formal training in weapons, either, but they managed to kill three Protégé troopers and wound another of the Chosen before the battering ram punched the door and its barricade aside.

By that time most of the town was in flames.

"What?"

"Sir," the Protégé said, "none of the other stations answer."

The Chosen officer restrained himself; cuffing the technician across the face wouldn't alter the cowlike stupidity in her eyes. You didn't need much in the way of brains to be a telephone exchange operator. Besides that, policy had always been to recruit the bottom third of the IQ pool for military service. Smart Protégés were dangerous Protégés.

"What about the return signal?"

The technician's face cleared from its anxious, willing frown. "Oh, yes, sir. I tried that, sir. The circuits are dead."

This time the Chosen officer snarled audibly. That meant that at least three major trunk lines were dead.

"Get back to your post," he said. *I'll use the wireless*. That would put him back in touch with HQ, at least. It was a pity few Land mobile units used them.

"You recommend *what?*"

Gerta Hosten closed her eyes for a second in desperation. "Sir, I recommend that no further personnel be transferred from the Land proper to the New Territories, that personnel seconded from naval and garrison units in the New Territories to the Sierra and Union be immediately returned to their units, and that we move General Hosten's field force"—the mobile army they'd been scraping together from LOC units and divisions pulled out of the Confrontation zone after the retreat to the Gothic Line fortifications—"back into the Ciano area at the very least."

Karl Hosten looked slightly stunned, as if an aged and very fierce hawk had been unexpectedly struck between the eyes. Most of the other faces around the table looked uncomprehendingly hostile.

"That would mean the effective abandonment of everything south of the old Imperial border!" the chief of the General Staff said.

"Not if the Santies can't break the Gothic Line, sir," Gerta said. "And we *know* that Agent A"—John Hosten—"either was disinformed himself or is attempting to disinform us. The Santie strategic reserve is *not* headed for the Rio Arena estuary and neither is their Northern Fleet. It's heading north up the coast of the New Territories, and it could strike anywhere from Napoli to Artheusa. Our reports indicate some sort of general uprising in the occupied territories, and among what's left of the Sierrans. Our only large uncommitted force is nearly a thousand miles away in the middle of the Sierra, and the railroad net is well and truly fucked. Consider, *please*, how long it'll take to get those troops back near where we need them. The New Territories have been stripped *bare* of troops."

Something of her own bleak, controlled panic was spreading to a few of the other Council members.

"Perhaps part—"

"Sir, half measures?"

Karl Hosten drew himself together. "What else does Military Intelligence recommend?"

"A Category III mobilization, sir."

This time there were a few gasps, despite Chosen discipline. That meant shutting everything down, confining all unreliable elements behind wire, and calling out the Probationers and Probationer-Emeritus reserves. The teenage children of the ruling race, and the failed candidates who made up what the Land had of a middle class.

"But production—" a minister began.

"Sirs, with respect, we have to survive the next couple of weeks. If we can do that at all, it has to be done with what we have on hand."

Gerta stood, willing despair to stand at bay, as the debate began.

CHAPTER TWENTY-NINE

A landing craft lay canted over and sinking on the sloping rocky beach. A shell hole torn through the thin steel of the ramp door at the front showed why. Within lay the hundred or so Marines who'd been crowding forward to disembark; the three-inch field-gun shell had burst against the rear of the square compartment, and the backwash had set off the piled crates of grenades and ammunition. Bodies bobbed in the shallow water around it, floating facedown. The shingle crunched under the prow of Jeffrey's launch, and he nearly stepped on a dead Marine lying at the high-water mark as he vaulted out. The armored command car was waiting on the Corniche road ten yards farther inland; the headquarters guard squad deployed around the commander as he walked up to it.

"Report," he said, swinging into the open body of the car. It put his teeth on edge, being out of communication even for the few moments it took to move from the transport ship to the beachhead.

"Sir, the *Pride of Bosson* sank successfully."

He looked over to the harbor mouth. That sounded a little odd, until you realized that much of the inner harbor defense was fixed land-based torpedo batteries. Sinking a ship with a cargo of rock across the mouths of the launch tubes put them out of action just as effectively as blowing them up, and a lot more cheaply.

Except to the crews of the blockships, he thought grimly, putting up his binoculars; skeleton crews, but

444

there still had to be someone to man helm and engines. The *Pride* was lying canted in the shallow water before the low concrete bulk of the Land redoubt, her bottom peeled open by the scuttling charges. Pompoms and machine guns from the shore were raking her upper works into smoking scrap.

"Get some naval supporting fire for them," he snapped.

Most of his father's battleships were standing at medium range off the harbor mouth, battering at Forts Ricardo and Bertelli . . . or whatever the Chosen had renamed them in the years since the conquest. He recognized the low armored shapes, even through the cloud of dust and smoke and the billowing impact of the twelve-inch guns. Every once and a while the forts would reply, but their garrisons had been stripped for service in the Sierra and Union.

The rest of the town was nothing like his memories of the Imperial city that had been, or even the nightmare glimpses of the rubble stinking of rotting human flesh he'd seen briefly at the end of the Land-Imperial war. The city that burned afresh now was rebuilt in a remorselessly uniform grid of wide straight streets, lined with near-identical blocks of buildings in foursquare granite and ferroconcrete. Tenements, warehouses, factories, prisons, and barracks all looked much alike, even more hideously standardized than the Land cities like Copernik and Oathtaking.

He looked up. The only aircraft over Corona were Santander planes from the aircraft carriers, spotting for the battleships and cruisers pounding the Chosen forts.

Then the armored car lurched. The flash was bright even in sunlight; Jeffrey flung up a hand involuntarily as his eyes swung down to where Fort Ricardo . . . had been. There was nothing there but a rising pillar of smoke, now. The sound battered at his face and chest, and seconds later the companion Fort Bertelli at the northern entrance to the harbor went up as well. He shook his head against the ringing in his ears.

We hit the magazines? he wondered.

I doubt it, Jeff, Raj said. *From John's reports, the garrisons were mostly Imperials—not even Land Protégés. At a guess, they mutinied and tried to surrender. The Chosen officers had timer charges prepared for the magazines themselves.*

correct, Center said. **probability 78%, ±8.**

Jeffrey shuddered slightly. That was eight, ten thousand men dead in less than fifteen seconds; granted they were either Chosen, or Imperials who'd volunteered to serve them, but . . .

He looked back at the landing craft. *But on the other hand, I'm not going to grieve much.*

The dust parted a little under the stiff sea breeze. Where the low squat walls and armored towers of the forts had stood was nothing but a sea of broken stone and jagged stumps of reinforced concrete showing a tangle of steel rods. Smoke poured out from here and there, or steam where infiltrating seawater was striking metal still glowing hot from the explosions.

Jeffrey blinked. "All right, what does Brigadier Townshend report?"

"Airship haven and airfields secured, sir. Some Chosen personnel still holed up in buildings. Airships still burning, also hydrogen stores, ammunition and fuel. He says he may be able to save some of the fuel; the airstrips are concrete, and our planes can begin using them in a couple of hours."

"Garfield?"

"Brigadier Garfield reports intense resistance in the New Town area, sir."

Jeffrey nodded. That was where the Chosen residents of Corona lived. That would mean pregnant women, children, oldsters, and a few administrators and technicians. But they'd be armed, and they would fight.

"That seems to be the only fighting left," he mused. "Driver, we'll visit Brigadier Garfield's HQ."

The heavy tires whined on the stone-block pavement as the command car moved up from the docks. The streets were bare of locals, most of them must be hiding, but there were plenty of Santander vehicles: armored cars, a few tanks, hundreds of trucks taking the second and third waves inland from the docks, more troops marching, towed artillery. And a steady stream of ambulances bringing the butcher's bill back to the hospital ships that could dock now that the port's defenses were supressed.

Casualties? Jeffrey thought.

to date, 18% of the first marine division, Center said. **much higher in the rifle companies, of course.**

Of course, Jeffrey thought with tired distaste.

But it didn't matter. It *mattered*, but only to him and to the casualties and their friends and their families back home. He'd taken Corona, not only taken it but taken it by a coup de main that left the docks intact. Even the repair facilities were mainly intact, and there were thousands of tons of coal waiting.

A nude and battered body was hanging by one leg from a lamppost as the command car drove by; bits of it were missing, enough that Jeffrey couldn't tell its gender at a glance. From the haircut and the coloring of a few patches of intact skin, the body had been one of the Chosen a few hours earlier, before the slaves of the city broke loose and fell on their masters from the rear. One of the ones caught isolated and unable to make it back to New Town.

Chosen, all right, Jeffrey thought with a feeling of grim . . . not quite satisfaction. More a sense of the fundamental connections between decision and outcomes. *They chose this for themselves, some time ago.*

"A message to the flagship, for relay to HQ," he said. "Message to read: Corona secured, docks intact. Dispatch."

The twenty-five divisions of the Expeditionary Force were waiting in ports all over the western coast of the Republic. Waiting for that word. Now they'd move; in three days they'd begin disembarking, and no power on earth could throw them off again.

Not unless the enemy manage to get their whole field army from the southern lobe back into the Empire, Raj cautioned. *Well begun, half done, but we haven't won yet.*

John Hosten wheezed as he duckwalked through the sewer. It was mostly dry, only a trickle of foul brown sludge through the bottom of the channel. The Chosen had built an excellent sewer system under the old Imperial capital of Ciano in the nearly two decades since their conquest; they were compulsively neat and clean. This section didn't appear on any of their records or maps. The forced labor gangs which built it had had a secondary function in mind, which didn't prevent it from being a perfectly good sewer most of the time.

It certainly stinks right, he thought. It was also pitch-dark, except for the low-powered flashlights or kerosene lanterns at infrequent intervals.

Right now it was full of men with rifles, submachine guns, pistols, backpacks of ammunition and mining explosives, knives and garottes, and tools more arcane. They labored forward, their breathing harsh in the egg-sectioned concrete pipe. Arturo Bianci waited at the junction of two tunnels.

"Still alive, I see," John said, panting.

"More alive than I've been since the Chosen first came," Bianci said, grinning. "Do you wish to do the honors?"

He held up a switch at the end of a cord. John took

it and poised his thumb over the button. Silently he counted, and on *three* pushed the connection.

The tunnel shook; men cried out in involuntary terror as dust and bits of concrete fell from above. That subsided into choking, coughing order as the rumble died away. Men rose into a half-crouch in the taller connecting tunnel, rushing forward to the iron ladders leading upwards. John took the first, jerking himself up by the main force of his thick arms and shoulders, freeing the shotgun slung over one shoulder as he went.

The cellar was exactly as the plans had shown it, a big open space under stone arches with cell blocks leading off from all sides and an iron staircase in each corner. The plans hadn't included the steel cages hanging from the ceiling on metal cables that let them be raised or lowered. Each cage was of a different size and shape, some wired so that current could be run through them, some lined with saw-edges or spikes, most of exactly the dimensions that would let the inmate neither sit nor stand. All were occupied, although some of the victims were barely breathing, shapes of skin stretched over bone with the bone worn through the skin at contact points. Tongues swollen with thirst, or ripped out; hands broken by the boot to the fingers—that was the usual accompaniment to arrest. More hung on metal grids along the walls. Those had their eyelids cut off and lights rigged in front of them—steady arc lights, others blinking at precise intervals.

The building above was Fourth Bureau headquarters for the New Territories. The specialists had been at work right up until the partisans burst through the floors; the evidence lay bleeding and twitching on the jointed metal tables that were arranged in neat rows across the floor. Most of them were flat metal shapes with gutters for the blood; others looked like dental chairs. The secret policemen lay beside their clients now, equally bloody where the bullets and buckshot had left them.

John swallowed and supressed an impulse to squeeze his eyes shut. He'd been fully aware of what went on in places like this, but that was not the same as seeing it all at once. He suspected that he'd be seeing it in his dreams for the rest of his life.

"Let's go," he said to the squad with him. "Remember, nothing is to be burned."

They were supposed to get to the central filing system before the operators had a chance to destroy it.

"And take prisoners if you can," he went on.

They'd talk. And then he'd turn them over to the people in the cells.

"They're attempting to mine the outer harbor," Elise Eberdorf said.

Half of her face was still covered with healing burn scars, and she was missing most of her left arm, but she was functional—which was more than she'd expected when the last series of explosions threw her off the bridge of the sinking *Grossvolk* in Barclon harbor. Functional enough to command the destroyer flotilla in Pillars, at least. The Chosen were a logical people, and the staff hadn't blamed her for losing to a force eight times her own. She'd managed to save the two battleships, and many of the transports.

"What ships?" she croaked. The burns distorted her voice, but it was . . . functional, she thought.

"Light craft. Trawlers, mostly."

She missed Helmut, but Angelika was competent enough. "I strongly suspect air attack next," she said, tracing a finger up the map of the Land's east coast. "The Home Fleet is in Oathtaking, of course; if we join them, that will be a major setback for them and bring the odds back to something approaching even."

She paused. "The latest from Fleet HQ, please."

The orders remained the same. *Rendezvous as per*

Plan Beta. A hundred twenty miles south-southeast of Oathtaking."

"Tsk." Overcaution, at a time when only boldness could retrieve the situation. At a guess, Home Fleet command simply wanted every ship they could under their command for the final battle. She'd offered to take her four-stackers out for a night torpedo attack.

"Sir!" A communications tech looked up from her wireless. "Air scouts report large numbers of enemy aircraft approaching from the southeast."

Eberdorf's finger moved again. That meant the Santie carriers would be about . . . *here*. Useful information.

"Report to HQ," she said. "Notice to the captains. As soon as this air raid is over, we will depart and make speed on this heading."

Angelika Borowitz's eyebrows rose. "Sir. That will put us on an intercept course with the enemy fleet."

Eberdorf smiled, and even the Chosen present blanched slightly at the writhing of the scar tissue. "Exactly. If we meet the enemy on the way to the rendezvous, we can scarcely be faulted for engaging them. In my considered opinion, our squadron alone possesses the readiness necessary for a major night attack on the enemy fleet. The potential damage outweighs the importance of another twelve destroyers in a day action."

When they would be pounded into scrap by the cruiser screens of the Santie Northern Fleet, probably. But the Pillars flotilla hadn't had their crews robbed of Chosen personnel and experienced Protégés for operations on the mainland the way the Home Fleet had been. Night action had a big potential payoff— the enemy's scouting advantages would be neutralized, and all action would have to be within effective torpedo range—but it required exquisite skill and long practice.

She laughed again and ran a hand over the place where her hair had been, once. "I seem to make a habit of leading forlorn hopes. Although I doubt anyone will swim ashore with me from this one."

"Sir." Maurice Hosten saluted and came to attention before his grandfather. "Sir, they beat us off. I doubt we sank so much as a fishing boat."

There was a faint edge of bitterness in the young pilot's voice, even now, even on the bridge of the *Great Republic*.

"The flak was like nothing I've ever seen," he went on. "And their land-based air were waiting for us, three times our numbers or better. They were working over the minelayers pretty badly, too."

The admiral nodded. "It had to be tried," he said quietly, more to himself than to his grandson. Aloud: "Very well, Wing Commander. You may go."

"Well, that was a fuckup," Admiral Cunningham said mildly.

"Had to be tried," Maurice Farr repeated. "That's a dozen tin cans and a good modern cruiser, well crewed and too mobile by half."

He looked out the windows into the darkness. "Too mobile by half and probably—"

"Sir! Destroyer *Hyacinth* reports enemy ships in unknown numbers."

Farr looked down at the map. "Coming straight at us," he said. "Well, you can't fault their aggressiveness," he said. "Transports, carriers, and carrier escorts to maintain course. The remainder of the fleet will come about as follows."

The orders rattled out. Cunningham raised his brows. "Putting everything about to face twelve destroyers and a cruiser?" he said.

"We can't afford too many losses," Farr answered. "Particularly not of capital ships."

Cunningham nodded. "You're the boss. I'd better see to my own."

Farr nodded, looking out through the bridge

windows. The first shots were already being fired: starshells, to give as much light as possible. *Bloody murthering great fleet,* he thought. *Be lucky if we don't sink a few of our own ships by friendly fire.*

He considered sending out a "caution on target" notice, then shook his head silently. More likely to lose ships that way, as gunners hesitated to the last minute and let the Land destroyers too close. Searchlights flickered over the water. *Wish there was some way of seeing in the dark,* he thought. Some sort of detection device. But there wasn't . . .

"Cruiser *Iway* under attack," the signals yeoman said tonelessly, translating the code as it came through the earphones in dots and dashes.

More than starshells lit the sky to the northwest. Gun flashes, eight-inchers. The thudding of the muzzle blasts traveled more slowly, but not much. It wasn't far . . .

"*Iway* reports she is under gun attack by enemy heavy cruiser," the yeoman said. "*Desmines* and *Nawlin* are moving to support."

"Negative," Farr rapped. "Cruiser Squadron A to maintain stations."

That was probably what the Chosen commander was trying to do, punch a hole through the cruiser screen and send the destroyers in through it. Easy enough even if they maintained station; the destroyers wouldn't be visible long enough to get most of them.

"Sir, *Iway* reports—"

There was a flash of light on the northwestern horizon, followed almost immediately by a huge dull boom.

"God damn," Farr said slowly and distinctly. *I never liked the magazine protection on those City-class cruisers,* he thought. They'd skimped on internal bulkheads to strengthen the main belt. . . .

"Sir." This time the yeoman's voice quavered a bit, just for an instant. "*Desmines* reports the *Iway* . . . she's *gone,* sir. Just gone. The stern section was all that's left and it sank like a rock."

"There's something wrong with our bloody cruisers today," Farr said, and lit a cigarette, looking at the map again and calculating distances and times. The captain of the *Great Republic* was the center of a flurry of activity; searchlights went on all over the superstructure.

"Here they come," he said, speaking loudly over the squeal of turrets training. Only the quick-firers and secondary armament; nobody was going to fire twelve-inch guns into the dark with dozens of Santander Navy ships around.

Long lean shapes were coming in, weaving between the cruiser squadrons, heading for the capital ships. Red-gold balls of light began to zip through the night, shells arching out to meet the enemy. The Chosen destroyers were throwing plumes back from their bows as high as their forward turrets, thirty knots and better.

"Here they come," repeated the captain. The battleship heeled sharply as it came about, presenting its bow to the destroyers and the smallest possible target to their torpedo sprays. "For what we are about to receive—"

"—may the Lord make us truly thankful," the bridge muttered with blasphemous piety.

Heinrich Hosten blinked. "He has said what?"

"Sir. Libert has announced that the Union is, ah, affirmatively neutral, as of one hundred hours today. Unionaise forces will not attempt to engage either Santander or Land forces except in direct self-defense. Sir, a number of our posts report that the Unionaise here in the Sierra are laagering and refusing contact. Shall I order activation of Plan Coat, sir?"

Heinrich stood stock-still for a full forty seconds. Sweat broke out on his expressionless face. "Not at the moment," he said very quietly. Plan Coat was the standing emergency option for the takeover of the Union.

Well, it looks like you were wrong for once, Gerta, he thought. Leaving Libert alive *had* been a mistake . . . although justified at the time.

"No, I don't think we'll distract ourselves just yet. Libert has two hundred and fifty thousand men. The Santies first, I'm afraid, tempting as it is. Attention, please."

His chief of staff bent forward. Heinrich looked down at the map. "Pending clarification from central HQ, the forces on the Confrontation Line are to stand in place." Selling their lives as dearly as they could. "All other forces in the Union are to retreat northward, destroying communications links behind them as far as possible, and catch us if they can."

"Catch us, sir?"

Heinrich tapped one thick finger on the center of the Sierra. "We're the only concentrated force the Land has left on the mainland. It's obvious what the Santies are doing: they've taken Corona, they're shipping their First Corps there as fast as they can, and they're going for our Home Fleet in the Passage."

His hand moved to the western shores of the Republic, and then swept up towards the Chosen homeland.

"Bold. Daring. It all turns on us, and on the Navy. If we can break their fleet and destroy their First Corps, then even losing the Union and the Sierra will be meaningless. We can retake them at our leisure and crush Santander next year."

And if we lose, or the Navy loses, the Chosen are doomed, he knew. By their faces, so did everyone else in the room.

"Sir, the communications grid is in very poor shape," the logistics chief warned.

Heinrich nodded. "Which means trains moving north are likely to go just as fast as the handcarts traveling ahead of the locomotives," he said. "That's still faster than oxcarts," he said. "Priorities: all light- and medium-armored fighting vehicles, then fuel, then artillery and artillery ammunition, and other supplies directly in tandem."

"What about the heavy armor?"

"Blow it in place."

"Sir!"

Heinrich tapped the map again. "Those monsters would be priceless if we could get them there. We can't. They take up too much space and effort. Better to have what we can in the right spot rather than what we can't halfway there at the crucial moment. Blow them."

"Zum behfel, Herr General."

"Aircraft, sir?"

"Coenraad, you and your staff get me an appreciation of how many we can shuttle back into the New Territories and refuel on the way. Blow the rest in place and assign the personnel to infantry units short of their quota of Chosen." Of which there were quite a few.

"Now, get me New Territories HQ."

"Sir . . . they haven't responded to signals for the past half hour. Last report was that insurgents had . . . emerged somehow . . . from Fourth Bureau headquarters and were attacking the administrative compound from within in conjunction with a general uprising of the animals."

Heinrich closed his eyes for a second, then shrugged. "All right, then let's do what we can with what we have. Next—"

The planning session went on. It was still going on when the vanguard of the last Chosen army moved north less than two hours later.

The last of her wingmates vanished in an orange globe of fire. Erika Hosten held the twin-engine biplane bomber straight and level until the last instant, then jerked on the stick. Wings screaming protest, the plane rose over the destroyer, clearing the stacks by less than six feet. Smoke and rising air buffeted at her for an instant, and then she was back on the surface, wheels almost touching the water.

A shape ahead of her. A long, flat, island superstructure to one side. Planes above it, a swarm of them—planes over the whole bowl of fire and smoke and ships that stretched to the horizon on either side, the others from the Land aircraft carriers, hundreds more on one-way trips from the Land itself. Pom-poms in gun tubs all the way along the edge of the carrier, and firing at her from behind, from the destroyer screen. Her gunner was slumped in the rear seat, and blood ran along the bottom of the cockpit and sloshed over the edges of her boots. Fabric was peeling off the wings.

"Just a little longer," she crooned to the aircraft. "Just a little."

Closer. Closer. *Now.*

She jerked the release toggle beside her seat. The biplane lurched as the torpedo released, and then again as something struck it. She yanked at the stick again, and—

Blackness.

"Welcome aboard, Admiral," the commander of the *Empire of Liberty* said. "We've notified the fleet you're transferring your flag."

Maurice Farr nodded as he moved to the front of the battleship's bridge. Forward, one of the eight-inch gun turrets was twisted wreckage. More twisted wreckage was being levered overside, the remains of a Land aircraft that had come aboard with its bombs still under the wings. That had caused surprisingly little damage, although the open-tub pom-poms on that side were silent, their barrels like surrealist sculpture.

"Status," he said crisply, despite the oil and water stains that soaked his uniform.

"Sir. Sixteen units of BatDivOne report full or nearly full operational status."

Two battleships lost last night to the torpedo attack and three cruisers. Three more this morning, running the gauntlet of Chosen air attacks from both sides of the Passage. That left him with an advantage of four, twice that in heavy cruisers, most of his destroyer screen still intact—less than a third of the enemy flotilla from Pillars had made it out—and with one crucial advantage. . . .

"Air?"

"Sir, we have the enemy main fleet under constant surveillance. The *Saunderton* is counterflooding to try and put out the fires, and the torpedo hit took out her rudder, but the *Lammas* and *Miller's Crossing* are still ready to retrieve aircraft."

They wouldn't be crowded. Most of the fighters were gone.

Maurice Farr looked at the horizon. All his life had been a preparation for this moment.

"Report movement."

"Sir, enemy destroyers are advancing at flank speed, followed by their battle line."

Which put them nose-on to his ships, which were advancing in exactly the same formation. There was one crucial difference: *his* heavy gun ships had aircraft to spot for them, and they'd honed the technique in years of practice. The Land fleet had excellent optical sights and good gunnery, but they couldn't use either until they came into sight. That was a long, long stretch of killing ground to run through, under the iron flail.

"The enemy carriers?"

"They've both broken off and are steaming northward at speed."

That puzzled him for an instant. *Ah. No more planes.* Without aircraft, they were as useless as merchantmen in a fleet engagement.

"Prepare to execute fleet turn; turn will be to port."

"Sir."

The Santander battleships were strung out like a line of sixteen beads, boiling forward at eighteen knots. The Land heavy ships were coming towards them at a knot or two better; some of his battlewagons had damage and weren't making their best speed.

"Turn."

The *Empire of Liberty* heeled, coming about to show her side to the enemy still beyond sight over the horizon. The turrets squealed as the long barrels of the twelve-inch guns came around. On either side her sisters did the same. Now the sixteen Santander battleships were moving west instead of north . . . and presenting the combined fire of their broadsides to their Land equivalents. If the enemy fleet tried to charge, close the range, they would be unable to reply with more than half their guns . . . and they would be firing blind for a long, long time anyway. If they duplicated his maneuver, they never would get within range. And if they withdrew, they'd never have an opportunity for a fleet engagement on anything like as favorable terms again. He could sail into Corona and refit, blockading the mainland under cover of land-based aircraft.

"Commence firing," he said.

One hundred and twenty heavy guns fired, and the Santander fleet disappeared for an instant in flame and smoke. Every man on the bridge opened his mouth and put his hands over his ears. The *Empire of Liberty* heeled over on her side, her structure screaming and flexing with the strain of the massive muzzle-horsepower of her four twelve-inch and four eight-inch broadside guns; for a brief instant he could see the shapes of the 800-pound shells at the top of their trajectory, and then they were falling towards the decks of the Land battlewagons. Towards the thinner deck armor, not the massive belts that protected their flanks.

"Splash," the signals yeoman said. "Forward air reports overshot. Range, correction—"

CHAPTER THIRTY

"General," the officer in the staff car said.

Jeffrey leaned down from the side of his armored car. Something went *CRACK* through the space he'd just vacated, far too loud for a bullet. He grabbed frantically for the railing at the side as the car lurched backwards.

That put them hull-down. "That was a tank gun, or I'm a snail-eater," the driver muttered.

Several Santander armored vehicles were advancing to either side of the road Jeffrey had been using. Four tanks, Whippet mediums with a 2.5-inch gun in their turrets; three troop carriers, Whippets with the turrets removed; a pom-pom Whippet, freed from its original tasking of antiaircraft work by the virtual absence of Land aircraft and doing fire support, instead. The Republic's armor clattered forward, halting with only the tank turrets showing over the hill and their guns at maximum depression. One fired, and a few seconds later there was a gout of smoke and fire in the middle distance, visible even over the ridge.

All across the rolling cropland to the west the Expeditionary Corps was advancing, infantry spread out in preparation for the engagement that seemed inevitable. A brace of ground-attack fighters flew by, their wheels less than fifty feet overhead, heading east for targets of opportunity.

"General," the breathless staff officer in the car said.

Jeffrey leaned down again. He grinned as he read the dispatches.

"Sir?" Henri said, his hands on the grips of the vehicle's machine gun. He didn't believe in taking unnecessary chances, and there still might be a few Chosen aircraft around. A couple of obvious command vehicles bunched right behind the front made a very tempting target.

"Message from Dad. Admiral Farr. *We have met the enemy and they are ours.*"

The Unionaise gave a soft whistle. "We hold the Passage, then?"

Jeffrey nodded. As long as the Expeditionary Force didn't get thrown back into the sea . . . which was looking increasingly unlikely.

He flipped to the other message and prevented his mouth falling open with an effort.

"Son of a *bitch.*"

Henri looked at him; that hadn't really been a curse.

"Libert. Libert has offered all the Chosen and Protégés remaining on Union or Sierran territory asylum. Union citizenship, land grants . . . the bastard's trying to get himself enough of an army so we won't feel like getting rid of him when this is all over."

Henri's face went white with rage around the nostrils and mouth. The Santander public hated Libert and his collaborationist regime almost as much as the Loyalist refugees did. The question of whether they hated him enough to fight another war was an entirely different one.

"Cheer up," Jeffrey said. "I haven't seen many of the Chosen surrendering yet."

He looked down at the map table. "All we have to do is hold them. They're out of supplies, out of fuel, out of hope."

The remnants of the force that had marched north out of the Sierra to meet him was strung out along the upper Pada River east of Ciano, fighting its way through swarms of guerillas. The few Chosen left alive in the Empire were laagered in the forts and towns that hadn't been overrun at the beginning of the uprising. There was nothing behind the last army of the Land but death.

"General message," he said to the signals technician. "All we have to do is hold their first attack. Hold them. The Protégés have already started to turn on their masters. If we can hold this attack, they'll disintegrate."

Heinrich Hosten looked around the position. There were six of them left, all of his remaining staff. Probably thousands left alive elsewhere, scattered pockets isolated where the fury of their attack had left them deep in the Santander positions. He checked the magazine of his automatic.

The Santies were ahead, in among the trees that lined the road. Probably a platoon of them, and certainly an armored car.

Heinrich estimated distances. *At least I don't have to make any more decisions*, he thought. He laughed, feeling the weight on his shoulders lighten. Nothing good had come of that. Just one more. He laughed again, feeling young. Young as he had been at the beginning of the war, young and confident and happy.

"*Sturm!*" he shouted. "Charge!"

Knife in one hand, pistol in the other, he went forward at a pounding run with the others at his heels. Muzzle flashes winked through the twilight at him, rifles from among the trees. Then a continuous blinking flicker from the half-seen shape of the armored car.

Something hit him, spinning him around. He staggered and came on, squeezing off the last three rounds in the pistol. Had he hit someone? No way of telling. On. Another impact, somewhere in a body that felt far away. He fell, crawled forward, digging his free hand into the dirt and holding the knife tighter as his fingers went numb. Boots ahead of him, and the tip of a bayonet. Heinrich scrabbled half-erect, lunging forward, swinging the long curved knife where he knew a body must be. Something struck him between the shoulderblades, and he was floating.

Gerta. Wetness spilled out of his mouth. Nothing.

"Jesus," the Santander soldier said, looking down at the knife that had missed his crotch by inches. "Jesus. This bastid must've ten holes in him and he wouldn't fuckin' *stop*. I put a whole clip into him. Jesus."

Jeffrey Farr looked down at Heinrich's face. The lips were still twisted in a snarl, or perhaps a smile; it was difficult to tell, with the blood. He reached down and closed the staring blue eyes.

"Sir, this is fuckin' *stupid*."

John Hosten nodded. "Yes, it is, Barrjen," he said. "Smith, all of you, you've been with me a long time, but this is personal. He's my father, not yours."

Oathtaking was burning. The Santander gunboat had come in unopposed, unless the wild random fire of looters counted. The harbor was empty, but the great naval dockyards in the center of the drowned caldera were the scene of a battle—who against who was hard to tell, but the volume of fire was considerable. What was going on in the streets wasn't a battle; it was halfway between orgy and massacre, as the slave laborers and Protégé rebels hunted down stray Chosen and anyone associated with them.

"I'm going," John said, hefting his machine pistol. "I can't stop you from coming too, but I wish you wouldn't."

They looked at him in silence; he smiled wryly and headed down the street. Stray bands of looters parted before their guns and obvious discipline; the smoke was thick enough to keep visibility down to twenty yards or less, and thick enough to make each breath painful. Fires were burning on both sides, licking tongues of flame out of the windows of the buildings.

"That's a barricade, sir. Careful," Smith said.

John shook his head. "I don't think anyone's alive behind it," he said.

There were plenty of dead before it, in the striped uniforms of the labor camps or drab Protégé issue clothing. First a thick scattering, then piles two and three deep. Gray Land uniforms and weapons showed here and there among them, soldiers or police turned against their masters. Before the line of furniture and upturned handcarts the dead lay in layers waist-high, the granite pavement running with viscous red; the Santander party had to climb over them, breathing through their mouths. Where the barrels of the machine guns had been covered by the curtain of falling dead, the smell was of cooked meat. Broiled by the red-hot metal, boiled by the steam escaping from the ruptured water jackets. Most of the dead behind the barricade were Chosen; mostly children, in the plain gray school uniforms of Probationers. The adults among them were white-haired, probably teachers. Most of the dead children looked to have died quickly, the mutilations done afterwards. Most.

"You bastard," Barrjen breathed at the bald man whose age-spotted hands were still locked around a dead Protégé's throat. The knife in the Protégé's hand was buried in the schoolmaster's gut. "You *bastard*."

"Keep moving," John said sharply.

The fires got worse as they moved through Old Town. A housemaid fled screaming past them, her naked body streaked with blood. Half a dozen Protégé soldiers chased her at an easy lope, the insignia torn from their uniforms, bottles in their hands. One or two of them halted to stare at the Santander party; were was no mind in the shaven heads, but enough animal caution to send them reeling on again.

"Where'll he be, sir?" Barrjen asked.

John replied without turning or halting his steady trot. "I think I know."

They were elbowing their way through crowds now, turning south to Monument Point. The crackle of small-arms fire sounded. The downslope of an avenue let them see the square around the Founders Monument, the bronze figures still raising their weapons in the Oath. A barricade of vehicles surrounded it, some of them tanks or armored cars.

"He'll be there, if he's alive at all," John said tonelessly. "There are bunkers under the monument, old ones, but they're always kept up, the magazines kept full, it's a ritual—"

A wave moved forward from the streets and buildings around the square, a wave that screamed and fired as it ran, ran over a carpet of bodies that covered the pavement too thickly for the stone to show. Bullets lashed out into the wave and it absorbed them, piling up as if on a breakwater. In a minute or less the edge of the wave was piled against the muzzles of the guns, stabbing and shooting and tearing flesh with its bare hands.

"*Vater* . . ." John whispered, in the tongue of his youth.

Something prompted Barrjen to dive for John's legs. They went down in a tangle of limbs; the others went prone with old-soldier reflex before they were consciously aware of what had happened. Even over a thousand yards and the screaming of the attacking horde the explosion was loud. Bronze and stone and human flesh erupted upwards. No un-Chosen hand would ever touch the Monument of the Oath.

"*Vater!*" John screamed, knowing exactly who had touched off that last fuse.

"Oh, Jesus fuckin' *Christ*, sir, stay down!" Barrjen shouted.

Barrjen and Smith wrestled with him. Then he grunted and collapsed into their arms.

"Damn, damn!" Smith said, hands scrabbling for the wound. "Damn, give me a bandage here, put some pressure on!"

Barrjen left them to their work, looking out over the square with a silent whistle. The crater was a hundred yards across, and he ran a quick calculation.

There can't be that many dead people in that small a space, he thought. Then he looked around at the burning chaos that stretched on either side around the harbor, farther than the eye could penetrate, up the sides of the mountains where the flames marked every plantation manor and village.

I guess there can be.

"Okay, let's get the boss back to the ship," he said aloud.

"*Nein,*" Gerta Hosten said tonelessly.

"But sir, we have to strike quickly, before the enemy land-troops in the Land itself. We have half the area under control, and hundreds of thousands of armed—"

"Shut. Up." Gerta told her son, looking down over the harbor of Westhavn. The fires were out, and the ships that crowded the roadstead were moving towards the docks. Occasionally a shot crackled, but nothing like yesterday when the local issue was still in doubt. She went on in the same flat mechanical voice:

"We have *pockets* of control in the north and east of the island. We have hundreds of thousands of *children*, Probationers; if it weren't for the fact that they'd been called up and concentrated, we'd all be dead by now. I doubt there are more than two divisions worth of Chosen adults left in areas we control. Perhaps a division's worth of Protégés who didn't mutiny. Now let me give you some arithmetic; there were more than two *million* slave laborers in the camps around Oathtaking and Copernik alone. And enough arms in the warehouses waiting shipment to the mainland to equip ten divisions. So there are at least a million armed rebels in the southern and eastern lowlands, not counting several divisions of Protégés who've killed their officers.

Suppose that our children—and some of them are shorter than the weapons they're carrying—could retake that part of the Land, which they can't possibly do, what do you think the Sanye army would make of them? And they'll be ready to put troops ashore here in fairly short order."

"Their . . . their navy was heavily damaged in the battle of the Passage."

Gerta nodded, her face still to the window. "They have six intact battleships. None of ours survived. The aircraft carriers are without aircraft. Perhaps two dozen other warships, all damaged, and several hundred merchantmen. We have no repair facilities, and no hope of restarting the industries—we had to kill nine tenths of the labor force over the past six days, or didn't you notice?"

"Then—"

Gerta turned. Johan Hosten was standing rigidly, but tears were trickling down his cheeks.

Smack. The flat of her palm took him across the side of the face. "Attention!"

"Yes, sir!"

She could see him gather himself. "Now, you will hear what we are going to do, and then you will assist me in preparing the necessary orders. Those who wish to do so will entrench here in Westhavn and in Konugsburg, and surrender to the Santander forces. They will live, at least. Those who do *not* wish do do so will board ship."

"Ship?" Johann asked. "For where, sir?"

"The Western Isles, of course," Gerta said. "It's our only remaining possession. The wireless reports that conditions are stable"—as much as they could be in a clutch of small jungle islands halfway around the world—"and it's rather far for the enemy to get around to anytime soon. We'll load all possible industrial equipment."

"But sir . . . how will . . . even if only half our

remaining population . . . the Western Isles don't have any agriculture to speak of."

"Then we'll eat a lot of fish, won't we?" Gerta said.

"But there aren't enough Protégés there to support us!"

Gerta sighed, closed her eyes and put two fingers to her brow. *We just don't* learn *very fast,* she thought bitterly.

"Then we'll have to learn how to fish, ourselves, won't we? You have your orders, *Hauptman.*"

"*Zum behfel, Herr General.*" Johann remained standing. "May I speak further, General?" he said.

Gerta felt cold. "You may," she said.

"General," said the boy. There were tears on his cheeks. "I will be among those who remain in Westhavn. With your permission, sir."

"Permission granted," Gerta said tonelessly. "Now, bring me the file on the merchant vessels available."

"*Mi Mutti?* I will never surrender!"

Gerta looked at her son: perfectly trained to be what she wanted him to be. Her ultimate failure. "No," she said, "I don't suppose you will. Now, bring me the file."

EPILOGUE

John Hosten smiled at his wife from the hospital bed. "Yes, Pia, I agree. A holiday . . . when things are settled a bit."

She put her hands on her hips. "They will never be settled. Already they are talking of drafting you as a candidate for premier in the next election."

John sat upright and winced at the pain in his leg. The doctors had saved it—and him—but it had been touch and go for a while. "Not a chance, by God!"

Pia sighed and smiled. "They will tell you it is for the public good—"

correct, Center said.

Shut up, John hissed mentally.

"—and you will rise to it like a trout to a fly."

She gathered her cloak. "Now they tell me you must rest. But you will see our son married—"

Maurice Hosten put his free arm around his fiancée; Alexandra Farr was still in Auxiliary uniform, and he in Air Corps sky-blue. The left arm was in a sling, but the cast was due to come off any day now. With luck, he might be able to fly an aircraft again, although not a fighter.

"—and you will rest for one year. If I have to hit you over the head with a hammer to make you do it."

She swept out, her son in her wake. Jeffrey sat on the edge of John's bed, and offered him a cigarillo. John leaned forward carefully.

"I feel like someone who's been climbing up a

469

staircase all my life," he said, blowing smoke towards the open window. A spray of blossoming crab apple waved across it in the mild spring breeze; the warm season came early to Dubuk. "Suddenly I'm at the top, and there's a whole new staircase."

eliminating the chosen menace was the first step towards restoring visager to the second federation, Center said. **every journey begins with a first step. yet that is only the beginning.**

Images spun through his mind: universities, trade treaties . . .

And Jeff will have a fair bit of fighting to do still, Raj said, with cheerful resignation. *I fought all my major wars on Bellevue before I was thirty, and damned if the mopping up didn't take the rest of my days.*

Jeffrey sighed and trickled smoke from his nostrils. "Some of what we're doing is harder to stomach than the war," he said. "Santander troops have had to fire on Imperials to keep them from slaughtering Chosen trying to surrender to us. They're finally doing that in some numbers, and your friend Arturo doesn't like it at all. He thinks their national destiny is fertilizer."

John shrugged, remembering the cellars in Ciano. "He's got his reasons. Still, he won't push it. We'll probably have to stop calling it the Empire, by the way. A republic? We'll see."

"The Premier is talking about a protectorate," Jeffrey said.

John laughed, and winced at the jar to his leg. "When iron floats. I know the Santander electorate, and they want complete demobilization, yesterday if possible."

"Damned right. We had a mutiny in Salini, just last week—troops demanding we disband them."

John scowled. "Which means we won't be able to do anything about Libert. Damn, but I hate to see that slimy bastard getting away with it. He's not as bad as the Chosen, but that's not saying much."

But he's popular in the Union now, Raj said to both of them. *He kept them out of war, and grabbed off a big chunk of territory from their traditional enemies. Are you ready to fight a major war and lose another hundred thousand dead to topple him?*

"If Gerard were alive, yes," Jeffrey said. "As it is—" He sighed. "But are we storing up trouble for the future? An awful lot of Chosen took Libert's amnesty, as many as surrendered to us. It didn't make it easier to get the Settlement Act through the Congress."

Which allowed the Chosen refugees resident status and citizenship for their children. Not quite as generous as Libert's offer, although the Republic was a more advanced country. Most of the Chosen were highly educated, highly intelligent people. They'd be an asset . . . provided they assimilated.

they will, Center said. **the overwhelming majority. the events of the past generation were sufficient to destroy even the most intensive cultural conditioning.**

And the real irreconcilables died rather than surrender, Raj said.

correct. the chosen elements in the union will also be assimilated to their surroundings, albeit more slowly. they will, however, serve as a nucleus of resistance to santander hegemony . . . which is a positive factor, in this context. remember, we must think in terms of planetary welfare, not national. this world has been severely damaged; more than one-tenth of the planetary population has died, and there will be further extensive losses from famine and disease in the immediate aftermath of the wars. the former imperial territories are in chaos and will, with a high degree of probability, splinter politically. there will be wars of succession there and in the unoccupied areas of the

sierra. the former land is likely to decivilize entirely, as protégés and slave laborers fight over the spoils—and the land was dependent on imported food supplies and a highly advanced agriculture, neither of which still exist. some degree of long-term cultural damage and demoralization will also result from the brutalizing effects of the conflict. we must ensure a long period of relative stability to ensure a regenerative process.

"Yeah, it was a damned hard war," Jeffrey agreed, flicking the butt of his cigarillo out the window. "You're right; the complete hardasses among the Chosen are pushing up the daisies. We can deal with the others."

John nodded. "Except, perhaps, Gerta's?"

the western isles lack the area and resource base to support a major military power, Center said, then slowly added: from a eugenic point of view, the settlement there will supply material for valuable study. existance without a slave base will lead to rapid cultural change, however. the maximum probability is a reorientation of effort from military to commercial-scientific endeavor.

John shrugged. "Good luck to Gerta, then," he said. "Probably better for her than winning would have been, when you think about it."

Jeffrey snorted laughter. "I doubt she'd agree."

"True. But it's our opinion that matters, isn't it? That's what winning means. Not killing your opponents, but converting their children's children. The Chosen made tools of human beings, and that had to be stopped. But we're all the tools of humankind."

The brothers sat in silence for a long moment, looking down the years ahead.

"Well, I've got a wedding to plan," Jeffrey said at last. "Which is the future incarnate. That's what it was all about, wasn't it?"

"Amen," John said softly. "Amen, brother."